Charlotte Mary Yonge

The Young Step-Mother

Outlook

Charlotte Mary Yonge

The Young Step-Mother

1. Auflage | ISBN: 978-3-73261-976-4

Erscheinungsort: Paderborn, Deutschland

Erscheinungsjahr: 2018

Outlook Verlag GmbH, Paderborn.

Reproduction of the original.

THE YOUNG STEP-MOTHER

or, A CHRONICLE OF MISTAKES

By Charlotte M Yonge

Fail—yet rejoice, because no less
The failure that makes thy distress
May teach another full success.

Nor with thy share of work be vexed
Though incomplete and even perplexed
It fits exactly to the next.
ADELAIDE A PROCTOR

CHAPTER I.

'Have you talked it over with her?' said Mr. Ferrars, as his little slender wife met him under the beeches that made an avenue of the lane leading to Fairmead vicarage.

'Yes!' was the answer, which the vicar was not slow to understand.

'I cannot say I expected much from your conversation, and perhaps we ought not to wish it. We are likely to see with selfish eyes, for what shall we do without her?'

'Dear Albinia! You always taunted me with having married your sister as much as yourself.'

'So I shall again, if you cannot give her up with a good grace.'

'If I could have had my own way in disposing of her.'

'Perhaps the hero of your own composition might be less satisfactory to her than is Kendal.'

'At least he should be minus the children!'

'I fancy the children are one great attraction. Do you know how many there are?'

'Three; but if Albinia knows their ages she involves them in a discreet haze. I imagine some are in their teens.'

'Impossible, Winifred, he is hardly five-and-thirty.'

'Thirty-eight, he said yesterday, and he married very early. I asked Albinia if her son would be in tail-coats; but she thought I was laughing at her, and would not say. She is quite eager at the notion of being governess to the girls.'

'She has wanted scope for her energies,' said Mr. Ferrars. 'Even spoiling her nephew, and being my curate, have not afforded field enough for her spirit of usefulness.'

'That is what I am afraid of.'

'Of what, Winifred?'

'That it is my fault. Before our marriage, you and she were the whole world to each other; but since I came, I have seen, as you say, that the craving for work was strong, and I fear it actuates her more than she knows.'

'No such thing. It is a case of good hearty love. What, are you afraid of that, too?'

'Yes, I am. I grudge her giving her fresh whole young heart away to a man who has no return to make. His heart is in his first wife's grave. Yes, you may smile, Maurice, as if I were talking romance; but only look at him, poor man! Did you ever see any one so utterly broken down? She can hardly beguile a smile from him.'

'His melancholy is one of his charms in her eyes.'

'So it may be, as a sort of interesting romance. I am sure I pity the poor man heartily, but to see her at three-and-twenty, with her sweet face and high spirits, give herself away to a man who looks but half alive, and cannot, if he would, return that full first love—have the charge of a tribe of children, be spied and commented on by the first wife's relations—Maurice, I cannot bear it.'

'It is not what we should have chosen,' said her husband, 'but it has a bright side. Kendal is a most right-minded, superior man, and she appreciates him thoroughly. She has great energy and cheerfulness, and if she can comfort him, and rouse him into activity, and be the kind mother she will be to his poor children, I do not think we ought to grudge her from our own home.'

'You and she have so strong a feeling for motherless children!'

'Thinking of Kendal as I do, I have but one fear for her.'

'I have many—the chief being the grandmother.'

'Mine will make you angry, but it is my only one. You, who have only known her since she has subdued it, have probably never guessed that she has that sort of quick sensitive temper—'

'Maurice, Maurice! as if I had not been a most provoking, presuming sister-in-law. As if I had not acted so that if Albinia ever had a temper, she must have shown it.'

'I knew you would not believe me, and I really am not afraid of her doing any harm by it, if that is what you suspect me of. No, indeed; but I fear it may make her feel any trials of her position more acutely than a placid person would.'

'Oho! so you own there will be trials!'

'My dear Winifred, as if I had not sat up till twelve last night laying them before Albinia. How sick the poor child must be of our arguments, when there is no real objection, and she is so much attached! Have you heard anything about these connexions of his? Did you not write to Mrs. Nugent? I wish she were at home.'

'I had her answer by this afternoon's post, but there is nothing to tell. Mr. Kendal has only been settled at Bayford Bridge a few years, and she never visited any one there, though Mr. Nugent had met Mr. Kendal several times before his wife's death, and liked him. Emily is charmed to have Albinia for a neighbour.'

'Does she know nothing of the Meadows' family?'

'Nothing but that old Mrs. Meadows lives in the town with one unmarried daughter. She speaks highly of the clergyman.'

'John Dusautoy? Ay, he is admirable—not that I have done more than see him at visitations when he was curate at Lauriston.'

'Is he married?'

'I fancy he is, but I am not sure. There is one good friend for Albinia any way!'

'And now for your investigations. Did you see Colonel Bury?'

'I did, but he could say little more than we knew. He says nothing could be more exemplary than Kendal's whole conduct in India, he only regretted that he kept so much aloof from others, that his principle and gentlemanly feeling did not tell as much as could have been wished. He has always been wrapped up in his own pursuits—a perfect dictionary of information.'

'We had found out that, though he is so silent. I should think him a most elegant scholar.'

'And a deep one. He has studied and polished his acquirements to the utmost. I assure you, Winifred, I mean to be proud of my brother-in-law.'

'What did you hear of the first wife?'

'It was an early marriage. He went home as soon as he had sufficient salary, married her, and brought her out. She was a brilliant dark beauty, who became quickly a motherly, housewifely, common-place person—I should think there had been a poet's love, never awakened from.'

'The very thing that has always struck me when, poor man, he has tried to be civil to me. Here is a man, sensible himself, but who has never had the hap to live with sensible women.'

'When their children grew too old for India, she came into some little property at Bayford Bridge, which enabled him to retire. Colonel Bury came home in the same ship, and saw much of them, liked him better and better, and seems to have been rather wearied by her. A very good woman, he says, and Kendal most fondly attached; but as to comparing her with Miss Ferrars, he could not think of it for a moment. So they settled at Bayford, and there, about two years ago, came this terrible visitation of typhus fever.'

'I remember how Colonel Bury used to come and sigh over his friend's illness and trouble.'

'He could not help going over it again. The children all fell ill together—the two eldest were twin boys, one puny, the other a very fine fellow, and his father's especial pride and delight. As so often happens, the sickly one was spared, the healthy one was taken.'

'Then Albinia will have an invalid on her hands!'

'The Colonel says this Edmund was a particularly promising boy, and poor Kendal felt the loss dreadfully. He sickened after that, and his wife was worn out with nursing and grief, and sank under the fever at once. Poor Kendal has never held up his head since; he had a terrible relapse.'

'And,' said Winifred, 'he no sooner recovers than he goes and marries our Albinia!'

'Two years, my dear.'

'Pray explain to me, Maurice, why, when people become widowed in any unusually lamentable way, they always are the first to marry again.'

'Incorrigible. I meant to make you pity him.'

'I did, till I found I had wasted my pity. Why could not these Meadowses look after his children! Why must the Colonel bring him here? I believe it was with malice prepense!'

'The Colonel went to see after him, and found him so drooping and wretched, that he insisted on bringing him home with him, and old Mrs. Meadows and her daughter almost forced him to accept the invitation.'

'They little guessed what the Colonel would be at!'

'You will be better now you have the Colonel to abuse,' said her husband.

'And pray what do you mean to say to the General?'

'Exactly what I think.'

'And to the aunts?' slyly asked the wife.

'I think I shall leave you all that correspondence. It will be too edifying to see you making common cause with the aunts.'

'That comes of trying to threaten one's husband; and here they come,' said Winifred. 'Well, Maurice, what can't be cured must be endured. Albinia'a heart is gone, he is a very good man, and spite of India, first wife, and melancholy, he does not look amiss!'

Mr. Ferrars smiled at the chary, grudging commendation of the tall, handsome man who advanced through the beech-wood, but it was too true that his clear olive complexion had not the line of health, that there was a world of oppression on his broad brow and deep hazel eyes, and that it was a dim, dreamy, reluctant smile that was awakened by the voice of the lady who walked by his side, as if reverencing his grave mood.

She was rather tall, very graceful, and well made, but her features were less handsome than sweet, bright, and sensible. Her hair was nut-brown, in long curled waves; her eyes, deep soft grey, and though downcast under the new sympathies, new feelings, and responsibilities that crowded on her, the smile and sparkle that lighted them as she blushed and nodded to her brother and sister, showed that liveliness was the natural expression of that engaging face.

Say what they would, it was evident that Albinia Ferrars had cast in her lot with Edmund Kendal, and that her energetic spirit and love of children animated her to embrace joyfully the cares which such a choice must impose on her.

As might have been perceived by one glance at the figure, step, and bearing of Mr. Ferrars, perfectly clerical though they were, he belonged to a military family. His father had been a distinguished Peninsular officer, and his brother, older by many years, held a command in Canada. Maurice and Albinia, early left orphans, had, with a young cousin, been chiefly under the charge of their aunts, Mrs. Annesley and Miss Ferrars, and had found a kind home in their house in Mayfair, until Maurice had been ordained to the family living of Fairmead, and his sister had gone to live with him there, extorting the consent of her elder brother to her spending a more real and active life than her aunts' round of society could offer her.

The aunts lamented, but they could seldom win their darling to them for more than a few weeks at a time, even after their nephew Maurice had—as they considered—thrown himself away on a little lively lady of Irish parentage, no equal in birth or fortune, in their opinion, for the grandson of Lord Belraven.

They had been very friendly to the young wife, but their hopes had all the more been fixed on Albinia; and even Winifred could afford them some generous pity in the engagement of their favourite niece to a retired East India Company's servant—a widower with three children.

CHAPTER II.

The equinoctial sun had long set, and the blue haze of March east wind had deepened into twilight and darkness when Albinia Kendal found herself driving down the steep hilly street of Bayford. The town was not large nor modern enough for gas, and the dark street was only lighted here and there by a shop of more pretension; the plate-glass of the enterprising draper, with the light veiled by shawls and ribbons, the 'purple jars,' green, ruby, and crimson of the chemist; and the modest ray of the grocer, revealing busy heads driving Saturday-night bargains.

'How well I soon shall know them all,' said Albinia, looking at her husband, though she knew she could not see his face, as he leant back silently in his corner, and she tried to say no more. She was sure that coming home was painful to him; he had been so willing to put it off, and to prolong those pleasant seaside days, when there had been such pleasant reading, walking, musing, and a great deal of happy silence.

Down the hill, and a little way on level ground—houses on one side, something like hedge or shrubbery on the other—a stop—a gate opened—a hollow sound beneath the carriage, as though crossing a wooden bridge—trees—bright windows—an open door—and light streaming from it.

'Here is your home, Albinia,' said that deep musical voice that she loved the better for the subdued melancholy of the tones, and the suppressed sigh that could not be hidden.

'And my children,' she eagerly said, as he handed her out, and, springing to the ground, she hurried to the open door opposite, where, in the lamp-light, she saw, moving about in shy curiosity and embarrassment, two girls in white frocks and broad scarlet sashes, and a boy, who, as she advanced, retreated with his younger sister to the fireplace, while the elder one, a pretty, and rather formal looking girl of twelve, stood forward.

Albinia held out her arms, saying, 'You are Lucy, I am sure,' and eagerly kissed the girl's smiling, bright face.

'Yes, I am Lucy,' was the well-pleased answer, 'I am glad you are come.'

'I hope we shall be very good friends,' said Albinia, with the sweet smile that few, young or old, could resist. 'And this is Gilbert,' as she kissed the blushing cheek of a thin boy of thirteen—'and Sophia.'

Sophia, who was eleven, had not stirred to meet her. She alone inherited her father's fine straight profile, and large black eyes, but she had the heaviness of feature that sometimes goes with very dark complexions. The white frock did not become her brown neck and arms, her thick black hair was arranged in too womanly a manner, and her head and face looked too large; moreover, there was no lighting-up to answer the greeting, and Albinia was disappointed.

Poor child, she thought, she is feeling deeply that I am an interloper, it will be different now her father is coming.

Mr. Kendal was crossing the hall, and as he entered he took the hand and kissed the forehead of each of the three, but Sophia stood with the same half sullen indifference—it might be shyness, or sensibility.

'How much you are grown!' he said, looking at the children with some surprise.

In fact, though Albinia knew their ages, they were all on a larger scale than she had expected, and looked too old for the children of a man of his youthful appearance. Gilbert had the slight look of rapid growth; Lucy, though not so tall, and with a small, clear, bright face, had the air of a little woman, and Sophia's face might have befitted any age.

'Yes, papa,' said Lucy; 'Gilbert has grown an inch-and-a-half since October, for we measured him.'

'Have you been well, Gilbert?' continued Mr. Kendal, anxiously.

'I have the toothache, said Gilbert, piteously.

'Happily, nothing more serious,' thrust in Lucy; 'Mr. Bowles told Aunt Maria that he considers Gilbert's health much improved.'

Albinia asked some kind questions about the delinquent tooth, but the answers were short; and, to put an end to the general constraint, she asked Lucy to show her to her room.

It was a pretty bay-windowed room, and looked cheerful in the firelight. Lucy's tongue was at once unloosed, telling that Gilbert's tutor, Mr. Salsted, had insisted on his having his tooth extracted, and that he had refused, saying it was quite well; but Lucy gave it as her opinion that he much preferred the toothache to his lessons.

'Where does Mr. Salsted live?'

'At Tremblam, about two miles off; Gilbert rides the pony over there every day, except when he has the toothache, and then he stays at home.'

'And what do you do?'

'We went to Miss Belmarche till the end of our quarter, and since that we have been at home, or with grandmamma. Do you *really* mean that we are to study with you?'

'I should like it, my dear. I have been looking forward very much to teaching you and Sophia.'

'Thank you, mamma.'

The word was said with an effort as if it came strangely, but it thrilled Albinia's heart, and she kissed Lucy, who clung to her, and returned the caress.

'I shall tell Gilbert and Sophy what a dear mamma you are,' she said. 'Do you know, Sophy says she shall never call you anything but Mrs. Kendal; and I know Gilbert means the same.'

'Let them call me whatever suits them best,' said Albinia; 'I had rather they waited till they feel that they like to call me as you have done—thank you for it, dear Lucy. You must not fancy I shall be at all hurt at your thinking of times past. I shall want you to tell me of them, and of your own dear mother, and what will suit papa best.'

Lucy looked highly gratified, and eagerly said, 'I am sure I shall love you just like my own mamma.'

'No,' said Albinia, kindly; 'I do not expect that, my dear. I don't ask for any more than you can freely give, dear child. You must bear with having me in that place, and we will try and help each other to make your papa comfortable; and, Lucy, you will forgive me, if I am impetuous, and make mistakes.'

Lucy's little clear black eyes looked as if nothing like this had ever come within her range of observation, and Albinia could sympathize with her difficulty of reply.

Mr. Kendal was not in the drawing-room when they re-entered, there was only Gilbert nursing his toothache by the fire, and Sophy sitting in the middle of the rug, holding up a screen. She said something good-natured to each, but neither responded graciously, and Lucy went on talking, showing off the room, the chiffonieres, the ornaments, and some pretty Indian ivory carvings. There was a great ottoman of Aunt Maria's work, and a huge cushion with an Arab horseman, that Lucy would uncover, whispering, 'Poor mamma worked it,' while Sophy visibly winced, and Albinia hurried it into the chintz cover again, lest Mr. Kendal should come. But Lucy had full time to be communicative about the household with such a satisfied, capable manner, that Albinia asked if she had been keeping house all this time.

'No; old Nurse kept the keys, and managed till now; but she went this morning.'

Sophy's mouth twitched.

'She was so very fond—' continued Lucy.

'Don't!' burst out Sophy, almost the first word Albinia had heard from her; but no more passed, for Mr. Kendal came in, and Lucy's conversation instantly was at an end.'

Before him she was almost as silent as the others, and he seldom addressed himself to her, only inquiring once after her grandmamma's health, and once calling Sophy out of the way when she was standing between the fire and— He finished with the gesture of command, whether he said 'Your mamma,' none could tell.

It was late, and the meal was not over before bed-time, when Albinia lingered to find remedies for Gilbert's toothache, pleased to feel herself making a commencement of motherly care, and to meet an affectionate glance of thanks from Mr. Kendal's eye. Gilbert, too, thanked her with less shyness than before, and was hopeful about the remedy; and with the feeling of having made a beginning, she ran down to tell Mr. Kendal that she thought he had hardly done justice to the children—they were fine creatures—something so sweet and winning about Lucy—she liked Gilbert's countenance—Sophy must have something deep and noble in her.

He lifted his head to look at her bright face, and said, 'They are very much obliged to you.'

'You must not say that, they are my own.'

'I will not say it again, but as I look at you, and the home to which I have brought you, I feel that I have acted selfishly.'

Albinia timidly pressed his hand, 'Work was always what I wished,' she said, 'if only I could do anything to lighten your grief and care.'

He gave a deep, heavy sigh. Albinia felt that if he had hoped to have lessened the sadness, he had surely found it again at his own door. He roused himself, however, to say, 'This is using you ill, Albinia; no one is more sensible of it than I am.'

'I never sought more than you can give,' she murmured; 'I only wish to do what I can for you, and you will not let me disturb you.'

'I am very grateful to you,' was his answer; a sad welcome for a bride. 'And these poor children will owe everything to you.'

'I wish I may do right by them,' said Albinia, fervently.

'The flower of the flock'—began Mr. Kendal, but he broke off at once.

Albinia had told Winifred that she could bear to have his wife's memory first with him, and that she knew that she could not compensate to him for his loss, but the actual sight of his dejection came on her with a chill, and she had to call up all her energies and hopes, and, still better, the thought of strength not her own, to enable her to look cheerfully on the prospect. Sleep revived her elastic spirits, and with eager curiosity she drew up her blind in the morning, for the first view of her new home.

But there was a veil—moisture made the panes resemble ground glass, and when she had rubbed that away, and secured a clear corner, her range of vision was not much more extensive. She could only see the grey outline of trees and shrubs, obscured by the heavy mist; and on the lawn below, a thick cloud that seemed to hang over a dark space which she suspected to be a large pond.

'There is very little to be gained by looking out here!' Albinia soliloquized. 'It is not doing the place justice to study it on a misty, moisty morning. It looks now as if that fever might have come bodily out of the pond. I'll have no more to say to it till the sun has licked up the fog, and made it bright! Sunday morning—my last Sunday without school-teaching I hope! I famish to begin again—and I will make time for that, and the girls too! I am glad he consents to my doing whatever I please in that way! I hope Mr. Dusautoy will! I wish Edmund knew him better—but oh! what a shy man it is!'

With a light step she went down-stairs, and found Mr Kendal waiting for her in the dining-room, his face brightening as she entered.

'I am sorry Bayford should wear this heavy cloud to receive you,' he said.

'It will soon clear,' she answered, cheerfully. 'Have you heard of poor Gilbert this morning?'

'Not yet.' Then, after a pause, 'I have generally gone to Mrs. Meadows after the morning service,' he said, speaking with constraint.

'You will take me?' said Albinia. 'I wish it, I assure you.'

It was evidently what he wished her to propose, and he added, 'She must never feel herself neglected, and it will be better at once.'

'So much more cordial,' said Albinia. 'Pray let us go!'

They were interrupted by the voices of the girls—not unpleasing voices, but loud and unsubdued, and with a slight tone of provincialism, which seemed to hurt Mr. Kendal's ears, for he said, 'I hope you will tune those voices to something less unlike your own.'

As he spoke, the sisters appeared in the full and conscious rustling of new lilac silk dresses, which seemed to have happily carried off all Sophy's sullenness, for she made much more brisk and civil answers, and ran across the room in a boisterous manner, when her father sent her to see whether Gilbert were up.

There was a great clatter, and Gilbert chased her in, breathless and scolding, but the tongues were hushed before papa, and no more was heard than that the tooth was better, and had not kept him awake. Lucy seemed disposed to make conversation, overwhelming Albinia with needless repetitions of 'Mamma dear,' and plunging into what Mrs. Bowles and Miss Goldsmith had said of Mr. Dusautoy, and how he kept so few servants, and the butcher had no orders last time he called. Aunt Maria thought he starved and tyrannized over that poor little sickly Mrs. Dusautoy.

Mr. Kendal said not one word, and seemed not to hear. Albinia felt as if she had fallen into a whirlpool of gossip; she looked towards him, and hoped to let the conversation drop, but Sophy answered her sister, and, at last, when it came to something about what Jane heard from Mrs. Osborn's Susan, Albinia gently whispered, 'I do not think this entertains your papa, my dear,' and silence sank upon them all.

Albinia's next venture was to ask about that which had been her Sunday pleasure from childhood, and she turned to Sophy, and said, 'I suppose you have not begun to teach at the school yet!'

Sophy's great eyes expanded, and Lucy said, 'Oh dear mamma! nobody does that but Genevieve Durant and the monitors. Miss Wolte did till Mr. Dusautoy came, but she does not approve of him.'

'Lucy, you do not know what you are saying,' said Mr. Kendal, and again there was an annihilating silence, which Albinia did not attempt to disturb.

At church time, she met the young ladies in the hall, in pink bonnets and sea-green mantillas over the lilac silks, all evidently put on for the first time in her honour, an honour of which she felt herself the less deserving, as, sensible that this was no case for bridal display, she wore a quiet dark silk, a Cashmere shawl, and plain straw bonnet, trimmed with white.

With manifest wish for reciprocity, Lucy fell into transports over the shawl, but gaining nothing by this, Sophy asked if she did not like the mantillas? Albinia could only make civility compatible with truth by saying that the colour was pretty, but where was Gilbert? He was on a stool before the dining-room fire, looking piteous, and pronouncing his tooth far too bad for going to church, and she had just time for a fresh administration of camphor before Mr. Kendal came forth from his study, and gave her his arm.

The front door opened on a narrow sweep, the river cutting it off from the road, and crossed by two wooden bridges, beside each of which stood a weeping-willow, budding with fresh spring foliage. Opposite were houses of various pretentious, and sheer behind them rose the steep hill, with the church nearly at the summit, the noble spire tapering high above, and the bells ringing out a cheerful chime. The mist had drawn up, and all was fresh and clear.

'There go Lizzie and Loo!' cried Lucy, 'and the Admiral and Mrs. Osborn. I'll run and tell them papa is come home.'

Sophy was setting off also, but Mr. Kendal stopped them, and lingered a moment or two, making an excuse of looking for a needless umbrella, but in fact to avoid the general gaze. As if making a desperate plunge, however, and looking up and down the broad street, so as to be secure that no acquaintance was near, he emerged with Albinia from the gate, and crossed the road as the chime of the bells changed.

'We are late,' he said. 'You will prefer the speediest way, though it is somewhat steep.'

The most private way, Albinia understood, and could also perceive that the girls would have liked the street which sloped up the hill, and thought the lilac and green insulted by being conducted up the steep, irregular, and not very clean bye-lane that led directly up the ascent, between houses, some meanly modern, some picturesquely ancient, with stone steps outside to the upper story, but all with far too much of pig-stye about them for beauty or fragrance. Lucy held up her skirts, and daintily picked her way, and Albinia looked with kindly eyes at the doors and windows, secretly wondering what friends she should find there.

The lane ended in a long flight of more than a hundred shallow steps cut out in the soft stone of the hill, with landing-places here and there, whence views were seen of the rich meadow-landscape beyond, with villages, orchards, and farms, and the blue winding river Baye in the midst, woods rising on the opposite side under the soft haze of distance. On the other side, the wall of rock was bordered by gardens, with streamers of ivy or periwinkle here and there hanging down.

The ascent ended in an old-fashioned stone stile; and here Sophy, standing on the step, proclaimed, with unnecessary loudness, that Mr. Dusautoy was carrying Mrs. Dusautoy across the churchyard. This had the effect of making a pause, but Albinia saw the rector, a tall, powerful man, rather supporting than actually carrying, a little fragile form to the low-browed door leading into the chancel on the north side. The church was handsome, though in the late style, and a good deal misused by eighteenth-century taste; and Albinia was full of admiration as Mr. Kendal conducted her along the flagged path.

She was rather dismayed to find herself mounting the gallery stairs, and to emerge into a well-cushioned abode, with the shield-bearing angel of the corbel of an arch all to herself, and a very good view of the cobwebs over Mr. Dusautoy's sounding-board. It seemed to suit all parties, however, for Lucy and Sophia took possession of the forefront, and their father had the inmost corner, where certainly nobody could see him.

Just opposite to Albinia was a mural tablet, on which she read what revealed to her more of the sorrows of her household than she had guessed before:

```
'To the memory of Lucy, the beloved wife of Edmund Kendal.
      Died February 18th, 1845, aged 35 years.

   Edmund Meadows Kendal, born January 20th, 1834.
      Died February 10th, 1845.

   Maria Kendal, born September 5th, 1840.
      Died September 14th, 1840.

   Sarah Anne Kendal, born October 3rd, 1841.
      Died November 20th, 1843.

   John Augustus Kendal, born January 4th, 1842.
      Died July 6th, 1842.

   Anne Maria Kendal, born June 12th, 1844.
      Died June 19th, 1844.'
```

Then followed, in the original Greek, the words, 'Because I live, ye shall live also.'

Four infants! how many hopes laid here! All the English-born children of the family had died in their cradles, and not only did compassion for the past affect Albinia, as she thought of her husband's world of hidden grief, but a shudder for the future came over her, as she remembered having read that such mortality is a test of the healthiness of a locality. What could she think of Willow Lawn? It was with a strong effort that she brought her attention back to Him Who controlleth the sickness that destroyeth at noon-day.

But Mr. Dusautoy's deep, powerful intonations roused her wandering thoughts, and she was calmed and reassured by the holy Feast, in which she joined with her husband.

Mr. Kendal's fine face was calm and placid, as best she loved to look upon it, when they came out of church, and she was too happy to disturb the quiet by one word. Lively and animated as she was, there was a sort of repose and enjoyment in the species of respect exacted by his grave silent demeanour.

If this could only have lasted longer! but he was taking her along an irregular street, and too soon she saw a slight colour flit across his cheek, and his eyebrows contract, as he unlatched a green door in a high wall, and entered a little flagged court, decorated by a stand destined for flowers.

Albinia caught the blush, and felt more bashful than she had believed was in her nature, but she had a warm-hearted determination that she would work down prejudices, and like and be liked by all that concerned him and his children. So she smiled at him, and went bravely on into the matted hall and up the narrow stairs, and made a laughing sign when he looked back at her ere he tapped at the sitting-room door.

It was opened from within before he could turn the handle, and a shrill voice, exaggerating those of the girls, showered welcomes with such rapidity, that Albinia was seated at the table, and had been helped to cold chicken, before she could look round, or make much answer to reiterations of 'so very kind.'

It was a small room, loaded with knicknacks and cushions, like a repository of every species of female ornamental handiwork in vogue for the last half century, and the luncheon-tray in the middle of all, ready for six people, for the two girls were there, and though Mr. Kendal stood up by the fire, and would not eat, he and his black image, reflected backwards and forwards in the looking-glass and in the little round mirror, seemed to take up more room than if he had been seated.

Mrs. Meadows was slight, shrunken, and gentle-looking, with a sweet tone in her voice, great softness of manner, and pretty blue eyes. Albinia only wished that she had worn mourning, it would have been so much more becoming than bright colours, but that was soon overlooked in gratitude for her affectionate reception, and in the warmth of feeling excited by her evident fondness and solicitude for Mr. Kendal.

Miss Meadows was gaily dressed in youthful fashion, such as evidently had set her off to advantage when she had been a bright, dark, handsome girl; but her hair was thin, her cheeks haggard, the colour hardened, and her forty years apparent, above all, in an uncomfortable furrow on the brow and round the mouth; her voice had a sharp distressed tone that grated even in her lowest key, and though she did not stammer, she could never finish a sentence, but made half-a-dozen disjointed commencements whenever she spoke. Albinia pitied her, and thought her nervous, for she was painfully assiduous in waiting on every one, scarcely sitting down for a minute before she was sure that pepper, or pickle, or new bread, or stale bread, or something was wanted, and squeezing round the table to help some one, or to ring the bell every third minute, and all in a dress that had a teasing stiff silken rustle. She offered Mr. Kendal everything in the shape of food, till he purchased peace by submitting to take a hard biscuit, while Albinia was not allowed her glass of water till all manner of wines, foreign and domestic, had been tried upon her in vain.

Conversation was not easy. Gilbert was inquired after, and his aunt spoke in her shrill, injured note, as she declared that she had done her utmost to persuade him to have the tooth extracted, and began a history of what the dentist ought to have done five years ago.

His grandmother softly pitied him, saying poor little Gibbie was such a delicate boy, and required such careful treatment; and when Albinia hoped that he was outgrowing his ill-health, she was amused to find that desponding compassion would have been more pleasing.

There had been a transaction about a servant in her behalf: and Miss Meadows insisted on hunting up a note, searching all about the room, and making her mother and Sophy move from the front of two table-drawers, a disturbance which Sophy did not take with such placid looks as did her grandmother.

The name of the maid was Eweretta Dobson, at which there was a general exclamation.

'I wonder what is the history of the name,' said Albinia; 'it sounds like nothing but the diminutive of ewer. I hope she will not be the little pitcher with long ears.'

Mr. Kendal looked as much amused as he ever did, but no one else gave the least token of so much as knowing what she meant, and she felt as if she had been making a foolish attempt at wit.

'You need not call her so,' was all that Mrs. Meadows said.

'I do not like calling servants by anything but their true names,' answered Albinia; 'it does not seem to me treating them with proper respect to change their names, as if we thought them too good for them. It is using them like slaves.

Lucy exclaimed, 'Why! grandmamma's Betty is really named Philadelphia.'

Albinia laughed, but was disconcerted by finding that she had really given annoyance. 'I beg your pardon,' she said. 'It is only a fancy of my own. I am afraid that I have many fancies for my friends to bear with. You see I have so fine a name of my own, that I have a fellow-feeling for those under the same affliction; and I believe some servants like an alias rather than be teased for their finery, so I shall give Miss Eweretta her choice between that and her surname.

The old lady looked good-natured, and that matter blew over; but Miss Meadows fell into another complication of pros and cons about writing for the woman's character, looking miserably harassed whether she should write, or Mrs. Kendal, before she had been called upon.

Albinia supposed that Mrs. Wolfe might call in the course of the week; but this Miss Meadows did not know, and she embarked in so many half speeches, and looked so mysterious and significant at her mother, that Albinia began to suspect that some dreadful truth was behind.

'Perhaps,' said the old lady, 'perhaps Mrs. Kendal might make it understood through you, my dear Maria, that she is ready to receive visits.'

'I suppose they must be!' said Albinia.

'You see, my dear, people would be most happy, but they do not know whether you have arrived. You have not appeared at church, as I may say.'

'Indeed,' said Albinia, much diverted by her new discoveries in the realms of etiquette, 'I was rather in a cupboard, I must allow. Ought we to have sailed up the aisle in state in the Grandison pattern? Are you ready?' and she glanced up at her husband, but he only half heard.

'No,' said Miss Meadows, fretfully; 'but you have not appeared as a bride. The straw bonnet—you see people cannot tell whether you are not incog, as yet—'

To refrain from laughing was impossible. 'My tarn cap,' she exclaimed; 'I am invisible in it! What shall I do? I fear I shall never be producible, for indeed it is my very best, my veritable wedding-bonnet!'

Lucy looked as if she thought it not worth while to be married for no better a bonnet than that.

'Absurdity!' said Mr. Kendal.

If he would but have given a good hearty laugh, thought Albinia, what a consolation it would be! but she considered herself to have had a lesson against laughing in that house, and was very glad when he proposed going home. He took a kind, affectionate leave of the old lady, who again looked fondly in big face, and rejoiced in his having recovered his looks.

As they arrived at home, Lucy announced that she was just going to speak to Lizzie Osborn, and Sophy ran after her to a house of about the same degree as their own, but dignified as Mount Lodge, because it stood on the hill side of the street, while Mr. Kendal's house was for more gentility called 'Willow Lawn.' Gilbert was not to be found; but at four o'clock the whole party met at dinner, before the evening service.

Gilbert could eat little, and on going back to the fire to roast his cheek instead of going to church, was told by his father, 'I cannot have this going on. You must go to Mr. Bowles directly after breakfast to-morrow, have the tooth drawn, and then go on to Mr. Salsted's.

The tone was one that admitted of no rebellion. If Mr. Kendal interfered little, his authority was absolute where he did interfere, and Albinia could only speak a few kind words of encouragement, but the boy was vexed and moody, seemed half asleep when they came home, and went to bed as soon as tea was over.

Sophy went to bed too, Mr. Kendal went to his study, and Albinia, after this day of novelty and excitement, drew her chair to the fire, and as Lucy was hanging wearily about, called her to her side, and made her talk, believing that there was more use in studying the girl's character than even in suggesting some occupation, though that was apparently the great want of the whole family on Sunday.

Lucy's first confidence was that Gilbert had not been out alone, but with that Archibald Tritton. Mr. Tritton had a great farm, and was a sort of gentleman, and Gilbert was always after that Archy. She thought it 'very undesirable,' and Aunt Maria had talked to him about it, but he never listened to Aunt Maria.

Albinia privately thought that it must be a severe penance to listen to Aunt Maria, and took Gilbert's part. She supposed that he must be very solitary; it must be a melancholy thing to be a twin left alone.

'And Edmund, dear Edmund, was always so kind and so fond of Gilbert!' said Lucy. 'You would not have thought they were twins, Edmund was so much the tallest and strongest. It seemed so odd that Gilbert should have got over it, when he did not. Should you like to hear all about it, mamma?'

It was Albinia's great wish to lift that dark veil, and Lucy began, with as much seriousness and sadness as could co-exist with the satisfaction and importance of having to give such a narration, and exciting emotion and pity. It was remarkable how she managed to make herself the heroine of the story, though she had been sent out of the house, and had escaped the infection. She spoke in phrases that showed that she had so often told the story as to have a set form, caught from her elders, but still it had a deep and intrinsic interest for the bride, that made her sit gazing into the fire, pressing Lucy's hand, and now and then sighing and shuddering slightly as she heard how there had been a bad fever prevailing in that lower part of the town, and how the two boys were both unwell one damp, hot autumn morning, and Lucy dwelt on the escape it had been that she had not kissed them before going to school. Sophy had sickened the same day, and after the tedious three weeks, when father and mother were spent with attendance on the three, Edmund, after long delirium, had suddenly sunk, just as they had hopes of him; and the same message that told Lucy of her brother's death, told her of the severe illness of both parents.

The disease had done the work rapidly on the mother's exhausted frame, and she was buried a week after her boy. Lucy had seen the procession from the window, and thought it necessary to tell how she had cried.

Mr. Kendal's had been a long illness; the first knowledge of his loss had caused a relapse, and his recovery had long been doubtful. As soon as the children were able to move, they were sent with Miss Meadows to Ramsgate, and Lucy had joined them there.

'The day before I went, I saw papa,' she said. 'I had gone home for some things that I was to take, and his room door was open, so he saw me on the stairs, and called me, for there was no fear of infection then. Oh, he was so changed! his hair all cut off, and his cheeks hollow, and he was quite trembling, as he lay back on pillows in the great arm-chair. You can't think what a shock it was to me to see him in such a state. He held out his arms, and I flung mine round his neck, and sobbed and cried. And he just said, so faintly, "Take her away, Maria, I cannot bear it." I assure you I was quite hysterical.'

'You must have wished for more self-command,' said Albinia, disturbed by Lucy's evident pleasure in having made a scene.

'Oh, but it was such a shock, and such a thing to see the house all empty and forlorn, with the windows open, and everything so still! Miss Belmarche cried too, and said she did not wonder my feelings overcame me, and *she* did not see papa.'

'Ah! Lucy,' said Albinia, fervently, 'how we must try to make him happy after all that he has gone through!'

'That is what grandmamma said when she got his letter. "I would be glad of anything," she said, "that would bring back a smile to him." And Aunt Maria said she had done her best for him, but he must consult his own happiness; and so I say. When people talk to me, I say that papa is quite at liberty to consult his own happiness.'

'Thank you.'

Lucy did not understand the tone, and went on patronizing. 'And if they say you look younger than they expected, I don't object to that at all. I had rather you were not as old as Aunt Maria, or Miss Belmarche.'

'Who thinks me so young?'

'Oh! Aunt Maria, and grandmamma, and Mrs. Osborn, and all; but I don't mind that, it is only Sophy who says you look like a girl. Aunt Maria says Sophy has an unmanageable temper.'

'Don't you think you can let me find that out for myself?'

'I thought you wanted me to tell you about everybody.'

'Ah! but tell me of the good in your brother and sister.'

'I don't know how,' said Lucy. 'Gilbert is so tiresome, and so is Sophy. I heard Mary telling Jane, "I'm sure the new missus will have a heavy handful of those two."'

'And what of yourself?' said Albinia.

'Oh! I don't know,' said Lucy, modestly.

Mr. Kendal came in, and as Albinia looked at his pensive brow, she was oppressed by the thought of his sufferings in that dreary convalescence. At night, when she looked from her window, the fog hung white, like mildew over the pond, and she could not reason herself out of a spectral haunting fancy that sickness lurked in the heavy, misty atmosphere. She dreamt of it and the four babies, started, awoke, and had to recall all her higher trust to nable her vigour to chase off the oppressive imagination.

CHAPTER III.

Fog greeted Mrs. Kendal's eyes as she rose, and she resolved to make an attack on the pond without loss of time. But Mr. Kendal was absorbed nearly all breakfast-time in a letter from India, containing a scrap in some uncouth character. As he finished his last cup of tea, he looked up and said, 'A letter from my old friend Penrose, of Bombay—an inscription in the Salsette caves.'

'Have you seen the Salsette caves?

'Yes.'

She was longing to hear about them, but his horse was announced.

'You said you would be engaged in the morning while I ride out, Albinia?' he said, 'I shall return before luncheon. Gilbert, you had better go at once to Mr. Bowles. I shall order your pony to be ready when you come back.'

There was not a word of remonstrance, though the boy looked very disconsolate, and began to murmur the moment his father had gone. Albinia, who had regarded protection at a dentist's one of the offices of the head of a family, though dismayed at the task, told Gilbert that she would come with him in a moment. The girls exclaimed that no one thought of going with him, and fearing she had put an affront on his manliness, she asked what he would like, but could get no answer, only when Lucy scolded him for lingering, he said, 'I thought *she* was going with me.'

'Amiable,' thought Albinia, as she ran up to put on her bonnet; 'but I suppose toothache puts people out of the pale of civilization. And if he is thankless, is not that treating me more like a mother?'

Perhaps he had accepted her escort in hopes of deferring the evil hour, for he seemed discomfited to see her so quickly ready, and not grateful to his sisters, who hurried them by saying that Mr. Bowles would be gone out upon his rounds.

Mr. Bowles was amazed at the sight of Mrs. Kendal, and so elaborate in compliments and assurances that Mrs. Bowles would do herself the honour of calling, that Albinia, pitying Gilbert, called his attention back.

With him the apothecary was peremptory and facetious. 'He had expected that he should soon see him after his papa's return!' And with a 'soon be over,' he set him down, and Albinia bravely stood a desperate wringing of her hand at the tug of war. She was glad she had come, for the boy suffered a good deal, and was faint, and Mr. Bowles pronounced his mouth in no state for a ride to Tremblam.

'I must go,' said Gilbert, as they walked home, 'I wish papa would listen to anything.'

'He would not wish you to hurt yourself.'

'When papa says a thing—' began Gilbert.

'Well, Gilbert, you are quite right, and I hope you don't think I mean to teach you disobedience. But I do desire you, on my own responsibility, not to go and catch an inflammation in your jaw. I'll undertake papa.'

Gilbert at once became quite another creature. He discoursed so much, that she had to make him restore the handkerchief to his mouth; he held open the gate, showed her a shoal of minnows, and tried to persuade her to come round the garden before going in, but she clapped her hands at him, and hunted him back into the warm room, much impressed and delighted by his implicit obedience to his father. With Lucy and Sophy, his remaining seemed likewise to make a great sensation; they looked at Mrs. Kendal and whispered, and were evidently curious as to the result of her audacity. Albinia, who had grown up with her brother Maurice and cousin Frederick, was more used to boys than to girls, and was already more at ease with her son than her daughters.

Gilbert lent a ready hand with hammer and chisel, and boxes were opened, to the great delight and admiration of the girls. They were all very happy and busy setting things to rights, but Albinia was in difficulty how to bestow her books. There was an unaccountable scarcity both of books and book-cases; none were to be seen except that, in a chiffoniere in the drawing-room, there was a row in gilded bindings, chiefly Pope, Gray, and the like; and one which Albinia took out had pages which stuck together, a little pale blue string, faded at the end, and in the garlanded fly-leaf the inscription, 'To Miss Lucy Meadows, the reward of good conduct, December 20th, 1822.' The book seemed rather surprised at being opened, and Albinia let it close itself as Lucy said, 'Those are poor mamma's books, all the others are in the study. Come in, and I'll show you.'

She threw open the door, and Albinia entered. The study was shaded with a mass of laurels that kept out the sun, and made it look chill and sad, and the air in it was close. The round library-table was loaded with desks, pocket- books, and papers, the mantelpiece was covered with letters, and book- shelves mounted to the ceiling, filled with the learned and the poetical of new and old times.

Over the fireplace hung what it needed not Lucy's whisper to point out, as 'Poor mamma's picture.' It represented a very pretty girl, with dark eyes, brilliant colour, and small cherry mouth, painted in the exaggerated style usually called 'ridiculously like.'

Albinia's first feeling was that there was nothing in herself that could atone for the loss of so fair a creature, and the thought became more oppressive as she looked at a niche in the wall, holding a carved sandal-wood work-box, with a silver watch lying on it.

'Poor Edmund's watch,' said Lucy. 'It was given to him for a reward just before he was ill.'

Albinia tried to recover composure by reading the titles of the books. Suddenly, Lucy started and exclaimed, 'Come away. There he is!'

'Why come away?' said Albinia.

'I would not have him find me there for all the world.'

In all her vexation and dismay, Albinia could not help thinking of Bluebeard's closet. Her inclination was to stay where she was, and take her chance of losing her head, yet she felt as if she could not bear to be found invading a sanctuary of past recollections, and was relieved to find that it was a false alarm, though not relieved by the announcement that Admiral and Mrs. Osborn and the Miss Osborns were in the drawing-room.

'Before luncheon—too bad!' she exclaimed, as she hurried upstairs to wash off the dust of unpacking.

Ere she could hurry down, there was another inundation streaming across the hall, Mrs. Drury and three Miss Drurys, who, as she remembered, when they began to kiss her, were some kind of cousins.

There was talk, but Albinia could not give entire attention; she was watching for Mr. Kendal's return, that she might guard Gilbert from his displeasure, and the instant she heard him, she sprang up, and flew into the hall. He could not help brightening at the eager welcome, but when she told him of Mr. Bowles' opinion, he looked graver, and said, 'I fear you must not always attach credit to all Gilbert's reports.'

'Mr. Bowles told me himself that he must run no risk of inflammation.'

'You saw Mr. Bowles?'

'I went with Gilbert.'

'You? I never thought of your imposing so unpleasant a task on yourself. I fear the boy has been trespassing on your kindness.'

'No, indeed, he never asked me, but—' with a sort of laugh to hide the warmth excited by his pleased, grateful look, 'I thought it all in the day's work, only natural—'

She would have given anything to have had time to enjoy his epanchement de coeur at those words, bit she was obliged to add, 'Alas! there's all the world in the drawing-room!'

'Who?'

'Osborns and Drurys.'

'Do you want me?'

'I ran away on the plea of calling you.'

'I'll never do so again,' was her inward addition, as his countenance settled into the accustomed fixed look of abstraction, and as an unwilling victim he entered the room with her, and the visitors were 'dreadful enough' to congratulate him.

Albinia knew that it must be so unpleasant to him, that she blushed up to the roots of her hair, and could not look at anybody.

When she recovered, the first comers were taking leave, but the second set stayed on and on till past luncheon-time, and far past her patience, before the room was at last cleared.

Gilbert hurried in, and was received by his father with, 'You are very much obliged to her!'

'Indeed I am,' said Gilbert, in a winning, pleasant manner.

'I don't want you to be,' said Albinia, affectionately laying her arm on his shoulder. 'And now for luncheon—I pitied you, poor fellow; I thought you must have been famished.'

'Anything not to have all the Drurys at luncheon,' said Gilbert, confidentially, 'I had begun to wish myself at Tremblam.'

'By the bye,' said Mr. Kendal, waking as he sat down at the bottom of the table, 'how was it that the Drurys did not stay to luncheon?'

'Was that what they were waiting for?' exclaimed Albinia. 'Poor people, I had no notion of that.'

'They do have luncheon here in general,' said Mr. Kendal, as if not knowing exactly how it came to pass.

'O yes,' said Lucy; 'Sarah Anne asked me whether we ate wedding-cake every day.'

'Poor Miss Sarah Anne!' said Albinia, laughing. 'But one cannot help feeling inhospitable when people come so unconscionably early, and cut up all one's morning.'

The door was again besieged by visitors, just as they were all going out to make the round of the garden, and it was not till half-past four that the succession ceased, and Albinia was left to breathe freely, and remember how often Maurice had called her to order for intolerance of morning calls.

'And not the only people I cared to see,' she said, 'the Dusautoys and Nugents. But they have too much mercy to call the first day.'

Mr. Kendal looked as if his instinct were drawing him study-wards, but Albinia hung on his arm, and made him come into the garden. Though devoid of Winifred's gardening tastes, she was dismayed at the untended look of the flower-beds. The laurels were too high, and seemed to choke the narrow space, and the turf owed its verdant appearance to damp moss. She had made but few steps before the water squished under her feet, and impelled her to exclaim, 'What a pity this pond should not be filled up!'

'Filled up!—'

'Yes, it would be so much less damp. One might drain it off into the river, and then we should get rid of the fog.'

And she began actively to demonstrate the convenient slope, and the beautiful flower-bed that might be made in its place. Mr. Kendal answered with a few assenting sounds and complacent looks, and Albinia, accustomed to a brother with whom to assent was to act, believed the matter was in train, and that pond and fever would be annihilated.

The garden opened into a meadow with a causeway leading to a canal bank, where there was a promising country walk, but the cruel visitors had left no time for exploring, and Albinia had to return home and hurry up her arrangements before there was space to turn round in her room—even then it was not what Winifred could have seen without making a face.

Mr. Kendal had read aloud to his wife in the evening during the stay at the sea-side, and she was anxious not to let the habit drop. He liked it, and read beautifully, and she thought it good for the children. She therefore begged him to read, catching him on the way to his study, and coaxing him to stay no longer than to find a book. He brought Schlegel's Philosophy of History. She feared that it was above the young ones, but it was delightful to herself, and the custom had better be established before it was perilled by attempts to adapt it to the children. Lucy and Sophy seemed astonished and displeased, and their whispers had to be silenced, Gilbert learnt his lessons apart. Albinia rallied her spirits, and insisted to herself that she did not feel discouraged.

Monday had gone, or rather Albinia had been robbed of it by visitors—now for a vigorous Tuesday. Her unpacking and her setting to rights were not half over, but as the surface was habitable, she resolved to finish at her leisure, and sacrifice no more mornings of study.

So after she had lingered at the door, to delight Gilbert by admiring his pony, she returned to the dining-room, where the girls were loading a small table in the window with piles of books and exercises, and Lucy was standing, looking all eagerness to show off her drawings.

'Yes, my dear, but first we had better read. I have been talking to your papa, and we have settled that on Wednesdays and Fridays we will go to church; but on these days we will begin by reading the Psalms and Lessons.'

'Oh,' said Lucy, 'we never do that, except when we are at grandmamma's.'

'Pray are you too old or too young for it?' said Albinia.

'We did it to please grandmamma,' said Sophy.

'Now you will do it to please me,' said Albinia, 'if for no better reason. Fetch your Bibles and Prayerbooks.'

'We shall never have time for our studies, I assure you, mamma,' objected Lucy.

'That is not your concern,' said Albinia, her spirit rising at the girls' opposition. 'I wish for obedience.'

Lucy went, Sophy leant against the table like a post. Albinia regretted that the first shot should have been fired for such a cause, and sat perplexing herself whether it were worse to give way, or to force the girls to read Holy Scripture in such a mood.

Lucy came flying down with the four books in her hands, and began officiously opening them before her sister, and exhorting her not to give way to sullenness—she ought to like to read the Bible—which of course made Sophy look crosser. The desire to establish her authority conquered the scruple about reverence. Albinia set them to read, and suffered for it. Lucy road flippantly; Sophy in the hoarse, dull, dogged voice of a naughty boy. She did not dare to expostulate, lest she should exasperate the tempers that she had roused.

'Never mind,' she thought, 'when the institution is fixed, they will be more amenable.'

She tried a little examination afterwards, but not one answer was to be extracted from Sophy, and Lucy knew far less than the first class at Fairmead, and made her replies wide of the mark, with an air of satisfaction that nearly overthrew the young step-mother's patience.

When Albinia took her Bible upstairs, she gave Sophy time to say what Lucy reported instantly on her entrance.

'Dear me, mamma, here is Sophy declaring that you ought to be a charity-schoolmistress. You wont be angry with her, but it is so funny!'

'If you were at my charity school, Lucy,' said Albinia, 'the first lesson I should give you would be against telling tales.'

Lucy subsided.

Albinia turned to Sophy. 'My dear,' she said, 'perhaps I pressed this on when you were not prepared for it, but I have always been used to think of it as a duty.'

Sophy made no answer, but her moody attitude relaxed, and Albinia took comfort in the hope that she might have been gracious if she had known how to set about it.

'I suppose Miss Belmarche is a Roman Catholic,' she said, wishing to account for this wonderful ignorance, and addressing herself to Sophy; but Lucy, whom she thought she had effectually put down, was up again in a moment like a Jack-in-a-box.

'O yes, but not Genevieve. Her papa made it his desire that she should be brought up a Protestant. Wasn't it funny? You know Genevieve is Madame Belmarche's grand-daughter, and Mr. Durant was a dancing-master.'

'Madame Belmarche's father and brother were guillotined,' continued Sophy.

'Ah! then she is an emigrant?'

'Yes. Miss Belmarche has always kept school here. Our own mamma, and Aunt Maria went to school to her, and Miss Celeste Belmarche married Mr. Durant, a dancing-master—she was French teacher in a school in London where he taught, and Madame Belmarche did not approve, for she and her husband were something very grand in France, so they waited and waited ever so long, and when at last they did marry, they were quite old, and she died very soon; and they say he never was happy again, and pined away till he really did die of grief, and so Genevieve came to her grandmamma to be brought up.'

'Poor child! How old is she?'

'Fifteen,' said Lucy. 'She teaches in the school. She is not at all pretty, and such a queer little thing.'

'Was her father French?'

'No,' said Sophy.

'Yes,' said Lucy. 'You know nothing about it, Sophy. He was French, but of the Protestant French sort, that came to England a great many years ago, when they ran away from the Sicilian Vespers, or the Edict of Nantes, I don't remember which; only the Spitalfields weavers have something to do with it. However, at any rate Genevieve has got something in a drawer up in her own room that she is very secret about, and wont show to anybody.'

'I think it is something that somebody was killed with,' said Sophy, in a low voice.

'Dear me, if it is, I am sure it is quite wicked to keep it. I shall be quite afraid to go into her room, and you know I slept there all the time of the fever.'

'It did not hurt you,' said Sophy.

Albinia had been strongly interested by the touching facts, so untouchingly narrated, and by the characteristic account of the Huguenot emigration, but it suddenly occurred to her that she was promoting gossip, and she returned to business. Lucy showed off her attainments with her usual self-satisfaction. They were what might be expected from a second-rate old-fashioned young ladies' school, where nothing was good but the French pronunciation. She was evidently considered a great proficient, and her glib mediocrity was even more disheartening than the ungracious carelessness or dulness—there was no knowing which—that made her sister figure wretchedly in the examination. However, there was little time—the door-bell rang at a quarter to twelve, and Mrs. Wolfe was in the drawing-room.

'I told you so,' whispered Lucy, exultingly.

'This is unbearable,' cried Albinia. 'I shall give notice that I am always engaged in the morning.'

She desired each young lady to work a sum in her absence, and left them to murmur, if they were so disposed. Perhaps it was Lucy's speech that made her inflict the employment; at any rate, her spirit was not as serene as she could have desired.

Mr. Kendal was quite willing that she should henceforth shut her door against company in the morning; that is to say, he bowed his head assentingly. She was begging him to take a walk with her, when, at another sound of the bell, he made a precipitate retreat into his study. The visitors were the Belmarche family. The old lady was dark and withered, small, yet in look and air, with a certain nobility and grandeur that carried Albinia back in a moment to the days of hoops and trains, of powder and high-heeled shoes, and made her feel that the sweeping courtesy had come straight from the days of Marie Antoinette, and that it was an honour and distinction conferred by a superior —superior, indeed, in all the dignity of age, suffering, and constancy.

Albinia blushed, and took her hand with respect very unlike the patronizing airs of Bayford Bridge towards 'poor old Madame Belmarche,' and with downcast eyes, and pretty embarrassment, heard the stately compliments of the ancien regime.

Miss Belmarche was not such a fine specimen of Sevres porcelain as her mother. She was a brown, dried, small woman, having lost, or never possessed, her country's taste in dress, and with a rusty bonnet over the tight, frizzly curls of her front, too thin and too scantily robed to have any waist, and speaking English too well for the piquant grace of her mother's speech. Poor lady! born an exile, she had toiled, and struggled for a whole lifetime to support her mother; but though care had worn her down, there was still vivacity in her quick little black eyes, and though her teeth were of a dreadful colour, her laugh was so full of life and sweetness, that Albinia felt drawn towards her in a moment.

Silent and demure, plainly dressed in an old dark merino, and a white-ribboned faded bonnet, sat a little figure almost behind her grandmother. Her face had the French want of complexion, but the eyes were of the deepest, most lustrous hue of grey, almost as dark as the pupils, and with the softness of long dark eyelashes—beautiful eyes, full of light and expression—and as she moved towards the table, there was a finish and delicacy about the whole form and movements, that made her a most pleasing object.

But Albinia could not improve her acquaintance, for in flowed another party of visitors, and Madame curtsied herself out again, Albinia volunteering that she would soon come to see her, and being answered, 'You will do me too much honour.'

Another afternoon devoured by visitors! Every one seemed to have come except the persons who would have been most welcome, Mr. Dusautoy, and Winifred's friends, the Nugents.

When, at four o'clock, she had shaken hands with the last guest, she gave a hearty yawn, jumped up and shook herself, as she exclaimed, 'There! There! that is done! I wonder whether your papa would come out now?'

'He is in his study,' said the girls.

Albinia thought of knocking and calling at the door, but somehow it seemed impossible, and she decided on promenading past his window to show that she was ready for him. But alas! those evergreens! She could not see in, and probably he could not see out.

'Ha!' cried Lucy, as they pursued their walk into the kitchen garden, 'here are some asparagus coming up. Grandmamma always has our first asparagus.'

Albinia was delighted to find such an opening. Out came her knife—they would cut the heads and take them up at once; but when the tempting white-stalked, pink-tipped bundle had been made up and put into a basket, a difficulty arose.

'I'll call the boy to take it,' said Lucy.

'What, when we are going ourselves?' said Albinia.

'Oh! but we can't.'

'Why? Do you think we shall break down under the weight?'

'O no, but people will stare.'

'Why—what should they stare at?'

'It looks *so* to carry a basket—'

Albinia burst into one of her merriest peals of laughing.

'Not carry a basket! My dear, I have looked *so* all the days of my life. Bayford must endure the spectacle, so it may as well begin at once.'

'But, dear mamma—'

'I'm not asking you to carry it. O no, I only hope you don't think it too ungenteel to walk with me. But the notion of calling a boy away from his work, to carry a couple of dozen asparagus when an able-bodied woman is going that way herself!'

Albinia was so tickled that she could hardly check herself, even when she saw Lucy looking distressed and hurt, and little laughs would break out every moment as she beheld the young lady keeping aloof, as if ashamed of her company, turning towards the steep church steps, willing at least to hide the dreadful sight from the High Street.

Just as they had entered the narrow alley, they heard a hasty tread, and almost running over them with his long strides, came Mr. Dusautoy. He brought himself up short, just in time, and exclaimed, 'I beg your pardon—Mrs. Kendal, I believe. Could you be kind enough to give me a glass of brandy?'

Albinia gave a great start, as well she might.

'I was going to fetch one,' quickly proceeded Mr. Dusautoy, 'but your house is nearer. A poor man—there—just come home—been on the tramp for work—quite exhausted—' and he pointed to one of the cottages.

'I'll fetch it at once,' cried Albinia.

'Thank you,' he said, as they crossed the street. 'This poor fellow has had nothing all day, has walked from Hadminster—just got home, sank down quite worn out, and there is nothing in the house but dry bread. His wife wants something nearly as much as he does.'

In the excitement, Albinia utterly forgot all scruples about 'Bluebeard's closet.' She hurried into the house, and made but one dash, standing before her astonished husband's dreamy eyes, exclaiming, 'Pray give me the key of the cellaret; there's a poor man just come home, fainting with exhaustion, Mr. Dusautoy wants some brandy for him.'

Like a man but half awake, obeying an apparition, Mr. Kendal put his hand into his pocket and gave her the key. She was instantly opening the cellaret, seeking among the bottles, and asking questions all the time. She proposed taking a jug of the kitchen-tea then in operation, and Mr. Dusautoy caught at the idea, so that poor Lucy beheld the dreadful spectacle of the vicar bearing a can full of steaming tea, and Mrs. Kendal a small cup with the 'spirituous liquor.' What was the asparagus to this?

Albinia told her to go on to Mrs. Meadows', and that she should soon follow. She intended to have gone the moment that she had carried in the cup, leaving Mr. Dusautoy in the cottage, but the poor trembling frightened wife needed woman's sympathy and soothing, and she waited to comfort her, and to see the pair more able to enjoy the meeting, in their tidy, but bare and damp-looking cottage. She promised broth for the morrow, and took her leave, the vicar coming away at the same time.

'Thank you,' he said, warmly, as they came out, and turned to mount the hill together.

'May I go and call on them again?'

'It will be very kind in you. Poor Simkins is a steady, good sort of fellow, but a clumsy workman, down-hearted, and with poor health, and things have been untoward with him.'

'People, who do not prosper in the world are not always the worst,' said Albinia.

'No, indeed, and these are grateful, warm-hearted people that you will like, if you can get over the poor woman's lackadaisical manner. But you are used to all that,' he added, smiling. 'I see you know what poor folk are made of.'

'I have been living among them nearly all my days,' said Albinia. 'I hope you will give me something to do, I should be quite forlorn without it;' and she looked up to his kind, open face, as much at home with him as if she had known, him for years.

'Fanny—my wife—shall find work for you,' he said. 'You must excuse her calling on you, she is never off the sofa, but—' And what a bright look he gave! as much as to say that his wife *on* the sofa was better than any one else *off*. 'I was hoping to call some of these afternoons,' he continued, 'but I have had little time, and Fanny thought your door was besieged enough already.'

'Thank you,' said Albinia; 'I own I thought it was your kindness in leaving me a little breathing time. And would Mrs. Dusautoy be able to see me if I were to call?'

'She would be delighted. Suppose you were to come in at once.'

'I wish I could, but I must go on to Mrs. Meadows'. If I were to come to-morrow?'

'Any time—any time,' he said. 'She is always at home, and she has been much better since we came here. We were too much in the town at Lauriston.'

Mr. Dusautoy, having a year ago come out of the diocese where had been Albinia's home, they had many common friends, and plunged into 'ecclesiastical intelligence,' with a mutual understanding of the topics most often under discussion, that made Albinia quite in her element. 'A great Newfoundland dog of a man in size, and countenance, and kindness,' thought she. 'If his wife be worthy of him, I shall reck little of all the rest.'

Her tread the gayer for this resumption of old habits, she proceeded to Mrs. Meadows', where the sensation created by her poor little basket justified Lucy's remonstrance. There were regrets, and assurances that the girl could have come in a moment, and that she need not have troubled herself, and her laughing declarations that it was no trouble were disregarded, except that the old lady said, in gentle excuse to her daughter, that Mrs. Kendal had always lived in the country, where people could do as they pleased.

'I mean to do as I please here,' said Albinia, laughing; but the speech was received with silent discomfiture that made her heartily regret it. She disdained to explain it away; she was beginning to hold Mrs. and Miss Meadows too cheap to think it worth while.

'Well,' said Mrs. Meadows, as if yielding up the subject, 'things may be different from what they were in my time.'

'Oh! mamma—Mrs. Kendal—I am sure—' Albinia let Maria flounder, but she only found her way out of the speech with 'Well! and is not it the most extraordinary!—Mr. Dusautoy—so rude—'

'I should not wonder if you found me almost as extraordinary as Mr. Dusautoy,' said Albinia.

Why would Miss Meadows always nettle her into saying exactly the wrong thing, so as to alarm and distress the old lady? That want of comprehension of playfulness was a strangely hard trial. She turned to Mrs. Meadows and tried to reassure her by saying, 'You know I have been always in the clerical line myself, so I naturally take the part of the parson.'

'Yes, my dear,' said Mrs. Meadows. 'I dare say Mr. Dusautoy is a very good man, but I wish he would allow his poor delicate wife more butcher's meat, and I don't think it looks well to see the vicarage without a man- servant.'

Albinia finally made her escape, and while wondering whether she should ever visit that house without tingling with irritation with herself and with the inmates, Lucy exclaimed, 'There, you see I was right. Grandmamma and Aunt Maria were surprised when I told them that you said you were an able- bodied woman.'

What would not Albinia have given for Winifred to laugh with her? What to do now she did not know, so she thought it best not to hear, and to ask the way to a carpenter's shop to order some book-shelves.

She was more uncomfortable after she came home, for by the sounds when Mr. Kendal next emerged from his study, she found that he had locked himself in, to guard against further intrusion. And when she offered to return to him the key of the cellaret, he quietly replied that he should prefer her retaining it,—not a formidable answer in itself, but one which, coupled with the locking of the door, proved to her that she might do anything rather than invade his privacy.

Now Maurice's study was the thoroughfare of the household, the place for all parish preparations unpresentable in the drawing-room, and Albinia was taken by surprise. She grew hot and cold. Had she done anything wrong? Could he care for her if he could lock her out?

'I will not be morbid, I will not be absurd,' said she to herself, though the tears stood in her eyes. 'Some men do not like to be rushed in upon! It may be only habit. It may have been needful here. It is base to take petty offences, and set up doubts.'

And Mr. Kendal's tender manner when they were again together, his gentle way of addressing her, and a sort of shy caress, proved that he was far from all thought of displeasure; nay, he might be repenting of his momentary annoyance, though he said nothing.

Albinia went to inquire after the sick man at her first leisure moment, and while talking kindly to the wife, and hearing her troubles, was surprised at the forlorn rickety state of the building, the broken pavement, damp walls, and door that would not shut, because the frame had sunk out of the perpendicular.

'Can't you ask your landlord to do something to the house?'

'It is of no use, ma'am, Mr. Pettilove never will do nothing. Perhaps if you would be kind enough to say a word to him, ma'am—'

'Mr. Pettilove, the lawyer? I'll try if Mr. Kendal can say anything to him. It really is a shame to leave a house in this condition.'

Thanks were so profuse, that she feared that she was supposed to possess some power of amelioration. The poor woman even insisted on conducting her up a break-neck staircase to see the broken ceiling, whence water often streamed in plentifully from the roof.

Her mind full of designs against the cruel landlord, she speeded up the hill, exhilarated by each step she took into the fresh air, to the garden-gate, which she was just unhasping when the hearty voice of the Vicar was heard behind her. 'Mrs. Kendal! I told Fanny you would come.'

Instead of taking her to the front door he conducted her across a sloping lawn towards a French window open to the bright afternoon sunshine.

'Here she is, here is Mrs. Kendal!' he said, sending his voice before him, as they came in sight of the pretty little drawing-room, where through the gay chintz curtains, she saw the clear fire shining upon half-a-dozen school girls, ranged opposite to a couch. 'Ah!' as he perceived them, 'shall I take her for a turn in the garden while you finish your lesson?'

'One moment, if you please. I did not know it was so late,' and a face as bright as all the rest was turned towards the window.

'Ah! give her her scholars, and she never knows how time passes,' said Mr. Dusautoy. 'But step this way, and I'll show you the best view in Bayford.' He took her up a step or two, to a little turfed mound, where there was a rustic seat commanding the whole exquisite view of river, vale, and woodland, with the church tower rising in the foreground. The wind blew pleasantly, chasing the shadows of the clouds across the open space. Albinia was delighted to feel it fan her brow, and her eager exclamations contented Mr. Dusautoy. 'Yes,' he said, 'it was all Fanny's notion. She planned it all last summer when I took her round the garden. It is wonderful what an eye she has! I only hope when the dry weather comes, that I shall be able to get her up there to enjoy it.'

On coming down they found that Mrs. Dusautoy had dismissed her class, and come out to a low, long-backed sloping garden-seat at the window. She was very little and slight, a mere doll in proportion to her great husband, who could lift her as easily and tenderly as a baby, paying her a sort of reverential deference and fond admiration that rendered them a beautiful sight, in such full, redoubled measure was his fondness repaid by the little, clever, fairy-looking woman, with her playful manner, high spirits, keen wit, and the active habits that even confirmed invalidism could not destroy. She had small deadly white hands, a fair complexion, that varied more than was good for her, pretty, though rather sharp and irregular features, and hazel eyes dancing with merriment, and face and figure at some years above thirty, would have suited a girl of twenty. To see Mr. Dusautoy bringing her footstools, shawls, and cushions, and to remember the accusation of starvation, was almost irresistibly ludicrous.

'Now, John, you had better have been giving Mrs. Kendal a chair all this time.'

'Mrs. Kendal will excuse,' said Mr. Dusautoy, as he brought her a seat.

'Mrs. Kendal has excused,' said Mrs. Dusautoy, bursting into a merry fit of laughter. 'Oh, I never heard anything more charming than your introduction! I beg your pardon, but I laughed last evening till I was worn out, and waked in the night laughing again.'

It was exhilarating to find that any one laughed at Bayford, and Albinia partook of the mirth with all her heart. 'Never was an address more gratifying to me!' she said.

'It was like him! so unlike Bayford! So bold a venture!' continued Mrs. Dusautoy amid peals of laughter.

'What is there to laugh at?' said Mr. Dusautoy, putting on a look between merriment and simplicity. 'What else could I have done? I should have done the same whoever I had met.'

'Ah! now he is afraid of your taking it as too great a compliment! To do him justice I believe he would, but the question is, what answer he would have had.'

'Nobody could have refused—' began Albinia.

'Oh!' cried Mrs. Dusautoy. 'Little you know Bayford.

'Fanny! Fanny! this is too bad. Madame Belmarche—'

'Would have had nothing but eau sucre! No, John, decidedly you and Simkins fell upon your legs, and you had better take credit for your "admirable sagacity."'.

'I like the people,' said Albinia, 'but they never can be well while they live in such a shocking place. It is quite a disgrace to Bayford.'

'It is in a sad state,' said Mr. Dusautoy.

'I know I should like to set my brother upon that Mr. Pettilove, who they say will do nothing,' exclaimed Albinia.

The Vicar was going to have said something, but a look from his wife checked him. Albinia was sorry for it, as she detected a look of suppressed amusement on Mrs. Dusautoy's face. 'I mean to ask Mr. Kendal what can be done,' she said; 'and in the meantime, to descend from what we can't do to what we can. Mr. Dusautoy told me to come to you for orders.'

'And I told Mr. Dusautoy that I should give you none.'

'Oh! that is hard.'

'If you could have heard him! He thought he *had* got a working lady at last, and he would have had no mercy upon you. One would have imagined that Mr. Kendal had brought you here for his sole behoof!'

'Then I shall look to you, Mr. Dusautoy.'

'No, I believe she is quite right,' he said. 'She says you ought to undertake nothing till you have had time to see what leisure you have to give us.'

'Nay, I have been used to think the parish my business, home my leisure.'

'Yes,' said Mrs. Dusautoy, 'but then you were the womankind of the clergy, now you are a laywoman.'

'I think you have work at home,' said the Vicar.

'Work, but not work *enough!*' cried Albinia. 'The girls will help me; only tell me what I may do.'

'I say, "what you can,"' said Mrs. Dusautoy. 'You see before you a single-handed man. Only two of the ladies here can be called coadjutors, one being poor little Genevieve Durant, the other the bookseller's daughter, Clarissa Richardson, who made all the rest fly off. All the others do what good they mean to do according to their own sweet will, free and independent women, and we can't have any district system, so I think you can only do what just comes to hand.'

Most heartily did Albinia undertake all that Mrs. Dusautoy would let her husband assign to her.

'Yes, John is a strong temptation,' said the bright little invalid, 'but you must let Mrs. Kendal find out in a month's time whether she has work enough.'

'I could think my wise brother Maurice had been cautioning you,' said Albinia, taking leave as of an old friend, for indeed she felt more at home with Mrs. Dusautoy than with any acquaintance she had made in Bayford.

Albinia told her husband of the state of the cottages, and railed at Mr. Pettilove much to her own satisfaction. Mr. Kendal answered, 'He would see about it,' an answer of which Albinia had yet to learn the import.

CHAPTER IV.

There are some characters so constituted, that of them the old proverb, that Love is blind, is perfectly true; they can see no imperfection in the mind or body of those dear to them. There are others in whom the strongest affections do not destroy clearness of vision, who see their friends on all sides, and perceive their faults and foibles, without loving them the less.

Albinia Kendal was a person of the latter description. It might almost be called her temptation, that her mind beheld all that came before it in a clear, and a humorous light, such as only a disposition overflowing with warm affection and with the energy of kindness, could have prevented from bordering upon censoriousness. She had imagination, but it was not such as to make an illusion of the present, or to interfere with her almost satirical good sense. Happily, religion and its earthly manifestation—charity regulated her, taught her to fear to judge lest she should be judged, strengthened her naturally fond affections, and tempered the keenness that disappointment might soon have turned to sourness. The tongue, the temper, and the judgment knew their own tendencies, and a guard was set over them; and if the sentinel were ever torpid or deceived, repentance paid the penalty.

She had not long seen her husband at home before she had involuntarily completed her view of his character. Nature must have designed him for a fellow of a college, where, apart from all cares, he might have collected fragments of forgotten authors, and immortalized his name by some edition of a Greek Lyric poet, known by four poems and a half, and two-thirds of a line quoted somewhere else. In such a controversy, lightened by perpetually polished poems, by a fair amount of modern literature, select college friendships, and methodical habits, Edmund Kendal would have been in his congenial element, lived and died, and had his portrait hung up as one of the glories of his college.

But he had been carried off from school, before he had done more than prove his unusual capacity. All his connexions were Indian, and his father, who had not seen him since his earliest childhood, offered him no choice but an appointment in the civil service. He had one stimulus; he had seen Lucy Meadows in the radiant glory of girlish beauty, and had fastened on her all a poet's dreams, deepening and becoming more fervid in the recesses of a reserved heart, which did not easily admit new sensations. That stimulus carried him out cheerfully to India, and quickened his abilities, so that he exerted himself sufficiently to obtain a lucrative situation early in life. He married, and his household must have been on the German system, all the learning on one side, all the domestic cares on the other. The understanding and refinement wanting in his wife, he believed to be wanting in all women. As resident at a small remote native court in India, he saw no female society such as could undeceive him; and subsequently his Bayford life had not raised his standard of womankind. A perfect gentleman, his superiority was his own work, rather than that of station or education, and so he had never missed intercourse with really ladylike or cultivated, female minds, expected little from wife, or daughters, or neighbours; had a few learned friends, but lived within himself. He had acquired a competence too soon, and had the great misfortune of property without duties to present themselves obviously. He had nothing to do but to indulge his naturally indolent scholarly tastes, which, directed as they had been to Eastern languages, had even less chance of sympathy among his neighbours than if they had been classical. Always reserved, and seldom or never meeting with persons who could converse with him, he had lapsed into secluded habits, and learnt to shut himself up in his study and exclude every one, that he might have at least a refuge from the gossip and petty cares that reigned everywhere else. So seldom was anything said worth his attention, that he never listened to what was passing, and had learnt to say 'very well'—'I'll see about it,' without even knowing what was said to him.

But though his wife had been no companion, the illusion had never died away, he had always loved her devotedly, and her loss had shattered all his present rest and comfort; as entirely as the death of his son had taken from him hope and companionship.

What a home it must have been, with Lucy reigning over it in her pert self-sufficiency, Gilbert and Sophy running riot and squabbling, and Maria Meadows coming in on them with her well-meant worries and persecutions!

When taken away from the scene of his troubles, his spirits revived; afraid to encounter his own household alone, he had thought Albinia the cure for everything. But at home, habit and association had proved too strong for her presence—the grief, which he had tried to leave behind, had waited ready to meet him on the threshold, and the very sense that it was a melancholy welcome added to his depression, and made him less able to exert himself. The old sorrows haunted the walls of the house, and above all the study, and tarried not in seizing on their unresisting victim. Melancholy was in his nature, his indolence gave it force, and his habits were almost ineffaceable, and they were habits of quiet selfishness, formed by a resolute, though inert will, and fostered by an adoring wife. A youth spent in India had not given him ideas of responsibilities beyond his own family, and his principles, though sound, had not expanded the views of duty with which he had started in life.

It was a positive pleasure to Albinia to discover that there had been an inefficient clergyman at Bayford before Mr. Dusautoy, and to know that during half the time that the present vicar had held the living, Mr. Kendal had been absent, so that his influence had had no time to work. She began to understand her line of action. It must be her effort, in all loving patience and gentleness, to raise her husband's spirits and rouse his faculties; to make his powers available for the good of his fellow-creatures, to make him an active and happy man, and to draw him and his children together. This was truly a task to make her heart throb high with hope and energy. Strong and brave was that young heart, and not self-confident—the difficulty made her only the more hopeful, because she saw it was her duty. She was secure of her influence with him. If he did exclude her from his study, he left her supreme elsewhere, and though she would have given the world that their sovereignty might be a joint one *everywhere*, still she allowed much for the morbid inveterate habit of dreading disturbance. When he began by silence and not listening, she could always rouse him, and give him animation, and he was so much surprised and pleased whenever she entered into any of his pursuits, that she had full hope of drawing him out.

One day when the fog, instead of clearing off had turned to violent rain, Albinia had been out on parish work, and afterwards enlivening old Mrs. Meadows by dutifully spending an hour with her, while Maria was nursing a nervous headache—she had been subject to headaches ever since…an ominous sigh supplied the rest.

But all the effect of Albinia's bright kindness was undone, when the grandmother learnt that Gilbert was gone to his tutor, and would have to come home in the rain, and she gave such an account of his exceeding delicacy, that Albinia became alarmed, and set off at once that she might consult his father about sending for him.

Her opening of the hall door was answered by Mr. Kendal emerging from his study. He was looking restless and anxious, came to meet her, and uncloaked her, while he affectionately scolded her for being so venturesome. She told him where she had been, and he smiled, saying, 'You are a busy spirit! But you must not be too imprudent.'

'Oh, nothing hurts me. It is poor Gilbert that I am anxious about.'

'So am I. Gilbert has not a constitution fit for exposure. I wish he were come home.'

'Could we not send for him? Suppose we sent a fly.'

He was consenting with a pleased smile, when the door opened, and there stood the dripping Gilbert, completely wet through, pale and chilled, with his hair plastered down, and his coat stuck all over with the horse's short hair.

'You must go to bed at once, Gilbert,' said his father. 'Are you cold?'

'Very. It was such a horrid driving wind, and I rode so fast,' said Gilbert; violently shivering, as they helped to pull him out of his great coat; he put his hand to his mouth, and said that his face ached. Mr. Kendal was very anxious, and Albinia hurried the boy up to bed, and meantime ordered quickly a basin of the soup preparing for dinner, warmed some worsted socks at the fire, and ran upstairs with them.

He seemed to have no substance in him; he had hardly had energy to undress himself, and she found him with his face hidden on the pillow, shivering audibly, and actually crying. She was aghast.

The boys with whom she had been brought up, would never have given way so entirely without resistance; but between laughing, cheering, scolding, covering him up close, and rubbing his hands with her own, she comforted him, so that he could be grateful and cheerful when his father himself came up with the soup. Albinia noticed a sort of shudder pass over Mr. Kendal as he entered, and he stood close by Gilbert, turning his back on everything else, while he watched the boy eat the soup, as if restored by every spoonful. 'That was a good thought,' was his comment to his wife, and the look of gratitude brought a flush of pleasure into her cheek.

Of all the dinners, this was the most pleasant; he was more gentle and affectionate, and she made him tell her about the Persian poets, and promise to show her some specimens of the Rose Garden of Saadi—she had never before been so near having his pursuits opened to her.

'What a favourite Gilbert is!' Lucy said to Sophia, as Albinia lighted a candle and went up to his room.

'He makes such a fuss,' said Sophy. 'What is there in being wet through to cry about?'

Albinia heard a little shuffle as she opened the door, and Gilbert pushed a book under his pillow. She asked him what he had been reading. 'Oh,' he said, 'he had not been doing it long, for the flickering of the candle hurt his eyes.'

'Yes, you had better not,' said Albinia, moving the flaring light to a less draughty part of the dingy whitewashed attic. 'Or shall I read to you?'

'Are you come to stay with me?' cried the boy, raising himself up to look after her, as she moved about the room and stood looking from the window over the trees at the water meadows, now flooded into a lake, and lighted by the beams of a young moon.

'I can stay till your father is ready for tea,' said Albinia, coming nearer. 'Let me see whether your hands are hot.'

She found her own hand suddenly clasped, and pressed to his lips, and then, as if ashamed, he turned his face away; nor would she betray her pleasure in it, but merely said, 'Shall I go on with your book!'

'No,' said he, wearily turning his reddened cheek to the other side. 'I only took it because it is so horrid lying here thinking.'

'I am very sorry to hear it. Do you know, Gibbie, that it is said there is nothing more lamentable than for a man not to like to have his own thoughts for his company,' said she, gaily.

'Ah! but—!' said Gilbert. 'If I lie here alone, I'm always looking out there,' and he pointed to the opposite recess. She looked, but saw nothing. 'Don't you know?' he said.

'Edmund?' she asked.

He grasped her hands in both his own. 'Aye! Ned used to sleep there. I always look for him there.'

'Do you mean that you would rather have another room? I would manage it directly.'

'O no, thank you, I like it for some things. Take the candle—look by the shutter—cut out in the wood.'

The boys' scoring of 'E. & G. K.,' was visible there.

'Papa has taken all he could of Edmund's,' said Gilbert, 'but he could not take that! No, I would not have any other room if you were to give me the best in the house.'

'I am sure not! But, my dear, considering what Edmund was, surely they should be gentle, happy thoughts that the room should give you.'

He shuddered, and presently said, 'Do you know what?' and paused; then continued, with an effort, getting tight hold of her hand, 'Just before Edmund died—he lay out there—I lay here—he sat up all white in bed, and he called out, clear and loud, "Mamma, Gilbert"—I saw him—and then—he was dead! And you know mamma did die—and I'm sure I shall!' He had worked himself into a trembling fit, hid his face and sobbed.

'But you have not died of the fever.'

'Yes—but I know it means that I shall die young! I am sure it does! It was a call! I heard Nurse say it was a call!'

What was to be done with such a superstition? Albinia did not think it would be right to argue it away. It might be in truth a warning to him to guard his ways—a voice from the twin-brother, to be with him through life. She knelt down by him, and kissed his forehead.

'Dear Gilbert,' she said, 'we all shall die.'

'Yes, but I shall die young.'

'And if you should. Those are happy who die young. How much pain your baby-brother and sisters have missed! How happy Edmund is now!'

'Then you really think it meant that I shall' he cried, tremblingly. 'O don't! I can't die!'

'Your brother called on what he loved best,' said Albinia. 'It may mean nothing. Or rather, it may mean that your dear twin-brother is watching for you, I am sure he is, to have you with him, for what makes your mortal life, however long, seem as nothing. It was a call to you to be as pure on earth as he is in heaven. O Gilbert, how good you should be!'

Gilbert did not know whether it frightened him or soothed him to see his superstition treated with respect—neither denied, nor reasoned away. But the ghastliness was not in the mere fear that death might not be far off.

The pillow had turned a little on one side—Albinia tried to smooth it—the corner of a book peeped out. It was a translation of The Three Musqueteers, one of the worst and most fascinating of Dumas' romances.

'You wont tell papa!' cried Gilbert, raising himself, in far more real and present terror than he had previously shown.

'How did you get it? Whose is it?'

'It is my own. I bought it at Richardson's. It is very funny. But you wont tell papa? I never was told not; indeed I was not.'

'Now, Gilbert dear, will you tell me a few things? I do only wish what is good for you. Why don't you wish that papa should hear of this book?'

Gilbert writhed himself.

'You know he would not like it?'

'Then why did you take to reading it?'

'Oh!' cried the boy, 'if you only did know how stupid and how miserable it has been! More than half myself gone, and Sophy always glum, and Lucy always plaguing, and Aunt Maria always being a torment, you would not wonder at one's doing anything to forget it!'

'Yes, but why do what you knew to be wrong?'

'Nobody told me not.'

'Disobedience to the spirit, then, if not to the letter. It was not the way to be happier, my poor boy, nor nearer to your brother and mother.'

'Things didn't use to be stupid when Ned was there!' sobbed Gilbert, bursting into a fresh flood of tears.

'Ah! Gilbert, I grieved most of all for *you* when first I heard your story, before I thought I should ever have anything to do with you,' said Albinia, hanging over him fondly. 'I always thought it must be so forlorn to be a twin left solitary. But it is sadder still than I knew, if grief has made you put yourself farther from him instead of nearer.'

'I shall be good again now that I have you,' said Gilbert, as he looked up into that sweet face.

'And you will begin by making a free confession to your father, and giving up the book.'

'I don't see what I have to confess. He would be so angry, and he never told me not. Oh! I cannot tell him.'

She felt that this was not the right way to begin a reformation, and yet she feared to press the point, knowing that the one was thought severe, the other timid.

'At least you will give up the book,' she said.

'O dear! if you would let me see whether d'Artagnan got to England. I must know that! I'm sure there can't be any harm in that. Do you know what it is about?'

'Yes, I do. My brother got it by some mistake among some French books. He read some of the droll unobjectionable parts to my sister and me, but the rest was so bad, that he threw it into the fire.'

'Then you think it funny?'

'To be sure I do.'

'Do you remember the three duels all at once, and the three valets? Oh! what fun it is. But do let me see if d'Artagnan got the diamonds.'

'Yes, he did. But will this satisfy you, Gilbert? You know there are some exciting pleasures that we must turn our backs on resolutely. I think this book is one of them. Now you will let me take it? I will tell your father about it in private, and he cannot blame you. Then, if he will give his consent, whenever you can come home early, come to my dressing-room, out of your sisters' way, and I will read to you the innocent part, so as to get the story out of your brain.'

'Very well,' said Gilbert, slowly. 'Yes, if you will not let papa be angry with me. And, oh dear! must you go?'

'I think you had better dress yourself and come down to tea. There is nothing the matter with you now, is there?'

He was delighted with the suggestion, and promised to come directly; and Albinia carried off her prize, exceedingly hopeful and puzzled, and wondering whether her compromise had been a right one, or a mere tampering with temptation—delighted with the confidence and affection bestowed on her so freely, but awe-struck by the impression which the boy had avowed, and marvelling how it should be treated, so as to render it a blessed and salutary restraint, rather than the dim superstitious terror that it was at present. At least there was hope of influencing him, his heart was affectionate, his will on the side of right, and in consideration of feeble health and timid character, she would overlook the fact that he had not made one voluntary open confession, and that the partial renunciation had been wrung from him as a choice of evils. She could only feel how much he was to be pitied, and how he responded to her affection.

She was crossing the hall next day, when she heard a confusion of tongues through the open door of the dining-room, and above all, Gilbert's. 'Well, I say there are but two ladies in Bayford. One is Mrs. Kendal, and the other is Genevieve Durant!'

'A dancing-master's daughter!' Lucy's scornful tone was unmistakeable, and so was the ensuing high-pitched querulous voice, 'Well, to be sure, Gilbert might be a little more—a little more civil. Not that I've a word to say against—against your—your mamma. Oh, no!—glad to see—but Gilbert might be more civil.'

'I think so indeed,' said Albinia. 'Good morning, Miss Meadows. You see Gilbert has come home quite alive enough for mischief.'

'Ah! I thought I might be excused. Mamma was so uneasy—though I know you don't admit visitors—my just coming to see—We've been always so anxious about Gilbert. Gibbie dear, where is that flannel I gave you for your throat?'

She advanced to put her finger within his neck-tie and feel for it. Gilbert stuck his chin down, and snapped with his teeth like a gin. Lucy exclaimed, 'Now, Gilbert, I know mamma will say that is wrong.'

'Ah! we are used to Gilbert's tricks. Always bear with a boy's antics,' said Miss Meadows, preventing whatever she thought was coming out of Mrs. Kendal's month. Albinia took the unwise step of laughing, for her sympathies were decidedly with resistance both to flannels and to the insertion of that hooked finger.

'Mr. Bowles has always said it was a case for great care. Flannel next the skin—no exposure,' continued Miss Meadows, tartly. 'I am sure—I know I am the last person to wish to interfere—but so delicate—You'll excuse—but my mother was uneasy; and people who go out in all weathers—'

'I hope Mrs. Meadows had my note this morning.'

'O yes! I am perfectly aware. Thank you. Yes, I know the rule, but you'll excuse—My mother was still anxious—I know you exclude visitors in lesson-time. I'm going. Only grandmamma would be glad—not that she wishes to interfere—but if Gilbert had on his piece of flannel—'

'Have you, Gilbert?' said Albinia, becoming tormented.

'I have been flannel all over all my life,' said Gilbert, sulkily, 'one bit more or less can make no odds.'

'Then you have not that piece? said Albinia.

'Oh, my dear! Think of that! New Saxony! I begged it of Mr. Holland. A new remnant—pink list, and all! I said it was just what I wanted for Master Gilbert. Mr. Holland is always a civil, feeling man. New Saxony—three shillings the yard—and trimmed with blue sarsenet! Where is it, Gilbert?'

'In a soup dish, with a crop of mustard and cress on it,' said Gilbert, with a wicked wink at Albinia, who was unable to resist joining in the girls' shout of laughing, but she became alarmed when she found that poor Miss Meadows was very near crying, and that her incoherency became so lachrymose as to be utterly incomprehensible.

Lucy, ashamed of her laughter, solemnly declared that it was very wrong of Gilbert, and she hoped he would not suffer from it, and Albinia, trying to become grave, judicial, and conciliatory, contrived to pronounce that it was very silly to leave anything off in an east wind, and hoping to put an end to the matter, asked Aunt Maria to sit down, and judge how they went on with their lessons.

O no, she could not interrupt. Her mother would want her. She knew Mrs. Kendal never admitted visitors. She had no doubt she was quite right. She hoped it would be understood. She would not intrude. In fact, she could neither go nor stay. She would not resume her seat, nor let anything go on, and it was full twenty minutes before a series of little vibrating motions and fragmentary phrases had borne her out of the house.

'Well!' cried Gilbert, 'I hoped Aunt Maria had left off coming down upon us.'

'O, mamma!' exclaimed Lucy, 'you never sent your love to grandmamma.'

'Depend upon it she was waiting for that,' said Gilbert.

I'm sure I wish I had known it,' said Albinia, not in the most judicious manner. 'Half-past eleven!'

'Aunt Maria says she can't think how you can find time for church when you can't see visitors in the morning,' said Lucy. 'And oh! dear mamma, grandmamma says gravy soup was enough to throw Gilbert into a fever.'

'At any rate, it did not,' said Albinia.

'Oh! and, dear mamma, Mrs. Osborn is so hurt that you called on Mrs. Dusautoy before returning her visit; and Aunt Maria says if you don't call to-day you will never get over it, and she says that—'

'What business has Mrs. Osborn to ask whom I called on?' exclaimed Albinia, impatiently.

'Because Mrs. Osborn is the leading lady in the town,' said Lucy. 'She told Miss Goldsmith that she had no notion of not being respected.'

'And she can't bear the Dusautoys. She left off subscribing to anything when they came; and he behaved very ill to the Admiral and everybody at a vestry-meeting.'

'I shall ask your papa before I am in any hurry to call on the Osborns!' cried Albinia. 'I have no desire to be intimate with people who treat their clergyman in that way.'

'But Mrs. Osborn is quite the leader!' exclaimed Lucy. They keep the best society here. So many families in the county come and call on them.'

'Very likely—'

'Ah! Mrs. Osborn told Aunt Maria that as the Nugents called on you, and you had such connexions, she supposed you would be high. But you wont make me separate from Lizzie, will you? I suppose Miss Nugent is a fashionable young lady.'

'Miss Nugent is five years old. Don't let us have any more of this nonsense.'

'But you wont part me from Lizzie Osborn,' said Lucy, hanging her head pathetically on one side.

'I shall talk to your father. He said, the other day, he did not wish you to be so much with her.'

Lucy melted into tears, and Albinia was conscious of having been first indiscreet and then sharp, hurt at the comments, feeling injured by Lucy's evident habit of reporting whatever she said, and at the failure of the attempt to please Mrs. Meadows. She was so uneasy about the Osborn question, that she waylaid Mr. Kendal on his return from riding, and laid it before him.

'My dear Albinia,' he said, as if he would fain have avoided the appeal, 'you must manage your own visiting affairs your own way. I do not wish to offend my neighbours, nor would I desire to be very intimate with any one. I suppose you must pay them ordinary civility, and you know what that amounts to. As to the leadership in society here, she is a noisy woman, full of pretension, and thus always arrogates the distinction to herself. Your claims will establish themselves.'

'Oh, you don't imagine me thinking of that!' cried Albinia, laughing. 'I meant their behaving ill to Mr. Dusautoy.'

'I know nothing about that. Mr. Dusautoy once called to ask for my support for a vestry meeting, but I make it a rule never to meddle with parish skirmishes. I believe there was a very unbecoming scene, and that Mr. Dusautoy was in the minority.'

'Ah, Edmund, next time you'll see if a parson's sister can sit quietly by to see the parson beaten!'

He smiled, and moved towards his study.

'Then I am to be civil?'

'Certainly.'

'But is it necessary to call to-day?'

'I should suppose not;' and there he was, shut up in his den. Albinia went back, between laughing and vexation, and Lucy looked up from her exercise to say, 'Does papa say you must call on the Osborns?'

It was undignified! She bit her lip, and felt her false position, as with a quiver of the voice she replied, 'We shall make nothing but mischief if we talk now. Go on with your business.'

The sharp, curious eyes did not take themselves off her face. She leant over Sophy, who was copying a house, told her the lines were slanting, took the pencil from her hand, and tried to correct them, but found herself making them over-black, and shaky. She had not seen such a line since the days of her childhood's ill-temper. She walked to the fireplace and said, 'I am going to call on Mrs. Osborn to-day. Not that your father desires it, but because I have been indulging in a wrong feeling.'

'I'm sure you needn't,' cried Gilbert. 'It is very impertinent of Mrs. Osborn. Why, if he is an admiral, she was the daughter of an old lieutenant of the Marines, and you are General Sir Maurice Ferrars' first cousin.'

'Hush, hush, Gilbert!' said Albinia, blushing and distressed. 'Mrs. Osborn's standing in the place entitles her to all attention. I was thinking of nothing of the kind. It was because I gave way to a wrong feeling that I mean to go this afternoon.'

On the Sunday, when Mr. and Mrs. Kendal went to pay their weekly visit to Mrs. Meadows, they found the old lady taking a turn in the garden. And as they were passing by the screen of laurels, Gilbert's voice was heard very loud, 'That's too bad, Lucy! Grandmamma, don't believe one word of it!'

'Gilbert, you—you are, I'm sure, very rude to your sister.'

'I'll not stand to hear false stories of Mrs. Kendal!'

'What is all this?' said Mr. Kendal, suddenly appearing, and discovering Gilbert pirouetting with indignation before Lucy.

Miss Meadows burst out with a shower of half sentences, grandmamma begged that no notice might be taken of the children's nonsense, Lucy put on an air of injured innocence, and Gilbert was beginning to speak, but his father put him aside, saying, 'Tell me what has happened, Sophia. From you I am certain of hearing the exact truth.'

'Only,' growled Sophy, in her hoarse boy's voice, 'Lucy said mamma said she would not call on Mrs. Osborn unless you ordered her, and when you did, she cried and flew into a tremendous passion.'

'Sophy, what a story,' exclaimed Lucy, but Gilbert was ready to corroborate his younger sister's report.

'You know Lucy too well to attach any importance to her misrepresentations,' said Mr. Kendal, turning to Mrs. Meadows, 'but I know not what amends she can make for this most unprovoked slander. Speak, Lucy, have you no apology to make?'

For Lucy, in self-defence, had begun to cry, and her grandmother seemed much disposed to do the same. Miss Meadows had tears in her eyes, and incoherencies on her lips. The distress drove away all Albinia's inclination to laugh, and clasping her two hands over her husband's arm, she said, 'Don't, Edmund, it is only a misunderstanding of what really happened. I did have a silly fit, you know, so it is my fault.'

'I cannot forgive for you as you do for yourself,' said Mr. Kendal, with a look that was precious to her, though it might have given a pang to the Meadowses. 'I did not imagine that my daughter could be so lost to the sense of your kindness and forbearance. Have you nothing to say, Lucy?'

'Poor child! she cannot speak,' said her grandmother. 'You see she is very sorry, and Mrs. Kendal is too kind to wish to say any more about it.'

'Go home at once, Lucy,' said her father. 'Perhaps solitude may bring you to a better state of feeling. Go!'

Direct resistance to Mr. Kendal was never thought of, and Lucy turned to go. Her aunt chose to accompany her, and though this was a decided relief to the company she left, it was not likely to be the best thing for the young lady herself.

Mr. Kendal gave his arm to Mrs. Meadows, saying gravely that Lucy must not be encouraged in her habit of gossiping and inaccuracy. Mrs. Meadows quite agreed with him, it was a very bad habit for a girl, she was very sorry for it, she wished she could have attended to the dear children better, but she was sure dear Mrs. Kendal would make them everything desirable. She only hoped that she would remember their disadvantages, have patience, and not recollect this against poor Lucy.

The warm indignation and championship of her husband and his son were what Albinia chiefly wished to recollect; but it was impossible to free herself from a sense of pain and injury in the knowledge that she lived with a spy who would exaggerate and colour every careless word.

Mr. Kendal returned to the subject as they walked home.

'I hope you will talk seriously to Lucy about her intolerable gossiping,' he said. 'There is no safety in mentioning any subject before her; and Maria Meadows makes her worse. Some stop must be put to it.'

'I should like to wait till next time,' said Albinia.

'What do you mean?'

'Because this is too personal to myself.'

'Nay, your own candour is an example to which Lucy can hardly be insensible. Besides, it is a nuisance which must be abated.'

Albinia could not help thinking that he suffered from it as little as most people, and wondering whether it were this which had taught him silence.

They met Miss Meadows at their own gate, and she told them that dear Lucy was very sorry, and she hoped they would take no more notice of a little nonsense that could do no one any harm; she would be more on her guard next time.

Mr. Kendal made no answer. Albinia ventured to ask him whether it would not be better to leave it, since her aunt had talked to her.

'No,' he said; 'Maria has no influence whatever with the children. She frets them by using too many words about everything. One quiet remonstrance from you would have far more effect.'

Albinia called the culprit and tried to reason with her. Lucy tried at first to battle it off by saying that she had made a mistake, and Aunt Maria had said that she should hear no more about it. 'But, my dear, I am afraid you must hear more. It is not that I am hurt, but your papa has desired me to talk to you. You would be frightened to hear what he says.'

Lucy chose to hear, and seemed somewhat struck, but she was sure that she meant no harm; and she had a great deal to say for herself, so voluble and so inconsequent, that argument was breath spent in vain; and Albinia was obliged to wind up, as an ultimatum, with warning her, that till she should prove herself trustworthy, nothing interesting would be talked of before her.

The atmosphere of gossip certainly had done its part in cultivating Mr. Kendal's talent for silence. When Albinia had him all to herself, he was like another person, and the long drives to return visits in the country were thoroughly enjoyable. So, too, were the walks home from the dinner parties in the town, when the husband and wife lingered in the starlight or moonlight, and felt that the weary gaiety of the constrained evening was made up for.

Great was the offence they gave by not taking out the carriage!

It was disrespect to Bayford, and one of the airs of which Mrs. Kendal was accused. As granddaughter of a Baron, daughter of one General Officer and sister of another, and presented at Court, the Bayford ladies were prepared to consider her a fine lady, and when they found her peculiarly simple, were the more aggrieved, as if her contempt were ironically veiled. Her walks, her dress, her intercourse with the clergy, were all airs, and Lucy spared her none of the remarks. Albinia might say, 'Don't tell me all Aunt Maria says,' but it was impossible not to listen; and whether in mirth or vexation, she was sure to be harmed by what she heard.

And yet, except for the tale-bearing, Lucy was really giving less trouble than her sister, she was quick, observant, and obliging, and under Albinia's example, the more salient vulgarities of speech and manner were falling off. There had seldom been any collision, since it had become evident that Mrs. Kendal could and would hold her own; and that her address and air, even while criticised, were regarded as something superior, so that it was a distinction to belong to her. How many of poor Albinia'a so-called airs should justly have been laid to Lucy's account?

On the other hand, Sophy would attend to a word from her father, where she had obstinately opposed her step-mother's wishes, making her obedience marked, as if for the very purpose of enforcing the contrast. It was a character that Albinia could not as yet fathom. In all occupations and amusements, Sophy followed the lead of her elder sister, and in her lessons, her sole object seemed to be to get things done with as little trouble as possible, and especially without setting her mind to work, and yet in the very effort to escape diligence or exertion, she sometimes showed signs of so much ability as to excite a longing desire to know of what she would be capable when once aroused and interested; but the surly, ungracious temper rendered this apparently impossible, and whatever Albinia attempted, was sure, as if for the very reason that it came from her, to be answered with a redoubling of the growl of that odd hoarse voice.

On Lucy's birthday, there was an afternoon party of her young friends, including Miss Durant. Albinia, who, among the girlhood of Fairmead and its neighbourhood, had been so acceptable a playmate, that her marriage had caused the outcry that 'there would never be any fun again without Miss Ferrars,' came out on the lawn with the girls, in hopes of setting them to enjoy themselves. But they looked at her almost suspiciously, retained their cold, stiff, company manners, and drew apart into giggling knots. She relieved them of her presence, and sitting by the window, watched Genevieve walking up and down alone, as if no one cared to join her. Presently Lucy and Lizzie Osborn spoke to her, and she went in. Albinia went to meet her in the hall; she coloured and said, 'She was only come to fetch Miss Osborn's cloak.'

Albinia saw her disposing it over Lizzie's shoulders, and then running in again. This time it was for Miss Louisa's cloak, and a third time for Miss Drury's shawl, which Albinia chose to take out herself, and encountering Sophia, said, 'Next time, you had better run on errands yourself instead of sending your guests.'

Sophy gave a black look, and she retreated, but presently the groups coalesced, and Maria Drury and Sophy ran out to call Genevieve into the midst. Albinia hoped they were going to play, but soon she beheld Genevieve trying to draw back, but evidently imprisoned, there was an echo of a laugh that she did not like; the younger girls were skipping up in the victim's face in a rude way; she hastily turned round as in indignation, one hand raised to her eyes, but it was instantly snatched down by Maria Drury, and the pitiless ring closed in. Albinia sprang to her feet, exclaiming aloud, 'They are teasing her!' and rushed into the garden, hearing on her way, 'No, we wont let you go!— you shall tell us—you shall promise to show us—my papa is a magistrate, you know—he'll come and search—Jenny, you shall tell!'

Come with me, Genevieve,' said Albinia, standing in the midst of the tormentors, and launching a look of wrath around her, as she saw tears in the young girl's eyes, and taking her hand, found it trembling with agitation. Fondling it with both her own, she led Genevieve away, turning her back upon Lucy and her, 'We were only—'

The poor girl shook more and more, and when they reached the shelter of the house, gave way to a tightened, oppressed sob, and at the first kind words a shower of tears followed, and she took Albinia's hand, and clasped it to her breast in a manner embarrassing to English feelings, though perfectly natural and sincere in her. 'Ah! si bonne! si bonne! pardonnes-moi, Madame!' she exclaimed, sobbing, and probably not knowing that she was speaking French; 'but, oh, Madame, you will tell me! Is it true—can he?'

'Can who? What do you mean, my dear?'

'The Admiral,' said Genevieve, looking about frightened, and sinking her voice to a whisper. 'Miss Louisa said so, that he could send and search—'

'Search for what, my dear?'

'For my poor little secret. Ah, Madame, assuredly I may tell you. It is but a French Bible, it belonged to my martyred ancestor, Francois Durant, who perished at the St. Barthelemi—it is stained with his blood—it has been handed on, from one to the other—it was all that Jacques Durant rescued when he fled from the Dragonnades—it was given to me by my own dear father on his death-bed, with a charge to keep it from my grandmother, and not to speak of it—but to guard it as my greatest treasure. And now—Oh, I am not disobeying him,' cried Genevieve, with a fresh burst of tears. 'You can feel for me, Madame, you can counsel me. Can the magistrates come and search, unless I confess to those young ladies?'

'Most decidedly not,' said Albinia. 'Set your mind at rest, my poor child; whoever threatened you played you a most base, cruel trick.'

'Ah, do not be angry with them, Madame; no doubt they were in sport. They could not know how precious that treasure was to me, and they will say much in their gaiety of heart.'

'I do not like such gaiety,' said Albinia. 'What, they wished to make you confess your secret?'

'Yes. They had learnt by some means that I keep one of my drawers locked, and they had figured to themselves that in it was some relic of my Huguenot ancestors. They thought it was some instrument of death, and they said that unless I would tell them the whole, the Admiral had the right of search, and, oh! it was foolish of me to believe them for a moment, but I only thought that the fright would, kill my grandmother. Oh, you were so good, Madame, I shall never forget; no, not to the end of my life, how you rescued me!'

'We did not bring you here to be teased,' said Albinia, caressing her. 'I should like to ask your pardon for what they have made you undergo.'

'Ah, Madame!' said Genevieve, smiling, 'it is nothing. I am well used to the like, and I heed it little, except when it falls on such subjects as these.'

She was easily drawn into telling the full history of her treasure, as she had learnt from her father's lips, the Huguenot shot down by the persecutors, and the son who had fled into the mountains and returned to bury the corpse, and take the prized, blood-stained Bible from the breast; the escapes and dangers of the two next generations; the few succeeding days of peace; and, finally, the Dragonnade, when the children had been snatched from the Durant family, and the father and mother had been driven at length to fly in utter destitution, and had made their way to England in a wretched, unprovisioned open boat. The child for whose sake they fled, was the only one rescued from the hands of these enemies, and the tradition of their sufferings had been handed on with the faithfully preserved relic, down to the slender girl, their sole descendant, and who in early childhood had drunk in the tale from the lips of her father. The child of the persecutors and of the persecuted, Genevieve Durant did indeed represent strangely the history of her ancestral country; and as Albinia said to her, surely it might be hoped that the faith in which she had been bred up, united what was true and sound in the religion of both Reformed and Romanist.

The words made the brown cheek glow. 'Ah, Madame, did I not say I could talk with you? You, who do not think me a heretic, as my dear grandmother's friends do, and who yet can respect my grandmother's Church.'

Assuredly little Genevieve was one of the most interesting and engaging persons that Albinia had ever met, and she listened earnestly to her artless history, and pretty enthusiasms, and the story which she could not tell without tears, of her father's care, when the reward of her good behaviour had been the reading one verse in the quaint black letter of the old French Bible.

The conversation lasted till Gilbert made his appearance, and Albinia was glad to find that his greeting to Genevieve was cordial and affectionate, and free from all that was unpleasant in his sisters' manner, and he joined himself to their company when Albinia proposed a walk along the broad causeway through the meadows. It was one of the pleasantest walks that she had taken at Bayford, with both her companions so bright and merry, and the scene around in all the beauty of spring. Gilbert, with the courtesy that Albinia's very presence had infused into him, gathered a pretty wild bouquet for each, and Albinia talked of cowslip-balls, and found that neither Gilbert nor Genevieve had ever seen one; then she pitied them, and owned that she did not know how to get through a spring without one; and Gilbert having of course a pocketful of string, a delicious ball was constructed, over which Genevieve went into an inexpressible ecstasy.

All the evening, Gilbert devoted himself to Genevieve, though more than one of the others tried to attract him, playing off the follies of more advanced girlhood, to the vexation of Albinia, who could not bear to see him the centre of attention to silly girls, when he ought to have been finding his level among boys.

'Gilbert makes himself so ridiculous about Jenny Durant,' said his sisters, when he insisted on escorting her home, and thus they brought on themselves Albinia's pent-up indignation at their usage of their guest. Lucy argued in unsatisfactory self-defence, but Sophy, when shown how ungenerous her conduct had been, crimsoned deeply, and though uttering no word of apology, wore a look that gave her step-mother for the first time a hope that her sullenness might not be so much from want of compunction, as from want of power to express it.

Oh! for a consultation with her brother. But he and his wife were taking a holiday among their kindred in Ireland, and for once Albinia could have echoed the aunts' lamentation that Winifred had so many relations!

CHAPTER V.

Albinia needed patience to keep alive hope and energy, for a sore disappointment awaited her. Whatever had been her annoyances with the girls, she had always been on happy and comfortable terms with Gilbert, he had responded to her advances, accommodated himself to her wishes, adopted her tastes, and returned her affection. She had early perceived that his father and sisters looked on him as the naughty one of the family, but when she saw Lucy's fretting interference, and, Sophia's wrangling contempt, she did not wonder that an unjust degree of blame had often fallen to his share; and under her management, he scarcely ever gave cause for complaint. That he was evidently happier and better for her presence, was compensation for many a vexation; she loved him with all her heart, made fun with him, told legends of the freaks of her brother Maurice and cousin Fred, and grudged no trouble for his pleasure.

As long as The Three Musqueteers lasted, he had come constantly to her dressing-room, and afterwards she promised to find other pleasant reading; but after such excitement, it was not easy to find anything that did not appear dry. As the daughter of a Peninsular man, she thought nothing so charming as the Subaltern, and Gilbert seemed to enjoy it; but by the time he had heard all her oral traditions of the war by way of notes, his attendance began to slacken; he stayed out later, and always brought excuses—Mr. Salsted had kept him, he had been with a fellow, or his pony had lost a shoe. Albinia did not care to question, the evenings were light and warm, and the one thing she desired for him was manly exercise: she thought it much better for him to be at play with his fellow-pupils, and she could not regret the gain of another hour to her hurried day.

One morning, however, Mr. Kendal called her, and his look was so grave and perturbed, that she hardly waited till the door was shut to ask in terror, what could be the matter.

'Nothing to alarm you,' he said. 'It is only that I am vexed about Gilbert. I have reason to fear that he is deceiving us again; and I want you to help us to recollect on which days he should have been at Tremblam. My dear, do not look so pale!'

For Albinia had turned quite white at hearing that the boy, on whom she had fixed her warm affection, had been carrying on a course of falsehood; but a moment's hope restored her. 'I did keep him at home on Tuesday,' she said, 'it was so very hot, and he had a headache. I thought I might. You told me not to send him on doubtful days.'

'I hope you may be able to make out that it is right,' said Mr. Kendal, 'but I am afraid that Mr. Salsted has too much cause of complaint. It is the old story!'

And so indeed it proved, when Albinia heard what the tutor had come to say. The boy was seldom in time, often altogether missing, excusing himself by saying he was kept at home by fears of the weather; but Mr. Salsted was certain that his father could not know how he disposed of his time, namely, in a low style of sporting with young Tritton, the son of a rich farmer or half-gentleman, who was the pest of Mr. Salsted's parish. Ill-learnt, slurred-over lessons, with lame excuses, were nothing as compared with this, and the amount of petty deceit, subterfuge, and falsehood, was frightful, especially when Albinia recollected the tone of thought which the boy had seemed to be catching from her. Unused to duplicity, except from mere ignorant, unmanageable school-children, she was excessively shocked, and felt as if he must be utterly lost to all good, and had been acting a lie from first to last. After the conviction had broken on her, she hardly spoke, while Mr. Kendal was promising to talk to his son, threaten him with severe punishment, and keep a strict account of his comings and goings, to be compared weekly with Mr. Salsted's notes of his arrival. This settled, the tutor departed, and no sooner was he gone, than Albinia, hiding her face in her hands, shed tears of bitter grief and disappointment. 'My dearest,' said her husband, fondly, 'you must not let my boy's doings grieve you in this manner. You have been doing your utmost for him, if any one could do him good, it would be you.'

'O no, surely I must have made some dreadful mistake, to have promoted such faults.'

'No, I have long known him not to be trustworthy. It is an evil of long standing.'

'Was it always so?'

'I cannot tell,' said he, sitting down beside her, and shading his brow with one hand; 'I have only been aware of it since he has been left alone. When the twins were together, they were led by one soul of truth and generosity. What this poor fellow was separately no one could know, while he had his brother to guide and shield him. The first time I noticed the evil was when we were recovering. Gilbert and Sophia were left together, and in one of their quarrels injured some papers of mine. I was very weak, and had little power of self-control; I believe I terrified him too much. There was absolute falsehood, and the truth was only known by Sophia's coming forward and confessing the whole. It was ill managed. I was not equal to dealing with him, and whether the mischief began then or earlier, it has gone on ever since, breaking out every now and then. I had hoped that with your care—But oh! how different it would have been with his brother! Albinia, what would I not give that you had but seen *him!* Not a fault was there; not a moment's grief did he give us, till—O what an overthrow of hope!' And he gave way to an excess of grief that quite appalled her, and made her feel herself powerless to comfort. She only ventured a few words of peace and hope; but the contrast between the brothers, was just then keen agony, and he could not help exclaiming how strange it was, that Edmund should be the one to be taken.

'Nay,' he said, 'was not he ripe for better things? May not poor Gilbert have been spared that longer life may train him to be like his brother?'

'He never will be like him,' cried Mr. Kendal. 'No! no! The difference is evident in the very countenance and features.'

'Was he like you?'

'They said so, but you could not gather an idea of him from me,' said Mr. Kendal, smiling mournfully, as he met her gaze. 'It was the most beautiful countenance I ever saw, full of life and joy; and there were wonderful expressions in the eyes when he was thinking or listening. He used to read the Greek Testament with me every morning, and his questions and remarks rise up before me again. That text—You have seen it in church.'

'Because I live, ye shall live also,' Albinia repeated.

'Yes. A little before his illness we came to that. He rested on it, as he used to do on anything that struck him, and asked me, "whether it meant the life hereafter, or the life that is hidden here?" We went over it with such comments as I could find, but his mind was not satisfied; and it must have gone on working on it, for one night, when I had been thinking him delirious, he called me, and the light shone out of those bright dark eyes of his as he said, joyfully, "It is both, papa! It is hidden here, but it will shine out there," and as I did not catch his meaning, he repeated the Greek words.'

'Dear boy! Some day we shall be glad that the full life and glory came so soon.'

He shook his head, the parting was still too recent, and it was the first time he had been able to speak of his son. It was a great satisfaction to her that the reserve had once been broken; it seemed like compensation for the present trouble, though that was acutely felt, and not softened by the curious eyes and leading questions of the sisters, when she returned to give what attention she could to their interrupted lessons.

Gilbert returned, unsuspicious of the storm, till his father's stern gravity, and her depressed, pre-occupied manner, excited his attention, and he asked her anxiously whether anything were the matter. A sad gesture replied, and perhaps revealed the state of the case, for he became absolutely silent. Albinia left them together. She watched anxiously, and hurried after Mr. Kendal into the study, where his manner showed her not to be unwelcome as the sharer of his trouble. 'I do not know what to do,' he said, dejectedly. 'I can make nothing of him. It is all prevarication and sulkiness! I do not think he felt one word that I said.'

'People often feel more than they show.'

He groaned.

'Will you go to him?' he presently added. 'Perhaps I grew too angry at last, and I believe he loves you. At least, if he does not, he must be more unfeeling than I can think him. You do not dislike it, dearest.'

'O no, no! If I only knew what would be best for him!'

'He may be more unreserved with you,' said Mr. Kendal; and as he was anxious for her to make the attempt, she moved away, though in perplexity, and in the revulsion of feeling, with a sort of disgust towards the boy who had deceived her so long.

She found him seated on a wheelbarrow by the pond, chucking pebbles into the still black water, and disturbing the duckweed on the surface. His colour was gone, and his face was dark and moody, and strove not to relax, as she said, 'O Gilbert, how could you?'

He turned sharply away, muttering, 'She is coming to bother, now!'

It cut her to the heart. 'Gilbert!' was all she could exclaim, but the tone of pain made him look at her, as if in spite of himself, and as he saw the tears he exclaimed in an impatient voice of rude consolation, 'There's nothing to take so much to heart. No one thinks anything of it!'

'What would Edmund have thought?' said Albinia; but the appeal came too soon, he made an angry gesture and said, 'He was nearly three years younger than I am now! He would not have been kept in these abominable leading-strings.'

She was too much shocked to find an answer, and Gilbert went on, 'Watched and examined wherever I go—not a minute to myself—nothing but lessons at Tremblam, and bother at home; driven about hither and thither, and not allowed a friend of my own, nor to do one single thing! There's no standing it, and I won't!'

'I am very sorry,' said Albinia, struggling with choking tears. 'It has been my great wish to make things pleasant to you. I hope I have not teased or driven you to—'

'Nonsense!' exclaimed Gilbert, disrespectfully indeed, but from the bottom of his heart, and breaking at once into a flood of tears. 'You are the only creature that has been kind to me since I lost my mother and Ned, and now they have been and turned you against me too;' and he sobbed violently.

'I don't know what you mean, Gilbert. If I stand in your mother's place, I can't be turned against you, any more than she could,' and she stroked his brow, which she found so throbbing as to account for his paleness. 'You can grieve and hurt me, but you can't prevent me from feeling for you, nor for your dear father's grief.'

He declared that people at home knew nothing about boys, and made an uproar about nothing.

'Do you call falsehood nothing?'

'Falsehood! A mere trifle now and then, when I am driven to it by being kept so strictly.'

'I don't know how to talk to you, Gilbert,' said Albinia, rising; 'your conscience knows better than your tongue.'

'Don't go;' and he went off into another paroxysm of crying, as he caught hold of her dress; and when he spoke again his mood was changed; he was very miserable, nobody cared for him, he did not know what to do; he wanted to do right, and to please her, but Archie Tritton would not let him alone; he wished he had never seen Archie Tritton. At last, walking up and down with him, she drew from him a full confidence, and began to understand how, when health and strength had come back to him in greater measure than he had ever before enjoyed, the craving for boyish sports had awakened, just after he had been deprived of his brother, and was debarred from almost every wholesome manner of gratifying it. To fall in with young Tritton was as great a misfortune as could well have befallen a boy, with a dreary home, melancholy, reserved father, and wearisome aunt. Tritton was a youth of seventeen, who had newly finished his education at an inferior commercial school, and lived on his father's farm, giving himself the airs of a sporting character, and fast hurrying into dissipation.

He was really good-natured, and Gilbert dwelt on his kindness with warmth and gratitude, and on his prowess in all sporting accomplishments with a perfect effervescence of admiration. He evidently patronized Gilbert, partly from good-natured pity, and partly as flattered by the adherence of a boy of a grade above him; and Gilbert was proud of the notice of one who seemed to him a man, and an adept in all athletic games. It was a dangerous intimacy, and her heart sank as she found that the pleasures to which he had been introducing Gilbert, were not merely the free exercise, the rabbit-shooting and rat-hunting of the farm, nor even the village cricket-match, all of which, in other company, would have had her full sympathy. But there had been such low and cruel sports that she turned her head away sickened at the notion of any one dear to her having been engaged in such amusements, and when Gilbert in excuse said that every one did it, she answered indignantly, 'My brothers never!'

'It is no use talking about what swells do that hunt and shoot and go to school,' answered Gilbert.

'Do you wish you went to school?' asked Albinia.

'I wish I was out of it all!'

He was in a very different frame. He owned that he knew how wrong it had been to deceive, but he seemed to look upon it as a sort of fate; he wished he could help it, but could not, he was so much afraid of his father that he did not know what he said; Archie Tritton said no one could get on without.—There was an utter bewilderment in his notions, here and there showing a better tone, but obscured by the fancies imbibed from his companion, that the knowledge and practice of evil were manly. At one moment he cried bitterly, and declared that he was wretched; at another he defended each particular case with all his might, changing and slipping away so that she did not know where to take him. However, the conclusion was far more in pity than anger, and after receiving many promises that if she would shield him from his father and bear with him, he would abstain from all she disapproved, she caressed and soothed the aching head, and returned to his father hopeful and encouraged, certain that the evil had been chiefly caused by weakness and neglect and believing that here was a beginning of repentance. Since there was sorrow and confession, there surely must be reformation.

For a week Gilbert went on steadily, but at the end of that time his arrivals at home became irregular, and one day there was another great aberration. On a doubtful day, when it had been decided that he might go safely between the showers, he never came to Tremblam at all, and Mr. Salsted sent a note to Mr. Kendal to let him know that his son had been at the races—village races, managed by the sporting farmers of the neighbourhood. There was a sense of despair, and again a talk, bringing at once those ever-ready tears and protestations, sorrow genuine, but fruitless. 'It was all Archie's fault, he had overtaken him, persuaded him that Mr. Salsted would not expect him, promised him that he should see the celebrated 'Blunderbuss,' Sam Shepherd's horse, that won the race last year. Gilbert had gone 'because he could not help it.'

'Not help it!' cried Albinia, looking at him with her clear indignant eyes. 'How can you be such a poor creature, Gilbert?'

'It is very hard!' exclaimed Gilbert; 'I must go past Robble's Leigh twice every day of my life, and Archie will come out and be at me.'

'That is the very temptation you have to resist,' said Albinia. 'Fight against it, pray against it, resolve against it; ride fast, and don't linger and look after him.'

He looked desponding and miserable. If she could only have put a spirit into him!

'Shall I walk and meet you sometimes before you get to Robbie's Leigh!'

His face cleared up, but the cloud returned in a moment.

'What is it?' she asked. 'Only tell me. You know I wish for nothing so much as to help you.'

He did confess that there was nothing he should like better, if Archie would not be all the worse another time, whenever he should catch himalone.

'But surely, Gilbert, he is not always lying in ambush for you, like a cat for a mouse. You can't be his sole game.'

'No, but he is coming or going, or out with his gun, and he will often come part of the way with me, and he is such a droll fellow!'

Albinia thought that there was but one cure. To leave Gilbert daily exposed to the temptation must be wrong, and she laid the case before Mr. Kendal with so much earnestness, that he allowed that it would be better to send the boy from home; and in the meantime, Albinia obtained that Mr. Kendal should ride some way on the Tremblam road with his son in the morning, so as to convoy him out of reach of the tempter; whilst she tried to meet him in the afternoon, and managed so that he should be seldom without the hope of meeting her.

Albinia's likings had taken a current absolutely contrary to all her preconceived notions; Sophia, with her sullen truth, was respected, but it was not easy to like her even as well as Lucy, who, though pert and empty, had much good-nature and good-temper, and was not indocile; while Gilbert, in spite of a weak, shallow character, habits of deception, and low ungentlemanly tastes, had won her affection, and occupied the chief of her time and thoughts; and she dreaded the moment of parting with him, as removing the most available and agreeable of her young companions.

That moment of parting, though acknowledged to be expedient, did not approach. Gilbert, could not be sent to a public school without risk and anxiety which his father did not like, and which would have been horror to his grandmother; and Albinia herself did not feel certain that he was fit for it, nor that it was her part to enforce it. She wrote to her brother, and found that he likewise thought a tutor would be a safe alternative; but then he must be a perfect man in a perfect climate, and Mr. Kendal was not the man to make researches. Mr. Dusautoy mentioned one clergyman who took pupils, Maurice Ferrars another, but there was something against each. Mr. Kendal wrote four letters, and was undecided—a third was heard of, but the locality was doubtful, and the plan went off, because Mr. Kendal could not make up his mind to go thirty miles to see the place, and talk to a stranger.

Albinia found that her power did not extend beyond driving him from 'I'll see about it,' to 'Yes, by all means.' Action was a length to which he could not be brought. Mr. Nugent was very anxious that he should qualify as a magistrate since a sensible, highly-principled man was much wanted counterbalance Admiral Osborn's misdirected, restless activity and the lower parts of the town were in a dreadful state. Mrs. Nugent talked to Albinia, and she urged it in vain. To come out of his study, examine felons, contend with the Admiral, and to meet all the world at the quarter sessions, was abhorrent to him, and he silenced her almost with sternness.

She was really hurt and vexed, and scarcely less so by a discovery that she made shortly after. The hot weather had made the houses beneath the hill more close and unwholesome than ever, Simkins's wife had fallen into a lingering illness, and Albinia, visiting her constantly, was painfully sensible of the dreadful atmosphere in which she lived, under the roof, with a window that would not open. She offered to have the house improved at her own expense, but was told that Mr. Pettilove would raise the rent if anything were laid out on it. She went about talking indignantly of Mr. Pettilove's cruelty and rapacity, and when Mr. Dusautoy hinted that Pettilove was only agent, she exclaimed that the owner was worse, since ignorance alone could be excused. Who was the wretch? Some one, no doubt, who never came near the place, and only thought of it as money.

'Fanny,' said Mr. Dusautoy, 'I really think we ought to tell her.'

'Yes,' said Mrs. Dusautoy, 'I think it would be better. The houses belonged to old Mr. Meadows.'

'Oh, if they are Mrs. Meadows's, I don't wonder at anything.'

'I believe they are Gilbert Kendal's.'

They were very kind; Mr. Dusautoy strode out at the window, and his wife would not look at Albinia during the minute's struggle to regain her composure, under the mortification that her husband should have let her rave so much and so long about what must be in his own power. Her only comfort was the hope that he had never heard what she said, and she knew that he so extremely disliked a conference with Pettilove, that he would consent to anything rather than have a discussion.

She was, for the first time in her life, out of spirits. Gilbert was always upon her mind; and the daily walk to meet him was a burthen, consuming a great deal of time, and becoming trying on hot summer afternoons, the more so as she seldom ventured to rest after it, lest dulness should drive Gilbert into mischief, or, if nothing worse, into quarrelling with Sophia. If she could not send him safely out fishing, she must be at hand to invent pleasures and occupations for him; and the worst of it was, that the girls grudged her attention to their brother, and were becoming jealous. They hated the walk to Robble's Leigh, and she knew that it was hard on them that their pleasure should be sacrificed, but it was all-important to preserve him from evil. She had wished to keep the tutor-negotiations a secret, but they had oozed out, and she found that Mrs. and Miss Meadows had been declaring that they had known how it would be—whatever people said beforehand, it always came to the same thing in the end, and as to its being necessary, poor dear Gibbie was very different before the change at home.

Albinia could not help shedding a few bitter tears. Why was she to be always misjudged, even when she meant the best? And, oh! how hard, well- nigh impossible, to forgive and candidly to believe that, in the old lady, at least, it was partiality, and not spite.

In September, Mr. and Mrs. Ferrars returned from their journey. Albinia was anxious to see them, for if there was a sense that she had fallen short of her confident hopes of doing prosperously, there was also a great desire for their sympathy and advice. But Maurice had been too long away from his parish to be able to spare another day, and begged that the Kendals would come to Fairmead. Seeing that Albinia's heart was set on it, Mr. Kendal allowed himself to be stirred up to appoint a time for driving her over to spend a long day at Fairmead.

For her own pleasure and ease of mind, Albinia made a point of taking Gilbert, and the girls were to spend the day with their grandmother.

'Pretty old Fairmead!' she cried, as the beech-trees rose before her; and she was turning round every minute to point out to Gilbert some of the spots of which she had told him, and nodding to the few scattered children who were not at school, and who looked up with mouths from ear to ear, and flushed cheeks, as they curtsied to 'Miss Ferrars.' The 'Miss Ferrars' life seemed long ago.

They came to the little green gate that led to what had been 'home' for the happiest years of Albinia's life, and from the ivy porch there was a rush of little Willie and Mary, and close at hand their mamma, and Maurice emerging from the school. It was very joyous and natural. But there were two more figures, not youthful, but of decided style and air, and quiet but fashionable dress, and Albinia had only time to say quickly to her husband, 'my aunts,' before she was fondly embraced.

It was not at all what she had intended. Mrs. Annesley and Miss Ferrars were very kind aunts, and she had much affection for them; but there was an end of the hope of the unreserve and confidence that she wanted. She could get plenty of compassion and plenty of advice, but her whole object would be to avoid these; and, besides, Mr. Kendal had not bargained for strangers. What would become of his opportunity of getting better acquainted with Maurice and Winifred, and of all the pleasures that she had promised Gilbert?

At least, however, she was proud that her aunts should see what a fine-looking man her husband was, and they were evidently struck with his appearance and manner. Gilbert, too was in very good looks, and was altogether a bright, gentlemanly boy, well made, though with the air of growing too fast, and with something of uncertainty about his expression.

It was quickly explained that the aunts had only decided, two days before, on coming to Fairmead at once, some other engagement having failed them, and they were delighted to find that they should meet their dear Albinia, and be introduced to Mr. Kendal. Setting off before the post came in, Albinia had missed Winifred's note to tell her of their arrival.

'And,' said Winifred, as she took Albinia upstairs, 'if I did suspect that would be the case, I wont say I regretted it. I did not wish to afford Mr. Kendal the pleasures of anticipation.'

'Perhaps it was better,' said Albinia, smiling, 'especially as I suppose they will stay for the next six weeks, so that the days will be short before you will be free.'

'And now let me see you, my pretty one,' said Winifred, fondly. 'Are you well, are you strong? No, don't wriggle your head away, I shall believe nothing but what I read for myself.'

'Don't believe anything you read without the notes,' said Albinia. 'I have a great deal to say to you, but I don't expect much opportunity thereof.'

Certainly not, for Miss Ferrars was knocking at the door. She had never been able to suppose that the sisters-in-law could be more to each other than she was to her own niece.

So it became a regular specimen of a 'long day' spent together by relations, who, intending to be very happy, make themselves very weary of each other, by discarding ordinary occupations, and reducing themselves to needlework and small talk. Albinia was bent on liveliness, and excelled herself in her droll observations; but to Winifred, who knew her so well, this brilliancy did not seem like perfect ease; it was more like effort than natural spirits. This was no wonder, for not only had the sight of new people thrown Mr. Kendal into a severe access of shyness and silence, but he was revolving in fear and dread the expediency of asking them to Willow Lawn, and considering whether Albinia and propriety could make the effort bearable. Silent he sat, while the aunts talked of their wishes that one nephew would marry, and that the other would not, and no one presumed to address him, except little Mary, who would keep trotting up to him, to make him drink out of her doll's tea-cups.

Mr. Ferrars took pity on him, and took him and Gilbert out to call upon Colonel Bury; but this did not lessen his wife's difficulties, for there was a general expectation that she would proceed to confidences; whereas she would do nothing but praise the Dusautoys, ask after all the parishioners of Fairmead one by one, and consult about French reading-books and Italian grammars. Mrs. Annesley began a gentle warning against overtaxing her strength, and Miss Ferrars enforced it with such vehemence, that Winifred, who had been rather on that side, began to take Albinia's part, but perceived, with some anxiety, that her sister's attempts to laugh off the admonition almost amounted to an admission that she was working very hard. As to the step-daughters, no intelligence was attainable, except that Lucy would be pleased with a new crochet pattern, and that Sophy was like her father, but not so handsome.

The next division of time passed better. Albinia walked out at the window to meet the gentlemen when they came home, and materially relieved Mr. Kendal's mind by saying to him, 'The aunts are settled in here till they go to Knutsford. I hope you don't think—there is not the least occasion for asking them to stay with us.'

'Are you sure you do not wish it?' said Mr. Kendal, with great kindness, but an evident weight removed.

'Most certain!' she exclaimed, with full sincerity; 'I am not at all ready for them. What should I do with them to entertain?'

'Very well,' said Mr. Kendal, 'you must be the judge. If there be no necessity, I shall be glad to avoid unsettling our habits, and probably Bayford would hardly afford much enjoyment to your aunts.'

Albinia glanced in his face, and in that of her brother, with her own arch fun. It was the first time that day that Maurice had seen that peculiarly merry look, and he rejoiced, but he was not without fear that she was fostering Mr. Kendal's retiring habits more than was good for him. But it was not only on his account that she avoided the invitation, she by no means wished to show Bayford to her fastidious aunts, and felt as if to keep them satisfied and comfortable would be beyond her power.

Set free from this dread, and his familiarity with his brother-in-law renewed, Mr. Kendal came out to great advantage at the early dinner. Miss Ferrars was well read and used to literary society, and she started subjects on which he was at home, and they discussed new books and criticised critics, so that his deep reading showed itself, and even a grave, quiet tone of satire, such as was seldom developed, except under the most favourable circumstances. He and Aunt Gertrude were evidently so well pleased with each other, that Albinia almost thought she had been precipitate in letting him off the visit.

Gilbert had, fortunately, a turn for small children, and submitted to be led about the garden by little Willie; and as far as moderate enjoyment went, the visit was not unsuccessful; but as for what Albinia came for, it was unattainable, except for one little space alone with her brother.

'I meant to have asked a great deal,' she said, sighing.

'If you, want me, I would contrive to ride over,' said Maurice.

'No, it is not worth that. But, Maurice, what is to be done when one sees one's duty, and yet fails for ever for want of tact and temper! Ah, I know what you will say, and I often say it to myself, but whatever I propose, I always do either the wrong thing or in the wrong way!'

'You fall a hundred times a day, but are raised up again,' said Maurice.

'Maurice, tell me one thing. Is it wrong to do, not the best, but only the best one can?'

'It is the wrong common to us all,' said Maurice.

'I used to believe in "whatever is worth doing at all, is worth doing well." Now, I do everything ill, rather than do nothing at all.'

'There are only two ways of avoiding that.'

'And they are—?'

'Either doing nothing, or admiring all your own doings.'

'Which do you recommend?' said Albinia, smiling, but not far from tears.

'My dear,' said Maurice, 'all I can dare to recommend, is patience and self-control. Don't fret and agitate yourself about what you can't do, but do your best to do calmly what you can. It will be made up, depend upon it.'

There was no time for more, but the sound counsel, the sympathy, and playfulness had done Albinia wonderful good, and she was almost glad there had been no more privacy, or her friends might have guessed that she had not quite found a counsellor at home.

CHAPTER VI.

The Christmas holidays did indeed put an end to the walks to meet Gilbert, but only so as to make Albinia feel responsible for him all day long, and uneasy whenever he was not accounted for. She played chess with him, found books, and racked her brains to seek amusements for him; but knowing all the time that it was hopeless to expect a boy of fourteen to be satisfied with them. One or two boys of his age had come home for the holidays, and she tried to be relieved by being told that he was going out with Dick Wolfe or Harry Osborn, but it was not quite satisfactory, and she began to look fagged and unwell, and had lost so much of her playfulness, that even Mr. Kendal was alarmed.

Sophia's birthday fell in the last week before Christmas, and it had always been the family custom to drink tea with Mrs. Meadows. Albinia made the engagement with a sense of virtuous resignation, though not feeling well enough for the infliction, but Mr. Kendal put a stop to all notion of her going. She expected to enjoy her quiet solitary evening, but the result was beyond her hopes, for as she was wishing Gilbert good-bye, she heard the click of the study lock, and in came Mr. Kendal.

'I thought you were gone,' she said.

'No. I did not like to leave you alone for a whole evening.'

If it were only an excuse to himself for avoiding the Meadows' party, it was too prettily done for the notion to occur to his wife, and never had she spent a happier evening. He was so unusually tender and unreserved, so desirous to make her comfortable, and, what was far more to her, growing into so much confidence, that it was even better than what she used last year to picture to herself as her future life with him. It even came to what he had probably never done for any one. She spoke of a beautiful old Latin hymn, which she had once read with her brother, and had never seen adequately translated, and he fetched a manuscript book, where, written out with unrivalled neatness, stood a translation of his own, made many years ago, full of scholarly polish. She ventured to ask leave to copy it. 'I will copy it for you,' he said, 'but it must be for yourself alone.'

She was grateful for the concession, and happy in the promise. She begged to turn the page, and it was granted. There were other translations, chiefly from curious oriental sources, and there were about twenty original poems, elaborated in the same exquisite manner, and with a deep melancholy strain of thought, and power of beautiful description, that she thought finer and more touching than almost anything she had read.

'And these are all locked up for ever. No one has seen them.'

'So. When I was a young lad, my poor father put some lines of mine into a newspaper. That sufficed me,' and he shut the clasped book as if repenting of having revealed the contents.

'No, I was not thinking of anything you would dislike with regard to those verses. I don't like to let in the world on things precious, but (how could she venture so far!) I was thinking how many powers and talents are shut up in that study! and whether they might not have been meant for more. I beg your pardon if I ought not to say so.'

'The time is past,' he replied, without displeasure; 'my youth is gone, and with it the enterprise and hopefulness that can press forward, insensible to annoyance. You should have married a man with freshness and energy more responsive to your own.'

'Oh, Edmund, that is a severe reproach for my impertinent speech.'

'You must not expect too much from me,' he continued. 'I told you that I was a broken, grief-stricken man, and you were content to be my comforter.'

'Would that I could be so!' exclaimed Albinia, 'but to try faithfully, I must say what is on my mind. Dear Edmund, if you would only look out of your books, and see how much good you could do, here in your own sphere, how much the right wants strengthening, how much evil cries out to be repressed, how sadly your own poor suffer—oh! if you once began, you would be so much happier!'

She trembled with earnestness, and with fear of her own audacity, but a resounding knock at the door prevented her from even discovering whether he were offended. He started away to secure his book, and the two girls came in. Albinia could hardly believe it late enough for their return, but they accounted for having come rather earlier by saying that Gilbert had been making himself so ridiculous when he had come at last, that grandmamma had sent him home.

'At last!' said Albinia. 'He set off only ten minutes after you, as soon as he found that papa was not coming.'

'All I know,' said Lucy, 'is, that he did not come till half-past nine, and said he had come from home.'

'And where can he be now?'

'Gone to bed,' growled Sophy.

'I don't know what he has been doing,' said Lucy, who since the suspicion of favouritism, had seemed to find especial pleasure in bringing forward her brother's faults; 'but he came in laughing like a plough-boy, and talking perfect nonsense. And when Aunt Maria spoke to him, he answered quite rudely, that he wasn't going to be questioned and called to order, he had enough of petticoat government at home.'

'No,' said Sophy, breaking in with ungracious reluctance, as if against her will conveying some comfort to her step-mother for the sake of truth, 'what he said was, that if he bore with petticoat government at home, it was because Mrs. Kendal was pretty and kind, and didn't torment him out of his life for nothing, and what he stood from her, he would not stand from any other woman.'

'But, Sophy, I am sure he did say Mrs. Kendal knew what she was going to say, and said it, and it was worth hearing, and he laughed in Aunt Maria's face, and told her not to make so many bites at a cherry.'

'He must have been beside himself,' said Albinia, in a bewilderment of consternation, but Mr. Kendal's return put a stop to all, for the sisters never told tales before him, and she would not bring the subject under his notice until she should be better informed. His suffering was too great, his wrath too stern, to be excited without serious cause; but she spent a wakeful, anxious night, revolving all imaginable evils into which the boy could have fallen, and perplexing herself what measures to take, feeling all the more grieved and bound to him by the preference that, even in this dreadful mood, he had expressed for her. She fell into a restless sleep in the morning, from which she wakened so late as to have no time to question Gilbert before breakfast. On coming down, she found that he had not made his appearance, and had sent word that he had a bad headache, and wanted no breakfast. His father, who had made a visit of inspection, said he thought it was passing off, smiling as he observed upon Mrs. Meadows's mince-pie suppers and home-made wine.

Lucy said nothing, but glanced knowingly at her sister and at Albinia, from neither of whom did she get any response.

Albinia did not dare to take any measures till Mr. Kendal had ridden out, and then she went up and knocked at Gilbert's door. He was better, he said, and was getting up, he would be down-stairs presently. She watched for him as he came down, looking still very pale and unwell. She took him into her room, made him sit by the fire, and get a little life and warmth into his chilled hands before she spoke. 'Yes, Gilbert, I don't wonder you cannot lift up your head while so much is on your mind.'

Gilbert started and hid his face.

'Did you think I did not know, and was not grieved?'

'Well,' he cried, peevishly, 'I'm sure I have the most ill-natured pair of sisters in the world.'

'Then you meant to deceive us again, Gilbert.'

He had relapsed into the old habit—as usual, a burst of tears and a declaration that no one was ever so badly off, and he did not know what to do.

'You *do* know perfectly well what to do, Gilbert. There is nothing for it but to tell me the whole meaning of this terrible affair, and I will see whether I can help you.'

It was always the same round, a few words would always bring the confession, and that pitiful kind of helpless repentance, which had only too often given her hope.

Gilbert assured her that he had fully purposed following his sisters, but that on the way he had unluckily fallen in with Archie Tritton and a friend, who had driven in to hear a man from London singing comic songs at the King's Head, and they had persuaded him to come in. He had been uneasy and tried to get away, but the dread of being laughed at about his grandmother's tea had prevailed, and he had been supping on oysters and porter, and trying to believe himself a fast man, till Archie, who had assured him that he was himself going home in 'no time,' had found it expedient to set off, and it had been agreed that he should put a bold face on it, and profess that he had never intended to do more than come and fetch his sisters home.

That the porter had anything to do with his extraordinary manner to his grandmother and aunt, was so shocking a notion, and the very hint made him cry so bitterly, and protest so earnestly that he had only had one pint, which he did not like, and only drank because he was afraid of being teased, that Albinia was ready to believe that he had been so elevated by excitement as to forget himself, and continue the style of the company he had left. It was bad enough, and she felt almost overpowered by the contemplation of the lamentable weakness of the poor boy, of the consequences, and of what was incumbent on her.

She leant back and considered a little while, then sighed heavily, and said, 'Gilbert, two things must be done. You must make an apology to your grandmother and aunt, and you must confess the whole to your father.'

He gave a sort of howl, as if she were misusing his confidence.

'It must be,' she said. 'If you are really sorry, you will not shrink. I do not believe that it could fail to come to your father's knowledge, even if I did not know it was my duty to tell him, and how much better to confess it yourself.'

For this, however, Gilbert seemed to have no force; he cried piteously, bewailed himself, vowed incoherently that he would never do so again, and if she had not pitied him so much, would have made her think him contemptible.

She was inexorable as to having the whole told, though dreading the confession scarcely less than he did; and he finally made a virtue of necessity, and promised to tell, if only she would not desert him, declaring, with a fresh flood of tears, that he should never do wrong when she was by. Then came the apology. It was most necessary, and he owned that it would be much better to be able to tell his father that his grandmother had forgiven him; but he really had not nerve to set out alone, and Albinia, who had begun to dread having him out of sight, consented to go and protect him.

He shrank behind her, and she had to bear the flood of Maria's surprises and regrets, before she could succeed in saying that he was very sorry for yesterday's improper behaviour, and had come to ask pardon.

Grandmamma was placable; Gilbert's white face and red eyes were pleading enough, and she was distressed at Mrs. Kendal having come out, looking pale and tired. If she had been alone, the only danger would have been that the offence would be lost in petting; but Maria had been personally wounded, and the jealousy she already felt of the step-mother, had been excited to the utmost by Gilbert's foolish words. She was excessively grieved, and a great deal more angry with Mrs. Kendal than with Gilbert; and the want of justification for this feeling, together with her great excitement, distress, and embarrassment, made her attempts to be dry and dignified ludicrously abortive. She really seemed to have lost the power of knowing what she said. She was glad Mrs. Kendal could walk up this morning, since she could not come at night.

'It was not my fault,' said Albinia, earnestly; 'Mr. Kendal forbade me. I am sure I wish we had come.'

The old lady would have said something kind about not reproaching herself, but Miss Meadows interposed with, 'It was very unlucky, to be sure— Mr. Kendal never failed them before, not that she would wish—but she had always understood that to let young people run about late in the evening by themselves—not that she meant anything, but it was very unfortunate—if she had only been aware—Betty should have come down to walk up with them.'

Gilbert could not forbear an ashamed smile of intense affront at this reproach to his manliness.

'It was exceedingly unfortunate,' said Albinia, trying to repress her vexation; 'but Gilbert must learn to have resolution to guard himself. And now that he is come to ask your forgiveness, will you not grant it to him?'

'Oh, yes, yes, certainly, I forgive him from my heart. Yes, Gilbert, I do, only you must mind and beware—it is a very shocking thing—low company and all that—you've made yourself look as ill—and if you knew what a cake Betty had made—almond and citron both—"but it's for Master Gilbert," she said, "and I don't grudge"—and then to think—oh, dear!'

Albinia tried to express for him some becoming sorrow at having disappointed so much kindness, but she brought Miss Meadows down on her again.

'Oh, yes—she grudged nothing—but she never expected to meet with gratitude—she was quite prepared—' and she swallowed and almost sobbed, 'there had been changes. She was ready to make every excuse—she was sure she had done her best—but she understood—she didn't want to be assured. It always happened so—she knew her homely ways were not what Mrs. Kendal had been used to—and she didn't wonder—she only hoped the dear children —' and she was absolutely crying.

'My dear Maria,' said her mother, soothingly, 'you have worked yourself into such a state, that you don't know what you are saying. You must not let Mrs. Kendal think that we don't know that she is leading the dear children to all that is right and kind towards as.'

'Oh, no, I don't accuse any one. Only if they like to put me down under their feet and trample on me, they are welcome. That's all I have to say.'

Albinia was too much annoyed to be amused, and said, as she rose to take leave, 'I think it would be better for Gilbert, as well as for ourselves, if we were to say no more till some more cool and reasonable moment.'

'I am as cool as possible,' said Miss Meadows, convulsively clutching her hand; 'I'm not excited. Don't excite yourself, Mrs. Kendal—it is very bad for you. Tell her not, Mamma—oh! no, don't be excited—I mean nothing—I forgive poor dear Gibbie whatever little matters—I know there was excuse— boys with unsettled homes—but pray don't go and excite yourself—you see how cool I am—'

And she pursued Albinia to the garden-gate, recommending her at every step not to be excited, for she was as cool as possible, trembling and stammering all the time, with flushed cheeks, and tears in her eyes.

'I wonder who she thinks is excited?' exclaimed Albinia, as they finally turned their backs on her.

It was hardly in human nature to help making the observation, but it was not prudent. Gilbert took licence to laugh, and say, 'Aunt Maria is beside herself.'

'I never heard anything so absurd or unjust!' cried Albinia, too much irritated to remember anything but the sympathy of her auditor. 'If I am to be treated in this manner, I have done striving to please them. Due respect shall be shown, but as to intimacy and confidence—'

'I'm glad you see it so at last!' cried Gilbert. 'Aunt Maria has been the plague of my life, and I'm glad I told her a bit of my mind!'

What was Albinia's consternation! Her moment's petulance had undone her morning's work.

'Gilbert,' she said, 'we are both speaking very wrongly. I especially, who ought to have helped you.'

Spite of all succeeding humility the outburst had been fatal, and argue and plead as she might, she could not restore the boy to anything like the half satisfactory state of penitence in which she had led him from home. The giving way to her worse nature had awakened his, and though he still allowed that she should prepare the way for his confession to his father, all real sense of his outrageous conduct towards his aunt was gone.

Disheartened and worn out, Albinia did not feel equal even to going to take off her walking things, but sat down in the drawing-room on the sofa, and tried to silence the girls' questions and chatter, by desiring Lucy to read aloud.

By-and-by Mr. Kendal was heard returning, and she rose to arrest him in the hall. Her looks began the story, for he exclaimed, 'My dear Albinia, what is the matter?'

'Oh, Edmund, I have such things to tell you! I have been doing so wrong.'

She was almost sobbing, and he spoke fondly. 'No, Albinia, I can hardly believe that. Something has vexed you, and you must take time to compose yourself.'

He led her up to her own room, tried to soothe her, and would not listen to a word till she should be calm. After lying still for a little while, she thought she had recovered, but the very word 'Gilbert' brought such an expression of anxiety and sternness over his brow as overcame her again, and she could not speak without so much emotion that he silenced her; and finding that she could neither leave the subject, nor mention it without violent agitation, he said he would leave her for a little while, and perhaps she might sleep, and then be better able to speak to him. Still she held him, and begged that he would say nothing to Gilbert till he had heard her, and to pacify her he yielded, passed his promise, and quitted her with a kiss.

CHAPTER VII.

There was a messenger at Fairmead Parsonage by sunrise the next morning, and by twelve o'clock Mr. and Mrs. Ferrars were at Willow Lawn.

Mr. Kendal's grave brow and depressed manner did not reassure Winifred as he met her in the hall, although his words were, 'I hope she is doing well.'

He said no more, for the drawing-room door was moving to and fro, as if uneasy on the hinges, and as he made a step towards it, it disclosed a lady with black eyes and pinched features, whom he presented as 'Miss Meadows.'

'Well, now—I think—since more efficient—since I leave Mrs. Kendal to better—only pray tell her—my love and my mother's—if I could have been of any use—or shall I remain?—could I be of any service, Edmund?—I would not intrude when—but in the house—if I could be of any further use.'

'Of none, thank you,' said Mr. Kendal, 'unless you would be kind enough to take home the girls.'

'Oh, papa!' cried Lucy, I've got the keys. You wont be able to get on at all without me. Sophy may go, but I could not be spared.'

'Let it be as you will,' said Mr. Kendal; 'I only desire quiet, and that you should not inconvenience Mrs. Ferrars.'

'You will help me, will you not!' said Winifred, smiling, though she did not augur well from this opening scene. 'May I go soon to Albinia?'

'Presently, I hope,' said Mr. Kendal, with an uneasy glance towards Miss Meadows, 'she has seen no one as yet, and she is so determined that you cannot come till after Christmas, that she does not expect you.'

Miss Meadows began one of her tangled skeins of words, the most tangible of which was excitement; and Mr. Kendal, knowing by long experience that the only chance of a conclusion was to let her run herself down, held his tongue, and she finally departed.

Then he breathed more freely, and said he would go and prepare Albinia to see her sister, desiring Lucy to show Mrs. Ferrars to her room, and to take care not to talk upon the stairs.

This, Lucy, who was in high glory, obeyed by walking upon creaking tip-toe, apparently borrowed from her aunt, and whispering at a wonderful rate about her eagerness to see dear, dear mamma, and the darling little brother.

The spare room did not look expectant of guests, and felt still less so. It struck Winifred as very like the mouth of a well, and the paper showed patches of ancient damp. One maid was hastily laying the fire, the other shaking out the curtains, in the endeavour to render it habitable, and Lucy began saying, 'I must apologize. If papa had only given us notice that we were to have the pleasure of seeing you,' and then she dashed at the maid in all the pleasure of authority. 'Eweretta, go and bring up Mrs. Ferrars's trunks directly, and some water, and some towels.'

Winifred thought the greatest mercy to the hunted maid would be to withdraw as soon as she had hastily thrown off bonnet and cloak, and Lucy followed her into the passage, repeating that papa was so absent and forgetful, that it was very inconvenient in making arrangements. Whatever was ordinarily repressed in her, was repaying itself with interest in the pleasure of acting as mistress of the house.

Mrs. Ferrars beheld Gilbert sitting listlessly on the deep window-seat at the end of the passage, resting his head on his hand.

'Well!' exclaimed Lucy, 'if he is not there still! He has hardly stirred since breakfast! Come and speak to Mrs. Ferrars, Gilbert. Or,' and she simpered, 'shall it be Aunt Winifred?'

'As you please,' said Mrs. Ferrars, advancing towards her old acquaintance, whom she would hardly have recognised, so different was the pale, downcast, slouching figure, from the bright, handsome lad she remembered.

'How cold your hand is!' she exclaimed; 'you should not sit in this cold passage.'

'As I have been telling him all this morning,' said Lucy.

'How is she?' whispered the boy, rousing himself to look imploringly in Winifred's face.

'Your father seems satisfied about her.'

At that moment a door at some distance was opened, and Gilbert seemed to thrill all over as for the moment ere it closed a baby's cry was heard. He turned his face away, and rested it on the window. 'My brother! my brother!' he murmured, but at that moment his father turned the corner of the passage, saying that Albinia had heard their arrival, and was very eager to see her sister.

Still Winifred could not leave the boy without saying, 'You can make Gilbert happy about her, can you not? He is waiting here, watching anxiously for news of her.'

'Gilbert himself best knows whether he has a right to be made happy,' said

Mr. Kendal, gravely. 'I promised to ask no questions till she is able to explain, but I much fear that he has been causing her great grief and distress.'

He fixed his eyes on his son, and Winifred, in the belief that she was better out of their way, hurried to Albinia's room, and was seen very little all the rest of the day.

She was spared, however, to walk to church the next morning with her husband, Lucy showing them the way, and being quiet and agreeable when repressed by Mr. Ferrars's presence. After church, Mr. Dusautoy overtook them to inquire after Mrs. Kendal, and to make a kind proposal of exchanging Sunday duty. He undertook to drive the ponies home on the morrow, begged for credentials for the clerk, and messages for Willie and Mary, and seemed highly pleased with the prospect of the holiday, as he called it, only entreating that Mrs. Ferrars would be so kind as to look in on 'Fanny,' if Mrs. Kendal could spare her.

'I thought,' said Winifred to her husband, 'that you would rather have exchanged a Sunday when Albinia is better able to enjoy you?'

'That may yet be, but poor Kendal is so much depressed, that I do not like to leave him.'

'I have no patience with him!' cried Winifred; 'he does not seem to take the slightest pleasure in his baby, and he will hardly let poor Albinia do so either! Do you know, Maurice, it is as bad as I ever feared it would be. No, don't stop me, I must have it out. I always said he had no business to victimize her, and I am sure of it now! I believe this gloom of his has broken down her own dear sunny spirits! There she is—so unlike herself—so anxious and fidgety about her baby—will hardly take any one's word for his being as healthy and stout a child as I ever saw! And then, every other moment, she is restless about that boy—always asking where he is, or what he is doing. I don't see how she is ever to get well, while it goes on in this way! Mr. Kendal told me that Gilbert had been worrying and distressing her; and as to those girls, the eldest of them is intolerable with her airs, and the youngest—I asked her if she liked babies, and she growled, "No." Lucy said Gilbert was waiting in the passage for news of mamma, and she grunted, "All sham!" and that's the whole I have heard of her! He is bad enough in himself, but with such a train! My poor Albinia! If they are not the death of her, it will be lucky!'

'Well done, Winifred!'

'But, Maurice,' said his impetuous wife, in a curiously altered tone, 'are not you very unhappy about Albinia?'

'I shall leave you to find that out for me.'

'Then you are not?'

'I think Kendal thoroughly values and appreciates her, and is very uncomfortable without her.'

'I suppose so. People do miss a maid-of-all-work. I should not so much mind it, if she had been only *his* slave, but to be so to all those disagreeable children of his too! And with so little effect. Why can't he send them all to school?'

'Propose that to Albinia.'

'She did want the boy to go somewhere. I should not care where, so it were out of her way. What creatures they must be for her to have produced no more effect on them!'

'Poor Albinia! I am afraid it is a hard task: but these are still early days, and we see things at a disadvantage. We shall be able to judge whether there be really too great a strain on her spirits, and if so, I would talk to Kendal.'

'And I wonder what is to come of that. It seems to me like what John Smith calls singing psalms to a dead horse.'

'John Smith! I am glad you mentioned him; I shall desire Dusautoy to bring him here on Monday.'

'What! as poor Albinia would say, you can't exist a week without John Smith.'

'Even so. I want him to lay out a plan for draining the garden. That pond is intolerable. I suspect that all, yourself included, will become far more good-tempered in consequence.'

'A capital measure, but do you mean that Edmund Kendal is going to let you and John Smith drain his pond under his very nose, and never find it out? I did not imagine him quite come to that.'

'Not *quite*,' said Maurice; 'it is with his free consent, and I believe he will be very glad to have it done without any trouble to himself. He said that Albinia *thought it damp*, and when I put a few sanatory facts before him, thanked me heartily, and seemed quite relieved. If they had only been in Sanscrit, they would have made the greater impression.'

'One comfort is, Maurice, that however provoking you are at first, you generally prove yourself reasonable at last, I am glad you are not Mr. Kendal.'

'Ah! it will have a fine effect on you to spend your Christmas-day tete-a-tete with him.'

Mrs. Ferrars's views underwent various modifications, like all hasty yet candid judgments. She took Mr. Kendal into favour when she found him placidly submitting to Miss Meadows's showers of words, in order to prevent her gaining access to his wife.

'Maria Meadows is a very well-meaning person,' he said afterwards; 'but I know of no worse infliction in a sick-room.'

'I wonder,' thought Winifred, 'whether he married to get rid of her. I should have thought it justifiable had it been any one but Albinia!'

The call on Mrs. Dusautoy was consoling. It was delightful to find how Albinia was loved and valued at the vicarage. Mrs. Dusautoy began by sending her as a message, John's first exclamation on hearing of the event. 'Then she will never be of any more use.' In fact, she said, it was much to him like having a curate disabled, and she believed he could only be consoled by the hopes of a pattern christening, and of a nursery for his school-girls; but there Winifred shook her head, Fairmead had a prior claim, and Albinia had long had her eye upon a scholar of her own.

'I told John that she would! and he must bear it as he can,' laughed Mrs. Dusautoy; and she went on more seriously to say that her gratitude was beyond expression, not merely for the actual help, though that was much, but for the sympathy, the first encouragement they had met among their richer parishioners, and she spoke of the refreshment of the mirthfulness and playful manner, so as to convince Winifred that they had neither died away nor been everywhere wasted.

Winifred had no amenable patient. Weak and depressed as Albinia was, her restlessness and air of anxiety could not be appeased. There was a look of being constantly on the watch, and once, when her door was ajar, before Winifred was aware she exerted her voice to call Gilbert!

Pushing the door just wide enough to enter, and treading almost noiselessly, he came forward, looking from side to side as with a sense of guilt. She stretched out her hand and smiled, and he obeyed the movement that asked him to bend and kiss her, but still durst not speak.

'Let me have the baby,' she said.

Mrs. Ferrars laid it beside her, and held aloof. Gilbert's eyes were fixed intently on it.

'Yes, Gilbert,' Albinia said, 'I know what you will feel for him. He can't be what you once had—but oh, Gilbert, you will do all that an elder brother can to make him like Edmund!'

Gilbert wrung her fingers, and ventured to stoop down to kiss the little red forehead. The tears were running down his cheeks, and he could not speak.

'If your father might only say the same of him! that he never grieved him!' said Albinia; 'but oh, Gilbert—example,' and then, pausing and gazing searchingly in his face, 'You have not told papa.'

'No,' whispered Gilbert.

'Winifred,' said Albinia, 'would you be so kind as to ask papa to come?'

Winifred was forced to obey, though feeling much to blame as Mr. Kendal rose with a sigh of uneasiness. Gilbert still stood with his hand clasped in Albinia's, and she held it while her weak voice made the full confession for him, and assured his father of his shame and sorrow. There needed no such assurance, his whole demeanour had been sorrow all these dreary days, and Mr. Kendal could not but forgive, though his eye spoke deep grief.

'I could not refuse pardon thus asked,' he said. 'Oh, Gilbert, that I could hope this were the beginning of a new course!'

Albinia looked from Gilbert to his little brother, and back again to Gilbert.

'It *shall* be,' she said, and Gilbert's resolution was perhaps the more sincere that he spoke no word.

'Poor boy,' said Albinia, half to herself and half aloud, 'I think I feel more strong to love and to help him!'

That interview was a dangerous experiment, and she suffered for it. As her brother said, instead of having too little life, she had too much, and could not let herself rest; she had never cultivated the art of being still, and when she was weak, she could not be calm.

Still the strength of her constitution staved off the nervous fever of her spirits, and though she was not at all a comfortable patient, she made a certain degree of progress, so that though it was not easy to call her better, she was not quite so ill, and grew less irrational in her solicitude, and more open to other ideas. 'Do you know, Winifred,' she said one day, 'I have been thinking myself at Fairmead till I almost believed I heard John Smith's voice under the window.'

Winifred was obliged to look out at the window to hide her smile. Maurice, who was standing on the lawn with the very John Smith, beckoned to her, and she went down to hear his plans. He was wanted at home the next day, and asked whether she thought he had better take Gilbert with him. 'It is the wisest thing that has been said yet!' exclaimed she. 'Now I shall have a chance for Albinia!' and accordingly, Mr. Kendal having given a gracious and grateful consent, Albinia was informed; but Winifred thought her almost perverse when a perturbed look came over her, and she said, 'It is very kind in Maurice, but I must speak to him.'

He was struck by the worn, restless expression of her features, so unlike the calm contented repose of a young mother, and when she spoke to him, her first word was of Gilbert. 'Maurice, it is so kind, I know you will make him happy—but oh! take care—he is so delicate—indeed, he is—don't let him get wet through.'

Maurice promised, but Albinia resumed with minutiae of directions, ending with, 'Oh! if he should get hurt or into any mischief, what should we do? Pray, take care, Maurice, you are not used to such delicate boys.'

'My dear, I think you may rely on me.'

'Yes, but you will not be too strict with him—' and more was following, when her brother said, 'I promise you to make him my special charge. I like the boy very much. I think you may be reasonable, and trust him with me, without so much agitation. You have not let me see my own nephew yet.'

Albinia looked with her wistful piteous face at her brother as he took in his arms her noble-looking fair infant.

'You are a great fellow indeed, sir,' said his uncle. 'Now if I were your mamma, I would be proud of you, rather than—'

'I am afraid!' said Albinia, in a sudden low whisper.

He looked at her anxiously.

'Let me have him,' she said; then as Maurice bent over her, and she hastily gathered the babe into her arms, she whispered in quick, low, faint accents, 'Do you know how many children have been born in this house?'

Mr. Ferrars understood her, he too had seen the catalogue in the church, and guessed that the phantoms of her boy's dead brethren dwelt on her imagination, forbidding her to rejoice in him hopefully. He tried to say something encouraging of the child's appearance, but she would not let him go on. 'I know,' she said, 'he is so now—but—' then catching her breath again and speaking very low, 'his father does not dare look at him—I see that he is sorry for me—Oh, Maurice, it will come, and I shall be able to do nothing!'

Maurice felt his lip quivering as his sister's voice became choked—the sister to whom he had once been the whole world, and who still could pour out her inmost heart more freely to him than to any other. But it was a time for grave authority, and though he spoke gently, it was almost sternly.

'Albinia, this is not right. It is not thankful or trustful. No, do not cry, but listen to me. Your child is as likely to do well as any child in the world, but nothing is so likely to do him harm as your want of composure.'

'I tell myself so,' said Albinia, 'but there is no helping it.'

'Yes, there is. Make it your duty to keep yourself still, and not be troubled about what may or may not happen, but be glad of the present pleasure.'

'Don't you think I am?' said Albinia, half smiling; 'so glad, that I grow frightened at myself, and—' As if fain to leave the subject, she added, 'And it is what you don't understand, Maurice, but he can't be the first to Edmund as he is to me—never—and when I get almost jealous for him, I think of Gilbert and the girls—and oh! there is so much to do for them—they want a mother so much—and Winifred wont let me see them, or tell me about them!'

She had grown piteous and incoherent, and a glance from Winifred told him, 'this is always the way.'

'My dear,' he said, 'you will never be fit to attend to them if you do not use this present time rightly. You may hurt your health, and still more certainly, you will go to work fretfully and impetuously. If you have a busy life, the more reason to learn to be tranquil. Calm is forced on you now, and if you give way to useless nervous brooding over the work you are obliged to lay aside for a time, you have no right to hope that you will either have judgment or temper for your tasks.'

'But how am I to keep from thinking, Maurice? The weaker I am, the more I think.'

'Are you dutiful as to what Winifred there thinks wisest? Ah! Albinia, you want to learn, as poor Queen Anne of Austria did, that docility in illness may be self-resignation into higher Hands. Perhaps you despise it, but it is no mean exercise of strength and resolution to be still.'

Albinia looked at him as if receiving a new idea.

'And,' he added, bending nearer her face, and speaking lower, 'when you pray, let them be hearty faithful prayers that God's hand may be over your child—your children, not half-hearted faithless ones, that He may work out your will in them.'

'Oh, Maurice, how did you know? But you are not going? I have so much to talk over with you.'

'Yes, I must go; and you must be still. Indeed I will watch over Gilbert as though he were mine. Yes, even more. Don't speak again, Albinia, I desire you will not. Good-bye.'

That lecture had been the most wholesome treatment she had yet received;

she ceased to give way without effort to restless thoughts and cares, and was much less refractory.

When at last Lucy and Sophia were admitted, Winifred found perils that she had not anticipated. Lucy was indeed supremely and girlishly happy: but it was Sophy whose eye Albinia sought with anxiety, and that eye was averted. Her cheek was cold like that of a doll when Albinia touched it eagerly with her lips; and when Lucy admonished her to kiss the dear little brother, she fairly turned and ran out of the room.

'Poor Sophy!' said Lucy. 'Never mind her, mamma, but she is odder than ever, since baby has been born. When Eweretta came up and told us, she hid her face and cried; and when grandmamma wanted to make us promise to love him with all our hearts, and not make any difference, she would only say, "I wont!"'

'We will leave him to take care of that, Lucy,' said Albinia. But though she spoke cheerfully, Winifred was not surprised, after a little interval, to hear sounds like stifled weeping.

Almost every home subject was so dangerous, that whenever Mrs. Ferrars wanted to make cheerful, innocent conversation, she began to talk of her visit to Ireland and the beautiful Galway coast, and the O'Mores of Ballymakilty, till Albinia grew quite sick of the names of the whole clan of thirty-six cousins, and thought, with her aunts, that Winifred was too Irish. Yet, at any other time, the histories would have made her sometimes laugh, and sometimes cry, but the world was sadly out of joint with her.

There was a sudden change when, for the first time her eye rested on the lawn, and she beheld the work of drainage. The light glanced in her eye, the colour rose on her cheek, and she exclaimed, 'How kind of Edmund!'

Winifred must needs give her husband his share. 'Ah! you would never have had it done without Maurice.'

'Yes,' said Albinia, 'Edmund has been out of the way of such things, but he consented, you know.' Then as her eyes grew liquid, 'A duck pond is a funny subject for sentiment, but oh! if you knew what that place has been to my imagination from the first, and how the wreaths of mist have wound themselves into spectres in my dreams, and stretched out white shrouds now for one, now for the other!' and she shuddered.

'And you have gone through all this and never spoken. No wonder your nerves and spirits were tried.'

'I did speak at first,' said Albinia; 'but I thought Edmund did not hear, or thought it nonsense, and so did I at times. But you see he did attend; he always does, you see, at the right time. It was only my impatience.'

'I suspect Maurice and John Smith had more to do with it,' said Winifred.

'Well, we wont quarrel about that,' said Albinia. 'I only know that whoever brought it about has taken the heaviest weight off my mind that has been there yet.'

In truth, the terror, half real, half imaginary, had been a sorer burthen than all the positive cares for those unruly children, or their silent, melancholy father; and the relief told in all ways—above all, in the peace with which she began to regard her child. Still she would provoke Winifred by bestowing all her gratitude on Mr. Kendal, who began to be persuaded that he had made an heroic exertion.

Winifred had been somewhat scandalized by discovering Albinia's deficiencies in the furniture development. She was too active and stirring, and too fond of out-of-door occupation, to regard interior decoration as one of the domestic graces, 'her nest was rather that of the ostrich than the chaffinch,' as Winifred told her on the discovery that her morning-room had been used for no other purpose than as a deposit for all the books, wedding presents, lumber, etc., which she had never had leisure to arrange.

'You might be more civil,' answered Albinia. 'Remember that the ringdove never made half such a fuss about her nest as the magpie.'

'Well, I am glad you have found some likeness in yourself to a dove,' rejoined Winifred.

Mrs. Ferrars set vigorously to work with Lucy, and rendered the room so pretty and pleasant, that Lucy pronounced that it must be called nothing but the boudoir, for it was a perfect little bijou.

Albinia was laid on the sofa by the sparkling fire, by her side the little cot, and in her hand a most happy affectionate letter from Gilbert, detailing the Fairmead Christmas festivities. She felt the invigoration of change of room, admired and was grateful for Winifred's work, and looked so fair and bright, so tranquil and so contented, that her sister and husband could not help pausing to contemplate her as an absolutely new creature in a state of quiescence.

It did not last long, and Mrs. Ferrars felt herself the unwilling culprit. Attracted by sounds in the hall, she found the two girls receiving from the hands of Genevieve Durant a pretty basket choicely adorned with sprays of myrtle, saying mamma would be much obliged, and they would take it up at once; Genevieve should take home her basket, and down plunged their hands regardless of the garniture.

Genevieve's disappointed look caught Winifred's attention, and springing forward she exclaimed, 'You shall come to Mrs. Kendal yourself, my dear. She must see your pretty basket,' and yourself, she could have added, as she met the grateful glitter of the dark eyes.

Lucy remonstrated that mamma had seen no one yet, not even Aunt Maria, but Mrs. Ferrars would not listen, and treading airily, yet with reverence that would have befitted a royal palace, Genevieve was ushered upstairs, and with heartfelt sweetness, and timid grace, presented her etrennes.

Under the fragrant sprays lay a small white-paper parcel, tied with narrow blue satin bows, such as no English fingers could accomplish, and within was a little frock-body, exquisitely embroidered, with a breastplate of actual point lace in a pattern like frostwork on the windows. It was such work as Madame Belmarche had learnt in a convent in times of history, and poor little Genevieve had almost worn out her black eyes on this piece of homage to her dear Mrs. Kendal, grieving only that she had not been able to add the length of robe needed to complete her gift.

Albinia's kiss was recompense beyond her dreams, and she fairly cried for joy when she was told that she should come and help to dress the babe in it for his christening. Mrs. Ferrars would walk out with her at once to buy a sufficiency of cambric for the mighty skirts.

That visit was indeed nothing but pleasure, but Mrs. Ferrars had not calculated on contingencies and family punctilios. She forgot that it would be a mortal offence to let in any one rather than Miss Meadows; but the rest of the family were so well aware of it, that when she returned she heard a perfect sparrow's-nest of voices—Lucy's pert and eager, Miss Meadows's injured and shrill, and Albinia's, alas! thin and loud, half sarcasm, half fret.

There sat Aunt Maria fidgeting in the arm-chair; Lucy stood by the fire; Albinia's countenance sadly different from what it had been in the morning— weary, impatient, and excited, all that it ought not to be!

Winifred would have cleared the room at once, but this was not easy, and poor Albinia was so far gone as to be determined on finishing that endless thing, an altercation, so all three began explaining and appealing at once.

It seemed that Mrs. Osborn was requiting Mrs. Kendal's neglect in not having inquired after her when the Admiral's sister's husband died, by the omission of inquiries at present; whereat Albinia laughed a feeble, overdone giggle, and observed that she believed Mrs. Osborn knew all that passed in Willow Lawn better than the inmates; and Lucy deposed that Sophy and Loo were together every day, though Sophy knew mamma did not like it. Miss Meadows said if reparation were not made, the Osborns had expressed their intention of omitting Lucy and Sophy from their Twelfth-day party.

To this Albinia pettishly replied that the girls were to go to no Christmas parties without her; Miss Meadows had taken it very much to heart, and Lucy was declaiming against mamma making any condescension to Mrs. Osborn, or herself being supposed to care for 'the Osborn's parties,' where the boys were so rude and vulgar, the girls so boisterous, and the dancing a mere romp. Sophy might like it, but she never did!

Miss Meadows was hurt by her niece's defection, and had come to 'Oh, very well,' and 'things were altered,' and 'people used to be grateful to old friends, but there were changes.' And thereby Lucy grew personal as to the manners of the Osborns, while Albinia defended herself against the being grand or exclusive, but it was her duty to do what she thought right for the children! Yes, Miss Meadows was quite aware—only grandmamma was so nervous about poor dear Gibbie missing his Christmas dinner for the first time —being absent—Mrs. Ferrars would take great care, but damp stockings and all—

Winifred endeavoured to stem the tide of words, but in vain, between the meandering incoherency of the one, and the nervous rapidity of the other, and they had both set off again on this fresh score, when in despair she ran downstairs, rapped at the study door, and cried, 'Mr. Kendal, Mr. Kendal, will you not come! I can't get Miss Meadows out of Albinia's room.'

Forth came Mr. Kendal, walked straight upstairs, and stood in full majesty on the threshold. Holding out his hand to Maria with grave courtesy, he thanked her for coming to see his wife, but at the same time handed her down, saw her out safely at the hall door, and Lucy into the drawing-room.

It was a pity that he had not returned to Albinia's room, for she was too much excited to be composed without authority. First, she scolded Winifred; 'it was the thing she most wished to avoid, that he should fancy her teased by anything the Meadowses could say,' and she laughed, and protested she never was vexed, such absurdity did not hurt her in the least.

'It has tired you, though,' said Winifred. 'Lie quite down and sleep.'

Of course, however, Albinia would not believe that she was tired, and began to talk of the Osborns and their party—she was annoyed at the being thought too fine. 'If it were not such a penance, and if you would not be gone home, I really would ask you to take the girls, Winifred.'

'I shall not be gone home.'

'Yes, you will. I am well, and every one wants you.'

'Did you not hear Willie's complimentary message, that he is never naughty now, because Gilbert makes him so happy?'

'But, Winifred, the penny club! The people must have their things.'

'They can wait, or—'

'It is very well for us to talk of waiting,' cried Albinia, 'but how should we like a frosty night without cloaks, or blankets, or fire? I did not think it of you, Winifred. It is the first winter I have been away from my poor old dames, and I did think you would have cared for them.'

And thereupon her overwrought spirits gave way in a flood of tears, as she angrily averted her face from her sister, who could have cried too, not at the injustice, but with compassion and perplexity lest there should be an equally violent reaction either of remorse or of mirth.

It must be confessed that Albinia was very much the creature of health. Never having been ill before, the depression had been so new that it broke her completely down; convalescence made her fractious.

Recovery, however, filled her with such an ecstasy of animal spirits that her time seemed to be entirely passed in happiness or in sleep, and cares appeared to have lost all power. It was so sudden a change that Winifred was startled, though it was a very pleasant one, and she did not reflect that this was as far from the calm, self-restrained, meditative tranquillity enjoined by Maurice, as had been the previous restless, querulous state. Both were body more than mind, but Mrs. Ferrars was much more ready to be merry with Albinia than to moralize about her. And it was droll that the penny club was one of the first stages in her revival.

'Oh, mamma,' cried Lucy, flying in, 'Mr. Dusautoy is at the door. There is such a to do. All the women have been getting gin with their penny club tickets, and Mrs. Brock has been stealing the money, and Mr. Dusautoy wants to know if you paid up three-and-fourpence for the Hancock children.'

Albinia instantly invited Mr. Dusautoy to explain in person, and he entered, hearty and pleasant as ever, but in great haste, for he had left his Fanny keeping the peace between five angry women, while he came out to collect evidence.

The Bayford clothing-club payments were collected by Mrs. Brock, the sexton's wife, and distributed by tickets to be produced at the various shops in the town. Mrs. Brock had detected some women exchanging their tickets for gin, and the offending parties retaliated by accusing her of embezzling the subscriptions, both parties launching into the usual amount of personalities and exaggerations.

Albinia's testimony cleared Mrs. Brock as to the three-and-fourpence, but she 'snuffed the battle from afar,' and rushed into a scheme of taking the clothing-club into her own hands, collecting the pence, having the goods from London, and selling them herself—she would propose it on the very first opportunity to the Dusautoys. Winifred asked if she had not a good deal on her hands already.

'My dear, I have the work in me of a young giant.'

'And will Mr. Kendal like it?'

'He would never find it out unless I told him, and very possibly not then. Six months hence, perhaps, he may tell me he is glad that Lucy is inclined to useful pursuits, and that *is* approval, Winifred, much more than if I went and worried him about every little petty woman's matter.'

'Every one to her taste,' thought Winifred, who had begun to regard Mr. and Mrs. Kendal in the same relation as the king and queen at chess.

The day before the christening, Mr. Ferrars brought back Gilbert and his own little Willie.

Through all the interchange of greetings, Gilbert would hardly let go Albinia's hand, and the moment her attention was free, he earnestly whispered, 'May I see my brother?'

She took him upstairs at once. 'Let me look a little while,' he said, hanging over the child with a sort of hungry fondness and curiosity. 'My brother! my brother!' he repeated. 'It has rung in my ears every morning that I can say my brother once more, till I have feared it was a dream.'

It was the sympathy Albinia cared for, come back again! 'I hope he will be a good brother to you,' she said.

'He must be good! he can't help it! He has you!' said Gilbert. 'See, he is opening his eyes—oh! how blue! May I touch him?'

'To be sure you may. He is not sugar,' said Albinia, laughing. 'There— make an arm; you may have him if you like. Your left arm, you awkward man. Yes, that is right. You will do quite as well as I, who never touched a baby till Willie was born. There, sir, how do you like your brother Gilbert?'

Gilbert held him reverently, and gave him back with a sigh when he seemed to have satiated his gaze and touch, and convinced himself that his new possession was substantial. 'I say,' he added wistfully, 'did you think *that* name would bring ill-luck?

She knew the name he meant, and answered, 'No, but your father could not have borne it. Besides, Gibbie, we would not think him *instead* of Edmund.

No, he shall learn, to look up to his other brother as you do, and look to meeting and knowing him some day.'

Gilbert shivered at this, and made no opposition to her carrying him downstairs to his uncle, and then Gilbert hurried off for the basket of snowdrops that he had gathered early, from a favourite spot at Fairmead. That short absence seemed to have added double force to his affection; he could hardly bear to be away from her, and every moment when he could gain her ear, poured histories of the delights of Fairmead, where Mr. Ferrars had devoted himself to his amusement, and had made him happier than perhaps he had ever been in his life—he had had a taste of shooting, of skating, of snowballing—he had been useful and important in the village feasts, had dined twice at Colonel Bury's, and felt himself many degrees nearer manhood.

To hear of her old haunts and friends from such enthusiastic lips, delighted Albinia, and her felicity with her baby, with Mr. Kendal, with her brother and his little son, was one of the brightest things in all the world—the fresh young loving bloom of her matronhood was even sweeter and more beautiful than her girlish days.

Poor little frail, blighted Mrs. Dusautoy! Winifred could not help wondering if the contrast pained her, when in all the glory of her motherly thankfulness, Albinia carried her beautiful newly-christened Maurice Ferrars Kendal to the vicarage to show him off, lying so open-chested and dignified, in Genevieve's pretty work, with a sort of manly serenity already dawning on his baby brow.

Winifred need not have pitied the little lady. She would not have changed with Mrs. Kendal—no, not for that perfect health, usefulness, value—nor even for such a baby as that. No, indeed! She loved—she rejoiced in all her friend's sweet and precious gifts—but Mrs. Dusautoy had one gift that she prized above all.

Even grandmamma and Aunt Maria did justice to Master Maurice's attractions, at least in public, though it came round that Miss Meadows did not admire fat children, and when he had once been seen in Lucy's arms, an alarm arose that Mrs. Kendal would allow the girls to carry him about, till his weight made them crooked, but Albinia was too joyous to take their displeasure to heart, and it only served her for something to laugh at.

They had a very happy christening party, chiefly juvenile, in honour of little Willie and of Francis and Emily Nugent. Albinia was so radiantly lively and good-natured, and her assistants, Winifred, Maurice, and Mr. Dusautoy, so kind, so droll, so inventive, that even Aunt Maria forgot herself in enjoyment and novelty, and was like a different person. Mr. Kendal looked at her with a pleased sad wonder, and told his wife it reminded him of what she had been when she was nearly the prettiest girl at Bayford. Gilbert devoted himself as usual to making Genevieve feel welcome; and she had likewise Willie Ferrars and Francis Nugent at her feet. Neither urchin would sit two inches away from her all the evening, and in all games she was obliged to obviate jealousies by being partner to both at once. Where there was no one to oppress her, she came out with all her natural grace and vivacity, and people of a larger growth than her little admirers were charmed with her.

Lucy was obliging, ready, and useful, and looked very pretty, the only blot was the heavy dulness of poor Sophy, who seemed resolved to take pleasure in nothing. Winifred varied in opinion whether her moodiness arose from ill-health, or from jealousy of her little brother. This latter Albinia would not believe, especially as she saw that little Maurice's blue eyes were magnets that held the silent Sophy fast, but surly denials silenced her interrogations as to illness, and made her content to acquiesce in Lucy's explanation that Sophy was only cross because the Osborns and Drurys were not asked.

Albinia did her duty handsomely by the two families a day or two after, for whatever reports might come round, they were always ready to receive her advances, and she only took notice of what she saw, instead of what she heard. Her brother helped Mr. Kendal through the party, and Winifred made a discovery that excited her more than Albinia thought warranted by any fact relating to the horde of Irish cousins.

'Only think, Albinia, I have found out that poor Ellen O'More is Mr. Goldsmith's sister!'

'Indeed! But I am afraid I don't remember which Ellen O'More is. You know I never undertake to recollect any but your real cousins out of the thirty-six.'

'For shame, Albinia, I have so often told you about Ellen. I'm sure you can't forget. Her husband is my sister's brother-in-law's cousin.'

'Oh, Winifred, Winifred!'

'But I tell you, her husband is the third son of old Mr. O'More of Ballymakilty, and was in the army.'

'Oh! the half-pay officer with the twelve children in the cottage on the estate.'

'There now, I did think you would care when I told you of a soldier, a Waterloo man too, and you only call him a half-pay officer!'

'I do remember,' said Albinia, taking a little pity, 'that you used to be sorry for his good little English wife.'

'Of course. I knew she had married him very imprudently, but she has struggled gallantly with ill-health, and poverty, and Irish recklessness. I quite venerate her, and it seems these Goldsmiths had so far cast her off that they had no notion of the extent of her troubles.'

'Just like them,' said Albinia. 'Is that the reason you wish me to make the most of the connexion? Let me see, my sister-in-law's sister's wife—no, husband's brother's uncle, eh?'

'I don't want you to do anything,' said Winifred, a little hurt, 'only if you had seen Ellen's patient face you would be interested in her.'

'Well, I am interested, you know I am, Winifred. I hope you interested our respected banker, which would be more to the purpose.'

'I think I did,' said Winifred; 'at least he said "poor Ellen" once or twice. I don't want him to do anything for the captain, you might give him a thousand pounds and he would never be the better for it: but that fourth, boy, Ulick, is without exception the nicest fellow I ever saw in my life—so devoted to his mother, so much more considerate and self-denying than any of the others, and very clever. Maurice examined him and was quite astonished. We did get him sent to St. Columba for the present, but whether they will keep him there no one can guess, and it is the greatest pity he should run to waste. I told Mr. Goldsmith all this, and I really think he seemed to attend. I wonder if it will work.'

Albinia was by this time anxious that it should take effect, and they agreed that an old bachelor banker and his sister, both past sixty, were the very people to adopt a promising nephew.

What had become of the multitude of things which Albinia had to discuss with her brother? The floodtide of bliss had floated her over all the stumbling-blocks and shoals that the ebb had disclosed, and she had absolutely forgotten all the perplexities that had seemed so trying. Even when she sought a private interview to talk to him about Gilbert, it was in full security of hearing the praises of her darling.

'A nice boy, a very nice boy,' returned Maurice; 'most amiable and intelligent, and particularly engaging, from his feeling being so much on the surface.'

'Nothing can be more sincere and genuine,' she cried, as if this fell a little flat.

'Certainly not, at the time.'

'Always!' exclaimed Albinia. 'You must not distrust him because he is not like you or Fred, and has never been hardened and taught reserve by rude boys. Nothing was ever more real than his affection, poor dear boy,' and the tears thrilled to her eyes.

'No, and it is much to his credit. His love and gratitude to you are quite touching, poor fellow; but the worst of it is that I am afraid he is very timid, both physically and morally.'

Often as she had experienced this truth, the soldier's daughter could not bear to avow it, and she answered hastily, 'He has never been braced or trained; he was always ill till within the last few years—coddling at first, neglect afterwards, he has it all to learn, and it is too late for school.'

'Yes, he is too old to be laughed at or bullied out of cowardice. Indeed, I doubt whether there ever would have been substance enough for much wear and tear.'

'I know you have a turn for riotous, obstinate boys! You want Willie to be another Fred,' said Albinia, like an old hen, ruffling up her feathers. 'You think a boy can't be good for anything unless he is a universal plague!'

'I wonder what you will do with your own son,' said Maurice, amused, 'since you take Gilbert's part so fiercely.'

'I trust my boy will never be as much to be pitied as his brother,' said Albinia, with tenderness that accused her petulance. 'At least he can never be a lonely twin with that sore spot in his heart. Oh, Maurice, how can any one help dealing gently with my poor Gibbie?'

'Gentle dealing is the very thing he wants,' said Mr. Ferrars; 'and I am thinking how to find it for him. How did his going to Traversham fail?'

'I don't know; Edmund did not like to send him without having seen Traversham, and I could not go. But I don't think there is any need for his going away. His father has been quite enough tormented about it, and I can manage him very well now. He is always good and happy with me. I mean to try to ride with him, and I have promised to teach him music, and we shall garden. Never fear, I will employ him and keep him out of mischief—it is all pleasure to me.'

'And pray what are your daughters and baby to do, while you are galloping after Gilbert?'

'Oh! I'll manage. We can all do things together. Come, Maurice, I wont have Edmund teased, and I can't bear parting with any of them, or think that any strange man can treat Gibbie as I should.'

Maurice was edified by his sister's warm-hearted weakness, but not at all inclined to let 'Edmund' escape a 'teasing.'

Mr. Kendal's first impulse always was to find a sufficient plea for doing nothing. If Gilbert was to go to India, it was not worth while to give him a classical education.

'Is he to go to India? Albinia had not told me so.'

'I thought she was aware of it; but possibly I may not have mentioned it. It has been an understood thing ever since I came home. He will have a good deal of the property in this place, but he had better have seen something of the world. Bayford is no place for a man to settle down in too young.'

'Certainly,' said Mr. Ferrars, repressing a smile. 'Then are you thinking of sending him to Haileybury?'

He was pronounced too young, besides, it was explained that his destination in India was unfixed. On going home it had been a kind of promise that one of the twin brothers should have an appointment in the civil service, the other should enter the bank of Kendal and Kendal, and the survivor was unconsciously suspended between these alternatives, while the doubt served as a convenient protection to his father from making up his mind to prepare him for either of these or for anything else.

The prompt Ferrars temper could bear it no longer, and Maurice spoke out. 'I'll tell you what, Kendal, it is time to attend to your own concerns. If you choose to let your son run to ruin, because you will not exert yourself to remove him from temptation, I shall not stand by to see my sister worn out with making efforts to save him. She is willing and devoted, she fancies she could work day and night to preserve him, and she does it with all her heart; but it is not woman's work, she cannot do it, and it is not fit to leave it to her. When Gilbert has broken her heart as well as yours, and left an evil example to his brother, then you will feel what it is to have kept a lad whom you know to be well disposed, but weak as water, in the very midst of contamination, and to have left your young, inexperienced wife to struggle alone to save him. If you are unwarned by the experience of last autumn and winter, I could not pity you, whatever might happen.'

Maurice, who had run on the longer because Mr. Kendal did not answer immediately, was shocked at his own impetuosity; but a rattling peal of thunder was not more than was requisite.

'I believe you are right,' Mr. Kendal said. 'I was to blame for leaving him so entirely to Albinia; but she is very fond of him, and is one who will never be induced to spare herself, and there were considerations. However, she shall be relieved at once. What do you recommend?'

Mr. Ferrars actually made Mr. Kendal promise to set out for Traversham with him next morning, thirty miles by the railway, to inspect Mr. Downton and his pupils.

Albinia had just sense enough not to object, though the discovery of the Indian plans was such a blow to her that she could not be consoled by all her husband's representations of the advantages Gilbert would derive there, and of his belief that the Kendal constitution always derived strength from a hot climate, and that to himself going to India seemed going home. She took refuge in the hope that between the two Indian stools Gilbert might fall upon one of the professions which she thought alone worthy of man's attention, the clerical or the military.

Under Maurice's escort, Mr. Kendal greatly enjoyed his expedition; liked Traversham, was satisfied with the looks of the pupils, and very much pleased with the tutor, whom he even begged to come to Bayford for a conference with Mrs. Kendal, and this was received by her as no small kindness. She was delighted with Mr. Downton, and felt as if Gilbert could be safely trusted in his charge; nor was Gilbert himself reluctant. He was glad to escape from his tempter, and to begin a new life, and though he hung about Mrs. Kendal, and implored her to write often, and always tell him about his little brother—nay, though he cried like a child at the last, yet still he was happy and satisfied to go, and to break the painful fetters which had held him so long.

And though Albinia likewise shed some parting tears, she could not but own that she was glad to have him in trustworthy hands; and as to the additional time thus gained, it was disposed of in a million of bright plans for every one's service—daughters, baby, parish, school, classes, clubs, neighbours. It almost made Winifred giddy to hear how much she had undertaken, and yet with what zest she talked and acted.

'There's your victim, Winifred,' said Maurice, as they drove away, and looked back at Albinia, scandalizing Bayford by standing in the open gateway, her face all smiles of cheerful parting, the sun and wind making merry with her chestnut curls, her baby in one arm, the other held up to wave her farewell.

'That child will catch cold,' began Winifred, turning to sign her to go in. 'Well,' she continued, 'after all, I believe some people like an idol that sits quiet to be worshipped! To be sure she must want to beat him sometimes, as the Africans do their gods. But, on the whole, her sentiment of reverence is satisfied, and she likes the acting for herself, and reigning absolute. Yes, she is quite happy—why do you look doubtful? Don't you admire her?'

'From my heart.'

'Then why do you doubt? Do you expect her to do anything?'

'A little too much of everything.'

CHAPTER VIII.

Yes! Albinia was excessively happy. Her naturally high spirits were enhanced by the enjoyment of recovery, and reaction, from her former depression. Since the great stroke of the drainage, every one looked better, and her pride in her babe was without a drawback. He seemed to have inherited her vigour and superabundance of life, and 'that first wondrous spring to all but babes unknown,' was in him unusually rapid, so that he was a marvel of fair stateliness, size, strength, and intelligence, so unlike the little blighted buds which had been wont to fade at Willow Lawn, that his father watched him with silent, wondering affection, and his eldest sister was unmerciful in her descriptions of his progress; while even Sophia had not been proof against his smiles, and was proud to be allowed to carry him about and fondle him.

Neither was Mr. Kendal's reserve the trial that it had once been. After having become habituated to it as a necessary idiosyncrasy, she had become rather proud of his lofty inaccessibility. Besides, her brother's visit, her recovery, and the renewed hope and joy in this promising child, had not been without effect in rousing him from his apathy. He was less inclined to shun his fellow-creatures, had become friendly with the Vicar, and had even let Albinia take him into Mrs. Dusautoy's drawing-room, where he had been fairly happy. Having once begun taking his wife out in the carriage, he found this much more agreeable than his solitary ride, and was in the condition to which Albinia had once imagined it possible to bring him, in which gentle means and wholesome influence might lead him imperceptibly out of his morbid habits of self-absorption.

Unfortunately, in the flush of blitheness and whirl of activity, Albinia failed to perceive the relative importance of objects, and he had taught her to believe herself so little necessary to him that she had not learnt to make her pursuits and occupations subservient to his convenience. As long as the drive took place regularly, all was well, but he caught a severe cold, which lasted even to the setting in of the east winds, the yearly misery of a man who hardly granted that India was over-hot. Though Albinia had removed much listing, and opened various doors and windows, he made no complaints, but did his best to keep the obnoxious fresh air out of his study, and seldom crossed the threshold thereof but with a shiver.

His favourite atmosphere was quite enough to account for a return of the old mood, but Albinia had no time to perceive that it might have been prevented, or at least mitigated.

Few even of the wisest women are fit for authority and liberty so little restrained, and happily it seldom falls to the lot of such as have not previously been chastened by a life-long affliction. But Mrs. Kendal, at twenty-four, with the consequence conferred by marriage, and by her superiority of manners and birth, was left as unchecked and almost as irresponsible as if she had been single or a widow, and was solely guided by the impulses of her own character, noble and highly principled, but like most zealous dispositions, without balance and without repose.

Ballast had been given at first by bashfulness, disappointment, and anxiety, but she had been freed from her troubles with Gilbert, had gained confidence in herself, and had taken her position at Bayford. She was beloved, esteemed, and trusted in her own set, and though elsewhere she might not be liked, yet she was deferred to, could not easily be quarrelled with, so that she met with little opposition, and did not care for such as she did meet. In fact, very few persons had so much of their own way as Mrs. Kendal.

She was generally in her nursery at a much earlier hour than an old-established nurse would have tolerated, but the little Susan, promoted from Fairmead school and nursery, was trained in energetic habits. In passing the doors of the young ladies' rooms, Albinia gave a call which she had taught them not to resist, for, like all strong persons, she thought 'early to rise' the only way to health, wealth, or wisdom. Much work had been despatched before breakfast, after which, on two days in the week, Albinia and Lucy went to church. Sophy never volunteered to accompany them, and Albinia was the less inclined to press her, because her attitudes and attention on Sunday were far from satisfactory. On Tuesday and Thursday Albinia had a class at school, and so, likewise, had Lucy, who kept a jealous watch over every stray necklace and curl, and had begun thoroughly to enjoy the importance and bustle of charity. She was a useful assistant in the penny club and lending library, which occupied Albinia on other mornings in the week, until the hour when she came in for the girls' studies. After luncheon, she enjoyed the company of little Maurice, who indeed pervaded all her home doings and thoughts, for she had a great gift of doing everything at once.

A sharp constitutional walk was taken in the afternoon. She thought no one could look drooping or dejected but from the air of the valley, and that no cure was equal to rushing straight up one hill and on to the next, always walking rapidly, with a springy buoyant step, and surprised at any one who lagged behind. Parochial cares, visits, singing classes, lessons to Sunday- school teachers, &c., filled up the rest of the day. She had an endless number of 'excellent plans,' on which she always acted instantly, and which kept her in a state of perpetual haste. Poor Mrs. Dusautoy had almost learnt to dread her flashing into the room, full of some parish matter, and flashing out again before the invalid felt as if the subject had been fairly entered on, or her sitting down to impress some project with overpowering eagerness that generally carried away the Vicar into grateful consent and admiring approval, while his wife was feeling doubtful, suspecting her hesitation of being ungracious, or blaming herself for not liking the little she could do to be taken out of her hands.

There was nothing more hateful to Albinia than dawdling. She left the girls' choice of employments, but insisted on their being veritably occupied, and many a time did she encounter a killing glance from Sophia for attacking her listless, moody position in her chair, or saying, in clear, alert tones, 'My dear, when you read, read, when you work, work. When you fix your eye in that way, you are doing neither.'

Lucy's brisk, active disposition, and great good-humour, had responded to this treatment; she had been obliging, instead of officious; repeated checks had improved her taste; her love of petty bustle was directed to better objects, and though nothing could make her intellectual or deep, she was a really pleasant assistant and companion, and no one, except grandmamma, who thought her perfect before, could fail to perceive how much more lady-like her tones, manners, and appearance had become.

The results with Sophy had been directly the reverse. At first she had followed her sister's lead, except that she was always sincere, and often sulky; but the more Lucy had yielded to Albinia's moulding, the more had Sophy diverged from her, as if out of the very spirit of contradiction. Her intervals of childish nonsense had well nigh disappeared; her indifference to lessons was greater than ever, though she devoured every book that came in her way in a silent, but absorbed manner, a good deal like her father. Tales and stories were not often within her reach, but her appetite seemed to be universal, and Albinia saw her reading old-fashioned standard poetry—such as she had never herself assailed—and books of history, travels, or metaphysics. She wondered whether the girl derived any pleasure from them, or whether they were only a shield for doing nothing; but no inquiry produced an answer, and if Sophy remembered anything of them, it was not with the memory used in lesson-time. The attachment to Louisa Osborn was pertinacious and unaccountable in a person who could have so little in common with that young lady, and there was nothing comfortable about her except her fondness for her little brother, and that really seemed to be against her will. Her voice was less hoarse and gruff since the pond had been no more, and she had acquired an expression, so suffering, so concentrated, so thoughtful, that, together with her heavy black eyebrows, large face, profuse black hair, and unlustrous eyes, it gave her almost a dwarfish air, increased by her awkward deportment, which concealed that she was in reality tall, and on a large scale. She looked to so little advantage in bright delicate colours, that Albinia was often incurring her displeasure, and risking that of Lucy, by the deep blues and sober browns which alone looked fit to be seen with those beetle brows and sallow features. Her face looked many years older than that of her fair, fresh, rosy stepmother; nay, her father's clear olive complexion and handsome countenance had hardly so aged an aspect; and Gilbert, when he came home at Midsummer, declared that Sophy had grown as old as grandmamma.

The compliment could not be returned; Gilbert was much more boy-like in a good sense. He had brought home an excellent character, and showed it in every look and gesture. His father was pleased to have him again, took the trouble to talk to him, and received such sensible answers, that the habit of conversing was actually established, and the dinners were enlivened, instead of oppressed, by his presence. Towards his sisters he had become courteous, he was fairly amiable to Aunt Maria, very attentive to grandmamma, overflowing with affection to Mrs. Kendal, and as to little Maurice, he almost adored him, and awakened a reciprocity which was the delight of his heart.

At Midsummer came the grand penny-club distribution, the triumph for which Albinia had so long been preparing. One of Mrs. Dusautoy's hints as to Bayford tradesmen had been overruled, and goods had been ordered from a house in London, after Albinia and Lucy had made an incredible agitation over their patterns of calico and flannel. Mr. Kendal was just aware that there was a prodigious commotion, but he knew that all ladies were subject to linen-drapery epidemics, and Albinia's took a more endurable form than a pull on his purse for the sweetest silk in the world, and above all, it neither came into his study nor even into his house.

It was a grand spectacle, when Mr. Dusautoy looked in on Mrs. Kendal and her staff, armed with their yard-wands.

A pile of calico was heaped in wild masses like avalanches in one corner, rapidly diminishing under the measurements of Gilbert, who looked as if he took thorough good-natured delight in the frolic. Brown, inodorous materials for petticoats, blouses, and trowsers were dealt out by the dextrous hands of Genevieve, a mountain of lilac print was folded off by Clarissa Richardson, Lucy was presiding joyously over the various blue, buff, brown, and pink Sunday frocks, the schoolmistress helping with the other goods, the customers —some pleased with novelty, or hoping to get more for their money, others suspicious of the gentry, and secretly resentful for favourite dealers, but, except the desperate grumblers, satisfied with the quality and quantity of the wares—and extremely taken with the sellers, especially with Gilbert's wit, and with Miss Durant's ready, lively persuasions, varied to each one's taste, and extracting a smile and 'thank you, Miss,' from the surliest. And the presiding figure, with the light on her sunny hair, and good-natured, unfailing interest in her countenance, was at her central table, calculating, giving advice, considering of complaints, measuring, folding—here, there, and everywhere— always bright, lively, forbearing, however complaining or unreasonable her clients might be.

Mr. Dusautoy went home to tell his Fanny that Mrs. Kendal was worth her weight in gold; and the workers toiled till luncheon, when Albinia took them home for food and wine, to restore them for the labours of the afternoon.

'What have you been about all the morning, Sophy? Yes, I see your translation—very well—I wish you would come up and help this afternoon, Miss Richardson is looking so pale and tired that I want to relieve her.'

'I can't,' said Sophy,

'I don't order you, but you are losing a great deal of fun. Suppose you came to look on, at least.'

'I hate poor people.'

'I hope you will change your mind some day, but you must do something this afternoon. You had better take a walk with Susan and baby; I told her to go by the meadows to Horton.'

'I don't want to walk.'

'Have you anything to do instead? No, I thought not, and it is not at all hot to signify.—It will do you much more good. Yes, you must go.'

In the course of the summer an old Indian friend was staying at Fairmead Park, and Colonel Bury wrote to beg for a week's visit from the whole Kendal family. Even Sophy vouchsafed to be pleased, and Lucy threw all her ardour into the completion of a blue braided cape, which was to add immensely to little Maurice's charms; she declared that she should work at it the whole of the last evening, while Mr. and Mrs. Kendal were at the dinner that old Mr. and Mrs. Bowles annually inflicted on themselves and their neighbours, a dinner which it would have been as cruel to refuse as it was irksome to accept.

There was a great similarity in those Bayford parties, inasmuch as the same cook dressed them all, and the same waiters waited at them, and the same guests met each other, and the principal variety on this occasion was, that the Osborns did not come, because the Admiral was in London.

The ladies had left the dining-room, when Albinia's ear caught a sound of hurried opening of doors, and sound of steps, and saw Mrs. and Miss Bowles look as if they heard something unexpected. She paused, and forgot the end of what she was saying. The room door was pushed a little way open, but then seemed to hesitate. Miss Bowles hastened forward, and opening it, admitted a voice that made Albinia hurry breathlessly from the other side of the room, and push so that the door yielded, and she saw it had been Mr. Dusautoy who had been holding it while there was some kind of consultation round Gilbert. The instant he saw her, he exclaimed, 'Come to the baby, Sophy has fallen down with him.'

People pressed about her, trying to speak cheeringly, but she understood nothing but that her husband and Mr. Bowles were gone on, and she had a sense that there had been hardness and cruelty in hesitating to summon her. Without knowing that a shawl was thrown round her, or seeing Mr. Dusautoy's offered arm, she clutched Gilbert's wrist in her hand, and flew down the street.

The gates and front door were open, and there was a throng of people in the hall. Lucy caught hold of her with a sobbing, 'Oh, Mamma!' but she only framed the words with her lips—'where?'

They pointed to the study. The door was shut, but Albinia broke from Lucy, and pushed through it, in too much haste to dwell on the sickening doubt what it might conceal.

Two figures stood under the window. Mr. Kendal, who was holding the little inanimate form in his arms for the doctor to examine, looking up as she entered, cast on her a look of mute, pleading, despairing agony, that was as the bitterness of death. She sprang forward herself to clasp her child, and her husband yielded him in broken-hearted pity, but at that moment the little limbs moved, the features worked, the eyes unclosed, and clinging tightly to her, as she strained him to her bosom, the little fellow proclaimed himself alive by lusty roars, more welcome than any music. Partly stunned, and far more terrified, he had been in a sort of swoon, without breath to cry, till recalled to himself by feeling his mother's arms around him. Every attempt of Mr. Bowles to ascertain whether he were uninjured produced such a fresh panic and renewal of screams, that she begged that he might be left to her. Mr. Kendal took the doctor away, and gradually the terror subsided, though the long convulsive sobs still quivered up through the little frame, and as the twilight darkened on her, she had time to realize the past alarm, and rejoice in trembling over the treasure still her own.

The opening of the door and the gleaming of a light had nearly brought on a fresh access of crying, but it was his father who entered, and Maurice knew the low deep sweetness of his voice, and was hushed. 'I believe there is no harm done,' Albinia said; and the smile that she fain would have made reassuring gave way as her eyes filled with tears, on feeling the trembling of the strong arm that was put round her, when Mr. Kendal bent to look into the child's eyes.

'I thought my blight had fallen on you,' was all he said.

'Oh! the thankfulness—' she said; but she could not go on, she must stifle all that swelled within her, for the babe felt each throb of her beating heart; and she could barely keep from bursting into tears as his father kissed him; then, as he marked the still sobbing breath, said, 'Bowles must see him again.'

'I don't know how to make him cry again! I suppose he must be looked at, but indeed I think him safe.—See, this little bruise on his forehead is the only mark I can find. What was it? How did it happen?'

'Sophia thought proper to take him herself from the nursery to show him to Mrs. Osborn. In crossing the street, she was frightened by a party of men coming out of a public-house in Tibbs's Alley, and in avoiding them, slipped down and struck the child's head against a gate-post. He was perfectly insensible when I took him—I thought him gone. Albinia, you must let Bowles see him again!'

'Is any one there?' she said.

'Every one, I think,' he replied, looking oppressed—'Maria, and Mrs. Osborn, and Dusautoy—but I will call Bowles.'

Apparently the little boy had escaped entirely unhurt, but the surgeon still spoke of the morrow, and he was so startled and restless, that Albinia feared to move, and felt the dark study a refuge from the voices and sounds that she feared to encounter, lest they should again occasion the dreadful screaming. 'Oh, if they would only go home!' she said.

'I will send them,' said Mr. Kendal; and presently she heard sounds of leave-taking, and he came back, as if he had been dispersing a riot, announcing that the house was clear.

Gilbert and Lucy were watching at the foot of the stairs, the one pale, and casting anxious, imploring looks at her; the other with eyes red and swollen with crying, neither venturing near till she spoke to them, when they advanced noiselessly to look at their little brother, and it was not till they had caught his eye and made him smile, that Lucy bethought herself of saying she had known nothing of his adventure, and Albinia, thus recalled to the thought of the culprit, asked where Sophy was.

'In her own room,' said Mr. Kendal. 'I could not bear the sight of her obduracy. Even her aunt was shocked at her want of feeling.'

Low as he spoke, the sternness of his voice frightened the baby, and she was obliged to run away to the nursery, where she listened to the contrition of the little nursemaid, who had never suspected Miss Sophy's intention of taking him out of the house.

'And indeed, ma'am,' she said, 'there is not one of us servants who dares cross Miss Sophy.'

It was long before Albinia ventured to lay him in his cot, and longer still before she could feel any security that if she ceased her low, monotonous lullaby, the little fellow would not wake again in terror, but the thankfulness and prayer, that, as she grew more calm, gained fuller possession of her heart, made her recur the more to pity and forgiveness for the poor girl who had caused the alarm. Yet there was strong indignation likewise, and she could not easily resolve on meeting the hard defiance and sullen indifference which would wound her more than ever. She was much inclined to leave Sophy to herself till morning, but suspecting that this would be vindictive, she unclasped the arm that Lucy had wound round her waist, whispered to her to go on singing, and moved to Sophy's door. It was fastened, but before she could call, it was thrown violently back, and Sophy stood straight up before her, striving for her usual rigidity, but shaking from head to foot; and though there were no signs of tears, she looked with wistful terror at her step- mother's face, and her lips moved as if she wished to speak.

'Baby is gone quietly to sleep,' began Albinia in a low voice, beginning in displeasure; but as she spoke, the harshness of Sophy's face gave way, she sank down on the floor, and fell into the most overpowering fit of weeping that Albinia had ever witnessed. Kneeling beside her, she would have drawn the girl close to her, but a sharp cry of pain startled her, and she found the right arm, from elbow to wrist, all one purple bruise, the skin grazed, and the blood starting.

'My poor child! how you have hurt yourself!'

Sophy turned away pettishly.

'Let me look! I am sure it must be very bad. Have you done anything to it?'

'No, never mind. Go back to baby.'

'Baby does not want me. You shall come and see how comfortably he is asleep, if you will leave off crying, and let me see that poor arm. Did you hurt it in the fall?'

'The corner of the wall,' said Sophy. 'Oh! did it not hurt him?' but then, just as it seemed that she was sinking on that kind breast in exhaustion, she collected herself, and pushing Albinia off, exclaimed, 'I did it, I took him out, I fell down with him, I hurt his head, I've killed him, or made him an idiot for life. I did.'

'Who said so?' cried Albinia, transfixed.

'Aunt Maria said so. She said I did not feel. Oh, if I could only die before he grows up to let one see it. Why wont you begin to hate me?'

'My dear,' said Albinia, consoled on hearing the authority, 'people often say angry things when they are shocked. Your aunt had not seen Mr. Bowles, and we all think he was not in the least hurt, only terribly frightened. Dear, dear child, I am more distressed for you than for him!'

Sophy could hold out no longer, she let her head drop on the kind shoulder, and seemed to collapse, with burning brow, throbbing pulses, and sobs as deep and convulsive as had been those of her little brother. Hastily calling Lucy, who was frightened, subdued, and helpful, Albinia undressed the poor child, put her to bed, and applied lily leaves and spirits to her arm. The smart seemed to refresh her, but there had been a violent strain, as well as bruise, and each touch visibly gave severe pain, though she never complained. Lucy insisted on hearing exactly how the accident had happened, and pressed her with questions, which Albinia would have shunned in her present condition, and it was thus elicited that she had taken Maurice across the street to how him to Mrs. Osborn. He had resented the strange place, and strange people, and had cried so much that she was obliged to run home with him at once. A knot of bawling men came reeling out of one of the many beer shops in Tibbs's Alley, and in her haste to avoid them, she tripped, close to the gate- post of Willow Lawn, and fell, with only time to interpose her arm between Maurice's head and the sharp corner. She was lifted up at once, in the horror of seeing him neither cry nor move, for, in fact, he had been almost stifled under her weight, and all had since been to her a frightful phantom dream. Albinia was infinitely relieved by this history, showing that Maurice could hardly have received any real injury, and in her declarations that Sophy's presence of mind had saved him, was forgetting to whom the accident was owing. Lucy wanted to know why her sister could have taken him out of the house at all, but Albinia could not bear to have this pressed at such a moment, and sent the inquirer down to order some tea, which she shared with Sophy, and then was forced to bid her good-night, without drawing out any further confessions. But when the girl raised herself to receive her kiss, it was the first real embrace that had passed between them.

In the very early morning, Albinia was in the nursery, and found her little boy bright and healthy. As she left him in glad hope and gratitude, Sophy's door was pushed ajar, and her wan face peeped out. 'My dear child, you have not been asleep all night!' exclaimed Albinia, after having satisfied her about the baby.

'No.'

'Does your arm hurt you?'

'Yes.'

'Does your head ache?'

'Rather.'

But they were not the old sulky answers, and she seemed glad to have her arm freely bathed, her brow cooled, her tossed bed composed, and her window opened, so that she might make a fresh attempt at closing her weary eyes.

She was evidently far too much shaken to be fit for the intended expedition, even if her father had not decreed that she should be deprived of it. Albinia had never seen him so much incensed, for nothing makes a man so angry as to have been alarmed; and he was doubly annoyed when he found that she thought Sophy too unwell to be left, as he intended, to solitary confinement.

He would gladly have given up the visit, for his repugnance to society was in full force on the eve of a party; but Albinia, by representing that it would be wrong to disappoint Colonel Bury, and very hard on the unoffending Gilbert and Lucy, succeeded in prevailing on him to accept his melancholy destiny, and to allow her to remain at home with Sophy and the baby—one of the greatest sacrifices he or she had yet made. He was exceedingly vexed, and therefore the less disposed to be lenient. The more Albinia told him of Sophy's unhappiness, the more he hoped it would do her good, and he could not be induced to see her, nor to send her any message of forgiveness, for in truth it was less the baby's accident that he resented, than the eighteen months of surly resistance to the baby's mother, and at present he was more unrelenting than the generous, forgiving spirit of his wife could understand, though she tried to believe it manly severity and firmness.

'It would be time to pardon,' he said, 'when pardon was asked.'

And Albinia could not say that it had been asked, except by misery.

'She has the best advocate in you,' said Mr. Kendal, affectionately, 'and if there be any feeling in her, such forbearance cannot fail to bring it out. I am more grieved than I can tell you at your present disappointment, but it shall not happen again. If you can bring her to a better mind, I shall be the more satisfied in sending her from home.'

'Edmund! you do not think of it!'

'My mind is made up. Do you think I have not watched your patient care, and the manner in which it has been repaid? You have sufficient occupation without being the slave of those children's misconduct.'

'Sophy would be miserable. Oh! you must not! She is the last girl in the world fit to be sent to school.'

'I will not have you made miserable at home. This has been a long trial, and nothing has softened her.'

'Suppose this was the very thing.'

'If it were, what is past should not go unrequited, and the change will teach her what she has rejected. Hush, dearest, it is not that I do not think that you have done all for her that tenderness or good sense could devise, but your time is too much occupied, and I cannot see you overtasked by this poor child's headstrong temper. It is decided, Albinia; say no more.'

'I have failed,' thought Albinia, as he left the room. 'He decides that I have failed in bringing up his children. What have I done? Have I been mistaken? have I been careless? have I not prayed enough? Oh! my poor, poor Sophy! What will she do among strange girls? Oh! how wretched, how harsh, how misunderstood she will be! She will grow worse and worse, and just when I do think I might have begun to get at her! And it is for my sake! For me that her father is set against her, and is driving her out from her home! Oh! what shall I do? Winifred will promote it, because they all think I am doing too much! I wonder what put that in Edmund's head? But when he speaks in that way, I have no hope!'

Mr. Kendal's anger took a direction with which she better sympathized when he walked down Tibbs's Alley, and counted the nine beer shops, which had never dawned on his imagination, and which so greatly shocked it, that he went straight to the astonished Pettilove, and gave him a severe reprimand for allowing the houses to be made dens of iniquity and disorder.

He was at home in time to meet the doctor, and hear that Maurice had suffered not the smallest damage; and then to make another ineffectual attempt to persuade Albinia to consign Sophy to imprisonment with Aunt Maria; after which he drove off very much against his will with Lucy and Gilbert, both declaring that they did not care a rush to go to Fairmead under the present circumstances.

Albinia had a sad, sore sense of failure, and almost of guilt, as she lingered on the door-step after seeing them set off. The education of 'Edmund's children' had been a cherished vision, and it had resulted so differently from her expectations, that her heart sank. With Gilbert there was indeed no lack of love and confidence, but there was a sad lurking sense of his want of force of character, and she had avowedly been insufficient to preserve him from temptation; Lucy, whom externally she had the most altered, was not of a nature accordant enough with her own for her to believe the effects deep or permanent; and Sophia—poor Sophia! Had what was kindly called forbearance been really neglect and want of moral courage? Would a gentler, less eager person have won instead of repelling confidence? Had her multiplicity of occupations made her give but divided attention to the more important home duty. Alas! alas! she only knew that her husband thought his daughter beyond her management, and for that very reason she would have given worlds to retain the uncouth, perverse girl under her charge.

She stood loitering, for the sound of the river and the shade of the willows were pleasant on the glowing July day, and having made all her arrangements for going from home, she had no pressing employment, and thus she waited, musing as she seldom allowed herself time to do, and thinking over each phase of her conduct towards Sophy, in the endeavour to detect the mistake; and throughout came, not exactly answering her query, but throwing a light upon it, her brother's warning, that if she did not resign herself to rest quietly when rest was forced upon her, she would work amiss when she did work.

Just then came a swinging of the gate, a step on the walk, and Miss Meadows made her appearance. A message had been sent up in the morning, but grandmamma was so nervous, that Maria had trotted down in the heat so satisfy her.

Albinia was surprised to find that womanhood had thrown all their instincts on the baby's side, and was gratified by the first truly kind fellow-feeling they had shown her. She took Maria into the morning room, where she had left Sophy lying on the sofa, and ran up to fetch Maurice from the nursery.

When she came down, having left the nurse adorning him, she found that she had acted cruelly. Sophy was standing up with her hardest face on, listening to her aunt's well-meant rebukes on her want of feeling, and hopes that she did regret the having endangered her brother, and deprived 'her dear mamma of the party of pleasure at Fairmead; but Aunt Maria knew it was of no use to talk to Sophy, none—!'

'Pray don't, Aunt Maria,' said Albinia, gently drawing Sophy down on the sofa again; 'this poor child is in no state to be scolded.'

'You are a great deal too good to her, Mrs. Kendal—after such wilfulness as last night—carrying the dear baby out in the street—I never heard of such a thing—But what made you do it, Sophy, wont you tell me that? No, I know you won't; no one ever can get a word from her. Ah! that sulky disposition—it is a very nasty temper—can't you break through it, Sophy, and confess it all to your dear mamma? You would be so much better. But I know it is of no use, poor child, it is just like her father.'

Albinia was growing very angry, and it was well that Maurice's merry crowings were heard approaching. Miss Meadows was delighted to see him, but as he had a great aversion to her, the interview was not prolonged, since he could not be persuaded to keep the peace by being held up to watch a buzzing fly, as much out of sight of her as possible, wrinkling up his nose, and preparing to cry whenever he caught sight of her white bonnet and pink roses.

Miss Meadows bethought her that grandmamma was anxious, so she only waited to give an invitation to tea, but merely to Mrs. Kendal; she would say nothing about Sophy since disgrace—well-merited—if they could only see some feeling.

'Thank you,' said Albinia, 'some evening perhaps I may come, since you are so kind, but I don't think I can leave this poor twisted arm to itself.'

Miss Meadows evaporated in hopes that Sophy would be sensible of—and assurances that Mrs. Kendal was a great deal too—with finally, 'Good-bye, Sophy, I wish I could have told grandmamma that you had shown some feeling.'

'I believe,' said Albinia, 'that you would only be too glad if you knew how.'

Sophy gasped.

Albinia could not help feeling indignant at the misjudged persecution; and yet it seemed to render the poor child more entirely her own, since all the world besides had turned against her. 'Kiss her, Maurice,' she said, holding the little fellow towards her. That scratched arm of hers has spared your small brains from more than you guess.'

Sophy's first impulse was to hide her face, but he thought it was bo-peep, caught hold of her fingers, and laughed; then came to a sudden surprised stop, and looked up to his mother, when the countenance behind the screen proved sad instead of laughing.

'Ah! baby, you had better have done with me,' Sophy said, bitterly; 'you are the only one that does not hate me yet, and you don't know what I have done to you.'

'I know some one else that cares for you, my poor Sophy,' said Albinia, 'and who would do anything to make you feel it without distressing you. If you knew how I wish I knew what to do for you!'

'It is no use,' said Sophy, moodily; 'I was born to be a misery to myself and every one else.'

'What has put such a fancy in your head, my dear?' said Albinia, nearly smiling.

'Grandmamma's Betty said so, she used to call me Peter Grievous, and I know it is so. It is of no good to bother yourself about me. It can't be helped, and there's an end of it.'

'There is not an end of it, indeed!' cried Albinia. 'Why, Sophy, do you suppose I could bear to leave you so?'

'I'm sure I don't see why not.'

'Why not?' continued Albinia, in her bright, tender voice. 'Why, because I must love you with all my heart. You are your own dear papa's child, and this little man's sister. Yes, and you are yourself, my poor, sad, lonely child, who does not know how to bring out the thoughts that prey on her, and who thinks it very hard to have a stranger instead of her own mother. I know I should have felt so.'

'But I have behaved so ill to you,' cried Sophy, as if bent on repelling the proffered affection. 'I would not like you, and I did not like you. Never! and I have gone against you every way I could.'

'And now I love you because you are sorry for it.'

'I'm not'—Sophy had begun, but the words turned into 'Am I?'

'I think you are,' and with the sweetest of tearful smiles, she put an arm round the no longer resisting Sophy, and laying her cheek against the little brother's, she kissed first one and then the other.

'I can't think why you are so,' said Sophy, still struggling against the undeserved love, though far more feebly. 'I shall never deserve it.'

'See if you don't, when we pull together instead of contrary ways.'

'But,' cried Sophy, with a sudden start from her, as if remembering a mortal offence, 'you drained the pond!'

'I own I earnestly wished it to be drained; but had you any reason for regretting it, my dear?'

'Ah! you did not know,' said Sophy. 'He and I used to be always there.'

'He—?'

'Why, will you make me say it?' cried Sophy. 'Edmund! I mean Edmund! We always called it his pond. He made the little quay for his boats—he used to catch the minnows there. I could go and stand by it, and think he was coming out to play; and now you have had it dried up, and his dear little minnows are all dead,' and she burst into a passion of tears, that made Maurice cry till Albinia hastily carried him off and returned.

'My dear, I am sorry it seemed so unkind. I do not think we could have let the pond stay, for it was making the house unhealthy; but if we had talked over it together, it need not have appeared so very cruel and spiteful.'

'I don't believe you are spiteful,' said Sophy, 'though I sometimes think so.'

The filial compliment was highly gratifying.

'And now, Sophy,' she said, 'that I have told you why we were obliged to have the pond drained, will you tell me what you wanted with baby at Mrs. Osborn's?'

'I will tell,' said Sophy, 'but you wont like it.'

'I like anything better than concealment.'

'Mrs. Osborn said she never saw him. She said you kept him close, and that nobody was good enough to touch him; so I promised I would bring him over, and I kept my word. I know it was wrong—and—I did not think you would ever forgive me.'

'But how could you do it?'

'Mrs. Osborn and all used to be so kind to us when there was nobody else. I wont cast them off because we are too fine and grand for them.'

'I never thought of that. I only was afraid of your getting into silly ways, and your papa did not wish us to be intimate there. And now you see he was right, for good friends would not have led you to such disobedience—and by stealth, too, what I should have thought you would most have hated.'

Albinia had been far from intending these last words to have been taken as they were. Sophy hid her face, and cried piteously with an utter self-abandonment of grief, that Albinia could scarcely understand; but at last she extracted some broken words. 'False! shabby! yes—Oh! I have been false! Oh! Edmund! Edmund! Edmund! the only thing I thought I still was! I thought I was true! Oh, by stealth! Why couldn't I die when I tried, when Edmund did?'

'And has life been a blank ever since?'

'Off and on,' said Sophy. 'Well, why not? I am sure papa is melancholy enough. I don't like people that are always making fun, I can't see any sense in it.'

'Some sorts of merriment are sad, and hollow, and wrong, indeed,' said Albinia, 'but not all, I hope. You know there is so much love and mercy all round us, that it is unthankful not to have a cheerful spirit. I wish I could give you one, Sophy.'

Sophy shook her head. 'I can't understand about mercy and love, when Edmund was all I cared for.'

'But, Sophy, if life is so sad and hard to you, don't you see the mercy that took Edmund away to perfect joy? Remember, not cutting you off from him, but keeping him safe for you.'

'No, no,' cried Sophy, 'I have never been good since he went. I have got worse and worse, but I did think I was true still, that that one thing was left me—but now—' The sense of having acted a deception seemed to produce grief under which the stubborn pride was melting away, and it was most affecting to see the child weeping over the lost jewel of truth, which she seemed to feel the last link with the remarkable boy whose impress had been left so strongly on all connected with him.

'My dear, the truth is in you still, or you could not grieve thus over your failure,' said Albinia. 'I know you erred, because it did not occur to you that it was not acting openly by me; but oh! Sophy, there is something that would bring you nearer to Edmund than hard truth in your own strength.'

'I don't know what you mean,' said Sophy.

'Did you ever think what Edmund is about now?'

'I don't know,' said Sophy.

'I only know that the one thing which is carried with us to the other world is love, Sophy, and love that becomes greater than we can yet imagine. If you would think of Him who redeemed and saved your dear Edmund, and who is his happiness, his exceeding great reward, your heart would warm, and, oh! what hope and peace would come!'

'Edmund was good,' said Sophy, in a tone as if to mark the hopeless gulf between.

'And you are sorry. All human goodness begins from sorrow. It had even to be promised first for baby at his christening, you know. Oh, Sophy, God's blessing can make all these tears come to joy.'

Albinia's own tears were flowing so fast, that she broke off to hide them in her own room, her heart panting with hope, and yet with grief and pity for the piteous disclosure of so dreary a girlhood. After all, childhood, if not the happiest, is the saddest period of life—pains, griefs, petty tyrannies, neglects, and terrors have not the alleviation of the experience that 'this also shall pass away;' time moves with a tardier pace, and in the narrower sphere of interests, there is less to distract the attention from the load of grievances. Hereditary low spirits, a precocious mind, a reserved temper, a motherless home, the loss of her only congenial companion, and the long-enduring effect of her illness upon her health, had all conspired to weigh down the poor girl, and bring on an almost morbid state of gloomy discontent. Her father's second marriage, by enlivening the house, had rendered her peculiarities even more painful to herself and others, and the cultivation of mind that was forced upon her, made her more averse to the trifling and playfulness, which, while she was younger, had sometimes brightened and softened her. And this was the girl whom her father had resolved upon sending to the selfish, inconsiderate, frivolous world of school-girls, just when the first opening had been made, the first real insight gained into her feelings, the first appearance of having touched her heart! Albinia felt baffled, disappointed, almost despairing. His stern decree, once made, was, she knew, well-nigh unalterable; and though resolved to use her utmost influence, she doubted its power after having seen that look of decision. Nay, she tried to think he might be right. There might be those who would manage Sophy better. Eighteen months had been a fair trial, and she had failed. She prayed earnestly for whatever might be best for the child, and for herself, that she might take it patiently and submissively.

Sophy felt the heat of the day a good deal, but towards the evening she revived, and seemed so much cheered and refreshed by her tea, that, as the sound of the church bell came sweetly down in the soft air, Albinia said, 'Sophy, I am going to take advantage of my holiday and go to the evening service. I suppose you had rather not come?'

'I think I will,' returned Sophy, somewhat glumly, but Albinia hailed the answer joyfully, as the first shamefaced effort of a reserved character wishing to make a new beginning, and she took care that no remark, not even a look, should rouse the sullen sensitiveness that could so easily be driven back for ever.

Slowly they crept up the steps on the shady side of the hill, watching how, beyond the long shadow it cast over the town and the meadows, the trees revelled in the sunset light, and windows glittered like great diamonds, where in the ordinary daylight the distance was too great for distinct vision.

The church was cool and quiet, and there was something in Sophy's countenance and reverent attitude that seemed as if she were consecrating a newly-formed resolution; her eye was often raised, as though in spite of herself, to the name of the brother whose short life seemed inseparably interwoven with all the higher aspirations of his home.

In the midst of the Thanksgiving, a sudden movement attracted Albinia, and she saw Sophy resting her head, and looking excessively pale. She put her arm round her, and would have led her out, but could not persuade her to move, and by the time the Blessing was given, the power was gone, and she had almost fainted away, when a tall strong form stooped over her, and Mr. Dusautoy gathered her up in his arms, and bore her off as if she had been a baby, to the open window of his own drawing-room.

'Put me down! The floor, please!' said Sophy, feebly, for all her remaining faculties were absorbed in dislike to the mode of conveyance.

'Yes, flat on the floor,' said Mrs. Dusautoy, rising with full energy, and laying a cushion under Sophy's head, reaching a scent-bottle, and sending her husband for cold water and sal volatile; with readiness that astonished Albinia, unused to illness, and especially to faintings, and remorseful at having taken Sophy out. 'Was it the pain of her arm that had overcome her?'

'No,' said Sophy, 'it was only my back.'

'Indeed! you never told me you had hurt your back;' and Albinia began describing the fall, and declaring there must be a sprain.

'Oh, no,' said Sophy, 'kneeling always does it.'

'Does what, my dear?' said Albinia, sitting on the floor by her, and looking up to Mrs. Dusautoy, exceedingly frightened.

'Makes me feel sick,' said Sophy; 'I thought it would go off, as it always does, it didn't; but it is better now.'

'No, don't get up yet,' said Mrs. Dusautoy, as she was trying to move; 'I would offer you the sofa, it would be more hospitable, but I think the floor is the most comfortable place.'

'Thank you, *much*,' said Sophy, with an emphasis.

'Do you ever lie down on it when you are tired?' asked the lady, looking anxiously at Sophy.

'I always wish I might.'

Albinia was surprised at the interrogations that followed; she did not understand what Mrs. Dusautoy was aiming at, in the close questioning, which to her amazement did not seem to offend, but rather to be gratifying by the curious divination of all sensations. It made Albinia feel as if she had been carrying on a deliberate system of torture, when she heard of a pain in the back, hardly ever ceasing, aggravated by sitting upright, growing severe with the least fatigue, and unless favoured by day, becoming so bad at night as to take away many hours of sleep.

'Oh! Sophy, Sophy,' she cried, with tears in her eyes, 'how could you go on so? Why did you never tell me?'

'I did not like,' began Sophy, 'I was used to it.'

Oh, that barrier! Albinia was in uncontrollable distress, that the girl should have chosen to undergo so much suffering rather than bestow any confidence. Sophy stole her hand into hers, and said in her odd, short way, 'Never mind, it did not signify.'

'Yes,' said Mrs. Dusautoy, 'those things are just what one does get so much used to, that it seems much easier to bear them than to speak about them.'

'But to let oneself be so driven about,' cried Albinia. 'Oh! Sophy, you will never do so again! If I had ever guessed—'

'Please hush! Never mind!' said Sophy, almost crossly, and getting up from the floor quickly, as though resolved to be well.

'I have never minded long enough,' sighed Albinia. 'What shall I do, Mrs. Dusautoy? What do you think it is?'

This was the last question Mrs. Dusautoy wished to be asked in Sophy's presence. She had little doubt that it was spine complaint like her own, but she had not intended to let her perceive the impression, till after having seen Mrs. Kendal alone. However, Albinia's impetuosity disconcerted all precautions, and Sophy's two great black eyes were rounded with suppressed terror, as if expecting her doom. 'I think that a doctor ought to answer that question,' Mrs. Dusautoy began.

'Yes, yes,' exclaimed Albinia, 'but I never had any faith in old Mr. Bowles, I had rather go to a thorough good man at once.'

'Yes, certainly, by all means.'

'And then to whom! I will write to my Aunt Mary. It seems exactly like you. Do you think it is the spine?'

'I am afraid so. But, my dear,' holding out her hand caressingly to Sophy, 'you need not be frightened—you need not look at me as an example of what you will come to—I am only an example of what comes of never speaking of one's ailments.'

'And of having no mother to find them out!' cried Albinia.

'Indeed,' said Mrs. Dusautoy, anxious to console and encourage, as well as to talk the young step-mother out of her self-reproach, 'I do not think that if I had been my good aunt's own child, she would have been more likely to find out that anything was amiss. It was the fashion to be strong and healthy in that house, and I was never really ill—but I came as a little stunted, dwining cockney, and so I was considered ever after—never quite comfortable, often forgetting myself in enjoyment, paying for it afterwards, but quite used to it. We all thought it was "only Fanny," and part of my London breeding. Yes, we thought so in good faith, even after the largest half of my life had been spent in Yorkshire.'

'And what brought it to a crisis? Did they go on neglecting you?' exclaimed Albinia.

'Why, my dear,' said the little lady, a glow lighting on her cheek, and a smile awakening, 'my uncle took a new curate, whom it was the family custom to call "the good-natured giant," and whose approach put all of us young ladies in a state of great excitement. It was all in character with his good-nature, you know, to think of dragging the poor little shrimp up the hill to church, and I believe he did not know how she would get on without his strong arm; for do you know, when he had the curacy of Lauriston given him, he chose to carry the starveling off with him, instead of any of those fine, handsome prosperous girls. Dear Mary and Bessie! how good they were, and how kind and proud for me! I never could complain of not having sisters.'

'Well, and Mr. Dusautoy made you have advice?'

'Not he! Why, we all believed it cockneyism, you know, and besides, I was so happy and so well, that when we went to Scotland, I fairly walked myself off my legs, and ended the honeymoon laid up in a little inn on Loch Katrine, where John used regularly to knock his head whenever he came into the room. It was a fortnight before I could get to Edinburgh, and the journey made me as bad as ever. So the doctors were called in, and poor John learnt what a crooked stick he had chosen; but they all said that if I had been taken in hand as a child, most likely I should have been a sound woman. The worst of it was, that I was so thoroughly knocked up that I could not bear the motion of a carriage; besides, I suppose the doctors wanted a little amusement out of me, for they would not hear of my going home. So poor John had to go to Lauriston by himself, and those were the longest, dreariest six months I ever spent in my life, though Bessie was so good as to come and take care of me. But at last, when I had nearly made up my mind to defy the whole doctorhood, they gave leave, and between water and steam, John brought me to Lauriston, and ever since that, I don't see that a backbone would have made us a bit happier.'

Sophy had been intently reading Mrs. Dusautoy's face all through the narration, from under her thick black eyelashes, and at the end she drew a sigh of relief, and seemed to catch the smile of glad gratitude and affection. There was a precedent, which afforded incredible food to the tumultuous cravings of a heart that had been sinking in sullen gloom under the consciousness of an unpleasing exterior. The possibility of a 'good-natured giant' was far more present to her mind than the present probability of future suffering and restraint.

Ever rapid and eager, Albinia could think of nothing but immediate measures for Sophy's good, and the satisfaction of her own conscience. She could not bear even to wait for Mr. Kendal's return, but, as her aunts were still in London, she resolved on carrying Sophy to their house on the following day for the best advice. It was already late, and she knelt at the table to dash off two notes to put into the post-office as she went home. One to Mrs. Annesley, to announce her coming with Sophy, baby, and Susan, the other as follows:—

'July 10th, 9 p.m.

'Dearest Edmund,

'I find I have been cruelly neglectful. I have hunted and driven that poor child about till it has brought on spine complaint. The only thing I can do, is to take her to have the best advice without loss of time, so I am going to- morrow to my aunt's. It would take too long to write and ask your leave. You must forgive this, as indeed each word I have to say is, forgive! She is so generous and kind! You know I meant to do my best, but they were right, I was too young.

'Forgive yours,

'A. K.'

The Dusautoys were somewhat taken by surprise, but they knew too well the need of promptitude to dissuade her; and Sophia herself sat aghast at the commotion, excited by the habitual discomfort of which she had thought so little. The vicar, when he found Mrs. Kendal in earnest, offered to go with them and protect them; but Albinia was a veteran in independent railway travelling, and was rather affronted by being treated as a helpless female. Mrs. Dusautoy, better aware of what the journey might be to one at least of the travellers, gave advice, and lent air cushions, and Albinia bade her good night with an almost sobbing 'thank you,' and an entreaty that if Mr. Kendal came home before them, she would tell him all about it.

At home, she instantly sent the stupefied Sophy to bed, astonished the little nurse, ordered down boxes and bags, and spent half the night in packing, glad to be stirring and to tire herself into sleeping, for her remorse and her anticipations were so painful, that, but for fatigue, her bed would have been no resting-place.

CHAPTER IX.

Winifred Ferrars was surprised by Mr. Kendal's walking into her garden, with a perturbed countenance, begging her to help him to make out what could be the meaning of a note which he had just received. He was afraid that there was much amiss with the baby, and heartily wished that he had not been persuaded to leave home; but poor Albinia wrote in so much distress, that he could not understand her letter.

More accustomed to Albinia's epistolary habits, Winifred exclaimed at the first glance, 'What can you mean? There is not one word of the little one! It is only Sophy!'

The immediate clearing of his face was not complimentary to poor Sophy, as he said, 'Can you be quite sure? I had begun to hope that Albinia might at least have the comfort of seeing this little fellow healthy; but let me see—she says nursed and—and danced—is it? this poor child—'

'No, no; it is hunted and driven; that's the way she always *will* make her *h*'s; besides, what nonsense the other would be.'

'This poor child—' repeated Mr. Kendal, 'Going up to London for advice. She would hardly do that with Sophia.'

'Who ever heard of a baby of six months old having a spine complaint?' cried Mrs. Ferrars almost angrily.

'I have lost one in that way,' he replied.

A dead silence ensued, till Winifred, to her great relief, spied the feminine pronoun, but could not fully satisfy Mr. Kendal that the ups and downs were insufficient for the word *him*; and each scrawl was discussed as though it had been a cuneiform inscription, until he had been nearly argued into believing in the lesser evil. He then was persuaded that the Meadowses had been harassing and frightening Albinia into this startling measure. It was so contrary to his own nature, that he hardly believed that it had actually taken place, and that she must be in London by this time, but at any rate, he must join her there, and know the worst. He would take the whole party to an hotel, if it were too great a liberty to quarter themselves upon Mrs. Annesley.

Winifred was as much surprised as if the chess-king had taken a knight's move, but she encouraged his resolution, assured him of a welcome at what the cousinhood were wont to call the Family Office, and undertook the charge of Gilbert and Lucy. The sorrowful, almost supplicating tone of his wife's letter, would have sufficed to bring him to her, even without his disquietude for his child, whichever of them it might be; and though Albinia's merry blue-eyed boy had brought a renewed spring of hope and life, his crashed spirits trembled at the least alarm.

Thus, though the cheerful Winifred had convinced his reason, his gloomy anticipations revived before he reached London; and with the stern composure of one accustomed to bend to the heaviest blows, he knocked at Mrs. Annesley's door. He was told that Mrs. Kendal was out; but on further inquiry, learnt that Sophy was in the drawing-room, where he found her curled up in the corner of the sofa, reading intently.

She sprang to her feet with a cry of surprise, but did not approach, though he held out his arms, saying in a voice husky with anxiety, 'Is the baby well, Sophia?'

'Yes,' she cried, 'quite well; he is out in the carriage with them.' Then shrinking as he was stooping to kiss her, she reddened, reddening deeply, 'Papa, I did very wrong; I was sly and disobedient, and I might have killed him.'

'Do not let us speak of that now, my dear, I want to hear of—' and again he would have drawn her into his embrace, but she held out her hand, with her repelling gesture, and burst forth in her rude honesty, 'I can't be forgiven only because I am ill. Hear all about it, papa, and then say you forgive me if you can. I always was cross to mamma, because I was determined I would be; and I did not think she had any business with us. The more she was kind, the more I did not like it; and I thought it was mean in Gilbert and Lucy to be fond of her. No! I have not done yet! I grew naughtier and naughtier, till at last I have been false and sly, and—have done this to baby—and I would not have cared then—if—if she would not have been—oh! so good!'

Sophy made no farther resistance to the arm that was thrown round her, as her father said, 'So good, that she has overcome evil with good. My child, how should I not forgive when you are sensible of your mistake, and when she has so freely forgiven?'

Sophy did not speak, but she pressed his arm closer round her, and laid her cheek gratefully on his shoulder. She only wished it could last for ever; but he soon lifted her, that he might look anxiously at her face, while he said, 'And what is all this, my dear! I am afraid you are not well.'

Her energies were recalled; and, squeezing his hand, she said, 'Mind, you will not let them say it was mamma's fault.'

'Who is accusing her, my dear?' What is the matter?'

'It is only my back,' said Sophy; 'there always was a stupid pain there; but grandmamma's Betty said I made a fuss, and that it was all laziness, and I would not let any one say so again, and I never told of it, and it went on till the other night I grew faint at church, and Mrs. Dusautoy put mamma in such a fright, that we all came here yesterday; and there came a doctor this morning, who says my spine is not straight, and that I must lie on my back for a long time; but never mind, papa, it will be very comfortable to lie still and read, and I shall not be cross now,' she added reassuringly, as his grasp pressed her close, with a start of dismay.

'My dear, I am afraid you hardly know what you may have to go through, but I am glad you meet it bravely.'

'But you wont let them say mamma did it?'

'Who should say so?'

'Aunt Maria will, and mamma *will* go and say so herself,' cried Sophy; 'she *will* say it was taking walks and carrying baby, and it's not true. I told the doctor how my back ached long before baby came or she either, and he said that most likely the weakness had been left by the fever. So if it is any one's mismanagement, it is Aunt Maria's, and if you wont tell her so, I will.'

'Gently, Sophy, that would hardly be grateful, after the pains that she has taken with you, and the care she meant to give.'

'Her care was all worry,' said Sophy, 'and it will be very lucky if I don't tell her so, if she says her provoking things to mamma. But you wont believe them, papa.'

'Most certainly not.'

'Yes, you must tell her to be happy again,' continued Sophy; 'I cannot bear to see her looking sorrowful! Last night, when she fancied me asleep, she cried—oh! till it made me miserable! And to-day I heard Miss Ferrars say to Mrs. Annesley, that her fine spirits were quite gone. You know it is very silly, for I am the last person in all the world she ought to cry for.'

'She has an infinite treasure of love,' said Mr. Kendal, 'and we have done very little that we should be blessed with it.'

'There, they are come home!' exclaimed Sophy, starting up as sounds were heard on the stairs, and almost at the same moment Albinia was in the room, overflowing with contrition, gladness, and anxiety; but something of sweetness in the first hasty greeting made the trust overcome all the rest; and, understanding his uppermost wish, she stepped back to the staircase, and in another second had put Maurice into his arms, blooming and contented, and with a wide-mouthed smile for his papa. Mr. Kendal held him fondly through all the hospitable welcomes of the aunts, and his own explanations; but to Albinia it was all confusion, and almost annoyance, till she could take him upstairs, and tell her own story.

'I am afraid you have been very much alarmed,' were his first words.

'I have done everything wrong from beginning to end,' said Albinia. 'Oh, Edmund, I am so glad you are come! Now you will see the doctor, and know whether it was as bad as all the rest to bring her to London.'

'My dearest, you must calm yourself, and try to explain. You know I understand nothing yet, except from your resolute little advocate downstairs, and your own note, which I could scarcely make out, except that you were in great trouble.'

'Ah, that note; I wrote it in one of my impetuous fits. Maurice used to say I ran frantic, and grew irrational, and so I did not know what I was saying to you; and I brought that poor patient girl up here in all the heat, and the journey hurt her so much, that I don't know how we shall ever get her home again. Oh, Edmund, I am the worst wife and mother in the world; and I undertook it all with such foolish confidence.'

Mr. Kendal liked her impetuous fits as little as her brother did, and was not so much used to them; but he dealt with her in his quiet, straightforward way. 'You are exaggerating now, Albinia, and I do not wonder at it, for you have had a great deal to startle and to try you. Walking up and down is only heating and agitating you more; sit down here, and let me hear what gave you this alarm.'

The grave affection of his manner restrained her, and his presence soothed the flutter of spirits; though she still devoted herself with a sort of wilfulness to bear all the blame, until he said, 'This is foolish, Albinia; it is of no use to look at anything but the simple truth. This affection of the spine must be constitutional, and if neglect have aggravated the evil, it must date from a much earlier period than since she has been under your charge. If any one be to blame, it is myself, for the apathy that prevented me from placing the poor things under proper care, but I was hardly then aware that Maria's solicitude is always in the wrong place.'

'But everybody declares that it was always visible, and that no one could look at her without seeing that she was crooked.'

'Apres le coup,' said Mr. Kendal. 'I grant you that a person of more experience might perhaps have detected what was amiss sooner than you did, but you have only to regret the ignorance you shared with us all; and you did your utmost according to your judgment.'

'And a cruel utmost it was,' said Albinia; 'it is frightful to think what I inflicted, and she endured in silence, because I had not treated her so that she could bear to speak to me.'

'That is over now,' said Mr. Kendal, 'you have conquered her at last. Pride could not hold out against such sweetness.'

'It is her generosity,' said Albinia; 'I always knew she was the best of them all, if one could but get at her.'

'What have you done to her? I never heard her say half so much as she voluntarily said to me just now.'

'Poor dear! I believe the key of her heart was lost when Edmund died, and so all within was starved,' said Albinia. 'Yes,' as his eyes were suddenly raised and fixed on her, 'I got to that at last. No one has ever understood her, since she lost her brother.'

'She has a certain likeness to him. I knew she was his favourite sister; but such a child as she was—'

'Children have deeper souls than you give them credit for,' said Albinia. 'Yes, Edmund, you and Sophy are very much alike! You had your study, and poor Sophy enclosed herself in a perpetual cocoon of study atmosphere, and so you never found each other out till to-day.'

Perhaps it was the influence of the frantic fit that caused her to make so direct a thrust; but Mr. Kendal was not offended. There was a good deal in the mere absence from habitual scenes and associations; he always left a great deal of reserve behind him at Bayford.

'You may be right, Albinia,' he said; 'I sometimes think that amongst us you are like the old poet's "star confined into a tomb."'

Such a compliment was a pretty reward for her temerity.

Returning to business, she found that her journey was treated as more judicious than she deserved. The consequences had justified her decision. Mr. Kendal knew it was the right thing to be done, and was glad to have been spared the dreadful task of making up his mind to it. He sat down of his own accord to write a note to Winifred, beginning, 'Albinia was right, as she always is,' and though his wife interlined, 'Albinia had no right to be right, for she was inconsiderate, as she always is,' she looked so brilliantly pretty and bright, and was so full of sunny liveliness, that she occasioned one of the very few disputes between her good aunts. Miss Ferrars declared that poor Albinia was quite revived by the return to her old home, and absence of care, while Mrs. Annesley insisted on giving the credit to Mr. Kendal. They were perfectly agreed in unwillingness to part with their guests; and as the doctor wished to see more of his patient, the visit was prolonged, to the enjoyment of all parties.

Sophy had received her sentence so easily, that it was suspected that she did not realize the tedium of confinement, and was relieved by being allowed to be inactive. Until she should go home, she might do whatever did not fatigue her; but most sights, and even the motion of the carriage, were so fatiguing, that she was much more inclined to remain at home and revel in the delightful world of books. The kind, unobtrusive petting; the absence of customary irritations; the quiet high-bred tone of the family, so acted upon her, as to render her something as agreeably new to herself as to other people. The glum mask was cast aside, she responded amiably to kindness and attention, allowed herself to be drawn into conversation, and developed much more intelligence and depth than even Albinia had given her credit for.

One day, when Miss Ferrars was showing Mr. Kendal some illustrations of Indian scenery, a question arose upon the date of the native sovereign to whom the buildings were ascribed. Mr. Kendal could not recollect; but Sophia, looking up, quietly pronounced the date, and gave her reasons for it. Miss Ferrars asked how she could have learnt so much on an out-of-the-way topic.

'I read a book of the History of India, up in the loft,' said Sophy.

'That book!' exclaimed her father; 'I wish you joy! I never could get through it! It is the driest chronicle I ever read—a mere book of reference. What could induce you to read that?'

'I would read anything about India;' and her tone, though low and subdued, betrayed such enthusiasm as could find nothing dry, and this in a girl who had read aloud the reign of Edward III. with stolid indifference!

'Well, I think I can promise you more interesting reading about India when we go home,' said Mr. Kendal.

The colour rose on Sophy's cheek. Books out of papa's study! Could the world offer a greater privilege?' She could scarcely pronounce, 'Thank you.'

'Very faithful to her birth-place,' said Miss Ferrars; 'but she must have been very young when she came home.'

'About five years old, I believe,' said her father. 'You surely can remember nothing of Talloon.'

'I don't know,' said Sophy, mournfully; 'I used—'

'I thought Indian children usually lost their eastern recollections very early,' said Miss Ferrars; 'I never heard of one who could remember the sound of Hindostanee a year after coming home.'

Mr. Kendal, entertained and gratified, turned to his daughter; and, by way of experiment, began a short sentence in Hindostanee; but the first sound brought a glow to her cheeks, and, with a hurried gesture, she murmured, 'Please don't, papa.'

Albinia saw that feelings were here concerned which must not be played on in public; and she hastily plunged into the discussion, and drew it away from Sophy. Following her up-stairs at bed-time, she contrived to win from her an explanation.

Edmund had been seven years old at the time of the return to England. Fondly attached to some of the Hindoo servants, and with unusual intelligence and observation, the gorgeous scenery and oriental habits of his first home had dwelt vividly in his imagination, and he had always considered himself as only taken to England for a time, to return again to India. Thus, he had been fond of romancing of the past and of the future, and had never let his little sister's recollections fade entirely away. His father had likewise thought that it would save future trouble to keep up the boys' knowledge of the language, which would by-and-by be so important to them. Gilbert's health had caused his studies to be often intermitted, but Edmund had constantly received instructions in the Indian languages, and whatever he learnt had been imparted to Sophia. It was piteous to discover how much time the poor forlorn little girl had spent sitting on the floor in the loft, poring over old grammars, and phrase-books, and translations of missionary or government school-books there accumulated—anything that related to India, or that seemed to carry on what she had done with Edmund: and she had acquired just enough to give her a keen appetite for all the higher class of lore, which she knew to reside in the unapproachable study. Those few familiar words from her father had overcome her, because, a trivial greeting in themselves, they had been a kind of password between her and her brother.

Mr. Kendal was greatly touched, and very remorseful for having left such a heart to pine in solitude, while he was absorbed in his own lonely grief; and Albinia ventured to say, 'I believe the greatest pleasure you could give her would be to help her to keep up the language.'

He smiled, but said, 'Of what possible use could it be to her?'

'I was not thinking of future use. It would be of immense present use to her to do anything with you, and I can see that nothing would gratify her so much. Besides, I have been trying to think of all the new things I could set her to do. She must have lessons to fill up the day, and I want to make fresh beginnings, and not go back to the blots and scars of our old misunderstandings.'

'You want me to teach her Sanscrit because you cannot teach her Italian.'

'Exactly so,' said Albinia; 'and the Italian will spring all the better from the venerable root, when we have forgotten how cross we used to be to each other over our relative pronouns.'

'But there is hardly anything which I could let her read in those languages.'

'Very likely not; but you can pick out what there is. Do you remember the fable of the treasure that was to be gained by digging under the apple-tree, and which turned out not to be gold, but the fruit, the consequence of digging? Now, I want you to dig Sophy; a Sanscrit, or a Hindostanee, or a Persian treasure will do equally well as a pretext. If she had announced a taste for the differential calculus, I should have said the same. Only dig her, as Maurice dug me apropos to Homer. I wouldn't bother you, only you see no one else could either do it, or be the same to Sophy.'

'We will see how it is,' said Mr. Kendal.

With which Albinia was obliged to be content; but in the meantime she saw the two making daily progress in intimacy, and Mr. Kendal beginning to take a pride in his daughter's understanding and information, which he ascribed to Albinia, in spite of all her disclaimers. It was as if she had evoked the spirit of his lost son, which had lain hidden under the sullen demeanour of the girl, devoid indeed of many of Edmund's charms, but yet with the same sterling qualities, and with resemblance enough to afford infinite and unexpected joy and compensation.

Mr. Kendal enjoyed his stay in town. He visited libraries, saw pictures, and heard music, with the new zest of having a wife able to enter into his tastes. He met old friends, and did not shrink immoderately from those of his wife; nay, he found them extremely agreeable, and was pleased to see Albinia welcomed. Indeed, his sojourn in her former sphere served to make him wonder that she could be contented with Bayford, and to find her, of the whole party, by far the most ready to return home. Both he himself and Sophy had an unavowed dread of the influence of Willow Lawn; but Albinia had a spring of spirits, independent of place, and though happy, was craving for her duties, anxious to have the journey over, and afraid that London was making her little Maurice pale.

Miss Meadows was the first person whom they saw at Willow Lawn. Two letters had passed, both so conventionally civil, that her state of mind could not be gathered from them, but her first tones proved that coherence was more than ever wanting, and no one attempted to understand anything she said, while she enfolded Sophy in an agitated embrace, and marshalled them to the drawing-room, where the chief of the apologies were spent upon Sophy's new couch, which had been sent down the day before by the luggage-train, and which she and Eweretta had attempted to put together in an impossible way, failing which, they had called in the carpenter, who had made it worse.

It was an untold advantage that she had to take the initiative in excuses. Sophy was so meek with weariness, that she took pretty well all the kind fidgeting that could not be averted from her, and Miss Meadows's discourse chiefly tended to assurances that Mrs. Kendal was right, and grandmamma was nervous—and poor Mr. Bowles—it could not be expected—with hints of the wonderful commotion the sudden flight to London had excited at Bayford. As soon as Mr. Kendal quitted the room, these hints were converted into something between expostulation, condolence, and congratulation.

It was so very fortunate—so very lucky that dear Mr. Kendal had come home with her, for—she had said she would let Mrs. Kendal hear, if only that she might be on her guard—people were so ill-natured—there never was such a place for gossip—not that she heard it from any one but Mrs. Drury, who really now had driven in—not that she believed it, but to ascertain.—For Mrs. Drury had been told—mentioning no names—oh, no! for fear of making mischief— she had been told that Mrs. Kendal had actually been into Mr. Kendal's study, which was always kept locked up, and there she had found something which had distressed her so much that she had gone to Mr. Dusautoy, and by his advice had fled from home to the protection of her brother in Canada.

'Without waiting for Bluebeard's asking for the key! Oh, Maria!' cried Albinia, in a fit of laughter, while Sophia sat up on the sofa in speechless indignation.

'You may laugh, Mrs. Kendal, if you please,' said Maria, with tart dignity; 'I have told you nothing but the truth. I should have thought for my part, but that's of no consequence, it was as well to be on one's guard in a nest of vipers, for Edmund's sake, if not for your own.' And as this last speech convulsed Albinia, and rendered her incapable of reply, Miss Meadows became pathetic. 'I am sure the pains I have taken to trace out and contradict
—and so nervous as grandmamma has been—"I'm sure, Mrs. Drury," said I, "that though Edmund Kendal does lock his study door, nobody ever thought anything—the housemaids go in to clean it—and I've been in myself when the whitewashers were about the house—I'm sure Mrs. Kendal is a most amiable young woman, and you wouldn't raise reports." "No," she said, "but Mrs. Osborn was positive that Mrs. Kendal was nearly an hour shut up alone in the study the night of Sophy's accident—and so sudden," she said, "the

carriage being sent for—not a servant knew of it—and then," she said, "it was always the talk among the girls, that Mr. Kendal kept his study a forbidden place."'

'Then,' said Sophia, slowly, as she looked full at her aunt, 'it was the Osborns who dared to say such wicked things.'

'There now, I never meant you to be there. You ought to be gone to bed, child. It is not a thing for you to know anything about.'

'I only want to know whether it was the Osborns who invented these stories,' said Sophy.

'My dear,' exclaimed Albinia, 'what can it signify? They are only a very good joke. I did not think there had been so much imagination in Bayford.' And off she went laughing again.

'They are very wicked,' said Sophy, 'Aunt Maria, I will know if it was Mrs. Osborn who told the story.'

Sophy's *will* was too potent for Miss Meadows, and the admission was extracted in a burst of other odds and ends, in the midst of which Albinia beheld Sophy cross the room with a deliberate, determined step. Flying after her, she found her in the hall, wrapping herself up.

'Sophy, what is this? What are you about?'

'Let me alone,' said Sophy, straining against her detaining hand, 'I do not know when I shall recover again, and I will go at once to tell the Osborns that I have done with them. I stuck to them because I thought they were my mother's friends; I did not guess that they would make an unworthy use of my friendship, and invent wicked stories of my father and you.'

'Please don't make me laugh, Sophy, for I don't want to affront you. Yes, it is generous feeling; I don't wonder you are angry; but indeed silly nonsense like this is not worth it. It will die away of itself, it must be dead already, now they have seen we have not run away to Canada. Your heroics only make it more ridiculous.'

'I must tell Loo never to come here with her hypocrisy,' repeated Sophy, standing still, but not yielding an inch.

Miss Meadows pursued them at the same moment with broken protestations that they must forget it, she never meant to make mischief, &c., and the confusion was becoming worse confounded when Mr. Kendal emerged from the study, demanding what was the matter, to the great discomfiture of Maria, who began hushing Sophy, and making signs to Albinia that it would be dangerous for him to know anything about it.

But Albinia was already exclaiming, 'Here's a champion wanting to do battle with Louisa Osborn in our cause. Oh, Edmund! our neighbours could find no way of accounting for my taking French leave, but by supposing that I took advantage of being shut in there, while poor little Maurice was squalling so furiously, to rifle your secrets, and detect something so shocking, that away I was fleeing to William in Canada.'

'Obliging,' quietly said Mr. Kendal.

'Now, dear Edmund—I know—for my sake—for everything's sake, remember you are a family man, don't take any notice.'

'I certainly shall take no notice of such folly,' said Mr. Kendal, 'and I wish that no one else should. What are you about, Sophia?'

'Tell mamma to let me go, papa,' she exclaimed, 'I must and will tell Louisa that I hate her baseness and hypocrisy, and then I'll never speak to her again. Why will mamma laugh? It is very wicked of them.'

'Wrong in them, but laughing is the only way to treat it,' said Mr. Kendal. 'Go back to your sofa and forget it. Your aunt and I have heard Bayford reports before.'

Sophy obeyed unwillingly, she was far too much incensed to forget. On her aunt's taking leave, and Mr. Kendal offering his escort up the hill, she rose up again, and would have perpetrated a denunciation by letter, had not Albinia seriously argued with her, and finding ridicule, expediency, and Christian forgiveness all fail of hitting the mark, said, 'I don't know with what face you could attack Louisa, when you helped her to persecute poor Genevieve because you thought she had an instrument of torture in her drawer.'

'It was not I who said that,' said Sophy, blushing.

'You took part with those who did. And poor Genevieve was a much more defenceless victim than papa or myself.'

'I would not do so now.'

'It does not take much individual blackness of heart to work up a fine promising slander. A surmise made in jest is repeated in earnest, and all the other tale-bearers think they are telling simple facts. Depend upon it, the story did not get off from the Osborns by any means as it came back to Aunt Maria.'

'I should like to know.'

'Don't let us make it any worse; and above all, do not let us tell Lucy.'

'Oh, no!' said Sophy, emphatically.

To Albinia's surprise no innuendo from Mrs. or Miss Meadows ever referred to her management having caused Sophy's misfortune, and she secretly attributed this silence to Mr. Kendal's having escorted his sister-in- law to her own house.

Sophy's chief abode became the morning-room, and she seemed very happy and tranquil there—shrinking from visitors, but grateful for the kindness of parents, brother and sister.

Mr. Kendal, finding her really eager to learn of him, began teaching her Persian, and was astonished at her promptness and intelligence. He took increasing pleasure in her company, gave her books to read, and would sometimes tell the others not to stay at home for her sake, as he should be 'about the house.'

He really gave up much time to her, and used to carry her, when the weather served, to a couch in the garden, for she could not bear the motion of wheels, and was forbidden to attempt walking, though she was to be in the air as much as possible, so that Albinia spent more time at home. The charge of Sophy was evidently her business, and after talking the matter over with Mrs. Dusautoy, she resigned, though not without a pang, the offices she had undertaken in the time of her superfluous activity, and limited herself to occasional superintendence, instead of undertaking constant employment in the parish. Though she felt grieved and humiliated, Willow Lawn throve the better for it, and so did her own mind, yes, and even her temper, which was far less often driven by over-haste into quick censure, or unconsidered reply.

Her mistakes about Sophia had been a lesson against one-sided government. At first, running into the other extreme, she was ready to imagine that all the past ill-humour had been the effect of her neglect and cruelty; and Sophy's amiability almost warranted the notion. The poor girl herself had promised 'never to be cross again,' and fancied all temptation was over, since she had 'found out mamma,' and papa was so kind to her. But all on a sudden, down came the cloud again. Nobody could detect any reason. Affronts abounded— not received with an explosion that would have been combated, laughed at, and disposed of, but treated with silence, and each sinking down to be added to the weight of cruel injuries. There was no complaint; Sophy obeyed all orders with her old form of dismal submission, but everything proposed to her was distasteful, and her answers were in the ancient surly style. If attempts were made to probe the malady, her reserve was impenetrable—nothing was the matter, she wanted nothing, was vexed at nothing. She pursued her usual occupations, but as if they were hardships; she was sullen towards her mamma, snappishly brief with her aunt and sister, and so ungracious and indifferent even with her father, that Albinia trembled lest he might withdraw the attention so improperly received. When this dreary state of things had lasted more than a week, he did tell her that if she were tired of the lessons, it was not worth while to proceed; but that he had hoped for more perseverance.

The fear of losing these, her great pride and pleasure, overcame her. She maintained her grim composure till he had left her, but then fell into a violent fit of crying, in which Albinia found her, and which dissolved the reserve into complaints that every one was very cruel and unkind, and she was the most miserable girl in all the world; papa was going to take away from her the only one thing that made it tolerable!

Reasoning was of no use; to try to show her that it was her own behaviour that had annoyed him, only made her mamma appear equally hard-hearted, and she continued wretched all the rest of the day, refusing consolation, and only so far improved that avowed discontent was better than sullenness. The next morning, she found out that it was not the world that was in league against her, but that she had fallen into the condition which she had thought past for ever. This was worst of all, and her disappointment and dejection lasted not only all that long day, but all the next, making her receive all kindnesses with a broken-down, woebegone manner, and reply to all cheerful encouragements with despair about anything ever making her good. Albinia tried to put her in mind of the Source of all goodness; but any visible acceptance of personal applications of religious teaching had not yet been accomplished.

Gradually all cleared up again, and things went well till for some fresh trivial cause or no cause, the whole process was repeated—sulking, injured innocence, and bitter repentance. This time, Mr. Kendal pronounced, 'This is low spirits, far more than temper,' and he thenceforth dealt with these moods with a tender consideration that Albinia admired, though she thought at times that to treat them more like temper than spirits might be better for Sophy; but it was evident that the poor child herself had at present little if any power either of averting such an access, or of shaking it off. The danger of her father's treatment seemed to be, that the humours would be acquiesced in, like changes in the weather, and that she might be encouraged neither to repent, nor to struggle; while her captivity made her much more liable to the tedium and sinking of heart that predisposed her to them.

There seemed to be nothing to be done but to bear patiently with them while they lasted, to console the victim afterwards, lead her to prayer and resolute efforts, and above all to pray for her, as well as to avoid occasions of bringing them on; but this was not possible, since no one could live without occasional contradiction, and Sophy could sometimes bear a strong remonstrance or great disappointment, when at others a hint, or an almost imperceptible vexation, destroyed her peace for days.

Mr. Kendal bore patiently with her variations, and did his best to amuse away her gloom. It was wonderful how much of his own was gone, and how much more alive he was. He had set himself to attack the five public-houses and seven beer-shops in Tibbs's Alley, and since his eyes had been once opened, it seemed as if the disorders became more flagrant every day. At last, he pounced on a misdemeanour which he took care should come before the magistrates, and he was much annoyed to find the case dismissed for want of evidence. One Sunday he beheld the end of a fray begun during service-time; he caused an information to be laid, and went himself to the petty sessions to represent the case, but the result was a nominal penalty. The Admiral was a seeker of popularity, and though owning that the town was in a shocking state, and making great promises when talked to on general points, yet he could never make up his mind to punish any 'poor fellow,' unless he himself were in a passion, when he would go any length. The other magistrates would not interfere; and all the satisfaction Mr. Kendal obtained was being told how much he was wanted on the bench.

One of the few respectable Tibbs's Alleyites told him that it was of no use to complain, for the publicans boasted of their impunity, snapped their fingers at him, and drank Admiral Osborn's health as their friend. The consequence was, that Mr. Kendal took a magnanimous resolution, ordered a copy of Burn's Justice, and at the September Quarter Sessions actually rode over to Hadminster, and took the oaths.

On the whole, the expectation was more formidable than the reality. However much he disliked applying himself to business, no one understood it better. The value of his good sense, judgment, and acuteness was speedily felt. Mr. Nugent, the chairman, depended on him as his ally, and often as his adviser; and as he was thus made to feel himself of weight and importance, his aversion subsided, and he almost learnt to look forward to a chat with Mr. Nugent; or whether he looked forward to it or not, there could be no doubt that he enjoyed it. Though still shy, grave, silent, and inert, there was a great alteration in him since the time when he had had no friends, no interests, no pursuits beyond his study; and there was every reason to think that, in spite of the many severe shocks to his mauvaise honte, he was a much happier man.

His wife could not regret that his magisterial proceedings led to a coolness with the Osborns, augmented by a vestry-meeting, at which Mr. Dusautoy had begged him to be present. The Admiral and his party surpassed themselves in their virulence against whatever the vicar proposed, until they fairly roused Mr. Kendal's ire, and 'he came out upon them all like a lion;' and with force appearing the greater from being so seldom exerted, he represented Mr. Dusautoy's conduct in appropriate terms, showing full appreciation of his merits, and holding up their own course before them in its true light, till they had nothing to say for themselves. It was the vicar's first visible victory. The increased congregation showed how much way he had made with the poor, and Mr. Kendal taking his part openly, drew over many of the tradespeople, who had begun to feel the influence of his hearty nature and consistent uprightness, and had become used to what had at first appeared innovations. Mr. Dusautoy, in thanking Mr. Kendal, begged him to allow himself to be nominated his churchwarden next Easter, and having consented while his blood was up, there was no danger that, however he might dislike the prospect, he would falter when the time should come.

CHAPTER X.

It was 'a green Yule,' a Christmas like an April day, and even the lengthening days and strengthening cold of January attaining to nothing more than three slight hoar-frosts, each quickly melting into mud, and the last concluding in rain and fog.

'What would Willow Lawn have been without the drainage?' Albinia often thought when she paddled down the wet streets, and saw the fields flooded. The damp had such an effect upon Sophy's throat, temper, and whole nervous system, that her moods had few intervals, and Albinia wrote to the surgeon a detail of her symptoms, asking if she had not better be removed into a more favourable air. But he pronounced that the injury of the transport would outbalance the casual evils of the bad weather, and as the rain and fog mitigated, she improved; but there were others on whom the heavy moist air had a more fatal effect.

One morning, Mr. Kendal saw his wife descending the picturesque rugged stone staircase that led outside the house to the upper stories of the old block of buildings under the hill, nearly opposite to Willow Lawn. She came towards him with tears still in her eyes as she said, 'Poor Mrs. Simkins has just lost her little girl, and I am afraid the two boys are sickening.'

'What do you mean? Is the fever there again?' exclaimed Mr. Kendal in the utmost consternation.

'Did you not know it? Lucy has been very anxious about the child, who was in her class.'

'You have not taken Lucy to a house with a fever!'

'No, I thought it safer not, though she wanted very much to go.'

'But you have been going yourself!'

'It was a low, lingering fever. I had not thought it infectious, and even now I believe it is only one of those that run through an over-crowded family. The only wonder is, that they are ever well in such a place. Dear Edmund, don't be angry; it is what I used to do continually at Fairmead. I never caught anything; and there is plenty of chloride of lime, and all that. I never imagined you would disapprove.'

'It is the very place where the fever began before!' said Mr. Kendal, almost under his breath.

Instead of going into the house, he made her turn into the garden, where little Maurice was being promenaded in the sun. He stretched out from his nurse's arms to go to them, and Albinia was going towards him, but her husband held her fast, and said, 'I beg you will not take the child till you have changed your dress.'

Albinia was quite subdued, alarmed at the effect on him.

'You must go away at once,' he said presently. 'How soon can you be ready? You had better take Lucy and Maurice at once to your brother's. They will excuse the liberty when they know the cause.'

'And pray what is to become of poor Sophy?'

'Never going out, there may be the less risk for her. I will take care of her myself.'

'As if I was going to endure that!' cried Albinia. 'No, no, Edmund, I am not likely to run away from you and Sophy! You may send Lucy off, if you like, but certainly not me, or if you do I shall come back the same evening.'

'I should be much happier if you were gone.'

'Thank you, but what should I be? No, if it were to be caught here, which I don't believe, now the pond is gone, it would be of no use to send me away, after I have been into the house with it.'

Her resolution and Sophy's need prevailed, and most unwillingly Mr. Kendal gave up the point. She was persuaded that he was acting on a panic, the less to be wondered at after all he had suffered. She thought the chief danger was from the effect of his fears, and would fain have persuaded him to remain at Fairmead with Lucy, but she was not prepared to hear him insist on likewise removing Maurice. She had promised not to enter the sick room again, and pleaded that the little boy need never be taken into the street—that the fever was not likely to come across the running stream—that the Fairmead nursery was full enough already.

Mr. Kendal was inexorable. 'I hope you may never see what I have seen,' he said gravely, and Albinia was silenced.

A man who had lost so many children might be allowed to be morbidly jealous of the health of the rest. But it was a cruel stroke to her to be obliged to part with her noble little boy, just when his daily advances in walking and talking made him more charming than ever. Her eyes were full of tears, and she struggled to choke back some pettish rebellious words.

'You do not like to trust him with Susan,' said Mr. Kendal; 'you had better come with him.'

'No,' said Albinia, 'I ought to stay here, and if you judge it right, Maurice must go. I'll go and speak to Susan.'

And away she ran, for she had no power just then to speak in a wifely manner. It was not easy to respect a man in a panic so extremely inconvenient.

He was resolved on an immediate start, and the next few hours were spent in busy preparation, and in watching lest the excited Lucy should frighten her sister. Albinia tried to persuade Mr. Kendal at least to sleep at Fairmead that night, and after watching him drive off, she hurried, dashing away the tears that would gather again and again in her eyes, to hold council with the Dusautoys on the best means of stopping the course of the malady, by depriving it of its victims.

She had a quiet snug evening with Sophy, whom she had so much interested in the destitution of the sick children as to set her to work at some night-gear for them, and she afterwards sat long over the fire trying to read to silence the longing after the little soft cheek that had never yet been laid to rest without her caress, and foreboding that Mr. Kendal would return from his dark solitary drive with his spirits at the lowest ebb.

So late that she had begun to hope that Winifred had obeyed her behest and detained him, she heard his step, and before she could run to meet him, he had already shut himself into the study.

She was at the door in a moment; she feared he had thought her self-willed in the morning, and she was the more bent on rousing him. She knocked—she opened the door. He had thrown himself into his arm-chair, and was bending over the dreary, smouldering, sulky log and white ashes, and his face, as he raised his head, was as if the whole load of care and sorrow had suddenly descended again.

'I am sorry you sat up,' was of course his beginning, conveying anything but welcome; but she knew that this only meant that he was in a state of depression. She took hold of his hand, chilled with holding the reins, told him of the good fire in the morning-room, and fairly drew him up-stairs.

There the lamp burnt brightly, and the red fire cast a merry glow over the shining chintz curtains, and the two chairs drawn so cosily towards the fire, the kettle puffing on the hearth, and Albinia's choice little bed-room set of tea-china ready on the small table. The cheerfulness seemed visibly to diffuse itself over his face, but he still struggled to cherish his gloom, 'Thank you, but I would not have had you take all this trouble, my dear.'

'It would be a great deal more trouble if you caught a bad cold. I meant you to sleep at Fairmead.'

'Yes, they pressed me very kindly, but I could not bear not to come home.'

'And how did Maurice comport himself?'

'He talked to the horse and then went to sleep, and he was not at all shy with his aunt after the first. He watched the children, but had not begun to play with them. Still I think he will be quite happy with Lucy there, and I hope it will not be for long.'

It was a favourable sign that Mr. Kendal communicated all these particulars without being plied with questions, and Albinia went on with the more spirit.

'No, I hope it may not be for long. We have been holding a great council against the enemy, and I do hope that we have really done something. No, you need not be afraid, I have not been there again, but we have been routing out the nucleus, and hope we may starve out the fever for want of victims. You never saw such a swarm as we had to turn out. There were twenty-three people to be considered for.'

'Twenty-three! Have you turned out the whole block?'

'No, I wish we had; but that would have been seventy-five. This is only from those two tenements with one door!'

'Impossible!'

'I should have thought so; but the lawful inhabitants make up sixteen, and there were seven lodgers.'

Mr. Kendal gave a kind of groan, and asked what she had done; she detailed the measures.

'Twenty-three people in those two houses, and seventy-five in the whole block of building?'

'Too true. And if you could only see the rooms! The windows that wont open; the roofs that open too much; the dirt on the staircases, and, oh! the horrible smells!'

'It shall not go on,' said Mr. Kendal. 'I will look over the place.'

'Not till the fever is out of it,' hastily interposed Albinia.

He made a sign of assent, and went on: 'I will certainly talk to Pettilove, and have the place repaired, if it be at my own expense.'

Albinia lifted up her eyes, not understanding at whose expense it should be.

'The fact is,' continued Mr. Kendal, 'that there has been little to induce me to take interest in the property. Old Mr. Meadows was, as you know, a successful solicitor, and purchased these various town tenements bit by bit, and then settled them very strictly on his grandson. He charged the property with life incomes to his widow and daughters, and to me; but the land is in the hands of trustees until my son's majority, and Pettilove is the only surviving trustee.'

The burning colour mantled in Albinia's face, and almost inaudibly she said, 'I beg your pardon, Edmund; I have done you moat grievous injustice. I thought you *would* not see—'

'You did not think unjustly, my dear. I ought to have paid more attention to the state of affairs, and have kept Pettilove in order. But I knew nothing of English affairs, and was glad to be spared the unpleasant charge. The consequence of leaving a man like that irresponsible never occurred to me. His whole conscience in the matter is to have a large sum to put into Gilbert's hands when he comes of age. Why, he upholds those dens of iniquity in Tibbs's Alley on that very ground!'

'Poor Gilbert! I am afraid a large sum so collected is not likely to do him much good! and at one-and-twenty—! But that is one notion of faithfulness!'

Albinia was much happier after that conversation. She could better endure to regret her own injustice than to believe her husband the cruel landlord; and it was no small advance that he had afforded her an explanation which once he would have deemed beyond the reach of female capacity.

In spite of the lack of little Maurice's bright presence, which, to Albinia's great delight, his father missed as much as she did, the period of quarantine sped by cheerfully. Sophy had not a single sullen fit the whole time, and Albinia having persuaded Mr. Kendal that it would be a sanatory measure to whitewash the study ceiling, he was absolutely forced to turn out of it and live in the morning-room, with all his books piled up in the dining-room. And on that great occasion Albinia abstracted two fusty, faded, green canvas blinds from the windows, carried them off with a pair of tongs, and pushed them into a bonfire in the garden, persuaded they were the last relics of the old fever. She had the laurels cut, the curtains changed, the windows cleaned, and altogether made the room so much lighter, that when Mr. Kendal again took possession, he did not look at all sure whether he liked it; and though he was courteously grateful, he did not avail himself of the den half so much as when it had more congenial gloom. But then he had the morning-room as a resort, and it was one of Albinia's bargains with herself, that as far as her own influence could prevent it, neither he nor Sophy should ever render it a literal boudoir.

The sense of snugness that the small numbers produced was one great charm, and made Mr. Kendal come unusually far out of his shell. His chief sanatory precaution was to take Albinia out for a drive or walk every day, and these expeditions were greatly enjoyed.

One day, after a visit from her old nurse, Sophy received Albinia with the words,—

'Oh, mamma,' she said, 'old nurse has been telling me such things. I shall never be cross with Aunt Maria again. It is such a sad story, just like one in a book, if she was but that kind of person.'

'Aunt Maria! I remember Mrs. Dusautoy once saying she gave her the idea of happiness shattered, but—'

'Did she?' exclaimed Sophy. 'I never thought Aunt Maria could have done anything but fidget everybody that came near her; but old nurse says a gentleman was once in love with her, and a very handsome young gentleman too. Old Mr. Pringle's nephew it was, a very fine young officer in the army. I want you to ask papa if it is true. Nurse says that he wrote to make an offer for her, very handsomely, but grandpapa did not choose that both his daughters should go quite away; so he locked the letter up, and said no, and never told her, and she thought the captain had been trifling and playing her false, and pined and fretted, till she got into this nervous way, and fairly wore herself out, nurse says, and came to be what she is now, instead of the prettiest young lady in the town! And then, mamma, when grandpapa died, she found the letter in his papers, and one inside for her, that had never been given to her; and by that time there was no hope, for Captain Pringle had gone out with his regiment, and married a rich young lady in the Indies! Oh, mamma! you see she really is deserted, and it is all man's treachery that has broken her heart. I thought people always died or went into convents—I don't mean that Aunt Maria could have done that, but I did not think that way of hers was a broken heart!'

'If she has had such troubles, it should indeed make us try to be very forbearing with her,' said Albinia.

'Will you ask papa about it?' entreated Sophy.

'Yes, certainly; but you must not make sure whether he will think it right to tell us. Poor Aunt Maria; I do think some part of it must be true!'

'But, mamma, is that really like deserted love?'

'My dear, I don't think I ever saw deserted love,' said Albinia, rather amused. 'I suppose troubles of any kind, if not—I mean, I suppose, vexations —make people show their want of spirits in the way most accordant with their natural dispositions, and so your poor aunt has grown querulous and anxious.'

'If she has such a real grand reason for being unhappy, I shall not be cross about it now, except—'

Sophy gave a sigh, and Albinia bade her good night.

Mr. Kendal had never heard the story before, but he remembered many circumstances in corroboration. He knew that Mr. Pringle had a nephew in the army, he recollected that he had made a figure in Maria's letters to India; and that he had subsequently married a lady in the Mauritius, and settled down on her father's estate. He testified also to the bright gay youth of poor Maria, and his surprise at the premature loss of beauty and spirits; and from his knowledge of old Mr. Meadows, he believed him capable of such an act of domestic tyranny. Maria had always been looked upon as a mere child, and if her father did not choose to part with her, he would think it for her good, and his own peace, for her not to be aware of the proposal. He was much struck, for he had not suspected his sister-in-law to be capable of such permanent feeling.

'There was little to help her in driving it away,' said Albinia. 'Few occupations or interests, and very little change, to prevent it from preying on her spirits.'

'True,' said Mr. Kendal; 'a narrow education and limited sphere are sad evils in such cases.'

'Do you think anything can be a cure for disappointment?' asked Sophy, in such a solemn, earnest tone, that Albinia was disposed to laugh; but she knew that this would be a dire offence, and was much surprised that Sophy had so far broken through her reserve, as to mingle in their conversation on such a subject.

'Occupation,' said Mr. Kendal, but speaking rather as if from duty than from conviction. 'There are many sources of happiness, even if shipwreck have been made on one venture. Your aunt had few resources to which to turn her mind. Every pursuit or study is a help stored up against the vacuity which renders every care more corroding.'

'Well!' said Sophy, in her blunt, downright way, 'I think it would take all the spirit out of everything.'

'I hope you will never be tried,' said Mr. Kendal, with a mournful smile, as if he did not choose to confess that she had divined too rightly the probable effect of trouble upon her own temperament.

'I suppose,' said Albinia, 'that the real cure can be but one thing for that, as for any other trouble. I mean, "Thy will be done." I don't suppose anything else would give energy to turn to other duties. But it would be more to the purpose to resolve to be more considerate to poor Maria.'

'I shall never be impatient with her again,' said Sophy.

And though at first the discovery of so romantic a cause for poor Miss Meadows's fretfulness dignified it in Sophy's eyes, yet it did not prove sufficient to make it tolerable when she tormented the window-blinds, teased the fire, was shocked at Sophy's favourite studies, or insisting on her wishing to see Maria Drury. Nay, the bathos often rendered her petty unconscious provocations the more harassing, and Sophy often felt, in an agony of self-reproach, that she ought to have known herself too well to expect to show forbearance with any one when she was under the influence of ill-temper.

In Easter week Mr. Ferrars brought Lucy and Maurice home, and Gilbert came for a short holiday.

Gilbert was pleased when he was called to go over the empty houses with his father, Mr. Ferrars, and a mason.

Back they came, horrified at the dreadful disrepair, at the narrow area into which such numbers were crowded, and still more at the ill odours which Mr. Ferrars and the mason had gallantly investigated, till they detected the absence of drains, as well as convinced themselves that mending roofs, floors, or windows, would be a mere mockery unless the whole were pulled down.

Mr. Ferrars was more than ever thankful to be a country parson, and mused on the retribution that the miasma, fostered by the avarice of the grandfather and the neglect of the father, had brought on the family. Dives cannot always scorn Lazarus without suffering even in this life.

Gilbert, in the glory of castle-building, was talking eagerly of the thorough renovation that should take place, the sweep that should be made of all the old tenements, and the wide healthy streets and model cottages that should give a new aspect to the town.

Mr. Kendal prepared for the encounter with Pettilove, and his son begged to go with him, to which he consented, saying that it was time Gilbert should have an opinion in a matter that affected him so nearly.

Gilbert's opinion of the interview was thus announced on his return: 'If there ever was a brute in the world, it is that Pettilove!'

'Then he wont consent to do anything?'

'No, indeed! Say what my father or I would to him, it was all of not the slightest use. He smiled, and made little intolerable nods, and regretted—but there were the settlements, and his late lamented partner! A parcel of stuff. Not so much as a broken window will he mend! He says he is not authorized!'

'Quite true,' said Mr. Kendal. 'The man is warranted in his proceedings, and thinks them his duty, though I believe he has a satisfaction in the power of thwarting me.'

'I'm sure he has!' cried Gilbert. 'I am sure there was spite in his grin when he pulled out that horrid old parchment, with the lines a yard long, and read us out the abominable old crabbed writing, all about the houses, messuages, and tenements thereupon, and a lot of lawyer's jargon. I'm sure I thought it was left to Peter Pettilove himself. And when I came to understand it, one would have thought it took my father to be the worst enemy we had in the world, bent on cheating us!'

'That is the assumption on which settlements are drawn up, Gilbert,' said his father.

'Can nothing be done, then?' said Albinia.

'Thus much,' said Mr. Kendal. 'Pettilove will not object to our putting the houses somewhat in repair, as, in fact, that will be making a present to Gilbert; but he will not spend a farthing on them of the trust, except to hinder their absolute falling, nor will he make any regulation on the number of lodgers. As to taking them down, that is, as I always supposed, out of the question, though I think the trustees might have stretched a point, being certain of both my wishes and Gilbert's.'

'Don't you think,' said Mr. Ferrars, looking up from his book, 'that a sanatory commission might be got to over-ride Gilbert's guardian?'

'My guardian! do not call him so!' muttered Gilbert.

'I am afraid,' said Mr. Kendal, 'that unless your commission emulated of Albinia and Dusautoy they would have little perception of the evils. Our local authorities are obtuse in such matters.'

'Agitate! agitate!' murmured Mr. Ferrars, going on with his book.

'Well,' said Albinia, 'at least there is one beer-shop less in Tibbs's Alley. And if there are tolerable seasons, I daresay paint, whitewash, and windows to open, may keep the place moderately wholesome till—Are you sixteen yet, Gilbert? Five years.'

'Yes, and then—'

Gilbert came and sat down beside her, and they built a scheme for the almshouses so much wanted. Gilbert was sure the accumulation would easily cover the expense, and Albinia had many an old woman, who it was hoped might live to enjoy the intended paradise there.

'Yes, yes, I promise,' cried Gilbert, warming with the subject, 'the first thing I shall do—'

'No, don't promise,' said Albinia. 'Do it from your heart, or not at all.'

'No, don't promise, Gilbert,' said Sophy.

'Why not, Sophy?' he said good-humouredly.

'Because you are just what you feel at the moment,' said Sophy.

'You don't think I should keep it?'

'No.'

The grave answer fell like lead, and Albinia told her she was not kind or just to her brother. But she still looked steadily at him, and answered, 'I cannot help it. What is truth, is truth, and Gilbert cares only for what he sees at the moment.'

'What is truth need not always be fully uttered,' said Albinia. 'I hope you may find it untrue.'

But Sophy's words would recur, and weigh on her painfully.

CHAPTER XI.

The summer had just begun, when notice was given that a Confirmation would take place in the autumn; and Lucy's name was one of the first sent in to Mr. Dusautoy. His plan was to collect his candidates in weekly classes of a few at a time, and likewise to see as much as he could of them in private.

'Oh! mamma!' exclaimed Lucy, returning from her first class, 'Mr. Dusautoy has given us each a paper, where we are to set down our christening days, and our godfathers and godmothers. And only think, I had not the least notion when I was christened. I could tell nothing but that Mr. Wenlock was my godfather! It made me feel quite foolish not to know my godmothers.'

'We were in no situation to have things done in order,' said Mr. Kendal, gravely. 'If I recollect rightly, one of your godmothers was Captain Lee's pretty young wife, who died a few weeks after.'

'And the other?' said Lucy.

'Your mother, I believe,' he said.

Lucy employed herself in filling up her paper, and exclaimed, 'Now I do not know the date! Can you tell me that, papa?'

'It was the Christmas-day next after your birth,' he said. 'I remember that, for we took you to spend Christmas at the nearest station of troops, and the chaplain christened you.'

Lucy wrote down the particulars, and exclaimed, 'What an old baby I must have been! Six months old! And I wonder when Sophy was christened. I never knew who any of her godfathers and godmothers were. Did you, Sophy?'

'No—' she was looking up at her father.

A sudden flush of colour came over his face, and he left the room in haste.

'Why, Sophy!' exclaimed Lucy, 'one would think you had not been christened at all!'

Even the light Lucy was alarmed at the sound of her own words. The same idea had thrilled across Albinia; but on turning her eyes on Sophy, she saw a countenance flushed, anxious, but full rather of trembling hope than of dismay.

In a few seconds Mr. Kendal came back with a thick red pocket-book in his hand, and produced the certificate of the private baptism of Sophia, daughter of Edmund and Lucy Kendal, at Talloon, March 17th, 1838.

Sophy's face had more disappointment in it than satisfaction.

'I can explain the circumstances to you now,' said her father. 'At Talloon we were almost out of reach of any chaplains, and, as you know, were almost the only English. We always intended to take you to the nearest station, as had been done with Lucy, but your dear mother was never well enough to bear the journey; and when our next little one was born, it was so plain that he could not live, that I sent in haste to beg that the chaplain would come to us. It was then that you were both baptized, and before the week was over, he buried little Henry. It was the first of our troubles. We never again had health or spirits for any festive occasion while we continued in India, and thus the ceremony was never completed. In fact, I take shame to myself for having entirely forgotten that you had never been received into the congregation.'

'Then I have told a falsehood whenever I said the Catechism!' burst out Sophy. Lucy would have laughed, and Albinia could almost have been amused at the turn her displeasure had taken.

'It was not your fault,' said Mr. Kendal, quietly.

He evidently wished the subject to be at an end, excepting that in silence he laid before Albinia's eyes the certificate of the baptism of the twin-brothers, not long after the first arrival in India. He then put the book in his pocket, and began, as usual, to read aloud.

'Oh, don't go, mamma,' said Sophy, when she had been carried to her own room at bed-time, and made ready for the night.

Albinia was only too glad to linger, in the hope to be admitted into some of the recesses of that untransparent nature, and by way of assistance, said, 'I was not at all prepared for this discovery.'

Sophy drew a long sigh, and said, 'If I had never been christened, I should have thought there was some hope for me.'

'That would have been too dreadful. How could you imagine your papa capable—?'

'I thought I had found out why I am so horrid! exclaimed Sophy. 'Oh, if I could only make a fresh beginning! Mamma, do pray give me a Prayer Book.'

Albinia gave it to her, and she hastily turned the pages to the Order for Private Baptism.

'At least I have not made the promises and vows!' she said, as if her stern conscientiousness obtained some relief.

'Not formally made them,' said Albinia; 'but you cannot have a right to the baptismal blessings, except on those conditions.'

'Mamma, then I never had the sign of the cross on my forehead! It does not feel blest!' And then, hastily and low, she muttered,' Oh! is that why I never could bear the cross in all my life!'

'Nay, my poor Sophy, you must not think of it like a spell. Many bear the cross no better, who have had it marked on their brows.'

'Can it be done now?' cried Sophy, eagerly.

'Certainly; I think it ought to be done. We will see what your father says.'

'Oh, mamma, beg him, pray him!' exclaimed Sophy. 'I know it will make me begin to be good! I can't bear not to be one of those marked and sealed. Oh! and, mamma, you will be my godmother? Can't you? If the gleams of goodness and brightness do find me out, they are always from you.'

'I think I might be, dear child,' said Albinia, 'but Mr. Dusautoy must tell us whether I may. But, indeed, I am afraid to see you reckon too much on this. The essential, the regenerating grace, is yours already, and can save you from yourself, and Confirmation adds the rest—but you must not think of any of these like a charm, which will save you all further trouble with yourself. They do not kill the faults, but they enable you to deal with them. Even baptism itself, you know, has destroyed the guilt of past sin, but does not hinder subsequent temptation.'

Albinia hardly knew how far Sophy attended to this caution, for all she said was to reiterate the entreaty that the omitted ceremony might be supplied.

Mr. Kendal gave a ready consent, as soon as he was told that Sophy so ardently wished for it—so willing, indeed, that Albinia was surprised, until he went on to say, 'No one need be aware of the matter beyond ourselves. Your brother and sister would, I have no doubt, act as sponsors. Nay, if Ferrars would officiate, we need hardly mention it even to Dusautoy. It could take place in your sitting-room.'

'But, Edmund!' began Albinia, aghast, 'would that be the right thing? I hardly think Maurice would consent.'

'You are not imagining anything so preposterous or inexpedient as to wish to bring Sophia forward in church,' said Mr. Kendal; 'even if she were physically capable of it, I should not choose to expose her to anything so painful or undesirable.'

'I am afraid, then,' said Albinia, 'that it will not be done at all. It is not receiving her into the congregation to have this service read before half-a-dozen people in my sitting-room.'

'Better not have it done at all, then,' said Mr. Kendal. 'It is not essential. I will not have her made a spectacle.'

'Will you only consult Mr. Dusautoy?'

'I do not wish Mr. Dusautoy to interfere in my family regulations. I mean, that I have a great respect for him, but as a clergyman, and one wedded to form, he would not take into account the great evil of making a public display, and attracting attention to a girl of her age, station, and disposition. And, in fact,' added Mr. Kendal, with the same scrupulous candour as his daughter always showed, 'for the sake of my own position, and the effect of example, I should not wish this unfortunate omission to be known.'

'I suspect,' said Albinia, 'that the example of repairing it would speak volumes of good.'

'It is mere absurdity to speak of it!' said Mr. Kendal. 'The poor child is not to leave her couch yet for weeks.'

Sophy was told in the morning that the question was under consideration, and Lucy was strictly forbidden to mention the subject.

When next Mr. Kendal came to read with Sophy, she said imploringly, 'Papa, have you thought?'

'Yes,' he said, 'I have done so; but your mamma thinks, and, on examination of the subject, I perceive she is right, that the service has no meaning unless it take place in the church.'

'Yes,' said Sophy; 'but you know I am to be allowed to go about in July.'

'You will hardly be equal to any fatigue even then, I fear, my dear; and you would find this publicity extremely trying and unpleasant.'

'It would not last ten minutes,' said Sophy, 'and I am sure I should not care! I should have something else to think about. Oh! papa, when my forehead aches with surliness, it does feel so unblest, so uncrossed!' and she put her hand over it, 'and all the books and hymns seem not to belong to me. I think I shall be able to keep off the tempers when I have a right in the cross.'

'Ah! my child, I am afraid the tempers are a part of your physical constitution,' he returned, mournfully.

'You mean that I am like you, papa,' said Sophy. 'I think I might at least learn to be really like you, and if I must feel miserable, not to be unkind and sulky! And then I should leave off even the being unhappy about nothing.'

Her eyes brightened, but her father shook his head sadly, and said, 'You would not be like me, my dear, if depression never made you selfish. But,' he added, with an effort, 'you will not suffer so much from low spirits when you are in better health, and able to move about.'

'Oh, no!' exclaimed Sophy; 'I often feel so sick of lying here, that I feel as if I never could be sulky if only I might walk about, and go from one room to another when I please! But papa, you will let me be admitted into the Church when I am able, will you not?'

'It shall be well weighed, Sophy.'

Sophy knew her father too well, and had too much reticence to say any more. He was certainly meditating deeply, and reading too, indeed he would almost have appeared to have a fit of the study, but for little Maurice, a tyrannical little gentleman, who domineered over the entire household, and would have been grievously spoilt, if his mother had not taken all the crossing the stout little will upon herself. He had a gallant pair of legs, and the disposition of a young Centaur, he seemed to divide the world into things that could be ridden on, and that could not; and when he bounced at the study door, with 'Papa! gee! gee!' and lifted up his round, rosy face, and despotic blue eyes, Mr. Kendal's foot was at his service, and the study was brown no longer.

The result of Mr. Kendal's meditations was an invitation to his wife to drive with him to Fairmead.

That was a most enjoyable drive, the weather too hot and sunny, perhaps, for Albinia's preferences, but thoroughly penetrating, and giving energy to, her East-Indian husband, and making the whole country radiant with sunny beauty—the waving hay-fields falling before the mower's scythe, the ranks of hay-makers tossing the fragrant grass, the growing corn softly waving in the summer breeze, the river blue with reflected sky, the hedges glowing with stately fox-gloves, or with blushing wreaths of eglantine. And how cool, fresh, and fair was the beech-avenue at Fairmead.

Yet though Albinia came to it with the fond tenderness of old association, it was not with the regretful clinging of the first visit, when it seemed to her the natural home to which she still really belonged. Nor had she the least thought about producing an impression of her own happiness, and scarcely any whether 'Edmund' would be amused and at ease, though knowing he had a stranger to encounter in the person of Winifred's sister, Mary Reid.

That was not a long day. It was only too short, though Mr. and Mrs. Kendal stayed three hours longer than on the last occasion. Mr. Kendal faced Mary Reid without flinching, and she, having been previously informed that Albinia's husband was the most silent and shy man in existence, began to doubt her sister's veracity. And Albinia, instead of dealing out a shower of fireworks, to hide what, if not gloom, was at least twilight, was now 'temperately bright,' talking naturally of what most concerned her with the sprightliness of her happy temper, but without effort; and gratifying Winifred by a great deal more notice of the new niece and namesake than she had ever bestowed on either of her predecessors in their infant days. Moreover, Lucy's two long visits had made Mrs. Ferrars feel a strong interest in her, and, with a sort of maternal affection, she inquired after the cuttings of the myrtle which she had given her.

'Ah!' said Albinia, 'I never honoured gardening so much.'

'I know you would never respect it in me.'

'As you know, I love a walk with an object, and never could abide breaking my back, pottering over a pink with a stem that wont support it, and a calyx that wont hold it.'

'And Lucy converted you when I could not!'

'If you had known my longing for some wholesome occupation for her, such as could hurt neither herself nor any one else, and the pleasure of seeing her engrossed by anything innocent, making it so easy to gratify her. Why, a new geranium is a constant fund of ecstasy, and I do not believe she was ever so grateful to her father in her life as when he gave her a forcing-frame. Anything is a blessing that makes people contented at home, and takes them out of themselves.'

'Lucy is a very nice, pleasant inmate; her ready obligingness and facility of adapting herself make her very agreeable.'

'Yes,' said Albinia, 'she is the "very woman," taking her complexion from things around, and so she will go smoothly through the world, and be always preferred to my poor turbid, deep-souled Sophy.'

'Are you going to be very angry with me?'

'Ah! you do not know Sophy! Poor, dear child! I do so long that she could have—if it were but one day, one hour, of real, free, glowing happiness! I think it would sweeten and open her heart wonderfully just to have known it! If I could but see any chance of it, but I am afraid her health will always be against her, and oh! that dreadful sense of depression! Do you know, Winifred, I do think love would be the best chance. Now, don't laugh; I do assure you there is no reason Sophy should not be very handsome.'

'Quite as handsome as the owl's children, my dear.'

'Well, the owls are the only young birds fit to be seen. But I tell you,

Sophy's profile is as regular as her father's, and animation makes her eyes beautiful, and she has grown immensely since she has been lying down, so that she will come out without that disproportioned look. If her eyebrows were rather less marked, and her complexion—but that will clear.'

'Yes, we will make her a beauty when we are about it.'

'And, after all, affection is the great charm, and if she were attached, it would, be so intensely—and happiness would develop so much that is glorious, only hidden down so deep.'

'I hope you may find her a male Albinia,' said Winifred, a little wickedly, 'but take care. It might be kill or cure, and I fancy when sunshine is attracted by shadow, it is more often as it was in your case than vice versa.'

'Take care!' repeated Albinia, affronted. 'You don't fancy I am going beyond a vague wish, do you?'

'And rather a premature one. How old is Sophy?'

'Towards fourteen, but years older in thought and in suffering.'

Albinia did not hear the result of the conference with her brother till she had resumed her seat in the carriage, after having been surprised by Mr. Kendal handing in three tall theological tomes. They both had much to think over as they drove home in the lengthening shadows. Albinia was greatly concerned that Winifred's health had become affected, and that her ordinary home duties were beyond her strength. Albinia had formerly thought Fairmead parsonage did not give her enough to do, but now she saw the gap that she had left; and she had fallen into a maze of musings over schemes for helping Winifred, before Mr. Kendal spoke, telling her that he had resolved that Sophia's admission into the Church should take place as soon as she was equal to the exertion.

Albinia asked if she should speak to Mr. Dusautoy, but the manliness of Mr. Kendal's character revolted from putting off a confession upon his wife; so he went to church the next morning, and saw the vicar afterwards.

Mr. Dusautoy's first thought was gratitude for the effort that the resolution must have cost both Mr. Kendal and his daughter; his next, how to make the occasion as little trying to their feelings as was consistent with his duty and theirs. He saw Sophy, and tried to draw her out, but, though far from sullen, she did not reply freely. However, he was satisfied, and he wished her, likewise, to consider herself under preparation for Confirmation in the autumn. She did all that he wished quietly and earnestly, but without much remark, her confidence only came forth when her feelings were strongly stirred, and it was remarkable that throughout this time of preparation there was not the remotest shadow of ill-temper.

Mr. Kendal insisted that her London doctor should come to see her at the year's end. The improvement had not been all that had been hoped, but it was decided that though several hours of each day must still be spent on her back, she might move about, join the meals, and do whatever she could without over-fatigue. It seemed a great release, but it was a shock to find how very little she could do at first, now that she had lost the habit of exertion, and of disregard of her discomforts. She had quite shot up to more than the ordinary woman's height, and was much taller than her sister—but this hardly gave the advantage Albinia had hoped, for she had a weak, overgrown look, and could not help stooping. A number of people in a room, or even the sitting upright during a morning call, seemed quite to overcome and exhaust her: but still the return to ordinary life was such great enjoyment, that she endured all with good temper.

But now the church-going was possible, a fit of exceeding dread came upon her. Albinia found her with the tears silently rolling down her cheeks, almost as if she were unconscious of them.

'Oh, mamma, I can never do it! I know what I am. I can't let them say I will keep all the commandments always! It will not be true!'

'It will be true that you have the steadfast purpose, my dear.'

'How can it be steadfast when I know I can't?'

It was the old story, and all had to be argued through again how the obligation was already incurred at her baptism, and how it was needful that she should be sworn to her own side of the great covenant—how the power would be given, and the grace supplied, but that the will and purpose to obey was required—and then Sophy recurred to that blessing of the cross for which she longed so earnestly, and which again Albinia feared she was regarding in the light of a talisman.

Mr. Ferrars was to be her godfather. Mr. Kendal had wished Aunt Winifred, as Lucy called her, to be the godmother, but Sophy had begged earnestly for Mrs. Dusautoy, whose kindness had made a great impression.

There was not much liking between Mrs. Ferrars and Sophy. Perhaps Sophy had been fretted and angered by her quick, decided ways, and rather disgusted by the enthusiasm of her brother and sister about Fairmead; and she was not gratified by hearing that Winifred was to accompany her husband in order to try the experiment of a short absence from cares and children.

Albinia, on the contrary, was highly pleased to have Winifred to nurse, and desirous of showing off Sophy's reformation. Winifred arrived late in the day, with an invalid look, and a great inclination to pine for her baby. She was so much tired, that Albinia took her upstairs very soon, and put her to bed, sitting with her almost all the evening, hoping that downstairs all was going on well.

The next morning, too, went off very well. Mr. Ferrars sought a private talk with his old godchild, and though Sophy scarcely answered, she liked his kind, frank, affectionate manner, and showed such feeling as he wished, so that he fully credited all that his sister thought of her.

Otherwise, Sophy was kept quiet, to gave her strength and collect her thoughts.

At seven o'clock in the evening, there was not a formidable congregation. Miss Meadows, who had been informed as late as could save offence, had treated it as a freak of Mrs. Kendal, resented the injunction of secrecy, and would neither be present herself, nor let her mother come out. Genevieve, three old men, and a child or two, were the whole number present. The daily service at Bayford was an offering made in faith by the vicar, for as yet there was very little attendance. 'But,' said Mr. Dusautoy, 'it is the worship of God, not an entertainment to please man—it is all nonsense to talk of its answering or not answering.'

Mr. Kendal was in a state of far greater suffering from shame than his daughter, as indeed he deserved, but he endured it with a gallant, almost touching resignation. He was the only witness of her baptism, and it seemed like a confession, when he had to reply to the questions, by whom, and with what words this child had been baptized, when she stood beside him overtopping her little godmother. She stood with tightly-locked hands, and ebbing colour, which came back in a flood when Mr. Dusautoy took her by the hand, and said, 'We receive this child into the congregation,' and when he traced the cross on her brow, she stood tremblingly, her lips squeezed close together, and after she returned to her place no one saw her face.

Albinia, with her brother and Lucy, were at home by the short cut before the carriage could return. She met Sophy at the hall-door, kissed her, and said, 'Now, my dear, you had better lie down, and be quite quiet;' then followed Winifred into the drawing-room, and took her shawl and bonnet from her, lingering for a happy twilight conversation. Lucy came down, and went to water her flowers, and by-and-by tea was brought, the gentlemen came in from their walk, and Mr. Kendal asked whether Sophy was tired. Albinia went up to see. She found her on her couch in the morning room, and told her that tea was ready. There was something not promising in the voice that replied; and she said,

'No, don't move, my dear, I will bring it to you; you are tired.'

'No—I'll go down, thank you.' It was the gruff voice!

'Indeed you had much better not, my dear. It is only an hour to bed-time, and you would only tire yourself for nothing.'

'I'll go.'

'You are tired, Sophy,' said her father. 'You had better lie down while you have your tea.'

'No, thank you,' growled Sophy, as though hurt by being told to lie down before company.

Her father put a sofa-cushion behind her, but though she mumbled some acknowledgment, it was so surly, that Mrs. Ferrars looked up in surprise, and she would not lean back till fatigue gained the ascendancy. Mr. Kendal asking her, got little in reply but such a grunt, that Mrs. Ferrars longed to shake her, but her father fetched a footstool, and put it under her feet, and grew a little abstracted in his talk, as if watching her, and his eye had something of the old habitual melancholy.

So it went on. The night's rest did not carry off the temper. Sophy was monosyllabic, displeased if not attended to, but receiving attention like an affront, wanting nothing, but offended if it were not offered. Albinia was exceedingly grieved. She had some suspicion that Sophy might have been hurt by her going to Mrs. Ferrars instead of to her on their return from church, and made an attempt at an apology, but this was snubbed like an additional affront, and she could only bide the time, and be greatly disappointed at such an exhibition before the guests.

Winifred looked on, forbearing to hurt Albinia's feelings by remarks, but in private compensating by little outbreaks with her husband, teasing him about his hopeful goddaughter, laughing at Albinia's infatuation, and railing at Mr. Kendal's endurance of the ill-humour, which she declared he promoted.

Maurice, as usual, was provoking. He had no notion of giving up his godchild, he said, and he had no doubt that Edmund Kendal could manage his own child his own way.

'Because of his great success in that line.'

'He is not what he was. He uses his sense and principle now, and when they are fairly brought to bear, I know no one whom I would more entirely trust.'

'Well! it will be great good luck if I do not fall foul of Miss Sophy one of these days, if no one else will!'

Winifred was slightly irritable herself from weakness, and on the last morning of her stay she could bear the sight no longer. Sophy had twice been surly to Lucy's good offices, had given Albinia a look like thunder, and answered her father with a sulky displeasure that made Mrs. Ferrars exclaim, as soon as he had left the room, 'I should never allow a child of mine to peak to her father in that manner!'

Sophy swelled. She did not think Mrs. Ferrars had any right to interfere between her and her father. Her silence provoked Winifred to continue, 'I wonder if you have any compunction for having spoilt all your—all Mrs. Kendal's enjoyment of our visit.'

'I am not of consequence enough to spoil any one's pleasure.'

That was the last effort. Albinia came into the room, with little Maurice holding her hand, and flourishing a whip. He trotted up to the sofa, and began instantly to 'whip sister Sophy;' serve her right, if I had but the whip, thought Mrs. Ferrars, as his mother hurried to snatch him off. Leaning over Sophy's averted face, she saw a tear under her eyelashes, but took no notice.

Three seconds after, Sophy reared herself up, and with a rigid face and slow step walked out of the room.

'Have you said anything to her?' asked Albinia.

'I could not help it,' said Winifred, narrating what had past. 'Have I done wrong?'

'Edmund cannot bear to have anything harsh said to her in these moods, especially about her behaviour to himself. He thinks she cannot help it—but it may be well that she should know how it appears to other people, for I cannot bear to see his patient kindness spurned. Only, you know, she values it in her heart. I am afraid we shall have a terrible agony now.'

Albinia was right. It was the worst agony poor Sophy had ever undergone. She had been all this time ignorant that it was a cross fit, only imagining herself cruelly neglected and cast aside for the sake of Mrs. Ferrars; but the wakening time had either arrived, or had been brought by that reproach, and she beheld her conduct in the most abhorrent light. After having desired to be pledged to her share of the covenant, and earnestly longed to bear the cross, to be sworn in as soldier and servant, to have put her neck under the yoke of her old master ere the cross had dried upon her brow, to have been meanly jealous, ungrateful, disrespectful, vindictive!! oh! misery, misery! hopeless misery! She would take no word of comfort when Albinia tried to persuade her that it had been partly the reaction of a mind wrought up to an occasion very simple in its externals, and of a body fatigued by exertion; and then in warm-hearted candour professed that she herself had been thoughtless in neglecting Sophy for Winifred. Still less comfort would she take in her father's free forgiveness, and his sad entreaties that she would not treat these fits of low spirits as a crime, for they were not her fault, but that of her constitution.

'Then one can't help being hateful and wicked! Nothing is of any use! I had rather you had told me I was mad!' said poor Sophy.

She was so spent and exhausted with weeping, that she could not come down—indeed, between grief and nervousness she would not eat; and Albinia found Mr. Kendal mournfully persuading her, when a stern command would have done more good. Albinia spoke it: 'Sophy, you have put your father to a great deal of pain already; if you are really grieving over it, you will not hurt him more by making yourself ill.'

The strong will came into action on the right side, and Sophy sat up, took what was offered, but what was she that they should care for her, when she had spoilt mamma's pleasure? Better go and be happy with Mrs. Ferrars.

Sophy's next visitor came up with a manly tread, and she almost feared that she had made herself ill enough for the doctor; but it was Mr. Ferrars, with a kind face of pitying sympathy.

'May I come to wish my godchild good-bye?' he said.

Sophy did not speak, and he looked compassionately at the prone dejection of the whole figure, and the pale, sallow face, so piteously mournful. He took her hand, and began to tell her of the godfather's present, that he had brought her—a little book of devotions intended for the time when she should be confirmed. Sophy uttered a feeble 'thank you,' but a hopeless one.

'Ah! you are feeling as if nothing would do you any good,' said Mr. Ferrars.

'Papa says so!' she answered.

'Not quite,' said Mr. Ferrars. 'He knows that your low spirits are the effect of temperament and health, and that you are not able to prevent yourself from feeling unhappy and aggrieved. And perhaps you reckoned on too much sensible effect from Church ordinances. Now joy, help, all these blessings are seldom revealed to our consciousness, but are matters of faith; and you must be content to work on in faith in the dark, before you feel comfort. I cannot but hope that if you will struggle, even when you are hurt and annoyed, to avoid the expression of vexation, the morbid temper will wear out, and you will both be tempted and suffer less, as you grow older. And, Sophy—forgive me for asking—do you pray in this unhappy state?'

'I cannot. It is not true.'

'Make it true. Take some verse of a Psalm. Shall I mark you some? Repeat them, even if you seem to yourself not to feel them. There is a holy power that will work on you at last; and when you can truly pray, the dark hour will pass.'

'Mark them,' said Sophy.

There was some space, while she gave him the book, and he showed her the verses. Then he rose to go.

'I wish I had not spoilt the visit,' she said, wistfully, at last.

'We shall see you again, and we shall know each other better,' he said, kindly. 'You are my godchild now, Sophy, and you know that I must remember you constantly in prayer.'

'Yes,' she faintly said.

'And will you promise me to try my remedy? I think it will soften your heart to the graces of the Blessed Comforter. And even if all seems gloom within, look out, see others happy, try to rejoice with them, and peace will come in! Now, goodbye, my dear godchild, and the God of Peace bless you, and give you rest.

CHAPTER XII.

Mr. Dusautoy had given notice of the day of the Confirmation, when Mr. Kendal called his wife.

'I wonder,' he said, 'my dear, whether Sophia can spare you to take a walk with me before church.'

Sophy, who was well aware that a walk with him was the greatest and rarest treat to his wife, gave gracious permission, and in a few minutes they were walking by the bright canal-side, under the calm evening sunshine and deep blue sky of early autumn.

Mr. Kendal said not a word, and Albinia, leaning on his arm, listened, as it were, to the stillness, or rather to the sounds that marked it—the gurgling of the little streams let off into the water-courses in the meadows; the occasional plunge of the rat from the banks, the sounds from the town, softened by distance, and the far-off cawings of the rooks, which she could just see wheeling about as little black specks over the plantations of Woodside, or watching the swallows assembling for departure sitting in long ranks, like an ornament along the roof of a neighbouring barn.

Long, long it was before Mr. Kendal broke silence, but when at length he did speak, his words amazed her extremely.

'Albinia, poor Sophia's admission into the Church has not been the only neglect. I have never been confirmed. I intend to speak to Dusautoy this evening, but I thought you would wish to know it first.'

'Thank you. I suppose you went out to India too young.'

'Poor Maria says truly that no one thought of these things in our day, at least so far as we were concerned. I must explain to you, Albinia, how it is that I see things very differently now from the light in which I once viewed them. I was sent home from India, at six years old, to correspondents and relations to whom I was a burthen. I was placed at a private school, where the treatment was of the harsh style so common in those days. The boys always had more tasks than they could accomplish, and were kept employed by being always in arrears with their lessons. This pressed less heavily upon me than on most; but though I seldom incurred punishment, there was a sort of hard distrust of me, I believe because the master could not easily overwhelm me with work, so as to have me in his power. I know I was often unjustly treated, and I never was popular.'

'Yes, I can imagine you extremely miserable.'

'You can understand my resolution that my boys should not be sent to England to be homeless, and how I judged all schools by my own experience. I stayed there too late, till I was beyond both tormentors and masters, and was left to an unlimited appetite for books, chiefly poetry. Our religious instruction was a nullity, and I am only surprised that the results were not worse. India was not likely to supply what education had omitted. Looking back on old journals and the like, I am astonished to see how unsettled my notions were—my sublimity, which was really ignorant childishness, and yet my perfect unconsciousness of my want of Christianity.'

'I dare say you cannot believe it was yourself, any more than I can. What brought other thoughts!'

'Practical obligations made me somewhat less dreamy, and my dear boy, Edmund, did much for me, but all so insensibly, that I can remember no marked change. I do not know whether you will understand me, when I say that I had attained to somewhat of what I should call personal religion, such as we often find apart from the Church.'

'But, Edmund, you always were a Churchman.'

'I was; but I viewed the Church merely as an establishment—human, not divine. I had learnt faith from Holy Scripture, from my boy, from the infants who passed away so quickly, and I better understood how to direct the devotional tendencies that I had never been without, but the sacramental system had never dawned on my comprehension, nor the real meaning of Christian fellowship. Thence my isolation.'

'You had never fairly seen the Church.'

'Never. It might have made a great difference to me if Dusautoy had been here at the time of my trouble. When he did come, I had sunk into a state whence I could not rouse myself to understand his principles. I can hardly describe how intolerable my life had become. I was almost resolved on returning to India. I believe I should have done so if you had not come to my rescue.'

'What would you have done with the children?'

'To say the truth I had idolized their brother to such an exclusive degree, that I could not turn to the others when he was taken from me. I deserved to lose him; and since I have seen this unfortunate strain of melancholy developed in poor Sophia, who so much resembles him, I have been the more reconciled to his having been removed. I never understood what the others might be until you drew them out.'

Albinia paused, afraid to press his reserve too far; and the next thing she said was, 'I think I understand your distinction between personal religion and sacramental truth. It explains what has often puzzled me about good devout people who did not belong to the Church. The Visible Church cannot save without this individual personal religion but without having recourse to the Church, there is—' she could not find the word.

'There is a loss of external aid,' he said; 'nay, of much more. There is no certainty of receiving the benefits linked by Divine Power to her ordinances. Faith, in fact, while acknowledging the great Object of Faith, refuses or neglects to exercise herself upon the very subjects which He has set before her; and, in effect, would accept Him on her terms, not on His own.'

'It was not refusal on your part,' said Albinia.

'No, it was rather indifference and imaginary superiority. But I have read and thought much of late, and see more clearly. If I thought of this rite of Confirmation at all, it was only as a means of impressing young minds. I now see every evidence that it is the completion of Baptismal grace, and without, like poor Sophia, expecting that effects would ever have been perceptible, I think that had I known how to seek after the Spirit of Counsel and Ghostly Strength, I might have given way less to the infirmities of my character, and have been less wilfully insensible to obvious duties.'

'Then you have made up your mind?'

'Yes. I shall speak to Mr. Dusautoy at once.'

'And,' she said, feeling for his sensitive shyness, 'no one else need know it —at least—'

'I should not wish to conceal it from the children,' he answered, with his scrupulous candour. He was supine when thought more ill of than he deserved, but he always defended himself from undeserved credit.

'Whom do you think I have for a candidate?' said Mr. Dusautoy that evening.

'Another now! I thought you were talking to Mr. Kendal about the onslaught on the Pringle pew.'

'What do you think of my churchwarden himself?'

'You don't mean that he has never been confirmed!'

'So he tells me. He went out to India young, and was never in the way of such things. Well, it will be a great example.'

'Take care what you do. He will never endure having it talked of.'

'I think he has made up his mind, and is above all nonsense. I am sure it is well that I need not examine him. I should soon get beyond my depth.'

'And what good did his depth ever do to him,' indignantly cried Mrs. Dusautoy, 'till that dear good wife of his took him in hand? Don't you remember what a log he was when first we came—how I used to say he gave you subscriptions to get rid of you.'

'Well, well, Fanny, what's the use of recollecting all our foolish first impressions. I always told you he was the most able man in the parish.'

'Fanny' laughed merrily at this piece of sagacity, as she said 'Ay, the most able and the least practicable; and the best of it is, that his wife has not the most distant idea that she has been the making of him. She nearly quarrelled with me for hinting it. She would have it that "Edmund" had it all in him, and had only recovered his health and spirits.'

And, indeed, it was no wonder she was happy. This step taken of free will by Mr. Kendal, was an evidence not only of a powerful reasoning intellect bowed to an act of simple faith but of a victory over the false shame that had always been a part of his nature. Nor did it apparently cost him as much as his consent to Sophy's admission into the Church; the first effort had been the greatest, and he was now too much taken up with deep thoughts of devotion to be sensitive as to the eyes and remarks of the world. The very resolution to bend in faithful obedience to a rite usually belonging to early youth and not obviously enforced to human reason, nor made an express condition of salvation, was as a pledge that he would strive to walk for the future in the path of self-denying obedience. Who that saw the manly well-knit form kneeling among the slight youthful ones around, and the thoughtful, sorrow- marked brow bowed down beneath the Apostolic hand, could doubt that such faith and such humble obedience would surely be endowed with a full measure of the Spirit of Ghostly Might, to lead him on in his battle with himself? Those young ones needed the 'sevenfold veil between them and the fires of youth,' but surely the freshening and renewing came most blessedly to the man weary already with sin and woe, and tired out alike with himself and the world, because he had lived to himself alone.

CHAPTER XIII.

Old Mr. Pringle never stirred beyond his parlour, and was invisible to every one, except his housekeeper and doctor, but his tall, square, curtained pew was jealously locked up, and was a grievance to the vicar, who having been foiled in several attempts, was meditating a fresh one, if, as he told his wife, he could bring his churchwarden up to the scratch, when one Sunday morning the congregation was electrified by the sound of a creak and a shake, and beheld a stout hale sunburnt gentleman, fighting with the disused door, and finally gaining the victory by strength of hand, admitting himself and a boy among the dust and the cobwebs.

Had Mr. Pringle, or rather his housekeeper, made a virtue of necessity? and if so, who could it be?

Albinia hailed the event as a fertile source of conjecture which might stave off dangerous subjects in the Sunday call, but there was no opportunity for any discussion, for Maria was popping about, settling and unsettling everything and everybody, in a state of greater confusion than ever, inextricably entangling her inquiries for Sophy with her explanations about the rheumatism which had kept grandmamma from church, and jumping up to pull down the Venetian blind, which descended awry, and went up worse. The lines got into such a hopeless complication, that Albinia came to help her, while Mr. Kendal stood dutifully by the fire, in the sentry-like manner in which he always passed that hour, bending now and then to listen and respond to some meek remark of old Mrs. Meadows, and now and then originating one. As to assisting Maria in any pother, he well knew that would be a vain act of chivalry, and he generally contrived to be insensible to her turmoils.

‘Who could that have been in old Pringle’s seat?’ he presently began, appropriating Albinia’s cherished morsel of gossip; but he was not allowed to enjoy it, for Miss Meadows broke out,

‘Oh, Edmund! this blind, I beg your pardon, but if you would help—’

He was obliged to move to the window, and nervously clutching his arm, she whispered, ‘You’ll excuse it, I know, but don’t mention it—not a word to mamma.’ Mr. Kendal looked at Albinia to gather what could be this dreadful subject, but the next words made it no longer doubtful. ‘Ah, you were away, there’s no use in explaining—but not a word of Sam Pringle. It would only make her uneasy—’ she gasped in a floundering whisper, stopping suddenly short, for at that moment the stranger and his son were entering the garden, so near them, that they might have seen the three pairs of eyes levelled on them, through the wide open end of the unfortunate blind, which was now in the shape of a fan.

Albinia's cheeks glowed with sympathy, and she longed for the power of helping her, marvelling how a being so nervously restless and devoid of self-command could pass through a scene likely to be so trying. The bell sounded, and the loud hearty tones of a manly voice were heard. Albinia looked to see whether her help were needed, but Miss Meadows's whole face was brightened, and moving across the room with unusually even steps, she leant on the arm of her mother's chair, saying, 'Mamma, it is Captain Pringle. You remember Samuel Pringle? He settled in the Mauritius, you know, and he was at church this morning with his little boy.'

There was something piteous in the searching look of inquiry that Mrs. Meadows cast at her daughter's face, but Maria had put it aside with an attempt at a smile, as 'Captain Pringle' was announced.

He trod hard, and spoke loud, and his curly grizzled hair was thrown back from a bronzed open face, full of broad heartiness, as he walked in with outstretched hand, exclaiming, 'Well, and how do you do?' shaking with all his might the hand that Maria held out. 'And how are you, Mrs. Meadows? You see I could not help coming back to see old friends.'

'Old friends are always welcome, sir,' said the old lady, warmly. 'My son, Mr. Kendal, sir—Mrs. Kendal,' she added, with a becoming old-fashioned movement of introduction.

'Very glad to meet you,' said the captain, extending to each such a hearty shake of the hand, that Albinia suspected he was taking her on trust for Maria's sister.

'Your little boy?' asked Mrs. Meadows.

'Ay—Arthur, come and make the most of yourself, my man,' said he, thumping the shy boy on the back to give him courage. 'I've brought him home for his schooling—quite time, you see, though what on earth I'm to do without him—'

The boy looked miserable at the words. 'Ay, ay,' continued his father, 'you'll do well enough. I'm not afraid for you, master, but that you'll be happy as your father was before you, when once you have fellows to play with you. Here is Mr. Kendal will tell you so.'

It was an unfortunate appeal, but Mr. Kendal made the best of it, saying that his boy was very happy at his tutor's.

'A private tutor, eh?' said the rough captain, 'I'd not thought of that—

neither home nor school. I had rather do it thoroughly, and trust to numbers to choose friends from, and be licked into shape.'

Poor little Arthur looked as if the process would be severe; and by way of consolation, Mrs. Meadows suggested, a piece of cake. Maria moved to ring the bell. It was the first time she had stirred since the visitor came in, and he getting up at the same time, that she might not trouble herself, their eyes met. 'I'm very glad to see you again,' he exclaimed, catching hold of her hand for another shake; 'but, bless me! you are sadly altered! I'm sorry to see you looking so ill.'

'We all grow old, you know,' said Maria, endeavouring to smile, but half strangled by a tear, and looking at that moment as she might have done long ago. 'You find many changes.'

'I hope you find Mr. Pringle pretty well,' said Albinia, thinking this might be a relief, and accordingly, the kind-hearted captain began, ruefully to describe the sad alterations that time had wrought. Then he explained that he had had little correspondence with home, and had only landed three days since, so that he was ignorant of all Bayford tidings, and began asking after a multitude of old friends and acquaintance.

The Kendals thought all would go on the better in their absence, and escaped from the record of deaths and marriages, each observing to the other as they left the house, that there could be little doubt that nurse's story was true, but both amazed by the effect on Maria, who had never been seen before to sit so long quiet in her chair. Was his wife alive? Albinia thought not, but could not be certain. His presence was evidently happiness to Miss Meadows, but would this last? Would this renewal soothe her, or only make her more restless and unhappy?

Albinia found that Sophy's imagination bad been quicker than her own. Lucy had brought home the great news of the stranger, and she had leapt at once to the conclusion that it must be the hero of nurse's story, but she had had the resolution to keep the secret from her sister, who was found reproaching her with making mysteries. When Lucy heard that it was Captain Pringle, she was quite provoked.

'Only Mr. Pringle's nephew?' she said, disdainfully. 'What was the use of making a fuss? I thought it was some one interesting!'

Sophy was able to walk to church in the evening, but was made to go in to rest at the vicarage before returning home. While this was being discussed before the porch, Albinia felt a pressure on her arm, and looking round, saw Maria Meadows.

'Can you spare me a few moments?' she said; and Albinia turned aside with her to the flagged terrace path between the churchyard and vicarage garden, in the light of a half-moon.

'You were so kind this morning,' began Maria, 'that I thought—you see it is very awkward—not that I have any idea—but if you would speak to Edmund—I know he is not in the habit—morning visits and—'

'Do you wish him to call? He had been thinking of it.'

Maria would have been unbounded in her gratitude, but catching herself up, she disclaimed all personal interest—only she said Edmund knew nothing of anything that had passed—if he did, he would see they would feel—

'I think,' said Albinia, kindly, 'that we do know that you had some troubles on that score. Old nurse said something to Sophy, but no other creature knows it.'

'Ah!' exclaimed Maria, 'that is what comes of trusting any one. I was so ill when I found out how it had been, that I could not keep it from nurse, but from mamma I did—my poor father being just gone and all—I could not have had her know how much I felt it—the discovery I mean—and it is what I wish her never to do. But oh! Mrs. Kendal, think what it was to find out that when I had been thinking he had been only trifling with me all those years, to find that he had been so unkindly treated. There was his own dear letter to me never unsealed; and there was another to my father saying in a proud-spirited way that he did not know what he had done to be so served, and he wished I might find happiness, for I would never find one that loved me as well. I who had turned against him in my heart!'

'It was cruel indeed! And you kept it from your mother!' said Albinia, beginning to honour her.

'My poor father was just gone, you know, and I could not be grieving her with what was passed and over, and letting her know that my father had broken my heart, as indeed I think he did, though he meant it all for the best. But oh! I thought it hard when Lucy had married the handsomest man in the country, and gone out to India, without a word against it, that I might not please myself, because I was papa's favourite.'

'It was very hard not to be made aware of his intentions.'

'Yea,' said Maria; 'for it gave me such a bitter, restless feeling against him —though I ought to have known him better than to think he would give one minute's pain he could help; and then when I knew the truth, the bitterness all went to poor papa's memory, and yet perhaps he never meant to be unkind either.'

Albinia said some kind words, and Maria went on:

'But what I wanted to say was this—Please don't let mamma suspect one bit about it; and next, if Edmund would not mind showing him a little attention. Do you think he would, my dear? I do so wish that he should not think we were hurt by his marriage, and you see, two lone women can do nothing to make it agreeable; besides that, it would not be proper.'

'Is his wife living?'

'My dear, I could not make up my tongue to ask—the poor dear boy there and all—but it is all the same. I hope she is, for I would not see him unhappy, and you don't imagine I have any folly in my head—oh, no! for I know what a fright the fret and the wear of this have made me; and besides, I never could leave mamma. So I trust his wife is living to make him happy, and I shall be more at peace now I have seen him again, since he turned his horse at Bobble's Leigh, and said I should soon hear from him again.'

'Indeed I think you will be happier. There is something very soothing in taking up old feelings and laying them to rest. I hope even now there is less pain than pleasure.'

'I can't help it,' said Maria. 'I do hope it is not wrong; but his very voice has got the old tone in it, as if it were the old lullaby that my poor heart has been beating for all these years.'

Who would have thought of Maria speaking poetically? But her words did indeed seem to be the truth. In spite of the embarrassment of her situation and the flutter of her feelings, she was in a state of composure unexampled. Albinia had just gratified her greatly by a few words on Captain Pringle's evident good-nature, when a tread came behind them.

'Ha! you here?' exclaimed the loud honest voice.

'We were taking a turn in the moonlight,' said Albinia. 'A beautiful night.'

'Beautiful! Arthur and I have been a bit of the way home with old Goldsmith. There's an evergreen, to be sure; and now—are you bound homewards, Maria?'

Maria clung to Albinia's arm. Perhaps in the days of the last parting, she had been less careful to be with a chaperon.

'Ah! I forgot,' said the captain; 'your way lies the other side of the hill. I had very nearly walked into Willow Lawn this morning, only luckily I bethought me of asking.'

'I hope you will yet walk into Willow Lawn,' said Albinia.

'Ah! thank you; I should like to see the old place. I dare say it may be transmogrified now, but I think I could find my way blindfold about the old garden. I say, Maria, do you remember that jolly tea-party on the lawn, when the frog made one too many?'

'That I do——' Maria could not utter more, and Albinia said she was afraid he would miss a great deal.

'I reckoned on that when I came home. Changes everywhere; but after the one great change,' he added, mournfully, 'the others tell less. One has the less heart to care for an old tree or an old path.'

Albinia felt sure he could mean only one great change, but they were now at Mrs. Meadows's door, and Maria wished them good night, giving a most grateful squeeze of the hand to Mrs. Kendal.

'Where are you bound now?' asked the captain.

'Back to the vicarage, to take up my husband and the girls,' said Albinia, 'but good night. I am not afraid.'

The captain, however, chose to continue a squire of dames, and walked at her side, presently giving utterance to a sound of commiseration. 'Ah! well, poor Maria, I never thought to see her so altered. Why, she had the prettiest bloom—I dare say you remember—but, I beg your pardon, somehow I thought you were her *elder* sister.'

'Mr. Kendal's first wife was,' said Albinia, pitying the poor man; but Captain Pringle was not a man for awkwardness, and the short whistle with which he received her answer set her off laughing.

'I beg your pardon,' he said, recovering himself; 'but you see I am all astray, like a man buried and dug up again, so no wonder I make strange blunders; and my poor uncle is grown so childish, that he does not know one person from another, and began by telling me Maria Meadows had married and gone out to India. I had not had a letter these seven years, so I thought it was high time to bring my boy home, and renew old times, though how I am ever to go back without him—'

'Is he your only one?'

'Yes. I lost his mother when he was six years old, and we have been all the world to each other since, till I began to think I was spoiling him outright, and it was time he should see what Old England was made of.'

Albinia had something like a discovery to impart now; but she hated the sense of speculating on the poor man's intentions. He talked so much, that he saved her trouble in replying, and presently resumed the subject of Maria's looks.

'She has had a harassed life, I fear,' said Albinia.

'Eh! old Meadows was a terrible old tyrant, I believe; but she was his pet. I thought he refused her nothing—but there's no trusting such a Turk! Oh! ah! I dare say,' as if replying to something within. And then having come to the vicarage wicket, Albinia took leave of him and ran indoors, answering the astonished queries as to how she had been employed, 'Walking home with Aunt Maria and Captain Pringle!'

It was rather a relief at such a juncture that Lucy's curious eyes should be removed. Mr. Ferrars came to talk his wife's state over with his sister. Her children were too much for Winifred, and he wished to borrow Lucy for a few weeks, till a governess could be found for them.

It struck Albinia that this would be an excellent thing for Genevieve Durant, and she at once contrived to ask her to tea, and privately propound the plan.

Genevieve faltered much of thanks, and said that Madame was very good; but the next morning a note was brought in, which caused a sudden change of countenance:

'My dear Madame,

'I was so overwhelmed with your kindness last night, and so unwilling to appear ungrateful, that perhaps I left you under a false impression. I entreat you not to enter on the subject with my grandmamma or my aunt. They would grieve to prevent what they would think for my advantage, and would, I am but too sure, make any sacrifice on my account; but they are no longer young, and though my aunt does not perceive it, I know that the real work of the school depends on me, and that she could not support the fatigue if left unassisted. They need their little Genevieve, likewise, to amuse them in their evenings; and, forgive me, madame, I could not, without ingratitude, forsake them now. Thus, though with the utmost sense of your kindness, I must beg of you to pardon me, and not to think me ungrateful if I decline the situation so kindly offered to me by Mr. Ferrars, thanking you ten thousand times for your too partial recommendation, and entreating you to pardon

'Your most grateful and humble servant,

'GENEVIEVE CELESTE DURANT.'

'There!' said Albinia, tossing the note to her brother, who was the only person present excepting Gilbert.

'Poor Albinia,' he said, 'it is hard to be disappointed in a bit of patronage.'

'I never meant it as patronage,' said Albinia, slightly hurt. 'I thought it would help you, and rescue her from that school. There will she spend the best years of her life in giving a second-rate education to third-rate girls, not one of whose parents can appreciate her, till she will grow as wizened and as wooden as Mademoiselle herself.'

'Happily,' said Mr. Ferrars, 'there are worse things than being spent in one's duty. She may be doing an important work in her sphere.'

'So does a horse in a mill,' exclaimed Albinia; 'but you would not put a hunter there. Yes, yes, I know, education, and these girls wanting right teaching; but she, poor child, has been but half educated herself, and has not time to improve herself. If she does good, it is by force of sheer goodness, for they all look down upon her, as much as vulgarity can upon refinement.'

'I told her so,', exclaimed Gilbert; 'I told her it was the only way to teach them what she was worth.'

'What did you know of the matter?' asked Albinia; and the colour mounted in the boy's face as he muttered, 'She was overcome when she came down, she said you had been so kind, and we were obliged to walk up and down before she could compose herself, for she did not want the old ladies to know anything about it.'

'And did she not wish to go?'

'No, though I did the best I could. I told her what a jolly place it was, and that the children would be a perfect holiday to her. And I showed her it would not be like going away, for she might come over here whenever she pleased; and when I have my horse, I would come and bring her word of the old ladies once a week.'

'Inducements, indeed!' said Mr. Ferrars. 'And she could not be incited by any of these?'

'No,' said Gilbert, 'she would not hear of leaving the old women. She was only afraid it would vex Mrs. Kendal, and she could not bear not to take the advice of so kind a friend, she said. You are not going to be angry with her,' he added.

'No,' said Albinia, 'one cannot but honour her motives, though I think she is mistaken; and I am sorry for her; but she knows better than to be afraid of me.'

With which assurance Gilbert quitted the room, and the next moment, hearing the front door, she exclaimed, 'I do believe he is gone to tell her how I took the announcement.'

Maurice gave a significant 'Hem!' to which his sister replied, 'Nonsense!'

'Very romantic consolations and confidences.'

'Not at all. They have been used to each other all their lives, and he used to be the only person who knew how to behave to her, so no wonder they are great friends. As to anything else, she is nineteen, and he not sixteen.'

'One great use of going to school is to save lads from that silly pastime. I advise you to look to these moonlight escortings!'

'One would think you were an old dowager, Maurice. I suppose Colonel Bury may not escort Miss Mary.'

'Ah, Albinia, you are a very naughty child still.'

'Of course, when you are here to keep me in order, I wish I never were so at other times when it is not so safe.'

Mr. Kendal was kind and civil to Captain Pringle, and though the boisterous manner seemed to affect him like a thunderstorm, Maria imagined they were delighted with one another.

Maria was strangely serene and happy; her querulous, nervous manner smoothed away, as if rest had come to her at last; and even if the renewed intercourse were only to result in a friendship, there was hope that the troubled spirit had found repose now that misunderstandings were over, and the sore sense of ill-usage appeased.

Yet Albinia was startled when one day Mr. Kendal summoned her, saying, 'It is all over, she has refused him!'

'Impossible; she could only have left half her sentence unsaid.'

'Too certain. She will not leave her mother.'

'Is that all?'

'Of course it is. He told me the whole affair, and certainly Mr. Meadows was greatly to blame. He let Maria give this man every encouragement, believing his property larger, and his expectations more secure than was the case; and when the proposal was made, having discovered his mistake, he sent a peremptory refusal, giving him reason to suppose her a party to the rejection. Captain Pringle sailed in anger; but it appears that his return has revived his former feelings, and that he has found out that poor Maria was a greater sufferer than himself.'

'Why does he come to you?'

'To consult me. He wishes me to persuade poor old Mrs. Meadows to go out to the Mauritius, which is clearly impossible, but Maria must not be sacrificed again. Would the Drurys make her comfortable? Or could she not live alone with her maid?'

'She might live here.'

'Albinia! Think a little.'

'I can think of nothing else. Let her have the morning room, and Sophy's little room, and Lucy and I would do our best for her.'

'No, that is out of the question. I would not impose such charge upon you on any consideration!'

Albinia's face became humble and remorseful. 'Yes,' she said, 'perhaps I am too impatient and flighty.'

'That was not what I meant,' he said; 'but I do not think it right that a person with no claims of relationship should be made a burthen on you.'

'No claims, Edmund,' said she, softly. 'In whose place have you put me?'

He was silent: then said, 'No, it must not be, my kind Albinia. She is a very good old lady, but Sophy and she would clash, and I cannot expose the child to such a trial.'

'I dare say you are right,' pensively said Albinia, perceiving that her plan had been inconsiderate, and that it would require the wisdom, tact, and gentleness of a model woman to deal with such discordant elements. 'What are you going to do?' as he took up his hat. 'Are you going to see Maria? May I come with you?'

'If you please; but do not mention this notion. There is no necessity for such a tax on you; and such arrangement should never be rashly made.'

He asked whether Miss Meadows could see him, and awaited her alone in the dining-room, somewhat to the surprise of his wife; but either he felt that there was a long arrear of kindness owing, or feared to trust Albinia's impulsive generosity.

Meantime Albinia found the poor old lady in much uneasiness and distress. Her daughter fancied it right to keep her in ignorance of the crisis; but Maria was not the woman to conceal her feelings, and her nervous misery had revealed all that she most wished to hide. Too timid to take her confidence by storm, her mother had only exchanged surmises and observations with Betty, and was in a troubled condition of affectionate curiosity and anxiety. Albinia was a welcome visitor since it was a great relief to hear what had really taken place and to know that Mr. Kendal was with Maria.

'Ah! that is kind,' she said; 'but he must tell her not to think of me. I am an old woman, good for nothing but to be put out of the way, and she has gone through quite enough! You will not let her give it up! Tell her I have not many more years to live, and anything is good enough for me.'

'That would hardly comfort her,' said Albinia, affectionately; 'but indeed, dear grandmamma, I hope we shall convince her that we can do something to supply her place.'

'Ah! my dear, you are very kind, but nobody can be like a daughter! But don't tell Maria so—poor dear love—she may never have another chance. Such a beautiful place out there, and Mr. Pringle's property must come to him at last! Bless me, what will Sarah Drury say? And such a good attentive man —besides, she never would hear of any one else—her poor papa never knew —Oh! she must have him! it is all nonsense to think of me! I only wish I was dead out of the way!'

There was a strong mixture of unselfish love, and fear of solitude; of the triumph of marrying a daughter, and dread of separation; of affection, and of implanted worldliness; touching Albinia at one moment, and paining her at another; but she soothed and caressed the old lady, and was a willing listener to what was meant for a history of the former transaction; but as it started from old Mr. Pringle's grandfather, it had only proceeded as far as the wedding of the Captain's father and mother, when it was broken off by Mr. Kendal's entrance.

'Oh! my dear Mr. Kendal, and what does poor Maria say? It is so kind in you. I hope you have taken her in hand, and told her it is quite another thing now, and her poor dear papa would think so. She must not let this opportunity pass, for she may never have another. Did you tell her so?'

'I told her that, under the circumstances, she has no alternative but to accept Captain Pringle.'

'Oh! thank you. And does she?'

'She has given me leave to send him to her.'

'I am so much obliged. I knew that nobody but you could settle it for her, poor dear girl; she is so young and inexperienced, and one is so much at a loss without a gentleman. But this is very kind; I did not expect it in you, Mr. Kendal. And will you see Mr. Pettilove, and do all that is proper about settlements, as her poor dear papa would have done. Poor Pettilove, he was once very much in love with Maria!'

In this mood of triumph and felicity, the old lady was left to herself and her daughter. Albinia, on the way home, begged to hear how Mr. Kendal had managed Maria; and found that he had simply told her, in an authoritative tone, that after all that had passed, she had no choice but to accept Captain Pringle, and that he had added a promise, equally vague and reassuring, of being a son to Mrs. Meadows. Such injunctions from such a quarter had infused new life into Maria; and in the course of the afternoon, Albinia met the Captain with the mother and daughter, one on each arm, Maria in recovered bloom and brilliancy, and Mrs. Meadows's rheumatism forgotten in the glory of exhibiting her daughter engaged.

For form's sake, secrecy had been mentioned; but the world of Bayford had known of the engagement a fortnight before took place. Sophy had been questioned upon it by Mary Wolfe two hours ere she was officially informed, and was sore with the recollection of her own ungracious professions of ignorance.

'So it is true,' she said. 'I don't mind, since Arthur is not a girl.'

Mr. Kendal laughed so heartily, that Sophy looked to Albinia for explanation; but even on the repetition of her words, she failed to perceive anything ridiculous in them.

'Why, mamma,' she said, impressively, 'if you had been like Aunt Maria, I should—' she paused and panted for sufficient strength of phrase—'I should have run away and begged! Papa laughs, but I am sure he remembers when grandmamma and Aunt Maria wanted to come and live here!'

He looked as if he remembered it only too well.

'Well, papa,' pursued Sophy, 'we heard the maids saying that they knew it would not do, for all Mr. Kendal was so still and steady, for Miss Meadows would worret the life out of a lead pincushion.'

'Hem!' said Mr. Kendal. 'Albinia, do you think after all we are doing Captain Pringle any kindness?'

'He is the best judge.'

'Nay, he may think himself bound in honour and compassion—he may be returning to an old ideal.'

'People like Captain Pringle are not apt to have ideals,' said Albinia; 'nor do I think Maria will be so trying. Do you remember that creeper of Lucy's, all tendrils and catching leaves, which used to lie sprawling about, entangling everything till she gave it a prop, when it instantly found its proper development, and offered no further molestation?'

All was not, however, smooth water as yet. The Captain invaded Mr. Kendal the next morning in despair at Maria having recurred to the impossibility of leaving her mother, and wanting him to wait till he could reside in England. This could not be till his son was grown up, and ten years were a serious delay. Mr. Kendal suspected her of a latent hope that the Captain would end by remaining at home; but he was a man sense and determination, who would have thought it unjustifiable weakness to sacrifice his son's interests and his own usefulness. He would promise, that if all were alive and well, he would bring Maria back in ten or twelve years' time; but he would not sooner relinquish his duties, and he was very reluctant to become engaged on such terms.

'No one less silly than poor Maria would have thought of such a proposal,' was Mr. Kendal's comment afterwards to his wife. 'Twelve years! No one would be able to live with her by that time!'

'I cannot help respecting the unselfishness,' said Albinia.

'One sided unselfishness,' quoth Mr. Kendal. 'I am sick of the whole business, I wish I had never interfered. I cannot get an hour to myself.'

He might be excused for the complaint on that day of negotiations and counter-negotiations, which gave no one any rest, especially after Mrs. Drury arrived with all the rights of a relation, set on making it evident, that whoever was to be charged with Mrs. Meadows, it was not herself; and enforcing that nothing could be more comfortable than that Lucy Kendal should set up housekeeping with her dear grandmamma. Every one gave advice, and nobody took it; Mrs. Meadows cried, Maria grew hysterical, the Captain took up his hat and walked out of the house; and Albinia thought it would be very good in him ever to venture into it again.

The next morning Mr. Kendal ordered his horse early, and hastened his breakfast; told Albinia not to wait dinner for him, and rode off by one gate, without looking behind him, as the other opened to admit Captain Pringle. She marvelled whither he had fled, and thought herself fortunate in having only two fruitless discussions in his absence. Not till eight o'clock did he make his appearance, and then it was in an unhearing, unseeing mood, so that nothing could be extracted, except that he did not want any dinner; and it was not till late in the evening that he abruptly announced, 'Lucy is coming home on Wednesday. Colonel Bury will bring her to Woodside.'

What? have you heard from Maurice?'

'No; I have been at Fairmead.'

You! To-day! How was Winifred?'

'Better—I believe.'

'How does she like the governess?'

'I did not hear.'

Gradually something oozed out about Lucy having been happy and valuable, and after Sophy had gone to bed, he inquired how the courtship was going on?

'Worse than ever,' Albinia said.

'I suppose it must end in this?'

'In what!'

'If there is no more satisfactory arrangement, I suppose we must receive Mrs. Meadows.'

If Albinia could but have heard what a scolding her brother was undergoing from his vivacious wife!

'As if poor Albinia had not enough on her hands! Of all inmates in the world! When Mr. Kendal himself did not like it! Well! Maurice would certainly have advised Sinbad to request the honour of taking the Old Man of the Sea for a promenade a cheval. There was an end of Albinia. There would never be any room in her house, and she would never be able to come from home. And after having seen her worked to death, he to advise—'

'I did not advise, I only listened. What he came for was to silence his conscience and his wife by saying, "Your brother thinks it out of the question." Now to this my conscience would not consent.'

'More shame for it, then!'

'I could not say I thought these two people's happiness should be sacrificed, or the poor old woman left desolate. Albinia has spirits and energy for a worse infliction, and Edmund Kendal himself is the better for every shock to his secluded habits. If it is a step I would never dare advise, still less would I dare dissuade.'

'Well! I thought Mr. Kendal at least had more sense.'

'Ay, nothing is so provoking as to see others more unselfish than ourselves.'

'All I have to say,' concluded Mrs. Ferrars, walking off, 'is, I wish there was a law against people going and marrying two wives.'

Albinia was in no haste to profit by her husband's consent to her proposal. The more she revolved it, the more she foresaw the discomfort for all parties. She made every effort to devise the 'more satisfactory arrangement,' but nothing would occur. The Drurys would not help, and the poor old lady could not be left alone. Her maid Betty, who had become necessary to her comfort, was not a trustworthy person, and could not be relied on, either for honesty, or for not leaving her mistress too long alone; and when the notion was broached of boarding Mrs. Meadows with some family in the place, the conviction arose, that when she had grandchildren, there was no reason for leaving her to strangers.

Finally, the proposal was made, and as instantly rejected by Maria. It was very kind, but her mother could never be happy at Willow Lawn, never; and the tone betrayed some injury at such a thing being thought possible. But just as the Kendals had begun to rejoice at having cleared their conscience at so slight a cost, Captain Pringle and Miss Meadows made their appearance, and Maria presently requested that Mrs. Kendal would allow her to say a few words.

'I am afraid you thought me very rude and ungrateful,' she began, 'but the truth was, I did not think dear mamma would ever bear to live here, my poor dear sister and all; but since that, I have been talking it over with the dear Captain—thinks that since you are so kind, and dear Edmund—more than I could ever have dared to expect—that I could not do better than just to sound mamma.'

There was still another vicissitude. Mrs. Meadows would not hear of being thrust on any one, and was certain that Maria had extorted an invitation; she would never be a burden upon any one; young people liked company and amusement, and she was an old woman in every one's way; she wished she were in her coffin with poor dear Mr. Meadows, who would have settled it all. Maria fell back into the depths of despair, and all was lugubrious, till Mr. Kendal, in the most tender and gentle manner, expressed his hopes that Mrs. Meadows would consider the matter, telling her that his wife and children would esteem it a great privilege to attend on her, and that he should be very grateful if she would allow them to try to supply Maria's place. And Albinia, in her coaxing tone, described the arrangement; how the old furniture should stand in the sitting-room, and how Lucy would attend to her carpet-work, and what nice walks the sunny garden would afford, and how pleasant it would be not to have the long hill between them, till grandmamma forgot all her scruples in the fascination of that sweet face and caressing manner, she owned that poor old Willow Lawn always was like home, and finally promised to come. Before the evening was over the wedding-day was fixed.

What Sophy briefly termed 'the fuss about Aunt Maria,' had been so tedious, that it almost dispelled all poetical ideas of courtship. If Captain Pringle had been drowned at sea, and Aunt Maria pined herself into her grave, it would have been much more proper and affecting.

Sophy heard of the arrangement without remark, and quietly listened to Albinia's explanation that she was not to be sent up to the attics, but was to inhabit the spare room, which was large enough to serve her for a sitting- room. But in the evening Mr. Kendal happened in her absence to take up the book which she had been reading, and did not perceive at once on her entrance that she wanted it. When he did so, he yielded it with a few kind words of apology, but this vexation had been sufficient to bring down the thunder-cloud which had been lowering since the morning. There were no signs of clearance the next day; but Albinia had too much upon her hands to watch the symptoms, and was busy making measurements for the furniture in the morning-room when Mr. Kendal came in.

'I have been thinking,' he said, 'that it is a pity to disturb this room. I dare say Mrs. Meadows would prefer that below-stairs. It used to be her parlour, where she always sat when I first knew the house.'

'The dining-room? How could we spare that?'

'No, the study.'

Albinia remained transfixed.

'We could put the books here and in the dining-room,' he continued, 'until next spring, when, as your brother said, we can build a new wing on the drawing-room side.'

'And what is to become of you?' she continued.

'Perhaps you will admit me here,' he said, smiling, for he was pleased with himself. 'Turn me out when I am in the way.'

'Oh! Edmund, how delightful! See, we shall put your high desk under the window, and your chair in your own corner. This will be the pleasantest place in the house, with you and your books! Dear Winifred! she did me one of her greatest services when she made me keep this room habitable!'

'And I think Sophy will not object to give up her present little room for my dressing-room. Shall you, my dear?' said he, anxious to judge of her temper by her reply.

'I don't care,' she said; 'I don't want any difference made to please me; I think that weak.'

'Sophy!'began Albinia, indignantly, but Mr. Kendal stopped her, and made her come down, to consider of the proposal in the study.

That study, once an oppressive rival to the bride, now not merely vanquished, but absolutely abandoned by its former captive!

'Don't say anything to her,' said Mr. Kendal, as they went downstairs. 'Of course her spirits are one consideration, but were it otherwise, I could not see you give up your private room.'

'It is very kind in you, but indeed I can spare mine better than you can,' said Albinia. 'I am afraid you will never feel out of the whirl.'

'Yours would be a loss to us all,' said Mr. Kendal. 'The more inmates there are in a house, the more needful to have them well assorted.'

'Just so; and that makes me afraid—'

'Of me? No, Albinia, I will try not to be a check on your spirits.'

'You! Oh! I meant that we should disturb you.'

'You never disturb me, Albinia; and it is not what it was when the children's voices were untrained and unsubdued.'

'I can't say much for Master Maurice's voice.'

He smiled, he had never yet found those joyous notes de trop, and he continued, 'Your room is of value and use to us all; mine has been of little benefit to me, and none to any one else. I wish I could as easily leave behind me all the habits I have fostered there.'

'Edmund, it is too good! When poor Sophy recovers her senses she will feel it, for I believe that morning room would have been a great loss to her.'

'It was too much to ask in her present state. I should have come to the same conclusion without her showing how much this plan cost her, for nothing can be plainer than that while she continues subject to these attacks, she must have some retreat.'

'Yet,' ventured Albinia, 'if you think solitude did you no good, do you think letting these fits have their swing is good for Sophy?'

'I *cannot* drive her about! They must not be harshly treated,' he answered quickly. 'Resistance can only come from within; compulsion is worse than useless. Poor child, it is piteous to watch that state of dull misery! On other grounds, I am convinced this is the best plan. The communication with the offices will prevent that maid from being always on the stairs. Mrs. Meadows will have her own visitors more easily, and will get out of doors sooner, and I think she will be better pleased.'

'Yes, it will be a much better plan for every one but Mr. Kendal himself,' said Albinia; 'and if he can be happy with us, we shall be all the happier. So this was the old sitting-room!' 'Yes, I knew them first here,' he said. 'It used to be cheerful then, and I dare say you can make it the same again. We must dismantle it before Mrs. Meadows or Maria come to see it, or it will remind them of nothing but the days when I was recovering, and anything but grateful for their attention. Yes,' he added, 'poor Mrs. Meadows bore most gently and tenderly with a long course of moroseness. I am glad to have it in my power to make any sort of amends, though it is chiefly through you.'

Albinia might well be very happy! It was her moment of triumph, and whatever might be her fears for the future, and uneasiness at Sophy's discontent, nothing could take away the pleasure of finding herself deliberately preferred to the study.

Sophy did not fail to make another protest, and when told that 'it was not solely on her account,' the shame of having fancied herself so important, rendered her ill-humour still more painful and deplorable. It was vain to consult her about the arrangements, she would not care about anything, except that by some remarkable effect of her perverse condition, she had been seized with a penchant for maize colour and blue for the bridesmaids, and was deeply offended when Albinia represented that they would look like a procession of macaws, and her aunt declared that Sophy herself would be the most sacrificed by such colours. She made herself so grim that Maria broke up the consultation by saying good-humouredly, 'Yes, we will settle it when Lucy comes home.'

'Yes,' muttered Sophy, 'Lucy is ready for any sort of nonsense.'

Mr. and Mrs. Kendal went to Woodside to meet Lucy, hoping that solitude would be beneficial. Albinia grieved at the manifestations of these, her sullen fits, if only because they made Lucy feel herself superior. In truth, Lucy was superior in temper, amiability, and all the qualities that smooth the course of life, and it was very pleasant to greet her pretty bright face, so full of animation.

'Dear grandmamma going to live with us? Oh, how nice! I can always take care of her when you are busy, mamma.'

That accommodating spirit was absolute refreshment, and long before Albinia reached home the task of keeping the household contented seemed many degrees easier.

A grand wedding was 'expected,' so all the Bayford flys were bespoken three deep, a cake was ordered from Gunter, and so many invitations sent out, that Albinia speculated how all were to come alive out of the little dining-room.

And Mr. Kendal the presiding gentleman!

He had hardly seemed aware of his impending fate till the last evening, when, as the family were separating at night, he sighed disconsolately, and said, 'I am as bad as you are, Sophy.'

It awoke her first comfortable smile.

Experience had, however, shown him that such occasions might be survived, and he was less to be pitied than his daughter, who felt as if she and her great brown face would be the mark of all beholders. Poor Sophy! all scenes were to her like daguerreotypes in a bad light, she saw nothing but herself distorted!

And yet she was glad that the period of anticipation had consumed itself and its own horrors, and found herself not insensible to the excitement of the occasion. Lucy was joyous beyond description, looking very pretty, and solicitously decorating her sister, while both bestowed the utmost rapture on their step-mother's appearance.

Having learnt at last what Bayford esteemed a compliment, she had commissioned her London aunts to send her what she called 'an unexceptionable garment,' and so well did they fulfil their orders, that not only did her little son scream, 'Mamma, pretty, pretty!' and Gilbert stand transfixed with admiration, but it called forth Mr. Kendal's first personal remark, 'Albinia, you look remarkably well;' and Mrs. Meadows reckoned among the honours done to her Maria, that Mrs. Kendal wore a beautiful silk dress, and a lace bonnet, sent down on purpose from London!

Maria Meadows made a very nice bride, leaning on her brother-in-law, and not more agitated than became her well. The haggard restless look had long been gone, repose had taken away the lean sharpness of countenance, the really pretty features had fair play, and she was astonishingly like her niece Lucy, and did not look much older. Her bridegroom was so beaming and benignant, that it might fairly be hoped that even if force of habit should bring back fretfulness, he had a stock of happiness sufficient for both. The chairs were jammed so tight round the table, that it was by a desperate struggle that people took their seats, and Mr. Dusautoy's conversation was a series of apologies for being unable to keep his elbows out of his neighbours' way while carving, and poor Sophy, whose back was not two feet from the fire, was soon obliged to retreat. She had gained the door before any one perceived her, and then her brother and sister both followed; Albinia was obliged to leave her to their care, being in the innermost recesses, where moving was impossible.

There was not much the matter, she only wanted rest, and Gilbert undertook to see her safely home.

'I shall be heartily glad to get away,' he said. 'There is no breathing in there, and they'll begin talking the most intolerable nonsense presently. Besides, I want to be at home to take baby down to the gate to halloo at the four white horses from the King's Head. Come along, Sophy.'

'Mind you don't make her walk too fast,' said the careful Lucy, 'and take care how you take off your muslin, Sophy, you had better go to the nursery for help.'

Gilbert did not seem inclined to hurry his sister as they came near Madame Belmarche's. He lingered, and presently said, 'Should you be too tired to come in here for a moment? it was an intolerable shame that none of them were asked.'

'Mamma did beg for Genevieve, but there was so little room, and the Drurys did not like it. Mrs. Drury said it would only be giving her a taste for things above her station.'

'Then Mrs. Drury should never come out of the scullery. I am sure she looks as if her station was to black the kettles!' cried Gilbert, with some domestic confusion in his indignation. 'Didn't she look like a housekeeper with her mistress's things on by mistake?'

'She did not look like mamma, certainly,' said Sophy. 'Mamma looked no more aware that she had on those pretty things than if she had been in her old grey—'

'Mamma—yes—Mrs. Drury might try seventy years to look like mamma, or Genevieve either! Put Genevieve into satin or into brown holland, you couldn't help her looking ten times more the lady than Mrs. Drury ever will! But come in, I have got a bit of the cake for them here, and they will like to see you all figged out, as they have missed all the rest of the show. Aunt Maria might have cared for her old mistress!'

Sophy wished to be amiable, and refrained from objecting.

It was a holiday in honour of cette chere eleve of five-and-twenty years since, and the present pupils were from their several homes watching for the first apparition of the four greys from the King's Head, with the eight white satin rosettes at their eight ears.

Madame Belmarche and her daughter were discovered in the parlour, cooking with a stew pan over the fire a concoction which Sophy guessed to be a conserve of the rose-leaves yearly begged of the pupils, which were chiefly useful as serving to be boiled up at any leisure moment, to make a cosmetic for Mademoiselle's complexion. She had diligently used it these forty-five years, but the effect was not encouraging, as brown, wrinkled, with her frizzled front awry, with not stainless white apron, and a long pewter spoon, she turned round to confront the visitors in their wedding finery.

But what Frenchwoman ever was disconcerted? Away went the spoon, forward she sprang, both hands outstretched, and her little black eyes twinkling with pleasure. 'Ah! but this is goodness itself,' said she, in the English wherein she flattered herself no French idiom appeared. 'You are come to let us participate in your rejoicing. Let me but summon Genevieve, the poor child is at every free moment trying to perfectionnate her music in the school-room.'

Madame Belmarche had arisen to receive the guests with her dignified courtesy and heartfelt felicitations, which were not over when Genevieve tripped in, all freshness and grace, with her neat little collar, and the dainty black apron that so prettily marked her slender waist. One moment, and she had arranged a resting-place for Sophy, and as she understood Gilbert's errand, quickly produced from a corner-cupboard a plate, on which he handed it to the two other ladies, who meanwhile paid their compliments in the most perfect style.

The history of the morning was discussed, and Madame Belmarche described her sister's wedding, and the curiosity which she had shared with the bride for the first sight of 'le futur,' when the two sisters had been brought from their convent for the marriage.

'But how could she get to like him?' cried Sophy.

'My sister was too well brought up a young girl to acknowledge a preference,' replied Madame Belmarche. 'Ah! my dear, you are English; you do not understand these things.'

'No,' said Sophy, 'I can't understand how people can marry without loving. How miserable they must be!'

'On the contrary, my dear, especially if one continued to live with one's mother. It is far better to earn the friendship and esteem of a husband than to see his love grow cold.'

'And was your sister happy?' asked Sophy, abruptly.

'Ah, my dear, never were husband and wife more attached. My brother-in-law joined the army of the Prince de Conde, and never was seen after the day of Valmy; and my sister pined away and died of grief. My daughter and granddaughter go to the Catholic burying-ground at Hadminster on her fete day, to dress her grave with immortelles.'

Now Sophy knew why the strip of garden grew so many of the grey-leaved, woolly-stemmed, little yellow-and-white everlasting flowers. Good madame began to regret having saddened her on this day of joy.

'Oh! no,' said Sophy, 'I like sad things best.'

'Mais, non, my child, that is not the way to go through life,' said the old lady, affectionately. 'Look at me; how could I have lived had I not always turned to the bright side? Do not think of sorrow, it, is always near enough.'

This conversation had made an impression on Sophy, who took the first opportunity of expressing her indignation at the system of mariages de convenance.

'And, mamma, she said if people began with love, it always grew cold. Now, has not papa loved you better and better every day?'

Albinia could not be displeased, though it made her blush, and she could not answer such a home push. 'We don't quite mean the same things,' she said evasively. 'Madame is thinking of passion independent of esteem or confidence. But, Sophy, this is enough even for a wedding-day. Let us leave it off with our finery, and resume daily life.'

'Only tell me one thing, mamma.'

'Well?'

She paused and brought it out with an effort. It had evidently occupied her for a long time. 'Mamma, must not every one with feeling be in love once in their life?'

'Well done, reserve!' thought Albinia—'but she is only a child, after all; not a blush, only those great eyes seeming ready to devour my answer. What ought it to be? Whatever it is, she will brood on it till her time comes. I must begin, or I shall grow nervous: "Dear Sophy, these are not things good to think upon. There is quite enough to occupy a Christian woman's heart and soul without that—no need for her feelings to shrivel up for want of exercise. No, I don't believe in the passion once in the life being a fate, and pray don't you, my Sophy, or you may make yourself very silly, or very unhappy, or both."'

Sophy drew up her head, and her brown skin glowed. Albinia feared that she had said the wrong thing, and affronted her, but it was all working in the dark.

At any rate the sullenness was dissipated, and there were no tokens of a recurrence. Sophy set herself to find ways of making amends for the past, and as soon as she had begun to do little services for grandmamma, she seemed to have forgotten her gloomy anticipations, even while some of them were partly realized. For as it would be more than justice to human nature to say that Mrs. Meadows's residence at Willow Lawn was a perfect success, so it would be less than justice to call it a failure.

To put the darker side first. Grandmamma's interest in life was to know the proceedings of the whole household, and comment on each. Now Albinia could endure housewifely advice, some espionage on her servants, and even counsel about her child; but she could not away with the anxiety that would never leave Sophy alone, tried to force her sociability, and regretted all extra studies, unable to perceive the delicate treatment her disposition needed. And Sophy, in the intolerance of early girlhood, was wretched at hearing poor grandmamma's petty views, and narrow, ignorant prejudices. She might resolve to be filial and agreeable, but too often found herself just achieving a moody, disgusted silence, or else bursting out with some true but unbecoming reproof.

On the whole, all did well. Mrs. Meadows was happy; she enjoyed the animation of the larger party, liked their cheerful faces, grew fond of Maurice, and daily more dependent on Lucy and Mrs. Kendal. Probably she had never before had so much of her own way, and her gentle placid nature was left to rest, instead of being constantly worried. Her son-in-law was kind and gracious, though few words passed between them, and he gave her a sense of protection. Indeed, his patience and good-humour were exemplary; he never complained even when he was driven from the dining-room by the table- cloth, to find Maurice rioting in the morning-room, and a music lesson in the drawing-room, or still worse, when he heard the Drurys everywhere; and he probably would have submitted quietly for the rest of his life, had not Albinia insisted on bringing forward the plan of building.

When Captain and Mrs. Pringle returned to Bayford to take leave, they found grandmamma so thoroughly at home, that Maria could find no words to express her gratitude. Maria herself could hardly have been recognised, she had grown so like her husband in look and manner! If her sentences did not always come to their legitimate development, they no longer seemed blown away by a frosty wind, but pushed aside by fresh kindly impulses, and her pride in the Captain, and the rest in his support, had set her at peace with all the world and with herself. A comfortable, comely, happy matron was she, and even her few weeks beyond the precincts of Bayford had done something to enlarge her mind.

It was as if her education had newly begun. The fixed aim, and the union with a practical man, had opened her faculties, not deficient in themselves, but contracted and nipped by the circumstances which she had not known how to turn to good account. Such a fresh stage in middle life comes to some few, like the midsummer shoot to repair the foliage that has suffered a spring blight; but it cannot be reckoned on, and Mrs. Pringle would have been a more effective and self-possessed woman, a better companion to her husband, and with more root in herself, had Maria Meadows learnt to tune her nerves and her temper in the overthrow of her early hopes.

CHAPTER XIV.

Maurice Ferrars was a born architect, with such a love of brick and mortar, that it was meritorious in him not to have overbuilt Fairmead parsonage. With the sense of giving him an agreeable holiday, his sister wrote to him in February that Gilbert's little attic was at his service if he would come and give his counsel as to the building project.

Mr. Kendal disliked the trouble and disturbance as much as Maurice loved it; but he quite approved and submitted, provided they asked him no questions; he gave them free leave to ruin him, and set out to take Sophy for a drive, leaving the brother and sister to their calculations. Of ruin, there was not much danger, Mr. Kendal had a handsome income, and had always lived within it; and Albinia's fortune had not appeared to her a reason for increased expense, so there was a sufficient sum in hand to enable Mr. Ferrars to plan with freedom.

A new drawing-room, looking southwards, with bedrooms over it, was the matter of necessity; and Albinia wished for a bay-window, and would like to indulge Lucy by a conservatory, filling up the angle to the east with glass doors opening into the drawing-room and hall. Maurice drew, and she admired, and thought all so delightful, that she began to be taken with scruples as to luxury.

'No,' said Maurice, 'these are not mere luxuries. You have full means, and it is a duty to keep your household fairly comfortable and at ease. Crowded as you are with rather incongruous elements, you are bound to give them space enough not to clash.'

'They don't clash, except poor Sophy. Gilbert and Lucy are elements of union, with more plaster of Paris than stone in their nature.'

'Pray, has Kendal made up his mind what to do with Gilbert?'

'I have heard nothing lately; I hope he is grown too old for India.'

'Gilbert is rather too well off for his good,' said Mr. Ferrars; 'the benefit of a profession is not evident enough.'

'I know what I wish! If he could but be Mr. Dusautoy's curate, in five or six years' time, what glorious things we might do with the parish!'

'Eh! is that his wish?'

'I have sometimes hoped that his mind is taking that turn. He is ready to help in anything for the poor people. Once he told me he never wished to look beyond Bayford for happiness or occupation; but I did not like to draw him out, because of his father's plans. Why, what have you drawn? The alms-houses?'

'I could do no other when I was improving Gilbert's house for him.'

'That would be the real improvement! How pretty! I will keep them for him.'

The second post came in, bringing a letter from Gilbert to his father, and Albinia was so much surprised, that her brother asked whether Gilbert were one of the boys who only write to their father with a reason.

'He can write more freely to me,' said Albinia; 'and it comes to the same thing. I am not in the least afraid of anything wrong, but perhaps he may be making some proposal for the future. I want to know how he is. Fancy his being so foolish as to go out bathing. I am afraid of his colds.'

Many times during the consultation did Mr. Ferrars detect Albinia's eye stealing wistfully towards that 'E. Kendal, Esq.;' and when the proper owner came in, he was evidently as much struck, for he paused, as if in dread of opening the letter. Her eyes were on his countenance as he read, and did not gather much consolation. 'I am afraid this is serious,' at last he said.

'His cold?' exclaimed Albinia.

'Yes,' said Mr. Kendal, reading aloud sentence by sentence, with gravity and consideration.

'I do not wish to alarm Mrs. Kendal, and therefore address myself at once to you, for I do not think it right to keep you in ignorance that I have had some of the old symptoms. I do not wish to make any one uneasy about me, and I may have made light of the cold I caught a month since; but I cannot conceal from myself that I have much painful cough, an inclination to shortness of breath, and pain in the back and shoulders, especially after long reading or writing. I thought it right to speak to Mr. Downton, but people in high health can understand nothing short of a raging fever; however, at last he called in the parish surgeon, a stupid, ignorant fellow, who understands my case no more than his horse, and treats me with hyoscyamus, as if it were a mere throat-cough. I thought it my duty to speak openly, since, though I am quite aware that circumstances make little difference in constitutional cases, I know you and dear Mrs. Kendal will wish that all possible means should be used, and I think it—'

Mr. Kendal broke down, and handed the letter to his wife, who proceeded,

'I think it best you should be prepared for the worst, as I wish and endeavour to be; and truly I see so much trial and disappointment in the course of life before me, that it would hardly be the worst to me, except—'

That sentence finished Albinia's voice, and stealing her hand into her husband's, she read on in silence,

'for the additional sorrow to you, and my grief at bringing pain to my more than mother, but she has long known of the presentiment that has always hung over me, and will be the better prepared for its realization. If it would be any satisfaction to you, I could easily take a ticket, and go up to London to see any physician you would prefer. I could go with Price, who is going for his sister's birthday, and I could sleep at his father's house; but, in that case, I should want three pounds journey money, and I should be very glad if you would be so kind as to let me have a sovereign in advance of my allowance, as Price knows of a capital secondhand bow and arrows. With my best love to all,

'Your affectionate son,

'GILBERT KENDAL.'

Albinia held the letter to her brother, to whom she looked for something cheering, but, behold! a smile was gaining uncontrollably on the muscles of his cheeks, though his lips strove hard to keep closely shut. She would not look at him, and turning to her husband, exclaimed, 'We will take him to London ourselves!'

'I am afraid that would be inconvenient,' observed Maurice.

'That would not signify,' continued Albinia; 'I must hear myself what is thought of him, and how I am to nurse him. Oh! taking it in time, dear Edmund, we need not be so much afraid! Maurice will not mind making his visit another time.'

'I only meant inconvenient to the birthday party,' drily said her brother.

'Maurice!' cried she, 'you don't know the boy!'

'I have no doubt that he has a cold.'

'And I know there is a great deal more the matter!' cried Albinia. 'We have let him go away to be neglected and badly treated! My poor, dear boy! Edmund, I will fetch him home to-morrow.'

'You had better send me,' said Maurice, mischievously, for he saw he was diminishing Mr. Kendal's alarm, and had a brotherly love of teasing Albinia, and seeing how pretty she looked with her eyes flashing through wrathful tears, and her foot patting impetuously on the carpet.

'You!' she cried; 'you don't believe in him! You fancy all boys are made of iron and steel—you would only laugh at him—you made us send him there—I wish—'

'Gently, gently, my dear Albinia,' said her husband, dismayed at her vehemence, just when it most amused her brother. 'You cannot expect Maurice to feel exactly as we do, and I confess that I have much hope that this alarm may be more than adequate.'

'He thinks it all a scheme!' said Albinia, in a tone of great injury.

'No, indeed, Albinia,' answered her brother, seriously, 'I fully believe that Gilbert imagines all that he tells you, but you cannot suppose that either the tutor or doctor could fail to see if he were so very ill.'

'Certainly not,' assented Mr. Kendal.

'And low spirits are more apt to accompany a slight ailment, than such an illness as you apprehend.'

'I believe you are right,' said Mr. Kendal. 'Where is the letter?'

Albinia did not like it to come under discussion, but could not withhold it, and as she read it again, she felt that neither Maurice nor her cousin Fred could have written the like, but she was only the more impelled to do battle, and when she came to the unlucky conclusion, she exclaimed, 'I am sure that was an afterthought. I dare say Price asked him while he was writing.'

'What's this?' asked Mr. Kendal, coming to the 'presentiment.'

She hesitated, afraid both of him and of Maurice, but there was no alternative. 'Poor Gilbert!' she said. 'It was a cry or call from his brother just at last. It has left a very deep impression.'

'Indeed!' said his father, much moved. 'Yes. Edmund gave a cry such as was not to be forgotten,' and the sigh told how it had haunted his own pillow; 'but I had not thought that Gilbert was in a condition to notice it. Did he mention it to you?'

'Yes, not long after I came, he thinks it was a call, and I have never known exactly how to deal with it.'

'It is a case for very tender handling,' said Maurice.

'I should have desired him never to think of it again,' said Mr. Kendal, decidedly. 'Mere nonsense to dwell on it. Their names were always in Edmund's mouth, and it was nothing but accident. You should have told him so, Albinia.'

And he walked out of the room.

'Ah! it will prey upon him now,' said Albinia.

'Yes, I thought he only spoke of driving it away because it was what he would like to be able to do. But things do not prey on people of his age as they do on younger ones.'

'I wonder if I did right,' said Albinia. 'I never liked to ask you, though I wished it. I could not bear to treat it as a fancy. How was I to know, if it may not have been intended to do him good? And you see his father says it was very remarkable.'

'Do you imagine that it dwells much upon his mind?'

'Not when he is well—not when it would do him good,' said Albinia; 'it rather haunts him the instant he is unwell.'

'He makes it a superstition, then, poor boy! You thought me hard on him, Albinia; but really I could not help being angry with him for so lamentably frightening his father and you.'

'Let us see how he is before you find fault with him,' said Albinia.

'You're as bad as if you were his mother, or worse!' exclaimed Maurice.

'Oh! Maurice, I can't help it! He had no one to care for him till I came, and he is such a very dear fellow—he wants me so much!'

Mr. Ferrars agreed to go with Mr. Kendal to Traversham. He thought his father would be encouraged by his presence, and he was not devoid of curiosity. Albinia would not hear of staying at home; in fact, Maurice suspected her of being afraid to trust Gilbert to his mercy.

With a trembling heart she left the train at the little Traversham station, making resolutions neither to be too angry with the negligent tutor, nor to show Gilbert how much importance she attached to his illness.

As they walked into the village, they heard a merry clamour of tongue, and presently met five or six boys, and, a few paces behind them, Mr. Downton.

'Ah!' he exclaimed, 'I am glad you are come. I would have written yesterday, but that I found your boy had done so. I shall be very glad to have him cheered up about himself. I will turn back with you. You go on, Price. They are setting out for one of Hullah's classes, so we shall have the house clear.'

'I hope there is not much amiss?' said Mr. Kendal.

'A tedious cold,' said the tutor; 'but the doctor assures me that there is nothing wrong with his chest, and I do believe he would not cough half so much, if he were not always watching himself.'

'Who has been attending him?'

'Lee, the union doctor, a very good man, with a large family,' (Albinia could have beaten him). 'Indeed,' he continued perceiving some dissatisfied looks, 'I think you will find that a little change is all that he wants.'

'I hope you can give a good account of him in other respects?' said Mr. Kendal.

'Oh! yes, in every way; he is the most good-natured lad in the world, and quite the small boys' friend. Perhaps he has been a little more sentimental of late, but that may be only from being rather out of order. I'll call him.'

The last words were spoken as they entered the parsonage, where opening a door, he said, 'Here, Kendal, here's a new prescription for you.'

Albinia had a momentary view of a tabby-cat and kitten, a volume of poetry, a wiry-haired terrier, and Gilbert, all lying promiscuously on the hearth-rug, before the two last leaped up, the one to bark, and the other to come forward with outstretched hand, and glad countenance.

He looked flushed and languid, but the roaring fire and close room might account for that, and though, when the subject was mentioned, he gave a short uncomfortable cough, Albinia's mind was so far relieved, that she was in doubt with whom to be angry, and prepared to stand on the defensive, should her brother think him too well.

The gentlemen went away together, and Gilbert, grasping her hand, gave way to one of his effusions of affection—'So kind to come to him—he knew he had her to trust to, whatever happened'—and he leant his cheek on his hand in a melancholy mood.

'Don't be so piteous, Gibbie,' she said. 'You were quite right to tell us you were not well, only you need not have been so very doleful, I don't like papa to be frightened.'

'I thought it was no use to go on in this way,' said Gilbert, with a cough: 'it was the old thing over again, and nobody would believe I had anything the matter with me.'

And he commenced a formidable catalogue of symptoms which satisfied her that Maurice would think him fully justified. Just at a point where it was not easy to know what next to say, the kitten began to play tricks with her mother's tail, and a happy diversion was made; Gilbert began to exhibit the various drolleries of the animals, to explain the friendship between dog and cat, and to leave off coughing as he related anecdotes of their sagacity; and finally, when the gentlemen returned, laughing was the first sound they heard, and Mrs. Kendal was found sitting on the floor at play with the livestock.

They had come to fetch her to see the church and schools, and on going out, she found that Mr. Ferrars had moved and carried that Gilbert should be taken home at once, and, on the way, be shown to a physician at the county town. From this she gathered that Maurice was compassionate, and though, of course, he would make no such admission, she had reason afterwards to believe that he had shown Mr. Downton that the pupil's health ought to have met with a shade more attention.

With Gilbert wrapped up to the tip of his nose, they set off, and found the doctor at home. Nothing could have been more satisfactory to Albinia, for it gave her a triumph over her brother, without too much anxiety for the future. The physician detected the injury to the lungs left by an attack that the boy had suffered from in his first English winter, and had scarcely outgrown when Albinia first knew him. The recent cold had so far renewed the evil, that though no disease actually existed, the cough must be watched, and exposure avoided; in fact, a licence for petting to any extent was bestowed, and therewith every hope of recovery.

Albinia and her son sat in their corners of the carriage in secret satisfaction, while Mr. Kendal related the doctor's opinion to Mr. Ferrars, but one of them, at least, was unprepared for the summing-up. 'Under the circumstances, Gilbert is most fortunate. A few years in his native climate will quite set him up.'

'Oh! but he is too old for Haileybury,' burst out Albinia, in her consternation.

'Nearly old enough for John Kendal's bank, eh, Gilbert?'

'Oh!' cried Albinia, 'pray don't let us talk of that while poor Gilbert is so ill.'

'Hm!' said Mr. Kendal with interrogative surprise, almost displeasure, and no more was said.

Albinia felt guilty, as she remembered that she had no more intended to betray her dislike to the scheme, than to gratify Gilbert by calling him 'so ill.' Aristocratic and military, she had no love for the monied interest, and had so sedulously impressed on her friends that Mr. Kendal had been in the Civil Service, and quite unconnected with the bank, that Mr. Ferrars had told her she thought his respectability depended on it, and she was ashamed that her brother should hear her give way again so foolishly to the weakness.

Gilbert became the most talkative as they drew near home, and was the first to spring out and open the hall door, displaying his two sisters harnessed tandem-fashion with packthread, and driven at full speed by little Maurice, armed with the veritable carriage whip! The next moment it was thrown down, with a rapturous shout, and Maurice was lost to everything but his brother!

'Oh! girls, how could you let him serve you so?' began the horrified Albinia. 'Sophy will be laid up for a week!'

'Never mind,' said Sophy, dropping on a chair. 'Poor little fellow, he wished it so much!'

'I tried to stop her, mamma,' said Lucy, 'but she will do as Maurice pleases.'

'See, this is the way they will spoil my boy, the instant my back is turned!' said Albinia. 'What's the use of all I can do with him, if every one else will go and be his bond-slave! I do believe Sophy would let him kill her, if he asked her!'

'It is no real kindness,' said Mr. Kendal. 'Their good-nature ought not to go beyond reason.'

The elder Maurice could hardly help shrugging his shoulders. Well did he know that Mr. Kendal would have joined the team if such had been the will of that sovereign in scarlet merino, who stood with one hand in Gilbert's, and the whip in the other.

'Come here, Maurice,' quoth Albinia; 'put down the whip,' and she extracted it from his grasp, with grave resolution, against which he made no struggle, gave it to Lucy to be put away, and seated him on her knee. 'Now listen, Maurice; poor sister Sophy is tired, and you are never to make a horse of her. Do you hear?'

'Yes,' said Maurice, fidgeting.

'Mind, if ever you make a horse of Sophy, mamma will put you into the black cupboard. You understand?'

'Sophy shan't be horse,' said Maurice. 'Sophy naughty, lazy horse. Boy has Gibbie—'

'There's gratitude,' said Mr. Ferrars, as 'Boy' slid off his mamma's knee, stood on tiptoe to pull the door open, and ran after Gilbert to grandmamma's room.

'Yes,' said Albinia, 'no one is grateful for services beyond all reason. So, Sophy, mind, into the cupboard he goes, the very next time you are so silly as to be a horse.'

'To punish which of them?' asked her brother.

'Sophy knows,' said Albinia.

Sophy was too miserable to smile. Sarah Anne Drury had been calling, and on hearing of Gilbert's indisposition, had favoured them with 'mamma's remarks,' and when Mrs. Kendal was blamed, Sophy had indignantly told Sarah Anne that she knew nothing about it, and had no business to interfere. Then followed the accusation, that Mrs. Kendal had set the whole family against their old friends, and Sophy had found all her own besetting sins charged upon her step-mother.

'My dear!' said Albinia, 'don't you know that if a royal tiger were to eat up your cousin John in India, the Drurys would say Mrs. Kendal always let the tigers run about loose! Nor am I sure that your faults are not my fault. I helped you to be more exclusive and intolerant, and I am sure I tried your temper, when I did not know what was the matter with you—'

'No—no,' said the choked voice. It would have been an immense comfort to cry, or even to be able to return the kiss; but she was a great deal too wretched to be capable of any demonstration; physically exhausted by being driven about by Maurice; mentally worn out by the attempts to be amiable, which had degenerated into wrangling, full of remorse for having made light of her brother's illness, and, for that reason, persuaded that she was to be punished by seeing it become fatal. Not a word of all this did she say, but, dejected and silent, she spent the evening in a lonely corner of the drawing-room, while her brother, in the full pleasure of returning home, and greatly enjoying his invalid privileges, was discussing the projected improvements.

Talking at last brought back his cough with real violence, and he was sent to bed; Albinia went up with him to see that his fire burnt. He set Mr. Ferrars's drawing of the alms-houses over his mantelshelf. 'I shall nail it up to-morrow,' he said. 'I always wanted a picture here, and that's a jolly one to look to.'

'It would be a beautiful beginning,' she said. 'I think your life would go the better for it, Gibbie.'

'I suppose old nurse would be too grand for one,' he said, 'but I should like to have her so near! And you must mind and keep old Mrs. Baker out of the Union for it. And that famous old blind sailor! I shall put him up a bench to sit in the sun, and spin his yarns on, and tell him to think himself at Greenwich.'

Albinia went down, only afraid that his being so very good was a dangerous symptom.

Sophy was far from well in the morning, and Albinia kept her upstairs, and sent her godfather to make her a visit. He always did her good; he knew how to probe deeply, and help her to speak, and he gave her advice with more experience than his sister, and more encouragement than her father.

Sophy said little, but her eyes had a softened look.

'One good thing about Sophy,' said he afterwards to his sister, 'is, that she will never talk her feelings to death.'

'That reserve is my great pain. I don't get at the real being once in six months.'

'So much the better for people living together.'

'Well, I was thinking that you and I are a great deal more intimate and confidential when we meet now, than we used to be when we were always together.'

'People can't be often confidential from the innermost when they live together,' said Maurice.

'Since I have been a Kendal, such has been my experience.'

'It was the same before, only we concealed it by an upper surface of chatter,' said Maurice. '"As iron sharpeneth iron, so doth a man the countenance of his friend;" but if the mutual sharpening went on without intermission, both irons would wear away, and no work would be done. Aren't you coming with me? Edmund is going to drive me to Woodside to meet the pony-carriage from home.'

'I wish I could; but you see what happens when I go out pleasuring!'

'Well, you can take one element of mischief with you—that imp, Maurice.'

'Ye—es. Papa would like it, if you do.'

'I should like you to come on worse terms.'

'Very well, then; and Sophy is safe; I had already asked Genevieve to come and read to her this afternoon. If Gilbert can spare me, I will go.'

Gilbert did not want her, and begged Lucy not to think of staying indoors on his account. He was presently left in solitary possession of the drawing- room, whereupon he rose, settled his brown locks at the glass, arranged his tie, brushed his cuffs, leisurely walked upstairs, and tapped at the door of the morning-room, meekly asking, 'May I come in?' with a cough at each end of the sentence.

'Oh! Gilbert!' cried his anxious sister, starting up. 'Are you come to see me?' and she would have wheeled round her father's arm-chair for him, but Genevieve was beforehand with her, and he sank into it, saying pathetically, 'Ah! thank you, Miss Durant; you are come to a perfect hospital. Oh! this is too much,' as she further gave him a footstool. 'Oh! no, thank you, Sophy,' for she would have handed Genevieve her own pillow for his further support; 'this is delightful!' reclining pathetically in his chair. 'This is not like Traversham.'

'Where they would not believe he was ill!' said Sophy.

'I hope he does not look so very ill,' said Genevieve, cheerfully, but this rather hurt the feelings of both; the one said, 'Oh! but he is terribly pale,' the other coughed, and said, 'Looks are deceitful.'

'That is the very reason,' said Genevieve. 'You don't look deceitful enough to be so ill—so ill as Miss Sophie fears; now you are at home, and well cared for, you will soon be well.'

'Care would have prevented it all,' said Sophy.

'And not brought me home!' said Gilbert. 'Home is home on any terms. No one there had the least idea a fellow could ever be unwell or out of spirits!'

'Ah! you must have been ill,' cried his sister, 'you who never used to be miserable!'

Gilbert gave a sigh. 'They were such mere boys,' he said.

'Monsieur votre Precepteur?' asked Genevieve.

'Ah! he was otherwise occupied!'

'There is some mystery beneath,' said Genevieve, turning to Sophy, who exclaimed abruptly, 'Oh! is he in love?'

'Sophy goes to the point,' said Gilbert, smiling, the picture of languid comfort; 'but I own there are suspicious circumstances. He always has a photograph in his pocket, and Price has seen him looking at it.'

'Ah! depend upon it, Miss Sophy, it is all a romance of these young gentlemen,' said Genevieve, turning to her with a droll provoking air of confidence; 'ce pauvre Monsieur had the portrait of his sister!'

'Catch me carrying Sophy's face in my waistcoat pocket, cried Gilbert, forgetting his languor.

'Speak for yourself, Mr. Gilbert,' laughed Genevieve.

'And he writes letters every day, and wont let any of us put them into the post for him; but we know the direction begins with Miss—'

'Oh! the curious boys!' cried Genevieve. 'If I could only hint to this poor tutor to let them read Miss Downton on one!'

'I assure you,' cried Gilbert, 'Price has laid a bet that she's an heiress with forty thousand pounds and red hair.'

'Mr. Price is an impertinent! I hope you will inform me how he looks when he is the loser.'

'But he has seen her! He met Mr. Downton last Christmas in Regent Street, in a swell carriage, with a lady with such carrots, he thought her bonnet was on fire; and Mr. Downton never saw Price, though he bowed to him, and you know nobody would marry a woman with red hair unless she was an heiress.'

'Miss Sophy,' whispered Genevieve, 'prepare for a red-haired sister-in-law. I predict that every one of the pupils of the respectable Mr. Downton will marry ladies with lively chestnut locks.'

'What, you think me so mercenary, Genevieve?' said Gilbert.

'I only hope to see this school-boy logic well revenged!' said Genevieve. 'Mrs. Price shall have locks of orange red, and for Mrs. Gilbert Kendal—ah! we will content ourselves with her having a paler shade—sandy gold.'

'No,' said Gilbert, speaking slowly, turning round his eyes. 'I could tell you what Mrs. G. Kendal's hair will be—'

Genevieve let this drop, and said, 'You do not want me: good-bye, Miss Sophie.'

'Going! why, you came to read to me, Genevieve,' exclaimed Sophy.

'Ah! I beg your pardon, I have been interrupting you all this time,' cried Gilbert; 'I never meant to disturb you. Pray let me listen.'

And Genevieve read while Gilbert resumed his reclining attitude, with half-closed eyes, listening to the sweet intonations and pretty refined accent of the ancien regime.

Sophy enjoyed this exceedingly, she made it her especial occupation to take care of Gilbert, and enter into his fireside amusements. This indisposition had drawn the two nearer together, and essentially unlike as they were, their two characters seemed to be fitting well one into the other. His sentiment accorded with her strain of romance, and they read poetry and had discussions as they sat over the fire, growing constantly into greater intimacy and confidence. Sophy waited on him, and watched him perpetually, and her assiduity was imparting a softness and warmth quite new to her, while the constant occupation kept affronts and vexations out of her sight, and made her amiable.

Gilbert's health improved, though with vicissitudes that enforced the necessity of prudence. Rash when well, and desponding at each renewal of illness, he was not easy to manage, but he was always so gentle, grateful, and obliging, that he endeared himself to the whole household. It was no novelty for him to be devoted to his step-mother and his little brother, but he was likewise very kind to Lucy, and spent much time in helping in her pursuits; he was becoming companionable to his father, and could play at chess sufficiently well to be a worthy antagonist in Mr. Kendal's scientific and interminable games. He would likewise play at backgammon with grandmamma, and could entertain her for hours together by listening to her long stories of the old Bayford world. He was a favourite in her little society, and would often take a hand at cards to make up a rubber, nay, even when not absolutely required, he was very apt to bestow his countenance upon the little parties, where he had the pleasure of being treated as a great man, and which, at least, had the advantage of making a variation in his imprisonment during the east winds.

Madame Belmarche and her daughter and grandchild were sometimes of the party, and on these occasions, Sophy always claimed Genevieve, and usually succeeded in carrying her off when Gilbert would often join them. Their books and prints were a great treat to her; Gilbert had a beautiful illustrated copy of Longfellow's poems, and the engravings and 'Evangeline' were their enjoyment; Gilbert regularly proffering the loan of the book, and she as regularly refusing it, and turning a deaf ear to gentle insinuations of the pleasure of knowing that an book of his was in her hands. Gilbert had never had much of the schoolboy manner, and he was adopting a gentle, pathetic tone, at which Albinia was apt to laugh, but in her absence was often verged upon tendresse, especially with Genevieve. She, however, by her perfect simplicity and lively banter, always nipped the bud of his sentiment, she had known him from a child, and never lost the sense of being his elder, treating him somewhat as a boy to be played with. Perfectly aware of her own position, her demeanour, frank and gracious as it was, had something in it which kept in check other Bayford youths less gentlemanlike than Gilbert Kendal. If she never forgot that she was dancing-master's daughter, she never let any one else forget that she was a lady.

When the building began, Gilbert had a wholesome occupation, saving his father some trouble and—not quite so much expense by overlooking the workmen. Mr. Kendal was glad to be spared giving orders and speaking to people, and would always rather be overcharged than be at the pains of bargaining or inquiring. 'It was Gilbert's own house,' he said, 'and it was good for the boy to take an interest in it, and not to be too much interfered

with.' So the bay window and the conservatory were some degrees grander than Mr. Ferrars had proposed but all was excused by the pleasure and experience they afforded Gilbert, and it was very droll to see Maurice following him about after the workmen, watching them most knowingly, and deep in mischief at every opportunity. Once he had been up to his knees in a tempting blancmanger-like lake of lime, many times had he hammered or cut his fingers, and once his legs had gone through the new drawing-room ceiling, where he hung by the petticoats screaming till rescued by his brother. The room was under these auspices finished, and was a very successful affair
—the conservatory, in which the hall terminated, and into which a side door of the drawing-room opened, gave a bright fragrant, flowery air to the whole house; and the low fireplace and comfortable fan-shaped fender made the room very cheerful. Fresh delicately-tinted furniture, chosen con amore by the London aunts, had made the apartment very unlike old Willow-Lawn, and Albinia had so much enjoyed setting it off to the best advantage, that she sent word to Winifred that she was really becoming a furniture fancier.

It was a very pretty paper, and some choice prints hung on it, but Albinia and Sophy had laid violent hands on all the best-looking books, and kept them for the equipment of one of the walls. The rest were disposed, for Mr. Kendal's delectation, in the old drawing-room, henceforth to be named the library. Lucy thought it sounded better, and he was quite as willing as Albinia was that the name of study should be extinct. Meantime Mr. Downton had verified the boys' prediction by writing to announce that he was about to marry and give up pupils.

Gilbert was past seventeen, and it was time to decide on his profession. Albinia had virtuously abstained from any hint adverse to the house of Kendal and Kendal, for she knew it hurt her husband's feelings to hear any disparagement of the country where he had spent some of his happiest years. He was fond of his cousins, and knew that they would give his son a safe and happy home, and he believed that the climate was exactly what his health needed.

Sophy fired at the idea. Her constant study of the subject and her vivid imagination had taken the place of memory, which could supply nothing but the glow of colouring and the dazzling haze which enveloped all the forms that she would fain believe that she remembered. She and her father would discuss Indian scenery as if they had been only absent from it a year, she envied Gilbert his return thither, but owned that it was the next thing to going herself, and was already beginning to amass a hoard of English gifts for the old ayahs and bearers who still lived in her recollection, in preparation for the visit which on his first holiday her brother must pay to her birthplace and first home.

Gilbert, however, took no part in this enthusiasm, he made no opposition, but showed no alacrity; and at last his father asked Albinia whether she knew of any objection on his part, or any design which he might be unwilling to put forward. With a beating heart she avowed her cherished scheme.

'Is this his own proposal?' asked Mr. Kendal.

'No; he has never spoken of it, but your plan has always seemed so decided that perhaps he thinks he has no choice.'

'That is not what I wish,' said his father. 'If his inclinations be otherwise, he has only to speak, and I will consider.'

'Shall I sound him?' suggested Albinia, dreading the timidity that always stood between the boy and his father.

'Do not inspire him with the wish and then imagine it his own,' said Mr. Kendal; and then thinking he had spoken sternly, added 'I know you would be the last to wish him to take holy orders inconsiderately, but you have such power over him, that I question whether he would know his wishes from yours.'

Albinia began to disavow the desire of actuating him.

'You would not intend it, but he would catch the desire from you, and I own I would rather he were not inspired with it. If he now should express it, I should fear it was the unconscious effort to escape from India. If it had been his brother Edmund, I would have made any sacrifice, but I do not think Gilbert has the energy or force of character I should wish to see in a clergyman, nor do I feel willing to risk him at the university.'

'Oh! Edmund, why will you distrust Oxford? Why will you not believe what I know through Maurice and his friends?'

'If my poor boy had either the disposition or the discipline of your brother, I should not feel the same doubt.'

'Maurice had no discipline except at school and when William licked him,' cried Albinia. 'You know he was but eleven years old when my father died, and my aunts spoilt us without mitigation.'

'I said the disposition,' repeated Mr. Kendal; 'I can see nothing in Gilbert marking him for a clergyman, and I think him susceptible to the temptations that you cannot deny to exist at any college. Nor would I desire to see him fixed here, until he has seen something of life and of business, for which this bank affords the greatest facilities with the least amount of temptation. He would also be doing something for his own support; and with the life-interests upon his property, he must be dependent on his own exertions, unless I were to do more for him than would be right by the other children.'

'Then I am to say nothing to him?'

'I will speak to him myself. He is quite old enough to understand his prospects and decide for himself.'

'But, Edmund,' cried Albinia, with sudden vehemence, 'you are not sacrificing Gilbert for Maurice's sake?'

She had more nearly displeased him than she had ever done before, though he looked up quietly, saying, 'Certainly not. I am not sacrificing Gilbert, and I should do the same if Maurice were not in existence.'

She was too much ashamed of her foolish fancy to say more, and she cooled into candour sufficient to perceive that he was wise in distrusting her tact where her preference was so strong. But she foresaw that Gilbert would shrink and falter before his father, and that the conference would lead to no discovery of his views, and she was not surprised when her husband told her that he could not understand the boy, and believed that the truth was, that he would like to do nothing at all. It had ended by Mr. Kendal, in a sort of despair, undertaking to write to his cousin John for a statement of what would be required, after which the decision was to be made.

Meantime Mr. Kendal advised Gilbert to attend to arithmetic and book-keeping, and offered to instruct him in his long-forgotten Hindostanee. Sophy learnt all these with all her heart, but Gilbert always had a pain in his chest if he sat still at any kind of study!

CHAPTER XV.

Colonel Bury was the most open-hearted old bachelor in the country. His imagination never could conceive the possibility of everybody not being glad to meet everybody, his house could never be too full, his dinner-parties of 'a few friends' overflowed the dining-room, and his 'nobody' meant always at least six bodies. Every season was fertile in occasions of gathering old and young together to be made happy, and little Mary Ferrars, at five years old, had told her mamma that 'the Colonel's parties made her quite dissipated.'

One bright summer day, his beaming face appeared at Willow-Lawn with a peremptory invitation. His nephew and heir had newly married a friend of Albinia's girlhood, and was about to pay his wedding visit. Too happy to keep his guests to himself, the Colonel had fixed the next Thursday for a fete, and wanted all the world to come to it—the Kendals, every one of them—if they could only sleep there—but Albinia brought him to confession that he had promised to lodge five people more than the house would hold; and the aunts were at the parsonage, where nobody ventured to crowd their servants.

But there was a moon—and though Mr. Kendal would not allow that she was the harvest moon, the hospitable Colonel dilated on her as if she had been bed, board, and lodging, and he did not find much difficulty in his persuasions.

Few invitations ever gave more delight; Albinia appreciated a holiday to the utmost, and the whole family was happy at Sophy's chance of at length seeing Fairmead, and taking part in a little gaiety. And if Mr. Kendal's expectations of pleasure were less high, he submitted very well, smiled benignantly at the felicity around him, and was not once seen to shudder.

Sarah Anne Drury had been invited to enliven grandmamma, and every one augured a beautiful day and perfect enjoyment. The morning was beautiful, but alas! Sophy was hors de combat, far too unwell to think of making one of the party. She bore the disappointment magnanimously, and even the pity. Every one was sorry, and Gilbert wanted her to go and wait at Fairmead Parsonage for the chance of improving, promising to come and fetch her for any part of the entertainment; and her father told her that he had looked to her as his chief companion while the gay people were taking their pleasure. No one was uncomfortably generous enough to offer to stay at home with her; but Lucy suggested asking Genevieve to come and take care of her.

'Nay,' said Sophy, 'it would be much better if she were to go in my stead.'

Gilbert and Lucy both uttered an exclamation; and Sophy added, 'She would have so much more enjoyment than I could! Oh, it would quite make up for my missing it!'

'My dear,' said grandmamma, 'you don't know what you are talking of. It would be taking such a liberty.'

'There need be no scruples on that score,' said Albinia; 'the Colonel would only thank me if I brought him half Bayford.'

'Then,' cried Sophy, 'you think we may ask her? Oh, I should like to run up myself;'—and a look of congratulation and gratitude passed between her and her brother.

'No, indeed, you must not, let me go,' said Lucy, 'I'll just finish this cup of tea—'

'My dear, my dear,' interposed Mrs. Meadows, 'pray consider. She is a very good little girl in her way, but it is only giving her a taste for things out of her station.'

'Oh! don't say that, dear grandmamma,' interposed Albinia, 'one good festival does carry one so much better through days of toil!'

'Ah, well! my dear, you will do as you think proper; but considering who the poor child is, I should call it no kindness to bring her forward in company.'

Something passed between the indignant Gilbert and Sophy about French counts and marquises, but Lucy managed much better. 'Dear me, grandmamma, nobody wishes to bring her forward. She will only play with the children, and see the fireworks, and no one will speak to her.'

Albinia averted further discussion till grandmamma had left the breakfast-table, when all four appealed with one voice to Mr. Kendal, who saw no objection, whereupon Lucy ran off, while Albinia finished her arrangements for the well-being of grandmamma, Sophy, and Maurice, who were as difficult to manage as the fox, goose, and cabbage. At every turn she encountered Gilbert, touching up his toilette at each glass, and seriously consulting her and Sophy upon the choice between lilac and lemon-coloured gloves, and upon the bows of his fringed neck-tie.

'My dear Gilbert,' said Albinia, on the fifth anxious alternative, 'it is of no use. No living creature will be the wiser, and do what you will, you will never look half so well as your father.'

Gilbert flung aside, muttering something about 'fit to be seen,' but just then Lucy hurried in. 'Oh! mamma, she wont go—she is very much obliged, but she can't go.'

'Can't! she must,' cried Albinia and Gilbert together.

'She says you are very kind, but that she cannot. I said everything I could; I told her she should wear Sophy's muslin mantle, or my second best polka.'

'No doubt you went and made a great favour of it,' said Gilbert.

'No, I assure you I did not; I persuaded her with all my might; I said mamma wished it, and we all wished it; and I am sure she would really have been very glad if she could have gone.'

'It can't be the school, it is holiday time,' said Gilbert. 'I'll go and see what is the matter.'

'No, I will go,' said Albinia, 'I will ask the old ladies to luncheon here, and that will make her happy, and make it easier for Sophy to get on with Sarah Anne Drury.'

Lucy had seen Genevieve alone; Albinia took her by storm before Madame Belmarche, whose little black eyes sparkled as she assured Mrs. Kendal that the child merited that and every other pleasure; and when Genevieve attempted to whisper objections, silenced her with an embrace, saying, 'Ah! my love, where is your gratitude to Madame? Have no fears for us. Your pleasure will be ours for months to come.'

The liquid sweetness of Genevieve's eyes spoke of no want of gratitude, and with glee which she no longer strove to repress, she tripped away to equip herself, and Albinia heard her clear young voice upstairs, singing away the burthen of some queer old French ditty.

Albinia found Gilbert and Sophy in disgrace with Lucy for having gathered the choicest flowers, which they were eagerly making up into bouquets. Genevieve's was ready before she arrived in the prettiest tremor of gratitude and anticipation, and presented to her by Gilbert, whilst Sophy looked on, and blushed crimson, face, neck, and all, as Genevieve smelt and admired the white roses that had so cruelly been reft from Lucy's beloved tree.

With every advantage of pretty features, good complexion, and nice figure, the English Lucy, in her blue-and-white checked silk, worked muslin mantle, and white chip bonnet with blue ribbons, was eclipsed by the small swarthy French girl, in that very old black silk dress, and white trimmed coarse straw bonnet, just enlivened by little pink bows at the neck and wrists. It had long been acknowledged that Genevieve was unrivalled in the art of tying bows, and those pink ones were paragons, redolent of all her own fresh sprightly archness and refinement. Albinia herself was the best representative of

English good looks, and never had she been more brilliant, her rich chestnut hair waving so prettily on the rounded contour of her happy face, her fair cheek tinted with such a healthy fresh bloom, her grey eyes laughing with merry softness, her whole person so alert and elastic with exuberant life and enjoyment, that grandmamma was as happy in watching her as if she had been her own daughter, and stroked down the broad flounces of her changeable silk, and admired her black lace, as if she felt the whole family exalted by Mrs. Kendal's appearance.

It was a merry journey, through the meadows and corn-fields, laughing in the summer sunshine, and in due time they saw the flag upon Fairmead steeple, and Albinia nodded to curtseying old friends at the cottage doors. The lodge gate swung open wide, and the well-known striped marquee was seen among the trees in the distance, as they went up the carriage road; but at the little iron gate leading to the shrubbery there was a halt; Mr. Ferrars called to the carriage to stop, and opened the door. At the same moment Albinia gave a cry of wonder, and exclaimed, 'Why, Fred? is William here?'

'No; at Montreal, but very well,' was the answer, with a hearty shake of the hand.

'Edmund, it is Fred Ferrars,' said Albinia. 'Why, Maurice, you never told us.'

'He took us by surprise yesterday.'

'Yes; I landed yesterday morning, went to the Family Office, found Belraven was nowhere, and the aunts at Fairmead, and so came on here,' explained Fred, as he finished shaking hands with all the party, and walked on beside Albinia. He was tall, fresh-coloured, a good deal like her, with a long fair moustache, and light, handsome figure; and Lucy, though rather disconcerted at Genevieve being taken for one of themselves, began eagerly to whisper her conviction that he was Lord Belraven's brother, mamma's first cousin, captain in the 25th Lancers, and aide-de-camp to General Ferrars.

It was the first meeting since an awkward parting. The only son of a foolish second marriage, and early left an orphan, Frederick Ferrars bad grown up under the good aunts' charge, somewhat neglected by his half-brother, by many years his senior. He was little older than Albinia, and a merry, bantering affection had always subsisted between them, till he had begun to give it the air of something more than friendship. Albinia was, however, of a nature to seek for something of depth and repose, on which to rely for support and anchorage. Fred's vivacious disposition had never for a moment won her serious attachment; she was 'very fond of him,' but no more; her heart was set on sharing her brother's life as a country pastor. She went to Fairmead, Fred was carried off by the General to Canada, and she presently heard of his hopeless attachment to a lovely Yankee, whom he met on board the steamer. All this was now cast behind the seven most eventful years of Albinia's life; and in the dignity of her matronhood, she looked more than ever on 'poor Fred' as a boy, and was delighted to see him again, and to hear of her brother William.

A few steps brought them to the shade of the large cedar-tree, where was seated Winifred, and Mrs. Annesley was with her. The greetings had hardly been exchanged before the Colonel came upon them in all his glory, with his pretty shy bride niece on his arm, looking very like the Alice Percy of the old times, when Fred used to tease the two girls.

Genevieve was made heartily welcome, and Sophia's absence deplored, and then the Colonel carried off the younger ones to the archery, giving his arm to the much-flattered Lucy, and followed by Gilbert and Genevieve, with Willie and Mary adhering to them closely, and their governess in sight.

Mr. Ferrars and Mr. Kendal fell into one of their discussions, and paced up and down the shady walk, while Albinia sat, in the complete contentment, between Alice and Winifred, with Fred Ferrars on the turf at their feet, living over again the bygone days, laughing over ancient jokes, resuscitating past scrapes, tracing the lot of old companions, or telling mischievous anecdotes of each other, for the very purpose of being contradicted. They were much too light-hearted to note the lapse of time, till Maurice came to take his wife home, thinking she had had fatigue enough. Mrs. Annesley went with her, and Albinia, on looking for her husband, was told that he had fallen in with some old Indian acquaintances; and Charles Bury presently came to find his wife, and conduct the party to luncheon. There was no formal meal, but a perpetual refection laid out in the dining-room, for relays of guests. Fred took care of Albinia and here they met Miss Ferrars, who had been with one of her old friends, to whom she was delighted to exhibit her nephew and niece in their prime of good looks.

'But I must go,' said Albinia; 'having found the provisions, I must secure that Mr. Kendal and the children are not famished.'

Fred came with her, and she turned down the long alley leading to the archery-ground. He felt old times so far renewed as to resume their habits of confidence, and began, 'I suppose the General has not told you what has brought me home?'

'He has not so much as told me you were coming.'

'Ay, ay, of course you know how he treats those things.'

'Oh—h!' said Albinia, perfectly understanding.

'But,' continued Frederick, eagerly, 'even he confesses that she is the very sweetest—I mean,' as Albinia smiled at this evident embellishment, 'even he has not a word of objection to make except the old story about married officers.'

'And who is *she*, Fred?'

'Oh, mamma, there you are!' and Lucy joined them as they emerged on the bowling-green, where stood the two bright targets, and the groups of archers, whose shafts, for the most part, flew far and wide.

'Where are the rest, my dear? are they shooting?'

'Yes; Gilbert has been teaching Genevieve—there, she is shooting now.'

The little light figure stood in advance. Gilbert held her arrows, and another gentleman appeared to be counselling her. There seemed to be general exultation when one of her arrows touched the white ring outside the target.

'That has been her best shot,' said Lucy. 'I am sure I would not shoot in public unless I knew how!'

'Do you not like shooting?' asked Captain Ferrars; and Lucy smiled, and lost her discontented air.

'It hurts my fingers, she said; 'and I have always so much to do in the garden.'

Albinia asked if she had had anything to eat.

'Oh, yes; the Colonel asked Gilbert to carve in the tent there, for the children and governesses,' said Lucy, 'he and Genevieve were very busy there, but I found I was not of much use so, I came away with the Miss Bartons to look at the flowers, but now they are shooting, and I could not think what had become of you.'

And Lucy bestowed her company on Albinia and the Captain, reducing him to dashing, disconnected talk, till they met Mr. Kendal, searching for them in the same fear that they were starving, and anxious to introduce his wife to his Indian friends. When at the end of the path, Albinia looked round, the Lancer had disappeared, and Lucy was walking by her father, trying to look serenely amused by a discussion on the annexation of the Punjaub.

The afternoon was spent in pleasant loitering, chiefly with Miss Ferrars, who asked much after Sophy, lamented greatly over Winifred's delicate health, and was very anxious to know what could have brought Fred home, being much afraid it was some fresh foolish attachment.

Ominous notes were heard from the band, and the Colonel came to tell them that there was to be dancing till it was dark enough for the fireworks, his little Alice had promised him her first country-dance. Fred Ferrars emerged again with a half-laughing, half-imploring, 'For the sake of old times, Albinia! We've been partners before!'

'You'll take care of Lucy,' said Albinia, turning to her aunt; but Mr. Winthrop had already taken pity on her, and Albinia was led off by her cousin to her place in the fast lengthening rank. How she enjoyed it! She had cared little for London balls after the first novelty, but these Fairmead dances on the turf had always had an Arcadian charm to her fancy, and were the more delightful after so long an interval, in the renewal of the old scene, and the recognition of so many familiar faces.

With bounding step and laughing lips, she flew down the middle, more exhilarated every moment, exchanging merry scraps of talk with her partner or bright fragments as she poussetted with pair after pair; and when the dance was over, with glowing complexion and eyes still dancing, she took Fred's arm, and heard the renewal of his broken story—the praise of his Emily, the fairest of Canadians, whom even the General could not dislike, though, thorough soldier as he was, he would fain have had all military men as devoid of encumbrances as himself, and thought an officer's wife one of the most misplaced articles in the world. Poor Fred had been in love so often, that he laboured under the great vexation of not being able to persuade any of his friends to regard his passion seriously, but Albinia was quite sisterly enough to believe him this time, and give full sympathy to his hopes and fears. Far less wealth had fallen to his lot than to that of his cousins, and his marriage must depend on what his brother would 'do for him,' a point on which he tried to be sanguine, and Albinia encouraged him against probability, for Lord Belraven was never liberal towards his relations, and had lately married an expensive wife, with whom he lived chiefly abroad.

This topic was not exhausted when Fred fell a prey to the Colonel, who insisted on his dancing again, and Albinia telling him to do his duty, he turned towards a group that had coalesced round Miss Ferrars, consisting of Lucy, Gilbert, Genevieve, and the children from the parsonage, and at once bore off the little Frenchwoman, leaving more than one countenance blank. Lucy and Willie did their best for mutual consolation, while Albinia undertook to preside over her niece and a still smaller partner in red velvet, in a quadrille. It was amusing to watch the puzzled downright motions of the sturdy little bluff King Hal, and the earnest precision of the prim little damsel, and Albinia hovering round, now handing one, now pointing to the other, keeping lightly out of every one's way, and far more playful than either of the small performers in this solemn undertaking. As it concluded she found that Mr. Kendal had been watching her, with much entertainment, and she was glad to take his arm, and assure herself that he had not been miserable, but had been down to the parsonage, where he had read the newspaper in peace, and had enjoyed a cup of tea in quiet with Winifred and Mrs. Annesley.

The dancing had been transferred to the tent, which presented a very pretty scene from without, looking through the drooping festoons of evergreens at the lamps and the figures flitting to and fro in their measured movements, while the shrubs and dark foliage of the trees fell into gloom around; and above, the sky assumed the deep tranquil blue of night, the pale bright stars shining out one by one. The Kendals were alone in the terrace, far enough from the gay tumult to be sensible of the contrast.

'How beautiful!' said Albinia: 'it is like a poem.'

'I was just thinking so,' he answered.

'This is the best part of all,' she said, feeling, though hardly expressing to herself the repose of his lofty, silent serenity, standing aloof from gaiety and noise. She could have compared him and her lively cousin to the evening stillness contrasted with the mirthful scene in the tent; and though her nature seemed to belong to the busy world, her best enjoyment lay with what calmed and raised her above herself; and she was perfectly happy, standing still with her arm upon that of her silent husband.

'These things are well imagined,' said he. 'The freedom and absence of formality give space for being alone and quiet.'

'Yes,' said Albinia, saucily, 'when that is what you go into society for.'

'You have me there,' he said, smiling; 'but I must own how much I enjoyed coming back from the parsonage by myself. I am glad we brought that little Genevieve; she seems to be so perfectly in her element. I saw her amusing a set of little children in the prettiest, most animated way; and afterwards, when the young people were playing at some game, her gestures were so sprightly and graceful, that no one could look at the English girls beside her. Indeed I think she was making quite a sensation; your cousin seemed to admire her very much. If she were but in another station, she would shine anywhere.'

'How much you have seen, Edmund!'

'I have been a spectator, you an actor,' he said, smiling.

Her quiescence did not long continue, for the poor people had begun to assemble on the gravel road before the front door to see the fireworks, and she hurried away to renew her acquaintance with her village friends, guessing at them in the dark, asking after old mothers and daughters at service, inquiring the names of new babies, and whether the old ones were at school, and excusing herself for having become 'quite a stranger.'

In the midst—whish—hiss, with steady swiftness, up shot in the dark purple air the first rocket, bursting and scattering a rain of stars. There was an audible gasp in the surrounding homely world, a few little cries, and a big boy clutched tight hold of her arm, saying, 'I be afeard.' She was explaining away his alarms, when she heard her brother's voice, and found her arm drawn into his.

'Here you are, then,' he said; 'I thought I heard your voice.'

'Oh! Maurice, I have hardly seen you. Let us have a nice quiet turn in the park together.'

He resisted, saying, 'I don't approve of parents and guardians losing themselves. What have you done with all your children?'

'What have you done with yours?' retorted she.

'I left Willie and Mary at the window with their governess, I came to see that these other children of mine were orderly.'

'Most proper, prudential, and exemplary Maurice!' his sister laughed. 'Now I have an equally hearty belief in my children being somewhere, sure to turn up when wanted. Come, I want to get out from the trees to look for Colonel Bury's harvest moon, for I believe she is an imposition.'

'No, I'm not coming. You, don't understand your duties. Your young ladies ought always to know where to find you, and you where to find them.'

'Oh! Maurice, what must you have suffered before you imported Winifred to chaperon me!'

'You are in so mad a mood that I shall attempt only one moral maxim, and that is, that no one should set up for a chaperon, till she has retired from business on her own account.'

'That's a stroke at my dancing with poor Fred, but it was his only chance of speaking to me.'

'Not particularly at the dancing.'

'Well, then—'

'You'll see, by-and-bye. It was not your fault if those girls were not in all sorts of predicaments.'

'I believe you think life is made up of predicaments. And I want to hear whether William has written to you anything about poor Fred.'

'Only that he is more mad than ever, and that he let him go, thinking that there is no chance of Belraven helping him, but that it may wear itself out on the journey.'

A revolving circle shedding festoons of purple and crimson jets of fire made all their talk interjectional, and they had by this time reached the terrace, where all the company were assembled, the open windows at regular intervals casting bewildering lights on the heads and shoulders in front of them. Then out burst a grand wheat-sheaf of yellow flame with crimson ears and beards, by whose light Albinia recognised Gilbert standing close to her in the shadow, and asked him where the rest where.'

'I can't tell; Lucy and my father were here just now.'

'Are you feeling the chill, Gilbert?' asked Albinia, struck by something in his tone. 'You had better look from the window.'

He neither moved nor made answer, but a great illumination of Colonel Bury's coat-of-arms, with Roman candles and Chinese trees at the four corners, engrossed every eye, and flashing on every face, enabled Albinia to join Mr. Kendal, who was with Lucy and Miss Ferrars. No one knew where Genevieve was, but Albinia was confident that she could take good care of herself, and was not too uneasy to enjoy the grand representation of Windsor Castle, and the finale of interlaced ciphers amidst a multitude of little fretful sputtering tongues of flame. Then it was, amid good nights, donning of shawls, and announcing of carriages, that Captain Ferrars and Miss Durant made their appearance together, having been 'looking everywhere for Mrs. Kendal,' and it was not in the nature of a brother not to look a little arch, though Albinia returned him as resolute and satisfied a glance as could express 'Well, what of that?'

In consideration of the night air, Mr. Kendal put Gilbert inside the carriage, and mounted the box, to revel in the pleasures of silence. The four within talked incessantly and compared adventures. Lucy had been gratified by being patronized by Miss Ferrars, and likewise had much to say of the smaller fry, and went into raptures about many a 'dear little thing,' none of whom would, however, stand a comparison with Maurice; Gilbert was critical upon every one's beauty; and Genevieve was more animated than all, telling anecdotes with great piquancy, and rehearsing the comical Yankee stories she had heard from Captain Ferrars. She had enjoyed with the zest and intensity of a peculiarly congenial temperament, and she seemed not to be able to cease from working off her excitement in repetitions of her thanks, and in discussing the endless delights the day had afforded.

But the day had begun early, and the way was long, so remarks became scanty, and answers were brief and went astray, and Albinia thought she was travelling for ever to Montreal, when she was startled by a pettish exclamation from Lucy, 'Is that all! It was not worth while to wake me only to see the moon.'

'I beg your pardon,' said Genevieve, 'but I thought Mrs. Kendal wished to see it rise.'

'Thank you, Genevieve,' said Albinia, opening her sleepy eyes; 'she is as little worth seeing as a moon can well be, a waning moon does well to keep untimely hours.'

'Why do you think she is so much more beautiful in the crescent, Mrs. Kendal?' said Genevieve, in the most wakeful manner.

'I'm sure I don't know,' said Albinia, subsiding into her corner.

'Is it from the situation of the mountains in the moon?' continued the pertinacious damsel.

'In Africa!' said Albinia, well-nigh asleep, but Genevieve's laugh roused her again, partly because she thought it less mannerly than accorded with the girl's usual politeness. No mere sleep was allowed her; an astronomical passion seemed to have possessed the young lady, and she dashed into the tides, and the causes of the harvest-moon, and volcanoes, and thunderbolts, and Lord Rosse's telescope, forcing her tired friend to reply by direct appeals, till Albinia almost wished her in the moon herself; and was rejoiced when in the dim greyness of the early summer dawn, the carriage drew up at Madame Belmarche's house. As the light from the weary maid's candle flashed on Genevieve's face, it revealed such a glow of deep crimson on each brown cheek, that Albinia perceived that the excitement must have been almost fever, and went to bed speculating on the strange effects of a touch of gaiety on the hereditary French nature, startling her at once from her graceful propriety and humility of demeanour, into such extraordinary obtrusive talkativeness.

She heard more the next morning that vexed her. Lucy was seriously of opinion that Genevieve had not been sufficiently retiring. She herself had heedfully kept under the wing of Mary's governess, mamma, or Miss Ferrars, and nobody had paid her any particular attention; but Genevieve had been with Gilbert half the day, had had all the gentlemen round her at the archery and in the games, had no end of partners in the dances, and had walked about in the dark with Captain Ferrars. Lucy was sure she was taken for her sister, and whenever she had told people the truth, they had said how pretty she was.

'You are jealous, Lucy,' Sophy said.

Lucy protested that it was quite the reverse. She was glad poor little Jenny should meet with any notice, there was no cause for jealousy of *her*, and she threw back her head in conscious beauty; 'only she was sorry for Jenny, for they were quite turning her head, and laughing at her all the time.'

Albinia's candour burst out as usual, 'Say no more about it, my dear; it was a mistake from beginning to end. I was too much taken up with my own diversion to attend to you, and now you are punishing me for it. I left you to take care of yourselves, and exposed poor little Genevieve to unkind remarks.'

'I don't know what I said,' began Lucy. 'I don't mean to blame her; it was just as she always is with Gilbert, so very French.'

That word settled it—Lucy pronounced it with ineffable pity and contempt —she was far less able to forgive another for being attractive, than for trying to attract.

Sophy looked excessively hurt and grieved, and in private asked her step-mother what she thought of Genevieve's behaviour.

'My dear, I cannot tell; I think she was off her guard with excitement; but all was very new to her, and there was every excuse. I was too happy to be wise, so no wonder she was.'

'And do you think Captain Ferrars was laughing at her? I wish you would tell her, mamma. Gilbert says he is a fine, flourishing officer in moustaches, who, he is sure, flirts with and breaks the heart of every girl he meets. If he is right, mamma, it would cure Genevieve to tell her so, and you would not mind it, though he is your cousin.'

'Poor Fred!' said Albinia. 'I am sorry Gilbert conceived such a notion. But Genevieve's heart is too sensible to break in that way, even if Fred wished it, and I can acquit him of such savage intentions. I never should have seen any harm in all that Genevieve did last night if she had not talked us to death coming home! Still I think she was off her balance, and I own I am disappointed. But we don't know what it is to be born French!'

CHAPTER XVI.

'Mrs. Kendal, dear Madame, a great favour, could you spare me a few moments?'

A blushing face was raised with such an expression of contrite timidity, that Albinia felt sure that the poor little Frenchwoman had recovered from her brief intoxication, and wanted to apologize and be comforted, so she said kindly,

'I was wishing to see you, my dear; I was afraid the day had been too much for you; I was certain you were feverish.'

'Ah! you were so good to make excuses for me. I am so ashamed when I think how tedious, how disagreeable I must have been. It was why I wished to speak to you.'

'Never mind apologies, my dear; I have felt and done the like many a time —it is the worst of enjoying oneself.'

'Oh! that was not all—I could not help it—enjoyment—no!' stammered Genevieve. 'If you would be kind enough to come this way.'

She opened her grandmother's back gate, the entrance to a slip of garden smothered in laurels, and led the way to a small green arbour, containing a round table, transformed by calico hangings into what the embroidered inscription called 'Autel a l'Amour filial et maternel,' bearing a plaster vase full of fresh flowers, but ere Albinia had time to admire this achievement of French sentiment, Genevieve exclaimed, clasping her hands, 'Oh, madame, pardon me, you who are so good! You will tell no one, you will bring on him no trouble, but you will tell him it is too foolish—you will give him back his billet, and forbid him ever to send another.'

Spite of the confidence about Emily, spite of all unreason, such was the family opinion of Fred's propensity to fall in love, that Albinia's first suspicion lighted upon him, but as her eye fell on the pink envelope the handwriting concerned her even more nearly.

'Gilbert!' she cried. 'My dear, what is this? Do you wish me to read it?'

'Yes, for I cannot.' Genevieve turned away, as in his best hand, and bad it was, Albinia read the commencement—

"My hope, my joy, my Genevieve!"

In mute astonishment Albinia looked up, and met Genevieve's eyes. 'Oh, madame, you are displeased with me!' she cried in despair, misinterpreting the look, 'but indeed I could not help it.'

'My dear child,' said Albinia, affectionately putting her arm round her waist, and drawing her down on the seat beside her, 'indeed I am not displeased with you; you are doing the very best thing possible by us all. Think I am your sister, and tell me what is the meaning of all this, and then I will try to help you.'

'Oh, madame, you are too good,' said Genevieve, weeping; and kindly holding the trembling hand, Albinia finished the letter, herself. 'Silly boy! Genevieve, dear girl, you must set my mind at rest; this is too childish—this is not the kind of thing that would touch your affections, I am sure.'

'Oh! pour cela non,' said Genevieve. 'Oh! no; I am grateful to Mr. Gilbert Kendal, for, even as a little boy, he was always kind to me, but for the rest— he is so young, madame, even if I could forget—'

'I see,' said Albinia. 'I am sure that you are much too good and sensible at your age to waste a moment's thought or pain on such a foolish boy, as he certainly is, Genevieve, though not so foolish in liking you, whatever he may be in the way of expressing it. Though of course—' Albinia had floundered into a dreadful bewilderment between her sense of Genevieve's merits and of the incompatibility of their station, and she plunged out by asking, 'And how long has this been going on?'

Genevieve hesitated. 'To speak the truth, madame, I have long seen that, like many other youths, he would be—very attentive if one were not guarded; but I had known him so long, that perhaps I did not soon enough begin, to treat him en jeune homme.

'And this is his first letter?'

'Oh! yes, madame.'

'He complains that you will not hear him? Do you dislike to tell me if anything had passed previously?'

'Thursday,' was slightly whispered.

'Thursday! ah! now I begin to understand the cause of your being suddenly moon-struck.'

'Ah! madame, pardon me!'

'I see—it was the only way to avoid a tete-a-tete!' said Albinia. 'Well done, Genevieve. What had he been saying to you, my dear?'

Poor Genevieve cast about for a word, and finally faltered out, 'Des sottises, Madame.'

'That I can well believe,' said Albinia. 'Well, my dear—'

'I think,' pursued Genevieve, 'that he was vexed because I would not let him absorb me exclusively at Fairmead; and began to reproach me, and protest—'

'And like a wise woman you waked the sleeping dragon,' said Albinia. 'Was this all?'

'No, madame; so little had passed, that I hoped it was only the excitement, and that he would forget; but on Saturday he met me in the flagged path, and oh! he said a great deal, though I did my best to convince him that he could only make himself be laughed at. I hoped even then that he was silenced, and that I need not mention it, but I see he has been watching me, and I dare not go out alone lest I should meet him. He called this morning, and not seeing me left this note.'

'Do your grandmother and aunt know?'

'Oh, no! I would far rather not tell them. Need I? Oh! madame, surely you can speak to him, and no one need ever hear of it?' implored Genevieve. 'You have promised me that no one shall be told!'

'No one shall, my dear. I hope soon to tell you that he is heartily ashamed of having teased you. No one need be ashamed of thinking you very dear and good—you can't help being loveable, but Master Gibbie has no right to tell you so, and we'll put an end to it. He will soon be in India out of your way. Good-bye!'

Albinia kissed the confused and blushing maiden, and walked away, provoked, yet diverted.

She found Gilbert alone, and was not slow in coming to the point, endeavouring to model her treatment on that of her brother, the General, towards his aide-de-camp in the like predicaments.

'Gilbert, I want to speak to you. I am afraid you have been making yourself troublesome to Miss Durant. You are old enough to know better than to write such a note as this.'

He was all one blush, made an inarticulate exclamation, and burst out, 'That abominable treacherous old wooden doll of a mademoiselle.'

'No, Miss Belmarche knows nothing of it. No one ever shall if you will promise to drive this nonsense out of your head.'

'Nonsense! Mrs. Kendal!' with a gesture of misery.

'Gilbert, you are making yourself absurd.'

He turned about, and would have marched out of the room, but she pursued him. 'You must listen to me. It is not fit that you should carry on this silly importunity. It is exceedingly distressing to her, and might lead to very unpleasant and hurtful remarks.' Seeing him look sullen, she took breath, and considered. 'She came to me in great trouble, and begged me to restore your letter, and tell you never to repeat the liberty.'

He struck his hand on his brow, crying vehemently, 'Cruel girl! She little knows me—you little know me, if you think I am to be silenced thus. I tell you I will never cease! I am not bound by your pride, which has sneered down and crushed the loveliest—'

'Not mine,' said Albinia, disconcerted at his unexpected violence.

'Yes!' he exclaimed. 'I know you could patronize! but a step beyond, and it is all the same with you as with the rest—you despise the jewel without the setting.'

'No,' said Albinia, 'so far from depreciating her, I want to convince you that it is an insult to pursue her in this ridiculous underhand way.'

'You do me no justice,' said Gilbert loftily; 'you little understand what you are pleased to make game of,' and with one of his sudden alternations, he dropped into a chair, calling himself the most miserable fellow in the world, unpitied where he would gladly offer his life, and his tenderest feelings derided, and he was so nearly ready to cry, that Albinia pitied him, and said, 'I'll laugh no more if I can help it, Gibbie, but indeed you are too young for all this misery to be real. I don't mean that you are pretending, but only that this is your own fancy.'

'Fancy!' said the boy solemnly. 'The happiness of my life is at stake. She shall be the sharer of all that is mine, the moment my property is in my own hands.'

'And do you think so high-minded a girl would listen to you, and take advantage of a fancy in a boy so much younger, and of a different class?'

'It would be ecstasy to raise her, and lay all at her feet!'

'So it might, if it were worthy of her to accept it. Gilbert, if you knew what love is, you would never wish her to lower herself by encouraging you now. She would be called artful—designing—'

'If she loved me—' he said disconsolately.

'I wish I could bring you to see how unlikely it is that a sensible, superior woman could really attach herself to a mere lad. An unprincipled person might pretend it for the sake of your property—a silly one might like you because you are good-looking and well-mannered; but neither would be Genevieve.'

'There is no use in saying any more,' he said, rising in offended dignity.

'I cannot let you go till you have given me your word never to obtrude your folly on Miss Durant again.'

'Have you anything else to ask me?' cried Gilbert in a melodramatic tone.

'Yes, how would you like your father to know of this? It is her secret, and I shall keep it, unless you are so selfish as to continue the pursuit, and if so, I must have recourse to his authority.'

'Oh! Mrs. Kendal,' he said, actually weeping, 'you have always pitied me hitherto.'

'A man should not ask for pity,' said Albinia; 'but I am sorry for you, for she is an admirable person, and I see you are very unhappy; but I will do all I can to help you, and you will get over it, if you are reasonable. Now understand me, I will and must protect Genevieve, and I shall appeal to your father unless you promise me to desist from this persecution.'

The debate might have been endless, if Mr. Kendal had not been heard coming in. 'You promise?' she said. 'Yes,' was the faint reply, in nervous terror of immediate reference to his father; and they hurried different ways, trying to look unconcerned.

'Never mind,' said Albinia to herself. 'Was not Fred quite as bad about me, and look at him now! Yes, Gilbert must go to India, it will cure him, or if it should not, his affection will be respectable, and worth consideration. If he were but older, and this were the genuine article, I would fight for him, but—'

And she sat down to write a loving note to Genevieve. Her sanguine disposition made her trust that all would blow over, but her experience of the cheerful buoyant Ferrars temperament was no guide to the morbid Kendal disposition, Gilbert lay on the grass limp and doleful till the fall of the dew, when he betook himself to a sofa; and in the morning turned up his eyes reproachfully at her instead of eating his breakfast.

About eleven o'clock the Fairmead pony-carriage stopped at the door, containing Mr. Ferrars, the Captain, Aunt Gertrude, and little Willie. Albinia, her husband, and Lucy, were soon in the drawing-room welcoming them; and Lucy fetched her little brother, who had been vociferous for three days about Cousin Fred, the real soldier, but now, struck with awe at the mighty personage, stood by his mamma, profoundly silent, and staring. He was ungracious to his aunt, and still more so to Willie, the latter of whom was despatched under Lucy's charge to find Gilbert, but they came back unsuccessful. Nor did Sophy make her appearance; she was reported to be reading to grandmamma—Mrs. Meadows preferred to Miss Ferrars! there was more in this than Albinia could make out, and she sat uneasily till she could exchange a few words with Lucy. 'My dear, what is become of the other two?'

'I am sure I don't know what is the matter with them,' said Lucy. 'Gilbert is gone out—nobody knows where—and when I told Sophy who was here, she said Captain Ferrars was an empty-headed coxcomb, and she did not want to see him!'

'Oh! the geese!' murmured Albinia to herself, till the comical suspicion crossed her mind that Gilbert was jealous, and that Sophy was afraid of falling a victim to the redoubtable lady killer.

Luncheon-time produced Sophy, grave and silent, but no Gilbert, and Mr. Kendal, receiving no satisfactory account of his absence, said, 'Very strange,' and looked annoyed.

Captain Ferrars seemed to have expected to see his bright little partner of Thursday, for he inquired for her, and Willie imparted the information that Fred had taken her for Sophy all the time! Fred laughed, and owned it, but asked if she were not really the governess? 'A governess,' said Albinia, 'but not ours,' and an explanation followed, during which Sophy blushed violently, and held up her head as if she had an iron bar in her neck.

'A pity,' said the Lancer, when he had heard who she was, and under his moustache he murmured to Albinia, 'She is rather in Emily's style.'

'Oh, Fred,' thought Albinia, 'after all, it may be lucky that you aren't going to stay here!'

When Albinia was alone with her brother, she could not help saying, 'Maurice, you were right to scold me; I reproached you with thinking life made up of predicaments. I think mine is made of blunders!'

'Ah! I saw you were harassed to-day,' said her brother kindly.

'Whenever one is happy, one does something wrong!'

'I guess—'

'You are generous not to say you warned me months ago. Mind, it is no fault of hers, she is behaving beautifully; but oh! the absurdity, and the worst of it is, I have promised not to tell Edmund.'

'Then don't tell me. You have a judgment quite good enough for use.'

'No, I have not. I have only sense, and that only serves me for what other people ought to do.'

'Then ask Albinia what Mrs. Kendal ought to do.'

Gilbert came in soon after their departure, with an odd, dishevelled, abstracted look, and muttering something inaudible about not knowing the time. His depression absolutely courted notice, but as a slight cough would at any time reduce him to despair, he obtained no particular observation, except from Sophy, who made much of him, flushed at Genevieve's name, and looked reproachful, that it was evident that she was his confidante. Several times did Albinia try to lead her to enter on the subject, but she set up her screen of silence. It was disappointing, for Albinia had believed better things of her sense, and hardly made allowance for the different aspect of the love- sorrows of seventeen, viewed from fifteen or twenty-six—vexatious, too, to be treated with dry reserve, and probably viewed as a rock in the course of true love; and provoking to see perpetual tete-a-tetes that could hardly fail to fill Sophy's romantic head with folly.

At the end of another week, Albinia received the following note:—

'Dear and most kind Madame,

'I would not trouble you again, but this is the third within four days. I returned the two former ones to himself, but he continues to write. May I ask your permission to speak to my relatives, for I feel that I ought to hide this no longer from them, and that we must take some measures for ending it. He does me the honour to wait near the house, and I never dare go out, since—for I will confess all to you, madame—he met me by the river on Monday. I am beginning to fear that his assiduities have been observed, and I should be much obliged if you would tell me how to act. Your kind perseverance in your goodness towards me is my greatest comfort, and I hope that you will still continue it, for indeed it is most unwillingly that I am a cause of perplexity and vexation to you. Entreating your pardon,

What was to be done? That broken pledge overpowered Albinia with a personal sense of shame, and though it set her free to tell all to her husband, she shrank from provoking his stern displeasure towards his son, and feared he might involve Genevieve in his anger. She dashed off a note to her poor little friend, telling her to do as she thought fit by her aunt and grandmother, and then sought another interview with the reluctant Gilbert, to whom she returned the letter, saying, 'Oh, Gilbert, at least I thought you would keep your word.'

'I think,' he said, angrily, trying for dignity, though bewrayed by his restless eyes and hands—'I think it is too much to accuse me of—of—when I never said—What word did I ever give?'

'You promised never to persecute her again.'

'There may be two opinions as to what persecution means,' said Gilbert.

'I little thought of subterfuges. I trusted you.'

'Mrs. Kendal! hear me,' he passionately cried. 'You knew not the misery you imposed. To live so near, and not a word, not a look! I bore it as long as I could; but when Sophy would not so much as take one message, human nature could not endure.'

'Well, if you cannot restrain yourself like a rational creature, some means must be taken to free Miss Durant from a pursuit so injurious and disagreeable to her.'

'Ay,' he cried, 'you have filled her with your own prejudices, and inspired her with such a dread of the hateful fences of society, that she does not dare to confess—'

'For shame, Gilbert, you are accusing her of acting a part.'

'No!' he exclaimed, 'all I say is, that she has been so thrust down and forced back, that she cannot venture to avow her feelings even to herself!'

'Oh!' said Albinia, 'you conceited person!'

'Well!' cried the boy, so much nettled by her sarcasm that he did not know what he said, 'I think—considering—considering our situations, I might be worth her consideration!'

'Who put that in your head?' asked Albinia. 'You are too much a gentleman for it to have come there of its own accord.'

He blushed excessively, and retracted. 'No, no! I did not mean that! No, I only mean I have no fair play—she will not even think. Oh! if I had but been born in the same station of life!'

Gilbert making entrechats with a little fiddle! It had nearly overthrown her gravity, and she made no direct answer, only saying, 'Well, Gilbert, these talks are useless. I only thought it right to give you notice that you have released me from my engagement not to make your father aware of your folly.'

He went into an agony of entreaties, and proffers of promises, but no more treaties of secrecy could he obtain, she would only say that she should not speak immediately, she should wait and see how things turned out. By which she meant, how soon it might be hoped that he would be safe in the Calcutta bank, where she heartily wished him.

She sought a conference with Genevieve, and took her out walking in the meadows, for the poor child really needed change and exercise, the fear of Gilbert had made her imprison herself within the little garden, till she looked sallow and worn. She said that her grandmother and aunt had decided that she should go in a couple of days to the Convent at Hadminster, to remain there till Mr. Gilbert went to India—the superior was an old friend of her aunt, and Genevieve had often been there, and knew all the nuns.

Albinia was startled by this project. 'My dear, I had much rather send you to stay at my brother's, or—anywhere. Are you sure you are not running into temptation?'

'Not of that kind,' said Genevieve. 'The priest, Mr. O'Hara, is a good-natured old gentleman, not in the least disposed to trouble himself about my conversion.'

'And the sisters?'

'Good old ladies, they have always been very kind to me, and petted me exceedingly when I was a little child, but for the rest—' still seeing Albinia's anxious look—'Oh! they would not think of it; I don't believe they could argue; they are not like the new-fashioned Roman Catholics of whom you are thinking, madame.'

'And are there no enthusiastic young novices?'

'I should think no one would ever be a novice there,' said Genevieve.

'You seem to be bent on destroying all the romance of convents, Genevieve!'

'I never thought of anything romantic connected with the reverend mothers,' rejoined Genevieve, 'and yet when I recollect how they came to

Hadminster, I think you will be interested. You know the family at Hadminster Hall in the last century were Roman Catholics, and a daughter had professed at a convent in France. At the time of the revolution, her brother, the esquire, wrote to offer her an asylum at his house. The day of her arrival was fixed—behold! a stage-coach draws up to the door—black veils inside—black veils clustered on the roof—a black veil beside the coachman, on the box—eighteen nuns alight, and the poor old infirm abbess is lifted out. They had not even figured to themselves that the invitation could be to one without the whole sisterhood!'

'And what did the esquire do with the good ladies?'

'He took them as a gift from Providence, he raised a subscription among his friends, and they were lodged in the house at Hadminster, where something like a sisterhood had striven to exist ever since the days of James II.'

'Are any of these sisters living still?'

'Only poor old Mother Therese, who was a little pensionnaire when they came, and now is blind, and never quits her bed. There are only seven sisters at present, and none of them are less than five-and-forty.'

'And what shall you do there, Genevieve?'

'If they have any pupils from the town, perhaps I may help to teach them French. And I shall have plenty of time for my music. Oh! madame, would you lend me a little of your music to copy?'

'With all my heart. Any books?'

'Oh! that would be the greatest kindness of all! And if it were not presuming too much, if madame would let me take the pattern of that beautiful point lace that she sometimes wears in the evening, then I should make myself welcome!'

'And put out your eyes, my dear! But you may turn out my whole lace-drawer if you think anything there will be a pleasure to the old ladies.'

'Ah! you do not guess the pleasure, madame. Needlework and embroidery is their excitement and delight. They will ask me closely about all I have seen and done for months past, and the history of the day at Fairmead will be a fete in itself.'

'Well! my dear, it is very right of you; and I do feel very thankful to you for treating the matter thus. Pray tell your grandmamma and aunt to pardon the sad revolution we have made in their comfort, and that I hope it will soon be over!'

Genevieve took no leave. Albinia sent her a goodly parcel of books and work-patterns, and she returned an affectionate note; but did not attempt to see Lucy and Sophy.

The next Indian mail brought the expected letter, giving an exact account of the acquirements and habits that would be required of Gilbert, with a promise of a home where he would be treated as a son, and of admission to the firm after due probation. The letter was so sensible and affectionate, that Mr. Kendal congratulated his son upon such an advantageous outset in life.

Gilbert made slight reply, but the next morning Sophy sought Albinia out, and with some hesitation began to tell her that Gilbert was very anxious that she would intercede with papa not to send him to Calcutta.

'You now, Sophy!' cried Albinia. 'You who used to think nothing equal to India!'

'I wish it were I,' said Sophy, 'but you know—'

'Well,' said Albinia, coldly.

Sophy was too shy to begin on that tack, and dashed off on another.

'Oh, mamma, he is so wretched. He can't bear to thwart papa, but he says it would break his heart to go so far away, and that he knows it would kill him to be confined to a desk in that climate.'

'You know papa thinks that nothing would confirm his health so much as a few years without an English winter.'

'One's own instinct—' began Sophy; then breaking off, she added, 'Mamma, you never were for the bank.'

'I used not to see the expediency, and I did not like the parting; but now I understand your father's wishes, and the sort of allegiance he feels towards India, so that Gilbert's reluctance will be a great mortification to him.'

'So it will,' said Sophy, mournfully, 'I am sure it is to me. I always looked forward to Gilbert's going to Talloon, and seeing the dear old bearer, and taking all my presents there, but you see, of course, mamma, he cannot bear to go—'

'Sophy, dear,' said Albinia, 'you have been thinking me a very hard-hearted woman this last month. I have been longing to have it out.'

'Not hard-hearted,' said Sophy, looking down, 'only I had always thought you different from other people.'

'And you considered that I was worldly, and not romantic enough. Is that it, Sophy?'

'I thought you knew how to value her for herself, so good and so admirable —a lady in everything—with such perfect manners. I thought you would have been pleased and proud that Gilbert's choice was so much nobler than beauty, or rank, or fashion could make it,' said Sophy, growing enthusiastic as she went on.

'Well, my dear, perhaps I am.'

'But, mamma, you have done all you could to separate them: you have shut Genevieve up in a convent, and you want to banish him.'

'It sounds very grand, and worthy of a cruel step-dame,' said Albinia; 'but, my dear, though I do think Genevieve in herself an admirable creature, worthy of any one's love, what am I to think of the way Gilbert has taken to show his admiration?'

'And is it not very hard,' cried Sophy, 'that even you, who own all her excellences, should turn against him, and give in to all this miserable conventionality, that wants riches and station, and trumpery worldly things, and crushes down true love in two young hearts?'

'Sophy dear, I am afraid the love is not proved to be true in the one heart, and I am sure there is none in the other!'

'Mamma! 'Tis her self-command—'

'Nonsense! His attentions are nothing but distress to her! Sensible grown-up young women are not apt to be flattered by importunity from silly boys. Has he told you otherwise?'

'He thinks—he hopes, at least—and I am sure—it is all stifled by her sense of duty, and fear of offending you, or appearing mercenary.'

'All delusion!' said Albinia; 'there's not a spark of consciousness about her! I see you don't like to believe it, but it is my great comfort. Think how she would suffer if she did love him! Nay, think, before you are angry with me for not promoting it, how it would bring them into trouble and disgrace with all the world, even if your father consented. Have you once thought how it would appear to him?'

'You can persuade papa to anything!'

'Sophy! you ought to know your father better than to say that!' cried Albinia, as if it had been disrespect to him.

'Then you think he would never allow it! You really think that such a creature as Genevieve, as perfect a lady as ever existed, must always be a victim to these hateful rules about station.'

'No,' said Albinia, 'certainly not; but if she were in the very same rank, if all else were suitable, Gilbert's age would make the pursuit ridiculous.'

'Only three years younger,' sighed Sophy. 'But if they were the same age? Do you mean that no one ever ought to marry, if they love ever so much, where the station is different?'

'No, but that they must not do so lightly, but try the love first to see whether it be worth the sacrifice. If an attachment last through many years of adverse circumstances, I think the happiness of the people has been shown to depend on each other, but I don't think it safe to disregard disparities till there has been some test that the love is the right stuff, or else they may produce ill- temper, regrets, and unhappiness, all the rest of their lives.'

'If Gilbert went on for years, mamma?'

'I did not say that, Sophy.'

'Suppose,' continued the eager girl, 'he went out to Calcutta, and worked these five years, and was made a partner. Then he would be two-and-twenty, nobody could call him too young, and he would come home, and ask papa's consent, and you—'

'I *should* call that constancy,' said Albinia.

'And he would take her out to Calcutta, and have no Drurys and Osborns to bother her! Oh! It would be beautiful! I would watch over her while he was gone! I'll go and tell him!'

'Stop, Sophy, not from me—that would never do. I don't think papa would think twenty-two such a great age—'

'But he would have loved her five years!' said Sophy. 'And you said yourself that would be constancy!'

'True, but, Sophy, I have known a youth who sailed broken-hearted, and met a lady "just in the style" of the former one, on board the steamer—'

Sophy made a gesture of impatient disdain, and repeated, 'Do you allow me to tell Gilbert that this is the way?'

'Not from me. I hold out no hope. I don't believe Genevieve cares for him, and I don't know whether his father would consent—' but seeing Sophy's look of disappointment, 'I see no harm in your suggesting it, for it is his only chance with either of them, and would be the proof that his affection was good for something.'

'And you think her worth it?'

'I think her worth anything in the world—the more for her behaviour in this matter. I only doubt if Gilbert have any conception how much she is worth.'

Away went Sophy in a glow that made her almost handsome, while Albinia, as usual, wondered at her own imprudence.

At luncheon Sophy avoided her eye, and looked crestfallen, and when afterwards she gave a mute inquiring address, shook her head impatiently. It was plain that she had failed, and was too much pained and shamed by his poorness of spirit to be able as yet to speak of it.

Next came Gilbert, who pursued Albinia to the morning-room to entreat her interference in his behalf, appealing piteously to her kindness; but she was obdurate. If any remonstrance were offered to his father, it must be by himself.

Gilbert fell into a state of misery, threw himself about upon the chairs, and muttered in the fretfulness of childish despair something about its being very hard, when he was owner of half the town, to be sent into exile—it was like jealousy of his growing up and being master.

'Take care, Gilbert!' said Albinia, with a flash of her eye that he felt to his backbone.

'I don't mean it,' cried Gilbert, springing towards her in supplication. 'I've heard it said, that's all, and was as angry as you, but when a fellow is beside himself with misery at being driven away from all he loves—not a friend to help him—how can he keep from thinking all sorts of things?'

'I wonder what people dare to say it!' cried Albinia wrathfully; but he did not heed, he was picturing his own future misfortunes—toil—climate—fevers—choleras—Thugs—coups de soleil—genuine dread and repugnance working him up to positive agony.

'Gilbert,' said Albinia, 'this is trumpery self-torture! You know this is a mere farrago that you have conjured up. Your father would neither thrust you into danger, nor compel you to do anything to which you had a reasonable aversion. Go and be a man about it in one way or the other! Either accept or refuse, but don't make these childish lamentations. They are cowardly! I should be ashamed of little Maurice if he behaved so!'

'And you will not speak a word for me!'

'No! Speak for yourself!' and she left the room.

Days passed on, till she began to think that, after all, Gilbert preferred Calcutta, cholera, Thugs, and all, to facing his father; but at last, he must have taken heart from his extremity, for Mr. Kendal said, with less vexation than she had anticipated, 'So our plans are overthrown. Gilbert tells me he has an invincible dislike to Calcutta. Had you any such idea?'

'Not till your cousin's letter arrived. What did you say to him?'

'He was so much afraid of vexing me that I was obliged to encourage him to speak freely, and I found that he had always had a strong distaste to and dread of India. I told him I wished he had made me aware of it sooner, and desired to know what profession he really preferred. He spoke of Oxford and the Bar, and so I suppose it must be. I do not wonder that he wishes to follow his Traversham friends, and as they are a good set, I hope there may not be much temptation. I see you are not satisfied, Albinia, yet your wishes were one of my motives.'

'Thank you—once I should,' said Albinia; 'but, Edmund, I see how wrong it was to have concealed anything from you;' and thereupon she informed him of Gilbert's passion for Genevieve Durant, which astonished him greatly, though he took it far less seriously than she had expected, and was not displeased at having been kept in ignorance and spared the trouble of taking notice of it, and thus giving it importance.

'It will pass off,' he said. 'She has too much sense and principle to encourage him, and if you can get her out of Bayford for a few years he will be glad to have it forgotten.'

'Poor Genevieve! She must break up her grandmother's home after all!'

'It will be a great advantage to her. You used to say that it would be most desirable for her to see more of the world. Away from this place she might marry well.'

'Any one's son but yours,' said Albinia, smiling.

'The connexion would be worse here than anywhere else; but I was not thinking of any one in our rank of life. There are many superior men in trade with whom she might be very happy.'

'Poor child!' sighed Albinia. 'I cannot feel that it is fair that she should be banished for Gilbert's faults; and I am sorry for the school; you cannot think how much the tone was improving.'

'If it could be done without hurting her feelings, I should gladly give her a year at some superior finishing school, which might either qualify her for a governess, or enable her to make this one more profitable.'

'Oh! thank you!' cried Albinia; 'yet I doubt. However, her services would be quite equivalent in any school to the lessons she wants. I'll write to Mrs. Elwood—' and she was absorbed in the register-office in her brain, when Mr. Kendal continued—

'This is quite unexpected. I could not have supposed the boy so foolish! However, if you please, I will speak to him, tell him that I was unaware of his folly, and insist on his giving it up.'

'I should be very glad if you would.'

Gilbert was called, and the result was more satisfactory than Albinia thought that Genevieve deserved. His frenzy had tended to wear itself out, and he had been so dreadfully alarmed about India and his father, that in his relief, gratitude, and fear of being sent out, he was ready to promise anything. Before his father he could go into no rhapsodies, and could only be miserably confused.

'Personally,' said Mr. Kendal, 'it is creditable that you should be attracted by such estimable qualities, but these are not the sole consideration. Equality of station is almost as great a requisite as these for producing comfort or respectability, and nothing but your youth and ignorance could excuse your besetting any young woman with importunities which she had shown to be disagreeable to her.'

There was no outcry of despair, only a melancholy muttering. Then Mr. Kendal pronounced his decree in terms more explicit than those in which Albinia had exacted the promise. He said nothing about persecution, nor was he unreasonable enough to command an instant immolation of the passion; he only insisted that Gilbert should pay no marked attention, and attempt no unsanctioned or underhand communication. Unless he thought he had sufficient self-command to abstain, his father must take 'further measures.'

As if fearing that this must mean 'Kendal and Kendal,' he raised his head, and with a deep sigh undertook for his own self-command. Mr. Kendal laid his hand on his shoulder with kind pity, told him he was doing right, and that while he acted openly and obediently, he should always meet with sympathy and consideration.

Two difficult points remained—the disposing of the young people. Gilbert was still over young for the university, as well as very backward and ill-prepared, and the obstinate remains of the cough made his father unwilling to send him from home. And his presence made Genevieve's absence necessary.

The place had begun to loom in the distance. A former governess of Albinia's, who would have done almost anything to please her, had lately been left a widow, and established herself in a suburb of London, with a small party of pupils. She had just begun to feel the need of an additional teacher, and should gladly receive Genevieve, provided she fulfilled certain requisites, of which, luckily, French pronunciation stood the foremost. The terms were left to Albinia, who could scarcely believe her good fortune, and went in haste to discuss the matter with the Belmarches.

It almost consoled her for what she had been exceedingly ashamed to announce, the change of purpose with regard to Gilbert, which was a sentence of banishment to the object of his folly. Nothing pained her more than the great courtesy and kindness of the two old ladies to whom it was such a cruel stroke, they evidently felt for her, and appeared to catch at Mrs. Elwood's offer, and when Albinia proposed that her salary should be a share in the instructions of the masters, agreed that this was the very thing they had felt it their duty to provide for her, if they had been able to bring themselves to part with her.

'So,' said good Madame Belmarche, smiling sadly, 'you see it has been for the dear child's real good that our weakness has been conquered.'

Genevieve was written to, and consented to everything, and when Mr. Kendal took Gilbert away to visit an old friend, his wife called for Genevieve at the convent to bring her home. Albinia could not divest herself of some curiosity and excitement in driving up to the old-fashioned red brick house, with two tall wings projecting towards the street, and the front door in the centre between them, with steps down to it. She had not been without hopes of a parlour with a grille, or at least that a lay sister would open the door; but she saw nothing but a very ordinary-looking old maid-servant, and close behind her was Genevieve, with her little box, quite ready—no excuse for seeing anything or anybody else.

If Genevieve were sad at the proposal of leaving home and going among strangers, she took care to hide all that could pain Mrs. Kendal, and her cheerful French spirit really enjoyed the prospect of new scenes, and bounded with enterprise at the hope of a new life and fresh field of exertion.

'Perhaps, after all,' she said, smiling, 'they may make of me something really useful and valuable, and it will all be owing to you, dear madame. Drawing and Italian! When I can teach them, I shall be able to make grandmamma easy for life!'

Genevieve skipped out of the carriage and into her aunt's arms, as if alive only to the present delight of being at home again. It was a contrast to Sophy's dolorous visage. Poor Sophy! she was living in a perpetual strife with the outward tokens of sulkiness, forcing herself against the grain to make civil answers, and pretend to be interested when she felt wretched and morose. That Gilbert, after so many ravings, should have relinquished, from mere cowardice, that one hope of earning Genevieve by honourable exertion, had absolutely lowered her trust in the exalting power of love, and her sense of justice revolted against the decision that visited the follies of the guilty upon the innocent. She was yearning over her friend with all her heart, pained at the separation, and longing fervently to make some demonstration, but the greater her wish, the worse was her reserve. She spent all her money upon a beautiful book as a parting gift, and kept it beside her, missing occasion after occasion of presenting it, and falling at each into a perfect agony behind that impalpable, yet impassable, barrier of embarrassment.

It was not till the very last evening, when Genevieve had actually wished her good-bye and left the house, that she grew desperate. She hastily put on bonnet and cloak, and pursued Genevieve up the street, overtaking her at last, and causing her to look round close to her own door.

'My dear Miss Sophy,' cried Genevieve, 'what is the matter? You are quite overcome.'

'This book—' said Sophy—it was all she could say.

'Love—yes,' said Genevieve. 'Admiration—no.'

'You shall not say that,' cried Sophy. 'I have found what is really dignified and disinterested, and you must let me admire you, Jenny, it makes me comfortable.'

Genevieve smiled. 'I would not commit an egoism,' she said; but if the sense of admiration do you good, I wish it had a worthier cause.'

'There's no one to admire but you,' said Sophy. 'I think it very unfair to send you away, and though it is nobody's fault, I hate good sense and the way of the world!'

'Oh! do not talk so. I am only overwhelmed with wonder at the goodness I have experienced. If it had happened with any other family, oh! how differently I should have been judged! Oh! when I think of Mrs. Kendal, I am ready to weep with gratitude!'

'Yes, mamma is mamma, and not like any one else, but even she is obliged to be rational, and do the injustice, whatever she feels,' said Sophy.

'Oh! not injustice—kindness! I shall be able to earn more for grandmamma!'

'It is injustice!' said Sophy, 'not hers, perhaps, but of the world! It makes me so angry, to think that you—you should never do anything but wear yourself out in drudging over tiresome little children—'

'Little children are my brothers and sisters, as I never had any,' said Genevieve. 'Oh! I always loved them, they make a home wherever they are. I am thankful that my vocation is among them.'

In dread of a token from Gilbert, Genevieve would not notice it, but pursued, 'You must come in and rest—you must have my aunt's salts.'

'No—no—' said Sophy, 'not there—' as Genevieve would have taken her to the little parlour, but opening the door of the school-room, she sank breathless into a sitting position on the carpetless boards.

Genevieve shut the door, and kneeling down, found Sophy's arms thrown round her, pressing her almost to strangulation.

'Oh! I wanted to do it—I never could wont you have the book, Genevieve? It is my keepsake—only I could not give it because—'

'Is it your keepsake, indeed, dear Miss Sophy?' said Genevieve. 'Oh! if it is yours—how I shall value it—but it is too beautiful—'

'Nothing is too beautiful for you, Genevieve,' said Sophy fervently.

'And it is your gift! But I am frightened—it must have cost—!' began Genevieve, still a little on her guard. 'Dear, dear Miss Sophy, forgive me if I do seem ungrateful, but indeed I ought to ask—if—if it is all your own gift?'

'Mine? yes!' said Sophy, on the borders of offence. 'I know what you mean, Genevieve, but you may trust me. I would not take you in.'

Genevieve was blushing intensely, but taking courage she bestowed a shower of ardent embraces and expressions of gratitude, mingled with excuses for her precaution. 'Oh! it was so very kind in Miss Sophy,' she said; 'it would be such a comfort to remember, she had feared she too was angry with her.'

'Angry? oh, no!' cried Sophy, her heart quite unlocked; 'but the more I loved and admired, the more I could not speak. And if they drive you to be a governess? If you had a situation like what we read of?'

'Perhaps I shall not,' said Genevieve, laughing. 'Every one has been so good to me hitherto! And then I am not reduced from anything grander. I shall always have the children, you know.'

'How I should hate them!' quoth Sophy.

'They are my pleasure. Besides I have always thought it a blessing that my business in life, though so humble, should be what may do direct good. If only I do not set them a bad example, or teach them any harm.'

'Not much danger of that,' said Sophy, smiling. 'Well, I can't believe it will be your lot all your life. You will find some one who will know how to love you.'

'No,' said Genevieve, 'I am not in a position for marriage—grandmamma has often told me so!'

'Things sometimes happen,' pursued Sophy. 'Mamma said if Gilbert had been older, or even if—if he had been in earnest and steady enough to work for you in India, then it might—And surely if Gilbert could care for you—people higher and deeper than he would like you better still.'

'Hush,' said Genevieve; 'they would only see the objections more strongly. No, do not put these things in my head. I know that unless a teacher hold her business as her mission, and put all other schemes out of her mind, she will work with an absent, distracted, half-hearted attention, and fail of the task that the good God has committed to her.'

'Then you would never even wish—'

'It would be seeking pomps and vanities to wish,' said Genevieve; 'a school-room is a good safe cloister, probably less dull than the convent. If I wish at all, it will be that I may be well shut up there, for I know that in spite of myself my manners are different from your English ones. I cannot make them otherwise, and that amuses people; and I cannot help liking to please, and so I become excited. I enjoy society so much that it is not safe for me! So don't be sorry, dear Sophy, it is a fit penance for the vanity that elated me too much that evening at Fairmead!'

Mademoiselle Belmarche was here attracted by the voices. Sophy started up from the ground, made some unintelligible excuse, and while Mademoiselle was confounded with admiration at the sight of the book, inflicted another boa-constrictor embrace, and hurried away.

CHAPTER XVII.

Planets hostile to the tender passion must have been in the ascendant, for the result of Captain Ferrars's pursuit of his brother to Italy was the wholesome certainty that his own slender portion was all he had to reckon upon. Before returning to Canada, he came to Bayford to pour out his troubles to his cousin, and to induce her, if he could induce no one else, to advise his immediate marriage. It was the first time he had been really engaged, and his affection had not only stood three months' absence, but had so much elevated his shatter-brained though frank and honest temperament, that Albinia conceived a high opinion of 'Emily,' and did her best to persuade him to be patient, and wait for promotion.

Sophy likewise approved of him this time, perhaps because he was so opposite a specimen of the genus lover from that presented by her brother. Gilbert had not been able to help enjoying himself while from home, but his spirits sank on his return; he lay about on the grass in doleful dejection, studied little but L. E. L., lost appetite, and reproachfully fondled his cough; but Albinia was now more compassionate than Sophy, whom she was obliged to rebuke for an unsisterly disregard toward his woes.

'I can't help it,' said Sophy; 'I can't believe in himnow!'

'Yes, you ought to believe that he is really unhappy, and be more gentle and considerate with him.'

'If it had been earnest, he would have sacrificed himself instead of Genevieve.'

'Ah! Sophy, some day you will learn to make excuses for other people, and not be so intolerant.'

'I never make excuses.'

'Except for Maurice,' said Albinia. 'If you viewed other people as you do him, your judgments would be gentler.'

Sophy's conscientiousness, like her romance, was hard, high, and strict; but while she had as little mercy on herself as on others, and while there were some soft spots in her adamantine judgment, there was hope that these would spread, and, without lowering her tone, make her more merciful.

She corresponded constantly with Genevieve, who seemed very happily placed; Mrs. Elwood was delighted with her, and she with Mrs. Elwood; and her lively letters showed no signs of pining for home. Sophy felt as if it were a duty to her friend, to do what in her lay to prevent the two old ladies from being dull, and spent an hour with them every week, not herself contributing much to their amusement, but pleasing them by the attention, and hearing much that was very curious of their old-world recollections.

Ever since that unlucky penny-club-day, when she had declared that she hated poor people, she had been let alone on that subject; and though principle had made her use her needle in their behalf, shyness and reserve had kept her back from all intercourse with them; but in her wish to compensate for Genevieve's absence, she volunteered to take charge of her vacant Sunday-school class, and obtained leave to have the girls at home on the afternoons for an hour and a half. This was enough for one who worked as she did, making a conscience of every word, and toiling to prepare her lessons, writing out her questions beforehand, and begging for advice upon them.

'My dear,' said Albinia, 'you must alter this—you see this question does not grow out of the last answer.'

'Yes,' said Sophy, 'that must have been what puzzled them last Sunday: they want connexion.'

'Nothing like logic to teach one to be simple,' said Albinia.

'I can't see the use of all this trouble,' put in Lucy. 'Why can't you ask them just what comes into your head, as I always do?'

'Suppose mistakes came into my head.'

'Oh! they would not find it out if they did! I declare!—what's this— Persian? Are you going to teach them Persian?'

'No; it is Greek. You see it is a piece of a Psalm, a quotation rather different in the New Testament. I wrote it down to ask papa what it is in Hebrew.'

'By-the-bye, Sophy,' continued Lucy, 'how could you let Susan Price come to church with lace sleeves—absolute lace sleeves!'

'Had she?'

'There—you never see anything! Mamma, would not it be more sensible to keep their dress in order, than to go poking into Hebrew, which can't be of use to any one?'

There was more reason than might appear in what Lucy said: the girls of her class were more orderly, and fonder of her than Sophy's of the grave young lady whose earnestness oppressed them, and whose shyness looked dislike and pride. As to finding fault with their dress, she privately told

Albinia that she could not commit such a discourtesy, and was answered that no one but Mrs. Dusautoy need interfere.

'I will go and ask Mrs. Dusautoy what she wishes,' said Albinia. 'I should be glad if she would modify Lucy's sumptuary laws. To fall foul of every trifle only makes the girls think of their dress.'

Albinia found Mrs. Dusautoy busied in writing notes on mourning paper.

'Here is a note I had written to you,' she said. 'I am sending over to Hadminster to see if any of the curates can take the services to-morrow.'

Albinia looked at the note while Mrs. Dusautoy wrote on hurriedly. She read that there could be no daily services at present, the Vicar having been summoned to Paris by the sudden death of Mrs. Cavendish Dusautoy. As the image of a well-endowed widow, always trying to force her way into higher society, arose before Albinia, she could hardly wait till the letter was despatched, to break out in amazement,

'Was she a relation of yours? Even the name never made me think of it!'

'It is a pity she cannot have the gratification of hearing it, poor woman,' said Mrs. Dusautoy, 'but it is a fact that she did poor George Dusautoy the honour to marry him.'

'Mr. Dusautoy's brother?'

'Ay—he was a young surgeon, just set up in practice, exactly like John— nay, some people thought him still finer-looking. She was a Miss Greenaway Cavendish, a stock-broker's heiress of a certain age.'

'Oh!' expressively cried Albinia.

'You may say so,' returned Mrs. Dusautoy. 'She made him put away his profession, and set up for taste and elegant idleness.'

'And he submitted?'

'There was a great deal of the meek giant in him, and he believed implicitly in the honour she had done him. It would have been very touching, if it had not been so provoking, to see how patiently and humbly that fine young man gave up all that would have made him happy, to bend to her caprices and pretensions.'

'Did you ever see them together?'

'No, I never saw her at all, and him only once. I never knew John really savage but once, and that was at her not letting him come to our wedding; but she did give him leave of absence for one fortnight, when we were at Lauriston. How happy the brothers were! It did one good to hear their great voices about the house; and they were like boys on a stolen frolic, when John took him to prescribe for some of our poor people. He used to talk of bringing us his little son—the one pleasure of his life—but he never was allowed. Oh, how I used to long to stir up a mutiny!' cried Mrs. Dusautoy, quite unknowing that she ruled her own lion with a leash of silk. 'If she had appreciated him, it would have been bearable; but to her he was no more than the handsome young doctor, whom she had made a gentleman, and not a very good piece of work of it either! Little she recked of the great loving heart that had thrown itself away on her, and the patience that bore with her; and she tried to hinder all the liberal bountiful actions that were all he cared to do with his means! I wish the boy may remember him!'

'How long has he been dead?'

'These ten years. He was drowned in a lake storm in Switzerland—people clung to him, and he could not swim. It was John's one great grief—he cannot mention him even now. And really,' she added, smiling, 'I do believe he has brought himself to fancy it was a very happy marriage. She has always been very civil; but she has been chiefly abroad, and never would take his advice about sending her boy to school.'

'What becomes of him now?'

'He is our charge. She was on the way home from Italy, when she was taken ill at Paris, and died at the end of the week.'

'How old is he?'

'About nineteen, I fancy. He must have had an odd sort of education; but if he is a nice lad, it will be a great pleasure to John to have something young about the house.'

'I was thinking that Mr. Dusautoy hardly wanted more cares.'

'So have I,' said her friend, smiling, 'and I have been laying a plot against him. You see, he is as strong as a lion, and never yet was too tired to sleep; but it is rather a tempting of Providence to keep 3589 people and fourteen services in a week resting upon one man!'

'Exactly what his churchwarden has preached to him.'

'Moreover, he cannot be in two places at once, let alone half-a-dozen. Now, my Lancashire people have written in quest of a title for holy orders for a young man who has just gone through Cambridge with great credit, and it strikes me that he might at once help John, and cram Master Algernon.'

'And Gilbert!' cried Albinia. 'Oh, if you will import a tutor for Gilbert, we shall be for ever beholden to you!'

'I had thought of him. I have no doubt that he is much better taught than Algernon; but I am not afraid of this poor fellow bringing home bad habits, and they will be good companions. I reckon upon you and Mr. Kendal as great auxiliaries, and I don't think John will be able to withstand our united forces.'

On the way home, on emerging from the alley, Albinia encountered Gilbert, just parting with another youth, who walked off quickly on the Tremblam road, while she inquired who it was.

'That?' said Gilbert; 'oh! that was young Tritton. He has been away learning farming in Scotland. We speak when we meet, for old acquaintance sake and that.'

The Bayford mind was diverted from the romance of Genevieve, by the enormous fortune of the Vicar's nephew, whose capital was in their mouths and imaginations swelled into his yearly income. Swarms of cards of inquiry were left at the vicarage; and Mrs. Meadows and Lucy enjoyed the reflected dignity of being able to say that Mrs. Kendal was continually there. And so she was, for Mrs. Dusautoy was drooping, though more in body than visibly in spirit, and needed both companionship and assistance in supporting the charge left by her absent Atlas.

He was not gone a moment longer than necessary, and took her by surprise at last, while Albinia and Sophy were sitting on the lawn with her, when she welcomed the nephew and the Vicar, holding out a hand to each, and thanked them for taking care of 'Fanny.' 'Here, Algernon,' he continued, 'here are two of our best friends, Mrs. Kendal and Miss Sophy.'

There was a stiff bow from a stiff altitude. The youth was on the gigantic Dusautoy scale, looking taller even than his uncle, from his manner of holding himself with his chin somewhat elevated. He had a good ruddy sun- burnt complexion, shining brown hair, and regular features; and Albinia could respond heartily to the good Vicar's exclamation, as he followed her down to the gate for the sake of saying,

'Well-grown lad, isn't that? And a very good-hearted fellow too, poor boy —the very picture of his dear father. Well, and how has Fanny been?'

He stayed to be reassured that his return was all his Fanny wanted, and then hurried back to her, while Albinia and Sophy pursued their way down the hill.

'News for grandmamma. We must give her a particular description of the hero.'

'How ugly he thought me!' said Sophy, quaintly.

'My dear, I believe that is the first thing you think of when you meet a stranger!'

'I saw it this time,' returned Sophy. 'His chin went up in the air at once. He set me down for Mrs. Kendal, and you for Miss Sophy.'

'Nonsense,' said Albinia, for the inveterate youthfulness of her bright complexion and sunny hair was almost a sore subject with her. 'Your always fancying that every one is disgusted with you, is as silly as if you imagined yourself transcendently beautiful. It is mere self-occupation, and helps to make you blunt and shy.'

'Mamma,' said Sophy, 'tell me one thing. Did you ever think yourself pretty?'

'I have thought myself looking so, under favourable circumstances, but that's all. You are as far from ugliness as I am, and have as little need to think of it. As far as features go, there's the making of a much handsomer woman in you than in me.'

Sophy laughed. A certain yearning for personal beauty was a curious part of her character, and she would have been ashamed to own the pleasure those few words had given her, or how much serenity and forbearance they were worth; and her good-humour was put to the proof that evening, for grandmamma had a tea-party, bent on extracting the full description of the great Algernon Greenaway Cavendish Dusautoy, Esquire. Lucy's first sight was less at her ease. Elizabeth Osborn, with whom she kept up a fitful intimacy, summoned her mysteriously into her garden, to show her a peep- hole through a little dusty window in the tool-house, whence could be descried the vicarage garden, and Mr. Cavendish Dusautoy, as, with a cigar in his mouth, and his hands in his pockets,

Lucy was so much amused, that she could not help reporting it at home, where Gilbert forgot his sorrows, in building up a mischievous romance in honour of the hole in the 'sweet and lovely wall.'

But the parents' feud did not seem likely to hold out. A hundred thousand pounds on one side of the wall, and three single daughters on the other, Mrs. Osborn was not the woman to trust to the 'wall's hole;' and so Mr. Dusautoy's enemy laid down her colours; and he was too kind-hearted to trace her sudden politeness to the source.

Mr. Dusautoy acceded to the scheme devised by his wife, and measures were at once taken for engaging the curate. When Albinia went to talk the matter over at the parsonage, Lucy accompanied her; but the object of her curiosity was not in the room; and when she had heard that he was fond of drawing, and that his horses were to be kept at the King's Head stables, the conversation drifted away, and she grew restless, and begged Mrs. Dusautoy to allow her to replenish the faded bouquets on the table. No sooner was she in the garden, than Mrs. Dusautoy put on an arch look, and lowering her voice, said,

'Oh! it is such fun! He does despise us so immensely.'

'Despise—you?'

'He is a good, boy, faithful to his training. Now his poor mother's axioms were, that the English are vulgar, country English more vulgar, Fanny Dusautoy the most vulgar! I wish we always as heartily accepted what we are taught.'

'He must be intolerable.'

'No, he is very condescending and patronizing to the savages. He really is fond of his uncle; and John is so much hurt it I notice his peculiarities, that I have been dying to have my laugh out.'

'Can Mr. Dusautoy bear with pretension?'

'It is not pretension, only calm faith in the lessons of his youth. Look,' she added, becoming less personal at Lucy's re-entrance, and pointing to a small highly-varnished oil-painting of a red terra cotta vase, holding a rose, a rhododendron before it, and half a water-melon grinning behind, newly severed by a knife.

'Is that what people bring home from Italy now-a-days?' said Albinia.

'That is an original production.'

'Did Mr. Cavendish Dusautoy do that?' cried Lucy.

'Genre is his style,' was the reply. 'His mother was resolved he should be an amateur, and I give his master great credit.'

'Especially for that not being a Madonna,' said Albinia. 'I congratulate you on his having so safe an amusement.'

'Yes; it disposes of him and of the spare room. He cannot exist without an atelier.'

Just then the Vicar entered.

'Ah! Algernon's picture,' began he, who had never been known to look at one, except the fat cattle in the Illustrated News. 'What do you think of it? Has he not made a good hand of the pitcher?'

Albinia gratified him by owning that the pitcher was round; and Lucy was in perfect rapture at the 'dear little spots' in the rhododendron.

'A poor way of spending a lad's time,' said the uncle; 'but it is better than nothing; and I call the knife very good: I declare you might take it up,' and he squeezed up his eyes to enhance the illusion.

A slow and wide opening of the door admitted the lofty presence of Algernon Cavendish Dusautoy, with another small picture in his hand. Becoming aware of the visitors, he saluted them with a dignified movement of his head, and erecting his chin, gazed at them over it.

'So you have brought us another picture, Algernon,' said his uncle. 'Mrs. Kendal has just been admiring your red jar.'

'Have you a taste for art?' demanded Mr. Cavendish Dusautoy, turning to her with magnificent suavity.

'I used to be very fond of drawing.'

'Genre is my style,' he pursued, almost overthrowing her gravity by the original of his aunt's imitation. 'I took lessons of old Barbouille—excellent master. Truth and nature, those were his maxims; and from the moment I heard them, I said, "This is my man." We used positively to live in the Borghese. There!' as he walked backwards, after adjusting his production in the best light.

'A snipe,' said Albinia.

'A snipe that I killed in the Pontine marshes.'

'There is very good shooting about Anxur,' said Albinia.

'You have been at Rome?' He permitted himself a little animation at discovering any one within the pale of civilization.

'For one fortnight in the course of a galloping tour with my two brothers,' said Albinia. 'All the Continent in one long vacation!'

'That was much to be regretted. It is my maxim to go through every museum thoroughly.'

'I can't regret,' said Albinia. 'I should be very sorry to give up my bright indistinct haze of glorious memories, though I was too young to appreciate all I saw.'

'For my part, I have grown up among works of art. My whole existence has been moulded on them, and I feel an inexpressible void without them. I shall be most happy to introduce you into my atelier, and show you my notes on the various Musees. I preserved them merely as a trifling memorial; but many connoisseurs have told me that I ought to print them as a Catalogue raisonnee, for private circulation, of course. I should be sorry to interfere with Murray, but on the whole I decided otherwise: I should be so much bored with applications.'

Mrs. Dusautoy's wicked glance had so nearly demolished the restraint on her friend's dimples, that she turned her back on her, and commended the finish of a solitary downy feather that lay detached beside the bird.

'My maxim is truth to nature, at any cost of pains,' said the youth, not exactly gratified, for homage was his native element, but graciously proceeding to point out the merits of the composition.

Albinia's composure could endure no more, and she took her leave, Mr. Dusautoy coming down the hill with her to repeat, and this time somewhat wistfully,

'A fine lad, is he not, poor fellow?'

With perfect sincerity, she could praise his good looks.

'He has had a quantity of sad stuff thrust on him by the people who have been about his poor mother,' said Mr. Dusautoy. 'She could never bear to part with him, and no wonder, poor thing; and she must have let a very odd sort of people get about her abroad—they've flattered that poor lad to the top of his bent, you see, but he's a very good boy for all that, very warm-hearted.'

'He must be very amiable for his mother to have been able to manage him all this while.'

'Just what I say!' cried the Vicar, his honest face clearing. 'Many youths would have run into all that is bad, brought up in that way; but only consider what disadvantages he has had! When we get him to see his real standing a little better—I say, could not you let us have your young people to come up this evening, have a little music, and make it lively? I suppose Fanny and I are growing old, though I never thought so before. Will you come, Lucy, there's a good girl, and bring your brother and sister? The lads must be capital friends.'

Lucy promised with sparkling eyes, and the Vicar strode off, saying he should depend on the three.

Gilbert 'supposed he was in for it,' but 'did not see the use of it,' he was sick of the name of 'that polysyllable,' and 'should see enough of him when Mr. Hope came, worse luck.'

The result of the evening was, that Lacy was enraptured at the discovery that this most accomplished hero sang Italian songs to the loveliest guitar in the world, and was very much offended with Sophy for wishing to know whether mamma really thought him so very clever.

Immediately after the Ordination arrived Mr. Hope, a very youthful, small, and delicate-looking man, whom Mr. Dusautoy could have lifted as easily as his own Fanny, with short sight, timid nature, scholarly habits, weak nerves, and an inaudible voice.

Of great intellect, having read deeply, and reading still more deeply, he had the utmost dread of ladies, and not even his countrywoman, Mrs. Dusautoy, could draw him out. He threw his whole soul into the work, winning the hearts of the infant-school and the old women, but discomfiting the congregation by the weakness of his voice, and the length and depth of his sermons. There was one in especial which very few heard, and no one entered into except Sophy, who held an hour's argument over it with her father, till they arrived at such lengthy names of heresies, that poor grandmamma asked if it were right to talk Persian on a Sunday evening.

He conscientiously tutored his two pupils, but there was no common ground between him and them. Excepting his extra intellect, there was no boyhood in him. A town-bred scholar, a straight constitutional upon a clean road was his wildest dream of exercise; he had never mounted a horse, did not know a chicken from a partridge, except on the table, was too short-sighted for pictures, and esteemed no music except Gregorians.

The two youths were far more alive to his deficiencies than to his endowments: Algernon contemned him for being a book-seller's son, with nothing to live on but his fellowship and curacy, and Gilbert looked down on his ignorance of every matter of common life, and excessive bashfulness. Mr. Dusautoy would have had less satisfaction in the growing intimacy between the lads, had he known that it had been cemented by inveigling poor Mr. Hope into a marsh in search of cotton-grass, which, at Gilbert's instigation,

Algernon avouched to be a new sort of Indian corn, grown in Italy for feeding silkworms.

An intimacy there was, rather from constant intercourse than from positive liking. Gilbert saw through and disdained young Dusautoy's dulness and self-consequence; but good-natured, kindly, and unoccupied, he had no objection to associate with him, showing him English ways, trying to hinder him from needlessly exposing himself, and secretly amused with his pretension. Algernon, with his fine horses, expensive appointments, and lofty air, was neither a discreditable nor unpleasing companion. Mr. Kendal had given his son a horse, which, without costing the guineas that Algernon had 'refused' for each of his steeds, was a very respectable-looking animal, and the two young gentlemen, starting on their daily ride, were a grand spectacle for more than little Maurice.

Gilbert had suffered some eclipse. Once he had been the grand parti, the only indisputable gentleman, but now Mr. Cavendish Dusautoy had entirely surpassed him both in self-assertion and in the grounds for it. His incipient dandyisms faded into insignificance beside the splendours of the heir of thousands; and he, who among all his faults had never numbered conceit or forwardness, had little chance beside such an implicit believer in his own greatness.

Nor was Bayford likely to diminish that faith. The non-adorers might be easily enumerated—his uncle and aunt, his tutor, his groom, Mr. and Mrs. Kendal, Gilbert and Sophy; the rest all believed in him as thoroughly as he did in himself. His wealth was undoubted, his accomplishments were rated at his own advertisement, and his magnanimous condescension was esteemed at full value. Really handsome, good-natured and sociable, he delighted to instruct his worshippers by his maxims, and to bend graciously to their homage. The young ladies had but one cynosure! Few eyes were there that did not pursue his every movement, few hearts that did not bound at his approach, few tongues that did not chronicle his daily comings and goings.

'It would save much trouble,' said Albinia, 'if a court circular could be put into the Bayford paper.'

The Kendals were the only persons whom Algernon regarded as in any way on a footing with him. Finding that the lady was a Ferrars, and had been in Italy, he regarded her as fit company, and whenever they met, favoured her with the chief and choicest of his maxims, little knowing how she and his aunt presumed to discuss him in private.

Without being ill-disposed, he had been exceedingly ill taught; his mother, the child of a grasping vulgar father, had little religious impression, and that little had not been fostered by the lax habits of a self-expatriated Englishwoman, and very soon after his arrival at Bayford his disregard of ordinary English proprieties had made itself apparent. On the first Sunday he went to church in the morning, but spent the evening in pacing the garden with a cigar; and on the afternoon of that day week his aunt was startled by the sound of horse's hoofs on the road. Mr. Dusautoy was at school, and she started up, met the young gentleman, and asked him what strange mistake could have been made. He made her a slight bow, and loftily said he was always accustomed to ride at that hour! 'But not on Sunday!' she exclaimed. He was not aware of any objection. She told him his uncle would be much displeased, he replied politely that he would account to his uncle for his conduct, begged her pardon, but he could not keep his horse waiting.

Mrs. Dusautoy went back, fairly cried at the thought of her husband's vexation, and the scandal to the whole town.

The Vicar was, of course, intensely annoyed, though he still could make excuses for the poor boy, and laid all to the score of ignorance and foreign education. He made Algernon clearly understand that the Sunday ride must not be repeated. Algernon mumbled something about compromising his uncle and offending English prejudices, by which he reserved to himself the belief that he yielded out of magnanimity, not because he could not help it; but he could not forgive his aunt for her peremptory opposition; he became unpleasantly sullen and morose as regularly as the Sunday came round, and revenged himself by pacing the verandah with his cigar, or practising anything but sacred music on his key-bugle in his painting-room.

The youth was really fond of his uncle, but he had imbibed all his mother's contempt for her sister-in-law. Used to be wheedled by an idolizing mother, and to reign over her court of parasites, he had no notion of obeying, and a direct command or opposition roused his sullen temper of passive resistance. When he found 'that little nobody of a Mrs. John Dusautoy' so far from being a flatterer, or an adorer of his perfections, inclined to laugh at him, and bent on keeping him in order, all the enmity of which he was capable arose in his mind, and though in general good-natured and not aggressive, he had a decided pleasure in doing what she disapproved, and thus asserting the dignity of a Greenaway Cavendish Dusautoy.

The atelier was a happy invention. Certainly wearisome noises, and an aroma of Havannahs would now and then proceed therefrom, but he was employed there the chief part of the day, and fortunately his pictures were of small size, and took an infinite quantity of labour, so that they could not speedily outrun all the Vicarage walls.

He favoured the University of Oxford by going up with Gilbert for matriculation, when, to the surprise of Mr. Hope, he was not plucked. They were to begin their residence at the Easter term. Mrs. Dusautoy did not confess even to Albinia how much she looked forward to Easter.

In early spring, a sudden and short illness took away Madame Belmarche's brave spirit to its rest, after sixty years of exile and poverty, cheerfully borne.

There had been no time to summon Genevieve, and her aunt would not send for her, but decided on breaking up the school, which could no longer be carried on, and going to live in the Hadminster convent. And thus, as Mr. Kendal hoped, all danger of renewed intercourse between his son and Genevieve ended. Gilbert looked pale and wretched, and Sophy hoped it was with compunction at having banished Genevieve at such a moment, but not a word was said—and that page of early romance was turned!

CHAPTER XVIII.

It was a beautiful July afternoon, the air musical with midsummer hum, the flowers basking in the sunshine, the turf cool and green in the shade, and the breeze redolent of indescribable freshness and sweetness compounded of all fragrant odours, the present legacy of a past day's shower. Like the flowers themselves, Albinia was feeling the delicious repose of refreshed nature, as in her pretty pink muslin, her white drapery folded round her, and her bright hair unbonnetted, she sat reclining in a low garden chair, at the door of the conservatory, a little pale, a little weak, but with a sweet happy languor, a soft tender bloom.

There was a step in the conservatory, and before she could turn round, her brother Maurice bent over her, and kissed her.

'Maurice! you have come after all!'

'Yes, the school inspection is put off. How are you?' as he sat down on the grass by her side.

'Oh, quite well! What a delicious afternoon we shall have! Edmund will be at home directly. Mrs. Meadows has absolutely let Gilbert take her to drink tea at the Drurys! Only I am sorry Sophy should miss you, for she was so good about going, because Lucy wanted to do something to her fernery. Of course you are come for Sunday, and the christening?'

'Yes,—that is, to throw myself on Dusautoy's mercy.'

'We will send Mr. Hope to Fairmead,' said Albinia, 'and see whether Winifred can make him speak. We can't spare the Vicar, for he is our godfather, and you must christen the little maiden.'

'I thought the three elder ones were to be sponsors.'

'Gilbert is shy,' said Albinia, 'afraid of the responsibility, and perhaps he is almost too near, the very next to ourselves. His father would have preferred Mr. Dusautoy from the first, and only yielded to my wish. I wish you had come two minutes sooner, she was being paraded under that wall, but now she is gone in asleep.'

'Her father writes grand things of her.'

'Does he?' said Albinia, colouring and smiling at what could not be heard too often; 'he is tolerably satisfied with the young woman! And he thinks her like Edmund, and so she must be, for she is just like him. She will have such beautiful eyes. It is very good of her to take after him, since Maurice won't!'

'And she is to be another Albinia.'

'I represented the confusion, and how I always meant my daughter to be Winifred, but there's no doing anything with him! It is only to be a second name. A. W. K.! Think if she should marry a Mr. Ward!'

'No, she would not be awkward, if she were so a-warded.'

'It wont spell, Maurice,' cried Albinia, laughing as their nonsense, as usual, rose to the surface, 'but how is Winifred?'

'As well as could be hoped under the affliction of not being able to come and keep you in order.'

'She fancied me according to the former pattern,' said Albinia, smiling, 'I could have shown her a better specimen, not that it was any merit, for there were no worries, and Edmund was so happy, that it was pleasure enough to watch him.'

'I was coming every day to judge for myself, but I thought things could not be very bad, while he wrote such flourishing accounts.'

'No, there were no more ponds!' said Albinia, 'and grandmamma happily was quite well, cured, I believe, by the excitement. Lucy took care of her, and Sophy read to me—how we have enjoyed those readings! Oh! and Aunt Gertrude has found a delightful situation for Genevieve, a barrister's family, with lots of little children—eighty pounds a year, and quite ready to value her, so she is off my mind.'

'Maurice, boy! come here,' she called, as she caught sight of a creature prancing astride on one stick, and waving another. On perceiving a visitor, the urchin came careering up, bouncing full tilt upon her, and clasping her round with both his stalwart arms. 'Gently, gently, boy,' she said, bending down, and looking with proud delight at her brother, as she held between her hands a face much like her own, as fair and freshly tinted, but with a peculiar squareness of contour, large blue eyes, with dark fringes, brimming over with mischief and fun, a bold, broad brow, and thick, light curls. There was a spring and vigour as of perpetual irrepressible life about the whole being, and the moment he had accepted his uncle's kiss, he poised his lance, and exclaimed, 'You are Bonaparte, I'm the Duke!'

'Indeed,' said Mr. Ferrars, at once seizing a wand, and bestriding the nearest bench. Two or three charges rendered the boy so uproarious, that presently he was ordered off, and to use the old apple tree as Bonaparte.

'What a stout fellow!' said Mr. Ferrars, as he went off at a plunging gallop, 'I should have taken him for at least five years old!'

'So he might be,' said Albinia, 'for strength and spirit—he is utterly fearless, and never cries, much as he knocks himself about! He will do anything but learn. The rogue! he once knew all his letters, but no sooner did he find they were the work of life, than he forgot every one, and was never so obstreperous as when called upon to say them. I gave up the point, but I foresee some fine scenes.'

'His minding no one but you is an old story. I hope at least the exception continues.'

'I have avoided testing it. I want all my forces for a decisive battle. I never heard of such a masterful imp,' she continued, with much more exultation than anxiety, 'his sisters have no chance with him, he rules them like a young Turk. There's the pony! Sophy will let him have it as a right, and it is the work of my life to see that she is not defrauded of her rides.'

'You don't mean that that child rides anything but a stick.'

'One would think he had been born in boots and spurs. Legitimately he only rides with some one leading the pony, but I have my suspicions that by some preternatural means he has been on the pony's back, and round the yard alone, and that papa prudentially concealed it from me!'

'I confess I should not like it,' said her brother gravely.

'Oh! I don't mind that kind of thing. A real boy can't be hurt, and I don't care how wild he runs, so long as he is obedient and truthful. And true I think he is to the backbone, and I know he is reverend. We had such a disturbance because he would not say his prayers.'

'Proof positive!'

'Yes, it was,' said Albinia. 'It did not seem to him orthodox without me, and when he was let into my room again, it was the prettiest sight! When he had been told of his little sister, all he said was that he did not want little girls —girls were stupid—'

'Ah! that came of your premature introduction to my Albinia,'

'Not at all. It was partly as William's own nephew, and partly because pleasure was expected from him. But when he actually saw the little thing, that sturdy face grew so very soft and sweet, and when we told him he was her protector, he put both his hands tight together, and said, "I'll be so good!" When he is with her, another child seems to shine out under the bluff pickle he generally is—he walks so quietly, and thinks it such an honour to touch her.'

'She will be his best tutor,' said Maurice, smiling, but breaking off—

A sudden shriek of deadly terror rang out over the garden from the river! A second or two sufficed to show them Lucy at the other end of the foot-bridge, that led across the canal to the towing-path. She did not look round, till Albinia, clutching her, demanded, 'Where is he?'

Unable to speak, Lucy pointed down the towing-path, along which a horse was seen rushing wildly—a figure pursuing it. 'It was hitched up here—he must have scrambled up by the gate! Oh! mamma! mamma! He has run after him, but oh!'

Mr. Ferrars gave Lucy's arm a squeeze, a hint not to augment the horror. Something he said of 'Let me—and you had better—' but Albinia heard nothing, and was only bent on pressing forward.

The canal and path took a wide sweep round the meadow, and the horse was still in sight, galloping at full speed, with a small heap on its back, as they trusted, but the rapid motion, and their eyes strained and misty with alarm, caused an agony of uncertainty.

Albinia pointed across the meadows in anguish at not being able to make herself understood, and hoarsely said, 'The gate!'

Mr. Ferrars caught her meaning, and the next moment had leaped over the gutter, and splashed into the water meadow, but in utter hopelessness of being beforehand with the runaway steed! How could that gate be other than fatal? The horse was nearing it—the pursuer far behind—Mr. Ferrars not half way over the fields.

There was a loud cry from Lucy.—'He is caught! caught!'

A loud shout came back, was caught up, and sent on by both the pursuers, 'All right!'

Albinia had stood in an almost annihilation of conscious feeling. Even when her brother strode back to her repeating 'All safe, thanks be to God,' she neither spoke nor relaxed that intensity of watching. A few seconds more, and she sprang forward again as the horse was led up by a young man at his side; and on his back, laughing and chattering, sat Master Maurice. Algernon Dusautoy strode a few steps behind, somewhat aggrieved, but that no one saw.

The elder Maurice lifted down the younger one, who, as he was clasped by his mother, exclaimed, 'Oh! mamma, Bamfylde went so fast! I am to ride home again! He said so—he's my cousin!'

Albinia scarcely heard; her brother however had turned to thank the stranger for her, and exclaimed, 'I should say you were an O'More.'

'I'm Ulick, from the Loughside Lodge,' was the answer. 'Is cousin Winifred here?'

'No, this is my sister, Mrs. Kendal, but—'

Albinia held out her hand, and grasped his; 'I can't—Maurice, speak,' she said.

The little Maurice persisted in his demand to be remounted for the twelve yards to their own gate, but nobody heard him; his uncle was saying a few words of explanation to the stranger, and Algernon Dusautoy was enunciating something intended as a gracious reception of the apologies which no one was making. All Albinia thought of was that the little unruly hand was warm and struggling, prisoned in her own; all her brother cared for was to have her safely at home. He led her across the bridge, and into the garden, where they met Mr. Kendal, who had taken alarm from her absence; Lucy ran up with her story, and almost at the same moment, Albinia, springing to him, murmured, 'Oh! Edmund, the great mercy—Maurice;' but there she found herself making a hoarse shriek; with a mingled sense of fright and shame, she smothered it, but there was an agony of suffocation, she felt her husband's arms round her, heard his voice, and her boy's scream of terror—felt them all unable to help her, and sank into unconsciousness.

Mr. Ferrars helped Mr. Kendal to carry his wife's inanimate form to her room. They used all means of restoration, but it was a long, heavy swoon, and a slow, painful revival. Mr. Kendal would have been in utter despair at hearing that the doctor was out, but for his brother, with his ready resources and cheerful encouragement; and finally, she lifted her eyelids, and as she felt the presence of her two dearest guardians, whispered, 'Where is he?'

Lucy reported that he was with Susan, and Albinia, after hearing her husband again assure her that he was quite safe, lay still from exhaustion, but so calm, that her brother thought them best alone, and drew Lucy away.

In about a quarter of an hour Mr. Kendal came down, saying that she was quietly asleep, and he had left the nurse with her. He had yet to hear the story, and when he understood that the child had been madly careering along the towing-path, on the back of young Dusautoy's most spirited hunter, and had been only stopped when the horse was just about to leap the tall gate, he was completely overcome. When he spoke again, it was with the abrupt exclamation, 'That child! Lucy, bring him down!'

In marched the boy, full of life and mischief, though with a large red spot beneath each eye.

'Maurice!' Gilbert had often heard that tone, but Maurice never, and he tossed back his head with an innocent look of fearless wonder. 'Maurice, I find you have been a very naughty, disobedient boy. When you rode the pony round the yard, did not I order you never to do so again?'

'I did not do it again,' boldly rejoined Maurice.

'Speak the truth, sir. What do you mean by denying what you have done?' exclaimed his father, angrily.

'I didn't ride the pony,' indignantly cried the child, 'I rode a horse, saddled and bridled!'

'Don't answer me in that way!' thundered Mr. Kendal, and much incensed by the nice distinction, and not appreciating the sincerity of it, he gave the child a shake, rough enough to bring the red into his face, but not a tear. 'You knew it was very wrong, and you were as near as possible breaking your neck. You have frightened your mamma, so as to make her very ill, and I am sorry to find you most mischievous and unruly, not to be trusted out of sight. Now, listen to me, I shall punish you very severely if you act in this disobedient way again.'

Papa angry, was a novel spectacle, at which Maurice looked as innocently and steadily as ever, so completely without fear or contrition, that he provoked a stern, 'Do you hear me, sir?' and another shake. Maurice flushed, and his chest heaved, though he did not sob, and his father, uncomfortable at such sharp dealing with so young a child, set him aside, with the words, 'There now, recollect what I have told you!' and walked to the window, where he stood silent for some seconds, while the boy stood with rounded shoulders, perplexed eye, and finger on his pouting lip, and Mr. Ferrars, newspaper in hand, watched him under his eyelids, and speculated what would be the best sort of mediation, or whether the young gentleman yet deserved it. He knew that his own Willie would have been a mere quaking, sobbing mass of terror, under such a shake, and he would like to have been sure whether that sturdy silence were obstinacy or fortitude.

The sound of the door-bell made Mr. Kendal turn round, and laying his hand on the little fellow's fair head, he said, 'There, Maurice, we'll say no more about it if you will be a good boy. Run away now, but don't go into your mamma's room.'

Maurice looked up, tossed his curls out of his eyes, shook himself, felt the place on his arm where the grip of the hand had been, and galloped off like the young colt that he was.

Albinia awoke, refreshed, though still shaken and feeble, and surprised to find that dinner was going on downstairs. Her own meal presently put such new force into her, that she felt able to speak Maurice's name without bursting into tears, and longing to see both her little ones beside her, she told the nurse to fetch the boy, but received for answer, 'No, Master Maurice said he would not come,' and the manner conveyed that it had been defiantly said. Master Maurice was no favourite in the nursery, and he was still less so, when his mamma, disregarding all mandates, set out to seek him. Already she heard from the stairs the wrangling with Susan that accompanied all his toilettes, and she found him the picture of firm, solid fairness, in his little robe de nuit, growling through the combing of his tangled locks. Though ordinarily scornful of caresses, he sprang to her and hugged her, as she sat down on a low chair, and he knelt in her lap, whispering with his head on her shoulder, and his arms round her neck, 'Mamma, were you dead?'

'No, Maurice,' she answered with something of a sob, 'or I should not have my dear, dear little boy throttling me now! But why would you not come down to me?'

'Papa said I must not.'

Oh, that was quite right, my boy;' and though she unclasped the tight arms, she drew him nestling into her bosom. 'Oh, Maurice, it has been a terrible day! Does my little boy know how good the great God has been to him, and how near he was never seeing mamma nor his little sister again.'

Her great object was to make him thankful for his preservation, but with a child, knowing nothing of death and heedless of fear, this was very difficult. The rapid motion had been delightful excitement, or if there had been any alarm, it was forgotten in the triumph. She had to change her note, and represent how the poor horse might have run into the river, or against a post! Maurice looked serious, and then she came to the high moral tone—mounting strangers' horses without leave—would papa, would Gilbert, think of such a thing? The full lip was put out, as though under conviction, and he hung his head. 'You wont do it again?' said she.

'No.'

She told him to say his prayers, guiding the confession and thanksgiving that she feared he did not fully follow. As he rose up, and saw the tears on her cheeks, he whispered, 'Mamma, did it make you *so*?'

Cause and effect were a great puzzle to him, but that swoon was the only thing that brought home to him that he had been guilty of something enormous, and when she owned that his danger had been the occasion, he stood and looked; then, standing bolt upright, with clasped hands, and rosy feet pressed close together, he said, with a long breath, 'I'll never get on Bamfylde again till I'm a big boy.'

As he spoke, Mr. Kendal pushed open the half-closed door, and Albinia, looking up, said, 'Here's a boy who knows he has done wrong, papa.'

Never was more welcome excuse for lifting the gallant child to his breast, and lavishing caresses that would have been tender but for the strong spirit of riot which turned them into a game at romps, cut short by Mr. Kendal, as soon as the noise grew very outrageous. 'That's enough to-night; good night.' And when they each had kissed the monkey face tossing about among the clothes, Maurice might have heard more pride than pain in the 'I never saw such a boy!' with which they shut the door.

'This is not prudent!' said Mr. Kendal.

'Do you think I could have rested till I had seen him? and he said you had told him not to come down.'

'I would have brought him to you. You are looking very ill; you had better go to bed at once.'

'No, I should not sleep. Pray let me grow quiet first. Now you know you trust Maurice,—old Maurice, and I'll lie on the sofa like any mouse, if you'll bring him up and let him talk. You know it will be an interesting novelty for you to talk, and me to listen! and he has not seen the baby.'

Albinia gained her point, but Mr. Kendal and Lucy first tucked her up upon the sofa, till she cried out, 'You have swathed me hand and foot. How am I to show off that little Awk?'

'I'll take care of that,' said Mr. Kendal; and so he did, fully doing the honours of the little daughter, who had already fastened on his heart.

'But,' cried Albinia, breaking into the midst, 'who or what are we, ungrateful monsters, never to have thought of the man who caught that dreadful horse!'

'You shall see him as soon as you are strong enough,' said Mr. Kendal; 'your brother and I have been with him.'

'Oh, I am glad; I could not rest if he had not been thanked. And can anything be done for him? What is he? I thought he was a gentleman.'

Maurice smiled, and Mr. Kendal answered, 'Yes, he is Mr. Goldsmith's nephew, and I am pleased to find that he is a connexion of your brother.'

'One of the O'Mores,' cried Albinia. 'Oh, Maurice, is it really one of Winifred's O'Mores?'

'Even so,' replied Mr. Ferrars; the very last person I should have expected to meet on the banks of the Baye! It was that clever son of the captain's for whose education Mr. Goldsmith paid, and it seems had sent for, to consider of his future destination. He only arrived yesterday.'

'A very fine young man,' said Mr. Kendal. 'I was particularly pleased with his manner, and it was an act of great presence of mind and dexterity.'

'It is all a maze and mystery to me,' said Albinia; 'do tell me all about it. I can't make out how the horse came there.'

'I understood that young Dusautoy was calling here,' said Mr. Kendal; 'I wondered at even his coolness in coming in by that way, and at your letting him in.'

'I saw nothing of him,' said Albinia. 'Perhaps he was looking for Gilbert.'

'No,' said Lucy, looking up from her work, with a slight blush, and demure voice of secret importance; 'he had only stepped in for a minute, to bring me a new fern.'

'Indeed,' said her father; 'I was not aware that he took interest in your fernery.'

'He knows everything about ferns,' said Lucy. 'Mrs. Cavendish Dusautoy once had a conservatory filled with the rarest specimens, and he has given me a great many directions how to manage them.'

'Oh! if he could get you to listen to his maxims, I don't wonder at anything,' exclaimed Albinia.

'He had only just come in with the Adiantium, and was telling me how hydraulic power directed a stream of water near the roots among his mother's Fuci,' said Lucy, rather hurt. 'He had fastened up his horse quite securely, and nobody could have guessed that Maurice could have opened that gate to cross the bridge, far less have climbed up the rail to the horse's back. I never shall forget my fright, when we heard the creature's feet, and Mr. Cavendish Dusautoy began to run after it directly.'

'As foolish a thing as he could have done,' said Mr. Kendal, not impressed with Mr. Cavendish Dusautoy's condescension in giving chase. 'It was well poor little Maurice was not abandoned to your discretion, and his resources.'

'It seems,' continued Mr. Ferrars, 'that young O'More was taking a walk on the towing-path, and was just so far off as to see, without being able to prevent it, this little monkey scramble from the gate upon the horse's neck. How it was that he did not go down between, I can't guess; the beast gave a violent start, as well it might, jerked the reins loose, and set off full gallop. Seeing the child clinging on like a young panther, he dashed across the meadow, to cut him off at the turn of the river; and it was a great feat of swiftness, I assure you, to run so lightly through those marshy meadows, so as to get the start of the runaway; then he crept up under cover of the hedge, so as not to startle the horse, and had hold of the bridle, just as he paused before leaping the gate! He said he could hardly believe his eyes when he saw the urchin safe, and looking more excited than terrified.'

'Yes, he was exceedingly struck with Maurice's spirit,' said Mr. Kendal, who, when the fright and anger were over, could begin to be proud of the exploit.

'They fraternized at once,' said Mr. Ferrars. 'Maurice imparted that his name was Maurice Ferrars Kendal, and Ulick, in all good faith and Irish simplicity, discovered that they were cousins!'

'Oh! Edmund, he must come to the christening dinner!'

'Mind,' said Maurice, 'you, know he is not even my wife's cousin; only nephew to her second cousin's husband.'

'For shame, Maurice, cousin is that cousinly does!'

'Very well, only don't tell the aunts that Winifred saddled all the O'Mores upon you.'

'Not an O'More but should be welcome for his sake!'

'Nor an Irishman,' said Mr. Ferrars.

Albinia suffered so much from the shock, that she could not make her appearance till noon on the following day. Then, after sitting a little while in the old study, to hear that grandmamma had not been able to sleep all night for thinking of Maurice's danger, and being told some terrible stories of accidents with horses, she felt one duty done, and moved on to the drawing- room in search of her brother.

She found herself breaking upon a tete-a-tete. A sweet, full voice, with strong cadences, was saying something about duty and advice, and she would have retreated, but her brother and the stranger both sprang up, and made her understand that she was by no means to go away. No introduction was wanted; she grasped the hand that was extended to her, and would have said something if she could, but she found herself not strong enough to keep from tears, and only said, 'I wish little Maurice were not gone out with his brother, but you will dine with us, and see him to-morrow.'

'With the greatest pleasure, if my uncle and aunt will spare me.'

'They must,' said Albinia, 'you must come to meet your old friend and *cousin*,' she added, mischievously glancing at Maurice, but he did not look inclined to disavow the relationship, and the youth was not a person whom any one would wish to keep at a distance. He seemed about nineteen or twenty years of age, not tall, but well made, and with an air of great ease and agility, rather lounging and careless, yet alert in a moment. The cast of his features at once betrayed his country, by the rounded temples, with the free wavy hair; the circular form of the eyebrow; the fully opened dark blue eye, looking almost black when shaded; the short nose, and the well-cut chin and lips, with their outlines of sweetness and of fun, all thoroughly Irish, but of the best style, and with a good deal of thought and mind on the brow, and determination in the mouth. Albinia had scarcely a minute, however, for observation, for he seemed agitated, and in haste to take leave, nor did her brother press him to remain, since she was still looking very white and red, and too fragile for anything but rest. With another squeeze of the hand she let him go, while he, with murmured thanks, and head bent in enthusiastic honour to the warm kindness of one so sweet and graceful, took leave. Mr. Ferrars followed him into the hall, leaving the door open, so that she heard the words, 'Good-bye, Ulick; I'll do my best for you. All I can say is, that I respect you.'

'Don't respect me too soon,' he answered; 'maybe you'll have to change your mind. The situation may like me no better than I the situation.'

'No, what you will, you can do; I trust to your perseverance.'

'As my poor mother does! Well, with patience the snail got to Rome, and if it is to lighten her load, I must bear it. Many thanks, Mr. Ferrars. Good morning.'

'Good morning; only, Ulick, excuse me, but let me give you a hint; if the situation is to like you, you must mind your Irish.'

'Then you must not warm my heart with your kindness,' was the answer. 'No, no, never fear, when I'm not with any one who has seen Ballymakilty, I can speak English so that I could not be known for a Galway man. Not that I'm ashamed of my country,' he added; and the next moment the door shut behind him.

'How could you scold him for his Irish?' exclaimed Albinia, as her brother re-entered; 'it sounds so pretty and characteristic.'

'I fear Mr. Goldsmith may think it too characteristic!'

'I am sure Edmund might well call him prepossessing. I hope Mr. Goldsmith is going to do something handsome for him!'

'Poor lad! Mr. Goldsmith considers that he has purchased him for a permanent fixture on a high stool. It is a sad disappointment, for he had been doing his utmost to prepare himself for college, and he has so far distinguished himself at school, that I see that a very little help would soon enable him to maintain himself at the University. I could have found it in my heart to give it to him myself; it would please Winifred.'

'Oh, let us help; I am sure Edmund would be glad.'

'No, no, this is better for all. Remember this is the Goldsmith's only measure of conciliation towards their sister since her marriage, and it ought not to be interfered with. Poor Ulick says he knows this is the readiest chance of being of any use to his family, and that his mother has often said she should be happy if she could but see one of the six launched in a way to be independent! There are those three eldest, little better than squireens, never doing a thing but loafing about with their guns. I used to long for a horse- whip to lay about them, till they spoke to me, and then not one of the rogues but won my heart with his fun and good-nature.'

'Then I suppose it is a great thing to have one in the way of money- making.'

'Hem! The Celtic blood is all in commotion! This boy's business was to ask my candid opinion whether there were anything ungentlemanlike in a clerkship in a bank. It was well it was not you!'

'Now, Maurice, don't you know how glad I should have been if Gilbert would have been as wise!'

'Yes, you have some common sense after all, which is more than Ulick attributes to his kith and kin. When I had proved the respectability of banking to his conviction, I'll not say satisfaction, he made me promise to write to his father. He is making up his mind to what is not only a great vexation to himself, and very irksome employment, but he knows he shall be looked down upon as having lost caste with all his family!'

'It really is heroism!' cried Albinia.

'It is,' said Mr. Ferrars; 'he does not trust himself to face the clan, and means to get into harness at once, so as to clench his resolution, and relieve his parents from his maintenance immediately.'

'Is he to live with that formal Miss Goldsmith?'

'No. In solitary lodgings, after that noisy family and easy home! I can't think how he will stand it. I should not wonder if the Galwegian was too strong after all.'

'We must do all we can for him,' cried Albinia; 'Edmund likes him already. Can't he dine with us every Sunday?'

'I know you will be kind,' said Mr. Ferrars. 'Only see how things turn out before you commit yourself. Ah! I have said the unlucky word which always makes you fly off!'

There was little fear that Ulick O'More would not win his way with Mr. and Mrs. Kendal, recommended as he was, and with considerable attractions in the frankness and brightness of his manner. He was a very pleasant addition to the party who dined at Willow Lawn, after the christening. No one had time to listen to Mr. Cavendish Dusautoy's maxims, and he retired rather sullenly, to lean against the mantelpiece, and marvel why the Kendals should invite an Irish banker's clerk to meet *him*. Gilbert likewise commented on the guest with a muttered observation on his sisters' taste; 'Last year it was all the Polysyllable, now it would be all the Irishman!'

CHAPTER XIX.

There was a war of supremacy in the Kendal household. Albinia and her son were Greek to Greek, and if physical force were on her side, her own tenderness was against her. As to allies, Maurice had by far the majority of the household; the much-tormented Susan was her mistress's sole supporter; Mr. Kendal and Sophy might own it inexpedient to foster his outrecuidance, but they so loved to do his bidding, so hated to thwart him, and so grieved at his being punished, that they were little better than Gilbert, Lucy, grandmamma, or any of the maids or men.

The moral sense was not yet stirred, and the boy seemed to be trying the force of his will like the strength of his limbs. Even as he delighted to lift a weight the moment he saw that it was heavy, so a command was to him a challenge to see how much he would undergo rather than obey, but his resistance was so open, gay, and free, that it could hardly be called obstinacy, and he gloried in disappointing punishment. The dark closet lost all terror for him; he stood there blowing the horn through his hand, content to follow an imaginary chase, and when untimely sent to bed, he stole Susan's scissors, and cut a range of stables in the sheets. The short, sharp infliction of pain answered best, but his father, though he could give a shake when angry, could *not* strike when cool, and Albinia was forced to turn executioner, though with such tears and trembling that her culprit looked up reassuringly, saying, 'Never mind, mamma, I shan't!' He did, however, *mind* her tears, they bore in upon him the sense of guilt; and after each transgression, he could not be at peace till he had marched up to her, holding out his hand for the blow, and making up his face not to wince, and then would cling round her neck to feel himself pardoned. Justice came to him in a most fair and motherly shape! The brightest, the merriest of all his playmates was mamma; he loved her passionately, and could endure no cloud between himself and her, so that he was slowly learning that submission to her was peace and pleasure, and rebellion mere pain to both. She established ten minutes of daily lessons, but even she could not reach beyond the capture of his restless person, his mind was out of reach, and keen as he was in everything else, towards "a + b = ab" he was an unmitigated dunce. Nor did he obey any one who did not use authority and force of will, and though perfectly simple and sincere, he was too young to restrain himself without the assistance of the controlling power, so that in his mother's absence he was tyrannical and violent, and she never liked to have him out of her sight, and never was so sure that he was deep in mischief as when she had not heard his voice for a quarter of an hour.

'Albinia,' said Mr. Kendal, one relenting autumn day, when November strove to look like April, 'I thought of walking to pay Farmer Graves for the corn. Will you come with me?'

'Delightful, I want to see what Maurice will say to the turkey-cock.'

'Is it not too far for him?'

'He would run quite as many miles in the garden,' said Albinia, who would have walked in dread of a court of justice on her return, had not the scarlet hose been safely prancing on the road before her.

'This way, then,' said Mr. Kendal; 'I must get this draft changed at the bank. Come, Maurice, you will see a friend there.'

'Do you know, Edmund,' said Albinia, as they set forth, 'my conscience smites me as to that youth; I think we have neglected him.'

'I cannot see what more we could have done. If his uncle does not bring him forward in society, we cannot interfere.'

'It must be a forlorn condition,' said Albinia; 'he is above the other clerks, and he seems to be voted below the Bayford Elite, since the Polysyllable has made it so very refined! One never meets him anywhere now it is too dark to walk after the banking hours. Cannot we ask him to come in some evening?'

'We cannot have our evenings broken up,' said Mr. Kendal. 'I should be glad to show him any kindness, but his uncle seems to have ruled it that he is to be considered more as his clerk than as one of his family, and I doubt if it would be doing him any service to interfere.'

They were now at the respectable old freestone building, with 'Goldsmith' inscribed on the iron window-blinds, and a venerable date carved over the door. Inside, those blinds came high, and let in but little light over the tall desks, at which were placed the black-horsehair perches of the clerks, old Mr. Goldsmith himself occupying a lower throne, more accessible to the clients. One of the high stools stood empty, and Albinia making inquiry, Mr. Goldsmith answered, with a dry, dissatisfied cough, that More, as he called him, had struck work, and gone home with a headache.

'Indeed,' said Albinia, 'I am sorry to hear it. Mr. Hope said he thought him not looking well.'

'He has complained of headache a good deal lately,' said Mr. Goldsmith. 'Young men don't find it easy to settle to business.'

Albinia's heart smote her for not having thought more of her son's rescuer, and she revolved what could or what might have been done. It really was not easy to show him attention, considering Gilbert's prejudice against his accent, and Mr. Kendal's dislike to an interrupted evening, and all she could devise was a future call on Miss Goldsmith. But for Maurice, it would have been a silent walk, and though her mind was a little diverted by his gallant attempt to bestride the largest pig in the farm-yard, she was sure Mr. Kendal was musing on the same topic, and was not surprised when, as they returned, he exclaimed, 'I have a great mind to go and see after that poor lad.'

'This way, then,' said Albinia, turning down a narrow muddy street parallel with the river.

'Impossible!' said Mr. Kendal; 'he can never live at the Wharves?'

'Yes,' said Albinia; 'he told me that he lodged with an old servant of the Goldsmiths, Pratt's wife, at the Lower Wharf.'

She pointed to the name of Pratt over a shop-window in a house that had once seen better days, but which looked so forlorn, that Mr. Kendal would not look the slatternly maid in the face while so absurd a question was asked as whether Mr. O'More lived there.

The girl, without further ceremony, took them up a dark stair, and opened the door of a twilight room, where Albinia's first glimpse showed her the young man with his head bent down on his arms on the table, as close as possible to the forlorn, black fire, of the grim, dull, sulky coal of the county, which had filled the room with smoke and blacks. The window, opened to clear it, only admitted the sickly scent of decaying weed from the river to compete with the perfume of the cobbler's stock-in-trade. Ulick started up pale and astonished, and Mr. Kendal, struck with consternation, chiefly thought of taking away his wife and child from the infected atmosphere, and made signs to Albinia not to sit down; but she was eagerly compassionate.

'It was nothing,' said Ulick, 'only his head was rather worse than usual, and he thought it time to give in when the threes put lapwings' feathers in their caps just like the fives.'

'Are you subject to these headaches?'

'It is only home-sickness,' he said. 'I'll have got over it soon.'

'I must come and see after you, my good friend,' said Mr. Kendal, with suppressed impatience and anxiety. 'I shall return in a moment or two, but I am sure you are not well enough for so many visitors taking you by surprise. Come.'

He was so peremptory, that Albinia found herself on the staircase before she knew what she was about. The fever panic had seized Mr. Kendal in full force; he believed typhus was in the air, and insisted on her taking Maurice home at once, while he went himself to fetch Mr. Bowles. She did not in the least credit fever to be in the chill touch of that lizard hand, and believed that she could have been the best doctor; but there was no arguing while he was under this alarm, and she knew that she might be thankful not to be ordered to observe a quarantine.

When Mr. Kendal returned home he looked much discomposed, though his first words were, 'Thank Heaven, it is no fever! Albinia, we must look after that poor lad; he is positively poisoned by that pestiferous river and bad living! Bowles said he was sure he was not eating meat enough. I dare say that greasy woman gives him nothing fit to eat! Albinia, you must talk to him —find out whether old Goldsmith gives him a decent salary!'

'He ought not to be in those lodgings another day. I suppose Miss Goldsmith had no notion what they were. I fancy she never saw the Lower Wharf in her life.'

'I never did till to-day,' said Mr. Kendal. 'It was all of a piece—the whole street—the room—the furniture—why the paper was coming off the walls! What could they be dreaming of! And there he was, trying to read a little edition of Prodentius, printed at Salamanca, which he picked up at a bookstall at Galway. It must have belonged to some priest educated in Spain. He says any Latin book was invaluable to him. He is infinitely too good for his situation, and the Goldsmiths are neglecting him infamously. Look out some rooms fit for him, Albinia.'

'I will try. Let me see—if I could only recollect any; but Mr. Hope has the only really nice ones in the place.'

'Somewhere he must be, if it is in this house.'

'There is poor old Madame Belmarche's still empty, with Bridget keeping it. I wish he could have rooms there.'

'Well, why not? Pettilove told me it must be let as two tenements. If the old woman could take half, a lodger would pay her rent,' said Mr. Kendal, promptly. 'You had better propose it.'

'And the Goldsmiths?' asked Albinia.

'I will show him the Lower Wharf.'

The next afternoon Mr. Kendal desired his wife to go to the Bank and borrow young O'More for her walking companion.

'Really I don't know whether I have the impudence.'

'I will come and do it for you. You will do best alone with the lad; I want you to get into his confidence, and find out whether old Goldsmith treats him properly. I declare, but that I know John Kendal so well, this would be enough to make me rejoice that Gilbert is not thrown on the world!'

Albinia knew herself to be so tactless, that she saw little hope other doing anything but setting him against his relations; but her husband was in no frame to hear objections, so she made none, and only trusted she should not be very foolish. At least, the walk would be a positive physical benefit to the slave of the desk.

Ulick O'More was at his post, and said his head was well, but his hair stuck up as if his fingers had been many times run through it; he was much thinner, and the wearied countenance, whitened complexion, and spiritless sunken eyes, were a sad contrast to the glowing freshness and life that had distinguished him in the summer.

Mr. Kendal told the Banker that it had been decided that his nephew needed exercise, and that Mrs. Kendal would be glad of his company in a long walk. Mr. Goldsmith seemed rather surprised, but consented, whereupon the young clerk lighted up into animation, and bounded out of his prison house, with a springy step learnt upon mountain heather. Mr. Kendal only waited to hear whither they were bound.

'Oh! as far as we can go on the Woodside road,' said Albinia. 'I think the prescription I used to inflict on poor Sophy will not be thrown away here. I always fancy there is a whiff of sea air upon the hill there.'

Ulick smiled at such a fond delusion, bred up as he had been upon the wildest sea-coast, exposed to the full sweep of the Atlantic storm! She set him off upon his own scenery, to the destruction of his laborious English, as he dwelt on the glories of his beloved rocks rent by fierce sea winds and waves into fantastic, grotesque, or lovely shapes, with fiords of exquisite blue sea between, the variety of which had been to him as the gentle foliage of tamer countries. Not a tree stood near the 'town' of Ballymakilty, but the wild crags, the sparkling waters, the broad open hills, and the bogs, with their intensely purple horizon, held fast upon his heart; and he told of white sands, reported to be haunted by mermaids, and crevices of rock where the tide roared, and gave rise to legends of sea monsters, and giants turned to stone. He was becoming confidential and intimate when, in a lowered voice, he mentioned the Banshee's crag, where the shrouded messenger of doom never failed to bewail each dying child of the O'More, and where his own old nurse had actually beheld her keening for the uncle who was killed among the Caffres. Albinia began to know how she ought to respect the O'Mores.

They were skirting the side of the hill, with a dip of green meadow-land below them, rising on the other side into coppices. The twang of the horn, and the babbling cry of the hounds, reminded Albinia that the hunting season had begun, and looking over a gate, she watched the parti-coloured forms of the dogs glancing among the brushwood opposite, and an occasional red coat gleaming out through the hedge above. Just then the cry ceased, the dogs became silent, and scattered hither and thither bewildered. Ulick looked eagerly, then suddenly vaulted over the gate, went forward a few steps, looked again, pointed towards some dark object which she could barely discern, put his finger in his ear, and uttered an unearthly screech, incomprehensible to her, but well understood by the huntsman, and through him by the dogs, which at once simultaneously dashed in one direction, and came pouring into the meadow over towards him, down went their heads, up went their curved tails, the clatter and rushing of hoofs, and the apparition of red coats, showed the hunters all going round the copse, while at the same moment, away with winged steps bounded her companion, flying headlong like the wind, so as to meet the hunt.

laughed Albinia to herself. 'Well done, speed! Edmund might be satisfied there's not much amiss! Through the hedge—over the meadow—a flying leap over the stream—it is more like a bird than a man—up again. Does he mean to follow the hunt all the rest of the way? Rather Irish, I must say! And I do believe they will all come down this lane! I must walk on; it wont do to be overtaken here between these high hedges. Ah! I thought he was too much of a gentleman to leave me—here he comes. How much in his way I must be! I never saw such a runner; not a bit does he slacken for the hill—and what bright cheeks and eyes! What good it must have done him!'

'I beg ten thousand pardons!' cried he, as he came up, scarcely out of breath. 'I declare I forgot you, I could not help it, when I saw them at a check!'

'You feel for the hunter as I do for the fox,' said Albinia. 'Is yours one of the great hunting neighbourhoods?'

'That it is!' he cried. 'My grandfather had the grand stud! He and his seven sons were out three times in the week, and there was a mount for whoever wanted it!'

'And this generation is not behind the last?'

'Ah! and why would it be?' exclaimed the boy, the last remnant of English pronunciation forsaking him. 'My Uncle Connel has the best mare on this side the bridge of Athlone! I mean that side.'

'And how is it with you?' asked Albinia.

'We've got no horses—that is, except my father's mare, and the colt, and Fir Darrig—the swish-tailed pony—and the blind donkey that brings in the turf. So we younger ones mostly go hunting on foot; and after all I believe that's the best sport. Bryan always comes in before any of the horses, and we all think it a shame if we don't!'

'I see where you learnt the swiftness of foot that was so useful last July,' said Albinia.

'That? oh! but Bryan would have been up long before me,' said Ulick. 'He'd have made for the lock, not the gate! You should see what sport we have when the fox takes to the Corrig Dearg up among the rocks—and little Rosie upon Fir Darrig, with her hair upon the wind, and her colour like the morning cloud, glancing in and out among the rocks like the fairy of the glen. There are those that think her the best part of the hunt; they say the English officers at Ochlochtimore would never think it worth coming out but for her. I don't believe that, you know,' he added, laughing, 'though I like to fetch a rise out of Ulick at the great house by telling him of it.'

'How old is she?'

'Fifteen last April, and she is like an April wind, when it comes warm and frolicking over the sea! So wild and free, and yet so gentle and soft! Ellen and Mary are grave and steady, and work hard—every stitch of my stockings was poor Mary's knitting, except what poor old Peggy would send up for a compliment; but Rosie—I don't think she does a thing but sing, and ride, and row the boat, and keep the house alive! My mother shakes her head, but I don't know what she'll say when she gets my aunt's letter. My Aunt Goldsmith purses up her lips, and says, "I'll write to advise my sister to send her daughters to some good school." Ellen, maybe, might bear one, but ah! the thought of little Rosie in a good school!'

'Like her brother Ulick in a good bank, eh?'

'Why,' he cried, 'they always called me the steady Englishman!'

Albinia laughed, but at that moment the sounds of the hunt again occupied them, and all were interpreted by Ulick with the keenest interest, but he would not run away again, though she exhorted him not to regard her. Presently it swept on out of hearing, and by-and-bye they reached the summit of the hill, and looked forth on the dark pine plantations on the opposite undulation, standing out in black relief against a sky golden with a pale, pure, pearly November sunset, a 'daffodil sky' flecked with tiny fleeces of soft bright-yellow light, reminding Albinia of Fouque's beautiful dream of Aslauga's golden hair showing the gates of Heaven to her devoted knight. She looked for her companion's sympathy in her admiration, but the woods seemed to oppress him, and his panting sigh showed how real a thing was *he-men.*

'Oh! my poor sun!' he broke out, 'I pity you for having to go down before your time into these black, stifling woods that rise up to smother you like giants—and not into your own broad, cool Atlantic, laughing up your own sparkles of light.'

'We inland people can hardly appreciate your longing for space.'

'It's a very prison,' said Ulick; 'the horizon is choked all round, and one can't breathe in these staid stiff hedges and enclosures!' And he threw out his arms and flapped them over his breast with a gesture of constraint.

'You seem no friend to cultivation.'

'Why, your meadows would be pretty things if they were a little greener,' said Ulick; 'but one gets tired of them, and of those straight lines of ploughed field. There's no sense of liberty; it is like the man whose prison walls closed in upon him!' And he gave another weary sigh, his step lost elasticity, and he moved on heavily.

'You are tired; I have brought you too far.'

'Tired by a bit of a step like this?' cried the boy, disdainfully, as he straightened himself, and resumed his brisk tread. But it did not last.

'I had forgotten that you had not been well,' she said.

'Pshaw!' muttered Ulick; then resumed, 'Aye, Mr. Kendal brought in the doctor upon me—very kind of him—but I do assure you 'tis nothing but home sickness; I was nearly as bad when I went to St. Columba, but I got over it then, and I will again!'

'It may be so in part,' said Albinia, kindly; 'but let me be impertinent, Ulick, for my sister Winifred told me to look after you; surely you give it every provocation. Such a change of habits is enough to make any one ill. Should you not ask your uncle for a holiday, and go home for a little while?'

'Don't name it, I beg of you,' cried the poor lad in an agitated voice, 'it would only bring it all over again! I've promised my mother to do my part, and with His help I *will*! Let the columns run out to all eternity, and the figures crook themselves as spitefully as they will, I've vowed to myself not to stir till I've got the better of the villains!'

'Ah!' said Albinia, 'they have blackened your eyes like the bruises of material antagonists! Yes, it is a gallant battle, but indeed you must give yourself all the help you can, for it would be doing your mother no good to fall ill.'

'I've no fears,' said Ulick; 'I know very well what is the matter with me, and that if I don't give way, it will go off in time. You've given it a good shove with your kindness, Mrs. Kendal,' he added, with deep emotion in his sensitive voice; 'only you must not talk of my going home, or you'll undo all you have done.'

'Then I won't; we must try to make you a home here. And in the first place, those lodgings of yours; you can never be comfortable in them.'

'Ah! you saw my fire smoking. I never shall learn to make a coal fire burn.'

'Not only that,' said Albinia, 'but you might easily find rooms much better furnished, and fitter for you.'

'I do assure you,' exclaimed Ulick, 'you scarcely saw it! Why, I don't think there's a room at the big house in better order, or so good!'

'At least,' said Albinia, repressing her deduction as to the big house of Ballymakilty, 'you have no particular love for the locality—the river smell— the stock of good leather, &c.'

'It's all Bayford and town smell together,' said Ulick; 'I never thought one part worse than another, begging your pardon, Mrs. Kendal.'

'And I am sure,' she continued, 'that woman can never make your meals comfortable. Yes, I see I am right, and I assure you hard head-work needs good living, and you will never be a match for the rogues in black and white without good beef-steaks. Now confess whether she gives you dinners of old shoe-leather.'

'A man can't sit down to dinner by himself,' cried Ulick, impatiently. 'Tea with a book are all that is bearable.'

'And you never go out—never see any one.'

'I dine at my uncle's every Sunday,' said Ulick.

'Is that all the variety you have?'

'Why, my uncle told me he would not have me getting into what he calls idle company. I've dined once at the vicarage, and drunk tea twice with Mr. Hope, but it is no use thinking of it—I couldn't afford it, and that's the truth.'

'Have you any books? What can you find to do all the evening?'

'I have a few that bear reading pretty often, and Mr. Hope as lent me some. I've been trying to keep up my Greek, and then I do believe there's some way of simplifying those accounts by logarithms, if I could but work it out. But my mother told me to walk, and I assure you I do take a constitutional as soon as I come out at half-past four every day.'

'Well, I have designs, and mind you don't traverse them, or I shall have to report you at home. I have a lodging in my eye for you, away from the river, and a nice clean, tidy Irishwoman to keep you in order, make your fires, and cram you, if you wont eat, and see if she does not make a man of you—'

'Stop, stop, Mrs. Kendal!' cried Ulick, distressed. 'You are very kind, but it can't be.'

'Excuse me, it is economy of the wrong sort to live in a gutter, and catch agues and fevers. Only think, if it was my boy Gilbert, should I not be obliged to any one that would tyrannize over him for his good! Besides, what I propose is not at all beyond such means as Mr. Kendal tells me are the least Mr. Goldsmith ought to give you. Do you dislike going into particulars with me? You know I am used to think for Gilbert, and I am a sort of cousin.'

'You are kindness itself,' said Ulick; 'and there! I suppose I must go to the bottom of it, and it is no news that pence are not plenty among the O'Mores, though it is no fault of my uncle. See there what my poor dear mother says.'

He drew a letter from his pocket, and gave a page to her.

'I miss you sorely, my boy,' it said; 'I know the more what a support and friend you have been to me now that you are so far away; but all is made up to me in knowing you to be among my own people, and the instrument of reconciliation with my brother, as you well know how great has been the pain of the estrangement caused by my own pride and wilfulness. I cannot tell you how glad I am that he approves of you, and that you are beginning to get used to the work that was my own poor father's for so long. Bred up as you have been, my mountain lad, I scarcely dared to hope that you would be able to sit down quietly to it, with all our hopes of making you a scholar so suddenly frustrated; but I might have put faith in your loving heart and sense of duty to carry you through anything. I feel as if a load were off my mind since you and Bryan are so happily launched. The boy has not once applied for money since he joined; and if you write to him, pray beg him to be careful, for it would well-nigh drive your father mad to be pressed any more—the poor mare has been sold at a dead loss and the Carrick-humbug quarry company pays no dividends, so how we are to meet the Christmas bills I cannot guess. But, as you remember, we have won over worse times, and now Providence has been so good to you and Bryan, what have I to do but be thankful and hope the best.'

Ulick watched her face, and gave her another note, saying mournfully, 'You see they all, but my mother, think, that if I am dragging our family honour through the mire, I've got something by it. Poor Bryan, he knows no better— he's younger than me by two years.'

The young ensign made a piteous confession of the first debt he had been able to contract, for twenty pounds, with a promise that if his brother would help him out of this one scrape, he would never run into another.

'I am very sorry for you, Ulick,' said Albinia, 'and I hate to advise you to be selfish, but it really is quite impossible for you to be paymaster for all your brothers' debts.'

'If it were Connel, I know it would be of no use,' said Ulick. 'But Bryan—you see he has got a start—they gave him a commission, and he is the finest fellow of us all, and knows what his word is, and keeps it! Maybe, if I get on, I may be able to save, and help him to his next step, and then if Redmond could get to college, my mother would be a happy woman, and all thanks to my uncle.'

'Then it is this twenty pounds that is pinching you now? Is that it?'

'You see my uncle said he would give me enough to keep me as a gentleman and his nephew, but not enough to keep all the family, as he said. After my Christmas quarter I shall be up in the world again, and then there will be time to think of the woman you spoke of—a Connaught woman, did you say?'

When Albinia reported this dialogue to her husband, he was much moved by this simple self-abnegation.

'There is nothing for it,' he said, 'but to bring him here till Christmas, and by that time we will take care that the new lodgings are cheap enough for him. He must not be left to the mercy of old Goldsmith and his sister!'

Even Albinia was astonished, but Mr. Kendal carried out his intentions, and went in quest of his new friend; while no one thought of objecting except grandmamma.

'I suppose, my dear,' she said, 'that you know what Mr. Goldsmith means to do for this young man.'

'I am sure I don't,' said Albinia.

'Really! Ah! well, I'm an old woman, and I may be wrong, but my poor dear Mr. Meadows would never encourage a banker's clerk about the house unless he knew what were his expectations. Irish too! If there was a thing Mr. Meadows disliked more than another, it was an Irishman! He said they were all adventurers.'

However, Ulick's first evening at Willow Lawn was on what he called 'a headache day.' He could not have taken a better measure for overcoming grandmamma's objections. Poor dear Mr. Meadows' worldly wisdom was not sufficiently native to her to withstand the sight of anything so pale and suffering, especially as he did not rebel against answering her close examination, which concluded in her pronouncing these intermitting attacks to be agueish, and prescribing quinine. To take medicines is an effectual way of gaining an old lady's love. Ulick was soon established in her mind as 'a very pretty behaved young gentleman.'

In the evenings, when Mr. Kendal read aloud, Ulick listened, and enjoyed it from the corner where he sheltered his eyes from the light. He was told that he ought to go to bed quickly, but after the ladies were in their rooms, a long buzzing murmur was heard in the passage, and judicious peeping revealed the two gentlemen, each, candle in hand, the one with his back against the wall at the top of the stairs, the other leaning upon the balusters three steps below, and there they stayed, till the clock struck one, and Ulick's candle burnt out.

'What could you be talking about?' asked the aggrieved Albinia.

'Prometheus Vinctus,' composedly returned Mr. Kendal.

Ulick's eagerness in collecting every crumb of scholarship was a great bond of union; but there was still more in the bright, open, demonstrative nature of the youth, which had a great attraction for the reserved, serious Mr. Kendal, and scarcely a day had passed before they were on terms of intimacy, almost like an elder and younger brother. Admitted into the family as a connexion, Ulick at once viewed the girls as cousins, and treated them with the same easy grace of good-natured familiarity as if they had been any of the nineteen Miss O'Mores around Ballymakilty.

'How is your head now?' asked Mr. Kendal. 'You are late this evening.'

'Yes,' said Ulick, entering the drawing-room, which was ruddy with firelight, and fragrant with the breath of the conservatory, and leaning over an arm-chair, as he tried to rub the aching out of his brow; 'there were some accounts to finish up and my additions came out different every time.'

'A sure sign that you ought to have left off.'

'I was just going to have told my uncle I was good for nothing to-day, when I heard old Johns mumbling something to him about Mr. More being unwell, and looking up, I saw that cold grey eye twinkling at me, as much as to say he was proud to see how soon an Irishman could be beaten. So what could I do but give him look for look, and go on with eight and seven, and five and two, as unconcerned as he was.'

'Well,' said Mr. Kendal, 'you know I think that your uncle's apparent indifference may be his fashion of being your best friend.'

'I'd take it like sunshine in May from a stranger, and be proud to disappoint him,' said Ulick, 'but to call himself my uncle, and use my mother's own eyes to look at me that way, that's the stroke! and to think that I'm only striving to harden myself by force of habit to be exactly like him! I'd rather enlist to-morrow, if that would not be his greatest triumph!' he cried, pressing his hands hard on his temple. 'It is very childish, but I could forgive him anything but using my mother's eyes that way!'

'You will yet rejoice in the likeness,' said Mr. Kendal. 'You must believe in more than you can trace, and when your perseverance has conquered his esteem, the rest will follow.'

'Follow? The rest, as you call it, would go before at home,' sighed Ulick, wearily. 'Esteem is like fame! what I want begins without it, and lives as well with or without it!'

'Perhaps,' said his friend, 'Mr. Goldsmith would think it weakness to show preference to a relation before it was earned.'

'Ah then,' cried Ulick, in a quaint Irish tone, 'Heaven have mercy on the little children!'

'Yes, the doctrine can only be consistently held by a solitary man.'

'Where would we be but for inconsistency?' exclaimed Ulick.

'I do not like to hear you talk in that manner,' said Sophy. 'Inconsistency is mere weakness.'

'Ah! then you are the dangerous character,' said Ulick, with a droll gesture of sheltering himself behind the chair.

'I did not call myself consistent, I wish I were,' she said, gravely.

'How she must love the French!' returned Ulick, confidentially turning to her father.

'Not at all, I detest them.'

'Then you are inconsistent, for they're the very models of uncompromising consistency.'

'Yes, to bad principles,' said Sophy.

'Robespierre was a prime specimen of consistency to good principle!'

Sophy turned to her father, and with an odd dubious look, asked him, 'Is be teasing me?'

'He'd be proud to have the honour,' Ulick made answer, so that Mr. Kendal's smile grew broad. It was the funniest thing to see Ulick sporting with Sophy's gravity, constraining her to playfulness, with something of the compulsion exercised by a large frolicsome puppy upon a sober old dog of less size and strength.

'I do not like to see powers wasted on paradox,' she said, even as the grave senior might roll up his lip and snarl.

'I'm in earnest, Sophy,' pursued Ulick, changing his note to eagerness. 'La grande nation herself finds that logic was her bane. Consistency was never made for man! Why where would this world be if it did not go two ways at once?'

Sophy did laugh at this Irish version of the centripetal and centrifugal forces, but she held out. 'The earth describes a circle; I like straight lines.'

'Much we shall have of the right direction, unless we are content to turn right about face,' said Ulick. 'The best path of life is but a herring-bone pattern.'

'What does he know of herring-boning?' asked Mrs. Kendal, coming in at the moment, with a white cashmere cloak folded picturesquely over her delicate blue silk. Ulick in a moment assumed a less careless attitude, as he answered—

'I found my poetical illustration on the motion of the earth too much for her, so I descended to the herring-bone as more suited to her capacity.'

'There he is, mamma,' said Sophy, 'pleading that consistency is the most ruinous thing in the world.'

'I thought as much,' said Albinia. 'Prometheus and his kin do most abound when Ulick's head is worst, and papa is in greatest danger of being late.'

Mr. Kendal turned round, looked at the time-piece, and marched off.

'But mamma!' continued Sophy, driving straight at her point, 'what do you think of consistency?'

'Oh, mamma!' cried Lucy, coming into the room in a flutter of white; 'there you are in your beautiful blue! Have you really put it on for the Drurys?'

Sophy bit her lip, neither pleased at the interruption, nor at the taste.

'Have you a graduated scale of dresses for all your friends, Lucy? asked Ulick.

'Everybody has, I suppose,' said Lucy.

'Ah! then I shall know how to judge how I stand in your favour. I never knew so well what the garb of friendship meant.'

'You must know which way her scale goes,' said Albinia, laughing at Sophy's evident affront at the frivolous turn the conversation had taken.

'That needs no asking,' quoth Ulick, 'Unadorned, adorned the most for the nearest the hearth.'

'That's all conceit,' said Lucy. 'Maybe familiarity breeds contempt.'

'No, no, when young ladies despise, they use a precision that says, "'Tis myself I care for, and not you."'

'What an observer!' cried Lucy. 'Now then, interpret my dress to-night!'

'How can you, Lucy!' muttered the scandalized Sophy.

'Well, Sophy, as you will have him to torment with philosophy this whole evening, I think you might give him a little respite,' said Lucy, good-humouredly. 'I want to know what my dress reveals to him!' and drawing up her head, where two coral pins contrasted with her dark braids, and spreading out her full white skirts and cerise trimmings, she threw her figure into an attitude, and darted a merry challenge from her lively black eyes, while Ulick availed himself of the permission to look critically, and Sophy sank back disgusted.

'Miss Kendal can, when she is inclined, produce as much effect with her beams of the second order as with all her splendours displayed.'

'Stuff,' said Lucy.

'Stuff indeed,' more sincerely murmured Sophy.

'Say something in earnest,' said Lucy. 'You professed to tell what I thought of the people.'

'I hope you'll never put on such new white gloves where I'm the party chiefly concerned.'

'What do you mean?'

'They are a great deal too unexceptionable.'

If there were something coquettish in the manner of these two, it did not give Albinia much concern. It was in him 'only Irish;' and Fred Ferrars had made her believe that it was rather a sign of the absence of love than of its presence. She saw much more respect and interest in his mischievous attacks on Sophy's gravity, and though Lucy both pitied him and liked chattering with him, it was all the while under the secret protest that he was only a banker's clerk.

Sophy was glad of the presence of a third person to obviate the perils of her evenings with grandmamma, and she beheld the trio set off to their dinner-party, without the usual dread of being betrayed into wrangling. Mr. O'More devoted himself to the old lady's entertainment, he amused her with droll stories, and played backgammon with her. Then she composed herself to her knitting, and desired them not to mind her, she liked to hear young people talk cheerfully; whereupon Sophy, by way of light and cheerful conversation, renewed the battle of consistency with a whole broadside of heavy metal.

When the diners-out came home, they found the war raging as hotly as ever; a great many historical facts and wise sayings having been fired off on both sides, and neither having found out that each meant the same thing.

However, the hours had gone imperceptibly past them, which could not be said for the others. The half-yearly dinners at Mr. Drury's were Albinia's dread nearly as much as Mr. Kendal's aversion. He was certain, whatever he might intend, to fall into a fit of absence, and she was almost equally sure to hear something unpleasant, and to regret her own reply. On the whole, however, Mr. Kendal came away on this evening the least dissatisfied, for Mr. Goldsmith had asked him with some solicitude, whether he thought 'that lad, young More,' positively unwell; and had gone the length of expressing that he seemed to be fairly sharp, and stuck to his work. Mr. Kendal seized the moment for telling his opinion, of Ulick, and though Mr. Goldsmith coughed and looked dry and almost contemptuous, he was perceptibly gratified, and replied with a maxim evidently intended both as an excuse for himself and as a warning to the Kendals, that young men were always spoilt by being made too much of—in his younger days—&c.

Lucy, meantime, was undergoing the broad banter of her unrefined cousins on the subject of the Irish clerk. A very little grace in the perpetration would have made it grateful to her vanity, but this was far too broad raillery, and made her hold up her head with protestations of her perfect indifference, to which her cousins manifested incredulity, visiting on her with some petty spite their small jealousies of her higher pretensions, and of the attention which had been paid to her by Mr. Cavendish Dusautoy.

'Not that he will ever look at you again, Lucy, you need not flatter yourself,' said the amiable Sarah Anne. 'Harry Wolfe writes that he was flirting with a beautiful young lady who came to see Oxford, and that he is spending quantities of money.'

'It is nothing to me, I am sure,' retorted Lucy. 'Besides, Gilbert says no such thing.'

'Gilbert! oh, no!' exclaimed Miss Drury; 'why, he is just as bad himself. Papa said, from what Mrs. Wolfe told him, he would not take 500 pounds to pay Mr. Gilbert's bills.'

Albinia had been hearing much the same story from Mrs. Drury, though not so much exaggerated, and administered with more condolence. She did not absolutely believe, and yet she could not utterly disbelieve, so the result was a letter to Gilbert, with an anxious exhortation to be careful, and not to be deluded into foolish expenditure in imitation of the Polysyllable; and as no special answer was returned, she dismissed the whole from her mind as a Drury allegation.

The horse chanced to be lame, so that Gilbert could not be met at Hadminster on his return from Oxford, but much earlier than the omnibus usually lumbered into Bayford, he astonished Sophy, who was lying on the sofa in the morning-room, by marching in with a free and easy step, and a loose coat of the most novel device.

'No one else at home?' he asked.

'Only grandmamma. We did not think the omnibus would come in so soon, but I suppose you took a fly, as there were three of you.'

'As if we were going to stand six miles of bus with the Wolfe cub! No, Dusautoy brought his horse down with him, and I took a fly!' said Gilbert. 'Well, and what's the matter with Captain; has the Irishman been riding him?'

Sophy bit her lip to prevent an angry answer, and was glad that Maurice rushed in, fall of uproarious joy. 'Hollo! boy, how you grow! What have you got there?'

'It's my new pop-gun, that Ulick made me, I'll shoot you,' cried Maurice, retiring to a suitable distance.

'I declare the child has caught the brogue! Is the fellow here still?'

'What fellow?' coldly asked Sophy.

'Why, this pet of my father's.'

'Bang!' cried Maurice, and a pellet passed perilously close to Gilbert's eyes.

'Don't, child. Pray is this banker's clerk one of our fixtures, Sophy?'

'I don't know why you despise him, unless it is because it is what you ought to be yourself,' Sophy was provoked into retorting.

'Apparently my father has a monomania for the article.' Gilbert intended to speak with provoking coolness; but another fraternal pellet hit him fall in the nose, and the accompanying shout of glee was too much for an already irritated temper. With passion most unusual in him, he caught hold of the child, and exclaiming, 'You little imp, what do you mean by it?' he wrenched the weapon out of his hand, and dashed it into the fire, in the midst of an energetic 'For shame!' from his sister. Maurice, with a furious 'Naughty Gilbert,' struck at him with both his little fists clenched, and then precipitated himself over the fender to snatch his treasure from the grate, but was instantly captured and pulled back, struggling, kicking, and fighting with all his might, till, to the equal relief of both brothers, Sophy held up the pop-gun in the tongs, one end still tinged with a red glow, smoky, blackened, and perfumed. Maurice made one bound, she lowered it into his grasp as the last red spark died out, and he clasped it as Siegfried did the magic sword!

'There, Maurice, I didn't mean it,' said Gilbert, heartily ashamed and sorry; 'kiss and make it up, and then put on your hat, and we'll come up to old Smith's and get such a jolly one!'

The forgiving child had already given the kiss, glad to atone for his aggressions, but then was absorbed in rubbing the charred wood, amazed that while so much black came off on his fingers, the effect on the weapon was not proportionate, and then tried another shot in a safer direction. 'Come,' said Gilbert, 'put that black affair into the fire, and come along.'

'No!' said Maurice; 'it is my dear gun that Ulick made me, and it shan't be burnt.'

'What, not if I give you a famous one—like a real one, with a stock and barrel?' said Gilbert, anxious to be freed from the tokens of his ebullition.

'No! no!' still stoutly said the constant Maurice. 'I don't want new guns; I've got my dear old one, and I'll keep him to the end of his days and mine!' and he crossed his arms over it.

'That's right, Maurice,' said Sophy; 'stick to old friends that have borne wounds in your service!'

'Well, it's his concern if he likes such a trumpery old thing,' said Gilbert. 'Come here, boy; you don't bear malice! Come and have a ride on my back.'

The practical lesson, 'don't shoot at your brother's nose,' would never have been impressed, had not mamma, on coming in, found Maurice and his pop-gun nearly equally black, and by gradual unfolding of cause and effect, learnt his forgotten offence. She reminded him of ancient promises never to aim at human creatures, assured him that Gilbert was very kind not to have burnt it outright; and to the great displeasure, and temporary relief of all the family, sequestrated the weapon for the rest of the evening.

Sophy told her in confidence that Gilbert had been the most to blame, which she took as merely an instance of Sophy's blindness to Maurice's errors; for the explosion had so completely worked off the Oxford dash, that he was perfectly meek and amiable. Considering the antecedents, such a contrast to himself as young O'More could hardly fail to be an eyesore, walking tame about the home, and specially recommended to his friendship; but so good-natured was he, and so attractive was the Irishman, that it took much influence from Algernon Dusautoy to keep up a thriving aversion. Albinia marvelled at the power exercised over Gilbert by one whose intellect and pretensions he openly contemned, but perceived that obstinacy and undoubting self-satisfaction overmastered his superior intelligence and principle, and that while perceiving all the follies of the Polysyllable, Gilbert had a strange propensity for his company, and therein always resumed the fast man, disdainful of the clerk. He did not like Ulick better for being the immediate cause of the removal of the last traces of the Belmarche family from their old abode, which had been renovated by pretty shamrock chintz furniture, the pride of the two Irish hearts. Indeed it was to be feared that Bridget would assist in the perpetuation of those rolling R's which caused Mr. Goldsmith's brow to contract whenever his nephew careered along upon one.

His departure from Willow Lawn was to take place at Christmas. The Ferrars party were coming to keep the two consecutive birthdays of Sophy and Maurice at Bayford, would take him back for Christmas-day to Fairmead, and on his return he would take possession of his new rooms.

Maurice's fete was to serve as the occasion of paying off civilities to a miscellaneous young party; but as grandmamma's feelings would have been hurt, had not Sophy's been equally distinguished, it was arranged that Mrs. Nugent should then bring her eldest girl to meet the Ferrarses at an early tea.

Just as Albinia had descended to await her guests, Gilbert came down, and presently said, with would-be indifference, 'Oh, by-the-by, Dusautoy said he would look in.'

'The Polysyllable!' cried Albinia, thunderstruck; 'what possessed you to ask him, when you knew I sacrificed Mr. Dusautoy rather than have him to spoil it all?'

'I didn't ask him exactly,' replied Gilbert; 'it was old Bowles, who met us, and tried to nail us to eat our mutton with him, as he called it. I had my answer, and Dusautoy got off by saying he was engaged to us, and desired me to tell you he would make his excuses in person.'

'He can make no excuse for downright falsehood.'

'Hem!' quoth Gilbert. 'You wouldn't have him done into drinking old Bowles's surgery champagne.'

'One comfort is that he wont get any dinner,' said Albinia, vindictively. 'I hope he'll be ravenously hungry.'

'He may not come after all,' said Gilbert; and Albinia, laying hold of that hope, had nearly forgotten the threatened disaster, as her party appeared by instalments, and Winifred owned to her that Sophy had grown better-looking than could have been expected. Her eyes had brightened, the cloudy brown of her cheeks was enlivened, she held herself better, and the less childish dress was much to her advantage. But above all, the moody look of suffering was gone, and her face had something of the grave sweetness and regular beauty of that of her father.

'Seventeen,' said Mrs. Ferrars; 'by the time she is seventy, she may be a remarkably handsome woman!'

The tea-drinking was in lively operation, when after a thundering knock, Mr. Cavendish Dusautoy was ushered in, with the air of a prince honouring the banquet of his vassals, saying, 'I told Kendal I should presume on your hospitality, I beg you will make no difference on my account.'

Of which gracious permission Albinia was resolved to avail herself. She left all the insincerity to her husband, and would by no means allow grandmamma to abdicate the warm corner. She suspected that he wanted an introduction to Mrs. Nugent, and was resolved to defeat this object, unless he should condescend to make the request, so she was well satisfied to see him wedged in between papa and Sophy, while a prodigious quantity of Irish talk was going on between Mrs. Nugent and Mr. O'More, with contributions of satire from Mr. Ferrars which kept every one laughing except little Nora Nugent and Mary Ferrars, who were deep in the preliminaries of an eternal friendship, and held the ends of each other's crackers like a pair of doves. Lucy, however, was ill at ease at the obscurity which shrouded the illustrious guest, and in her anxiety, gave so little attention to her two neighbours, that Willie Ferrars, affronted at some neglect, exclaimed, 'Why, Lucy, what makes you screw your eyes about so! you can't attend to any one.'

'It is because Polly Silly is there,' shouted Master Maurice from his throne beside his mamma.

To the infinite relief of the half-choked Albinia, little Mary Ferrars, with whom her cousin had been carrying on a direful warfare all day, fitted on the cap, shook her head gravely at him, and after an appealing look of indignation, first at his mamma, then at her own, was overheard confiding to Nora Nugent that Maurice was a very naughty boy—she was sorry to say, a regular spoilt child.

'But how should you hinder Miss Kendal from attending?'

'I'll tell you, darling. Poor Lucy! she is very fond of me, and I dare say she wanted me to sit next to her, but you know she will have me for three days, and I have you only this one evening. I'll go and speak to her after tea, when we go into the drawing-room, and then she wont mind.'

Lucy, after an agony of blushes, had somewhat recovered on finding that no one seemed to apply her brother's speech, and when the benevolent Mary made her way to her, and thrust a hand into hers, only a feeble pressure replied to these romantic blandishments, so anxious was she to carry to Mrs. Kendal the information that Mr. Cavendish Dusautoy had been so obliging as to desire his servant to bring his guitar and key-bugle.

'We are much obliged,' said Albinia, 'but look at that face!' and she turned Lucy towards Willie's open-mouthed, dismayed countenance. You must tell him the company are not sufficiently advanced in musical science.'

'But mamma, it would gratify him!'

'Very likely'—and without listening further, Albinia turned to Willie, who had all day been insisting that papa should introduce her to the new game of the Showman.

Infinitely delighted to be relieved from the fear of the guitar, Willie hunted all who would play into another room; whence they were to be summoned, one by one, back to the drawing-room by the showman, Mr. Ferrars, who shrugged his shoulders at the task, but undertook it, and first called for Mrs. Kendal.

She found him stationed before the red curtains, which were closely drawn, and her husband and the three elder ladies sitting by as audience.

'Pray, madam, may I ask what animal you would desire to have exhibited to you, out of the vast resources that my menagerie contains. Choose freely, I undertake that whatever you may select, you shall not be disappointed.'

'What, not if I were to ask for a black spider monkey?' said Albinia, to whom it was very charming to be playing with Maurice again.

Mr. Kendal looked up in entertained curiosity, Mrs. Nugent smiled as if she thought the showman's task impossible, and Winifred stretched out to gain a full view.

'A black spider monkey,' he said, slowly. 'Allow me to ask, madam, if you are acquainted with the character of the beast?'

'It doesn't scratch, does it?' said she, quickly.

'That is for you to answer.'

'I never knew it do so. It does chatter a great deal, but it never scratched that I knew of.'

'Nor I,' said the showman, 'since it was young. Do you think age renders it graver and steadier?'

'Not a bit. It is always frisky and troublesome, and I never knew it get a bit better as it grew older.'

Winifred laughed outright. Mr. Kendal's lips were parted by his smile. 'I wonder what sort of a mother it would make?' said the showman.

'All animals are good mothers, of course.'

'I meant, is it a good disciplinarian?'

'If you mean cuffing its young one for playing exactly the same tricks as itself.'

'Exactly; and what would be the effect of letting it and its young one loose in a great scholar's study?'

'There wouldn't be much study left.'

'And would it be for his good?'

'Really, Mr. Showman, you ask very odd questions. Shall we try?' said Albinia, with a skip backward, so as to lay her hand on the shoulder of her own great scholar, while the showman drew back the curtain, observing—'I wish, ma'am, I could show "it and its young one" together, but the young specimen is unfortunately asleep. Behold the original black spider monkey!'

There stood the monkey, with sunny brown locks round the laughing glowing face, and one white paw still lying on the scholar's shoulder—while his face made no assurance needful that it was very good for him! The mirror concealed behind the curtains was the menagerie! Albinia clapped her hands with delight, and pronounced it the most perfect of games.

'And now let us have Willie,' said Mrs. Ferrars; 'it will conduce to the harmony of the next room.'

Willie, already initiated, hoped to puzzle papa as a platypus ornithoryncus, but was driven to allow that it was a nondescript animal, neither fish, flesh, nor good red-herring, useless, and very fond of grubbing in the mud; and if it were not at Botany Bay, it ought to be! The laughter that hailed his defence of its nose as 'well, nothing particular,' precipitated the drawing up of the curtain and his apparition in the glass: and then Nora Nugent being called, the inseparable Mary accompanied her, arm-in-arm, simpering an announcement that they liked nothing so well as a pair of dear little love-birds.

Oh, unpitying papa! to draw from the unsuspicious Nora the admission that they were very dull little birds, of no shape at all, who always sat hunched up in a corner without any fun, and people said their love was all stupidity and pretence; in fact, if she had one she should call it Silly Polly or Polly Silly!

To silence Willie's exultation in his sister's discomfiture, he was sent to fetch Lucy, whose impersonation of an argus pheasant would not have answered well but for a suggestion of Albinia, that she was eyes all over for any delinquency in school. Ulick O'More, owning with a sigh that he should like to see no beast better than a snipe, gave rise to much ingenuity by being led to describe it as of a class migratory, hard to catch, food for powder, given to long bills. There he guessed something, and stood on the defensive, but could not deny that its element was bogs, but that it had been seen skimming over water meadows, and finding sustenance in banks, whereupon the curtain rose. Ulick rushed upon the battles of his nation, and was only reduced to quiescence by the entrance of Sophy, who expressed a desire to see a coral worm, apparently perplexing the showman, who, to gain time, hemmed, and said, 'A very unusual species, ma'am,' which set all the younger ones in a double giggle, such as confused Sophy, to find herself standing up, with every one looking at her, and listening for her words. 'I thought you undertook for any impossibility in earth air or water.'

'Well, ma'am, do you take me for a mere mountebank? But when ladies and gentlemen take such unusual fancies—and for an animal that—you would not aver that it is often found from home?'

'Never, I should say.'

'Nor that it is accessible?'

'Certainly not.'

'And why is it so, ma'am?'

'Why,' said Sophy, bewildered into forgetting her natural history, 'it lives at the bottom of the sea; that's one thing.'

'Where Truth lives,' said a voice behind.

'I beg to differ,' observed Albinia. 'Truth is a fresh water fish at the bottom of a well; besides, I thought coral worms were always close to the surface.'

'But below it—not in everybody's view,' said Sophy—an answer which seemed much to the satisfaction of the audience, but the showman insisted on knowing why, and whether it did not conceal itself. 'It makes stony caves for itself, out of sight,' said Sophy, almost doubting whether she spoke correctly. 'Well, surely it does so.'

'Most surely,' said an acclamation so general that she did not like it. If she had been younger, she would have turned sulky upon the spot, and Mr. Ferrars almost doubted whether to bring ont his final query. 'Pray, ma'am, do you think this creature out of reach in its self-made cave, at the bottom—no, below the surface of the sea, would be popular enough to repay the cost of procuring it.'

'Ah! that's too bad,' burst out the Hibernian tones. 'Why, is not the best of everything hidden away from the common eye? Out of sight—stony cave—It is the secret worker that lays the true solid foundation, raises the new realms, and forms the precious jewels.' The torrent of r's was irresistible!

'Police! order!' cried the showman. 'An Irish mob has got in, and there's an end of everything.' So up went the curtain, and the polyp appeared, becoming rapidly red coral as she perceived what the exhibition was, and why the politeness of the Green Isle revolted from her proclaiming her own unpopularity. But all she did was to turn gruffly aside, and say, 'It is lucky there are no more ladies to come, Mr. Showman, or the mob would turn everything to a compliment.'

Gilbert's curiosity was directed to the Laughing Jackass, and with too much truth he admitted that it took its tone from whatever it associated with, and caught every note, from the song of the lark to the bray of the donkey; then laughed good-humouredly when the character was fitted upon himself.

'That is all, is it not?' asked the showman. 'I may retire into private life.'

'Oh no,' cried Willie; 'you have forgotten Mr. Dusautoy.'

'I was afraid you had,' said Lucy, 'or you could not have left him to the last.'

'I am tempted to abdicate,' said Mr. Ferrars.

'No,' Albinia said. 'He must have his share, and no one but you can do it. Where can he be? the pause becomes awful!'

'Willie is making suggestions,' said Gilbert; 'his imagination would never stretch farther than a lion. It's what he thinks himself and no mistake.'

'He is big enough to be the elephant,' said little Mary.

'The half-reasoning!' said Ulick, softly; 'and I can answer for his trunk, I saw it come off the omnibus.'

'Ladies and gentlemen, if you persist in such disorderly conduct, the exhibition will close,' cried the showman, waving his wand as Willie trumpeted Mr. Cavendish Dusautoy in, and on the demand what animal he wanted to see, twitched him as Flibbertigibbet did the giant warder, and caused him to respond—'The Giraffe.'

'Has it not another name, sir? A short or a long one, more or less syllables!'

'Camelopard. A polysyllabic word, certainly,' said Algernon, looking with a puzzled expression at the laughers behind; and almost imagining it possible that he could have made an error, he repeated, 'Camel-le-o-pard. Yes, it is a polysyllable'—as, indeed, he had added an unnecessary syllable.

'Most assuredly,' said the showman, looking daggers at his suffocating sister. 'May I ask you to describe the creature?'

'Seventeen feet from the crown to the hoof, but falls off behind,' said the accurate Mr. Dusautoy; 'beautiful tawny colour.'

'Nearly as good as a Lion,' added Gilbert; but Algernon, fancying the game was by way of giving useful instruction to the children, went on in full swing. 'Handsomely mottled with darker brown; a ruminating animal; so gentle that in spite of its size, none of my little friends need be alarmed at its vicinity. Inhabits the African deserts, but may be bred in more temperate latitudes. I myself saw an individual in the Jardin des Plantes, which was popularly said never to bend its neck to the ground, but I consider this a vulgar delusion, for on offering it food, it mildly inclined its head.'

'Let us hope the present specimen is equally condescending,' said Mr. Ferrars.

'Eh! what! I see myself!' said Mr. Cavendish Dusautoy, with a tone so inappreciably grand in mystification, that the showman had no choice but to share the universal convulsion of laughter, while Willie rolling on the floor with ecstasy, shouted, 'Yes, it is you that are the thing with such a long name that it can't bend its head to the ground!'

'But too good-natured to be annoyed at folly,' said Mr. Ferrars, perceiving that it was no sport to him.

'This is the way my mischievous uncle has served us all in turn,' said Lucy, advancing; 'we have all been shown up, and there was mamma a monkey, and I an argus pheasant—'

'Ah! I see,' said the gentleman. 'These are your rural pastimes of the season. Yes, I can take my share in good part, just as I have pelted the masks at the Carnival.'

'Even a giraffe can bend his head and do at Rome as Rome does,' murmured Ulick. But instead of heeding the audacious Irishman, Algernon patronized the showman by thanks for his exhibition; and then sitting down by Lucy, asked if he had ever told her of the tricks that he and il Principe

Odorico Moretti used to play at Ems on the old Baron Sprawlowsky, while Mr. Ferrars, leaning over his sister's chair, said aside, 'I beg your pardon, Albinia; I should not have yielded to Willie. This "rural pastime" is only in season en famille.'

'Never mind, it served him right.'

'It may have served him right, but had we the right to serve him?'

'I forgive your prudence for the sake of your folly. Could not Oxford have lessened his pomposity?'

'It comes too late,' said Maurice.

Before Ulick went to bed his pen and ink had depicted the entire caravan. The love-birds were pressed up together, with the individual features of the two young ladies, and completely little parrots; the snipe ran along the bars of the cage, looking exactly like all the O'Mores. The monkey showed nothing but the hands, but one held Maurice, and the other was clenched as if to cuff him, and grandest of all was, as in duty bound, Camelopardelis giraffa, thrown somewhat backwards, with such a majestic form, such a stalking attitude, loftily ruminating face, and legs so like the Cavendish Dusautoy's last new pair of trousers, that Albinia could not help reserving it for the private delectation of his Aunt Fanny.

'It and its young one,' said Mr. Kendal, as he looked at her portrait; and the name delighted him so much, that he for some time applied it with a smile whenever his wife gave him cause to remember how much there was of the monkey in her composition.

It was the merriest Christmas ever known at Willow Lawn, and the first time there had been anything of the atmosphere of family frolic and fun. The lighting up of Sophy was one great ingredient; hitherto mirth had been merely endured by her, whereas now, improved health and spirits had made her take her share, amuse others and be amused, and cease to be hurt by the jarring of chance words. Lucy was lively as usual, but rather more excited than Albinia altogether liked; she was doubly particular about her dress; more disdainful of the common herd, and had a general air of exaltation that made Albinia rejoice when the Polysyllable, the horses, the key-bugle, and genre painting disappeared from the Bayford horizon.

CHAPTER XX.

If the end of the vacation were a relief on Lucy's account, Albinia would gladly have lengthened it on Gilbert's. Letters from his tutor had disquieted his father; there had been an expostulation followed by promises, and afterwards one of the usual scenes of argument, complaint, excuse, lamentation, and wish to amend; but lastly, a murmur that it was no use to talk to a father who had never been at the University, and did not know what was expected of a man.

The aspect of Oxford had changed in Albinia's eyes since the days of her brother. Alma Mater had been a vision of pealing bells, chanting voices, cloistered shades, bright waters—the source of her most cherished thoughts, the abode of youth walking in the old paths of pleasantness and peace; and she knew that to faithful hearts, old Oxford was still the same. But to her present anxious gaze it had become a field of snares and temptations, whither she had been the means of sending one, unguarded and unstable.

Once under the influence of a good sound-hearted friend, he might have been easily led right, but his intimacy with young Dusautoy seemed to cancel all hope of this, and to be like a rope about his neck, drawing him into the same career, and keeping aloof all better influences. Algernon, with his pride, pomposity, and false refinement, was more likely to run into ostentations expenditure, than into coarse dissipation, and it might still be hoped that the two youths would drag through without public disgrace; but this was felt to be a very poor hope by those who felt each sin to be a fatal blot, and trembled at the self-indulgent way of life that might be a more fatal injury than even the ban of the authorities.

She saw that the anxiety pressed heavily on Mr. Kendal, and though both shrank from giving their uneasiness force by putting it into words, each felt that it was ever-present with the other. Mr. Kendal was deeply grieving over the effects, for the former state of ignorance and apathy of the evils of which he had only recently become fully sensible. Living for himself alone, without cognizance of his membership in one great universal system, he had needed the sense of churchmanship to make him act up to his duties as father, neighbour, citizen, and man of property; and when aroused, he found that the time of his inaction had bound him about with fetters. A tone of mind had grown up in his family from which only Sophy had been entirely freed; seeds of ineradicable evil had been sown, mischiefs had grown by neglect, abuses been established by custom; and his own personal disadvantages, his mauvaise honte, his reserved, apparently proud manner, his slowness of speech, dislike to interruption, and over-vehemence when excited, had so much increased upon him, as, in spite of his efforts, to be serious hindrances. Kind, liberal, painstaking, and conscientious as he had become, he was still looked upon as hard, stern, and tyrannical. His ten years of inertness had strewn his path with thorns and briars, even beyond his own household; and when he looked back to his neglect of his son, he felt that even the worst consequences would be but just retribution.

Once such feelings would have wrapt him in morbid gloom; now he strove against his disposition to sit inert and hidden, he did his work manfully, and endeavoured not to let his want of spirits sadden the household.

Nor was he insensible to the cheerful healthy atmosphere of animation which had diffused itself there; and the bright discussions of the trifling interests of the day. Ulick O'More was also a care to him, which did him a great deal of good.

That young gentleman now lived at his lodgings, but was equally at home at Willow Lawn, and his knock at the library door, when he wished to change a book, usually led to some 'Prometheus' discussion, and sometimes to a walk, if Mr. Kendal thought him looking pale; or to dining and to spending the evening.

His scrapes were peculiar. He had thoroughly mastered his work, and his active mind wanted farther scope, so that he threw himself with avidity into deeper studies, and once fell into horrible disgrace for being detected with a little Plato on his desk. Mr. Goldsmith nearly gave him up in despair, and pronounced that he would never make a man of business. He made matters worse by replying that this was the best chance of his not being a man of speculation. If he were allowed to think of nothing but money, he should speculate for the sake of something to do!

Before Mr. Goldsmith had half recovered the shock, Mr. Dusautoy and Mr. Hope laid violent hands upon young O'More for the evening school twice a week, which almost equally discomposed his aunt. She had never got over the first blow of Mr. Dusautoy's innovations, and felt as if her nephew had gone over to the enemy. She was doubly ungracious at the Sunday dinner, and venomously critical of the choir's chanting, Mr. Hope's voice, and the Vicar's sermons.

The worst scrape came in March. The Willow Lawn ladies were in the lower end of the garden, which, towards the river, was separated from the lane that continued Tibb's Alley, by a low wall surmounted by spikes, and with a disused wicket, always locked, and nearly concealed by a growth of laurels; when out brake a horrible hullabaloo in that region of evil report, the shouts and yells coming nearer, and becoming so distinct that they were about to retreat, when suddenly a dark figure leapt over the gate, and into the garden, amid a storm of outcries. As he disappeared among the laurels, Albinia caught up Maurice, Lucy screamed and prepared to fly, and Sophy started forward, exclaiming, 'It is Ulick, mamma; his face is bleeding!' But as he emerged, she retreated, for she had a nervous terror of the canine race, and in his hand, at arm's length he held by the neck a yellow dog, a black pot dangling from its tail.

'Take care,' he shouted, as Albinia set down Maurice, and was running up to him; 'he may be mad.'

Maurice was caught up again, Lucy shrieked, and Sophy, tottering against an apple-tree, faintly said, 'He has bitten you!'

'No, not he; it was only a stone,' said Ulick, as best he might, with a fast bleeding upper lip. 'They were hunting the poor beast to death—I believe he's no more mad than I am—only with the fright—but best make sure.'

'Fetch some milk, Lucy,' said Albinia. 'Take Maurice with you. No, don't take the poor thing down to the river, he'll only think you are going to drown him. Go, Maurice dear.'

Maurice safe, Albinia was able to find ready expedients after Sir Fowell Buxton's celebrated example. She brought Ulick the gardener's thick gauntlets from the tool-house, and supplied him with her knife, with which he set the poor creature free from the instrument of torture, and then let him loose, with a pan of milk before him, in the old-fashioned summer-house, through the window of which he could observe his motions, and if he looked dangerous, shoot him.

Nothing could look less dangerous; the poor creature sank down on the floor and moaned, licked its hind leg, and then dragged itself as if famished to the milk, lapped a little eagerly, but lay down again whining, as if in pain. Ulick and Albinia called to it, and it looked up and tried to wag its tail, whining appealingly. 'My poor brute!' he cried, 'they've treated you worse than a heathen. That's all—let me see what I can do for you.'

'Yes, but yourself, Ulick,' said Albinia, as in his haste he took down his handkerchief from his mouth; 'I do believe your lip is cut through! You had better attend to that first.'

'No, no, thank you,' said Ulick, eagerly, 'they've broken the poor wretch's leg!' and he was the next moment sitting on the summer-house floor, lifting up the animal tenderly, regardless of her expostulation that the injured, frightened creature might not know its friends. But she did it injustice; it wagged its stumpy tail, and licked his fingers.

She offered to fetch rag for his surgery, and he farther begged for some slight bits of wood to serve as splints, he and his brothers had been dog- doctors before. As she hurried into the house, Sophy, who had sunk on a sofa in the drawing-room, looking deadly pale, called out, 'Is he bitten?'

'No, no,' cried Albinia, hurrying on, 'the dog is all safe. It has only got a broken leg.'

Maurice, with whom Lucy had all this time been fighting, came out with her to see the rest of the adventure; and thought it very cruel that he was not permitted to touch the patient, which bore the operation with affecting fortitude and gratitude, and was then consigned to a basket lined with hay, and left in the summer-house, Mr. Kendal being known to have an almost eastern repugnance to dogs.

Then Ulick had leisure to be conducted to the morning-room, and be rendered a less ghastly spectacle, by some very uncomfortable sticking- plaster moustaches, which hardly permitted him to narrate his battle distinctly. He thought the boys, even of Tibb's Alley, would hardly have ventured any violence after he had interfered, but for some young men who aught to have known better; he fancied he had seen young Tritton of Robbles Leigh, and he was sure of an insolent groom whom Mr. Cavendish Dusautoy, to the great vexation of his uncle, had recently sent down with a horse to the King's Head. They had stimulated the boys to a shout of Paddy and a shower of stones, and Ulick expected credit for great discretion, in having fled instead of fought. 'Ah! if Brian and Connel had but been there, wouldn't we have put them to the rout?'

Nothing would then serve him but going back to Tibb's Alley to trace the dog's history, and meantime Lucy, from the end of the passage, beckoned to Albinia, and whispered mysteriously that 'Sophy would not have any one know it for the world—but,' said Lucy, 'I found her absolutely fainting away on the sofa, only she would not let me call you, and ordered that no one should know anything about it. But, mamma, there was a red-hot knitting- needle sticking out of the fire, and I am quite sure that she meant if Ulick was bitten, to burn out the place.'

Albinia believed Sophy capable of both the resolution and its consequence; but she agreed with Lucy that no notice should be taken, and would not seem aware that Sophy was much paler than usual.

The dog, as well as Ulick could make out, was a waif or stray, belonging to a gipsy deported that morning by the police, and on whom its master's sins had been visited. So without scruple he carried the basket home to his lodgings, and on the way, had the misfortune to encounter his uncle, while shirtfront, coat, and waistcoat were fresh from the muddy and bloody fray, and his visage in the height of disfigurement.

Mr. Goldsmith looked on the whole affair as an insult to every Goldsmith of past ages! A mere street row! He ordered Mr. More to his lodgings, and said he should hear from him to-morrow. Ulick came down to Willow Lawn in the dark, almost considering himself as dismissed, not knowing whether to be glad or sorry; and wanting to consult Mr. Kendal whether it would be possible to work his way at college as Mr. Hope had done, or even wondering whether he might venture to beg for a recommendation to 'Kendal and Kendal.'

Mr. Kendal was so strongly affected, that he took up his hat and went straight to Mr. Goldsmith, 'to put the matter before him in a true light.'

True light or false, it was intolerable in the banker's eyes, and it took a great deal of eloquence to persuade him that his nephew was worth a second trial. Fighting in Tibb's Alley over a gipsy's dog, and coming back looking like a ruffian! Mr. Goldsmith wished him no harm, but it would be a disgrace to the concern to keep him on, and Miss Goldsmith, whom Mr. Kendal heartily wished to gag, chimed in with her old predictions of the consequences of her poor sister's foolish marriage. The final argument, was Mr. Kendal's declaration of the testimonials with which he would at once send him out to Calcutta, to take the situation once offered to his own son. No sooner did Mr. Goldsmith hear that his nephew had an alternative, than he promised to be lenient, and finally dispatched a letter to U. More, Esquire, with a very serious rebuke, but a promise that his conduct should be overlooked, provided the scandal were not repeated, and he should not present himself at the bank till his face should be fit to be seen.

Mr. Kendal mounted him the next morning on Gilbert's horse, and sent him to Fairmead. The dog was left in charge of Bridget, who treated it with abundant kindness, but failed to obtain the exclusive affection which the poor thing lavished upon its rescuer. By the time Ulick came home, it had arrived at limping upon three legs, and was bent on following him wherever he went. Disreputable and heinously ugly it was, of tawny currish yellow (whence it was known as the Orange-man), with a bull-dog countenance; and the legs that did not limp were bandy. Albinia called it the Tripod, but somehow it settled into the title of Hyder Ali, to which it was said to 'answer' the most readily, though it would in fact answer anything from Ulick, and nothing from any one else..

Ever at his heels, the 'brazen Tripod' contrived to establish an entrance at Willow Lawn; scratched till Mr. Kendal would interrupt a 'Prometheus talk' to let him in at the library door; and gradually made it a matter of course to come into the drawing-room, and repose upon Sophy's flounces.

This was by way of compensation for his misadventures elsewhere. He was always bringing Ulick into trouble; shut or tie him up as he might, he was sure to reappear when least wanted. He had been at church, he had been in Miss Goldsmith's drawing-room, he had been found times without number curled up under Ulick's desk. Mr. Goldsmith growled hints about hanging him, and old Mr. Johns, who really was fond of his bright young fellow clerk, gave grave counsel; but Ulick only loved his protege the better, and after having exhausted an Irish vocabulary of expostulation, succeeded in prevailing on him to come no farther than the street; except on very wet days, when he would sometimes be found on the mat in the entry, looking deplorably beseeching, and bringing on his master an irate, 'Here's that dog again!'

'Would that no one fell into worse scrapes,' sighed Mr. Dusautoy, when he heard of Ulick's disasters with Hyder Ali, and it was a sigh that the house of Kendal re-echoed.

Nobody could be surprised when, towards the long vacation, tidings came to Bayford, that after long forbearance on the part of the authorities, the insubordination and riotous conduct of the two young men could be endured no longer. It appeared that young Dusautoy, with his weak head and obstinate will, had never attempted to bend to rules, but had taken every reproof as an insult and defiance. Young men had not been wanting who were ready to take advantage of his lavish expenditure, and to excite his disdain for authorities. They had promoted the only wit he did understand, broad practical jokes and mischief; and had led him into the riot and gambling to which he was not naturally prone. Gilbert Kendal, with more sense and principle, had been led on by the contagion around him, and at last an outrageous wine party had brought matters to a crisis. The most guilty were the most cunning, and the only two to whom the affair could actually be brought home, were Dusautoy and Kendal. The sentence was rustication, and the tutor wrote to Mr. Dusautoy, as the least immediately affected, to ask him to convey the intelligence to Mr. Kendal.

The vicar was not a man to shrink from any task, however painful, but he felt it the more deeply, as, in spite of his partiality, he was forced to look on his own favourite Algernon as the misleader of Gilbert; and when he overtook the sisters on his melancholy way down the hill, he consulted them how their father would bear it.

'Oh! I don't know,' said Lucy; 'he'll be terribly angry. I should not wonder if he sent Gilbert straight off to India; should you, Sophy?'

'I hope he will do nothing in haste,' exclaimed Mr. Dusautoy. 'I do believe if those two lads were but separated, or even out of such company, they would both do very well.'

'Yes,' exclaimed Lucy; 'and, after all, they are such absurd regulations, treating men like schoolboys, wanting them to keep such regular troublesome hours. Mr. Cavendish Dusautoy told me that there was no enduring the having everything enforced.'

'If things had been enforced on poor Algernon earlier, this might never have been,' sighed his uncle.

'I'm sure I don't see why papa should mind it so much,' continued Lucy. 'Mr. Cavendish Dusautoy told me his friend Lord Reginald Raymond had been rusticated twice, and expelled at last.'

'What do you think of it, Sophy?' asked the vicar, anxiously.

'I don't feel as if any of us could ever look up again,' she answered very low.

'Why, no; not that exactly. It is not quite the right way to take these things, Sophy,' said Mr. Dusautoy. 'Boys may be very foolish and wrong-headed, without disgracing their family.'

Sophy did not answer—it was all too fresh and sore, and she did not find much consolation in the number of youths whom Lucy reckoned up as having incurred the like penalty. When they entered the house, and Mr. Dusautoy knocked at the library door, she followed Lucy into the garden, without knowing where she was going, and threw herself down upon the grass, miserable at the pain which was being inflicted upon her father, and with a hardened resentful feeling, between contempt and anger, against the brother, who, for very weakness, could so dishonour and grieve him. She clenched her hand in the intensity of her passionate thoughts and impulses, and sat like a statue, while Lucy, from time to time, between the tying up of flowers and watering of annuals, came up with inconsistent exhortations not to be so unhappy—for it was not expulsion—it was sure to be unjust—nobody would think the worse of them because young men were foolish—all men of spirit did get into scrapes—

It was lucky for Lucy that all this passed by Sophy's ear as unheeded as the babbling of the brook. She did not move, till roused by Ulick O'More, coming up from the bridge, telling that he had met some Irish haymakers in the meadows, and saying he wanted to beg a frock for one of their children.

'I think I can find you one,' said Lucy, 'if you will wait a minute; but don't go in, Mr. Dusautoy is there.'

'Is anything the matter?' he exclaimed.

'Every one must soon know,' said Lucy; 'it is of no use to keep it back, Sophy. Only my brother and Mr. Cavendish Dusautoy have got into a scrape about a wine party, and are going to be rusticated. But wait, I'll fetch the frock.'

Sophy had almost run away while her sister spoke, but the kind look of consternation and pity on Ulick's face deterred her, he in soliloquy repeated, as if confounded by the greatness of the misfortune, 'Poor Gilbert!'

'Poor Gilbert!' burst from Sophy in irritation at misplaced sympathy; 'I thought it would be papa and mamma you cared for!'

'With reason,' returned Ulick, 'but I was thinking how it must break his heart to have pained such as they.'

'I wish he would feel it thus,' exclaimed Sophy; 'but he never will!'

'Oh! banish that notion, Sophy,' cried Ulick, recoiling at the indignation in her dark eyes, 'next to grieving my mother, I declare nothing could crush me like meeting a look such as that from a sister of mine.'

'How can I help it?' she said, reserve breaking down in her vehemence, 'when I think how much papa has suffered—how much Gilbert has to make up to him—how mamma took him for her own—how they have borne with him, and set their happiness on him, and yielded to his fancies, only for him to disappoint them so cruelly, and just because he can't say No! I hope he wont come home; I shall never know how to speak to him!'

'But all that makes it so much the worse for him,' said Ulick, in a tone of amazement.

'Yes, you can't understand,' she answered; 'if he had had one spark of feeling like you, he would rather have died than have gone on as he has done.'

'Surely many a man may be overtaken in a fault, and never be wrong at heart,' said Ulick. 'There's many a worse sin than what the world sets a blot upon, and I believe that is just why homes were made.'

Lucy came back with the frock, and Ulick, thanking her, sped away; while Sophy slowly went upstairs and hid herself on her couch. For a woman to find a man thinking her over-hard and severe, is sure either to harden or to soften her very decidedly, and it was a hard struggle which would be the effect. There was an inclination at first to attribute his surprise to the lax notions and foolish fondness of his home, where no doubt far worse disorders than Gilbert's were treated as mere matters of course. But such strong pity for the offender did not seem to accord with this; and the more she thought, the more sure she became that it was the fresh charity and sweetness of an innocent spirit, 'believing all things,' and separating the fault from the offender. His words had fallen on her ear in a sense beyond what he meant. Pride and uncharitable resentment might be worse sins than mere weakness and excess. She thought of the elder son in the parable, who, unknowing of his brother's temptation and sorrow, closed his heart against his return; and if her tears would have come, she would have wept that she could not bring herself to look on Gilbert otherwise than as the troubler of her father's peace.

When her mother at last came upstairs, she only ventured to ask gently, 'How does papa bear it?'

'It did not come without preparation,' was the answer; 'and at first we were occupied with comforting Mr. Dusautoy, who takes to himself all the shame his nephew will not feel, for having drawn poor Gilbert into such a set.'

'And papa?' still asked Sophy.

'He is very quiet, and it is not easy to tell. I believe it was a great mistake, though not of his making, to send Gilbert to Oxford at all, and I doubt whether he will ever go back again.

'Oh, mamma, not conquer this, and live it down!' cried Sophy; but then changing, she sighed and said, 'If he would—'

'Yes, a great deal depends upon how he may take this, and what becomes of Algernon Dusautoy; though I suppose there is no lack of other tempters. Your papa has even spoken of India again; he still thinks he would be more guarded there, but all depends on the spirit in which we find him. One thing I hope, that I shall leave it all to his father's judgment, and not say one word.'

The next post brought a penitent letter from Gilbert, submitting completely to his father; only begging that he might not see any one at home until he should have redeemed his character, and promising to work very hard and deny himself all relaxation if he might only go to a tutor at a distance.

This did not at all accord with Mr. Kendal's views. He had an unavowed distrust of Gilbert's letters, he did not fancy a tutor thus selected, and believed the boy to be physically incapable of the proposed amount of study. So he wrote a very grave but merciful summons to Willow Lawn.

Albinia went to meet the delinquent at Hadminster, and was struck by the different deportment of the two youths. Algernon Dusautoy, whose servant had met him, sauntered up to her as if nothing had happened, carelessly hoped all were well at Bayford, and, in spite of her exceeding coldness, talked on with perfect ease upon the chances of a war with Russia, and had given her three or four maxims, before Gilbert came up with the luggage van, with a bag in his hand, and a hurried bewildered manner, unable to meet her eye. He handed her into the carriage, seated himself beside her, and drove off without one unnecessary word, while Algernon, mounting his horse, waved them a disengaged farewell, and cantered on. Albinia heard a heavy sigh, and saw her companion very wan and sorrowful, dejection in every feature, in the whole stoop of his figure, and in the nervous twitch of his hands. The contrast gave an additional impulse to her love and pity, and the first words she said were, 'Your father is quite ready to forgive.'

'I knew he would be so,' he answered, hardly able to command his voice; 'I knew you would all be a great deal too kind to me, and that is the worst of all.'

'No, Gilbert, not if it gives you resolution to resist the next time.'

He groaned; and it was not long before she drew from him a sincere avowal of his follies and repentance. He had been led on by assurances that 'every one' did the like, by fear of betraying his own timidity, by absurd dread of being disdained as slow; all this working on his natural indolence and love of excitement, had combined to involve him in habits which had brought on him this disgrace. It was a hopeful sign that he admitted its justice, and accused no one of partiality; the reprimand had told upon him, and he was too completely struck down even to attempt to justify himself; exceedingly afraid of his father, and only longing to hide himself. Such was his utter despair, that Albinia had no scruples in encouraging him, and assuring him with all her heart, that if taken rightly, the shock that brought him to his senses, might be the blessing of his life. He did not take comfort readily, though soothed by her kindness; he could not get over his excessive dread of his father, and each attempt at reassurance fell short. At last it came out that the very core of his misery was this, that he had found himself for part of the journey, in the same train with Miss Durant and two or three children. He could not tell her where he was going nor why, and he had leant back in the carriage, and watched her on the platform by stealth, as she moved about, 'lovelier and more graceful than ever!' but how could he present himself to her in his disgrace and misery? 'Oh, Mrs. Kendal, I forgive my father, but my life was blighted when I was cut off from her!'

'No, Gilbert, you are wrong. There is no blighting in a worthy, disinterested attachment. To be able to love and respect such a woman is a good substantial quality in you, and ought to make you a higher and better man.'

Gilbert turned round a face of extreme amazement. 'I thought,' he said, 'I thought you—' and went no farther.

'I respect your feeling for her more than when it was two years younger,' she said; 'I should respect it doubly if instead of making you ashamed, it had saved you from the need of shame.'

'Do you give me any hope?' cried Gilbert, his face gleaming into sudden eager brightness.

'Things have not become more suitable,' said Albinia; and his look lapsed again into despondency; but she added, 'Each step towards real manhood, force of character, and steadiness, would give you weight which might make your choice worth your father's consideration, and you worth that of Genevieve.'

'Oh! would you but have told me so before!'

'It was evident to your own senses,' said Albinia; and she thought of the suggestion that Sophy had made.

'Too late! too late!' sighed Gilbert.

'No, never too late! You have had a warning; you are very young, and it cannot be too late for winning a character, and redeeming the time!'

'And you tell me I may love her!' repeated Gilbert, so intoxicated with the words, that she became afraid of them.

'I do not tell you that you may importune her, or disobey your father. I only tell you that to look up and work and deny yourself, in honour of one so truly noble, is one of the best and most saving of secondary motives. I shall honour you, Gilbert, if you do so use it as to raise and support you, though of course I cannot promise that she can be earned by it, and even that motive will not do alone, however powerful you may think it.'

Neither of them said more, but Gilbert sighed heavily several times, and would willingly have checked their homeward speed. He grew pale as they entered the town, and groaned as the gates swung back, and they rattled over the wooden bridge. It was about four o'clock, and he said, hurriedly, as with a sort of hope, 'I suppose they are all out.'

He was answered by a whoop of ecstasy, and before he was well out of the carriage, he was seized by the joyous Maurice, shouting that he had been for a ride with papa, without a leading rein. Happy age for both, too young to know more than that the beloved playfellow was at home again!

Little Albinia studied her brother till the small memory came back, and she made her pretty signs for the well-remembered dancing in his arms. From such greetings, Gilbert's wounded spirit could not shrink, much as he dreaded all others; and, carrying the baby and preceded by Maurice, while he again muttered that of course no one was at home, he went upstairs.

Albinia meantime tapped at the library door. She knew Mr. Kendal to be there, yearning to forgive, but thinking it right to have his pardon sought; and she went in to tell him of his son's keen remorse, and deadly fear. Displeased and mournful, Mr. Kendal sighed. 'He has little to fear from me, would he but believe so! He ought to have come to me, but—'

That 'but' meant repentance for over-sternness in times past.

'Let me send him to you.'

'I will come,' said Mr. Kendal, willing to spare his son the terror of presenting himself.

There was a pretty sight in the morning-room. Gilbert was on the floor with the two children, Maurice intent on showing how nearly little Albinia could run alone, and between ordering and coaxing, drawing her gently on; her beautiful brown eyes opened very seriously to the great undertaking, and her round soft hands, with a mixture of confidence and timidity, trusted within the sturdy ones of her small elder, while Gilbert knelt on one knee, and stretched out a protecting arm, really to grasp the little one, if the more childish brother should fail her, and his countenance, lighted up with interest and affection, was far more prepossessing than when so lately it had been, full of cowering, almost abject apprehension.

Was it a sort of instinctive feeling that the little sister would be his best shelter, that made him gather the child into his arms, and hold her before his deeply blushing face as he rose from the floor? She merrily called out, 'Papa!' Maurice loudly began to recount her exploits, and thus passed the salutation, at the end of which Gilbert found that his father was taking the little one from him, and giving her to her mother, who carried her away, calling Maurice with her.

'Have you nothing to say to me?' said Mr. Kendal, after waiting for some moments; but as Gilbert only looked up to him with a piteous, scared, uncertain glance, be added; 'You need not fear me; I believe you have erred more from weakness than from evil inclinations, and I trust in the sincerity of your repentance.'

These kind words softened Gilbert; he assured his father of his thanks for his kindness, no one could grieve more deeply, or be more anxious to atone in any possible manner for what he had unwittingly done.

'I believe you, Gilbert,' said his father; 'but you well know that the only way of atoning for the past, as well as of avoiding such wretchedness and disgrace for the future, is to show greater firmness.'

'I know it is,' said Gilbert, sorrowfully.

'I cannot look into your heart,' added Mr. Kendal. 'I can only hope and believe that your grief for the sin is as deep, or deeper, than that for the public stigma, for which comparatively, I care little.'

Gilbert exclaimed that so indeed it was, and this was no more than the truth. Out of sight of temptation, and in that pure atmosphere, the loud revel and coarse witticisms that had led him on, were only loathsome and disgusting, and made him miserable in the recollection.

'I am ready to submit to anything,' he added, fervently. 'As long as you forgive me, I am ready to bear anything.'

'I forgive you from my heart,' said Mr. Kendal, warmly. 'I only wish to consider what may be most expedient for you. I should scarcely like to send you back to Oxford to retrieve your character, unless I were sure that you would be more resolute in resisting temptation. No, do not reply; your actions during this time of penance will be a far more satisfactory answer than any promises. I had thought of again applying to your cousin John, to take you into his bank, though you could not now go on such terms as you might have done when there was no error in the background, and I still sometimes question whether it be not the safer method.'

'Whatever you please,' said Gilbert; 'I deserve it all.'

'Nay, do not look upon my decision, whatever it may be, as punishment, but only as springing from my desire for your real welfare. I will write to your cousin and ask whether he still has a vacancy, but without absolutely proposing you to him, and we will look on the coming months as a period of probation, during which we may judge what may be the wisest course. I will only ask one other question, Gilbert, and you need not be afraid to answer me fully and freely. Have you any debts at Oxford?'

'A few,' stammered Gilbert, with a great effort.

'Can you tell me to whom, and the amount?'

He tried to recollect as well as he could, while completely frightened and confused by the gravity with which his father was jotting them down in his pocket-book.

'Well, Gilbert,' he concluded, 'you have dealt candidly with me, and you shall never have cause to regret having done so. And now we will only feel that you are at home, and dwell no longer on the cause that has brought you. Come out, and see what we have been doing in the meadow.'

Gilbert seemed more overthrown and broken down by kindness than by reproof. He hardly exerted himself even to play with Maurice, or to amuse his grandmother; and though his sisters treated him as usual, he never once lifted up his eyes to meet Sophy's glance, and scarcely used his voice.

Nothing could be more disarming than such genuine sorrow; and Sophy, pardoning him with all her heart, and mourning for her past want of charity, watched him, longing to do something for his comfort, and to evince her tenderness; but only succeeded in encumbering every petty service or word of intercourse with a weight of sad consciousness.

CHAPTER XXI.

'I had almost written to ask your pardon,' said Mrs. Dusautoy, as Albinia entered her drawing-room on the afternoon following. 'I should like by way of experiment to know what *would* put that boy out of countenance. He listened with placid graciousness to his uncle's lecture, and then gave us to understand that he was obliged for his solicitude, and that there was a great deal of jealousy and misrepresentation at Oxford; but he thought it best always to submit to authorities, however unreasonable. And this morning, after amiably paying his respects to me, he said he was going to inquire for Gilbert. I intimated that Willow Lawn was the last place where he would be welcome, but he was far above attending to me. Did Gilbert see him?'

'Gilbert was in the garden with us when we were told he was in the house. Poor fellow, he shuddered, and looked as if he wanted me to guard him, so I sent him out walking with Maurice while I went in, and found Lucy entertaining the gentleman. I made myself as cold and inhospitable as I could, but I am afraid he rather relishes a dignified retenue.'

'Poor boy! I wonder what on earth is to be done with him. I never before knew what John's love and patience were.'

'Do you think he will remain here?'

'I cannot tell; we talk of tutors, but John is really, I believe, happier for having him here, and besides one can be sure the worst he is doing is painting a lobster. However, much would depend on what you and Mr. Kendal thought. If he and Gilbert were doing harm to each other, everything must give way.'

'If people of that age will not keep themselves out of harm's way, nobody can do it for them,' said Albinia, 'and as long as Gilbert continues in his present mood, there is more real separation in voluntarily holding aloof, than if they were sent far apart, only to come together again at college.'

Gilbert did continue in the same mood. The tender cherishing of his home restored his spirits; but he was much subdued, and deeply grateful, as he manifested by the most eager and affectionate courtesy, such as made him almost the servant of everybody, without any personal aim or object, except to work up his deficient studies, and to avoid young Dusautoy. He seemed to cling to his family as his protectors, and to follow the occupations least likely to lead to a meeting with the Polysyllable; he was often at church in the week, rode with his father, went parish visiting with the ladies, and was responsible when Maurice fished for minnows in the meadows. Nothing could be more sincerely desirous to atone for the past and enter on a different course, and no conduct could be more truly humble or endearing.

The imaginary disdain of Ulick O'More was entirely gone, and perceiving that the Irishman's delicacy was keeping him away from Willow Lawn, Gilbert himself met him and brought him home, in the delight of having heard of a naval cadetship having been offered to his brother, and full of such eager joy as longed for sympathy.

'Happy fellow!' Gilbert murmured to himself.

Younger in years, more childish in character, poor Gilbert had managed to make his spirit world-worn and weary, compared with the fresh manly heart of the Irishman, all centered in the kindred 'points of Heaven and home,' and enjoying keenly, for the very reason that he bent dutifully with all his might to a humble and uncongenial task.

Yet somehow, admire and esteem as he would, there arose no intimacy or friendship between Gilbert and Ulick; their manners were frank and easy, but there was no spontaneous approach, no real congeniality, nor exchange of mind and sympathy as between Ulick and Mr. Kendal. Albinia had a theory that the friendship was too much watched to take; Sophy hated herself for the recurring conviction that 'Gilbert was not the kind of stuff,' though she felt day by day how far he excelled her in humility, gentleness, and sweet temper.

When the Goldsmiths gave their annual dinner-party, Albinia felt a sudden glow at the unexpected sight of Ulick O'More.

'I am only deputy for the Orange man,' he said; 'it is Hyder Ali who ought to be dining here! Yes, it is his doing, I'd back him against any detective!'

'What heroism have you been acting together?'

'We had just given Farmer Martin L120 in notes, when as he went out, we heard little Hyder growling and giving tongue, and a fellow swearing as if he was at the fair of Monyveagh, and the farmer hallooing thieves. I found little Hyder had nailed the rascal fast by the leg, just as he had the notes out of the farmer's pouch. I collared him, Johns ran for the police, and the rascal is fast.'

'What a shame to cheat Mr. Kendal of the committal.'

'The policeman said he was gone out, so we had the villain up to the Admiral with the greater satisfaction, as he was a lodger in one of the Admiral's pet public-houses in Tibb's Alley.'

'Ah, when Gilbert is of age,' said Albinia, 'woe to Tibb's! So you are a testimonial to the Tripod?'

'So I suspect, for I found an invitation when I came home, I would have run down to tell you, but I had been kept late, and one takes some getting up for polite society.'

There was a great deal of talk about Hyder's exploit, and some disposition to make Mr. O'More the hero of the day; but this was quickly nipped by his uncle's dry shortness, and the superciliousness with which Mr. Cavendish Dusautoy turned the conversation to the provision of pistols, couriers, and guards, for travelling through the Abruzzi. The polysyllabic courage, and false alarms on such a scale, completely eclipsed a real pick-pocket, caught by a gipsy's cur and a banker's clerk.

Not that Ulick perceived any disregard until later in the evening, when the young Kendals arrived, and of course he wanted each and all to hear of his Tripod's achievement. He met with ready attention from Sophy and Gilbert, who pronounced that as the cat was to Whittington, so was Hyder to O'More; but when in his overflowing he proceeded to Lucy, she had neither eyes nor ears for him, and when the vicar told her Mr. O'More was speaking to her, she turned with an air of petulance, so that he felt obliged to beg her pardon and retreat.

The Bayford parties never lasted later than a few minutes after ten, but when once Mr. Cavendish Dusautoy and Miss Kendal had possession of the piano and guitar, there was no conclusion. Song succeeded song, they wanted nothing save their own harmony, and hardly waited for Miss Goldsmith's sleepy thanks. The vicar hated late hours, and the Kendals felt every song a trespass upon their hosts, but the musicians had their backs to the world, and gave no interval, so that it was eleven o'clock before Mr. Kendal, in desperation, laid his hand on his daughter, and barbarously carried her off.

The flirtation was so palpable, that Albinia mused on the means of repressing it; but she believed that to remonstrate, would only be to give Lucy pleasure, and held her peace till a passion for riding seized upon the young lady. The old pony had hard service between Sophy's needs and Maurice's exactions, but Lucy's soul soared far above ponies, and fastened upon Gilbert's steed.

'And pray what is Gilbert to ride?'

'Oh! papa does not always want Captain, or Mr. Cavendish Dusautoy would lend him Bamfylde.'

'Thank you,' returned Gilbert, satirically.

Next morning Lucy, radiant with smiles, announced that all was settled. Mr. Cavendish Dusautoy's Lady Elmira would be brought down for her to try this afternoon, so Gilbert might keep his own horse and come too, which permission he received with a long whistle and glance at Mrs. Kendal, and then walked out of the room.

'How disobliging!' said Lucy. 'Well then, Sophy, you must make your old hat look as well as you can, for I suppose it will not quite do to go without anyone.'

Sophy, like her brother, looked at Mrs. Kendal, and with an eye of indignant appeal and entreaty, while Albinia's countenance was so full of displeasure, that Lucy continued earnestly, 'O, mamma, you can't object. You used to go out riding with papa when he was at Colonel Bury's.'

'Well, Lucy!' exclaimed her sister, 'I did not think even you capable of such a comparison.'

'It's all the same,' said Lucy tartly, blushing a good deal.

Sophy leapt up to look at her, and Albinia trying to be calm and judicious, demanded, 'What is the same as what?'

'Why, Algernon and *me*,' was the equally precise reply.

In stately horror, Sophy rose and seriously marched away, leaving, by her look and manner, a species of awe upon both parties, and some seconds passed ere, with crimson blushes, Albania ventured to invite the dreaded admission, by demanding, 'Now, Lucy, will you be so good as to tell me the meaning of this extraordinary allusion?'

'Why, to be sure—I know it was very different. Papa was so old, and *there were us*,' faltered Lucy, 'but I meant, you would know how it all is—how those things—'

'Stop, Lucy, am I to understand by those things, that you wish me to believe you and Mr. Cavendish Dusautoy are on the game terms as—No, I can't say it.'

'I don't know what you mean,' said Lucy, growing frightened, 'I never thought there could be such an uproar about my just going out riding.'

'You have led me to infer so much more, that it becomes my duty to have an explanation, at least,' she added, thinking this sounded cold, 'I should have hoped you would have given me your confidence.'

'O, but you always would make game of him!' cried Lucy.

'Not now; this is much too serious, if you have been led to believe that his attentions are not as I supposed, because you are the only girl about here whom he thinks worthy of his notice.'

'It's a great deal more,' said Lucy, with more feeling and less vanity than had yet been apparent.

'And what has he been making you think, my poor child?' said Albinia. 'I know it is very distressing, but it would be more right and safe if I knew what it amounts to.'

'Not much after all,' said Lucy, her tone implying the reverse, and though her cheeks were crimson, not averse to the triumph of the avowal, nor enduring as much embarrassment as her auditor, 'only he made me sure of it
—he said—(now, mamma, you have made me, so I must) that he had changed his opinion of English beauty—you know, mamma. And another time he said he had wandered Europe over to—to find loveliness on the banks of the Baye. Wasn't it absurd? And he says he does not think it half so much that a woman should be accomplished herself, as that she should be able to appreciate other people's talents—and once he said the Principessa Bianca di Moretti would be very much disappointed.'

'Well, my dear,' said Albinia, kindly putting her arm round Lucy's waist, 'perhaps by themselves the things did not so much require to be told. I can hardly blame you, and I wish I had been more on my guard, and helped you more. Only if he seems to care so little about disappointing this lady might he not do the same by you?'

'But she's an Italian, and a Roman Catholic,' exclaimed Lucy.

Albinia could not help smiling, and Lucy, perceiving that this was hardly a valid excuse for her utter indifference towards her Grandison's Clementina, continued, 'I mean—of course there was nothing in it.'

'Very possibly; but how would it be, if by-and-by he told somebody that Miss Kendal would be very much disappointed?'

'O, mamma,' cried Lucy, hastily detaching herself, 'you don't know!'

'I cannot tell, my poor Lucy,' said Albinia. 'I fear there must be grief and trouble any way, if you let yourself attend to him, for you know, even if he were in earnest, it would not be right to think of a person who has shown so little wish to be good.'

Lucy stood for a few moments before the sense reached her mind, then she dropped into a chair, and exclaimed,

'I see how it is! You'll treat him as grandpapa treated Captain Pringle, but I shall break my heart, quite!' and she burst into tears.

'My dear, your father and I will do our best for your happiness, and we would never use concealment. Whatever we do shall be as Christian people working together, not as tyrants with a silly girl.'

Lucy was pleased, and let Albinia take her hand.

'Then I will write to decline the horse. It would be far too marked.'

'But oh, mamma! you wont keep him away!'

'I shall not alter our habits unless I see cause. He is much too young for us to think seriously of what he may have said; and I entreat you to put it out of your mind, for it would be very sad for you to fix your thoughts on him, and then find him not in earnest, and even if he were, you know it would be wrong to let affection grow up where there is no real dependence upon a person's goodness.'

The kindness soothed Lucy, and though she shed some tears, she did not resist the decision. Indeed she was sensible of that calm determination of manner, which all the family had learnt to mean that the measures thus taken were unalterable, whereas the impetuous impulses often were reversed.

Many a woman's will is like the tide, ever fretting at the verge of the boundary, but afraid to overpass it, and only tempting the utmost limit in the certainty of the recall, and Lucy perhaps felt a kind of protection in the curb, even while she treated it as an injury. She liked to be the object of solicitude, and was pleased with Albinia's extra kindness, while, perhaps, there was some excitement in the belief that Algernon was missing her, so she was particularly amenable, and not much out of spirits.

The original Meadows character, and Bayford breeding, had for a time been surmounted by Albinia's influence and training; but so ingrain was the old disposition, that a touch would at once re-awaken it, and the poor girl was in a neutral state, coloured by whichever impression had been most recent. Albinia's hopes of prevailing in the end increased when Mrs. Dusautoy told her, with a look of intelligence, that Algernon was going to stay with a connexion of his mother, a Mr. Greenaway, with six daughters, very stylish young ladies.

Six stylish young ladies! Albinia could have embraced them all, and actually conferred a cordial nod on Mr. Cavendish Dusautoy when she met him on the way home.

But as she entered the house, so ominous a tone summoned her to the library, that she needed not to be told that Mr. Cavendish Dusautoy had been there.

'I told him,' said Mr. Kendal, 'that he was too young for me to entertain his proposal, and I intimated that he had character to redeem before presenting himself in such capacity.'

'I hope you made the refusal evident to his intellect.'

'He drove me to be more explicit than I intended. I think he was astonished. He stared at me for full three minutes before he could believe in the refusal. Poor lad, it must be real attachment, there could be no other inducement.'

'And Lucy is exceedingly pretty.'

Mr. Kendal glanced at the portrait over the mantelpiece smiled sadly, and shook his head.

'Poor dear,' continued Albinia, 'what a commotion there will be in her head; but she has behaved so well hitherto, that I hope we may steer her safely through, above all, if one of the six cousins will but catch him in the rebound! Have you spoken to her?'

'Is it necessary?'

'So asked her grandfather,' said Albinia, smiling, as he, a little out of countenance, muttered something of 'foolish affair—mere child—and turn her head—'

'That's done!' said Albinia, 'we have only to try to get it straight. Besides, it would hardly be just to let her think he had meant nothing, and I have promised to deal openly with her, otherwise we can hardly hope for plain dealing from her.'

'And you think it will be a serious disappointment?'

'She is highly flattered by his attention, but I don't know how deep it may have gone.'

'I wish people would let one's daughters alone!' exclaimed Mr. Kendal. 'You will talk to her then, Albinia, and don't let her think me more harsh than you can help, and come and tell me how she bears it.'

'Won't you speak to her yourself?'

'Do you think I must?' he said, reluctantly; 'you know so much better how to manage her.'

'I think you must do this, dear Edmund,' she said, between decision and entreaty. 'She knows that I dislike the man, and may fancy it my doing it she only hears it at second hand. If you speak, there will be no appeal, and besides there are moments when the really nearest should have no go-betweens.'

'We were not very near without you,' he said. 'If it were Sophy, I should know better what to be about.'

'Sophy would not put you in such a fix.'

'So I have fancied—' he paused, smiling, while she waited in eager curiosity, such as made him finish as if ashamed. 'I have thought our likings much the same. Have you never observed what I mean?'

'Oh! I never observe anything. I did not find out Maurice and Winifred till he told me. Who do you think it is? I always thought love would be the making of Sophy. I see she is another being. What is your guess, Mr. Hope?'

Mr. Kendal made a face of astonishment at such an improbable guess, and was driven into exclaiming, 'How could any one help thinking of O'More?'

'Oh! only too delightful!' cried Albinia. 'Why didn't I think of it—butthen his way is so free and cousinly with us all.'

'There may be nothing in it,' said Mr. Kendal; 'and under present circumstances it would hardly be desirable.'

'If old Mr. Goldsmith acts as he ought,' continued Albinia, 'we should never lose our Sophy—and what a son we should have! he has so exactly the bright temper that she needs.'

'Well, well, that is all in the clouds,' said Mr. Kendal. 'I wish the present were equally satisfactory.'

'Ah, I had better call poor Lucy.'

'Come back with her, pray,' called Mr. Kendal, nervously.

Albinia regretted her superfluous gossip when Lucy appeared with eyes so sparkling, and cheeks so flushed, that it was plain that she had been in all the miseries of suspense. Her countenance glowed with feeling, that lifted her beyond her ordinary doll-like prettiness. Albinia's heart sank with compassion as she held her hand, and her father stood as if struck by something more like the vision or his youth than he had been prepared for; each feeling that something genuine was present, and respecting it accordingly.

'Lucy,' said Mr. Kendal, tenderly, 'I see I need not tell you why I have sent for you. You are very young, my dear, and you must trust us to care for your happiness.'

'Yes.' Lucy looked up wistfully.

'This gentleman has some qualities such as may make him shine in the eyes of a young lady; but it is our duty to look farther, and I am afraid I know nothing of him that could justify me in trusting him with anything soprecious to me.'

Lucy's face became full of consternation, her hand lay unnerved in

Albinia'a pressure, and Mr. Kendal turned his eyes from her to his wife, as he proceeded,

'I have seen so much wretchedness caused by want of religious principle, that even where the morals appeared unblemished, I should feel no confidence where I saw no evidence of religion, and I should consider it as positively wrong to sanction an engagement with such a person. Now you must perceive that we have every means of forming an opinion of this young man, and that he has given us no reason to think he would show the unselfish care for your welfare that we should wish to secure.'

Albinia tried to make it comprehensible. 'You know, my dear, we have always seen him resolved on his own way, and not caring how he may inconvenience his uncle and aunt. We know his temper is not always amiable, and differently as you see him, you must let us judge.'

Wrenching her hand away, Lucy burst into tears. Her father looked at Albinia, as if she ought to have saved him this infliction, and she began a little whispering about not distressing papa, which checked the sobs, and enabled him to say, 'There, that's right, my dear, I see you are willing to submit patiently to our judgment, and I believe you will find it for the best. We will do all in our power to help you, and make you happy,' and bending down he kissed her, and left her to his wife.

In such family scenes, logic is less useful than the power of coming to a friendly conclusion; Lucy's awe of her father was a great assistance, she was touched with his unwonted softness, and did not apprehend how total was the rejection. But what he was spared, was reserved for Albinia. There was a lamentable scene of sobbing and weeping, beyond all argument, and only ending in physical exhaustion, which laid her on the bed all the rest of the day.

Gilbert and Sophy could not but be aware of the cause of her distress. The former thought it a great waste.

'Tell Lucy,' he said, 'that if she wishes to be miserable for life, she has found the best way! He is a thorough-bred tyrant at heart, pig-headed, and obstinate, and with the very worst temper I ever came across. Not a soul can he feel for, nor admire but himself. His wife will be a perfect slave. I declare I would as soon sell her to Legree.'

Sophy's views of the gentleman were not more favourable, but she was in terror lest Lucy should have a permanently broken heart, after the precedent of Aunt Maria. And on poor Sophy fell the misfortune of being driven up by grandmamma's inquiries, to own that the proposal had been rejected.

Shade of poor dear Mr. Meadows, didst thou not stand aghast! Five thousand a year refused! Grandmamma would have had a fit if she had not conceived a conviction, that imparted a look of shrewdness to her mild, simple old face. Of course Mr. Kendal was only holding off till the young man was a little older. He could have no intention of letting his daughter miss such a match, and dear Lucy would have her carriage, and be presented at court.

Sophy argued vehemently against this, and poor grandmamma, who had with difficulty been taught worldly wisdom as a duty, and always thought herself good when she talked prudently, began to cry. Sophy, quite overcome, was equally distressing with her apologies; Albinia found them both in tears, and Sophy was placed on the sick-list by one of her peculiar headaches of self-reproach.

It was a time of great perplexity. Lucy cried incessantly, bursting out at every trifle, but making no complaints, and submitting so meekly, that the others were almost as unhappy as herself.

She was first cheered by the long promised visit from Mrs. Annesley and Miss Ferrars. Albinia had now no fears of showing off home or children, and it was a great success.

The little Awk was in high beauty, and graciously winning, and Maurice's likeness to his Uncle William enchanted the aunts, though they were shocked at his mamma's indifference to his constant imperilling of life and limb, and grievously discomfited his sisters by adducing children who talked French and read history, whereas he could not read d-o-g without spelling, and had peculiar views as to b and d, p and q. However, if he could not read he could ride, and Mrs. Annesley scarcely knew the extent of the favour she conferred, when she commissioned Gilbert to procure for him a pony as his private property.

Miss Ferrars had not expected one of the thirty-six O'Mores to turn up here. She gave some good advice about hasty intimacies, and as it was received with a defence of the gentility of the O'Mores, the two good ladies agreed that dear Albinia was quite a child still, not fit for the care of those girls, and it would be only acting kindly to take Lucy to Brighton, and show her something of the world, or Albinia would surely let her fall a prey to that Irish clerk.

They liked Lucy's pretty face and obliging ways, and were fond of having a young lady in their house; they saw her looking ill and depressed, and thought sea air would be good for her, and though Lucy fancied herself past caring for gaiety, and was very sorry to leave home and mamma, she was not insensible to the refreshment of her wardrobe, and the excitement and honour of the invitation. At night she cried lamentably, and clung round Albinia'a neck, sobbing, 'Oh, mamma, what will become of me without you?' but in the morning she went off in very fair spirits, and Albinia augured hopefully that soon her type of perfection would be no longer Polysyllabic. Her first letters were deplorable, but they soon became cheerful, as her mornings were occupied by lessons in music and drawing, and her evenings in quiet parties among the friends whom the aunts met at Brighton. Aunt Gertrude wrote to announce that her charge had recovered her looks and was much admired, and this was corroborated by the prosperous complacency of Lucy's style. Albinia was more relieved than surprised when the letters dwindled in length and number, well knowing that the Family Office was not favourable to leisure; and devoid of the epistolary gift herself, she always wondered more at people's writing than at their silence, and scarcely reciprocated Lucy's effusions by the hurried notes which she enclosed in the well-filled envelopes of Gilbert and Sophy, who, like their father, could cover any amount of sheets of paper.

CHAPTER XXII.

'There!' cried Ulick O'More, 'I may wish you all good-bye. There's an end of it.'

Mr. Kendal stood aghast.

'He's insulted my father and my family,' cried Ulick, 'and does he think I'll write another cipher for him?'

'Your uncle?'

'Don't call him my uncle. I wish I'd never set eyes on his wooden old face, to put the family name and honour in the power of such as he.'

'What has he done to you?'

'He has offered to take me as his partner,' cried Ulick, with flashing eyes; and as an outcry arose, not in sympathy with his resentment, he continued vehemently, 'Stay, you have not heard! 'Twas on condition I'd alter my name, leave out the O that has come down to me from them that were kings and princes before his grandfathers broke stones on the road.'

'He offered to take you into partnership,' repeated Mr. Kendal.

'Do you think I could listen to such terms!' cried the indignant lad. 'Give up the O! Why, I would never be able to face my brothers!'

'But, Ulick—'

'Don't talk to me, Mr. Kendal; I wouldn't sell my name if you were to argue to me like Plato, nor if his bank were the Bank of England. I might as well be an Englishman at once.'

'Then this was the insult?'

'And enough too, but it wasn't all. When I answered, speaking as coolly, I assure you, as I'm doing this minute, what does he do, but call it a folly, and taunt us for a crew of Irish beggars! Beggars we may be, but we'll not be bought by him.'

'Well, this must have been an unexpected reception of such a proposal.'

'You may say that! The English think everything may be bought with money! I'd have overlooked his ignorance, poor old gentleman, if he would not have gone and spoken of my O as vulgar. Vulgar! So when I began to tell him how it began from Tigearnach, the O'More of Ballymakilty, that was Tanist of Connaught, in the time of King Mac Murrough, and that killed

Phadrig the O'Donoghoe in single combat at the fight of Shoch-knockmorty, and bit off his nose, calling it a sweet morsel of revenge, what does he do but tell me I was mad, and that he would have none of my nonsensical tales of the savage Irish. So I said I couldn't stand to hear my family insulted, and then—would you believe it? he would have it that it was I that was insolent, and when I was not going to apologize for what I had borne from him, he said he had always known how it would be trying to deal with one of our family, no better than making a silk purse out of a sow's ear. "And I'm obliged for the compliment," said I, quite coolly and politely, "but no Irish pig would sell his ear for a purse;" and so I came away, quite civilly and reasonably. Aye, I see what you would do, Mr. Kendal, but I beg with all my heart you won't. There are some things a gentleman should not put up with, and I'll not take it well of you if you call it my duty to hear my father and his family abused. I'll despise myself if I could. *You* don't—' cried he, turning round to Albinia.

'Oh, no, but I think you should try to understand Mr. Goldsmith's point of view.'

'I understand it only too well, if that would do any good. Point of view—why, 'tis the farmyard cock's point of view, strutting on the top of that bank of his own, and patronizing the free pheasant out in the woods. More fool I for ever letting him clip my wings, but he's seen the last of me. No, don't ask me to make it up. It can't be done—'

'What can be done to the boy?' asked Albinia; 'how can he be brought to hear reason?'

'Leave him alone,' Mr. Kendal said, aside; while Ulick in a torrent of eager cadences protested his perfect sanity and reason, and Mr. Kendal quietly left the room, again to start on a peace-making mission, but it was unpromising, for Mr. Goldsmith began by declaring he would not hear a single word in favour of the ungrateful young dog.

Mr. Kendal gathered that young O'More had become so valuable, and that cold and indifferent as Mr. Goldsmith appeared, he had been growing so fond and so proud of his nephew, as actually to resolve on giving him a share of the business, and dividing the inheritance which had hitherto been destined to a certain Andrew Goldsmith, brought up in a relation's office at Bristol. Surprised at his own graciousness, and anticipating transports of gratitude, his dismay and indignation at the reception of his proposal were extreme, especially as he had no conception of the offence he had given regarding the unfortunate O as a badge of Hibernianism and vulgarity. 'I put it to you, Mr. Kendal, as a sensible man, whether it would not be enough to destroy the credit of the bank to connect it with such a name as that, looking like an Irish haymaker's. I should be ashamed of every note I issued.'

'It is unlucky,' said Mr. Kendal, 'and a difficulty the lad could hardly appreciate, since it is a good old name, and the O is a special mark of nobility.'

'And what has a banker to do with nobility? Pretty sort of nobility too, at that dog-kennel of theirs in Ireland, and his father, a mere adventurer if ever there lived one! But I swore when he carried off poor Ellen that his speculation should do him no good, and I've kept my word. I wish I hadn't been fool enough to meddle with one of the concern! No, no, 'tis no use arguing, Mr. Kendal, I have done with him! I would not make him a partner, not if he offered to change his name to John Smith! I never thought to meet with such ingratitude, but it runs in the breed! I might have known better than to make much of one of the crew. Yet it is a pity too, we have not had such a clear-headed, trustworthy fellow about the place since young Bowles died; he has a good deal of the Goldsmith in him when you set him to work, and makes his figures just like my poor father. I thought it was his writing the other day till I looked at the date. Clever lad, very, but it runs in the blood. I shall send for Andrew Goldsmith.'

One secret of Mr. Kendal's power was that he never interrupted, but let people run themselves down and contradict themselves; and all he observed was, 'However it may end, you have done a great deal for him. Even if you parted now, he would be able to find a situation.'

'Why—yes,' said Mr. Goldsmith, 'the lad knew nothing serviceable when he came, we had an infinity of maggots about algebra and logarithms to drive out of his head; but now he really is nearly as good an accountant as old Johns.'

'You would be sorry to part with him, and I cannot help hoping this may be made up.'

'You don't bring me any message! I've said I'll listen to nothing.'

'No; the poor boy's feelings are far too much wounded,' said Mr. Kendal. 'Whether rightly or wrongly, he fancies that his father and family have been slightingly spoken of, and he is exceedingly hurt.'

'His father! I'm sure I did not say a tenth part of what the fellow richly deserves. If the young gentleman is so touchy, he had better go back to Ireland again.'

Nothing more favourable could Mr. Kendal obtain, though he thought Mr. Goldsmith uneasy, and perhaps impressed by the independence of his nephew's attitude.

It was an arduous office for a peace-maker, where neither party could comprehend the feelings of the other, but on his return he found that Ulick had stormed himself into comparative tranquillity, and was listening the better to the womankind, because they had paid due honour to the amiable ancestral Tigearnach and all his guttural posterity, whose savage exploits and bloody catastrophes acted as such a sedative, that by the time he had come down to Uncle Bryan of the Kaffir war, he actually owned that as to the mighty 'O,' Mr. Goldsmith might have erred in sheer ignorance.

'After all,' said Albinia, 'U. O'More is rather personal in writing to a creditor.'

'It might be worse,' said Ulick, laughing, 'if my name was John. I. O'More would be a dangerous confession. But I'll not be come round even by your fun, Mrs. Kendal, I'll not part with my father's name.'

'No, that would be base,' said Sophy.

'Who would wish to persuade you?' added Albinia. 'I am sure you are right in refusing with your feelings; I only want you to forgive your uncle, and not to break with him.'

'I'd forgive him his ignorance, but my mother herself could not wish me to forgive what he said of my father.'

'And how if he thinks this explosion needs forgiveness?'

'He must do without it,' said Ulick. 'No, I was cool, I assure you, cool and collected, but it was not fit for me to stand by and hear my father insulted.'

Albinia closed the difficult discussion by observing that it was time to dress, and Sophy followed her from the room burning with indignant sympathy. 'It would be meanly subservient to ask pardon for defending a father whom he thought maligned,' said Albinia, and Sophy took exception at the word 'thought.'

'Ah! of course *he* cannot be deceived!' said Albinia—but no sooner were the words spoken than she was half-startled, half-charmed by finding they had evoked a glow of colour.

'How do you think it will end?' asked Sophy.

'I can hardly fancy he will not be forgiven, and yet—it might be better.'

'Yes, I do think he would get on faster in India,' said Sophy eagerly; 'he could do just as Gilbert might have done.'

Was it possible for Albinia to have kept out of her eyes a significant glance, or to have disarmed her lips of a merry smile of amused encouragement! How she had looked she knew not, but the red deepened on Sophy's whole face, and after one inquiring gaze from the eyes they were cast down, and an ineffable brightness came over the expression, softening and embellishing.

'What have I done?' thought Albinia. 'Never mind—it must have been all there, or it would not have been wakened so easily—if he goes they will have a scene first.'

But when Mr. Kendal came back he only advised Ulick to go to his desk as usual the next day, as if nothing had happened.

And Ulick owned that, turn out as things might, he could not quit his work in the first ardour of his resentment, and with a great exertion of Christian forgiveness, he finally promised not to give notice of his retirement unless his uncle should repeat the offence. This time Albinia durst not look at Sophy.

Rather according to his friend's hopes than his own, he was able to report at the close of the next day, that he had not 'had a word from his uncle, except a nod;' and thus the days passed on, Andrew Goldsmith did not appear, and it became evident that he was to remain on sufferance as a clerk. Nor did Albinia and Sophy venture to renew the subject between themselves. At first there was consciousness in their silence; soon their minds were otherwise engrossed.

Mrs. Meadows was suddenly stricken with paralysis, and was thought to be dying. She recovered partial consciousness in the course of the next day, but was constantly moaning the name of her eldest and favourite granddaughter, and when telegraph and express train brought home the startled and trembling Lucy, she was led at once to the sick bed—where at her name there was the first gleam of anything like pleasure.

'And where have you been, my dear, this long time?'

'I've been at—at Brighton, dear grandmamma,' said Lucy, so much agitated as scarcely to be able to recall the name, or utter the words.

'And—I say, my dear love,' said Mrs. Meadows, earnestly and mysteriously, 'have you seen *him*?'

Poor Lucy turned scarlet with distress and confusion, but she was held fast, and grandmamma pursued, 'I'm sure he has not his equal for handsomeness and stateliness, and there must have been a pair of you.'

'Dear grandmamma, we must let Lucy go and take off her things; she shall come back presently, but she has had a long journey,' interposed Albinia, seeing her ready to sink into the earth.

But Mrs. Meadows had roused into eagerness, and would not let her go. 'I hope you danced with him, dear,' she went on; 'and it's all nonsense about his being high and silent. Your papa is bent on it, and you'll live like a princess in India.'

'She takes you for your mother—she means papa, whispered Albinia, not without a secret flash at once of indignation at perceiving how his first love had been wasted, yet of exultation in finding that no one but herself had known how to love him; but poor Lucy, completely and helplessly overcome, could only exclaim in a faltering voice: 'Oh, grandmamma, don't—' and Albinia was forced to disengage her, support her out of the room, and leaving her to her sister, hasten back to soothe the old lady, who had been terrified by her emotion. It had been a great mistake to bring her in abruptly, when tired with her journey, and not fully aware what awaited her. But there was at that time reason to think all would soon be over, and Albinia was startled and confused.

Albinia had hitherto been the only efficient nurse of the family. Sophy's presence seemed to stir up instincts of the old wrangling habits, and the invalid was always fretful when left to her, so that to her own exceeding distress she was kept almost entirely out of the sick room.

Lucy, on the other hand, was extremely valuable there, her bright manner and unfailing chatter always amused if needful, and her light step and tender hand made her useful, and highly appreciated by the regular nurse.

For the first few days, they watched in awe for the last dread summons, but gradually it was impossible not to become in a manner habituated to the suspense, so that common things resumed their interest, and though Sophy was pained by the incongruity, it could not have been otherwise without the spirits and health giving way under the strain. Nothing could be more trying than to have the mind wrought up to hourly anticipation of the last parting, and then the delay, without the reaction of recovery, the spirit beyond all reach of intercourse, and the mortal frame languishing and drooping. Mr. Kendal had from the first contemplated the possibility of the long duration of such lingering, and did his utmost to promote such enlivenment and change for the attendants as was consistent with their care of the sufferer. They never dared to be all beyond call at once, since a very little agitation might easily suffice to bring on a fatal attack, and Albinia and Lucy were forced to share the hours of exercise and employment between them, and often Albinia could not leave the house and garden at all.

Gilbert was an excellent auxiliary, and would devote many an hour to the cheering of the poor shattered mind. His entrance seldom failed to break the thread of melancholy murmurs, and he had exactly the gentle, bright attentive manner best fitted to rouse and enliven. Nothing could be more irreproachable, than his conduct, and his consideration and gentleness so much endeared him, that he had never been so much at peace. All he dreaded was the leaving what was truly to him the sanctuary of home, he feared alike temptation and the effort of resistance and could not bear to go away when his grandmother was in so precarious a state, and he could so much lighten Mrs. Kendal's cares both by being with her, and by watching over Maurice. His parents were almost equally afraid of trusting him in the world; and the embodiment of the militia for the county offered a quasi profession, which would keep him at home and yet give him employment. He was very anxious to be allowed to apply for a commission, and pleaded so earnestly and humbly that it would be his best hope of avoiding his former errors, that Mr. Kendal yielded, though with doubt whether it would be well to confine him to so narrow a sphere. Meantime the corps was quartered at Bayford, and filled the streets with awkward louts in red jackets, who were inveterate in mistaking the right for the left, Gilbert had a certain shy pride in his soldiership, and Maurice stepped like a young Field Marshal when he saw his brother saluted.

Nothing had so much decided this step as the finding that young Dusautoy was to return to his college after Easter. He was at the Vicarage again, marking his haughty avoidance of the Kendal family, and to their great joy, Lucy did not appear distressed, she was completely absorbed in her grandmother, and shrank from all allusion to her lover. Had the small flutter of vanity been cured by a glimpse beyond her own corner of the world?

But soon Albinia became sensible of an alteration in Gilbert. He had no sooner settled completely into his new employment, than a certain restless dissatisfaction seemed to have possessed him. He was fastidious at his meals, grumbled at his horse, scolded the groom, had fits of petulance towards his brother, and almost neglected Mrs. Meadows. No one could wonder at a youth growing weary of such attendance, but his tenderness and amiability had been his best points, and it was grievous to find them failing. Albinia would have charged the alteration on his brother officers, if they had not been a very steady and humdrum set, whose society Gilbert certainly did not prefer. She was more uneasy at finding that he sometimes saw Algernon Dusautoy, though for Lucy's sake, he always avoided bringing his name forward.

A woman was ill in the bargeman's cottage by the towing-path, and Albinia had walked to see her. As she came down-stairs, she heard voices, and beheld Mr. Hope evidently on the same errand with herself, talking to Gilbert. She caught the words, ere she could safely descend the rickety staircase, Gilbert was saying,

'Oh! some happy pair from the High Street!'

'I beg your pardon,' said Mr. Hope, 'I am so blind, I really took it for your sister, but our shopkeepers' daughters do dress so!'

Albinia looking in the same direction, beheld in a walk that skirted the meadow towards the wood, two figures, of which only one was clearly visible, it was nearly a quarter of a mile off, but there was something about it that made her exclaim, 'Why, that's Mr. Cavendish Dusautoy! whom can he be walking with?'

Gilbert started violently at hearing her behind him, and a word or two of greeting passed with Mr. Hope, then there was some spying at the pair, but they were getting further off, and disappeared in the wood, while Gilbert, screwing up his eyes, and stammering, declared he did not know; it might be, he did not think any one could be recognised at such a distance; and then saying that he had fallen in with Mr. Hope by chance, he hastened on. The curate made a brief visit, and walked home with her, examining her on her impression that the gentleman was young Dusautoy, and finally consulting her on the expediency of mentioning the suspicion to the vicar, in case he should be deluding some foolish tradesman's daughter. Albinia strongly advised his doing so; she had much faith in her own keen eyesight, and could not mistake the majestic mien of Algernon; she thought the vicar ought at once to be warned, but felt relieved that it was not her part to speak.

She was very glad when Mr. Hope took an opportunity of telling her that young Dusautoy was going to the Greenaways in a day or two.

As to Gilbert, it was as if this departure had relieved him from an incubus; he was in better spirits from that moment, and returned to his habits of kindness to both grandmamma and Maurice.

The manifold duties of head sick-nurse, governess, and housekeeper, were apt to clash, and valiant and unwearied as Albinia was, she was obliged perforce to leave the children more to others than she would have preferred. Little Albinia was all docility and sweetness, and already did such wonders with her ivory letters, that the exulting Sophy tried to abash Maurice by auguring that she would be the first to read; to which, undaunted, he replied, 'She'll never be a boy!' Nevertheless Maurice was developing a species of conscience, rendering him trustworthy and obedient out of sight, better, in fact, alone with his own honour and his mother's commands, than with any authority that he could defy. He knew when his father meant to be obeyed, and Gilbert managed him easily; but he warred with Lucy, ruled Sophy, and had no chivalry for any one but little Albinia, nor obedience except for his mother, and was a terror to maid-servants and elder children. With much of promise, he was anything but an agreeable child, and whilst no one but herself ever punished, contradicted, or complained of him, Albinia had a task that would have made her very uneasy, had not her mind been too fresh and strong for over-sense of responsibility. Each immediate duty in its turn was sufficient for her.

Maurice's shadow-like pursuit of Gilbert often took him off her hands. It might sometimes be troublesome to the elder brother, and now and then rewarded with a petulant rebuff, but Maurice was only the more pertinacious, and on the whole his allegiance was requited with ardent affection and unbounded indulgence. Nay, once when Maurice and his pony, one or both, were swept on by the whole hunt, and obliged to follow the hounds, Gilbert in his anxiety took leaps that he shuddered to remember, while the urchin sat the first gallantly, and though he fell into the next ditch, scrambled up on the instant, and was borne by his spirited pony over two more, amid universal applause. Mr. Nugent himself rode home with the brothers to tell the story; papa and mamma were too much elated at his prowess to scold.

The eventful year 1854 had begun, and General Ferrars was summoned from Canada to a command in the East. On his arrival in England, he wrote to his brother and sister to meet him in London, and the aunts, delighted to gather their children once more round them, sent pressing invitations, only regretting that there was not room enough in the Family Office for the younger branches.

Mr. Ferrars' first measure was to ride to Willow Lawn. Knocking at the door of his sister's morning-room, he found Maurice with a pouting lip, back rounded, and legs twisted, standing upon his elbows, which were planted upon the table on either side of a calico spelling-book. Mr. Kendal stood up straight before the fire, looking distressed and perplexed, and Albinia sat by, a little worn, a little irritable, and with the expression of a wilful victim.

All greeted the new-comer warmly, and Maurice exclaimed, 'Mamma, I may have a holiday now!'

'Not till you have learnt your spelling.' There was some sharpness in the tone, and Maurice's shoulder-blades looked sulky.

'In consideration of his uncle,' began Mr. Kendal, but she put her hand on the boy, saying, 'You know we agreed there were to be no holidays for a week, because we did not use the last properly.'

He moved off disconsolately, and his father said, 'I hope you are come to arrange the journey to London. Is Winifred coming with you?'

'No; a hurry and confusion, and the good aunts would be too much for her, you will be the only one for inspection.'

'Yes, take him with you, Maurice,' said Albinia, 'he must see William.'

'You must be the exhibitor, then,' her brother replied.

'Now, Maurice, I know what you are come for, but you ought to know better than to persuade me, when you know there are six good reasons against my going.'

'I know of one worth all the six.'

'Yes,' said Mr. Kendal; 'I have been telling her that she is convincing me that I did wrong in allowing her to burthen herself with this charge.'

'That's nothing to the purpose,' said Albinia; 'having undertaken it, when you all saw the necessity, I cannot forsake it now—'

'If Mrs. Meadows were in the same condition as she was in two months ago, there might be a doubt,' said Mr. Kendal; but she is less dependent on your attention, and Lucy and Gilbert are most anxious to devote themselves to her in your absence.'

'I know they all wish to be kind, but if anything went wrong, I should never forgive myself!'

'Not if you went out for pleasure alone,' said her brother; 'but relationship has demands.'

'Of course,' she said, petulantly, 'if Edmund is resolved, I must go, but that does not convince me that it is right to leave everything to run riot here.'

Mr. Kendal looked serious, and Mr. Ferrars feared that the winter cares had so far told on her temper, that perplexity made her wilful in self-sacrifice. There was a pause, but just as she began to perceive she had said something wrong, the lesser Maurice burst out in exultation,

'There, it is not indestructible!'

'What mischief have you been about?' The question was needless, for the table was strewn with snips of calico.

'This nasty spelling-book! Lucy said it was called indestructible, because nobody could destroy it, but I've taken my new knife to it. And see there!'

'And now can you make another?' said his uncle.

'I don't want *to*.'

'Nor *one* either, sir,' said Mr. Kendal. 'What shall we have to tell Uncle William about you! I'm afraid you are one of the chief causes of mamma not knowing how to go to London.'

Maurice did not appear on the way to penitence, but his mother said, 'Bring me your knife.'

He hung down his head, and obeyed without a word. She closed it, and laid it on the mantel-shelf, which served as a sort of pound for properties in sequestration.

'Now, then, go,' she said, 'you are too naughty for me to attend to you.'

'But when will you, mamma?' laying a hand on her dress.

'I don't know. Go away now.'

He slowly obeyed, and as the door shut, she said, 'There!' in a tone as if her view was established.

'You must send him to Fairmead,' said the uncle.

'To "terrify" Winifred? No, no, I know better than that; Gilbert can look after him. I don't so much care about that.'

The admission was eagerly hailed, and objection after objection removed, and having recovered her good humour, she was candid, and owned how much she wished to go. 'I really want to make acquaintance with William. I've never seen him since I came to my senses, and have only taken him on trust from you.'

'I wish equally that he should see you,' said her brother. 'It would be good for him, and I doubt whether he has any conception what you are like.'

'I'd better stay at home, to leave you and Edmund to depict for his benefit a model impossible idol—the normal woman.'

Maurice looked at her, and shook his head.

'No—it would be rather—it and its young one, eh?'

Maurice took both her hands. 'I should not like to tell William what I shall believe if you do not come.'

'Well, what—'

'That Edmund is right, and you have been overtasked till you are careful and troubled about many things.'

'Only too much bent on generous self-devotion,' said Mr. Kendal, eagerly; 'too unselfish to cast the balance of duties.'

'Hush, Edmund,' said Albinia. 'I don't deserve fine words. I honestly believe I want to do what is right, but I can't be sure what it is, and I have made quite fuss enough, so you two shall decide, and then I shall be made right anyway. Only do it from your consciences.'

They looked at each other, taken aback by the sudden surrender. Mr.

Ferrars waited, and her husband said, 'She ought to see her brother. She needs the change, and there is no sufficient cause to detain her.'

'She must be content sometimes to trust,' said Mr. Ferrars.

'Aye, and all that will go wrong, when my back is turned.'

'Let it,' said her brother. 'The right which depends on a single human eye is not good for much. Let the weeds grow, or you can't pull them up.'

'Let the mice play, that the cat may catch them,' said Albinia, striving to hide her care. 'One good effect is, that Edmund has not begun to groan.'

Indeed, in his anxiety that she should consent to enjoy herself, he had not had time to shrink from the introduction.

Outside the door they found Maurice waiting, his spelling learnt from a fragment of the indestructible spelling-book, and the question followed, 'Now, mamma, you wont say I'm too naughty for you to go to London and see Uncle William?'

'No, my little boy, I mean to trust you, and tell Uncle William that my young soldier is learning the soldier's first duty—obedience.'

'And may I have my knife, mamma?'

Papa had settled that question by himself taking it off the chimney-piece and restoring it. If mamma wished the penance to have been longer, she neither looked it nor said it.

The young people received the decision with acclamation, and the two elder ones vied with one another in attempts to set her mind at rest by undertaking everything, and promising for themselves and the children perfect regularity and harmony. Sophy, with a bluntness that King Lear would have highly disapproved, said, 'She was glad mamma was going, but she knew they should be all at sixes and sevens. She would do her best, and very bad it would be.'

'Not if you don't make up your mind beforehand that it must be bad,' said her uncle.

Sophy smiled, she was much less impervious to cheerful auguries, and spoke with gladness of the pleasure it would give her friend Genevieve to see Mrs. Kendal.

Mr. Ferrars had a short interview with Ulick, and was amused by observing that little Maurice had learnt as much Irish as Ulick had dropped. After the passing fever about his O had subsided, he was parting with some of his ultra-nationality. The whirr of his R's and his Irish idioms were far less perceptible, and though a word of attack on his country would put him on his mettle, and bring out the Kelt in full force, yet in his reasonable state, his good sense and love of order showed an evident development, and instead of contending that Galway was the most perfect county in the world, he only said it might yet be so.

'Isn't he a noble fellow?' cried Albinia, warmly.

'Yes,' said her brother; 'I doubt whether all the O'Mores put together have ever made such a conquest as he has.'

'It was fun to see how the aunts were dismayed to find one of the horde in full force here. I believe it was as a measure of precaution that they took Lucy away. I was very glad for Lucy to go, but hers was not exactly the danger.'

'Ha!' said Maurice; and Albinia blushed. Whereupon he said interrogatively, 'Hem?' which made her laugh so consciously that he added, 'Don't you go and be romantic about either of your young ladies, or there will be a general burning of fingers.'

'If you knew all our secrets, Maurice, you would think me a model of prudence and forbearance.'

'Ho!' was his next interjection, 'so much the worse. For my own part, I don't expect prudence will come to you naturally till the little Awk has a lover.'

'Won't it come any other way?'

'Yes, in *one* way,' he said, gravely.

'And that way is not easily found by those who have neither humility nor patience,' she said, sadly, 'who rush on their own will.'

'Nay, Albinia, it is being sought, I do believe; and remember the lines—

```
"Thine own mild energy bestow,
And deepen while thou bidst it flow,
More calm our stream of love."'
```

Forced to resign herself to her holiday, Albinia did so with a good grace, in imitation of her brother, who assured her that he had brought a bottle of Lethe, and had therein drowned wife, children, and parish. Mr. Kendal's spirits, as usual, rose higher every mile from Bayford, and they were a very lively party when they arrived in Mayfair.

The good aunts were delighted to have round them all those whom they called their children; all except Fred, whom the new arrangements had sent to rejoin his regiment in Ireland.

Sinewy, spare, and wiry, with keen gray eyes under straight brows, narrow temples, a sunburnt face, and alert, upright bearing and quick step, William Ferrars was every inch a soldier; but nothing so much struck Mr. and Mrs. Kendal as the likeness to their little Maurice, though it consisted more in air and gesture than in feature. His speech was brief and to the point, softened into delicately-polished courtesy towards womankind, in the condescension of strength to weakness—the quality he evidently thought their chief characteristic.

Albinia was amused as she watched him with grown-up eyes, and compared present with past impressions. She could now imagine that she had been an inconvenient charge to a young soldier brother, and that he had been glad to make her over to the aunts, only petting and indulging her as a child; looking down on her fancies, and smiling at her sauciness when she was an enthusiastic maiden—treatment which she had so much resented, that she had direfully offended Maurice by pronouncing William a mere martinet, when she was hurt at his neither reading the Curse of Kehama, nor entering into her plans for Fairmead school.

Having herself become a worker, she could better appreciate a man who had seen and acted instead of reading, recollected herself as an emanation of conceit, and felt shy and anxious, even more for her husband than for herself. How would the scholar and the soldier fare together? and could she and Maurice keep them from wearying of each other? She had little trust in her own fascinations, though she saw the General's eye approvingly fixed on her, and believing herself to be a more pleasing object in her womanly bloom than in her unformed girlhood.

'How does the Montreal affair go on?' she asked.

'What affair?'

'Fred and Miss Kinnaird.'

'I am sorry to say he has not put it out of his head.'

'Surely she is a very nice person.'

'Pshaw! He has no right to think of a wife these dozen years.'

'Not even think? When he is not to have one at any rate till he is a field officer!'

'And he is a fool to have one then. A mere encumbrance to himself and the entire corps.'

'Yes, I know,' said Albinia, 'she always gets the best cabin.'

'And that is no place for her! No man, as I have told Fred over and over again, ought to drag a woman into hardships for which she is not fitted, and where she interferes with his effectiveness and the comfort of every one else.'

The identical lecture of twelve years since, when he had feared Albinia's becoming this inconvenient appendage! If he had repeated it on all like occasions, she did not wonder that it had wearied his aide-de-camp.

'Perhaps,' she said, 'the backwoods may have fitted Miss Emily for the life; and I can't but be glad of Fred's having been steady to anything.'

Considering this speech like the Kehama days, the General went on to dilate on the damage that marriage was to the 'service,' removing the best officers, first from the mess, and then from the army.

'What a pity William was born too late to be a Knight of St. John!' said Albinia.

All laughed, but she doubted whether he were pleased, for he addressed himself to one of the aunts, while Maurice spoke to her in an under tone—'I believe he is quite right. Homes are better for the individual man, but not for the service. How remarkably the analogy holds with this other service!'

'You mean what St. Paul says of the married and unmarried?'

'I always think he and his sayings are the most living lessons I know on the requirements of the other army.'

Albinia mused on the insensible change in Maurice. He had not embraced his profession entirely by choice. It had always been understood that one of the younger branches must take the family living; and as Fred had spurned study, he had been bred up to consider it as his fate, and if he had ever had other wishes, he had entirely accepted his destiny, and sincerely turned to his vocation. The knowledge that he must be a clergyman had ruled him and formed him from his youth, and acting through him on his sister, had rendered her more than the accomplished, prosperous young lady her aunts meant to have made her. Yet, even up to a year or two after his Ordination, there had been a sense of sacrifice; he loved sporting, and even balls, and it had been an effort to renounce them. He had avoided coming to London because his keen enjoyment of society tended to make him discontented with his narrow sphere; she had even known him to hesitate to ride with the staff at a review, lest he should make himself liable to repinings. And now how entirely had all this passed away, not merely by outgrowing the enterprising temper and boyish habits, nor by contentment in a happy home, but by the sufficiency and rest of his service, the engrossment in the charge from his great Captain. Without being himself aware of it, he had ceased to distrust a holiday, because it was no longer a temptation; and his animation and mirth were the more free, because self-regulation was so thoroughly established, that restraint was no longer felt.

Mrs. Annesley was talking of the little Kendals, who she had ruled should be at Fairmead.

'No,' said Maurice, 'Albinia thought her son too mighty for Winifred. Our laudable efforts at cousinly friendship usually produce war-whoops that bring the two mammas each to snatch her own offspring from the fray, with a scolding for the sake of appearances though believing the other the only guilty party.'

'Now, Maurice,' cried Albinia, 'you confess how fond Mary is of setting people to rights.'

'Well—when Maurice bullies Alby.'

'Aye, you talk of the mammas, and you only want to make out poor Maurice the aggressor.'

'Never mind, they will work in better than if they were fabulous children. Ah, you are going to contend that yours is a fabulous child. Take care I don't come on you with the indestructible—'

'Take care I don't come on you with Mary's lessons to Colonel Bury on the game-law.'

'Does it not do one good to see those two quarrelling just like old times?' exclaimed one aunt to the other.

'And William looking on as contemptuous as ever?' said Albinia.

'Not at all. I rejoice to have this week with you. I should like to see your boy. Maurice says he is a thorough young soldier.'

Mr. Kendal looked pleased.

The man of study had a penchant for the man of action, and the brothers-in-law were drawing together. Mars, the great geographical master, was but opening his gloomy school on the Turkish soil, and the world was discovering its ignorance beyond the Pinnock's Catechisms of its youth. Maurice treated Mr. Kendal as a dictionary, and his stores of Byzantine, Othman, and Austrian lore, chimed in with the perceptions of the General, who, going by military maps, described plans of operations which Mr. Kendal could hardly believe he had not found in history, while he could as little credit that Mr. Kendal had neither studied tactics, nor seen the spots of which he could tell such serviceable minutiae.

They had their heads together over the map the whole evening, and the next morning, when the General began to ask questions about Turkish, his sister was proud to hear her husband answering with the directness and precision dear to a military man.

'That's an uncommonly learned man, Albinia's husband,' began the General, as soon as he had started with his brother on a round of errands.

'I never met a man of more profound and universal knowledge.'

'I don't see that he is so grave and unlike other people. Fred reported that he was silence itself, and she might as well have married Hamlet's ghost.'

'Fred saw him at a party,' said Maurice; then remembering that this might not be explanatory, he added, 'He shines most when at ease, and every year since his marriage has improved and enlivened him.'

'I am satisfied. I hardly knew how to judge, though I did not think myself called upon to remonstrate against the marriage, as the aunts wished. I knew I might depend on you, and I thought it high time that she should be settled.'

'I have been constantly admiring her discernment, for I own that at first his reserve stood very much in my way, but since she has raised his spirits, and taught him to exert himself, he has been a most valuable brother to me.

'Then you think her happy? I was surprised to see her such a fine-looking woman; my aunts had croaked so much about his children and his mother, that I thought she would be worn to a shadow.'

'Very happy. She has casual troubles, and a great deal of work, but that is what she is made for.'

'How does she get on with his children?'

'Hearty love for them has carried her through the first difficulties, which appalled me, for they had been greatly mismanaged. I am afraid that she has not been able to undo some of the past evil; and with all her good intentions, I am sometimes afraid whether she is old enough to deal with grown-up young people.'

'You don't mean that Kendal's children are grown up? I should think him younger than I am.'

'He is so, but civil servants marry early, and not always wisely; and the son is about twenty. Poor Albinia dotes on him, and has done more for him than ever his father did; but the lad is weak and tender every way, with no stamina, moral or physical, and with just enough property to do him harm. He has been at Oxford and has failed, and now he is in the militia, but what can be expected of a boy in a country town, with nothing to do? I did not like his looks last week, and I don't think his being there, always idle, is good for that little manly scamp of Albinia's own.'

'Why don't they put him into the service?'

'He is too old.'

'Not too old for the cavalry!'

'He can ride, certainly, and is a tall, good-looking fellow; but I should not have thought him the stuff to make a dragoon. He has always been puling and delicate, unfit for school, wanting force.'

'Wanting discipline,' said the General. 'I have seen a year in a good regiment make an excellent officer of that very stamp of youngster, just wanting a mould to give him substance.'

'The regiment should be a very good one,' said Mr. Ferrars; 'he would be only too easily drawn in by the bad style of subaltern.'

'Put him into the 25th Lancers,' said the General, 'and set Fred to look after him. Rattlepate as he is, he can take excellent care of a lad to whom he takes a fancy, and if Albinia asked him, he would do it with all his heart.'

'I wish you would propose it, though I am afraid his father will never consent. I would do a great deal to get him away before he has led little Maurice into harm.'

'This consideration moved the Rector of Fairmead himself to broach the subject, but neither Mr. Kendal nor Albinia could think of venturing their fragile son in the army, though assured that there was little chance that the 25th Lancers would be summoned to the east, and they would only hold out hopes of little Maurice by and by.

Albinia's martial ardour was revived as she listened with greater grasp of comprehension to subjects familiar in her girlhood. She again met old friends of her father, the lingering glories of the Peninsula and Waterloo, who liked her for her own sake as well as for her father's, while Maurice looked on, amused by her husband's silent pride in her, and her hourly progress in the regard of the General, who began to talk of making a long visit to Fairmead, after what he expected would be a slight demonstration on the Danube. He even began to regret the briefness of the time that he could spend in their society.

Much was crowded into that week, but Albinia contrived to find an hour for a call on her little French friend, to whom she had already forwarded the parcels she had brought from home—a great barm-brack from Biddy, and a store of delicate convent confections from Hadminster.

She was set down at a sober old house in the lawyers' quarter of the world, and conducted to a pretty, though rather littered drawing-room, where she found a delicate-looking young mamma, and various small children.

'I'm so glad,' said little Mrs. Rainsforth, 'that you have been able to come; it will be such a pleasure to dear Miss Durant; and while one of the children was sent to summon the governess, the lady continued, nervously but warmly, 'I hope you will think Miss Durant looking well; I am afraid she shuts herself up too much. I'm sure she is the greatest comfort, the greatest blessing to us.'

Albinia's reply was prevented by a rush of children, followed by the dear little trim, slight figure. There was no fear that Genevieve did not look well or happy. Her olive complexion was healthy; her dark eyes lustrous with gladness; her smile frank and unquelled; her movements full of elastic life.

She led the way to the back parlour, dingy by nature, but bearing living evidence to the charm which she infused into any room. Scratched table, desks, copybooks, and worn grammars, had more the air of a comfortable occupation than of the shabby haunt of irksome taskwork. There were flowers in the window, and the children's treasures were arranged with taste. Genevieve loved her school-room, and showed off its little advantages with pretty exultation. If Mrs. Kendal could only see how well it looked with the curtains down, after tea!

And then came the long, long talk over home affairs, and the history of half the population of Bayford, Genevieve making inquiries, and drinking in the answers as if she could not make enough of her enjoyment.

Not till all the rest had been discussed, did she say, with dropped eyelids, and a little blush, 'Is Mr. Gilbert Kendal quite strong?'

'Thank you, he has been much better this winter, and so useful and kind in nursing grandmamma!'

'Yes, he was always kind.'

'He was going to beg me to remember him to you, but he broke off, and said you would not care.'

'I care for all goodness towards me,' answered Genevieve, lifting her eyes with a flash of inquiry.

'I am afraid he is as bad as ever, poor fellow,' said Albinia, with a little smile and sigh; 'but he has behaved very well. I must tell you that you were in the same train with him on his journey from Oxford, and he was ashamed to meet your eye.'

'Ah, I remember well. I thought I saw him. I was bringing George and Fanny from a visit to their aunts, and I was sure it must be Mr. Gilbert.'

'As prudent as ever, Genevieve.'

'It would not have been right,' she said, blushing; 'but it was such a treat to see a Bayford face, that I had nearly sprung out of the waiting-room to speak to him at the first impulse.'

'My poor little exile!' said Albinia.

'No, that is not my name. Call me my aunt's bread-winner. That's my pride! I mean my cause of thankfulness. I could not have earned half so much at home.'

'I hope indeed you have a home here.'

'That I have,' she fervently answered. 'Oh, without being a homeless orphan, one does not learn what kind hearts there are. Mr. and Mrs. Rainsforth seemed only to fear that they should not be good enough to me.'

'Do you mean that you found it a little oppressive?'

'Fi donc, Madame! Yet I must own that with her timid uneasy way, and his so perfect courtesy, they did alarm me a little at first. I pitied them, for I saw them so resolved not to let me feel myself de trop, that I knew I was in their way.'

'Did not that vex you?'

'Why, I suppose they set their inconvenience against the needs of their children, and my concern was to do my duty, and be as little troublesome as possible. They pressed me to spend my evenings with them, but I thought that would be too hard on them, so I told them I preferred the last hours alone, and I do not come in unless there are others to prevent their being tete-a-tete.'

'Very wise. And do you not find it lonely?'

'It is my time for reading—my time for letters—my time for being at home!' cried Genevieve. 'Now however that I hope I am no longer a weight on them, Mrs. Rainsforth will sometimes ask me to come and sing to him, or read aloud, when he comes home so tired that he cannot speak, and her voice is weak. Alas! they are both so fragile, so delicate.'

Her soul was evidently with them and with her charges, of whom there was so much to say, that the carriage came all too soon to hurry Albinia away from the sight of that buoyant sweetness and capacity of happiness.

She was rather startled by Miss Ferrars saying, 'By-the-by, Albinia, how was it that you never told us of the development of the Infant prodigy?

'I don't know what you mean, Aunt Gertrude.'

'Don't you remember that boy, that Mrs. Dusautoy Cavendish's son, whom that poor little companion of hers used to call l'Enfant prodigue. I did not know he was a neighbour of yours, as I find from Lucy.'

'What did Lucy tell you about him? She did not meet him!' cried Albinia, endeavouring not to betray her alarm. 'I mean, did she meet him?'

'Indeed,' said Miss Ferrars, 'you should have warned us if you had any objection, my dear.'

'Well, but what did happen?'

'Oh, nothing alarming, I assure you. They met at a ball at Brighton; Lucy introduced him, and said he was your vicar's nephew; they danced together. I think only once.'

'I wish you had mentioned it. When did it happen?'

'I can hardly tell. I think she had been about a fortnight with us, but she seemed so indifferent that I should never have thought it worth mentioning. I remember my sister thought of asking him to a little evening party of ours, and Lucy dissuading her. Now, really, Albinia, don't look as if we had been betraying our trust. You never gave us any reason to think—'

'No, no. I beg your pardon, dear aunt. I hope there's no harm done. If I could have thought of his turning up, I would—But I hope it is all right.'

Such good accounts came from both homes, and the General was so unwilling to part with his brother and sister, that he persuaded them to accompany him to Southampton for embarkation. They all felt that these last days, precious now, might be doubly precious by-and-by, and alone with them and free from the kindly scrutiny of the good aunts, William expanded and evinced more warm fraternal feeling than he had ever manifested. He surprised his sister by thanking her warmly for having come to meet him. 'I am glad to have been with you, Albinia; I am glad to have seen your husband. I have told Maurice that I am heartily rejoiced to see you in such excellent hands.'

'You must come and see the children, and know him better.'

'I hope so, when this affair is over, and I expect it will be soon settled. Anyway, I am glad we have been together. If we meet again, we will try to see more of one another.'

He had said much more to his brother, expressing regret that he had been so much separated from his sister. Thorough soldier as he was, and ardent for active service, the sight of her and her husband had renewed gentler thoughts, and he was so far growing old that the idea of home and rest came invitingly before him. He was softened at the parting, and when he wrung their hands for the last time on the deck of the steamer, they were glad that his last words were, 'God bless you.'

There had been some uncertainty as to the time of his sailing, and Fairmead and Bayford had been told that unless their travellers arrived by the last reasonable train on Friday, they were not to be expected till the same time on Saturday, Maurice having concocted a scheme for crossing by several junction lines, so as to save waiting; but they had not reckoned on the discourtesies of two rival companies whose lines met at the same station, and the southern train was only in time to hear the parting snort of the engine that it professed to catch.

The Ferrars' nature, above all when sore with farewells, was not made to submit to having time wasted by treacherous trains on a cold wintry day, and at a small new station, with an apology for a waiting-room, no bookstall, and nothing to eat but greasy gingerbread and hard apples.

Maurice relieved his feelings by heartily rowing all the officials, but he could obtain no redress, as he knew full well the whole time, nor would any train pick them up for full three hours.

So indignant was he, that amusement rendered Albinia patient, especially when he took to striding up and down the platform, devising cases in which the delay might be actionable, and vituperating the placability of Mr. Kendal, who having wrapt up his wife in plaids and seated her on the top of the luggage, had set his back to the wall, and was lost to the present world in a book.

'Never mind, Maurice,' said Albinia; 'in any other circumstances we should think three hours of each other a great boon.'

'If anything could be an aggravation, it would be to see Albinia philosophical.'

'You make me so on the principle of the Helots and Spartans.'

It was possible to get to Hadminster by half-past seven, and on to Bayford by nine o'clock, but Fairmead lay further from the line, and the next train did not stop at the nearest station, so Maurice agreed to sleep at Bayford that night; and this settled, set out with his sister to explore the neighbourhood for eatables and church architecture. They made an ineffectual attempt to rouse Mr. Kendal to go with them, but he was far too deep in his book, and only muttered something about looking after the luggage. They found a stale loaf of bread, and a hideous church, but it was a merry walk, and brought them back in their liveliest mood, which lasted even to pronouncing it 'great fun' that the Hadminster flies were all at a ball, and that the omnibus must convey them home by the full moonlight.

CHAPTER XXIII.

Slowly the omnibus rumbled over the wooden bridge, and then with a sudden impulse it thundered up to the front door.

Albinia jumped out, and caught Sophy in her arms, exclaiming, 'And how are you all, my dear?'

'We had quite given you up,' Gilbert was saying. 'The fire is in the library,' he added, as Mr. Kendal was opening the drawing-room door, and closing it in haste at the sight of a pale, uninviting patch of moonlight, and the rush of a blast of cold wind.

'And how is grandmamma? and the children? My Sophy, you don't look well, and where's Lucy?'

Ere she could receive an answer, down jumped, two steps at a time, a half-dressed figure, all white stout legs and arms which were speedily hugging mamma.

'There's my man!' said Mr. Kendal, 'a good boy, I know.'

'No!' cried the bold voice.

'No?' (incredulously) what have you been doing?'

'I broke the conservatory with the marble dog, and—' he looked at Gilbert.

'There's my brave boy,' said Mr. Kendal, who had suffered so much from his elder son's equivocation as to be ready to overlook anything for the sake of truth. 'Here, Uncle Maurice, shake hands with your godson, who always tells truth.'

The urchin folded his arms on his bosom, and looked like a young Bonaparte.

'Where's your hand? said his uncle. 'Wont you give it to me?'

'No.'

'He will be wiser to-morrow, if you are so good as to try him again,' said Albinia, who knew nothing did him more harm than creating a commotion by his caprices; 'he is up too late, and fractious with sleepiness. Go to bed now, my dear.'

'I shall not be wiser to-morrow,' quoth the child, marching out of the room in defiance.

'Monkey! what's the matter now?' exclaimed Albinia; 'I suppose you have all been spoiling him. But what's become of Lucy?'

'Gilbert said she was at the Dusautoys,' replied Sophy; 'but if you would but come to grandmamma! She found out that you were expected, and she is in such a state that we have not known what to do.'

'I'll come, only, Sophy dear, please order tea and something to eat. Your uncle looks ravenous.'

She broke off, as there advanced into the room a being like Lucy, but covered with streams and spatters of flowing sable tears, like a heraldic decoration, over face, neck, and dress.

All unconscious, she came with outstretched hands and words of welcome, but an astonished cry of 'Lucy!' met her, and casting her eyes on her dress, she screamed, 'Oh goodness! it's ink!'

'Where can you have been? what have you been doing?'

'I—don't know—Oh! it was the great inkstand, and not the scent—Oh! it is all over me! It's in my hair!' shuddering. 'Oh, dear! oh dear! I shall never get it out!' and off she rushed, followed by Gilbert, and was soon heard calling the maids to bring hot water to her room.

'What is all this?' asked Mr. Kendal.

'I do not know,' mournfully answered Sophy.

Albinia left the library, and taking a candle, went into the empty drawing-room. The moonlight shone white upon the table, and showed the large cut-glass ink-bottle in a pool of its own contents; and the sofa-cover had black spots and stains as if it had partaken of the libation.

Sophy saw, and stood like a statue.

'You know nothing, I am sure,' said Albinia.

'Nothing!' repeated Sophy, with a blank look of wretchedness.

'If you please, ma'am,' said the nurse at the door, 'could you be kind enough to come to Mrs. Meadows, she will be quieter when she has seen you?'

'Sophy dear, we must leave it now,' said Albinia. 'You must see to their tea, they have had nothing since breakfast.'

She hastened to the sick room, where she found Mrs. Meadows in a painful state of agitation and excitement. The nurse said that until this evening, she had been as usual, but finding that Mrs. Kendal was expected, she had been very restless; Miss Kendal was out, and neither Miss Sophy nor Mr. Gilbert could soothe her.

She eagerly grasped the hand of Albinia who bent down to kiss her, and asked how she had been.

'Oh! my dear, very unwell, very. They should not leave me to myself so long, my dear. I thought you would never come back,' and she began to cry, and say, 'no one cared for an old woman.'

Albinia assured her that she was not going away, and restrained her own eager and bewildered feelings to tranquillize her, by prosing on in the lengthy manner which always soothed the poor old lady. It was a great penance, in her anxiety to investigate the mysteries that seemed to swarm in the house, but at last she was able to leave the bedside, though not till she had been twice summoned to tea.

Sophy, lividly pale, was presiding with trembling hands; Gilbert, flushed and nervous, waiting on every one, and trying to be lively and at ease, but secret distress was equally traceable in each.

She durst only ask after the children, and heard that her little namesake had been as usual as good and sweet as child could be. And Maurice?

'He's a famous fellow, went on capitally,' said Gilbert.

'Yes, till yesterday,' hoarsely gasped Sophy, sincerity wrenching out the protest by force.

'Ah, what has he been doing to the conservatory?'

'He let the little marble dog down from the morning-room window with my netting silk; it fell, and made a great hole,' said Sophy.

'What, as a form of dawdling at his lessons?'

'Yes, but he has not been at all tiresome about them except to-day and yesterday.'

'And he has told the exact truth,' said Mr. Kendal, 'his gallant confession has earned the little cannon I promised him.'

'I believe,' said Albinia, 'that it would be greater merit in Maurice to learn forbearance than to speak truth and be praised for it. I have never seen his truth really tried.'

'I value truth above all other qualities,' said Mr. Kendal.

'So do I,' said Albinia, 'and it is my greatest joy in that little fellow; but some time or other it must cost him something, or it will not be tested.'

Mr. Kendal did not like this, and repeated that he must have his cannon.

Albinia fancied that she heard something like a groan from Gilbert.

When they broke up for the night, she threw her arm round Sophy as they went upstairs, saying, 'My poor dear, you look half dead. Have things been going very wrong?'

'Only these two days,' said Sophy, 'and I don't know that they have either. I am glad you are come!'

'What kind of things?' said Albinia, following her into her room.

'Don't ask,' at first began Sophy, but then, frowning as if she could hardly speak, she added, 'I mean, I don't know whether it is my own horrid way, or that there is really an atmosphere of something I don't make out.'

'Didn't you tell me Lucy was at the Vicarage?' said Albinia, suddenly.

'Gilbert said yes, when I asked if she could be with the Dusautoys,' said Sophy, 'when grandmamma wanted her and she did not come. Mamma, please don't think of what I said, for very likely it is only that I am cross, because of being left alone with grandmamma so long this evening, and then Maurice being slow at his lessons.'

'You are not cross, Sophy; you are worn out, and perplexed, and unhappy.'

'Oh! not now you are come home,' and Sophy laid her head on her shoulder and cried with relief and exhaustion. Albinia caressed her, saying,

'My trust, my mainstay, my poor Sophy! There, go to bed and sleep, and don't think of it now. Only first tell me one thing, is that Algernon at home?'

'No!' said Sophy, vehemently, 'certainly not!'

Albinia breathed more freely.

'Everybody,' said Sophy, collecting herself, 'has gone on well, Gilbert and Lucy have been as kind as could be, and Maurice very good, but yesterday morning he went on in his foolish way at lessons, and Gilbert took him out riding before he had finished them. They came in very late, and I think Maurice must have been overtired, for he was so idle this morning, that I threatened to tell, and put him in mind of the cannon papa promised him; but somehow I must have managed badly for he only grew more defiant, and ended by letting the marble dog out of window, so that it went through the roof of the conservatory.'

'Yes, of course it was your fault, or the marble dog's,' said Albinia, smiling, and stroking her fondly. 'Ah! we ought to have come home at the fixed time, and not left you to their mercy; but one could not hurry away from William, when he was so much more sorry to leave us than we ever expected.'

'Oh! mamma, don't talk so! We were so glad. If only we could help being such a nuisance!'

Albinia contrived to laugh, and withdrew, intending to make a visit of inquiry to Lucy, but she could not refuse herself the refreshment of a kiss to the little darling who could have no guile to hide, no wrong to confess. She had never so much realized the value of the certainty of innocence as when she hung over the crib, and thought that when those dark fringed lids were lifted, the eyes would flash with delight at meeting her, without one drawback.

Suddenly a loud roar burst from the little room next to Gilbert's, in which Maurice had lately been installed. She hurried swiftly in that direction, but a passage and some steps lay between, and Gilbert had been beforehand with her.

She heard the words, 'I don't care! I don't care if it is manly! I will tell; I can't bear this!' then as his brother seemed to be hushing him, he burst out again, 'I wouldn't have minded if papa wouldn't give me the cannon, but he will, and that's as bad as telling a lie!' I can't sleep if you wont let me off my promise!'

Trembling from head to foot, her voice low and quivering with concentrated, incredulous wrath, Albinia advanced. 'Are you teaching my child falsehood?' she said; and Gilbert felt as if her look were worse to him than a thousand deaths.

'O mamma! mamma! Gilbert! let me tell her,' cried the child; and Albinia, throwing herself on her knees, clasped him in her arms, as though snatching him from the demon of deceit.

'Tell all, Maurice,' said Gilbert, folding his arms; 'it is to your credit, if you would believe so. I shall be glad to have this misery ended any way! It was all for the sake of others.'

'Mamma,' Maurice said, in the midst of these mutterings of his unhappy brother, 'I can't have the cannon without papa knowing it all. I couldn't shake hands with Uncle Maurice for telling the truth, for I had not told it.'

'And what is it, my boy?' tell me now, no one can hinder you.'

'I scratched and fought him—Mr. Cavendish Dusautoy—I kicked down the decanter of wine. They told me it was manly not to tell, and I promised.'

He was crying with the exceeding pain and distress of a child whose tears were rare, and Albinia rocked him in her arms.

Gilbert cautiously shut the door, and said sadly, 'Maurice behaved nobly, if he would only believe so. You would be proud of your son if you had seen him. They wanted to make him drink wine, and he was fighting them off.'

'And where were you, Gilbert, you to whom I trusted him?'

'I could not help it,' said Gilbert; then as her lip curled with contempt, and her eye spoke disappointment, he cast himself on the ground, exclaiming, 'Oh, if you knew how I have been mixed up with others, and what I have gone through, you would pity me. Oh, Maurice, don't cry, when I would give worlds to be like you. Why do you let him cry? why don't you tell him what a brave noble boy he is?'

'I don't know what to think or believe,' said Albinia, coldly, but returning vehemently to her child, she continued, 'Maurice, my dear, no one is angry with you! You, at least, I can depend on. Tell me where you have been, and what they have been doing to you.'

Even with Gilbert's explanations, she could hardly understand Maurice's narrative, but she gathered that on Thursday, the brothers had ridden out, and were about to turn homewards, when Archie Tritton, of whom to her vexation Maurice spoke familiarly, had told Gilbert that a friend was waiting for him at the inn connected with the training stables, three miles farther on. Gilbert had demurred, but was told the matter would brook no delay, and yielded on being pressed. He tried to suppress the friend's name, but Maurice had called him Mr. Cavendish Dusautoy.

While Gilbert was engaged with him, Tritton had introduced Maurice to the horses and stable boys, whose trade had inspired him with such emulation, that he broke off in the midst of his confession to ask whether he could be a jockey and also a gentleman. All this had detained them till so late, that they had been drawn into staying to dinner. Maurice had gone on very happily, secure that he was right in Gilbert's hands, and only laying up a few curious words for explanation; but when he was asked to drink wine, he stoutly answered that mamma did not allow it.

Idle mischief prompted Dusautoy and Tritton to set themselves to overpower his resistance. Gilbert's feeble remonstrances were treated as a jest, and Algernon, who could brook no opposition, swore that he would conquer the little prig. Maurice found himself pinioned by strong arms, but determined and spirited, he made a vigorous struggle, and so judiciously aimed a furious kick, that Mr. Cavendish Dusautoy staggered back, stumbling against the table, and causing a general overthrow.

The victory was with Maurice, but warned as he had often been against using his natural weapons, he thought himself guilty of a great crime. The others, including, alas! Gilbert, strove to persuade him it was a joke, and, above all, to bind him to silence, for Tritton and Dusautoy would never have ventured so far, could they have imagined the possibility of such terms as those on which he lived with his parents. They attacked the poor child on the score of his manly aspirations, telling him it was babyish to tell mamma and sisters everything, a practice fit for girls, not for boys or men. These assurances extracted a pledge of secrecy, which was kept as long as his mother was absent, and only rendered him reckless by the sense that he had forfeited the prize of good conduct; but the sight of her renewed the instinct of confidence, and his father's reliance on his truth so acted on his sense of honour, that he could not hold his peace.

'May I tell papa? and will he let me have the cannon?' he finished.

'You shall certainly tell him, my dear, dear little boy, and we will see what he says about the cannon,' she said, fervently kissing him. 'It will be some comfort for him to hear how you have behaved, my precious little man. I thank God with all my heart that He has saved you from putting anything before truth. I little thought I was leaving you to a tempter!'

The child did not fully understand her. His was a very simple nature, and he was tired out by conflicting emotions. His breast was relieved, and his mother caressed him; he cared for nothing more, and drawing her hand so as to rest his cheek on it, he looked up in her face with soft weary happiness in his eyes, then let the lids sink over them, and fell peacefully asleep, while the others talked on. 'At least you will do me the poor justice of believing it was not willingly,' said Gilbert.

'I wish you would not talk to me,' she answered, averting her face and speaking low as if to cut the heart; 'I don't want to reproach you, and I can't speak to you properly.'

'If you would only hear me, my only friend and helper! But it was all that was wanting! I have forfeited even your toleration! I wonder why I was born!'

He was taking up his light to depart, but Albinia's fear of her own temper made her suspect that she had spoken vindictively, and she said, 'What can I do, Gilbert? Here is this poor child, whom I trusted to you, who can never again be ignorant of the sound of evil words, and only owes it to God's mercy on his brave spirit that this has not been the beginning of destruction. I feel as if you had been trying to snatch away his soul!'

'And will you, can you not credit,' said Gilbert, nearly inaudibly, 'that I did not act by my free will? I had no notion that any such thing could befall him, and would never have let them try to silence him, but to shield others.'

'Others! Yes, Archie Tritton and Algernon Dusautoy! I know what your free-will is in their hands, and yet I thought you cared for your brother enough to guard him, if not yourself.'

'If you knew the coercion,' muttered Gilbert. 'I protest, as I would to my dying day, that I had no intention of going near the stables when I set out, and would never have consented could I have helped it.'

'And why could not you help it?'

Gilbert gasped. 'Tritton brought me a message from Dusautoy, insisting on my meeting him there. It was too late to take Maurice home, and I could not send him with Archie. I expected only to exchange a few words at the door. It was Tritton who took Maurice away to the stables.'

'I hear, but I do not see the compulsion, only the extraordinary weakness that leads you everywhere after those men.'

'I must tell you, I suppose,' groaned Gilbert; 'I can bear anything but this. There's a miserable money entanglement that lays me under a certain obligation to Dusautoy.'

'Your father believed you had told him of all your debts,' she said, in a tone of increased scorn and disappointment.

'I did—I mean—Oh! Mrs. Kendal, believe me, I intended to have told him the utmost farthing—I thought I had done so—but this was a thing— Dusautoy had persuaded me into half consenting to have some wine with him from a cheating Portuguese—then ordered more than ever I knew of, and the man went and became bankrupt, and sent in a great abominable bill that I no more owned, nor had reason to expect than my horse.'

'So you preferred intriguing with this man to applying openly to your father?'

'It was no doing of mine. It was forced upon me, and, in fact, the account was mixed up with his. It was the most evil hour of my life when I consented. I've not had a moment's peace or happiness since, and it was the promise of the bill receipted that led me to this place.'

'And why was this place chosen for the meeting? You and Mr. Cavendish Dusautoy live only too near one another.'

'He is not at the Vicarage,' faltered Gilbert.

Albinia suddenly grew pale with apprehension. 'Gilbert,' she said, 'there is only one thing that could make this business worse;' and as she saw his change of countenance, she continued, 'Then it is so, and Lucy is his object.'

'He did not speak, but his face was that of a convicted traitor, and fresh perceptions crowded on her, as she exclaimed, horror struck, 'The ink! Yes, when you said she was with the Dusautoys! I understand! He has been in hiding, he has been here! And this expedition was to arrange a clandestine meeting between them under your father's own roof! You conniving! you who said you would sooner see your sister sold to Legree!'

'It is all true,' said Gilbert, moodily, his elbows on the table and his face in his hands, 'and if the utmost misery for weeks past could be any atonement, it would be mine. But at least I have done nothing willingly to bring them together. I have only gone on in the hope and trust that I was some protection to poor Lucy.'

'Fine protection,' sighed Albinia. 'And how has it been? how does it stand?'

'Why, they met at Brighton, I believe. She used to walk on the chain pier before breakfast, and he met her there. If he chooses, he can make any one do what he likes, because he does not understand no for an answer. Then when she came home, he used to meet her on the bridge, when you sent her out for a turn in the evening, and sometimes she would make me take her out walking to meet him. Don't you see how utterly miserable it was for me; when they had volunteered this help all out of kindness, it was impossible for me to speak to you.'

Albinia made a sound of contempt, and said, 'Go on.'

'That time when you and Mr. Hope saw them, Lucy was frightened, and they had a quarrel, he went away, and I hoped and trusted it had died out. I heard no more till yesterday, when I was dragged into giving him this meeting. It seems that he had only just discovered your absence, and wanted to take the opportunity of seeing her. I was in hopes you would have come back; I assured him you would; but he chose to watch, till evening, and then Lucy was to meet him in the conservatory. Poor Lucy, you must not be very angry with her, for she was much averse to it, and I enclosed a letter from her to forbid him to come. I thought all was safe, till I actually heard their voices, and grandmamma got into an agitation, and Sophy was running about wild to find Lucy. When you came home, papa's opening the door frightened Lucy, and it seems that Dusautoy thought that she was going to faint and scream, and laid hold of the ink instead of the eau-de-cologne. There! I believe the ink would have betrayed it without me. Now you have heard everything, Mrs. Kendal, and can believe there is not a more wretched and miserable creature breathing than I am.'

Albinia slowly rose, and put her hand to her brow, as though confused with the tissue of deceit and double dealing.

'Oh! Mrs. Kendal, will you not speak to me?' I solemnly declare that I have told you all.'

'I am thinking of your father.'

With a gesture of acquiescent anguish and despair, he let her pass, held open the door, and closed it softly, so as not to awaken the happy sleeper.

'Good night,' she said, coldly, and turned away, but his mournful, resigned 'Good night,' was so utterly broken down that her heart was touched, and turning she said, 'Good night, Gilbert, I am sorry for you; I believe it is weakness and not wickedness.'

She held out her hand, but instead of being shaken, it was pressed to his lips, and the fingers were wet with his tears.

Feeling as though the bad dreams of a night had taken shape and life, Albinia stood by the fire in her sitting-room the next morning, trying to rally her judgment, and equally dreading the sight of those who had caused her grief, and of those who would share the shock she had last night experienced.

The first knock announced one whom she did not expect—Gilbert, wretchedly pale from a sleepless night, and his voice scarcely audible.

'I beg your pardon,' he said; 'but I thought I might have led you to be hard on Lucy: I do believe it was against her will.'

Before she could answer, the door flew wide, and in rushed Maurice, shouting, 'Good morning, mamma;' and at his voice Mr. Kendal's dressing-room door was pushed back, and he called, 'Here, Maurice.'

As the boy ran forward, he was met and lifted to his father's breast, while, with a fervency he little understood, though he never forgot it, the words were uttered,

'God bless you, Maurice, and give you grace to go on to withstand temptation, and speak the truth from your heart!'

Maurice was impressed for a moment, then he recurred to his leading thought—

'May I have the cannon, papa? I did kick—I broke the bottle, but may I have the cannon?'

'Maurice, you are too young to understand the value of your resistance. Listen to me, my boy, for you must never forget this: you have been taken among persons who, I trust, will never be your companions.'

'Oh!' interrupted Maurice, 'must I never be a jockey?'

'No, Maurice. Horses are perverted to bad purposes by thoughtless men, and you must keep aloof from such. You were not to blame, for you refused to do what you knew to be wrong, and did not know it was an improper place for you.'

'Gilbert took me,' said Maurice, puzzled at the gravity, which convinced him that some one was in fault, and of course it must be himself.

'Gilbert did very wrong,' said Mr. Kendal, 'and henceforth you must learn that you must trust to your own conscience, and no longer believe that all your brother tells you is right.'

Maurice gazed in inquiry, and perceiving his brother's downcast air, ran to his mother, crying, 'Is papa angry?'

'Yes,' said Gilbert, willing to spare her the pain of a reply, 'he is justly angry with me for having exposed you to temptation. Oh, Maurice, if I had been made such as you, it would have been better for us all!'

It was the first perception that a grown person could do wrong, and that person his dear Gilbert. As if the grave countenances were insupportable, he gave a long-drawn breath, hid his face on his mother's knee, and burst into an agony of weeping. He was lifted on her lap in a moment, father and mother both comforting him with assurances that he was a very good boy, and that papa was much pleased with him, Mr. Kendal even putting the cannon into his hand, as a tangible evidence of favour; but the child thrust aside the toy, and sliding down, took hold of his brother's languid, dejected hand, and cried, with a sob and stamp of his foot,

'You shan't say you are naughty: I wont let you!'

Alas! it was a vain repulsion of the truth that this is a wicked world. Gilbert only put him back, saying,

'You had better go away from me, Maurice: you cannot understand what I have done. Pray Heaven you may never know what I feel!'

Maurice did but cling the tighter, and though Mr. Kendal had not yet addressed the culprit, he respected the force of that innocent love too much to interfere. The bell rang, and they went down, Maurice still holding by his brother, and when his uncle met them, it was touching to see the generous little fellow hanging back, and not giving his own hand till he had seen Gilbert receive the ordinary greeting.

Though Mr. Ferrars had been told nothing, he could not but be aware of the symptoms of a family crisis—the gravity of some, and the pale, jaded looks of others. Lucy was not one of these; she came down with little Albinia in her arms, and began to talk rather airily, excusing herself for not having come down in the evening because that 'horrid ink' had got into her hair, and tittering a little over the absurdity of her having picked up the inkstand in the dark. Not a word of response did she meet, and her gaiety died away in vague alarm. Sophy, the most innocent, looked wretched, and Maurice absolutely began to cry again, at the failure of some manoeuvre to make his father speak to Gilbert.

His tears broke up the breakfast-party. His mother led him away to reason with him, that, sad as it was, it was better that people should be grieved when they had transgressed, as the only hope of their forgiveness and improvement. Maurice wanted her to reverse the declaration that Gilbert had done wrong; but, alas! this could not be, and she was obliged to send him out with his little sister, hoping that he would work off his grief by exercise. It was mournful to see the first shadow of the penalty of sin falling on the Eden of his childhood!

With an aching heart, she went in search of Lucy, who had taken sanctuary in Mrs. Meadows's room, and was not easily withdrawn from thence to a tete-a-tete. Fearful of falsehood, Albinia began by telling her she knew all, and how little she had expected such a requital of trust.

Lucy exclaimed that it had not been her fault, she had always wanted to tell, and gradually Albinia drew from her the whole avowal, half shamefaced, half exultant.

She had never dreamt of meeting Algernon at Brighton—it was quite by chance that she came upon him at the officers' ball when he was staying with Captain Greenaway. He asked her to dance, and she had said yes, all on a sudden, without thinking, and then she fancied he would go away; she begged him not to come again, but whenever she went out on the chain-pier before breakfast, there he was.

Why did she go thither? She hung her head. Mrs. Annesley had desired her to walk; she could not help it; she was afraid to write and tell what was going on—besides, he would come, though she told him she would not see him; and she could not bear to make him unhappy. Then, when she came home, she had been in hopes it was all over, but she had been very unhappy, and had been on the point of telling all about it many times, when mamma looked at her kindly; but then he came to the Vicarage, and he would wait for her at the bridge, and write notes to her, and she could not stop it; but she had always told him it was no use, she never would be engaged to him without papa's consent. She had only promised that she would not marry any one else, only because he was so very desperate, and she was afraid to break it off entirely, lest he should go and marry the Principessa Bianca, a foreigner and Papist, which would be so shocking for him and his uncle. Gilbert could testify how grieved she was to have any secrets from mamma; but Mr. Cavendish Dusautoy was so dreadful when she talked of telling, that she did not know what would happen.

When he went away, and she thought it was all over—mamma might recollect how hard it was for her to keep up, and what a force she put upon herself—but she would rather have pined to death than have said one word to bring him back, and was quite shocked when Gilbert gave her his note, to beg her to let him see her that evening, before the party returned; she said, with all her might, that he must not come, and when he did, she was begging him all the time to go away, and she was so dreadfully frightened when they actually came, that she had all but gone into hysterics, or fainted away, and that was the way he came to throw the ink at her—she was so very much shocked, and so would he be—and really she felt the misfortune to the beautiful new sofa-cover as a most serious calamity and aggravation of her offence.

It was not easy to know how to answer; Albinia was scornful of the sofa-cover, and yet it was hard to lay hold of a tangible subject on which to show Lucy her error, except in the concealment, which, by her own showing, she had lamented the whole time. She had always said no, but, unluckily, her noes were of the kind that might easily be made to mean yes, and she evidently had been led on partly by her own heart, partly by the force of the stronger will, though her better principles had filled her with scruples and misgivings at every stage. She had been often on the point of telling all, and asking forgiveness; and here it painfully crossed Albinia, that if she herself had been less hurried, and less disposed to take everything for granted, a little tenderness might have led to a voluntary confession.

Still Lucy defended herself by the compulsion exercised on her, and she would hear none of the conclusions Albinia drew therefrom; she would not see that the man who drove her to a course of disobedience and subterfuge could be no fit guide, and fired up at a word of censure, declaring that she knew that mamma had always hated him, and that now he was absent, she would not hear him blamed. The one drop of true love made her difficult to deal with, for the heart was really made over to the tyrant, and Albinia did not feel herself sufficiently guiltless of negligence and imprudence to rebuke her with a comfortable conscience.

Mr. Kendal had been obliged to attend to some justice business—better for him, perhaps, than acting as domestic magistrate—and meanwhile the Vicar of Fairmead found himself forgotten. He wanted to be at home, yet did not like to leave his sister in unexplained trouble, though not sure whether he might not be better absent.

Time passed on, he finished the newspaper, and wrote letters, and then, seeing no one, he had gone into the hall to send for a conveyance, when Gilbert, coming in from the militia parade, became the recipient of his farewells, but apparently with so little comprehension, that he broke off, struck by the dejected countenance, and wandering eye.

'I beg your pardon,' Gilbert said, passing his hand over his brow, 'I did not hear.'

'I was only asking you to tell my sister that I would not disturb her, and leaving my good-byes with you.'

'You are not going?'

'Thank you; I think my wife will grow anxious.'

'I had hoped'—Gilbert sighed and paused—'I had thought that perhaps—'

The wretchedness of his tone drove away Mr. Ferrars's purpose of immediate departure, and returning to the drawing-room he said, 'If there were any way in which I could be of use.'

'Then you do not know?' said Gilbert, veiling his face with his hand, as he leant on the mantel-shelf.

'I know nothing. I could only see that something was amiss. I was wishing to know whether my presence or absence would be best for you all.'

'Oh! don't go!' cried Gilbert. Nobody must go who can be any comfort to Mrs. Kendal.'

A few kind words drew forth the whole piteous history that lay so heavily on his heart. Reserves were all over now; and irregularly and incoherently he laid open his griefs and errors, his gradual absorption into the society with which he had once broken, and the inextricable complication of mischief in which he had been involved by his debt.

'Yet,' he said, 'all the time I longed from my heart to do well. It was the very thing that led me into this scrape. I thought if the man applied to my father, as he threatened, that I should be suspected of having concealed this on purpose, and be sent to India, and I was so happy, and thought myself so safe here. I did believe that home and Mrs. Kendal would have sheltered me, but my destiny must needs hunt me out here, and alienate even her!'

'The way to find the Devil behind the Cross, is to cower beneath it in weak idolatry, instead of grasping it in courageous faith,' said Mr. Ferrars. 'Such faith would have made you trust yourself implicitly to your father. Then you would either have gone forth in humble acceptance of the punishment, or else have stayed at home, free, pardoned, and guarded; but, as it was, no wonder temptation followed you, and you had no force to resist it.'

'And so all is lost! Even dear little Maurice can never be trusted to me again! And his mother, who would, if she could, be still merciful and pitying as an angel, she cannot forget to what I exposed him! She will never be the same to me again! Yet I could lay down my life for any of them!'

Mr. Ferrars watched the drooping figure, crouching on his chairs, elbows on knees, head bowed on the supporting hands, and face hidden, and, listening to the meek, affectionate hopelessness of the tone, he understood the fond love and compassion that had often surprised him in his sister, but he longed to read whether this were penitence towards God, or remorse towards man.

'Miserable indeed, Gilbert,' he said, 'but if all were irretrievably offended, there still is One who can abundantly pardon, where repentance is true.'

'I thought'—cried Gilbert—'I thought it had been true before! If pain, and shame, and abhorrence could so render it, I know it was when I came home. And then it was comparative happiness; I thought I was forgiven, I found joy and peace where they are promised'—the burning tears dropped between his fingers—'but it was all delusion; not prayers nor sacraments can shield me—I am doomed, and all I ask is to be out of the way of ruining Maurice!'

'This is mere despair,' said Mr. Ferrars. 'I cannot but believe your contrition was sincere; but steadfast courage was what you needed, and you failed in the one trial that may have been sent you to strengthen and prove you. The effects have been terrible, but there is every hope that you may retrieve your error, and win back the sense of forgiveness.'

'If I could dare to hope so—but I cannot presume to take home to myself those assurances, when I know that I only resolve, that I may have resolutions to break.'

'Have you ever laid all this personally before Mr. Dusautoy?'

'No; I have thought of it, but, mixed up as this is with his nephew and my sister, it is impossible! But you are a clergyman, Mr. Ferrars!' he added, eagerly.

Mr. Ferrars thought, and then said,

'If you wish it, Gilbert, I will gladly do what I can for you. I believe that I may rightly do so.'

His face gleamed for a moment with the light of grateful gladness, as if at the first ray of comfort, and then he said, 'I am sure none was ever more grieved and wearied with the burden of sin—if that be all.'

'I think,' said Mr. Ferrars, 'that it might be better to give time to collect yourself, examine the past, separate the sorrow for the sin from the disgrace of the consequences, and then look earnestly at the sole ground of hope. How would it be to come for a couple of nights to Fairmead, at the end of next week?'

Gilbert gratefully caught at the invitation; and Mr. Ferrars gave him some advice as to his reading and self-discipline, speaking to him as gently and tenderly as Albinia herself. Both lingered in case the other should have more to say, but at last Gilbert stood up, saying,

'I would thankfully go to Calcutta now, but the situation is filled up, and my father said John Kendal had been enough trifled with. If I saw any fresh opening, where I should be safe from hurting Maurice!'

'There is no reason you and your brother should not be a blessing to each other.'

'Yes, there is. Till I lived at home, I did not know how impossible it is to keep clear of old acquaintance. They are good-natured fellows—that Tritton and the like—and after all that has come and gone, one would be a brute to cut them entirely, and Maurice is always after me, and has been more about with them than his mother knows. Even if I were very different, I should be a link, and though it might be no great harm if Maurice were a tame mamma's boy— you see, being the fellow he is, up to anything for a lark, and frantic about horses—I could never keep him from them. There's no such great harm in themselves—hearty, good-natured fellows they are—but there's a worse lot that they meet, and Maurice will go all lengths whenever he begins. Now, so little as he is now, if I were once gone, he would never run into their way, and they would never get a hold of him.'

Mr. Ferrars had unconsciously screwed up his face with dismay, but he relaxed it, and spoke kindly.

'You are right. It was a mistake to stay at home. Perhaps your regiment may be stationed elsewhere.'

'I don't know how long it may be called out. If it were but possible to make a fresh beginning.'

'Did you hear of my brother's suggestion?'

'I wish—but it is useless to talk about that. I could not presume to ask my father for a commission—Heaven knows when I shall dare to speak to him!'

'You have not personally asked his pardon after full confession.'

'N-o—Mrs. Kendal knows all.'

'Did you ever do such a thing in your life?'

'You don't know what my father is.'

'Neither do you, Gilbert. Let that be the first token of sincerity.'

Without leaving space for another word, Mr. Ferrars went through the conservatory into the garden, where, meeting the children, he took the little one in his arms, and sent Maurice to fetch his mamma. Albinia came down, looking so much heated and harassed, that he was grieved to leave her.

'Oh, Maurice, I am sorry! You always come in for some catastrophe,' she said, trying to smile. 'You have had a most forlorn morning.'

'Gilbert has been with me,' he said. 'He has told me all, my dear, and I think it hopeful: I like him better than I ever did before.'

'Poor feather, the breath of your lips has blown him the other way,' said Albinia, too unhappy for consolation.

'Well, it seems to me that you have done more for him than I ever quite believed. I did not expect such sound, genuine religious feeling.'

'He always had plenty of religious sentiment,' said Albinia, sadly.

'I have asked him to come to us next week. Will you tell Edmund so?'

'Yes. He will be thankful to you for taking him in hand. Poor boy, I know how attractive his penitence is, but I have quite left off building on it.'

Mr. Ferrars defended him no longer. He could not help being much moved by the youth's self-abasement, but that might be only because it was new to him, and he did not even try to recommend him to her mercy; he knew her own heart might be trusted to relent, and it would not hurt Gilbert in the end to be made to feel the full weight of his offence.

'I must go,' he said, 'though I am sorry to leave you in perplexity. I am afraid I can do nothing for you.'

'Nothing—but feel kindly to Gilbert,' said Albinia. 'I can't do so yet. I don't feel as if I ever could again, when I think what he was doing with Maurice. Yes, and how easily he could have brought poor Lucy to her senses, if he had been good for anything! Oh! Maurice, this is sickening work! You should be grateful to me for not scolding you for having taken me from home!'

'I do not repent,' said her brother. 'The explosion is better than the subterranean mining.'

'It may be,' said Albinia, 'and I need not boast of the good I did at home!

My poor, poor Lucy! A little discreet kindness and watchfulness on my part would have made all the difference! It was all my running my own way with my eyes shut, but then, I had always lived with trustworthy people. Well, I wont keep you listening to my maundering, when Winifred wants you. Oh! why did that Polysyllable ever come near the place?'

Mr. Ferrars said the kindest and most cheering things he could devise, and drove away, not much afraid of her being unforgiving.

He was disposed to stake all his hopes of the young man on the issue of his advice to make a direct avowal to his father. And Gilbert made the effort, though rather in desperation than resolution, knowing that his condition could not be worse, and seeing no hope save in Mr. Ferrars' counsel. He was the first to seek Mr. Kendal, and dreadful to him as was the unaltering melancholy displeasure of the fixed look, the steadily penetrating deep dark eyes, and the subdued sternness of the voice, he made his confession fully, without reserve or palliation.

It was more than Mr. Kendal had expected, and more, perhaps, than he absolutely trusted, for Gilbert had not hitherto inspired faith in his protestations that he spoke the whole truth and nothing but the truth, nor had he always the power of doing so when overpowered by fright. The manner in which his father laid hold of any inadvertent discrepancy, treating it as a wilful prevarication, was terror and agony; and well as he knew it to be the meed of past equivocation, he felt it cruel to torture him by implied suspicion. Yet how could it be otherwise, when he had been introducing his little brother to his own corrupters, and conniving at his sister's clandestine correspondence with a man whom he knew to be worthless?'

The grave words that he obtained at last, scarcely amounted to pardon; they implied that he had done irreparable mischief and acted disgracefully, and such forgiveness as was granted was only made conditional on there being no farther reserves.

Alas! even with all tender love and compassion, no earthly parent can forgive as does the Heavenly Father. None but the Omniscient can test the fulness of the confession, nor the sincerity of 'Father, I have sinned against Heaven and before Thee, and am no more worthy to be called Thy son.' This interview only sent the son away more crushed and overwhelmed, and yearning towards the more deeply offended, and yet more compassionate Father.

Mr. Kendal, after this interview, so far relaxed his displeasure as to occasionally address Gilbert when they met at luncheon after this deplorable morning, while towards Lucy he observed a complete silence. It was not at first that she perceived this, and even then it struck more deeply on Sophia than it did on her.

Mr. Kendal shrank from inflicting pain on the good vicar, and it was decided that the wives should be the channel through which the information should be imparted. Albinia took the children, sending them to play in the garden while she talked to Mrs. Dusautoy. She found that keen little lady had some shrewd suspicions, but had discovered nothing defined enough to act upon, and was relieved to have the matter opened at last.

As to the ink, no mortal could help laughing over it; even Albinia, who had been feeling as if she could never laugh again, was suddenly struck by the absurdity, and gave way to a paroxysm of merriment.

'Properly managed, I do think it might put an end to the whole affair,' said Mrs. Dusautoy. 'He could not stand being laughed at.'

'I'm afraid he never will believe that he can be laughed at.'

'Yes, that is unlucky,' said Mrs. Dusautoy, gravely; but recollecting that she was not complimentary, she added, 'You must not think we undervalue Lucy. John is very fond of her, and the only objection is, that it would require a person of more age and weight to deal with Algernon.'

'Never mind speeches,' sighed Albinia; 'we know too well that nothing could be worse for either. Can't you give him a tutor and send him to travel.'

'I'll talk to John; but unluckily he is of age next month, and there's an end of our power. And John would never keep him away from hence, for he thinks it his only chance.'

'I suppose we must do something with Lucy. Heigh-ho! People used not to be always falling in love in my time, except Fred, and that was in a rational way; that could be got rid of!'

The effect of the intelligence on the vicar was to make him set out at once to the livery-stables in quest of his nephew, but he found that the young gentleman had that morning started for London, whither he proposed to follow him on the Monday. Lucy cried incessantly, in the fear that the gentle- hearted vicar might have some truculent intentions towards his nephew, and was so languid and unhappy that no one had the heart to scold her; and comforting her was still more impossible.

Mr. Kendal used to stride away from the sight of her swollen eyes, and ask Albinia why she did not tell her that the only good thing that could happen to her would be, that she should never see nor hear of the fellow again.

Why he did not tell her so himself was a different question.

CHAPTER XXIV.

'Well, Albinia,' said Mr. Kendal, after seeing Mr. Dusautoy on his return from London.

There was such a look of deprecation about him, that she exclaimed, 'One would really think you had been accepting this charming son-in-law.'

'Suppose I had,' he said, rather quaintly; then, as he saw her hands held up, 'conditionally, you understand, entirely conditionally. What could I do, when Dusautoy entreated me, with tears in his eyes, not to deprive him of the only chance of saving his nephew?'

'Umph,' was the most innocent sound Albinia could persuade herself to make.

'Besides,' continued Mr. Kendal, 'it will be better to have the affair open and avowed than to have all this secret plotting going on without being able to prevent it. I can always withhold my consent if he should not improve, and Dusautoy declares nothing would be such an incentive.'

'May it prove so!'

'You see,' he pursued, 'as his uncle says, nothing can be worse than driving him to these resorts, and when he is once of age, there's an end of all power over him to hinder his running straight to ruin. Now, when he is living at the Vicarage, we shall have far more opportunity of knowing how he is going on, and putting a check on their intercourse, if he be unsatisfactory.'

'If we can.'

'After all, the young man has done nothing that need blight his future life. He has had great disadvantages, and his steady attachment is much in his favour. His uncle tells me he promises to become all that we could wish, and, in that case, I do not see that I have the right to refuse the offer, when things have gone so far—conditionally, of course.' He dwelt on that saving clause like a salve for his misgivings.

'And what is to become of Gilbert and Maurice, with him always about the house?' exclaimed Albinia.

'We will take care he is not too much here. He will soon be at Oxford. Indeed, my dear, I am sorry you disapprove. I should have been as glad to avoid the connexion as you could be, but I do not think I had any alternative, when Mr. Dusautoy pressed me so warmly, and only asked that he should be taken on probation; and besides, when poor Lucy's affections are so decidedly involved.'

Albinia perceived that there had been temper in her tone, and could object no further, since it was too late, and as she could not believe that her husband had been weak, she endeavoured to acquiesce in his reasoning, and it was a strong argument that they should see Lucy bright again.

'I suppose,' he said, 'that you would prefer that I should announce my decision to her myself!'

It was a more welcome task than spreading gloom over her countenance, but she entered in great trepidation, prepared to sink under some stern mandate, and there was nothing at first to undeceive her, for her father was resolved to atone for his concession by sparing her no preliminary thunders, and began by depicting her indiscretion and deceit, as well as the folly of attaching herself to a man without other recommendations than figure and fortune.

How much Lucy heard was uncertain; she leant on a chair with drooping head and averted face, trembling, and suppressing a sob, apparently too much frightened to attend. Just when the exordium was over, and 'Therefore I lay my commands on you' might have been expected, it turned into, 'However, upon Mr. Dusautoy's kind representation, I have resolved to give the young man a trial, and provided he convinces me by his conduct that I may safely entrust your happiness to him, I have told his uncle that I will not withhold my sanction.'

With a shriek of irrepressible feeling, Lucy looked from father to mother, and clasped her hands, unable to trust her ears.

'Yes, Lucy,' said Albinia, 'your father consents, on condition that nothing further happens to excite his doubts of Mr. Cavendish Dusautoy. It rests with yourself now, it is not too late. After all that has passed, you would incur much deserved censure if you put an end to the affair; but even that would be better, far better, than entering into an engagement with a man without sound principle.'

'Your mother is quite right, Lucy,' said Mr. Kendal. 'This is the only time. Gratified vanity has led you too far, and you have acted as I hoped no child of mine would ever act, but you have not forfeited our tenderest care. You are not engaged to this man, and no word of yours would be broken. If you hesitate to commit yourself to him, you have only to speak, and we would gladly at once do everything that could conduce to make you happy.'

'You don't want me to give him up!' cried Lucy. 'Oh! mamma, did not he say he had consented?'

'I said it rested with yourself Lucy. Do not answer me now. Come to me at six o'clock, and tell me, after full reflection, whether I am to consider you as ready to pledge yourself to this young man.'

It was all that could be done. Albinia had a dim hope that the sense of responsibility, and dread of that hard will and selfish temper, might so rise upon Lucy as to startle her, but then, as Mr. Kendal observed, if she should decide against him, she would have used him so extremely ill, that they should feel nothing but shame.

'Yes,' said Albinia, 'but it would be better to be ashamed of a girl's folly, than to see her made miserable for life. Poor Lucy! if she decide against him, she will become a woman at once, if not, I'm afraid it will be the prediction about Marie Antoinette over again—very gay, and coming right through trial.'

They were obliged to tell Sophy of the state of things. She stood up straight, and said, slowly and clearly, 'I do not like the world at all.'

'I don't quite see what you mean.'

'Every one does what can't be helped, and it is not *the* thing.'

'Explain yourself, Sophy,' said her father, amused.

'I don't think Lucy ought to be making the decision at all,' said Sophy. She did that long ago, when first, she attended to what he said to her. If she does not take him now, it will be swearing to her neighbour, and disappointing him, because it is to her own hindrance.'

'Yes, Sophy; but I believe it is better to incur the sin of breaking a promise, than to go on when the fulfilment involves not only suffering, but mischief. Lucy has repeatedly declared there was no engagement.'

'I know it could not be helped; but Mr. Dusautoy ought not to have asked papa.'

'Nor papa to have consented, my Suleiman ben Daood,' said Mr. Kendal. 'Ah! Sophy, we all have very clear, straightforward views at eighteen of what other people ought to do.'

'Papa—I never meant—I did not think I was saying anything wrong. I only said I did not like the world.'

'And I heartily agree with you, Sophy, and if I had lived in it as short a time as you have, perhaps "considerations" would not affect my judgment.'

'I am always telling Sophy she will be more merciful as she grows older,' said Albinia.

'If it were only being more merciful, it would be very well,' said Mr.

Kendal; 'but one also becomes less thorough-going, because practice is more painful than theory, and one remembers consequences that have made themselves felt. It is just as well that there should be young people to put us in mind what our flights once were.'

Albinia and Sophy left Lucy to herself; they both wished to avoid the useless 'What shall I do?' and they thought that, driven back on her own resources, even *her* own mind might give her better counsel than the seven watchmen aloft in a high tower.

She came down looking exceedingly pale. Mr. Kendal regarded her anxiously, and held his hand out to her kindly.

'Papa,' she said, simply, 'I can't give it up. I do love him.'

'Very well, my dear,' he answered, 'there is no more to be said than that I trust he will merit your affection and make you happy.'

Good Mr. Dusautoy was as happy as a king; he took Lucy in his arms, and kissed her as if she had been his child, and with her hands folded in his own, he told her how she was to teach his dear Algernon to be everything that was good, and to lead him right by her influence. She answered with caresses and promises, and whoever had watched her eye, would have seen it in a happy day-dream of Algernon's perfection, and his uncle thanking her for it.

She had expected that grandmamma would have been very happy; but marriage had, with the poor old lady, led to so much separation, that her weakened faculties took the alarm, and she received the tidings by crying bitterly, and declaring that every one was going away and leaving her. Lucy assured her over and over again that she was never going to desert her, and as Mr. Kendal had made it a condition that Algernon should finish his Oxford career respectably, there was little chance that poor Mrs. Meadows would survive until the marriage.

All along Gilbert made no remark. Though he had been left out of the family conclaves, and his opinion not asked, he submitted with the utmost meekness, as one who knew that he had forfeited all right to be treated as son and heir. The more he was concerned at the engagement, the greater stigma he would place on his own connivance; so he said nothing, and only devoted himself to his grandmother, as though the attendance upon her were a refuge and relief. More gentle and patient than ever, he soothed her fretfulness, invented pleasures for her, and rendered her so placid and contented, that her health began to improve.

Not for a moment did he seem to forget his error; and Albinia's resolution to separate Maurice from him, could not hold when he himself silently assumed the mournful necessity, and put the child from him when clamorous for rides, till there was an appeal to papa and mamma. Mr. Kendal gave one look of inquiry at Albinia, and she began some matter-of-course about Gilbert being so kind—whereupon the brothers were together as before. When Albinia visited her little boy at night, she found that Gilbert had been talking to him of his eldest brother, and she heard more of Edmund's habits and tastes from the little fellow who had never seen him, than from either the twin- brother or the sister who had loved him so devotedly. It was as if Gilbert knew that he could be doing Maurice no harm when leading him to think of Edmund, and perhaps he felt some intrinsic resemblance in the deep loving strength of the two natures.

The invitation to Fairmead spared him the pain and shame of Algernon Dusautoy's first reception as Lucy's accepted lover. He went early on Saturday morning, and young Dusautoy, arriving in the evening, was first ushered into the library; while Albinia did her best to soothe the excited nerves and fluttering spirits of Lucy, who was exceedingly ashamed to meet him again under the eyes of others, after such a course of stolen interviews, and what she had been told of her influence doing him good only alarmed her the more.

Well she might, for if ever character resembled that of the iron pot borne down the stream in company with the earthen one, it was the object of her choice. Poor pipkin that Gilbert was, the contact had cost him a smashing blow, and for all clay of the more fragile mould, the best hope was to give the invulnerable material a wide berth. Talk of influence! Mr. Dusautoy might as well hope that a Wedgwood cream-jug would guide a copper cauldron and keep verdigris aloof.

His attraction for Lucy had always been a mystery to her family, who perhaps hardly did justice to the magnetism of mere force of purpose. Better training might have ennobled into resolution that which was now doggedness and obstinacy, and, even in that shape, the real element of strength had a tendency to work upon softer natures. Thus it had acted in different ways with the Vicar, with Gilbert, and with Lucy; each had fallen under the power of his determination, with more or less of their own consent, and with Lucy the surrender was complete; she no sooner sat beside Algernon than she was completely his possession, and his complacent self-satisfaction was reflected on her face in a manner that told her parents that she was their own no longer, but given up to a stronger master.

Albinia liked neither to see nor to think about it, and kept aloof as much as she could, dividing herself between grandmamma and the children. On Tuesday morning, during Maurice's lessons, there was a knock at the sitting-room door. She expected Gilbert, but was delighted to see her brother.

'I thought you were much too busy to come near us?'

'So I am; I can't stay; so if Kendal be not forthcoming you must give this fellow a holiday.'

'He is gone to Hadminster, so—'

'Where's Gilbert?' broke in little Maurice.

'He went to his room to dress to go up to parade,' said Mr. Ferrars, and off rushed the boy without waiting for permission.

Albinia sighed, and said, 'It is a perfect passion.'

'Don't mourn over it. Love is too good a thing to be lamented over, and this may turn into a blessing.'

'I used to be proud of it.'

'So you shall be still. I am very much pleased with that poor lad.'

She would not raise her eyes, she was weary of hoping for Gilbert, and his last offence had touched her where she had never been touchedbefore.

'Whatever faults he has,' Mr. Ferrars said, 'I am much mistaken if his humility, love, and contrition be not genuine, and what more can the best have?'

'Sincerity!' said Albinia, hopelessly. 'There's no truth in him!'

'You should discriminate between deliberate self-interested deception, and failure in truth for want of moral courage. Both are bad enough, but the latter is not "loving a lie," not such a ruinous taint and evidence of corruption as the former.'

'It is curious to hear you repeating my old excuses for him,' said Albinia, 'now that he has cast his glamour over you.'

'Not wrongly,' said her brother. 'He is in earnest; there is no acting about him.'

'Yes, that I believe; I know he loves us with all his heart, poor boy, especially Maurice and me, and I think he had rather go right than wrong, if he could only be let alone. But, oh! it is all "unstable as water." Am I unkind, Maurice? I know how it would be if I let him talk to me for ten minutes, or look at me with those pleading brown eyes of his!'

Mr. Ferrars knew it well, and why she was steeled against him, but he put this aside, saying that he was come to speak of the future, not of the past, and that he wanted Edmund to reconsider William's advice. He told her what Gilbert had said of the difficulty of breaking off old connexions, and the danger to Maurice from his acquaintance. An exchange into another corps of militia might be for the worse, the occupation was uncertain, and Mr. Ferrars believed that a higher position, companions of a better stamp, and the protection of a man of lively manners, quick sympathy, and sound principle, like their cousin Fred, might be the opening of a new life. He had found Gilbert most desirous of such a step, regarding it as his only hope, but thinking it so offensively presumptuous to propose it to his father under present circumstances, his Oxford terms thrown away, and himself disgraced both there and at home, that the matter would hardly have been brought forward had not Mr. Ferrars undertaken to press it, under the strong conviction that remaining at home would be destruction, above all, with young Dusautoy making part of the family.

'I declare,' said Mr. Ferrars, 'he looked so much at home in the drawing-room, and welcomed Gilbert with such an air of patronage, that I could have found it in my heart to have knocked him down!'

It was a treat to hear Maurice speak so unguardedly, and Albinia laughed, and asked whether he thought it very wrong to hope that the Polysyllable would yet do something flagrant enough to open Lucy's eyes.

'I'll allow you to hope that *if* he should, her eyes *may* be opened,' said Maurice.

Albinia began a vehement vindication for their having tolerated the engagement, in the midst of which her brother was obliged to depart, amused at her betrayal of her own sentiments by warfare against what he had never said.

She had treated his counsel as chimerical, but when she repeated it to her husband, she thought better of it, since, alas! it had become her great object to part those two loving brothers. Mr. Kendal first asked where the 25th Lancers were, then spoke of expense, and inquired what she knew of the cost of commissions, and of her cousin's means. All she could answer for was, that Fred's portion was much smaller than Gilbert's inheritance, but at least she knew how to learn what was wanted, and if her friends, the old Generals, were to be trusted, she ought to have no lack of interest at the Horse Guards.

Gilbert was taken into counsel, and showed so much right spirit and good sense, that the discussion was friendly and unreserved. It ended in the father and son resorting to Pettilove's office to ascertain the amount of ready money in his hands, and what income Gilbert would receive on coming of age. The investigation somewhat disappointed the youth, who had never thoroughly credited what his father told him of the necessity of his exerting himself for his own maintenance, nor understood how heavy a drain on his property were the life-interests of his father and grandmother, and the settlement on his aunt. By-and-by, he might be comparatively a rich man, but at first his present allowance would be little more than doubled, and the receipts would be considerably diminished by an alteration of existing system of rents, such as had so long been planned. It was plain that the almshouses were the unsubstantial fabric of a dream, but no one now dared to refer to them, and Mr. Kendal desired Albinia to write to consult her cousin.

Captain Ferrars was so much flattered at her asking his protection for anything, that he would have promised to patronize Cousin Slender himself for her sake. He praised the Colonel and lauded the mess to the skies, and economy being his present hobby, he represented himself as living upon nothing, and saving his pay. He further gave notice of impending retirements, and advised that the application should be made without loss of time, lamenting grievously himself that there was no chance for the 25th, of a touch at the Russians.

Something in his letter put every one into a hurry, and a correspondence began, which resulted in Gilbert's being summoned to Sandhurst for an examination, which he passed creditably. The purchase-money was deposited, and the household was daily thrown into a state of excitement by the arrival of official-looking envelopes, which turned out to contain solicitations from tailors and outfitters, bordered with portraits of camp-beds and portable baths, until, at last, when the real document appeared, Gilbert tossed it aside as from 'another tailor:' but Albinia knew the article too well to mistake it, and when the long blue cover was opened, it proved to convey more than they had reckoned upon.

Gilbert Kendal held a commission in the 25th Lancers, and the corps was under immediate orders for the East. The number of officers being deficient, he was to join the headquarters at Cork, without going to the depot, and would thence sail with a stated minimum of baggage.

Albinia could not look up. She knew her husband had not intended thus to risk the last of his eldest-born sons; and though her soldier-spirit might have swelled with exultation had her own brave boy been concerned, she dreaded the sight of quailing or dismay in Gilbert.

'Going really to fight the Russians,' shouted Maurice, as the meaning reached him. 'Oh! Gibbie, if I was but a man to go with you!'

'You will do your duty, my boy,' said his father.

'By God's help,' was the reverent answer which emboldened Albinia to look up at him, as he stood with Maurice clinging by both hands to him. She had done him injustice, and her heart bounded at the sight of the flush on his cheek, the light in his eyes, and the expression on his lips, making his face finer and more manly than she had ever seen it, as if the grave necessity, and the awe of the unseen glorious danger, were fixing and elevating his wandering purpose. To have no choice was a blessing to an infirm will, and to be inevitably out of his own power braced him and gave him rest. She held out her hand to him, and there was a grasp of inexpressible feeling, the first renewal of their old terms of sympathy and confidence.

There was no time to be lost; Mr. Kendal would go to London with him by the last train that day, to fit him out as speedily as possible, before he started for Cork.

Every one felt dizzy, and there was no space for aught but action. Perhaps Albinia was glad of the hurry, she could not talk to Gilbert till she had learnt to put faith in him, and she would rather do him substantial kindnesses than be made the sharer of feelings that had too often proved like the growth of the seed which found no depth of earth.

She ran about for him, worked for him, contrived for him, and gave him directions; she could not, or would not, perceive his yearning for an effusion of penitent tenderness. He looked wistfully at her when he was setting out to take leave at the Vicarage, but she had absorbed herself in flannel shirts, and would not meet his eye, nor did he venture to make the request that she would come with him.

Indeed, confidences there could be but few, for Maurice and Albinia hung on either side of him, so that he could hardly move, but he resisted all attempt to free him even from the little girl, who was hardly out of his arms for ten minutes together. It was only from her broken words that her mother understood that from the vicarage he had gone to the church. Poor little Albinia did not like it at all. 'Why was brother Edmund up in the church, and why did Gilbert cry?'

Maurice angrily enunciated, 'Men never cry,' but not a word of the visit to the church came from him.

Algernon Dusautoy had wisely absented himself, and the two sisters devoted themselves to the tasks in hand. Sophy worked as hard as did Mrs. Kendal, and spoke even less, and Lucy took care of Mrs. Meadows, whose nerves were painfully excited by the bustle in the house. It had been agreed that she should not hear of her grandson's intention till the last moment, and then he went in, putting on a cheerful manner, to bid her good-bye, only disclosing that he was going to London, but little as she could understand, there was an instinct about her that could not be deceived, and she began to cry helplessly and violently.

Mrs. Kendal and Lucy were summoned in haste; Gilbert lingered, trying to help them to restore her to composure. But time ran short; his father called him, and they hardly knew that they had received his last hurried embrace, nor that he was really gone, till they heard Maurice shouting like a Red Indian, as he careered about in the garden, his only resource against tears; and Sophy came in very still, very pale, and incapable of uttering a word or shedding a tear. Albinia was much concerned, for she could not bear to have sent him away without a more real adieu, and word of blessing and good augury; it made her feel herself truly unforgiving, and perhaps turned her heart back to him more fully and fondly than any exchange of sentiment would have done. But she had not much time to dwell on this omission, for poor Mrs. Meadows missed him sorely, and after two days' constant fretting after him, another paralytic stroke renewed the immediate danger, so that by the time Mr. Kendal returned from London she was again hovering between life and death.

Mr. Kendal, to his great joy, met Frederick Ferrars at the 'Family Office.' The changes in the regiment had given him his majority, and he had flashed over from Ireland to make his preparations for the campaign. His counsel had been most valuable in Gilbert's equipment, especially in the knotty question of horses, and he had shown himself so amiable and rational that Mr. Kendal was quite delighted, and rejoiced in committing Gilbert to his care. He had assumed the trust in a paternal manner, and, infected by his brilliant happiness and hopefulness, Gilbert had gone off to Ireland in excellent spirits.

'Another thing conduced to cheer him,' said Mr. Kendal afterwards to his wife, with a tone that caused her to exclaim, 'You don't mean that he saw Genevieve?'

'You are right. We came upon her in Rivington's shop, while we were looking for the smallest Bible. I saw who it was chiefly by his change of colour, and I confess I kept out of the way. The whole did not last five minutes; she had her pupils with her, and soon went away; but he thanked me, and took heart from that moment. Poor boy, who would have thought the impression would have been so lasting?'

'Well, by the time he is a field-officer, even William will let him please himself,' said Albinia, lightly, because her heart was too full for her to speak seriously.

She tried, by a kind letter, to atone for the omitted farewell, and it seemed to cheer and delight Gilbert. He wrote from Cork as if he had imbibed fresh hope and enterprise from his new companions, he liked them all, and could not say enough of the kindness of Major Ferrars. Everything went smoothly, and in the happiest frame he sailed from Cork, and was heard of again at Malta and Gallipoli, direfully sea-sick, but reviving to write most amusing long descriptive letters, and when he reached the camp at Yarna, he reported as gratefully of General Ferrars as the General did kindly of him.

Those letters were the chief pleasures in a harassing spring and summer. It was well that practice had trained Sophia in the qualities of a nurse, for Lucy was seldom available when Algernon Dusautoy was at home; she was sure to be riding with him, or sitting for her picture, or the good Vicar, afraid of her overworking herself, insisted on her spending the evening at the vicarage.

She yielded, but not with an easy conscience, to judge by her numerous apologies, and when Mr. Cavendish Dusautoy returned to Oxford, she devoted herself with great assiduity to the invalid. Her natural gifts were far more efficient than Sophy's laboriously-earned gentleness, and her wonderful talent for prattling about nothing had a revivifying influence, sparing much of the plaintive weariness which accompanied that mournful descent of life's hill.

Albinia had reckoned on a rational Lucy until the Oxford term should be over. She might have anticipated a failure in the responsions, (who, in connexion with the Polysyllable, could mention being plucked for the little-go?) but it was more than she did expect that his rejection would send him home in sullen resentment resolved to punish Oxford by the withdrawal of his august name. He had been quizzed by the young, reprimanded by the old, plucked by the middle-aged, and he returned with his mouth, full of sentences against blind, benighted bigotry, and the futility of classical study, and of declamations, as an injured orphan, against his uncle's disregard of the intentions of his dear deceased parent, in keeping him from Bonn, Jena, Heidelberg, or any other of the outlandish universities whose guttural names he showered on the meek Vicar's desponding head.

He was twenty-one, and could not be sent whither he would not go. His uncle's resource was Mr. Kendal, who strongly hoped that the link was about to snap, when, summoning the gentleman to the library, he gave him to understand that he should consider a refusal to resume his studies as tantamount to a dissolution of the engagement. A long speech ensued about dear mothers, amiable daughters, classics, languages, and foreign tours. That was all the account Mr. Kendal could give his wife of the dialogue, and she could only infer that Algernon's harangue had sent him into such a fit of abstraction, that he really could not tell the drift of it. However, he was clear that he had himself given no alternative between returning to Oxford and resigning Lucy.

That same evening, Lucy, all blushes and tears, faltered out that she was very unwilling, she could not bear to leave them all, nor dear grandmamma, but dear Algernon had prevailed on her to say next August!

When indignant astonishment permitted Albinia to speak, she reminded Lucy that a respectable career at Oxford had been the condition.

'I know,' said Lucy, 'but dear Algernon convinced papa of the unreasonableness of such a stipulation under the circumstances.'

Albinia felt the ground cut away under her feet, and all she could attempt was a dry answer. 'We shall see what papa says; but you, Lucy, how can you think of marrying with your grandmamma in this state, and Gilbert in that camp of cholera—'

'I told Algernon it was not to be thought of,' said Lucy, her tears flowing fast. But I don't know what to do, no one can tell how long it may go on, and we have no right to trifle with his feelings.'

'If he had any feelings for you, he would not ask it.'

'No, mamma, indeed!' cried Lucy, earnestly; 'it was his feeling for me; he said I was looking quite languid and emaciated, and that he could not allow my—good looks and vivacity to be diminished by my attendance in a sick chamber. I told him never to mind, for it did not hurt me; but he said it was incumbent on him to take thought for me, and that he could not present me to his friends if I were not in full bloom of beauty; yes, indeed, he said so; and then he said it would be the right season for Italy.'

'It is impossible you can think of going so far away! Oh, Lucy! you should not have consented.'

'I could not help it,' said Lucy, sobbing. 'I could not bear to contradict him, but please, mamma, let papa settle it for me. I don't want to go away; I told him I never would, I told him I had promised never to leave dear grandmamma; but you see he is so resolute, and he cannot bear to be without me. Oh! do get him to put it off—only if he is angry and goes to Italy without me, I know I shall die!'

'We will take care of you, my dear. I am sure we shall be able to show him how impossible a gay wedding would be at present; and I do not think he can press it,' said Albinia, moved into soothing the present distress, and relieved to find that there was no heartlessness on Lucy's side.

What a grand power is sheer obstinacy! It has all the momentum of a stone, or cannon-ball, or any other object set in motion without inconvenient sensations to obstruct its course!

Algernon Dusautoy had decided on being married in August, and taking his obedient pupil-wife through a course of lectures on the continental galleries of art; and his determined singleness of aim prevailed against the united objections and opposition of four people, each of double or quadruple his wisdom and weight.

His first great advantage was, that, as Albinia surmised, Mr. Kendal could not recal the finale of their interview, and having lost the thread of the rigmarole, did not know to what his silence had been supposed to assent. Next, Algernon conquered his uncle by representing Lucy as on the road to an atrophy, and persuading him that he should be much safer on the Continent with a wife than without one: and though the two ladies were harder to deal with in themselves, they were obliged to stand by the decision of their lords. Above all, he made way by his sincere habit of taking for granted whatever he wished, and by his magnanimous oblivion of remonstrance and denial; so that every day one party or the other found that assumed, as fixed in his favour, which had the day before been most strenuously refused.

'If you consented to this, I thought I could not refuse that.'

'I consent! I told him it was the last thing I could think of.'

'Well, I own I was surprised, but he told me you had readily come into his views.'

Such was the usual tenor of consultations between the authorities, until their marvel at themselves and each other came to a height when they found themselves preparing for the wedding on the very day originally chosen by Algernon.

Mr. Kendal's letter to Gilbert was an absolute apology. Gilbert in Turkey was a very different person from Gilbert at Bayford, and had assumed in his father's mind the natural rights of son and heir; he seemed happy and valued, and the heat of the climate, pestiferous to so many, seemed but to give his Indian constitution the vigour it needed. When his comrades were laid up, or going away for better air, much duty was falling on him, and he was doing it with hearty good-will and effectiveness. Already the rapid changes had made him a lieutenant, and he wrote in the highest spirits. Moreover, he had fallen in with Bryan O'More, and had been able to do him sundry kindnesses, the report of which brought Ulick to Willow Lawn in an overflow of gratitude.

It was a strange state of affairs there. Albinia was ashamed of the plea of 'could not help it,' and yet that was the only one to rest on; the adherence to promises alone gave a sense of duty, and when or how the promises had been given was not clear.

Besides, no one could be certain even about poor Lucy's present satisfaction; she sometimes seemed like a little bird fluttering under the fascination of a snake. She was evidently half afraid of Algernon, and would breathe more freely when he was not at hand; but then a restlessness would come on if he did not appear as soon as she expected, as if she dreaded having offended him. She had violent bursts of remorseful tears, and great outpourings of fondness towards every one at home, and she positively did look ill enough to justify Algernon in saying that the present condition of matters was hurtful to her. Still she could not endure a word that remotely tended towards advising her to break off the engagement, or even to retard the wedding, and her admiration of her intended was unabated.

Indeed, his affection could not be doubted; he liked her adoration of all his performances, and he regarded her with beneficent protection, as a piece of property; he made her magnificent presents, and conceded to her that the wedding tour should not be beyond Clifton, whence they would return to Willow Lawn, and judge ere deciding on going abroad.

He said that it would be 'de bon ton' to have the marriage strictly private. Even he saw the incongruity of festivity alongside of that chamber of decay and death; and besides, he had conceived such a distaste to the Drury family, that he had signified to Lucy that they must not make part of the spectacle.

Albinia and Sophy thought this so impertinent, that they manfully fought the battles of the Drurys, but without prevailing; Albinia took her revenge, by observing that this being the case, it was impossible to ask her brother and little Mary, whose well-sounding names she knew Algernon ambitionated for the benefit of the county paper.

Always doing what was most contrary to the theories with which she started in life, Albinia found herself taking the middle course that she contemned. She was marrying her first daughter with an aching, foreboding heart, unable either to approve or to prevent, and obliged to console and cheer just when she would have imagined herself insisting upon a rupture at all costs.

Sophy had said from the first that her sister could not go back. She expected her to be unhappy, and believed it the penalty of the wrongdoings in consenting to the clandestine correspondence; and treated her with melancholy kindness as a victim under sentence. She was very affectionate, but not at all consoling when Lucy was sad, and she was impatient and gloomy when the trousseau, or any of the privileges of a fiancee brought a renewal of gaiety and importance. A broken heart and ruined fortunes were the least of the consequences she augured, and she went about the house as if she had realized them both herself.

The wedding-day came, and grandmamma was torpid and only half conscious, so that all could venture to leave her. The bride was not allowed to see her, lest the agitation should overwhelm both; for the poor girl was indeed looking like the victim her sister thought her, pale as death, with red rings round her extinguished eyes, and trembling from head to foot, the more at the apprehension that Algernon would think her a fright.

After all that lavender and sal-volatile could do for her, she was such a spectacle, that when her father came to fetch her he was shocked, and said, tenderly, 'Lucy, my child, this must not be. Say one word, and all shall be over, and you shall never hear a word of reproach.'

But Lucy only cast a frightened glance around, and rising up with the accents of perfect sincerity, said, 'No, papa; I am quite ready; I am quite happy. I was only silly.'

Her mind was evidently made up, and it was past Albinia's divination whether her agitation were composed of fear of the future and remorse for the past, or whether it were mere love of home and hurry of spirits, exaggerated by belief that a bride ought to weep. Probably it was a compound of all, and the whole of her reply perfect truth, especially the final clause.

So they married her, poor child, very much as if they had been attending her to the block. Sophy's view of the case had infected them all beyond being dispelled by the stately complacency of the bridegroom, or the radiant joy and affection of his uncle.

They put her into a carriage, watched her away, and turned back to the task which she had left them, dreading the effects of her absence. She was missed, but less than they feared; the faculties had become too feeble for such strong emotion as had followed Gilbert's departure; and the void was chiefly perceptible by the plaintive and exacting clinging to Albinia, who had less and less time to herself and her children, and was somewhat uneasy as to the consequences as regarded Maurice. While Gilbert was at home, the child had been under some supervision; but now his independent and unruly spirit was left almost uncontrolled, except by his own intermittent young conscience, his father indulged him, and endured from him what would have been borne from no one else; and Sophy was his willing slave, unable to exact obedience, and never complaining, save under the most stringent necessity or sense of duty. He was too young for school, and there was nothing to be done but to go on, from day to day, in the trust that no harm could eventually ensue in consequence of so absolute a duty as the care of the sufferer; and that while the boy's truth and generosity were sound, though he might be a torment, his character might be all the stronger afterwards for that very indocility.

It was not satisfactory, and many mothers would have been miserable; but it was not in Albinia's nature to be miserable when her hands were full, and she was doing her best. She had heard her brother say that when good people gave their children sound principles and spoilt them, they gave the children the trouble of self-conquest instead of doing it for them. She had great faith in Maurice's undertaking this task in due time; and while she felt that she still had her hand on the rein she must be content to leave it loose for a while.

Besides, when his father and sisters, and, least of all, herself, did not find him a plague, did it much matter if other people did?

CHAPTER XXV.

Exulting peals rang out from the Bayford tower, and as Mr. and Mrs. Cavendish Dusautoy alighted from their carriage at Willow Lawn, the cry of the vicar and of the assembled household was, 'Have you heard that Sebastopol is taken?'

'Any news of Gilbert?' was Lucy's demand.

'No, the cavalry were not landed, so he had nothing to do with it.'

'I say, uncle,' said Algernon, 'shall I send up a sovereign to those ringers?'

'Eh! poor fellows, they will be very glad of it, thank you; only I must take care they don't drink it up. I'm sure they must be tired enough; they've been at it ever since the telegraph came in!'

'There!' exclaimed Algernon; 'Barton must have telegraphed from the station when we set out!'

'You? Did you think the bells were ringing for *you*,' exclaimed his uncle, 'when there's a great battle won, and Sebastopol taken?'

'Telegraphs are always lies!' quoth Mr. Cavendish Dusautoy, tersely, 'I don't believe anything has happened at all!' and he re-pocketed the sovereign.

Meantime Lucy was in a rapture of embracing. She was spread out with stiff silk flounces and velvet mantle, so as to emulate her husband's importance, and her chains and bracelets clattered so much, that Mr. Kendal could not help saying, 'You should have taken lessons of your Ayah, to learn how to manage your bangles.'

'Oh! papa,' said she, with a newly-learnt little laugh, 'I could not help it; Louise could not find room for them in my dressing-case.'

They were not, however, lost upon the whole of the family. Grandmamma's dim eyes lighted when she recognised her favourite grand-daughter in such gorgeous array, and that any one should have come back again was so new and delightful, that it constantly recurred as a fresh surprise and pleasure.

All were glad to have her again—their own Lucy, as she still was, though somewhat of the grandiose style and self-consequence of her husband had overlaid the original nature. She was as good-natured and obliging as ever, and though beginning by conferring her favours as condescensions, she soon would forget that she was the great Mrs. Cavendish Dusautoy, and quickly become the eager, helpful Lucy. She was in very good looks, and bright and happy, admiring Algernon, rejoicing to obey his behests, and enhancing his dignity and her own by her discourses upon his talents and importance. How far she was at ease with him, Albinia sometimes doubted; there now and then was an air of greater freedom when he left the room, and some of her favourite old household avocations were tenderly resumed by stealth, as though she feared he might think them unworthy of his wife.

She gave her spare time to the invalid, who was revived by her presence as by a sunbeam; and Albinia, in her relief and gratitude, did her utmost to keep Algernon happy and contented. She resigned a room to him as an atelier, and let the little Awk be captured to have her likeness taken, she promoted the guitar and key-bugle, and abstained from resenting his strictures on her dinners.

Such a guest reduced Mr. Kendal to absolute silence, but she did not think he suffered much therefrom, and he was often relieved, for all the neighbourhood asked the young couple to dinner. Mrs. Cavendish Dusautoy's toilette was as good as a play to the oldest and youngest inhabitants of the house, her little sister used to stand by the dressing-table with her small fingers straightened to sustain a column of rings threaded on them, and her arm weighed down with bracelets, and grandmamma's happiest moments were when she was raised up to contemplate the costly robes, jewelled neck, and garlanded head of her darling.

When it turned out that Sebastopol was anything but taken, Mr. Cavendish Dusautoy's incredulity was a precious confirmation of his esteem for his own sagacity, more especially as Ulick O'More and Maurice had worn out the little brass piece of ordnance in firing feux de joie.

'But,' said Maurice, 'papa always said it was not true. Now you only said so when you found the bells were ringing for that, and not for you.'

Maurice's observations were not always convenient. Algernon, with much pomp, had caused a horse to be led to the door, for which he had lately paid eighty guineas, and he was expatiating on its merits, when Maurice broke out, 'That's Macheath, the horse that Archie Tritton bought of Mr. Nugent's coachman for twenty pounds.'

'Hush, Maurice!' said his father, 'you know nothing of it; and Mr. Cavendish Dusautoy pursued, 'It was bred at Lord Lewthorp's, and sold because it was too tall for its companion. Laing was on the point of sending it to Tattersalls, where he was secure of a hundred, but he was willing to oblige me, as we had had transactions before.'

'Papa!' cried Maurice, 'I know it is Macheath, for Mr. Tritton showed him to Gilbert and me, when he had just got him, and said he was a showy beast, but incurably lame, so he should get what he could for him from Laing. Now, James, isn't it?' he called to the servant who was sedulously turning away a grinning face, but just muttered, 'Same, sir.'

Mr. Kendal charitably looked the other way, and Algernon muttered some species of imprecation.

Thenceforth Maurice took every occasion of inquiring what had become of Macheath, whether Laing had refunded the price, and what had been done to him for telling stories.

If the boy began in innocence, he went on in mischief; he was just old enough to be a most aggravating compound of simplicity and malice. He was fully aware that Mr. Cavendish Dusautoy was held cheap by his own favourites, and had been partly the cause of his dear Gilbert's troubles, and his sharp wits and daring nature were excited to the utmost by the solemn irritation that he produced. Not only was it irresistibly droll to tease one so destitute of fun, but he had the strongest desire to see how angry it was possible to make the big brother-in-law, of whom every one seemed in awe.

First, he had recourse to the old term Polysyllable, and when Lucy remonstrated, he answered, 'I've a right to call my brother what I please.'

'You know how angry mamma would be to hear you.'

'Mamma calls him the Polysyllable herself,' said Maurice, looking full at his victim.

Lucy, who would have given the world to hinder this epithet from coming to her husband's knowledge, began explaining something about Gilbert's nonsense before he knew him, and how it had been long disused.

'That's not true, Lucy,' quoth the tormentor. 'I heard mamma tell Sophy herself this morning to write for some fish-sauce, because she said that Polysyllable was so fanciful about his dinner.'

Lucy was ready to cry, and Algernon, endeavouring to recal his usual dignity, exclaimed, 'If Mrs. Kendal—I mean, Mrs. Kendal has it in her power to take liberties, but if I find you repeating such again, you little imp, it shall be at your risk.'

'What will you do to me?' asked the sturdy varlet.

'Dear Maurice, I hope you'll never know! Pray don't try!' cried Lucy; but if she had had any knowledge of character, she would have seen that she had only provoked the little Berserkar's curiosity, and had made him determined on proving the undefined threat. So the unfortunate Algernon seldom descended the stairs without two childish faces being protruded from the balusters of the nursery-flight over-head, pursuing him with hissing whispers of 'Polysyllable' and 'Polly-silly,' and if he ventured on indignant gestures, Maurice returned them with nutcracker grimaces and provoking assurances to his little sister that he could not hurt her.

Algernon could not complain without making himself ridiculous, and Albinia was too much engaged to keep watch over her son, so that the persecution daily became more intolerable, and barren indications of wrath were so diverting to the little monkey, that the presence of the heads of the family was the sole security from his tricks. Poor Lucy was the chief sufferer, unable to restrain her brother, and enduring the brunt of her husband's irritation, with the great disappointment of being unable to make him happy at her home, and fearing every day that he would fulfil his threat of not staying another week in the house with that intolerable child, for the sake of any one's grandmother.

Tidings came, however, that completely sobered Maurice, and made them unable to think of moving. It was the first rumour of the charge of Balaklava, with the report that the 25th Lancers were cut to pieces. In spite of Algernon's reiteration that telegraphs were lies, all the household would have been glad to lose the sense of existence during the time of suspense. Albinia's heart was wrung as she thought of the cold hurried manner of the last farewell, and every look she cast at her husband's calm melancholy face, seemed to be asking pardon that his son was not safe in India.

Late that evening the maid came hurriedly in with a packet of papers. 'A telegraph, ma'am, come express from Hadminster.'

It was to Mrs Kendal from one of her friends at the Horse Guards. She did not know how she found courage to turn her eyes on it, but her shriek was not of sorrow.

'Major the Honourable F. Ferrars, severely wounded—right arm amputated.'

'Lieutenant Gilbert Kendal, slightly wounded—contusion, rib broken.'

She saw the light of thankfulness break upon Mr. Kendal's face, and the next moment flew up to her boy's bed-side. He started up, half asleep, but crying out, Mamma, where's Gibbie?'

'Safe, safe! Maurice dearest, safe; only slightly wounded! Oh, Maurice, God has been very good to us!'

He flung his arms round her neck, as she knelt beside his crib in the dark, and thus Mr. Kendal found the mother and son. As he bent to kiss them, Maurice exclaimed, with a sort of anger, 'Oh, mamma, why have I got a bullet in my throat?'

Albinia laughed a little hysterically, as if she had the like bullet.

'It was very kind of Lord H——,' fervently exclaimed Mr. Kendal; 'you must write to thank him, Albinia. Gilbert may be considered safe while he is laid up. Perhaps he may be sent home. What should you say to that, Maurice?'

'Oh! I wouldn't come home to lose the fun,' said Maurice. 'Oh, mamma, let me get up to tell Awkey, and run up to Ulick! Gilbert will be the colonel when I'm a cornet! Oh! I must get up!'

His outspoken childish joy seemed to relieve Albinia's swelling heart, too full for the expression of thankfulness, and the excitement was too much even for the boy, for he burst into passionate sobs when forbidden to get up and waken his little sister.

The sobering came in Mr. Kendal's mention of Fred. Albinia was obliged to ask what had happened to him, and was shocked at having overlooked so terrible a misfortune; but Maurice seemed to be quite satisfied. 'You know, mamma, it said they were cut to pieces. Can't they make him a woodenarm?' evidently thinking he could be repaired as easily as the creatures in his sister's Noah's Ark. Even Algernon showed a heartiness and fellow-feeling that seemed to make him more like one of the family. Moreover, he was so much elevated at the receipt of a telegraph direct from the fountain-head, that he rode about the next day over all the neighbourhood with the tidings and comported himself as though he had private access to all Lord Raglan's secrets.

The unwonted emotion tamed Maurice for several days, and his behaviour was the better for his daily rides with papa to Hadminster, to forestall the second post. At last, on his return, his voice rang through the house. 'Mamma, where are you? The letter is come, and Gilbert shot two Russians, and saved Cousin Fred!'

'I opened your letter, Albinia,' said Mr. Kendal; and, as she took it from him, he said, 'Thank God, I never dared hope for such a day as this!'

He shut himself into the library, while Albinia was sharing with Sophy the precious letter, but with a moment's disappointment at finding it not from Gilbert, but from her brother William.

'Before you receive this,' he wrote, 'you will have heard of the affair of to-day, and that our two lads have come out of it better than some others. There are but nine officers living, and only four unhurt out of the 25th Lancers, and Fred's escape is entirely owing to your son.'

Then followed a brief narrative of the events of Balaklava, that fatal charge so well described as 'magnifique mais pas la guerre,' a history that seemed like a dream in connexion with the timid Gilbert. His individual story was thus:— He safely rode the 'half a league' forward, but when more than half way back, his horse was struck to the ground by a splinter of the same shell that overthrew Major Ferrars, at a few paces' distance from him. Quickly disengaging himself from his horse, Gilbert ran to assist his friend, and succeeded in extricating him from his horse, and supporting him through the remainder of the terrible space commanded by the batteries. Fred, unable to move without aid, and to whom each step was agony, had entreated Gilbert to relinquish his hold, and not peril himself for a life already past rescue; but Gilbert had not seemed to hear, and when several of the enemy came riding down on them, he had used his revolver with such effect, as to lay two of the number prostrate, and deter the rest from repeating the attack.

'All this I heard from Fred,' continued the General; 'he is in his usual spirits, and tells me that he feels quite jolly since his arm has been off, and he has been in his own bed, but I fear he has a good deal to suffer, for his right side is terribly lacerated, and I shall be glad when the next few days are over. He desires me to say with his love that the best turn you ever did him was putting young Kendal into the 25th. Tell your husband that I congratulate him on his son's conduct, and am afraid that his promotion without purchase is only too certain. Gilbert's only message was his love. Speaking seems to give him pain, and he is altogether more prostrated than so slight a wound accounts for; but when I saw him, he had just been told of the death of his colonel and several of his brother officers, among them young Wynne, who shared his tent; and he was completely overcome. There is, however, no cause for uneasiness; he had not even been aware that he was hurt, until he fainted while Fred was under the surgeon's hands, and was then found to have an ugly contusion of the chest, and a fracture of the uppermost rib on the left side. A few days' rest will set all that to rights, and I expect to see him on horseback before we can ship poor Fred for Scutari. In the meantime they are both in Fred's tent, which is fairly comfortable.'

Albinia understood whence came Gilbert's heroism. He had charged at first, as he had hunted with Maurice, because there was no doing otherwise, and in the critical moment the warm heart had done the rest, and equalled constitutional courage: but then, she saw the gentle tender spirit sinking under the slight injury, and far more at the suffering of his friend, the deadly havoc among his comrades, and his own share in the carnage. The General coolly mentioned the two enemies who had fallen by his pistol, and Maurice shouted about them as if they had been two rabbits, but she knew enough of Gilbert to be sure that what he might do in the exigency of self-defence, would shock and sicken him in recollection. Poor Fred! how little would she once have believed that his frightful wound could be a secondary matter with her, only enhancing her gratitude on account of another.

That was a happy evening; Maurice was sent to ask Ulick to dinner, and at dessert drank the healths of his soldier relatives, among whom Mr. Kendal with a smile at Ulick, included Bryan O'More.

In the universal good-will of her triumph, Albinia having read her precious letter to every one, resolved to let the Drurys hear it, before forwarding it to Fairmead. Lucy's neglect of that family was becoming flagrant, and Albinia was resolved to take her to make the call. Therefore, after promulgating her intentions too decidedly for Algernon to oppose them, she set out with Lucy in the most virtuous state of mind. Maurice was to ride out with his father, and Sophy was taking care of grandmamma, so she made her expedition with an easy mind, and absolutely enjoyed the change of scenery.

The war had drawn every one nearer together, and Mrs. Drury was really anxious about Gilbert, and grateful for the intelligence. Nor did Lucy meet with anything unpleasant. Mrs. Cavendish Dusautoy, in waist-deep flounces, a Paris bonnet, and her husband's dignity, impressed her cousins, and whatever use they might make of their tongues, it was not till after she was gone.

As the carriage stopped at the door, Sophy came out with such a perturbed an expression, as seemed to prelude fatal tidings; and Lucy was pausing to listen, when she was hastily summoned by her husband.

'Oh! mamma, he has struck Maurice such a blow!' cried Sophy.

'Algernon? where's Maurice? is he hurt?'

'He is in the library with papa.'

She was there in a moment. Maurice sat on his father's knee, listening to Pope's Homer, leaning against him, with eye, cheek, and nose exceedingly swelled and reddened; but these were symptoms of which she had seen enough in past days not to be greatly terrified, even while she exclaimed aghast.

'Aye!' said Mr. Kendal, sternly. 'What do you think of young Dusautoy's handiwork?'

'What could you have done to him, Maurice?'

'I painted his image.'

'The children got into the painting-room,' said Mr. Kendal, 'and did some mischief; Maurice ought to have known better, but that was no excuse for his violence. I do not know what would have been the consequence, if poor little

Albinia's screams had not alarmed me. I found Algernon striking him with his doubled fist.'

'But I gave him a dig in the nose,' cried Maurice, in exultation; 'I pulled ever so much hair out of his whiskers. I had it just now.'

'This sounds very sad,' said Albinia, interrupting the search for the trophy. 'What were you doing in the painting-room? You know you had no business there.'

'Why, mamma, little Awk wanted me to look at the pictures that Lucy shows her. And then, don't you know his image? the little white bare boy pulling the thorn out of his foot. Awkey said he was naughty not to have his clothes on, and so I thought it would be such fun to make a militiaman of him, and so the paints were all about, and so I gave him a red coat and black trousers.'

'Oh, Maurice, Maurice, how could you?'

'I couldn't help it, mamma! I did so want to see what Algernon would do!'

'Well.'

'So he came up and caught us. And wasn't he in a jolly good rage? that's all. He stamped, and called me names, and got hold of me to shake me, but I know I kicked him well, and I had quite a handful out of his whisker; but you see poor little Awkey is only a girl, and couldn't help squalling, so papa came up.'

'And in time!' said Mr. Kendal; 'he reeled against me, almost stunned, and was hardly himself for some moments. His nose bled violently. That fellow's fist might knock down an ox.'

'But he didn't knock *me* down,' said Maurice. 'You told me he did not, papa.'

'That's all he thinks of!' said Mr. Kendal, in admiration.

'Not a cry nor a tear from first to last. I told Sophy to let me know when Bowles came.'

'For a black eye?' cried the hard-hearted mother, laughing. 'You should have seen what Maurice and Fred used to do to each other.'

'Oh, tell me, mamma,' cried Maurice, eagerly.

'Not now, master,' she said, not thinking his pugnacity in need of such respectable examples. 'It would be more to the purpose to ask Mr. Cavendish Dusautoy's pardon for such very bad behaviour.'

Mr. Kendal looked at her in indignant surprise. 'Ours is not the side for the apology,' he said. 'If Dusautoy has a spark of proper feeling, he must excuse himself for such a brutal assault.'

'I am afraid Maurice provoked it; I hope my little boy is sorry for having been so mischievous, and sees that he deserves—'

Mr. Kendal silenced her by an impatient gesture, and feeling that anything was better than the discussion before the boy, she tried to speak indifferently, and not succeeding, left the room, much annoyed that alarm and indignation had led the indulgent father to pet and coax the spirit that only wanted to be taken down, and as if her discipline had received its first real shock.

Mr. Kendal followed her upstairs, no less vexed. 'Albinia, this is absurd,' he said. 'I will not have the child punished, or made to ask pardon for being shamefully struck.'

'It was shameful enough,' said Albinia; 'but, after all, I can't wonder that Algernon was in a passion; Maurice did behave very ill, and it would be much better for him if you would not make him more impudent than he is already.'

'I did not expect you to take part against your own child, when he has been so severely maltreated,' said he, with such unreasonable displeasure, that almost thinking it play, she laughed and said, 'You are as bad as the mothers of the school-children, when they wont have them beaten.'

He gave a look as if loth to trust his ears, walked into his room, and shut the door. The thrill of horror came over her that this was the first quarrel. She had been saucy when he was serious, and had offended him. She sprang to the door, knocked and called, and was in agony at the moment's delay ere he returned, with his face still stern and set. Pleading and earnest she raised her eyes, and surrendered unconditionally. 'Dear Edmund, don't be vexed with me, I should not have said it.'

'Never mind,' he said, affectionately; 'I do not wish to interfere with your authority, but it would be impossible to punish a child who has suffered so severely; and I neither choose that Dusautoy should be made to think himself the injured party, nor that Maurice should be put to the pain of apologizing for an offence, which the other party has taken on himself to cancel with interest.'

Albinia was too much demolished to recollect her two arguments, that pride on their side would only serve to make Algernon prouder, and that she did not believe that asking pardon would be so bitter a pill to Maurice as his father supposed. She could only feel thankful to have been forgiven for her own offence.

When they met at dinner, all were formal, Algernon stiff and haughty, ashamed, but too grand to betray himself, and Lucy restless and uneasy, her eyes looking as if she had been crying. When Maurice came in at dessert, the fourth part of his countenance emulating the unlucky cast in gorgeous hues of crimson and violet, Algernon was startled, and turning to Albinia, muttered something about 'never having intended,' and 'having had no idea.'

He might have said more, if Mr. Kendal, with Maurice on his knee, had not looked as if he expected it; and that look sealed Albinia's lips against expressing regret for the provocation; but Maurice exclaimed, 'Never mind, Algernon, it was all fair, and it doesn't hurt now. I wouldn't have touched your image, but that I wanted to know what you would do to me. Shake hands; people always do when they've had a good mill.'

Mr. Kendal looked across the table to his wife in a state of unbounded exultation in his generous boy, and Albinia felt infinitely relieved and grateful. Mr. Cavendish Dusautoy took the firm young paw, and said with an attempt at condescension, 'Very well, Maurice, the subject shall be mentioned no more, since you have received a severer lesson than I intended, and appear sensible of your error.'

'It wasn't you that made me so,' began Maurice, with defiant eye; but with a strong sense of 'let well alone,' his father cut him short with, 'That's enough, my man, you've said all that can be wished,' lifted him again on his knee, and stopped his mouth with almonds and raisins.

The subject was mentioned no more; Lucy considered peace as proclaimed, and herself relieved from the necessity of such an unprecedented deed as preferring an accusation against Maurice, and Albinia, unaware of the previous persecution, did not trace that Maurice considered himself as challenged to prove, that experience of his brother-in-law's fist did not suffice to make him cease from his 'fun.'

Two days after, Algernon was coming in from riding, when a simple voice upon the stairs observed, 'Here's such a pretty picture!'

'Eh! what?' said Algernon; and Maurice held it near to him as he stood taking off his great coat.

'Such a pretty picture, but you mustn't have it! No, it is Ulick's.'

'Heavens and earth!' thundered Algernon, as he gathered up the meaning. 'Who has dared—? Give it me—or—' and as soon as he was freed from the sleeves, he snatched at the paper, but the boy had already sprung up to the first landing, and waving his treasure, shouted, 'No, it's not for you, I'll not give you Ulick's picture.'

'Ulick!' cried Algernon, in redoubled fury. 'You're put up to this! Give it me this instant, or it shall be the worse for you;' but ere he could stride up the first flight, Maurice's last leg was disappearing round the corner above, and the next moment the exhibition was repeated overhead in the gallery. Thither did Algernon rush headlong, following the scampering pattering feet, till the door of Maurice's little room was slammed in his face. Bursting it open, he found the chamber empty, but there was a shout of elvish laughter outside, and a cry of dismay coming up from the garden, impelled him to mount the rickety deal-table below the deep sunk dormer window, when thrusting out his head and shoulders, he beheld his wife and her parents gazing up in terror from the lawn. No wonder, for there was a narrow ledge of leading without, upon which Maurice had suddenly appeared, running with unwavering steps till in a moment he stooped down, and popped through the similar window of Gilbert's room.

While still too dizzy with horror to feel secure that the child was indeed safe within, those below were startled by a frantic shout from Algernon: 'Let me out! I say, the imp has locked me in! Let me out!'

Albinia flew into the house and upstairs. Maurice was flourishing the key, and executing a war-dance before the captive's door, with a chant alternating of war-whoops, 'Promise not to hurt it, and I'll let you out!' and 'Pity poor prisoners in a foreign land!'

She called to him to desist, but he was too wild to be checked by her voice, and as she advanced to capture him, he shot like an arrow to the other end of the passage, and down the back-stairs. She promised speedy rescue, and hurried down, hoping to seize the culprit in the hall, but he had whipped out at the back-door, and was making for the garden gate, when his father hastened down the path to meet him, and seeing his retreat cut off, he plunged into the bushes, and sprang like a cat up a cockspur-thorn, too slender for ascent by a heavier weight, and thence grinned and waved his hand to his prisoner at the window.

'Maurice,' called his father, 'what does this mean?'

'I only want to take home Ulick's picture. Then I'll let him out.'

'What picture?'

'That's my secret.'

'This is not play, Maurice,' said Albinia. 'Attend to papa.'

The boy swung the light shrub about with him in a manner fearful to behold, and looked irresolute. Lucy put in her cry, 'You very naughty child, give up the key this moment,' and above, Algernon bawled appeals to Mr. Kendal, and threats to Maurice.

'Silence!' said Mr. Kendal, sternly. 'Maurice, this must not be. Come down, and give me the key of your room.'

'I will, papa,' said Maurice, in a reasonable voice. 'Only please promise not to let Algernon have Ulick's picture, for I got it without his knowing it.'

'I promise,' said Mr. Kendal. 'Let us put an end to this.'

Maurice came down, and brought the key to his father, and while Lucy hastened to release her husband, Mr. Kendal seized the boy, finding him already about again to take flight.

'Papa, let me take home Ulick's picture before he gets out,' said Maurice, finding the grasp too strong for him; but Mr. Kendal had taken the picture out of his hand, and looked at it with changed countenance.

It depicted the famous drawing-room scene, in its native element, the moon squinting through inky clouds at Lucy swooning on the sofa, while the lofty presence of the Polysyllable discharged the fluid from the inkstand.

'Did Mr. O'More give you this?' asked Mr. Kendal.

'No, it tumbled out of his paper-case. You know he said I might go to his rooms and get the Illustrated News with the picture of Balaklava, and so the newspaper knocked the paper-case down, and all the things tumbled out, so I picked this up, and thought I would see what Algernon would say to it, and then put it back again. Let me have it, papa, if he catches me, he'll tear it to smithereens.'

'Don't talk Irish, sir,' said his father. 'I see where your impertinence comes from, and I will put a stop to it.'

Maurice gave back a step, amazed at his father's unwonted anger, but far greater wrath was descending in the person of Mr. Cavendish Dusautoy, who came striding across the lawn, and planting himself before his father-in-law, demanded, 'I beg to know, sir, if it is your desire that I should be deliberately insulted in this house?'

'No one can be more concerned than I am at what has occurred.'

'Very well, sir; then I require that this intolerable child be soundly flogged, that beggarly Irishman kicked out, and that infamous libel destroyed!'

'Oh, papa,' cried Maurice, 'you promised me the picture should be safe!'

'I promise you, you impudent brat,' cried Algernon, 'that you shall learn what it is to insult your elders! You shall be flogged till you repent it!'

'You will allow me to judge of the discipline of my own family,' said Mr. Kendal.

'Ay! I knew how it would be! You encourage that child in every sort of unbearable impudence; but I have endured it long enough, and I give you warning that I do not remain another night under this roof unless I see the impertinence flogged out of him.'

'Papa never whips me,' interposed Maurice. 'You must ask mamma.'

Mr. Kendal bit his lips, and Albinia could have smiled, but their sense of the ludicrous inflamed Algernon, and like one beside himself, he swung round, and declaring he should ask his uncle if that were proper treatment, he marched across the lawn, while Mr. Kendal exclaimed, 'More childish than Maurice!'

'Oh, mamma, what shall I do?' was Lucy's woful cry, as she turned back, finding herself unable to keep up with his huge step, and her calls disregarded.

'My dear,' said Albinia, affectionately, 'you had better compose yourself and follow him. His uncle will bring him to reason, and then you can tell him how sorry we are.'

'You may assure him,' said Mr. Kendal, 'that I am as much hurt as he can be, that such an improper use should have been made of O'More's intimacy here, and I mean to mark my sense of it.'

'And,' said Lucy, 'I don't think anything would pacify him so much as Maurice being only a little beaten, not to hurt him, you know.'

'If Maurice be punished, it shall not be in revenge,' said Mr. Kendal.

'I'm afraid nothing else will do,' said Lucy, wringing her hands. 'He has really declared that he will not sleep another night here unless Maurice is punished; and whatever he says, he'll do, and I know it would kill me to go away in this manner.'

Her father confidently averred that he would do no such thing, but she cried so much as to move Maurice into exclaiming, 'Look here, Lucy, I'll come up with you, and let him give me one good punch, and then we shall all be comfortable again.'

'I don't know about the punching,' said Albinia; 'but I think the least you can do, Maurice, is to go and ask his forgiveness for having been so very naughty. You were not thinking what you were about when you locked him in.'

This measure was adopted, Mr. Kendal accompanying Lucy and the boy, while Albinia went in search of Sophy, whom she found in grandmamma's room, looking very pale. 'Well?' was the inquiry, and she told what had passed.

'I hope Maurice will be punished,' said Sophy; so unwonted a sentiment, that Albinia quite started, though it was decidedly her own opinion.

'That meddling with papers was very bad,' she said, with an extenuating smile.

'Fun is a perfect demon when it becomes master,' said Sophy. It was plain that it was not Maurice that she was thinking of, but the caricature. Her sister should have been sacred from derision.

'We must remember,' she said, 'that it was only through Maurice's meddling that we became aware of the existence of this precious work. It is not as if he had shown it to any one.'

'How many of the O'Mores have made game of it?' asked Sophy, bitterly. 'No, I am glad I know of it, I shall not be deceived any more.'

With these words she withdrew, evidently resolved to put an end to the subject. Her face was like iron, and Albinia grieved for the deep resentment that the man whom she had ventured to think of as devoted to herself, had made game of her sister. Poor Sophy, to her that tryste had been a subject of unmitigated affliction and shame, and it was a cruel wound that Ulick O'More should, of all men, have turned it into ridicule. What would be the effect on her?

In process of time Mr. Kendal returned. 'Albinia,' he said, 'this is a most unfortunate affair. He is perfectly impracticable, insists on starting for Paris to-morrow, and I verily believe he will.'

'Poor Lucy.'

'She is in such distress, that I could not bear to look at her, but he will not attend to her, nor to his uncle and aunt. Mrs. Dusautoy proposed that they should come to the vicarage, where there would be no danger of collisions with Maurice; but his mind can admit no idea but that he has been insulted, and that we encourage it, and he thinks his dignity concerned in resenting it.'

'Not much dignity in being driven off the field by a child of six years old.'

'So his aunt told him, but he mixes it up with O'More, and insists on my complaining to Mr. Goldsmith, and getting the lad dismissed for a libellous caricaturist, as he calls it. Now, little as I should have expected such conduct from O'More, it could not be made a ground of complaint to his uncle.'

'I should think not. No one with more wit than Algernon would have dreamt of it! But if Ulick came and apologized? Ah! but I forgot! Mr. Goldsmith sent him to London this morning. Well, it may be better that he should be out of the way of Algernon in his present mood.'

'Humph!' said Mr. Kendal. 'It is the first time I ever allowed a stranger to be intimate in my family, and it shall be the last. I never imagined him aware of the circumstance.'

'Nor I; I am sure none of us mentioned it.'

'Maurice told him, I suppose. It is well that we should be aware who has instigated the child's impertinence. I shall keep him as much as possible with me; he must be cured of Irish brogue and Irish coolness before they are confirmed.'

Mr. Kendal's conscience was evidently relieved by transferring to the Irishman the imputation of fostering Maurice's malpractices.

They were interrupted by Lucy's arrival. She was come to take leave of home, for her lord was not to be dissuaded from going to London by the evening's train. The greater the consternation, the sweeter his revenge. Never able to see more than one side of a question, he could not perceive how impossible it was for the Kendals to fulfil his condition with regard to Ulick O'More, and he sullenly adhered to his obstinate determination. Lucy was in an agony of grief, and perhaps the most painful blow was the perception how little he was swayed by consideration for her. Her maid packed, while her parents tried to console her. It was easier when she bewailed the terrors of the voyage, and the uncertainty of hearing of dear grandmamma and dear Gilbert, than when she sobbed about Algernon having no feeling for her. It might be only too true, but her wifely submission ought not to have acknowledged it, and they would not hear when they could not comfort; and so they were forced to launch her on the world, with a tyrant instead of a guide, and dreading the effect of dissipation on her levity of mind, as much as they grieved for her feeble spirit. It was a piteous parting—a mournful departure for a bride—a heavy penalty for vanity and weakness.

Unfortunately the result is to an action as the lens through which it is viewed, and the turpitude of the deed seems to increase or diminish according to the effect it produces.

Had it been in Algernon Dusautoy's nature to receive the joke good-humouredly, it might have been regarded as an audacious exercise of wit, and have been quickly forgotten, but when it had actually made a breach between him and his wife's family, and driven him from Bayford when everything conspired to make his departure unfeelingly cruel, the caricature was regarded as a serious insult and an abuse of intimacy. Even Mr. Kendal was not superior to this view, feeling the offence with all the sensitiveness of a hot- tempered man, a proud reserved guardian of the sanctities of home, and of a father who had seen his daughter's weakest and most faulty action turned into ridicule, and he seemed to feel himself bound to atone for not going to all the lengths to which Algernon would have impelled him, by showing the utmost displeasure within the bounds of common sense.

Albinia, better appreciating the irresistibly ludicrous aspect of the adventure, argued that the sketch harmlessly shut up in a paper-case showed no great amount of insolence, and that considering how the discovery had been made, it ought not to be visited. She thought the drawing had better be restored without remarks by the same hand that had abstracted it; but Mr.

Kendal sternly declared this was impossible, and Sophy's countenance seconded him.

'Well, then,' said Albinia, 'put it into my hands. I'm a bad manager in general, but I can promise that Ulick will come down so shocked and concerned, that you will not have the heart not to forgive him.'

'The question is not of forgiveness,' said Sophy, in the most rigid of voices, as she saw yielding in her father's face; if any one had to forgive, it was poor Lucy and Algernon. All we have to do, is to be on our guard for the future.'

'Sophy is right,' said Mr. Kendal; 'intimacy must be over with one who has so little discretion or good taste.'

'Then after his saving Maurice, he is to be given up, because he quizzed the Polysyllable?' cried Albinia.

'I do not give him up,' said Mr. Kendal. 'I highly esteem his good qualities, and should be happy to do him a service, but I cannot have my family at the mercy of his wit, nor my child taught disrespect. We have been unwisely familiar, and must retreat.'

'And what do you mean us to do?' exclaimed Albinia. 'Are we to cut him systematically?'

'I do not know what course you may adopt,' said Mr. Kendal, in a tone whose grave precision rebuked her half petulant, half facetious inquiry. 'I have told you that I do not mean to do anything extravagant, nor to discontinue ordinary civilities, but I think you will find that our former habits are not resumed.'

'And Maurice must not be always with him,' said Sophy.

'Certainly not; I shall keep the boy with myself.'

It was with the greatest effort that Albinia held her tongue. To have Sophy not only making common cause against her, but inciting her father to interfere about Maurice, was well-nigh intolerable, and she only endured it by sealing her lips as with a bar of iron.

By-and-by came the reflection that if poor Sophy had a secret cause of bitterness, it was she herself who had given those thoughts substance and consciousness, and she quickly forgave every one save herself and Algernon.

As to her little traitor son, she took him seriously in hand at bedtime, and argued the whole transaction with him, representing the dreadful consequences of meddling with people's private papers under trust. Here was poor Lucy taken away from home, and papa made very angry with Ulick, because Maurice had been meddlesome and mischievous; and though he had not been beaten for it, he would find it a worse punishment not to be trusted another time, nor allowed to be with Ulick.

Maurice turned round with mouth open at hearing of papa's anger with Ulick, and the accusation of having brought his friend into trouble.

'Why, Maurice, you remember how unhappy we were, Gilbert and all. It was because it was sadly wrong of Gilbert and Lucy to have let Algernon in without papa's knowing it, and it was not right or friendly in Ulick to laugh at what was so wrong, and grieved us all so much.'

'It was such fun,' said Maurice.

'Yes, Maurice; but fun is no excuse for doing what is unkind and mischievous. Ulick would not have been amused if he had cared as much for us as we thought he did, but, after all, his drawing the picture would have done no harm but for a little boy, whom he trusted, never thinking that an unkind wish to tease, would betray this foolish action, and set his best friends against him.'

'I did not know I should,' said Maurice, winking hard.

'No; you did not know you were doing what, if you were older, wouldhave been dishonourable.'

That word was too much! First he hid his face from his mother, and cried out fiercely, 'I've not—I've not been that and clenched his fist. 'Don't say it, mamma.'

'If you had known what you were doing, it would have been dishonourable,' she repeated, gravely. 'It will be a long time before you earn trust and confidence again.'

There was a great struggle with his tears. She had punished him, and almost more than she could bear to see, but she knew the conquest must be secured, and she tried, while she caressed him, to make him look at the real cause of his lapse; he declared that it was 'such fun' to provoke Algernon, and a little more brought out a confession of the whole course of persecution, the child's voice becoming quite triumphant as he told of the success of his tricks, and his mother, though appalled at their audacity, with great difficulty hindering herself from manifesting her amusement.

She did not wonder at Algernon's having found it intolerable, and though angry with him for having made himself such fair game, she set to work to impress upon Maurice his own errors, and the hatefulness of practical jokes, and she succeeded so far as to leave him crying himself to sleep, completely subdued, while she felt as if all the tears ought to have been shed by herself for her want of vigilance.

Conflicting duties! how hard to strike the balance! She had readily given up her own pleasures for the care of Mrs. Meadows, but when it came to her son's training, it was another question.

She much wished to see the note with which Mr. Kendal returned the unfortunate sketch, but one of the points on which he was sensitive, was the sacredness of his correspondence, and all that she heard was, that Ulick had answered 'not at all as Mr. Kendal had expected; he was nothing but an Irishman, after all.' But at last she obtained a sight of the note.

'I was much astonished at the contents of your letter of this morning, and greatly concerned that Mr. Cavendish Dusautoy should have done so much honour to any production of mine, as to alter his arrangements on that account.

'As the scrawl in question was not meant to meet the eye of any living being, I should, for my own part, have considered it proper to take no notice of what was betrayed by mere accident. I should have considered it more conducive to confidence between gentlemen. I fully acquiesce in what you say of the cessation of our former terms of acquaintance, and with many thanks for past kindness, believe me,

Nothing was more evidently written in a passion at the invasion of these private papers, and Albinia, though she had always feared he might consider himself the aggrieved party, had hardly expected so much proud irritation and so little regret. Mr. Kendal called him 'foolish boy,' and tried to put the matter aside, but he was much hurt, and Ulick put himself decidedly in the wrong by passing in the street with a formal bow, when Mr. Kendal, according to his purpose of ordinary civility without an open rupture, would have shaken hands.

Sophy looked white, stern, and cold, but said not a word; she deepened her father's displeasure quite sufficiently by her countenance. His was grave disappointment in a youth whom he found less grateful than he thought he had a right to expect; hers was the rankling of what she deemed an insult to her sister, and the festering of a wound of which she was ashamed. She meant to bear it well, but it made her very hard and rigid, and even the children could hardly extract a smile from her. She seemed to have made a determination to do all that Lucy or herself had ever done, and more too, and listened to no entreaties to spare herself. Commands were met with sullen resignation, entreaties were unavailing, and both in the sickroom and the parish, she insisted on working beyond her powers. It was a nightly battle to send her to bed, and Albinia suspected that she did not sleep. Meantime Lucy had sailed, and was presently heard of in a whirl of excitement that shortened her letters, and made them joyous and self-important.

'Ah!' said Sophy, 'she will soon forget that she ever had a home.'

'Poor dear! Wait till trouble comes, and she will remember it only too sadly,' sighed Albinia.

'Trouble is certain enough,' said Sophy; 'but I don't think what we deserve does us much good.'

Sophy could see nothing but the most ungentle and gloomy aspects. Gilbert had not yet written, and she was convinced that he was either very ill, or had only recovered to be killed at Inkermann, and she would only sigh at the Gazette that announced Lieutenant Gilbert Kendal's promotion to be Captain, and Major the Honourable Frederick Ferrars to be Lieutenant-Colonel.

The day after, however, came the long expected letter from the captain himself. It was to Mrs. Kendal, and she detected a shade of disappointment on her husband's face, so she would have handed it to him at once, but he said, 'No, the person to whom the letter is addressed, should always be the first to read it.'

The letter began with Gilbert's happiness in those from home, which he called the greatest pleasure he had ever known. He feared he had caused uneasiness by not writing sooner, but it had been out of his power while Fred Ferrars was in danger. Then followed the account of the severe illness from which Fred was scarcely beginning to rally, though that morning, on hearing that he was to be sent home as soon as he could move, he had talked about Canada and Emily. Gilbert said that not only time but strength had been wanting for writing, for attendance on Fred had been all that he could attempt, since moving produced so much pain and loss of breath, that he had been forced to be absolutely still whenever he was not wanted, but he was now much better. 'Though,' he continued, 'I do not now mind telling you that I had thought myself gone. You, who have known all my feelings, and have borne with them so kindly, will understand the effect upon me, when on the night previous to the 25th, I distinctly heard my own name, in Edmund's voice, at the head of my bed, just as he used to call me when he had finished his lessons, and wanted me to come out with him. As I started up, I heard it again outside the tent. I ran to the door, but of course there was nothing, nor did poor Wynne hear anything. I lay awake for some time, but slept at last, and had forgotten all by morning. It did not even occur to me when I saw the pleasant race they had cut out for us, nor through the whole affair. Do not ask me to describe it, the scene haunts me enough. When I found that I had not come off unhurt, and it seemed as if I could not ask for one of our fellows but to hear he was dead or dying, poor Wynne among them, then the voice seemed a summons. I was thoroughly done up, and could not even speak when General Ferrars came to me; I only wanted to be let alone to die in peace. I fancy I slept, for the next thing I heard was the Major's voice asking for some water, too feebly to wake the fellow who had been left in charge. I got up, and found him in a state of high fever and great pain, and from that time to the present, I have hardly thought of the circumstance, and know not why I have now written it to you. Did my danger actually bring Edmund nearer, or did its presence act on my imagination? Be that as it may, I think, after the first impression of awe and terror, the having heard the dear old voice braced me, and gave me a sense of being near home and less lonely. Not that my hurt has been for an instant dangerous, and I am mending every day; if it were warmer I should get on faster, but I cannot stir into the air without bringing on cough. Tell Ulick O'More that we entertained his brother at tea last evening, we were obliged to desire him to bring his own cup, and he produced the shell of a land tortoise; it was very like the fox and the crane. Poor fellow, it was the first good meal he had for weeks, and I was glad he came in for some famous bread that the General had sent us in. He made us much more merry than was convenient to either of us, not being in condition for laughing. He is a fine lad, and liked by all.' Then came a break, and the letter closed with such tidings of Inkermann as had reached the invalid's tent.

A few lines from General Ferrars spoke of the improvement in both patients, adding that Fred had had a hard struggle for his life, and had only been saved, by Gilbert's unremitting care by day and night.

Heroism had not transformed Gilbert, and Albinia's old fondness glowed with double ardour as she mused over his history of the battle-eve. His father attributed the impression to a mind full of presage and excitement, acted upon by strong memory; but woman-like, Albinia preferred the belief that the one twin might have been an actual messenger to cheer and strengthen the other for the coming trial. Sophy only said, 'Gilbert's fancies as usual.'

'This was not like fancy,' said Albinia. 'This is an unkind way of taking it.'

'It is common sense,' she bluntly answered. 'I don't see why he should think that Edmund has nothing better to do than to call him. It would be childish.'

Albinia did not reply, disturbed by this display of jealousy and harshness, as if every bud of tenderness had been dried up and withered, and poor Sophy only wanted to run counter to any obvious sentiment.

Albinia was grateful for the message which gave her an excuse for seeking Ulick out, and endeavouring to conciliate him. Mr. Kendal made no objection, and expressed a hope that he might have become reasonable. She therefore contrived to waylay him in the November darkness, holding out her hand so that he took it at unawares, as if not recollecting that he was offended, but in the midst his grasp relaxed, and his head went up.

'I have a message for you from Gilbert about your brother Bryan,' she said, and he could not defend himself from manifesting eager interest, as she told of the tea-party; but that over, it was in stiff formal English that he said, 'I hope you had a good account.'

It struck a chill, and she answered, almost imploringly, 'Gilbert is much better, thank you.'

'I am glad to hear it;' and he was going to bow and pass on, when she exclaimed,

'Ulick, why are we strangers?'

'It was agreed on all hands that things past could not be undone,' he frigidly replied.

'Too true,' she said; 'but I do not think you know how sorry we are for my poor little boy's foolish trick.'

'I owe no displeasure to Maurice. He knew no more what he was doing than if he had been a gust of wind; but if the wind had borne a private paper to my feet, I would never have acted on the contents.'

'Unhappily,' said Albinia, 'some revelations, though received against our will, cannot help being felt. We saw the drawing before we knew how he came by it, and you cannot wonder that it gave pain to find that a scene so distressing to us should have furnished you with amusement. It was absurd in itself, but we had hoped it was a secret, and it wounded us because we thought you would have been tender of our feelings.'

'You don't mean that it was fact!' cried Ulick, stopping suddenly; and as her silence replied, he continued, 'I give you my word and honour that I never imagined there was a word of truth in the farrago old Biddy told me, and I'll not deny that I did scrawl the scene down as the very picture of a bit of slander. I only wonder I'd not brought it to yourself.'

'Pray let me hear what she told you.'

'Oh! she said they two had been colloguing together by moonlight, and you came home in the midst, and Miss Kendal fainted away, so he catches up the ink and throws it over her instead of water, and you and Mr. Kendal came in and were mad entirely; and Mr. Kendal threatened to brain him with the poker if he did not quit it that instant, and sent Gilbert for a soldier for opening the door to him, but you and Lucy went down on your bare knees to get him to relent.'

'Well, I own the poker does throw an air of improbability over the whole. Minus that and the knees, I am afraid it is only too true. I suppose it got abroad through the servants.'

'It was an unlucky goose-quill that lay so handy,' exclaimed Ulick; 'but you may credit me, no eye but my own ever saw the scrawl, nor would have seen it.'

'Then, Ulick, if we all own that something is to be regretted, why do we stand aloof, and persist in quarrelling?'

'I want no quarrel,' said Ulick, stiffly. 'Mr. Kendal intimated to me that he did not wish for my company, and I'm not the man to force it.'

'Oh, Ulick, this is not what I hoped from you!'

'I'll tell you what, Mrs. Kendal, you could talk over the Giant's Causeway if you had a mind,' said Ulick, with much agitation; 'but you must not talk over me, for your own judgment would be against it. You know what I am, and what I came of, and what have I in the world except the honour of a gentleman? Mr. Kendal and yourself have been my kindest friends, and I'll be grateful to my dying day; but if Mr. Kendal thinks I can submit tamely when he resents what he never ought to have noticed, why, then, what have I to do but to show him the difference? If his kindness was to me as a gentleman and his equal, I love and bless him for it, but if it be a patronizing of the poor clerk, why, then, I owe it to myself and my people to show that I can stand alone, without cringing, and being thankful for affronts.'

'Did it ever occur to you to think whether pride be a sin?'

''Tis not pride!' cried Ulick. It is my duty to my family and my name. You'd say yourself, as you allowed before now, that it would be mere meanness and servility to swallow insults for one's own profit; and if I were to say "you're welcome, with many thanks, to shuffle over my private papers, and call myself to account," I'd better have given up my name at once, for I'd have left the gentleman behind me.'

'I do believe it is solely for the O'Mores that you are making a duty of implacability!'

'It is a duty not to run from one's word, and debase oneself for one's own advantage.'

'One would think some wonderful advantage was held out to you.'

'The pleasantest hours of my life,' murmured he sadly, under his breath.

'Well, Ulick,' she said, holding out her hand, 'I'm not quite dissatisfied; I think some day even an O'More will see that there is no exception from the law of forgiveness in their special favour, and that you will not be able to go on resenting what we have suffered from the young of the spider-monkey.'

Even this allusion produced no outward effect; he only shook hands gravely, saying, 'I never did otherwise than forgive, and regret the consequences: I am very thankful for all your past kindness.'

Worse than the Giant's Causeway, thought Albinia as she parted from him. Nothing is so hopeless as that sort of forgiveness, because it satisfies the conscience.

Mr. Kendal predicted that, the Keltic dignity having been asserted, good sense and principle would restore things to a rational footing. What this meant might be uncertain, but he certainly missed Prometheus, and found Maurice a poor substitute. Indulgence itself could hardly hold out in unmitigated intercourse with an obstreperous dunce not seven years old, and Maurice, deprived of Gilbert, cut off from Ulick, with mamma busy, and Sophy out of spirits, underwent more snubbing than had ever yet fallen to his lot. Not that he was much concerned thereat; and Mr. Kendal would resume his book after a lecture upon good manners, and then be roused to find his library a gigantic cobweb, strings tied to every leg of table or chair, and Maurice and the little Awk enacting spider and fly, heedless of the unwilling flies who might suffer by their trap. Such being the case, his magnanimity was the less amazing when he said, 'Albinia, there is no reason that O'More should not eat his Christmas dinner here.'

'Very well. I trust he will not think it needful still to be self-denying.'

'It is not our part to press advances which are repelled,' said Sophy.

'Indeed, Sophy,' said her father, smiling, 'I see nothing attractive in the attitude of rocks rent asunder.'

The undesigned allusion must have gone deep, for she coloured to a purple crimson, and said in a freezing tone, 'I thought you considered that to take him up again would be a direct insult to Lucy and her husband.'

'They do not show much consideration for us,' said Mr. Kendal. 'How long ago was the date of her last letter?'

'Nearly three weeks,' said Albinia. 'Poor child, how could she write with the catalogue raisonnee of the Louvre to learn by heart?'

The Dusautoys yearly gave a Christmas tea-party to the teachers in the Sunday-school, who had of late become more numerous, as Mr. Dusautoy's influence had had more time to tell. Mrs. Kendal was reckoned on as one of the chief supporters of the gaiety of the evening, but on this occasion she was forced to send Sophia alone.

Sophy regarded it as a duty and a penance, and submitted the more readily because it was so distasteful. It was, however, more than she had reckoned on to find that the party had been extended to the male teachers, an exceedingly good and lugubrious-looking youth lately apprenticed to Mr. Bowles, and Ulick O'More. It was the first time she had met the latter since his offence. She avoided seeing him as long as possible, though all his movements seemed to thrill her, and so confused the conversation which she was trying to keep up, that she found herself saying that Genevieve Durant had lost an arm, and that Gilbert would spend Christmas in London.

She felt him coming nearer; she knew he was passing the Miss Northover in the purple silk and red neck-ribbon; she heard him exchanging a few civil words with the sister with the hair strained off her face; she knew he was coming; she grew more eager in her fears for Mr. Rainsforth's chest.

Tea was announced. Sophy held back in the general move, Ulick made a step nearer, their eyes met, and if ever eyes spoke, hers ordered him to keep his distance, while he glanced affront for affront, bowed and stepped back.

Sophy sat by Miss Jane Northover, and endeavoured to make her talk. Anything would have been better than the echoes of the sprightliness at the lower end of the table, where Ulick was talking what he would have called blarney to Miss Susan Northover and Miss Mary Anne Higgins, both at once, till he excited them into a perpetual giggle. Mr. Dusautoy was delighted, and evidently thought this brilliant success; Mrs. Dusautoy was less at her ease—the mirth was less sober and more exclusive than she had intended; and Sophy, finding nothing could be made of Miss Jane, turned round to her other neighbour, Mr. Hope, and asked his opinion of the Whewell and Brewster controversy on the Plurality of Worlds.

Mr. Hope had rather a good opinion of Miss Sophia, and as she had never molested him, could talk to her, so he straightway became engrossed in the logical and theological aspects of the theory; and Mrs. Dusautoy could hardly suppress her smile at this unconscious ponderous attempt at a counter flirtation, with Saturn and Jupiter as weapons for light skirmishing.

Ulick received the invitation to dinner, and did not accept it. He said he had an engagement—Albinia wondered what it could be, and had reason afterwards to think that he had the silent young apothecary to a Christmas dinner in his own rooms—an act of charity at least, if not of forgiveness. Mr. Johns, the senior clerk, whose health had long been failing, was about to retire, and this announcement was followed by the appearance of a smart, keen-looking young man of six or seven-and-twenty, whom Miss Goldsmith paraded as her cousin, Mr. Andrew Goldsmith, and it was generally expected that he would be taken into partnership, and undertake old John's work, but in a fortnight he disappeared, and young O'More was promoted to the vacant post with an increase of salary. It was mortifying only to be informed through Mr. Dusautoy, instead of by the lad himself.

The Eastern letters were the chief comfort. First came tidings that Gilbert, not having yet recovered his contusion, was to accompany Colonel Ferrars to Scutari, and then after a longer interval came a brief and joyous note—Gilbert was coming home! On his voyage from the Crimea he had caught cold, and this had brought on severe inflammation on the injured chest, which had laid him by for many days at Scutari. The colonel had become the stronger of the two, in spite of a fragment of shell lodged so deeply in the side, that the medical board advised his going to London for its removal. Both were ordered home together with six months' leave, and Gilbert's note overflowed with glad messages to all, including Algernon, of whose departure he was still in ignorance.

Mr. Kendal knew not whether he was most gratified or discomfited by the insinuating ringer who touched his hat, hoping for due notice of the captain's arrival in time to welcome him with a peal of bells. Indeed, Bayford was so excited about its hero, that there were symptoms of plans for a grand reception with speeches, cheers, and triumphal arches, which caused Sophy to say she hoped that he would come suddenly without any notice, so as to put a stop to all that nonsense; while Albinia could not help nourishing a strange vague expectation that his return would be the beginning of better days.

At last, Sophia, with a touch of the old penny club fever, toiled over the school clothing wilfully and unnecessarily for two hours, kept up till evening without owning to the pain in her back, but finally returned so faint and dizzy that she was forced to be carried helpless to her room, and the next day could barely drag herself to the couch in the morning-room, where she lay quite prostrated, and grieved at increasing instead of lessening her mother's cares.

'Oh, mamma, don't stay with me. You are much too busy.'

'No, I am not. The children are out, and grandmamma asleep, and I am going to write to Lucy, but there's no hurry. Let me cool your forehead a little longer.'

'How I hate being another bother!'

'I like you much better so, than when you would not let me speak to you, my poor child.'

'I could not,' she said, stifling her voice on the cushion, and averting her head; but in a few moments she made a great effort, and said, 'You think me unforgiving, mamma. It was not entirely that. It was hating myself for an old fancy, a mere mistake. I have got over it; and I will not be in error again.'

'Sophy dear, if you find strength in pride, it will only wound yourself.'

'I do not think I am proud,' said Sophy, quietly. 'I may have been headstrong, but I despise myself too much for pride.'

'Are you sure it was mere fancy? It was an idea that occurred to more than to you.'

'Hush!' cried Sophy. 'Had it been so, could he have ridiculed Lucy? Could he have flown out so against papa? No; that caricature undeceived me, and I am thankful. He treated us as cousins—no more—he would act in the same manner by any of the Miss O'Mores of Ballymakilty, nay, by Jane Northover herself. We did not allow for Irish manner.'

'If so, he had no right to do so. I shall never wish to see him here again.'

'No, mamma, he did not know the folly he had to deal with. Next time I meet him, I shall know how to be really indifferent. Now, this is the last time we will mention the subject!'

Albinia obeyed, but still hoped. It was well that hope remained, for her task was heavier than ever; Mrs. Meadows was feebler, but more restless and wakeful, asking twenty times in an hour for Mrs. Kendal. The doctors thought it impossible that she should hold out another fortnight, but she lived on from day to day, and at times Albinia hardly could be absent from her for ten minutes together. Sophy was so completely knocked up that she could barely creep about the house, and was forbidden the sick-room; but she was softened and gentle, and was once more a companion to her father, while eagerly looking forward to devoting herself to Gilbert.

A letter with the Malta post-mark was eagerly opened, as the harbinger of his speedy arrival.

'Royal Hotel, Malta,
February 10th, 1855.

'Dearest Mrs. Kendal,

'I am afraid you will all be much disappointed, though your grief cannot equal mine at the Doctor's cruel decree. We arrived here the day before yesterday, but I had been so ill all the voyage with pain in the side and cough, that there was no choice but to land, and call in Dr.——, who tells me that my broken rib has damaged my lungs so much, that I must keep perfectly quiet, and not think of going home till warm weather. If I am well enough to join by that time, I shall not see you at all unless you and my father could come out. Am I nourishing too wild a hope in thinking it possible? Since Lucy has been so kind as to promise never to leave grandmamma, I cannot help hoping you might be spared. I do not think my proposal is selfish, since my poor grandmother is so little conscious of your cares; and Ferrars insists on remaining with me till he sees me in your hands, though they say that the splinter must be extracted in London, and every week he remains here is so much suffering, besides delaying his expedition to Canada. I have entreated him to hasten on, but he will not hear of it. He is like a brother or a father to me, and nurses me most tenderly, when he ought to be nursed himself. We are famishing for letters. I suppose all ours have gone up to Balaklava, and thence will be sent to England. If we were but there! We are both much better for the quiet of these two days, and are to move to-morrow to a lodging that a friend of Fred's has taken for us at Bormola, so as to be out of the Babel of these streets—we stipulated that it should be large enough to take in you and my father. I wish Sophy and the children would come too—it would do them all the good in the world; and Maurice would go crazy among the big guns; I am only afraid we should have him enlisting as a drummer. The happy pair would be very glad to have the house to themselves, and would persuade themselves that it was another honeymoon.

'Good-bye. Instead of looking for a letter, I shall come down to meet you at the Quarantine harbour. Love to all.

How differently Gilbert wrote when really ill, from his desponding style when he only fancied himself so, thought Albinia, as, perplexed and grieved, she handed the letter to her husband, and opened the enclosure, written in the laboured, ill-formed characters of a left-hand not yet accustomed to doing the offices of both.

'Dear Albinia,

'Come, if possible. His heart is set upon it, though he does not realize his condition, and I cannot bear to tell him. Only the utmost care can save him. I am doing my best for him, but my nursing is as left-handed as my writing.

His wife's look of horror was Mr. Kendal's preparation for this emphatic summons, perhaps a shock less sudden to him than to her, for he had not been without misgivings ever since he had heard of the situation of the injury. He read and spoke not, till the silence became intolerable, and she burst out almost with a scream, 'Oh! Edmund, I knew not what I did when I took grandmamma into this house!'

'This is very perplexing,' he said, his feelings so intense that he dared only speak of acting; 'I must set out to-night.'

'Order me to come with you,' she said breathlessly. 'That will cancel everything else.'

'Would Mrs. Drury take charge of her aunt?' said he, with a moment's hesitation; and Albinia felt it implied his impression that they were bound by her repeated promises never to quit the invalid, but she only spoke the more vehemently—

'Mrs Drury? She might—she would, under the circumstances. She could not refuse. If you desire me to come, I should not be doing wrong; and grandmamma might never even miss me. Surely—oh surely, a young life, full of hope and promise, that may yet be saved, is not to be set against what cannot be prolonged more than a few weeks.'

'As to that,' said Mr. Kendal, in the deliberate tone which denoted dissatisfaction, 'though of course it would be the greatest blessing to have you with us, I think you may trust Gilbert to my care. And we must consider poor Sophia.'

'She could not bear to be considered.'

'No; but it would be leaving her in a most distressing position, when she is far from well, and with most uncongenial assistants. You see, poor Gilbert reckons on Lucy being here, which would make it very different. But think of poor Sophia in the event of Mrs. Meadows not surviving till our return!'

'You are right! It would half kill her! My promise was sacred; I was a wretch to think of breaking it. But when I think of my boy—my Gilbert pining for me, and I deserting him—'

'For the sake of duty,' said her husband. 'Let us do right, and trust that all will be overruled for the best. I shall go with an easier mind if I leave you with the other children, and I can be the sooner with him.'

'I could travel as fast.'

'I may soon bring him home to you. Or you might bring the others to join us in the south of France. You will all need change.'

The decision was made, and her judgment acquiesced, though she could hardly have cast the balance for herself. She urged no more, even when relentings came over her husband at the thought of the trials to which he was leaving her, and of those which he should meet in solitude; yet not without a certain secret desire to make himself sufficient for the care and contentment of his own son. He cast about for all possible helpers for her, but could devise nothing except a note entreating her brother to be with her as much as possible, and commending her to the Dusautoys. It was a less decided kindness that he ordered Maurice's pony to be turned out to grass, so as to prevent rides in solitude, thinking the boy too young to be trusted, and warned by the example of Gilbert's temptations.

Going up to the bank to obtain a supply of gold, he found young O'More there without his uncle. The tidings of Gilbert's danger had spread throughout the town, and one heart at least was softened. Ulick wrung the hand that lately he would not touch, and Mr. Kendal forgot his wrath as he replied to the warm-hearted inquiry for particulars.

'Then Mrs. Kendal cannot go with you?'

'No, it is impossible. There is no one able to take charge of Mrs. Meadows.'

'Ah! and Mrs. Cavendish Dusautoy is gone! I grieve for the hour when my pen got the better of me. Mr. Kendal, this is worse than I thought. Your son will never forgive me when he knows I'm at the bottom of his disappointment.'

'There is something to forgive on all hands,' said Mr. Kendal. 'That meddlesome boy of mine has caused worse results than we could have contemplated. I believe it has been a lesson to him.'

'I know it has to some one else,' said Ulick. 'I wish I could do anything! It would be the greatest comfort you could give me to tell me of a thing I could do for Gilbert or any of you. If you'd send me to find Mr. Cavendish Dusautoy, and tell him 'twas all my fault, and bring them back—'

'Rather too wild a project, thank you,' said Mr. Kendal, smiling. 'No; the only thing you could do, would be—if that boy of mine have not completely forfeited your kindness—'

'Maurice! Ah! how I have missed the rogue.'

'Poor little fellow, I am afraid he may be a burthen to himself and every one else. It would be a great relief if you could be kind enough now and then to give him the pleasure of a walk.'

Maurice did not attend greatly to papa's permission to go out with Mr. O'More. Either it was clogged with too many conditions of discretion, and too many reminiscences of the past; or Maurice's mind was too much bent on the thought of his brother. Both children haunted the packing up, entreating to send out impossible presents. Maurice could hardly be persuaded out of contributing a perilous-looking boomerang, which he argued had some sense in it; while he scoffed at the little Awk, who stood kissing and almost crying over the china countenance of her favourite doll, entreating that papa would take dear Miss Jenny because Gibbie loved her the best of all, and always put her to sleep on his knees. At last matters were compromised by Sophy, who roused herself to do one of the few things for which she had strength, engrossing them by cutting out in paper an interminable hunt with horses and dogs adhering together by the noses and tails, which, when brilliantly painted according to their united taste, they might safely imagine giving pleasure to Gilbert, while, at any rate, it would do no harm in papa's pocket-book.

CHAPTER XXVI.

The day after Mr. Kendal's departure, Mrs. Meadows had another attack, but a fortnight still passed before the long long task was over and the weary spirit set free. There had been no real consciousness and no one could speak of regret; of anything but relief and thankfulness that release had come at last, when Albinia had redeemed her pledge and knew she should no more hear of the dreary 'very bad night,' nor be greeted by the low, restless moan. The long good-night was come, and, on the whole, there was peace and absence of self-condemnation in looking back on the past connexion. Forbearance and unselfishness were recompensed by the calm tenderness with which she could regard one who at the outset had appeared likely to cause nothing but frets and misunderstandings.

Had she and Sophy been left to themselves, there would have been nothing to break upon this frame of mind, but early the next day arrived Mr. and Mrs. Drury, upsetting all her arrangements, implying that it had been presumptuous to exert any authority without relationship. It did seem hard that the claims of kindred should be only recollected in order to unsettle her plans, and offend her unostentatious tastes.

Averse both to the proposals, and to the discussion, she felt unprotected and forlorn, but her spirit revived as she heard her brother's voice in the hall, and she hastened to put herself in his hands. He declined doing battle, he said it would be better to yield than to argue, and leave a grudge for ever. 'It will not vex Edmund,' he said, 'and though you and Sophy may be pained by incongruities, they will hurt you less than disputing.'

She felt that he was right, and by yielding the main points he contrived amicably to persuade Mr. Drury out of the numerous invitations and grand luncheon as well as to adhere to the day that she had originally fixed for the funeral, after which he hoped to take her and the young ones home with him and give her the thorough change and rest of which the over-energy of her manner betrayed the need.

Not that she consented. She could not bear not to meet her letters at once; or suppose Edmund and Gilbert should return to an empty, unaired house, and she thought herself selfish, when it might do so much good to Sophy, &c., &c., &c.—till Mr. Ferrars, going home for a night, agreed with Winifred, that domineering would be the only way to deal with her.

On his return he found Albinia on the stairs, and boxes and trunks carried down after her. Running to him, she exclaimed, abruptly, 'I am going to

Malta, Maurice, to-morrow evening!'

'Has Edmund sent for you?'

'Not exactly—he did not know—but Gilbert is dying, and wretched at my not coming. I never wished him good-by—he thinks I did not forgive him. Don't say a word—I shall go.'

He held her trembling hands, and said, 'This is not the way to be able to go. Come in here, sit down and tell me.'

'It is no use to argue. It is my duty now,' said Albinia; but she let him lead her into the room, where Sophy was changing the bright border of a travelling-cloak to crape, and Maurice stood watching, as if stunned.

'It is settled,' continued she, rapidly. 'Sophy and the children go to the vicarage. Yes, I know, you are very kind, but Maurice would be troublesome, and Winifred is not well enough, and the Dusautoys wish it.'

'Yes, that may be the best plan, as I shall be absent.'

She turned round, startled.

'I cannot let you go alone.'

'Nonsense—Winifred—Sunday—Lent—I don't want any one. Nothing could happen to me.'

Mr. Ferrars caught Sophy's eye beaming with sudden relief and gratitude, and repeated, 'If you go, I must take you.'

'I can't wait for Sunday,' she said.

'What have you heard?'

She produced the letter, and read parts of it. The whole stood thus:—

'Bormola, 11 p.m., February 28th, 1855.

'Dearest Albinia,

'I hope all has gone fairly well with you in my absence, and that Sophia is well again. Could I have foreseen the condition of affairs here, I doubt whether I could have resolved on leaving you at home, though you may be spared much by not being with us. I landed at noon to-day, and was met in the harbour by your cousin, who had come off in a boat in hopes of finding you on board. He did his best to prepare me for Gilbert's appearance, but I was more shocked than I can express. There can no longer be any doubt that it is a case of rapid decline, brought on by exposure, and, aggravated by the injury at Balaklava. Colonel Ferrars fancies that Gilbert's exertions on his behalf in the early part of his illness may have done harm, by preventing the broken bone from uniting, and causing it to press on the lungs; but knowing the constitutional tendency, we need not dwell on secondary causes, and there is no one to whom we owe a deeper debt of gratitude than to your cousin, for his most assiduous and affectionate attendance at a time when he is very little equal to exertion. They are like brothers together, and I am sure nothing has been wanting to Gilbert that he could devise for his comfort. They are in a tolerably commodious airy lodging, where I found Gilbert propped up with cushions on a large chair by the window, flushed with eager watching. Poor fellow, to see how his countenance fell when he found I was alone, was the most cutting reproach I ever received in my life. He was so completely overcome, that he could not restrain his tears, though he strove hard to command himself in this fear of wounding my feelings; but there are moments when the truth will have its way, and you have been more to him than his father has ever been. May it be granted that he may yet know how I feel towards him! His first impression was that you had never forgiven him for his unfortunate adventure with Maurice, and could never feel towards him as before; and though I trust I have removed this idea, perhaps such a letter as you can write might set his heart at rest. Ferrars says that hitherto his spirits have kept up wonderfully, though latterly he had been evidently aware of his condition, but he has been very much depressed this evening, probably from the reaction of excited expectation. On learning the cause of Lucy's desertion, he seemed to consider that his participation in the transactions of that night had recoiled upon himself, and deprived him of your presence. It was very painful to see how he took it. He was eager to be told of the children, and the only time I saw him brighten was when I gave him their messages. I am writing while I hope he sleeps. I am glad to be here to relieve the Colonel, who for several nights past has slept on the floor, in his room, not thinking the Maltese servant trustworthy. He looks very ill and suffering, but seems to have no thought but for Gilbert, and will not hear of leaving him; and, in truth, they cling together so affectionately, that I could not bear to urge their parting, even were Fred more fit to travel home alone. I will close my letter to-morrow after the doctor's visit.'

The conclusion was even more desponding; the physician had spoken of the case as hopeless, and likely to terminate rapidly; and Gilbert, who was always at the worst in the morning, had shown no symptom that could lead his father to retract his first impression.

Mr. Ferrars saw that it would be useless and cruel to endeavour to detain his sister, and only doubted whether in her precipitation, she might not cross and miss her husband in a still sadder journey homeward, and this made him the more resolved to be her escort. When she dissuaded him vehemently as though she were bent on doing something desperate, he replied that he was anxious about Fred, and if she and her husband were engrossed by their son, he should be of service in bringing him home; and this somewhat reconciled her to what was so much to her benefit. Only she gave notice that he must not prevent her from travelling day and night, to which he made no answer, while Sophy hoarsely said that but for knowing herself to be a mere impediment, she should have insisted on going, and her uncle must not keep mamma back. Then Maurice imitatively broke out, 'Mamma, take me to Gilbert, I wont be a plague, I promise you.' He was scarcely silenced before Mr. Dusautoy came striding in to urge on her that Fanny and himself should be much happier if he were permitted to conduct Mrs. Kendal to Malta (the fact being that Fanny was persuaded that Mr. Ferrars would obviate such necessity). Albinia almost laughed, as she had declared that she had set all the parsons in the country in commotion, and Mr. Dusautoy was obliged to limit his good offices to the care of the children, and the responsibility of the Fairmead Sunday services.

The good hard-worked brother had hardly time to eat his luncheon, before he started to inform his wife, and prepare for his journey. Winifred was a very good sister on an emergency; she had not once growled since poor Mrs. Meadows had been really ill; and though she had been feeding on hopes of Albinia's visit, and was far from strong, she quashed her husband's misgivings, and cheerily strove to convince him that he would be wanted by no one, least of all by herself. A slight vituperation of the polysyllabic pair was all the relief she permitted herself, and who could blame her for that, when even Mr. Dusautoy called the one 'that foolish fellow,' and the other 'poor dear Lucy?'

Albinia and Sophy safe over the fire that evening, after their sorrowful tasks unable to turn to anything else, wondering how and when they should meet again, and their words coming slowly, and with long intervals of silence.

'Dear child,' said Albinia, 'promise me to take care of yourself, and to let Mrs. Dusautoy judge what you can do.'

'I'm not worth taking care of,' muttered Sophy.

'We think you worth our anxiety,' said Albinia, tenderly.

'I will not make it worse for you,' meekly replied Sophy. 'I don't think I'm cross now, I could not be—'

'No, indeed you are not, my dear. We have leant on each other, and when we come home, you will make our welcome.'

'The children will.'

'Ah! I think Maurice will behave well. He is very much subdued. I told him he was to do no lessons, and he fairly burst out crying.'

'Oh, mamma!' exclaimed Sophy, hurt, indignant, and nearly ready to follow his example.

'I do not think he has mastery over himself, so as to help being unruly and idle, when he is chained to a spelling-book. I would not for the world set him and you to worry each other for an hour a day, and I shall start afresh with him all the better, when he knows what absence of lessons is, and has forgotten all the old associations.'

'How could you make him cry?' said Sophy, in reproach.

'I believe the tears only wanted an excuse. I *did* put it on his naughtiness, which usually would have elated him; but his heart was so full as to make even a long holiday a punishment. That boy often shows me what a thorough Kendal he is; things sink into him as they never did into us at the same age, when my aunts used to think I had no feeling. Oh, Sophy! how will you comfort him?'

'His will be an unstained sorrow,' said Sophy, from the depths of her heart. 'O, mamma, only tell Gilbert what you know I feel—no, you don't, no one can, but what I would not give, to change all I have felt towards him? If I had been like Edmund, and prized his gentleness and sweetness, and the humility that was the best worth of all, how different it would be! But I was proud of despising where truth was wanting.'

'I should have thought I should have done the same,' said Albinia; but there was no keeping from loving Gibbie. Besides, he was sincere, except when he was afraid, and he was miserable when he was deceiving.'

'Yes, after you came,' said Sophy; 'but I believe I helped him to think truth disagreeable. I showed my scorn for his want of boldness, instead of helping him. Think of my having fancied *he* had no courage.'

'Kindness taught him courage,' said Albinia. 'It might perhaps have earlier taught him moral courage. If you and he could have leant against each other, and been fused together, you would have made something like what Edmund was, I suppose.'

'I drove him off,' cried Sophy. 'I was no sister to him. Will you bring me his forgiveness?'

'Indeed I will; and you may feel sure of it already, dearest. It will make you gentler all your life.'

'No, I shall grow harder and harsher the longer I live, and the fewer I have to love me in spite of myself.'

'I think not,' said Albinia. 'Humility will make your severity more gentle, and you will soften, and win love and esteem.'

She looked up, but cried, 'I shall never make up to Gilbert nor to grandmamma!'

Albinia felt it almost as hard to leave her as the two little ones.

When once on her journey, and feeling each moment an advance towards the goal, Albinia was less unhappy than she could have thought possible; she trusted to her brother, and enjoyed the absence of responsibility, and while he let her go on, could give her mind to what pleased and interested him, and he, who was an excellent courier, so managed that there were few detentions to overthrow her equanimity on the way to Marseilles.

But when the Vectis came in sight of the rocky isle, with its white stony heights, the heart-sickness of apprehension grew over her, and she saw, as in a mist, the noble crescent-shaped harbour, the stately ramparts, mighty batteries, the lofty terraces of flat-roofed dwellings, apparently rather hewn out of, than built on, the dazzling white stone, between the intense blue of the sky above and of the sea below. Her eye roamed as in a dream over the crowds of gay boats with white awnings, and the motley crowds of English and natives, the boatmen screaming and fighting for the luggage, and beggars plaintively whining out their entreaties for small coins. Her brother Maurice had been at Malta as a little boy, and remembered the habits of the place enough, as soon as they had set foot on shore, to secure a brown-skinned loiterer, in Phrygian cap, loose trousers, and crimson sash, to act as guide and porter.

Along the Strada San Giovanni, a street of stairs, shut in by high stone walls, with doors opening on either side, they went not as fast as Albinia's quivering limbs would fain have moved, yet too fast when her breath came thick with anxiety—down again by the stone stairs called 'Nix Mangiare' (nothing to eat), from the incessant cry of the beggars that haunt them—then again in a boat, which carried them amid a strange world of shipping to the bottom of the dockyard creek, where, again landing, she was told she had but to ascend, and she would be at Bormola.

She could have paused, in dread; and she leant heavily on her brother's arm when they presently turned up a lane, no broader than a passage, with low stone steps at irregular intervals. They were come!

The summons at the door was answered by a dark-visaged Maltese, and while Maurice was putting the question whether Colonel Ferrars and Captain Kendal lived here, a figure appeared on the stairs, and beckoned, ascending noiselessly with languid steps and slippered feet, and leading the way into a slightly furnished room, with green balcony and striped blind. There he turned and held out his hand; but Albinia hardly recognised him till he said, 'I thought I heard your voice, Maurice;' and then the low subdued tone, together with the gaunt wasted form, haggard aged face, the long beard, and worn undress uniform, with the armless sleeve, made her so realize his sufferings, that, clasping his remaining hand in both her own, she could utter nothing but, 'Oh! Fred! Fred!'

He looked at her brother with such inquiry, perplexity, and compassion, that almost in despair Maurice exclaimed, 'We are not too late!'

'No, thank God!' said Frederick. 'We did hope you might come! Sit down, Albinia; I'll—'

'Edmund! Is he there!' she said, scarcely alive to what was passing, and casting another expressively sorrowful look at Maurice, Fred answered, 'Yes, I will tell him: I will see if you can come in.'

'Stay,' said Mr. Ferrars; 'she should compose herself, or she will only hurt herself and Gilbert.'

'I don't know,' murmured Fred, hastily leaving them.

Maurice understood that Gilbert was even then summoned by one who would brook no delays; but Albinia, too much agitated to notice slight indications, was about to follow, when her brother took her hand, and checked her like a child. 'Wait a minute, my dear, he will soon come back.'

'Where's Edmund? Why mayn't I go to Gilbert?' she said, still bewildered.

'Fred is gone to tell them. Sit down, my dear; take off your bonnet, you are heated, you will be better able to go to him, if you are quiet.'

She passively submitted to be placed on a chair, and to remove her bonnet; and seeing some dressing apparatus through an open door, Maurice brought her some cold water to refresh her burning face. She looked up with a smile, herself again. 'There thank you, Maurice: I wont be foolish now.'

'God support you, my dear!' said her brother, for the longer the Colonel tarried, the worse were his forebodings.

'Perhaps the doctor is there,' she proceeded. 'That will be well. Ask him everything, Maurice. But oh! did you ever see any one so much altered as poor Fred! He looks twenty years older! Ah! I am quite good now! I may go now!' she cried, as the door opened.

But as Frederick returned, there was that written on his brow, which lifted her out of the childishness of her agitation.

'My dear Albinia,' he said in a trembling voice, 'Mr. Kendal cannot leave him to come to you. He has been much worse since last night,' and as her face showed that she was gathering his meaning, he pursued in a lower and more awe-struck tone: 'We think he is sensible, but we cannot tell. It could not hurt him for you to come in, and perhaps he may know you, but are you able to bear it? Is she, Maurice?'

'Yes, I am,' she answered; and the calm firmness of her tone proved that she was a woman again. Her hand shook less than did that of her cousin, as silently and reverently he took it, and led her into another room on the same floor.

There, in the subdued light, she saw her husband, seated on the bed, holding in his arms his son, who lay lifted up and supported upon his breast, with head resting on his shoulder, and eyes closed. There was no greeting, no sound save the long, heavily drawn, gasping breaths. Mr. Kendal raised his eyes to her; she silently knelt down and took the wasted hand that lay helplessly on the coverlet, but it moved feebly from her as though harassed by the touch.

'Gilbert, dear boy,' said his father, earnestly, 'she is come! Speak to him, Albinia.'

She hardly knew her own voice as she said, 'Gilbert, Gibbie dear, here I am.'

Those large brown eyes were shown for a few moments beneath the heavy lids, and met hers. The mouth, hitherto only gasping for air, endeavoured to form a word; the hand sought hers. She kissed him, and his eyes opened wide and brightened, while he said, 'I think it is pardon now.'

'Pardon indeed!' said his father, with a greater look of relief than Albinia understood, 'you are resting in His Merits.'

Gilbert's look brightened, and he said, 'I know itnow.'

'Thank God,' said Mr. Kendal.

His eyes closed, and Fred whispered to the father, 'Maurice is here too.'

Again the light woke in the eye, with almost a smile, the look that always welcomed the little brother; and Albinia grieved to say, 'Not little Maurice, though he longed to come; it is my brother.' But the air of eagerness did not pass away, and he seemed satisfied when Mr. Ferrars came in. It was as a priest, speaking words not his own; and Albinia and Fred knelt with him. At the close of each prayer or psalm, Gilbert signed imploringly for more, even like our mighty dying queen; and at each short pause, the distressed agonized expression would again contract the brow, though in the sound of the holy words all was peace. The Psalm of the Good Shepherd with the Rod and Staff in the Valley of the Shadow of Death, recurred so strongly to Maurice, that he repeated it like a cadence after each penitential supplication, every time bringing a look of peace to the countenance of the sufferer.

They must have remained long thus, Fred had grown exhausted with kneeling and had been forced to sit on the floor, and Maurice's voice waxed low and hoarse; yet he durst not pause, though doubting whether Gilbert could follow the meaning. At length the eyes were again raised. With a start as of haste, Gilbert looked full at Albinia, and said, 'Thank you. Tell Maurice —' He could not finish, and there was an agony for breath, then as his father raised him, he contrived to say, 'Father—mother—kiss me; it is forgiven!'

Another look brought Fred to press his hand, and he smiled his thanks.

There were a few more terrible minutes, from which they would fain have led away Albinia, but suddenly his brow grew smooth, his eyes were eagerly fixed as on something before him, and as if replying to a call, he said, 'Yes!' with a start and a quiver of all his limbs, and then—

The first words were Mr. Kendal's. 'Edmund has come for him!'

It was to the rest as if the father had been in some manner conscious of the presence of the one twin-brother, and, were resigning the other to his charge, for he calmly kissed the forehead, closed the eyes, laid down the form, he had so long held in his arms, and after a few moments on his knees, with his face hidden, in his hands, he rose with composure, and said to his wife, 'I am glad you were in time.'

Had he given way, Albinia would have been strong, but there was no need to support to counteract the force of disappointment and grief, acting upon overwrought spirits, and a fatigued, exhausted frame. Were these half-conscious looks and broken words all she had come for, all she should ever have of Gilbert? This was the moment's predominant sensation; she was past thinking; and though she still controlled herself, she cast a wild, piteous eye on her husband, and as he lifted her up, she sank on his breast, not fainting, not sobbing, but utterly prostrated, and needing all his support as he led her out, and laid her on a couch in the next room, speaking softly as if hoping his voice would restore her. 'We had some faint hope of you; we knew you would wish it, so you see all is ready. But you have done too much, my dear: Maurice should not have let you travel so fast.'

'No, no,' said Albinia, catching her breath. 'Oh! not to have come sooner!' and she gave way to a violent burst of tears, during which he fondled and soothed her till she suddenly said, 'I did not come here to behave in this way! I came to help you! Edmund, what shall I do?' and she would have started up.

'Only lie still, and let me take care of you,' said he. 'Nothing could be to me like your coming,' and she was forced to believe his glistening eyes and voice of tenderness.

'Can you keep quiet a little while,' said Mr. Kendal, wistfully, 'while I go to speak to your brother? It was very good in him to come! Don't speak; I will come back directly.'

She did lie still, for she was too much spent to move, and the silence was good for her; for if the overwhelming sensation of grief would sweep over her, on the other hand, there was the remembrance of the look of peace, and the perception that her husband was not as yet so struck to the earth as she had feared. He was not long in returning, bringing some coffee for her and for himself, and speaking with the same dreamy serenity, though looking excessively pale. 'Your brother told me to give you this,' he said. 'I am glad the colonel is under such care, for he is terribly distressed and not at all fit to bear it. I could not make him go to bed all last night.'

'You were up all last night, and many nights before,' said Albinia; 'and all alone! Oh! why was I not here to help!'

'Fred was a great comfort,' said Mr. Kendal. 'I cannot describe my gratitude to him. And dearest—' He paused, and added with hesitation, 'I do not now regret the having come out alone. After the first disappointment, I think that my boy and I learnt to know each other better. If he had left me nothing but the recollection that I had been too severe and unsympathizing to win his confidence, I hardly know how I could have borne it.'

'He was able to talk to you, then?' cried Albinia. 'That was what I always wished! Yes, it *was* right, so it came right. I had got between you as I ought not to have done, and it was well you should have him to yourself.'

'Not as you ought not,' he fondly answered. 'You always were his better angel, and you came at last as a messenger of peace. There was relief and hope from the moment that he knew you.'

He told her what could scarcely have passed his lips save in those earlier hours of affliction. It had been a time of grievous mental distress. Neither natural temperament nor previous life had been such as to arm poor Gilbert to meet the King of Terrors; and as day by day he felt the cold grasp tightening on him, he had fluttered like a bird in the snare of the fowler, physically affrighted at the death-pang, shrinking from the lonely entrance into the unknown future, and despairing of the acceptableness of his own repentance. He believed that he had too often relapsed, and he could not take heart to grasp the hope of mercy and rest in the great atonement. The last Communion had been melancholy, the contrite spirit unable to lift itself up, and apparently only sunk the lower by the weight of love and gratitude, deepening the sense of how much had been disregarded. There had since been a few hopeful gleams, but dimmed by bodily suffering and terror; and doubly mournful had been the weary hours of the night and morning, while he lay gasping away his life upon his father's breast. Having at first taken the absence of his stepmother as a sign that she had not forgiven him, he had only laid aside this notion for a more morbid fancy that the deprivation was a token of wrath from above; and there could be little doubt that her final appearance was hailed as a seal of pardon not merely from her. Her brother, who had raised him up after his last fall, was likewise the person above all others to bring the message of mercy to speed him to the Unseen, where, as his look and gesture had persuaded his father, his brother, or some yet more blessed one, had received and welcomed the frail and trembling spirit.

That last farewell, that dawn of peace, so long prayed for, so ardently desired, had given Mr. Kendal such thankfulness and relief as sustained him, and enabled him to support his wife, who knew not how to meet her first home grief; whereas to him sorrow had long been a household guest more familiar than joy; and he was more at rest about his son than he had been for many a year. He could dwell on him together with Edmund, instead of connecting him with shame, grief, and pain; though how little could he have borne to think that thus it would end, when in the springtime of his manhood he had rejoiced over his beautiful twin boys.

He knew his son better than heretofore. After the first day's disappointment, Gilbert had found him all-sufficient, and had rested on his tenderness. All sternness had ceased on one side, all concealment on the other, and the sweetness of both characters had had full scope. Gilbert's ardent love of home had shown itself in every word, and his last exertion, had been to write a long letter to his little brother, which had been completed and despatched by a private hand a few days previously. He had desired that Maurice should have his sword, and mentioned the books which he wished his sisters to share, talking of Sophy as one whom he honoured much, and wished he had known better; but much pained by hearing nothing from Lucy, and lamenting his share in her union with Algernon. He had said something about his wish that the almshouses should be built, but his father had turned away the subject, knowing that in case of his dying intestate and unmarried, the property was settled on the sisters, and seeing little chance of any such work being carried out with the co-operation of Mr. Cavendish Dusautoy. Latterly he had spoken of Genevieve Durant; he knew better how unworthy of her he had been, and how harassing his pursuit must have appeared, but he could not help entreating that her pardon might be asked in his name, that she might hear that he had loved her to the last, and above all, that his father would never lose sight of her; and Mr. Kendal's promise to regard her as the next thing to his daughters had been requited with a look of the utmost gratitude and affection.

This was the substance of what Mr. Kendal told his wife as they sat together, unwitting of the lapse of time, and shrinking from any interruption that might mar their present peace and renew the sense of bereavement.

Mr. Ferrars was the first to knock at the door. He had been doing his utmost to spare both them and Fred, who needed all his care. These four months of mutual dependence had been even more endearing than the rescue of Fred's life on the battlefield; and he declared that Gilbert had done him more good than any one else. They had been so thrown together as to make the 'religious sentiment' of the younger tell upon the warm though thoughtless heart of the elder. They had been most fondly attached; and in his present state, reduced by wounds and exhausted by watching, Fred was more overpowered than those more closely concerned. He could hardly speak collectedly when an officer of the garrison called to consult him with regard to a military funeral, and it was for this that Maurice was obliged to refer to the father. There were indeed none of his regiment in the island, but there was a universal desire in the garrison to do honour to the distinguished young officer, for whom great interest had been felt and the compliment brought a glow of exultation to Mr. Kendal's face, as he expressed his warm thanks, but desired that the decision might rest with Fred himself, as his son's lieutenant-colonel.

Maurice felt himself fully justified in his expedition when he found that all devolved on him, even writing to Sophy, and making the most necessary arrangements; for the colonel was incapable of exertion, Albinia was prostrated by the shock, and Mr. Kendal appeared to be lulled into a strange calm by the effects of the excessive bodily weariness consequent on the exhausting attendance of the last few days. They all depended upon Mr. Ferrars, and recognised his presence as an infinite comfort.

In the morning Albinia came forth like one who had been knocked down and shattered, weary and gentle, and with the tears ever welling into her eyes, above all when she endeavoured to write to Sophy; and she showed her ordinary earnestness only when she entreated to see her boy once more. Her husband took her to look on the countenance settled into the expression of unearthly peace, but she was not satisfied; it was not her own Gilbert, boyish, sensitive, dependent, and shrinking. The pale brow, the marked manly features, the lower ones concealed by the brown moustache, belonged to the hero who had dared the deadly ride and borne his friend through the storm of shot and shell; the noble, settled, steadfast face was the face of a stranger, and gave her a thrill of disappointment. She gloried in the later Gilbert, but the last she had seen of him whom she loved for his weakness, had been when she had not heeded his farewell.

It made the pang the less when evening came and he was carried to his resting-place. They would have persuaded Frederick to spare himself, but as the only officer of the same corps, as well as for the sake of many closer ties, he would not hear of being absent, and made his cousin Maurice do his best to restore the smart soldierly air which he for the first time thought of regretting.

Gilbert's horse had perished at Balaklava, but his cap, sword, and spurs, were laid on the coffin, and from her shaded window Albinia watched it borne between the files of soldiers with arms reversed; and the procession of officers whose bright array contrasted with the colonel's war-worn dress, ghastly cheek, and empty sleeve, tokens of the reality of war amid its pageantry, as all moved slowly away to the deep tones of the solemn Dead March, music well befitting the calm grandeur of the face she had seen, and leaving her heart throbbing with the deep exulting awe and pathos of a soldier's funeral. She knelt alone, and followed the burial service in the stillness of the room overlooking the broad expanse of blue sea and sky; and by-and-by, through the window came the sound of the volley fired over the grave, the farewell of the army to the soldier at rest, his battles ended.

'There was peace, and there was glory; but she could not divest herself of a sense of unreality. She could not feel as if it were really and truly Gilbert, and she were mourning for him. All was like a dream—that solemn military spectacle—the serene, grave sunshine on the fortress-harbour stretching its mailed arms into the sea—the roofs of the knightly old monastic city rising in steps from the bay crowded with white sails—and even those around her were different, her husband pale and still, as in a region above common life, and her cousin like another man, without his characteristic joyousness and insouciance. She could hardly induce herself, in her drowsy state, to believe that all was indeed veritable and tangible.

There was nothing to detain them at Malta, and Mr. Ferrars, who arranged everything, thought the calm of a sea-voyage would be better for them all than the bustle and fatigue of a land journey.

'Kendal himself does not care about getting home,' he said to Fred, who was afraid this was determined on his account. 'I fear many annoyances are in store for him. His son-in-law will not be pleasant to deal with about the property.'

With an exclamation Fred started from the chairs on which he had been resting, and dived into his sabre-tasch which hung from the wall. 'I never liked to begin about it,' he said, 'but I ought to have given them this. It was done when he was so bad at Scutari. One night he worked himself into a fever lest he should not live till his birthday, and said a great deal about this Dusautoy making himself an annoyance, perhaps insisting on a sale and turning his father out. Nothing pacified him till, the very day he was of age, we got the vice-consul to draw up what he wanted, and witness it, and so did I and the doctor, and here it is. Afterwards he warned me to say nothing of it when Mr. Kendal came, for he said if the other fellow made a row, it would be better his father should be able to say he had known nothing of the matter.'

'Does he make his father his heir?'

'That's the whole of it. He said his sisters would see it was the only way to get things even, and I was to tell Albinia something about building cottages or almshouses. Ay, "his father was to do what ought to have been done."'

'Well, there's the best deed of poor Gilbert's life!'

'Thank you,' mumbled Fred, hall drolly, half gravely.

'Ay, Kendal and Albinia will do more good with that property than you have thought of in all your life, sir.'

'Their future and my past,' laughed Fred, adding more gravely, 'Scamp as I am, there's more responsibility coming on me now, and I have gone through some preparation for it. If I can get out to Canada—'

'You will not lessen your responsibilities,' said Maurice, smiling, 'nor your competency to meet them.'

'I *trust* not,' said Fred.

Mr. Ferrars read in his countenance far more than was implied by those words. The General, by treating him as a boy, had kept him one, and perhaps his levity had been prolonged by the rejection of his first love; but a really steady attachment had settled his character, and he had been undergoing much training through his own sufferings, Gilbert's illness, and the sense of the new position that awaited him as commanding officer; and for the first time Maurice, who had always been very fond of him, felt that he was talking to a high-principled and right-minded man instead of the family pet and laughing-stock.

'I suppose,' he said, 'that you cannot have heard often from Montreal since you have been in the East.'

'No. If my letters are anywhere, it is at the Family Office. I desired them to be forwarded thither from head-quarters, not expecting to be detained here. But,' cried Fred with animation, 'what think you of the General actually writing to Mr. Kinnaird from Balaklava?'

'It would have been too bad if he had not.'

'I believe he did so solely to make me sleep, but it is the first time he has deigned to treat the affair as anything but a delusion, and he can't retract now. Since that, poor Gilbert has made a scrap or two of mine presentable, and there's all that I have been able to accomplish; but I hope it may have set her mind at rest.'

'Shall I be secretary?'

'Thank you, I think not. She would only worry herself about what is before me; and if the doctors let me off easy, I had rather report of myself in person.'

His eyes danced, and Maurice thought his unselfishness deserved a reward.

'My poor Gilbert's last secret,' said Mr. Kendal, as he laid before his wife the brief document by which his son had designated him as his sole heir and executor. 'A gift to you, and a trust to me.'

Albinia looked up for explanation.

'While he intrusts his sisters to my justice, he tacitly commends to me the works which you wished to see accomplished.'

'The almshouses! The improvements! Do you mean to undertake them?'

'It shall be my most sacred duty.'

'Oh! that we could have planned it with him!'

'Perhaps I value this the more from the certainty that it is spontaneous,' said Mr. Kendal. 'It showed great consideration and forethought, that he said nothing of his intention to me. Had he mentioned it, I should have thought it right to suggest his leaving his sisters their share; and yet, as we are situated with young Dusautoy, it would have been awkward to have interfered. He did well and wisely to be silent.'

'You don't expect Algernon to be discontented. Impossible, at such a time, and so well off as he is!'

'I wish it may be impossible.'

'What do you mean, to do?'

'As far as I can see at present, I shall do this. I fear neither the mode of acquisition nor the management of that property was such as to bring a blessing, and I believe my poor boy has made it over to me in order to free his sisters from the necessity of winking at oppression and iniquity. Had it gone to them, matters must have been let alone till Sophia came of age, and even then, all improvements must have depended on Algernon's consent. The land

and houses we will keep, and sufficient ready money for the building and repairs; and to this, Sophia, at least, will gladly agree. The rest—something under twenty thousand, if I remember correctly—is the girls' right. I will settle Lucy's share on her so as to be out of her husband's power, and Sophia shall have hers when she comes of age.'

'I am sure that will take from Algernon all power of grumbling, though I cannot believe that even he could complain.'

'You approve, then?'

'How can you ask? It is the first thing that has seemed like happiness, if it did not make one long for him to talk it over!' The wound was still very recent, and her spirits very tender, and the more she felt the blessing of the association with Gilbert in the work of love, the more she wept, though not altogether in sorrow.

Mortified at having come so much overworked and weakened, as to occasion only trouble and anxiety, she yielded resignedly when forbidden to wear out strength and spirits by a visit to the burial-ground before her embarkation. She must content herself with Maurice's description of the locality, and carry away in her eye only the general picture of the sapphire ocean and white rock fortress of the holy warriors vowed to tenderness and heroism, as the last resting-place of her cherished Gilbert, when 'out of weakness he had been made strong' in penitence and love.

CHAPTER XXVII.

Had Sophia's wishes been consulted, she would have preferred nursing her sorrows at home; but no choice had been left, and at the vicarage the fatherly kindness of Mr. Dusautoy, and the considerate let-alone system of his wife, kept her at ease and not far from cheerful, albeit neither the simplicity of the one nor the keenness of the other was calculated to draw her into unreserve: comfort was in the children.

The children clung to her as if she made their home, little Albinia preferring her even to Uncle John, as he had insisted on being called ever since Lucy had become his niece, and Maurice invoking caresses, the bestowal of which was his mother's rare privilege. The boy was dull and listless, and though riot and mirth could be only too easily excited, his wildest shouts and most frantic gesticulations were like efforts to throw off a load at his heart. Time hung heavy on his hands, and he would lie rolling and kicking drearily on the floor, watching with some envy his little sister as she spelt her way prosperously through 'Little Charles,' or daintily and distinctly repeated her hymns. 'Nothing to do' was the burthen of his song, and with masculine perverseness he disdained every occupation suggested to him. Sophy might boast of his obedience and quiescence, but Mrs. Dusautoy pitied all parties, and wondered when he would be disposed of at school.

Permission to open letters had been left with Sophy, who with silent resignation followed the details of poor Gilbert's rapid decay. At last came the parcel by the private hand, containing a small packet for each of the family. Sophy received a silver Maltese Cross, and little Albinia a perfumy rose-leaf bracelet. There was a Russian grape-shot for Maurice, and with it a letter.

With childish secrecy, he refused to let any one look at so much as the envelope, and ran away with it, shouting 'It's mine.' Sophy was grieved that it should be treated like a toy, and fearing that, while playing at importance, he would lose or destroy it, without coming to a knowledge of the contents, she durst not betray her solicitude, lest she should give a stimulus to his wilfulness and precipitate its fate. However, when he had galloped about enough, he called imperatively, 'Sophy;' and she found him lying on his back on the grass, the black cat an unwilling prisoner on his chest.

'You may read it to Smut and me,' he said.

It bore date the day after his father's arrival, but it had evidently been continued at many different times; and as the handwriting became more feeble, the style grew more earnest, so that, but for her hoarse, indifferent voice, Sophy could hardly have accomplished the reading.

'My dear Maurice,

'Many, many thanks to you and dear little Awkey for your present. I have set it up like a picture, and much do I like to look at it, and guess who chose the colours and who are the hunters. I am sure the fat man in the red coat is the admiral. It makes the place seem like home to see what tells so plainly of you and baby.

'Kiss my little Awk for me, and thank her for wanting to send me Miss Jenny, dear little maid; I like to think of it. You will not let her quite forget me. You must show her my name if it is put up in church, like Edmund's and all the little ones'; and you will sometimes tell her about dear old Ned on a Sunday evening when you are both very good.

'I think you know that you and she will never again run out into the hall to pull Gibbie almost down between you. Perhaps by the time you read this, you will be the only son, with all the comfort and hope of the house resting upon you. My poor Maurice, I know what it is to be told so, and only to feel that one has no brother; but at least it cannot be to you as it was with me, when it was as if half myself were gone, and all my stronger, better, braver self.

'My father has been reading to me the Rich Man and Lazarus. Maurice, when you read of him and the five brethren, think of me, and how I pray that I may not have left seeds of temptation for you. In the time of my loneliness, Tritton was good-natured, but I ought to have avoided him; and that to which he introduced me has been the bane of my life. Nothing gives me such anguish as to think I have made you acquainted with that set. Keep out of their way! Never go near those pigeon-shootings and donkey-races; they seem good fun, but it is disobedience to go, and the things that happen there are like the stings of venomous creatures; the poison was left to fester even when your mother seemed to have cured me. Neither now nor when you are older resort to such things or such people. Next time you meet Tritton and Shaw tell them I desired to be remembered to them; after that have nothing to do with them; touch your hat and pass on. They meant it in good nature, and thought no harm, but they were my worst enemies; they led me astray, and taught me deception as a matter of course. Oh! Maurice, never think it manly to have the smallest reserve with your parents. I would give worlds to have sooner known that truth would have been freedom and rest. Thank Heaven, your faults are not my faults. If you go wrong, it will be with a high hand, but you would wring hearts that can ill bear further grief and disappointment. Oh! that I were more worthy to pray that you may use your strength and spirit the right way; then you will be gladness to our father and mother, and when you lie down to die, you will be happier than I am.

'I want to tell you more, but it hurts me to write long. If I could only see you—not only in my dreams. I wake, and my heart sickens with longing for a sight of my brave boy's merry face, till I almost feel as if it would make me well; but it is a blessing past hope to have my father with me, and know him as I have never done before. Give little Albinia these beads, with my love, and be a better brother to her than I was to poor Lucy.

'Good-by, Maurice. No one can tell what you have been to me since your mother put you into my arms, and I felt I had a brother again. God bless you and cancel all evil you may have caught from me. Papa will give you my sword. Perhaps you will wear it one day, and under my colonel. I have never been so happy as in the time it was mine. When you look at it, always say this to yourself: "Fear God, and fear nothing else." O that I had done so!

'Let your dear, dear mother be happy in you: it will be the only way to make her forgive me in her heart. Good-by, my own dear, brave boy,

'I say, Smut,' quoth Maurice, 'I think you and our Tabby would make two famous horses for Awkey's little cart. I shall take you home and harness you.'

Sophy sat breathless at his indifference. 'You mustn't,' she said in hasty anger; 'Smut is not yours.'

'Well, Jack said that our Tabby had two kittens up in the loft; I think they'll make better ponies. I shall go and try them!'

'Don't plague the kittens.'

'I'll not plague them; I'll only make ponies of them. Give me the letter.'

'No, not to play with the cats. I thought you would have cared about such a letter!'

'You have no right to keep it! It is mine; give it me!' cried Maurice, passionately.

'Promise to take real care of it.'

He only tore it from her, and was gone.

'I'm a fool to expect anything from such a child,' she thought.

At two o'clock the Vicar hurried into the bank. 'Good morning, Mr. Goldsmith, I beg your pardon; I wanted to ask if Mr. O'More has seen little Maurice Kendal.'

'Not since yesterday—what's the matter?'

'The child is not come in to dinner. He is nowhere at home or at Willow

Lawn.'

'Ha!' cried Ulick. 'Can he be gone to see his pony at Hobbs's!'

'No, it has been sent to Fairmead. Then you have no notion where the child can be? Sophy is nearly distracted. She saw him last about ten o'clock, bent on harnessing some kittens, but he's not in the hay-loft!'

'He may be gone to the toy-shop after the harness. Or has anyone looked in the church-tower—he was longing to go up it, and if the door were open—'

'The very thing!' cried the Vicar. 'I'll go this moment.'

'Or there's old Peter, the sailor,' called Ulick; 'if he wanted any tackle fitted, he might go to him.'

'You had better go yourself, More,' said Mr. Goldsmith. 'One would not wish to keep poor Miss Kendal in suspense, though I dare say the boy is safe enough.'

Mr. Goldsmith was thanked, and Ulick hurried out, Hyder Ali leaping up in amazement at his master being loose at that time of day.

Everybody had thought the child was with somebody else till dinner-time, and the state of the vicarage was one of dire alarm and self-reproach. Sophy was seeking and calling in every possible place, and had just brought herself to own the message of remembrance in Gilbert's letter, thinking it possible Maurice might have gone to deliver it at Robbles Leigh; and Mr. Hope had undertaken to go thither in quest of him. Ulick and Mr. Dusautoy, equally disappointed by the tower and the sailor, went again to Willow Lawn to interrogate the servants. The gardener's boy had heard Maurice scolding and the cat squalling, and the cook had heard his step in the house. They hurried into his little room—he was not there, but the drawers had been disturbed.

'He may be gone to Fairmead!' cried the Vicar.

'How?' said Ulick. 'Ha! Hyder, sir!' holding up a little shoe. 'Seek! That's my fine doggie—they only call you a mongrel because you have all the canine virtues united. See what you can do as sleuth hound. Ha! We'll nose him out for you in no time, Mr. Dusautoy!'

After sniffing round the drawers, the yellow tripod made an ungainly descent of the stairs, his nose down all the way, then across the hall and out at the gate; but when, after poking about, the animal set off on the turnpike-road, the Vicar demurred.

'Stay; the poor dog only wants to get you out for a walk. He is making for the Hadminster road.'

'And why wouldn't he, if the child is nowhere in Bayford?'

'I can't answer it to his mother wasting time in this way. You may do as you like. I shall go to the training-stables, where he has once been, if not on to Fairmead. I can't see Sophy till he is found!'

'I shall abide by my little Orangeman,' said Ulick; and they parted.

Hyder Ali pursued his way in the March dust, while Ulick eagerly scanned for the traces of a child's foot. Four miles did the dog go on, evidently following a scent, but Ulick's mind misgave him as Hadminster church-tower rose before him, and the dog took the ascent to the station.

Ulick made his way in as a train stood panting before the platform. He had a glimpse of a square face and curly hair at the window of a second-class carriage.

'Maurice, come back!' he cried. 'Here, guard! this little boy must come back!'

'Go on!' shouted Maurice. 'I've got my ticket. 'No one can stop me. I'm going to Malta!' and he tried to get to the other side of a stout traveller, who defended his legs from him, and said, 'Ha! Running away from school, young master! Here's your usher.'

'No, I'm not running away! I'm not at school! I'm Maurice Kendal! I'm going to my brother at Malta!'

'He is the son of Mr. Kendal of Bayford,' said Ulick to the station-master,' his parents are from home, and there will be dreadful distress if he goes in this way. Maurice, your sister has troubles enough already.'

'I've my ticket, and can't be stopped.'

But even as he spoke, the stout traveller picked him up by the collar, and dropped him like a puppy dog into Ulick's arms, just as the train was getting into motion; and a head protruded from every window to see the truant, who was pommelling Ulick in a violent fury, and roaring, 'Let me go; I will go to Gilbert!'

'Behave like a man,' said Ulick; 'don't disgrace yourself in that way.'

The boy coloured, and choking with passion and disappointment, and straining against Ulick's hold of his shoulder.

'Indeed, sir,' said the station-master, 'if we had recognised the young gentleman, we would have made more inquiries, but he asked so readily for his ticket, not seeming at a loss, and we have so many young travellers, that we thought of nothing amiss. Will you have a fly, sir?'

'I'm not going home,' said the boy, undaunted.

'You must submit, Maurice. You do not wish to make poor Sophy miserable.'

'I must go to Malta,' the boy persisted. 'Gilbert says it would make him well to see me. I know my way; I saw it in the map, and I've a roll, and the end of a cold tongue, and a clean shirt, and my own sovereign, and four shillings, and a half-crown, and a half-penny in my pocket; and I'm going!'

'But, Maurice, this gentleman will tell you that your whole sovereign would not carry you a quarter of the way to Malta.'

The station-master gave so formidable a description of the impossibilities of the route, that the hardy little fellow's look of decision relaxed into dejection, his muscles lost their tension, and he struggled hard with his tears.

He followed Ulick to the carriage, and hid his face in a corner, while orders were given to stop at the post-office in case there were fresh letters. There was one for Miss Kendal, in Mr. Ferrars' writing, and with black borders. Ulick felt too surely what it must be, and hardly could bear to address Maurice, who had shrunk from him with some remains of passion, but hearing suppressed sobs, he put his hand on him and said, 'My poor little man.'

'Get away,' said Maurice, shaking him off. 'Why did you come and bother?'

'I came because it would have almost killed your sister and mother for you to be lost. If you had seen Sophy's face, Maurice!'

'I don't care. Now I shall never see Gilbert again, and he did want me so!' Maurice hid his face, and his frame shook with sobs.

'Yes,' said Ulick, 'every one knew he wanted you; but if it had been possible for you to go, your mamma would have taken you. If your uncle had to take care of her how could you go alone?'

'I'd have got there somehow,' cried Maurice. 'I'd have seen and heard Gilbert. He's written me a letter to say he wants to see me, and I can't even make that out!'

'Has not your sister read it to you!'

'I hate Sophy's reading!' cried Maurice. 'It makes it all grumpy, like her. Take it, Ulick—you read it.'

That rich, sensitive, modulated voice brought out the meaning of the letter, though there were places where Ulick had nearly broken down; and Maurice pressed against him with the large tears in his eyes, and was some minutes without speaking.

'He does not think of your coming; he does not expect you, dear boy,' said Ulick. 'It is a precious letter to have. I hope you will keep it and read it often, and heed it too.'

'I can't read it,' said Maurice, ruefully. 'If I could, I shouldn't mind.'

'You soon will. You see how he tells you you are to be a comfort; and if you are a good boy, you'll quickly leave the dunce behind.'

'I can't,' said Maurice. 'Mamma said I should not do a bit of a lesson with Sophy, or I should tease her heart out. Would it come quite out?'

'Well, I think you've gone hard to try to-day,' said Ulick.

'Mamma said my being able to read would be a comfort, and papa says he never saw such an ignorant boy! so what's the use of minding Gilbert's letter? It wont let me.'

'What wont let you?'

'Fun!' said Maurice, with a sob.

'He is a rogue!' cried Ulick, vehemently; 'but a stout heart and good will can get him under yet. Think of what your brother says of making your father and mother happy!'

'If I could do something to please them very, very much! Oh! if I could but learn to read all at once.'

'You can read—anybody can read!' said Ulick, pulling a book out of his pocket. 'There! try.'

There was some laughing over this; and then Maurice leant out of window, and grew sleepy. They had descended into the wide basin of alluvial land through which the Baye dawdled its meandering course, and were just about to cross the first bridge about two miles from Bayford, when Maurice shouted, 'There's Sophy!—how funny.'

It was a tall figure, in deep mourning, slowly moving along the towing- path, intently gazing into the river; but so strange was it to see Sophy so far from home, that Ulick paused a moment ere calling to the driver to stop.

As he hastily wrenched open the door, she raised up her face, and he was shocked. She looked as if she had lived years of sorrow, and even Maurice was struck with consternation.

'Sophy! Sophy!' he cried, hanging round her. 'I wouldn't have gone without telling you, if I had thought you would mind it. Speak to me, Sophy!'

She could say nothing save a hoarse 'Where?' as with both arms she pressed him as if she could never let him go again.

'In the train—intending to go to Malta,' said Ulick.

'I didn't know I could not; I didn't mean to vex you, Sophy,' continued the child. 'I'm come home now, and I wont try again.'

'Oh! Maurice, what would have become of you?' She held out her hand to Ulick, the first time for months.

'And we've got a letter for you, proceeded Maurice.

Ulick would fain have withheld it, but he had not the choice. She caught at it, still holding Maurice fast, and ere he could propose her opening it in the carriage while he walked home she had torn it open, and the same moment she had sunk down, seated on the path, with an arm round her brother. 'Oh! Maurice, it is well you are here! You would not have found them—it is over!'

She had found one brother to lose the other; but the relief of Maurice's safety had so softened the blow, that her tears gushed forth freely.

The sense of Ulick's presence restrained her, but raising her head, she missed him, and felt lonely, desolate, deserted, almost fainting, and in a strange place.

'Is he dead?' said Maurice, in a solemn low voice, and she wept helplessly, while the little fellow stood sustaining her weight like a small pillar, perplexed and dismayed.

'Are you poorly, Sophy? What shall I do?' said he, as she almost fell back, but a stronger arm held her up.

'Lean on me, dear Sophy,' said Ulick, who had returned, bringing some water from a small house near at hand, and supported her and soothed her like a brother.

The mists cleared away, the sense of desertion was gone, and she rose, but could not stand without his arm, and he almost lifted her into the carriage, where her appealing eye and helpless gesture made him follow her, and take Maurice on his knee. No one spoke; Maurice nestled close to his friend; awe-struck but weighed down by weariness and excitement. The blow had in reality been given when he was forced to relinquish the hope of seeing his brother again, and the actual certainty of his death fell with less comparative force. Perhaps he did not enter into the fact enough to ask for particulars. After a short space Sophy recovered herself enough to take out the letter, and read it over with greater comprehension.

'They were come!' she said.

'In time. I am glad.'

'In time to bring him peace, my uncle says! He knew mamma. I could never have borne it if I had deprived him of her!'

'Nor I,' said Ulick, from his heart. 'Did one but know the upshot of one's idle follies!'

Sophy looked towards Maurice.

'Asleep!' said Ulick. 'No wonder. He has walked four miles! He has a heart that might have been born in Ireland;' and as he looked at the fair young face softened and sweetened by sleep, 'What an infant it is to have even fancied such an undertaking!'

'Poor child!' sighed Sophy. 'He will never be the same!'

'Nay, grief at that age does not check the spirits for life.'

'You have never known,' said Sophy.

'No; our number has never yet been broken; but for this little man, I trust that the sense of duty may be deepened, and with it his love to you all; and surely that is not what will quench the blithe temper.'

'May it be so!' said Sophy. 'He may have enough of his mother in him to be happy.'

'I must think that the recollection of so loving a brother, and his pride in him for a hero, may make the stream flow more deeply, but not more darkly.'

'There never was a cloud between them,' said Sophy.

'Clouds are all past and gone now between those who can with him "take part in that thanksgiving lay,"' answered Ulick, kindly.

'Yes,' said Sophy. 'My uncle says it was peace at last! Oh! if humbleness and penitence could win it, one might be sure it would be his.'

'True,' said Ulick. 'It was a beautiful thing to find the loving sweetness and kindness refined into self-devotion and patience, and growing into something brighter and purer as it came near the last. It will be a precious recollection.'

'To those who have no self-reproach,' sighed Sophy; and after a pause she abruptly resumed, 'You once blamed me for being hard with him. Nothing was more true.'

'Impossible—when could I have presumed?'

'When? You remember. After Oxford.'

'Oh! you should not have let what I said dwell with you. I was a very raw Irishman then, and thought it barbarity to look cold on a little indiscretion, but I have learnt to think differently,' and he sighed. 'The severity that leads to repentance is truer affection than is shown by making light of foolishness.'

'If it had been affection and not wounded pride.'

'The dross has been refined away, if there were any,' said Ulick. 'You will be able to love him better now than ever you did in life.'

His comprehension met her half way, and gave her more relief and soothing than anything she had experienced for months. There was that response and intercommunion of spirit for which her nature had yearned the more because of the inability to express the craving; the very turn of the dark blue eyes, and the inflexions of the voice, did not merely convey pity, but an entering into the very core of her sorrow, namely, that she had never loved her brother enough, nor forgiven him for not being his fellow-twin. Whatever he said tended to reveal to her that there had been more justice, rectitude, sisterly feeling, and wholesome training than she had given herself credit for, and, above all, that Gilbert had loved her all the time. She was induced to dwell on the exalting and touching circumstances of his last redeeming year, and her tears streamed calmly and softly, not with the harshness that had hitherto marred her grief. Neither could have believed that there had been so long and marked a separation in feeling, or that Ulick O'More had not always been one with the Kendal family. It was all too soon that the conversation ended, and Maurice wakened suddenly at the vicarage wicket. Mrs. Dusautoy herself came to meet them as the little boy was lifted out. She had never been seen on her own feet so far from the house before! But no one ever knew the terror she had suffered, when of all her three charges not one was safe but the little Albinia, whose 'poor Maurice' and 'all gone' were as trying as her alternations of merriment. The vicar, the curate, the parish clerk, the servants of the two establishments, and four policemen, were all gone different ways; and poor Mrs. Dusautoy's day had been spent in hearing the results of their fruitless researches, or in worse presages, in which, as it now appeared, the river had played its part.

She kissed Maurice, and he did not rebel! She kissed Sophy, and could have shaken off Ulick's hand, but he only waited to hold up Hyder Ali as the real finder, before he ran off to desire the school-bell to be rung—the signal for announcing a discovery. It was well that Maurice was too much stunned and fatigued to be sensible what a commotion he had excited, or he might have thought it good fun.

The tidings from Malta came in almost as something secondary. The case had been too hopeless for anything else to be looked for, and when Mrs. Dusautoy consigned her charge to a couch, with entreaties to her not to move, there was calm tenderness in Sophy's voice as she told what needed to be told, and did not shrink from sympathy. She was grateful and gentle, and lay all the rest of the day, sad and physically worn out, but quietly mournful, and no longer dwelling on the painful side of past transactions, her remorse had given way to resigned acquiescence, and desolation to a sense that there was one who understood her. The sweet tones, and, above all, those two words, '*dear Sophy*,' would come chiming back from some involuntary echo, and the turbid depths were at peace.

When Mr. Dusautoy came to her side, and held out his hand, his honest eyes brimming over, there was no repulsion in her manner of saying affectionately, 'You have had a great deal of trouble for my naughty little brother.' So different was her whole tone, that her kind friends thought how much better for some minds was any certainty than suspense. She bethought herself of sending to the Drurys, and showed rather gratification than her ordinary impatience at the manifold reports of the general sympathy, and of Bayford's grief for its hero. The poison was gone from her mind.

CHAPTER XXVIII.

The Family Office had been asked to receive the whole party on their return. Mr. Kendal had business in London, and could not bear to part with the colonel till he had seen him safely lodged, and heard the surgeon's opinion.

Mr. Ferrars was laying himself out to guard his brother-in-law from being oppressed by the sympathetic welcome of the good aunts; but though the good ladies never failed in kindness, all the excess was directed into a different channel; Albinia herself was but secondary to the wounded hero, for whom alone they had eyes and ears. They would hardly let him stand erect for a moment; easy-chairs and couches were offered, soup and wine, biscuits and coffee were suggested, and questions were crowded on him, while he, poor fellow, wistfully gazed at the oft-directed pile of foreign letters on the side-table, and in pure desperation became too fatigued to go down to luncheon.

When the others returned, he was standing on the rug, curling his moustaches. There was a glow of colour on his hollow cheek, and his eyes danced; he put out his hand, and catching Albinia's with boyish playfulness, he squeezed it triumphantly, with the words, 'Albinia, she's a brick!'

They went their several ways, Fred to rest, Maurice to make an appointment for him with the doctor, and Albinia to Genevieve, whom Mr. Kendal regarded like his son's widow, forgetting that the attachment had been neither sanctioned nor returned. He could not rest without seeing her, and delivering that last message, but he was glad to have the way prepared by his wife, and proposed to call for her when his law business should be over.

Albinia sent in her card, and asked whether Miss Durant were at liberty. Genevieve came hurrying to her with outstretched hands: 'Dear Mrs. Kendal, this is kind!' and led her to the back drawing-room, where they were with one impulse enfolded in each other's tearful embrace.

'Oh! madame, how much you have suffered!'

'You know all?' said Albinia.

'O no, very little. My aunt knows little of Bayford now, and her sight is too weak for much writing.'

Genevieve pushed back her hair; she looked ill and heavy-eyed, with the extinguished air that sorrow gave her. Gilbert had distressed, perplexed her, and driven her from home, but what could be remembered, save the warm affection he had lavished on her, and the pain she had inflicted? Uneasiness and sorrow, necessarily unavowed, had preyed on the poor girl for weeks in secret; and even now she hardly presumed to give way, relief, almost luxury, as it was to be pressed in those kind arms, and suffered to weep freely for the champion of her younger days. When she had heard how he had thought of her to the last, her emotion grew less controllable; and Albinia was touched by the idea that there had all along been a stifled preference. Embellished as Gilbert now was, she could not but wish to believe that his affection had not been wasted; and his constancy might well be touching in one of the heroes of the six hundred. At least, Genevieve had a most earnest and loving appetite for every detail, and though the afternoon was nearly gone, neither felt as if half an hour had passed when admittance was asked for Mr. Kendal.

It was a trying moment, but Genevieve was too simple, genuine, and grateful to pause in selfish embarrassment. Had she toyed with Gilbert's affection, she could not have met his father with such maidenly modesty, and sweet sympathy and respect in her blushing cheek and downcast, tearful eyes.

He took her hand, speaking in the kindest tone of his mellow voice: 'My dear, Mrs. Kendal has told you what brings us here, and how much we feel for and with you.'

'So kind in you,' said Genevieve, faltering.

'Poor child, she has suffered grievously for want of fuller tidings,' said Albinia; 'she has been keeping her sorrow pent up all this time.'

'She has acted, as she has done throughout, most consistently,' said Mr. Kendal. 'My dear, though it was inexpedient to show my sentiments, I always respected my son for having placed his affections so worthily, and though circumstances were unfortunately adverse, I cannot thank you enough for your course of action and the influence you exercised.'

'I never did,' murmured Genevieve.

'Not perhaps consciously; but unswerving rectitude of conduct is one of the strongest earthly influences. He was sensible of it. He bade me tell you that whenever higher and better thoughts came to him, you were connected with them; and when to his surprise, poor boy, he found that he was thought to have distinguished himself, his first thought was that it might be a step to your esteem. He desired me to thank you for all that you have been to him, to entreat you to pardon the annoyance of which he was the occasion, and to beg you to wear this for his sake, if you could think of his presumption with forgiveness and toleration. Those were his words; but I trust you do not retain displeasure, for though, perhaps, foolishly and obtrusively expressed, it was sincere and lasting affection.'

'Oh, sir!' exclaimed Genevieve, 'do not speak thus! What can I feel save that it will be my tenderest and deepest pride to have been so regarded. Oh! that I could thank him! but,'clasping her hands together, 'I cannot even thank you.'

'The best way to gratify us,' he said, 'will be always to remember that you have a home at Willow Lawn, and a daughter's place in our hearts. Think of me like a father, Genevieve;' and he kissed her drooping forehead.

'Oh! Mr. Kendal, this is goodness.'

He turned to Albinia to suggest, 'It must be intolerable to be here at present. Speak to Mrs. Rainsforth, let us take her home, if it be but for a week.'

Leaving him to make the proposition to Genevieve, Albinia gained admittance to the other drawing-room, which she found all over little children, and their mother looking unequal to dispensing with their deputy. She said she had feared Miss Durant was looking ill, and had something weighing on her spirits, though she was always so cheerful and helpful, but baby had not been well, and Mr. Rainsforth was not at all strong, and her views had evidently taken no wider range.

Albinia began to think her proposal cruel, and prefaced it by a few words on the state of the case. The little bit of romance touched the kind heart. Mrs. Rainsforth was shocked to think of the grief the governess must have suffered in secret while aiding to bear her burdens, and was resolved on letting her have this respite, going eagerly to assure her that she could well be spared; baby was better, and papa was better, and the children would be good.

But Genevieve knew too well how necessary she was, and had been telling Mr. Kendal of the poor little mother's anxieties with her many delicate children, and her husband's failing health. She could not leave them with a safe conscience; and she would not show how she longed after quiet, the country, and her aunt. She stood firm, and Albinia could not say that she was not right. Mrs. Rainsforth was distressed, though much relieved, and was only pacified by the engagement that Miss Durant should, when it was practicable, spend a long holiday with her friends.

'At home!' said Mr. Kendal, and the responsive look of mournful gratitude from beneath the black dewy eyelashes dispelled all marvel at his son's enduring attachment.

He was wonderfully patient when Mrs. Rainsforth could not be content without Mrs. Kendal's maternal and medical opinion of the baby, on the road to and from the nursery consulting her on all the Mediterranean climates, and telling her what each doctor had said of Mr. Rainsforth's lungs, in the course of which Miss Durant and her romance were put as entirely out of the little lady's mind as if she had never existed.

The next day the Kendals set their faces homewards, leaving Maurice till the surgeon's work should be done, and Fred, as the aunts fondly hoped, to be their nursling.

But, behold! Sunday and Monday Colonel Fred spent in bed, smiling incessantly; Tuesday and Wednesday on the sofa; Thursday in going about London; Friday he was off to Liverpool; Saturday had sailed for Canada.

Albinia was coming nearer to the home that was pulling her by the heart-strings. Hadminster was past, and she had heard the welcome wards, 'All well,' from the servant who brought the carriage; but how much more there was to know than Sophy's detailed letters could convey—Sophy, whose sincerity, though one of the most trustworthy things in the world, was never quite to be relied on as to her own health or Maurice's conduct.

At the gate there was a little chestnut curled being in a short black frock, struggling to pull the heavy gate open with her plump arms, and standing for one moment with her back to it, screaming 'Mamma! Papa!' then jumping and clapping her hands in ecstasy and oblivion that the swing of the gate might demolish her small person between it and the horse. But there was no time for fright. Sophy caught her and secured the gate together; and the first glimpse assured Albinia that the hard gloom was absent. And there was Maurice, leaning against the iron rail of the hall steps; but he hardly moved, and his face was so strangely white and set, that Albinia caught him in her arms, crying, 'Are you well, my boy? Sophy, is he well?'

'Quite well,' said Sophy; but the boy had wriggled himself loose, stood but for an instant to receive his father's kiss, and had hold of the sword. The long cavalry sabre was almost as tall as himself, and he stood with both arms clasped round it; but no sooner did he feel their eyes upon him, than he turned about and ran upstairs.

It was not gracious, but they excused it; they had their little Albinia comfortably and childishly happy, as yet without those troublesome Kendal feelings that always demonstrated themselves in some perverse manner.

And Sophy stood among them—that brighter, better Sophy who had so long been obscured, happy to have them at home; talking and asking questions eagerly about the journey, and describing the kindness of the Dusautoys and the goodness of the children.

'Have you heard from Lucy?' asked Mr. Kendal, as Albinia went in pursuit of her little boy. 'Yes—

poor Lucy?'

'Is there no letter from him?'

'Not for you, papa.'

'What? Did he write to his uncle?'

'No, papa—he wrote to me and to Mr. Pettilove. Cannot he be stopped, papa? Can he do any harm? Mr. Dusautoy and Mr. Pettilove think he can.'

'You mean that he wishes to question the will? You may be quite secure, my dear. Nothing can be more safe.'

'Oh, papa! I am so very glad. Not to be able to hinder him was so dreadful, when he wanted to pit Lucy and me against you. I could never have looked at you. I should always have felt that you had something to forgive me.'

'I could not well have confounded you with Algernon, my dear,' said Mr. Kendal. 'What did Pettilove mean? Do you know?'

'Not exactly; something about grandpapa's old settlement; which frightened the Vicar, though Mrs. Dusautoy said that it was only that he fancied nobody could do anything right without his help. Mr. Dusautoy is more angry with Algernon than I thought he could be with anybody.'

'No one but Algernon would have ever thought of it,' said Mr. Kendal. 'I am sorry he has molested you, my dear. Have you any objection to let me see his letter?'

'I kept it for you, papa, and a copy of my answer. I thought though I am not of age, perhaps my saying I would have nothing to do with it might do some good.'

Algernon magniloquently condoled with his sister-in-law on the injustice from which she and her sister had suffered, in consequence of the adverse influence which surrounded her brother, and generously informed her that she had a champion to defeat the machinations against their rights. He had little doubt of the futility of the document, and had written to the legal adviser of the late Mr. Meadows to inquire whether the will of that gentleman did not bar any power on the part of his grandson to dispose of the property. She might rely on him not to rest until she should be put in possession of the estate, unless it should prove to have been her grandfathers intention, in case of the present melancholy occurrence, that the elder sister should be the sole inheritrix, and he congratulated her on having such a protector, since, under the unfortunate circumstances, the sisters would have had no one to uphold their cause against their natural guardian.

Sophy's answer was—

'Dear Algernon,

'I prefer my *natural guardian* to any other whatever. I shall for my part owe you no thanks for attempting to frustrate my dear brother's wishes, and to raise an unbecoming dissension. I desire that no use of my name may be made, and you may rest assured that I should find nothing so difficult to forgive as any such interference in my behalf.

'Yours truly,

'SOPHIA KENDAL.'

'Certainly,' said Mr. Kendal, 'no family ill-will is complete unless money matters be brought in to aggravate it.'

'Do you think I did right, and spoke strongly enough, papa?'

'Quite strongly enough,' said Mr. Kendal, suppressing a smile. 'I hope you wrote kindly to Lucy at the same time.'

'One could not help that, papa; but I did say a great deal about the outrageous impropriety of raising the question, because I thought Algernon might be ashamed.'

'Riches kept for the owners thereof to their hurt,' said Mr. Kendal. 'Your grandfather's acquisitions have brought us little but evil hitherto, and now I fear that our dear Gilbert's endeavour to break the net which bound us into that system of iniquity and oppression, may cause alienation from poor Lucy. Sophy, you must allow no apparent coldness or neglect on her part to keep you from writing often and affectionately.'

Maurice here came down with his mother, and as soon as there was a moment's pause, laid hold of the first book he met with, and began:—

'I do not see the justness of the analogy to which Onuphrio refers, but there are many parts of that vision on which I should wish to hear the explanations of Philalethes.'

All broke out in amazement, 'Why, Maurice, has Mrs. Dusautoy been making a scholar of you?'

'Oh! Maurice, was this your secret?' cried Sophy.

He had hidden his face in his mother's lap, and when she raised it struggled to keep it down, and she felt him sobbing and panting for breath. Mr. Kendal stroked his hair, and they tried to soothe him, but he started up abruptly.

'I don't mean ever to be a plague again! So I did it. But there—when Ulick said it would be a comfort, you are all going to cry again, papa and all, and that's worse!' and stamping his foot passionately, he would have rushed out of the room, but was held fast in his father's arms, and indeed tears were flowing fast from eyes that his brother's death had left dry.

'My child! my dear child!' said Mr. Kendal, 'it is comfort. No one can rule you as by God's grace you can rule yourself, and your endeavours to do this are the greatest blessing I can ask.'

One more kiss from his mother, and she let him go. He did not know how to deal with emotion in himself, and hated the sight of it in others; so that it was better to let him burst away from them, while with one voice they admired, rejoiced, and interrogated Sophy.

'I know now,' she said, the rosy glow mantling in her cheek; 'it must have been Mr. O'More.'

'Ah! has he been with you?' said her father.

'Only once,' said Sophy, her colour deepening; 'but Maurice has been in a great hurry every day to go to him, and I saw there was some secret. One day, Susan asked me to prevent Master Maurice from teaching baby such ugly words, that she could not sleep—not bad words, but she thought they were Latin. So I watched, and I heard Maurice singing out some of the legend of Hiawatha, and insisting on poor little Awkey telling him what m-i-s-h-e-n-a-h-m-a, spelt. Poor little Awk stared, as well she might, and obediently made the utmost efforts to say after him, Mishenahma, king of fishes, but he was terribly discomposed at getting nothing but Niffey-ninny, king of fithes. I went to her rescue, and asked what they were about; but Maurice thundered down on me all the Delawares and Mohawks, and the Choctaws and Cameches; and baby squeaked after him as well as she could, till I fairly stopped my ears. I thought Ulick must be reading the legend to him. Now I see he must have been teaching him to read it.'

'Can it be possible?' said Mr. Kendal. 'He could not read words of five letters without spelling.'

'He always could do much more when he pleased than when he did not please,' said Albinia. 'I believe the impulse to use his understanding was all that was wanting, and I am very glad the impulse came from such a motive.'

Mr. Kendal ordained that Maurice's reward should be learning Latin from himself, a perilous trial; but it proved that Mr. Kendal was really a good teacher for a child of spirit and courage, and Maurice had early come to the age when boys do better with man than with woman. He liked the honour and the awe of papa's tutorship, and learnt so well, that his father never believed in his past dunceship; but over studies that he did not deem sufficiently masculine, he could be as troublesome as ever, his attention absent, and his restlessness most wearisome. To an ordinary eye, he was little changed; but his mother felt that the great victory of the will had been gained, and that his *self* was endeavouring to get the better of the spirit of insubordination and mischief. Night after night she found him sleeping with the Balaklava sword by his side, and his hand clasped over it; and he always crept out of the way of Crimean news, though that he gathered up the facts was plain when he committed his sovereign to Ulick, with a request that it might be devoted to the comforts preparing to be sent to the 25th Lancers.

Ulick wished him to consult his mother, but this he repelled. He could not endure the sight of a tear in her eye, and she could not restrain them when that chord was touched. It was a propensity she much disliked, the more because she thought it looked like affectation beside Sophy, whose feelings nevertook that course, but the more ill-timed the tears, the more they would come, at the most common-place condolence or remote allusion. It was the effect of the long strain on her powers, and the severe shock coming suddenly after so much pressure and fatigue; moreover, her habits had been so long disorganized that her time seemed blank, and she could not rouse herself from a feeling of languor and depression. Then Gilbert had been always on her mind, whether at home or absent; and it did not seem at first as if she had enough to fill up time or thoughts—she absolutely found herself doing nothing, because there was nothing she cared to do.

Mr. Kendal's first object was the fulfilment of Gilbert's wishes; but Albinia soon felt how much easier it is for women and boys to make schemes, than for men to bring them to effect, and how rash it is hastily to condemn those who tolerate abuses.

The whole was carefully looked over with a surveyor, and it was only then understood how complicated were the tenures, and how varied the covenants of the numerous small tenements which old Mr. Meadows had amassed. It was not possible to be free of the legal difficulties under at least a year, and plans of drainage might be impeded for want of other people's consent. Even if all had been smooth, the sacrifice of income, by destroying Tibb's Alley, and reducing the number of cottages, would be considerable. Meantime, the inspection had brought to light worse iniquities and greater wretchedness than Mr. Kendal had imagined, and his eagerness to set to work was tenfold. His table was heaped with sanitary reports, and his fits of abstraction were over the components of bad air or builder's estimates.

It only depended on Ulick to have resumed his intimacy at Willow Lawn; but the habit once broken was not resumed. He was often there, but never without invitation; and he was not always to be had. He had less leisure, he was senior clerk, and the junior was dull and untrained; and he often had work to do far into the evening. He looked bright and well, as though possessed of a sense of being valuable in his own place, more conducive to happiness than even congeniality of employment; and Sophy, though now and then disappointed at his non-appearance, always had a good reason for it, and continued to justify Mr. Dusautoy's boast that the air of the hill had made another woman of her.

Visiting cards had, of course, come in numbers to Willow Lawn, but Albinia seemed to have caught her husband's aversions, and it would be dangerous to say how long it was before she lashed herself into setting off for a round of calls.

Nothing surprised her more than Miss Goldsmith's reception. Conscious of her neglect, she expected the stiff manner to be more formal than ever; but the welcome was almost warm, and there was something caressing in her fears that Miss Kendal would be tired. Mr. Goldsmith was not quite well, there were threatenings of gout, and his sister had persuaded him to visit the relations at Bristol next week; everything might safely be trusted to young More, and therewith came such praise of his steadiness and ability, that Albinia did not know which way to look when all was ascribed to Mr. Kendal's great kindness to him.

It was too palpable to be altogether pleasant. Sophia Kendal was heiress enough to be a very desirable connexion for the bank. Albinia was afraid she should see through the lady's graciousness, and took her leave in haste; but Sophy only said, 'Do you remember, mamma, when the Goldsmiths thought we unsettled him?'

Before Albinia had disarmed her reply of the irony on the tip of her tongue, the omnibus came lumbering round the corner, and a voice proceeded from the rear, the door flew open, and there was a rapid exit.

Face and voice, light step, and gay bearing, all were Fred—the empty sleeve, the sole resemblance to the shattered convalescent of a few weeks back.

'There, Albinia! I said you should see her first. You haven't got any change, have you?' the last being addressed either to Albinia, the omnibus conductor, or a lady, who made a tender of two shillings, while Albinia ordered the luggage on to Willow Lawn, though something was faintly said about the inn.

'And there!' cried Fred, with an emphatic twist of his moustache, 'isn't she all I ever told you?'

'The last thing was a brick,' said Albinia, laughing, as she looked at the smiling, confiding, animated face, not the less pleasant for a French Canadian grace that recalled Genevieve.

'The right article for building a hut, I hope,' she said, merrily.

'But how and when could you have come?'

'This morning, from Liverpool. We did not mean to storm you in this manner; we meant to have settled ourselves at the inn, and walked down; Emily was very particular about it.'

'But you see, when he saw you, he forgot all my lectures!' said Emily, taking his welcome for granted.

'Very proper of him! But, Fred, I don't quite believe it yet. How long is it since we parted?'

'Six weeks; just enough to go to Canada and back, with a fortnight in the middle to spare.'

'And pray how long has Mrs. Fred existed?'

'Three weeks and two days;' and turning half round to give her the benefit of his words, 'it was on purely philanthropic principles, because I could not tie my own necktie.'

'Now could I,' said Emily pleadingly to Sophy—'now could I let him go back again alone, when he came so helpless, and looking so dreadfully ill?'

'And what are you going to do?' asked Albinia. 'You can't join again.'

'Join! why not? Here's a hand for a horse, and an arm for a wife, and the rest will be done much better for me than ever it was before.'

'But with her? and at Sebastopol!'

'That's the very thing' cried the colonel, again turning about. 'Nothing will serve her but to show how a backwoodsman's daughter can live in a hut.'

'And what will the general say?'

'The general,' cried Emily, 'will endure me better as a fact than as a prospect; and we will teach him that a lady is not all made of nerves and of fancies! See what he will say if we let him into our paradise!'

Fred brightened, though Albinia's inquiry had for a moment taken him a little aback. The one being whom he dreaded was General Ferrars, for whom he cared a thousand times more than for his own elder brother, and he was soon speculating, with his usual insouciance, as to how his announcement might have been received by his lordship, and whether the aunts would look at them as they went through London.

Mr. Kendal met them at the gate, amazed at the avalanche of luggage, but well pleased, for he had grown very fond of Fred, and had been very anxious about him, thinking him broken and enfeebled for life, and hardly expecting him to return from his mad expedition. He was slow to believe his eyes and ears when he beheld a hale, handsome, vigorous man, full of life and activity, but his welcome and congratulations were of the warmest. He could far better stand a sudden inroad than if he had had to meditate for a week on entertaining the bride. Not that the bride wanted entertainment, except waiting upon her husband, who let himself be many degrees less handy than at Malta, for the pleasure of her attentions.

Perhaps the person least gratified was Maurice; for the child shrank with shy reverence from him whom his brother had saved, and would as soon have thought of making a plaything of Gilbert's sword as of having fun with the survivor. The sight of such a merry man was a shock, and he abruptly repelled all attempts at playing with him, and kept apart with a big book on a chair before him, a Kendalism for which he amply compensated when familiarity had diminished his awe.

Mr. Kendal, though little disposed to exert himself to talk, liked to watch his wife reviving into animation, and Sophy taking a full share in the glee with which Emily enjoyed turning the laugh against the good-natured soldier. In the midst of their flush of joy there was a tender consideration about the young couple, such as to hinder their tone from jarring. Indeed, it was less consideration than fellow-feeling, for Gilbert Kendal had become enshrined in the depths of Fred's heart; while to Emily the visit was well-nigh a pilgrimage. All her hero-worship was directed to the youth who had guarded her soldier's life, nursed him in his sickness, and, as he averred, inspired him with serious thoughts. Poor, failing, timid, penitent Gilbert was to her a very St. George, and every relic of him was viewed with reverence; she composed a countenance for him from his father's fine features, and fitted the fragments of his history into an ideal, till Sophy, after being surprised and gratified, began to view Gilbert through a like halo, and to rank him with his twin brother. Friendship was a new and agreeable phase of life to Sophy, who found a suitable companion in such an open-hearted person, simpler in nature, and fresher than herself, free from English commonplaces, though older and of more standing. She expanded and brightened wonderfully, and Emily, imagining her a female Gilbert, was devoted to her, and thought her a marvel of learning, depth, goodness, and humility, the more striking for her tinge of grave pensiveness.

'Why, Albinia,' said the colonel, 'didn't I hear that it was your handsome daughter who is married?'

'Yes, poor Lucy was always called our pretty one.'

'More admired than her sister? Why, she never could have had a countenance!'

'Yes,' said Albinia, highly gratified by the opinion of such a connoisseur. 'I always told Winifred that Sophy was the beauty, but she has only lately had health or animation to set her off.'

'I declare, when we overtook you in the street, she looked a perfect Spanish princess, in her black robes and great shady hat. You ought always to keep her in black. Ha! Emily, what are you smiling at?'

His wife looked up into his face with mischievous shyness in her eyes, as if she wanted him to say what would be a liberty in her. Somebody else had overtaken the ladies nearly at the same moment, and Albinia exulted in perceiving that the embellishment had been observed by others besides herself. She did not look so severe but that Fred was encouraged to repeat, 'Only lately had health or animation? When Irish winds blow this way, I fancy—But what will the aunts say?'

'They are not Sophy's aunts, whatever they are to you.'

'What will Kendal say? which is more to the purpose.'

'Oh! he saw it first; he will be delighted; but you must not say a word to him, for it can't come to anything just now.'

Albinia was thus confirmed in her anticipations, and the bridal pair, only wishing everybody to be as happy as themselves, took the matter up with such vivid interest and amusement, that she was rather afraid of a manifestation such as to shock either her husband or the parties themselves; but Fred was too much of a gentleman, and Emily too considerate, for anything perilously marked. Only she thought Emily need not have been so decided in making room for Ulick next to Sophy, when they were all looking out at the young moon at the conservatory-door that evening.

And then Emily took her husband's arm, and insisted on going down the garden to be introduced to English nightingales; and though she was told they never had come there in the memory of man, she was bent on doing as she would be done by, and drew him alone the silvered paths, among the black shadows of the trees; and Ulick asked Sophy if she wished to go too. She looked as if she should like it very much; he fetched a couple of cloaks ont of the hall, put her into one, and ran after Mrs. Ferrars with the other.

'Well!' thought Albinia, as she stood at the conservatory-door, 'how much more boldness and tact some people have than others! If I had lived a hundred years, I should not have managed it so well!'

'What's become of them?' said Mr. Kendal, as she went back to the drawing-room.

'Gone to listen for nightingales!'

'Nightingales! How could you let them go into the river-fog?'

'Emily was bent upon it; she is too much of a bride not to have her way.'

'Umph! I wonder Sophy was so foolish.'

They came back in a quarter of an hour. No nightingales; and Fred was indulging in reminiscences of bull-frogs; the two ladies were rapturous on the effect of the moonbeams in the ripple of the waters, and the soft furry white mist rising over the meadows. Ulick shivered, and leant over the fire to breathe a drier air, bantering the ladies for their admiration, and declaring that Mrs. Ferrars had taken the moan of an imprisoned house-dog for the nightingale, which he disdainfully imitated with buzz, zizz, and guggle, assuring her she had had no loss; but he looked rather white and chilled. Sophy whispered something to her papa, who rang the bell, and ordered in wine and hot water.

'There, Emily,' said Albinia, when he had taken his leave; 'what shall we say to your nightingales, if Mr. O'More catches his ague again?'

'Oh, there are moments when people don't catch agues,' said Fred. 'He would be a poor fellow to catch an ague after all that, though, by-the-bye, it is not a place to go to at night without a cigar.'

Albinia was on thorns, lest Sophy should be offended; but though her cheeks lighted up, and she was certainly aware of some part of their meaning, either she did not believe in the possibility of any one bantering her, or else the assumption was more agreeable than the presumption was disagreeable. She endured with droll puzzled dignity, when Fred teased her anxiety the next day to know whether Mr. O'More had felt any ill effects; and it really appeared as if she liked him better for what might have been expected to be a dire affront; but then he was a man whose manner enabled to do and say whatever he pleased.

Emily never durst enter on the subject with her, but had more than one confidential little gossip with Albinia, and repeatedly declared that she hoped to be in England when 'it' took place. Indeed that week's visit made them all so intimate, that it was not easy to believe how recent was the acquaintance.

The aunts had been so much disappointed at Fred's desertion, so much discomfited at his recovery contrary to all predictions, and so much annoyed at his marriage, that it took all their kindness, and his Crimean fame, to make them invite him and his colonial wife to the Family Office, to be present at the royal distribution of medals. However, the good ladies did their duty; and Emily and Sophy parted with promises of letters.

The beginning of the correspondence was as full a description of the presentation of the medals as could be given by a person who only saw one figure wherever she went, and to whom the great incident of the day was, that the gracious and kindhearted Queen had herself fastened the left-handed colonel's medal as well as Emily could have done it herself! There was another medal, with two clasps, that came to Bayford, and which was looked at in pensive but not unhappy silence. 'You shall have it some day, Maurice, but not now,' said Mr. Kendal, and all felt that now meant his own lifetime. It was placed where Gilbert would well have liked to see it, beside his brother Edmund's watch.

Emily made Mrs. Annesley and Miss Ferrars more fond of her in three days, than eleven years had made them of Winifred; too fond, indeed, for they fell to preaching to Fred upon the horrors of Sebastopol, till they persuaded him that he was a selfish wretch, and brought him to decree that she should stay with them during his absence. But, as Emily observed, that was not what she left home for; she demolished his arguments with a small amount of playing at petulance, and triumphantly departed for the East, leaving Aunt Mary crying over her as a predestined victim.

The last thing Fred did before sailing, was to send Albinia a letter from his brother, that she might see 'how very kind and cordial Belraven was,' besides something that concerned her more nearly.

Lord Belraven was civil when it cost him nothing, and had lately regarded his inconvenient younger brother with favour, as bringing him distinction, and having gained two steps without purchase, removed, too, by his present rank, and the pension for his wound, from being likely to become chargeable to him; so he had written such brotherly congratulations, that good honest Fred was quite affected. He was even discursive enough to mention some connexions of the young man who had been with Fred in the Crimea, a Mr. Cavendish Dusautoy, a very good sort of fellow, who gave excellent dinners, and was a pleasant yachting companion. His wife was said to be very pretty and pleasing, but she had arrived at Genoa very unwell, had been since confined, and was not yet able to see any one. It was said to be the effect of her distress for the death of her brother, and the estrangement from her family, who had behaved very ill about his property. Had not Albinia Ferrars married into that family?

Albinia knew enough of her noble relative to be aware that good dinners and obsequiousness were the way to his esteem, and Algernon's was the sort of arrogance that would stoop to adore a coronet. All this was nothing, however, to the idea of Lucy, ill in that strange place, with no one to care for her but her hard master. Albinia sometimes thought of going to find her out at Genoa; but this was too utterly wild and impossible, and nothing could be done but to write letters of affectionate inquiry, enclosing them to Lord Belraven.

Algernon's answer was solemn, and as brief as he could make anything. He was astonished that the event bad escaped the notice of the circle at Bayford, since he believed it had appeared in all the principal European newspapers; and his time had been so fully occupied, that he had imagined that intimation sufficient, since it was evident from the tone of the recent correspondence, that the family of Bayford were inclined to drop future intercourse. He was obliged for the inquiries for Lucy, and was happy to say she was recovering favourably, though the late unfortunate events, and the agitation caused by letters from home, had affected her so seriously, that they had been detained at Genoa for nearly four months to his great inconvenience, instead of pushing on to Florence and Rome. It had been some compensation that he had become extremely intimate with that most agreeable and superior person, Lord Belraven, who had consented to become sponsor to his son.

Lucy wrote to Albinia. Poor thing, the letter was the most childishly expressed, and the least childishly felt, she had ever written; its whole aspect was weak and wobegone; yet there was less self-pity, and more endeavour to make the best of it, than before. She had the dearest little baby in the world; but he was very delicate, and she wished mamma would send out an English nurse, for she could not bear that Italian woman—her black eyes looked so fierce, and she was sure it was not safe to have those immense pins in her hair. Expense was nothing, but she should never be happy till she had an Englishwoman about him, especially now that she was getting better, and Algernon would want her to come out again with him. Dear Algernon, he had lost the Easter at Rome for her sake, but perhaps it was a good thing, for he was often out in Lord Belraven's yacht, and she could be quiet with baby. She did wish baby to have had her dear brothers' names, but Algernon would not consent. Next Tuesday he was to be christened; and then followed a string of mighty names, long enough for a Spanish princess, beginning with Belraven!!!

Lucy Dusautoy's dreary condition in the midst of all that wealth could give, was a contrast to Emily Ferrars' buoyant delight in the burrow which was her first married home, and proved a paradise to many a stray officer, aye, maybe, to Lieutenant-General Sir William Ferrars himself. Her letters were charming, especially a detail of Fred meeting Bryan O'More coming out of the trenches, grim, hungry, and tired, having recently kicked a newly alighted shell down from the parapet, with the cool words, 'Be off with you, you ugly baste you;' of his wolfish appetite after having been long reduced to simple rations, though he kept a curly black lamb loose about his hut, because he hadn't the heart to kill it; and it served him for bed if not for board, all his rugs and blankets having flown off in the hurricane, or been given to the wounded; he had been quite affronted at the suggestion that a Galway pig was as well lodged as himself— it was an insult to any respectable Irish animal!

Albinia sent Maurice to summon Ulick to enjoy the letter in store for him. He looked grave and embarrassed, and did not light up as usual at Bryan's praises. He said that his aunt, who had written to him on business, had given a bad account of Mr. Goldsmith, but Albinia hardly thought this accounted for his preoccupation, and was considering how to probe it, when her brother Maurice opened the door. 'Ulick O'More! that's right; the very man I was in search of!'

'How's Winifred, Maurice?'

'Getting on wonderfully well. I really think she is going to make a start, after all! and she is in such spirits herself.'

'And the boy?'

'Oh, a thumping great fellow! I promise you he'll be a match for your Maurice.'

'I do believe it is to reward Winifred for sparing you in the spring when we wanted you so much! Come, sit down, and wait for Edmund.'

'No; I've not a moment to stay. I'm to meet Bury again at Woodside at six o'clock, he drove me there, and I walked on, looking in at your lodgings by the way, Ulick.'

'I'm not there now. I am keeping guard at the bank.'

'So they told me. Well, I hope your guard is not too strict for you to come over to Fairmead on Sunday; we want you to do our boy the kindness to be his godfather!'

Sophy blushed with approving gratitude.

'I don't consider that it will be a sinecure—he squalls in such a characteristic manner that I am convinced he will rival his cousin here in all amiable and amenable qualities; so I consider it particularly desirable that he should be well provided with great disciplinarians.'

'You certainly could not find any one more accomplished in teaching dunces to read,' said Albinia.

'When their mammas have taught them already!' added Ulick, laughing. 'Thank you; but you know I can't sleep out; Hyder Ali and I are responsible for a big chest of sovereigns, and all the rest of it.'

'Nor could I lodge you at present; so we are agreed. My proposition is that you should drive my sister over on Sunday morning. My wife is wearying for a sight of her; and she has not been at Fairmead on a Sunday since she left it, eh, Albinia?'

'I suppose for such a purpose it is not wrong to use the horse,' she said, her eyes sparkling.

'And you might put my friend Maurice between you, if you can't go out pleasuring without him.'

'I scorn you, sir; Maurice is as good as gold; I shall leave him at home, I think, to prove that I can—'

'That's the reward of merit!' exclaimed Sophy.

'She expects my children to corrupt him!' quoth Mr. Ferrars.

'For shame, Maurice; that's on purpose to make me bring him. Well, we'll see what papa says, and if he thinks the new black horse strong enough, or to be trusted with Mr. O'More.'

'I only wish 'twas a jaunting car!' cried Ulick.

'And what's the boy's name to be? Not Belraven, I conclude, like my unfortunate grandson—Maurice, I hope.'

'No; the precedent of his namesake would be too dangerous. I believe he is to be Edmund Ulick. Don't take it as too personal, Ulick, for it was the name of our mutual connexion.'

'I take the personal part though, Maurice; and thank you, said Albinia, and Mr. Ferrars looked more happy and joyous than any time since his wife's health had begun to fail. Always cheerful, and almost always taking matters up in the most lively point of view, it was only by comparison that want of spirits in him could be detected; and it was chiefly by the vanishing of a certain careworn, anxious expression about his eyes, and by the ring of his merry laugh, that Albinia knew that he thought better of his wife's state than for the last five or six years.

Albinia and Ulick drove off at six o'clock on a lovely summer Sunday morning, with Maurice between them in a royal state of felicity. That long fresh drive, past summer hay-fields sleeping in their silver bath of dew, and villages tardily awakening to the well-earned Sunday rest, was not the least pleasant part of the day; and yet it was completely happy, not even clouded by one outbreak of Master Maurice. Luckily for him, Mary had a small class, who absorbed her superabundant love of rule; and little Alby was a fair- haired, apple-cheeked maiden of five, who awoke both admiration and chivalry, and managed to coquet with him and Ulick both at once, so that Willie had no disrespect to his sisters to resent.

He was exemplary at church, well-behaved at dinner, and so little on his mamma's mind, that she had a delightful renewal of her acquaintance with the Sunday-school, and a leisurable gossip with Mrs. Reid and the two Miss Reids, collectively and individually; but the best of all was a long quiet tete-a- tete with Winifred.

After the evening service, Mr. Ferrars himself carried his newly-christened boy back to the mother, and paused that his sister might come with him, and they might feel like the old times, when the three had been alone together.

'Yes,' said Winifred, when he had left them, 'it is very pretty playing at it; but one cannot be the same.'

'Nor would one exactly wish it,' said Albinia; 'though I think you are going to be more the same.'

'Perhaps,' said Winifred; 'the worst of being ill is that it does wear one's husband so! When he came in, and tried to make me fancy we were gone back to Willie's time, I could not help thinking how different you both looked.'

'Well, so much the better and more respectable,' said Albinia. 'You know I always wanted to grow old; I don't want to stop short like your sister Anne, who looks as much the child of the house as ever.

'I wish you had as few cares as Anne. Look; I declare that's a grey hair!'

'I know. I like it; now Sophy is growing young, and I'm growing old, it is all correct.'

'Old, indeed!' ejaculated Winifred, looking at her fair fresh complexion and bright features; 'don't try for that, when even Edmund is not grey.'

'Yes he is,' said Albinia, gravely; 'Malta sowed many white threads in his black head, and worry about those buildings has brought more.'

'Worry; I'm very sorry to hear of it.'

'Yes; the tenures are so troublesome, and everybody is so cantankerous. If he wanted to set up some pernicious manufacture, it could not be worse! The Osbornes, after having lived with Tibb's Alley close to them all their lives, object to the almshouses! Mr. Baron wont have the new drains carried through his little strip of land. The Town Council think we are going to poison the water; and Pettilove, and everybody else who owns a wretched tenement, that we shall increase the wants of their tenants, and lower their rents. If it be carried through, it will be by that sheer force in going his own way that Edmund can exert when he chooses.'

'And he will?'

'O, yes, no fear of that; he goes on, avoiding seeing or hearing what he has not to act upon; but worse than all are the people themselves; Tibb's Alley all has notice to quit, but none of them can be got rid of till Martinmas, and some not till Lady-day, and the beer-house people are in such a rage! The turn-out of the public-houses come and roar at our gate on Saturday nights; and they write up things on the wall against him! and one day they threw over into the garden what little Awkey called a poor dear dead pussy. I believe they tell them all sorts of absurd things about his tyranny; poor creatures.'

'Can't you get it stopped?'

'Edmund wont summon any one, because he thinks it would do more harm than good. He says it will pass off; but it grieves him more than he shows: he thinks he could once have made himself more popular: but I don't know, it is a horrid set.'

'I thought you said he was in good spirits.'

'And so he is: he never gets depressed and unwilling to be spoken to. He is ready to take interest in everything; and always so busy! When I remember how he never seemed to be obliged to attend to anything, I laugh at the contrast; and yet he goes about it all so gravely and slowly, that it never seems like a change.'

In this and other home talk nearly an hour had passed, when Mr. Ferrars returned. 'Are you come to tell me to go?' said Albinia.

'Not particularly,' he said, in a tone that made her laugh.

'No, no,' said Winifred. 'I want a great deal more of her. Where have you been?'

'I have been to see old Wilks; Ulick walked down with me. By-the-bye, Albinia, what nonsense has Fred's wife been talking to his brother?'

'Emily does not talk nonsense!' fired up Albinia, colouring, nevertheless.

'The worse for her, then! However, it seems Bryan has disturbed this poor fellow very much, by congratulating him on his prospects at Willow Lawn.'

'Oh! that is what made him so distant and cautious, is it?' laughed Albinia. 'I think Mrs. Emily might as well not have betrayed it.'

'Betrayed! What could have passed?'

'Oh! Emily and Fred saw it as plain as I did. Why, it does not do credit to your discernment, Maurice; papa found it out long ago, and told me.'

'Kendal did?'

'Yes, that he did, and did not mind the notion at all; rather liked it, in fact.'

'Well!' said Mr. Ferrars, in a different tone, 'it is a very queer business! I certainly did not think the lad showed any symptoms. He said he had heard gossip about it before, and had tried to be careful; his aunt talked to him once, but, as he said, it would be nothing but the rankest treason to think of such a thing, on the terms on which he is treated.'

'Ay, that's it!' said Albinia; 'he acts most perfectly.'

'Perfectly indeed, if that were acting,' said Mr. Ferrars.

'And what made him speak to you?' asked Winifred.

'He wanted to consult me. He said it was very hard on him, for all the pleasure he had came from his intercourse with Willow Lawn; and he could not bear to keep at a distance, because it looked as if he had not forgotten the old folly about the caricature; but he was afraid of the report coming to your ears or Mr. Kendal's, because you would think it so wrong and shameful an abuse of your kindness.'

'And that's his whole concern?'

'So he told me.'

'And what advice did you give him?'

'I told him Bayford was bent on gossip, and no one heeded it less than my respected brother and sister.'

'That was famous of you, Maurice. I was afraid you would have put it upon his honour and the state of his own heart.'

'Sooth to say, I did not think his heart appeared very ticklish.'

'Oh! Maurice, Maurice! But you've not been there to see the hot fits and the cold fits! It is a very fine thermometer whether he says Sophy or Miss Kendal.'

'And you say Edmund perceived this?'

'Much you would trust my unassisted 'cuteness! I tell you he did, and that it will make him happier than anything.'

'Very well; then my advice will have done no harm. I did not think there had been so much self-control in an Irishman.'

'Had he not better say, so much blindness in the rector of Fairmead?' laughed Albinia.

'And pray what course is the affair to take?'

'The present, I suppose. Some catastrophe will occur at last to prove to him that we honour him, and don't view it as outrageous presumption; and then— oh! there can be no doubt that he will have a share in the bank; and Sophy may buy toleration for his round O. After all, he has the best of it as to ancestry, and we Kendals need not turn up our noses at banking.'

'I think he will be too proud to address her, except on equality as to money matters.'

'Pride is sometimes quelled and love free,' said Albinia. 'No, no; content yourself with having given the best advice in the world, with your eyes fast shut!'

And Albinia went home in high spirits.

CHAPTER XXIX.

Not long afterwards, Ulick O'More was summoned to Bristol, where his uncle had become suddenly worse; but he had only reached Hadminster when a telegraph met him with the news of Mr. Goldsmith's death, and orders to remain at his post.

He came to the Kendals in the evening in great grief; he had really come to love and esteem his uncle, and he was very unhappy at having lost the chance of a reconciliation for his mother. As her chief friend and confidant, he knew that she regarded the alienation of her own family as the punishment of her disobedient marriage, and that his own appointment had been valued chiefly as an opening towards fraternal feeling, and reproached himself for not having made more direct efforts to induce his uncle to enter into personal intercourse with her.

'If I had only ventured it before he went to Bristol,' he said; 'I was a fool not to have done so; and there, the Goldsmiths detest the very name of us! Why could they not have telegraphed for me? I might have heard what would have done my mother's heart good for the rest of her life. I am sure my poor uncle wanted to ease his mind!'

'May he not have sent some communication direct to her?'

'I trust he did! I have long thought he only kept her aloof from habit, and felt kindly towards her all the time.'

'And never could persuade himself to make a move towards her until too late,' said Albinia.

'Yes. Nothing comes home to one more than the words, "Agree with thine adversary quickly whiles thou art in the way with him." If once one comes to think there's creditable pride in holding out, there's no end to it, or else too much end.'

'Mr. Goldsmith was persevering in the example his father had set him,' said Mr. Kendal.

'Ay! my mother never blamed either, and I'm afraid, if the truth were told, my father was hot enough too, though it would all have been bygones with him long ago, if they would have let it. But I was thinking just then of my own foolishness last winter, when I would not grant you it was pride, Mrs. Kendal, for fear I should have to repent of it.'

'What has brought you to see that it was?' asked she.

'One comes to a better mind when the fit is off,' he said. 'I hope I will not be as bad next time.'

'I hope we shall never give you a next time,' said Albinia; 'for neither party is comfortable, perched on a high horse.'

'And you see,' continued Ulick, 'it is hard for us to give up our pride, because it is the only thing we've got of our own, and has been meat, drink, and clothing to us for many a year.'

'So no wonder you make the most of it.'

'True; I think a very high born and very rich man might be humble,' said Ulick, so meditatively that they laughed; but Sophy said,

'No, that is not a paradox; the real difficulty is not in willingly yielding, but in taking what we cannot help.'

'Well,' said Ulick, 'I hope it is not pride not to intend working under Andrew Goldsmith.'

'Do you consider that as your fate?' asked Albinia.

'Never my fate,' said Ulick, quickly; 'hardly even my alternative, for he would like to put up a notice, "No Irish need apply." We had enough of each other last winter.'

'And do you suppose,' said Mr. Kendal, 'that Mr. Goldsmith has left your position exactly the same?'

'I've no reason to think otherwise. I refused all connexion with the bank if it was to interfere with my name. I don't think it unlikely that he may have left me a small compliment in the way of shares; but if so, I shall sell them, and make them keep me at Oxford. I'm not too old yet!'

'Then the work of these four years is wasted,' said Mr. Kendal, gravely.

'No, indeed,' cried Ulick; 'not if it takes me where I've always longed to be! Or, if not, I flatter myself I'm accountant enough to be an agent in my own country.'

'Anything to get away from here,' said Albinia, with a shade of asperity, provoked by the spirit of enterprise in his voice.

'After all, it is a bit of a place,' said Ulick; 'and the office parlour is not just a paradise! Then 'tis all on such a narrow scale, too little to absorb one, and too much to let one do anything else; I see how larger transactions might be engrossing, but this is mere cramping and worrying; I know I could do better for my family in the end than by what I can screw out of my salary now; and if it is no longer to give my poor mother a sense of expiation, as she calls it, why, then, the cage-door is open.'

His eyes glittered, and Sophy exclaimed, 'Yes; and now the training is over, it has made you fitter to fly.'

'It has,' he said; 'and I'm thankful for it. Without being here, I would never have learnt application—nor some better things, I hope.'

They scarcely saw him again till after the funeral, when late in the day he came into the drawing-room, and saying that his aunt was pretty well and composed, he knelt down on the floor with the little Awk, and silently built up a tower with her wooden bricks. His hand trembled nervously at first, but gradually steadied as the elevation became critical; and a smile of interest lighted his face as he became absorbed in raising the structure to the last brick, holding back the eager child with one hand lest she should overthrow it. Completion, triumph, a shock, a downfall!

'Well,' cried the elder Albinia, unable to submit to the suspense.

'Telle est la vie,' answered Ulick, smiling sadly as he passed his hand over his brow.

'It's too bad of him,' broke out Mrs. Kendal.

'I thought you were prepared,' said Sophy, severely, disappointed to see him so much discomposed.

'How should I be prepared,' said he, petulantly, 'for the whole concern, house, and bank, and all the rest of it?'

'Left to you?' was the cry.

'Every bit of it, and an annuity apiece charged on it to my mother and aunt for their lives! My aunt told me how it came about. It was all that fellow Andrew's fault.'

'Or misfortune,' murmured Albinia.

'My poor uncle had made a will in Andrew's favour long before my time, and at Bristol he wanted to make some arrangement for my mother and for me; but it seems Mr. Andrew took exception at me—would not promise to continue me on, nor to give me a share in the business, and at last my uncle was so much disgusted, that he sent for a lawyer and cut Andrew out of his will altogether. My aunt says he went on asking for me, and it was Andrew's fault that they wrote instead of telegraphing. You can't think what kind messages he sent to me;' and Ulick's eyes filled with tears. 'My poor uncle, away from home, and with that selfish fellow.'

'Did he send any message to your mother?'

'Yes! he told my aunt to write to her that he was sorry they had been strangers so long, and that—I'd been like a son to him. I'm sure I wish I had been. I dare say he would have let me if I had not flown out about my O. I could have saved changing it without making such an intolerable row, and then he might have died more at peace with the world.'

'At peace with you at least he did.'

'I trust so. But if I could only have been by his side, and felt myself a comfort, and thanked him with all my heart. Maybe he would have listened to me, and not have sown ill-will between Andrew and me, by giving neither what we would like.'

'Do you expect us to be sorry?'

'Nay, I came to be helped out of my ingratitude and discontent at finding the cage-door shut, and myself chained to the oar; for as things are left, I could not get it off my hands without giving up my mother's interests and my aunt's. Besides, my poor uncle left me an entreaty to keep things up creditably like himself, and do justice by the bank. It is as if, poor man, it was an idol that he had been high priest to, and wanted me to be the same—ay, and sacrifice too.'

'Nay, there are two ways of working, two kinds of sacrifice; and besides, you are still working for your mother.'

'So I am, but without the hope she had before. To be sure, it would be affluence at home, or would be if she could have it in her own hands. Little Redmond shall have the best of educations! And we must mind there is something in advance by the time Bryan wants to purchase his company.'

Albinia asked how his aunt liked the arrangement. It seemed that Andrew had offended her nearly as much as her brother, and that she was clinging to Ulick as her great comfort and support; he did not like to stay long away from her, but he had rushed down to Willow Lawn to avoid the jealous congratulations of the cousinhood.

'You will hardly keep from glad people,' said Albinia. 'You must shut yourself up if you cannot be congratulated. How rejoiced Mr. Dusautoy will be!'

'Whatever is, is best,' sighed Ulick. 'I shall mind less when the first is past! I must go and entertain all these people at dinner!' and he groaned. 'Good evening. Heigh ho! I wonder if our Banshee will think me worth keening for?'

'I hope she will have no occasion yet,' said Albinia, as he shut the door;

'but she will be a very foolish Banshee if she does not, for she will hardly find such another O'More! Well, Sophy, my dear.'

'We should have missed him,' said Sophy, as grave as a judge.

Albinia's heart beat high with the hope that Ulick would soon perceive sufficient consolation for remaining at Bayford, but of course he could make no demonstration while Miss Goldsmith continued with him. She made herself very dependent on him, and he devoted his evenings to her solace. He had few leisure moments, for the settlement of his affairs occupied him, and full attention was most important to establish confidence at this critical juncture, when it might be feared that his youth, his nation, and Andrew Goldsmith's murmurs might tell against him. Mr. Kendal set the example of putting all his summer rents into his hands, and used his influence to inspire trust; and fortunately the world had become so much accustomed to transacting affairs with him, that the country business seemed by no means inclined to fall away. Still there was much hard work and some perplexity, the Bristol connexion made themselves troublesome, and the ordinary business was the heavier from the clerks being both so young and inexperienced that he was obliged to exercise close supervision. It was guessed, too, that he was not happy about the effect of the influx of wealth at home, and that he feared it would only add to the number of horses and debts.

He soon looked terribly fagged and harassed, and owned that he envied Mr. Hope, who had just received the promise of a district church, in course of building under Colonel Bury's auspices, about four miles from Fairmead. To work his way through the University and take Holy Orders had been Ulick's ambition; he would gladly have endured privation for such an object, and it did seem hard that such aspirations should be so absolutely frustrated, and himself forced into the stream of uncongenial, unintellectual toil, in so obscure and uninviting a sphere. The resignation of all lingering hope of escape, and the effort to be contented, cost him more than even his original breaking in; and Mr. Kendal one day found him sitting in his little office parlour unable to think or to speak under a terrible visitation of his autumnal tormentor, brow-ague.

This made Mr. Kendal take to serious expostulation. It was impossible to go on in this way; why did he not send for a brother to help him?

Ulick could not restrain a smile at the fruitlessness of thinking of assistance of this kind from his elder brothers, and as to little Redmond, the only younger one still to be disposed of, he hoped to do better things for him.

'Then send for a sister.'

He hoped he might bring Rose over when his aunt was gone, but he could not shut those two up together at any price.

Then,' said Mr. Kendal, rather angrily, 'get an experienced, trustworthy clerk, so as to be able to go from home, or give yourself some relaxation.'

'Yes, I inquired about such a person, but there's the salary; and where would be the chance of getting Redmond to school?'

'I think your father might see to that.'

Ulick had no answer to make to this. The legacy to Mrs. O'More might nearly as well have been thrown into the sea.

'Well,' said Mr. Kendal, walking about the room, 'why don't you keep a horse?'

'As a less costly animal than brother, sister, or clerk?' said Ulick, laughing.

'Your health will prove more costly than all the rest if you do not take care.'

'Well, my aunt told me it would be respectable and promote confidence if I lived like a gentleman and kept my horse. I'll see about it,' said Ulick, in a more persuadable tone.

The seeing about it resulted in the arrival of a genuine product of county Galway, a long-legged, raw-boned hunter, with a wild, frightened eye, quivering, suspicious-looking ears, and an ill-omened name compounded of kill and of kick, which Maurice alone endeavoured to pronounce; also an outside car, very nearly as good as new. This last exceeded Ulick's commission, but it had been such a bargain, that Connel had not been able to resist it, indeed it cost more in coming over than the original price; but Ulick nearly danced round it, promising Mrs. and Miss Kendal that when new cushioned and new painted they would find it beat everything.

He was not quite so envious of Mr. Hope when he devoted the early morning hours to Killye-kickye, as the incorrect world called his steed, and, if the truth must be told, he first began to realize the advantages of wealth, when he set his name down among the subscribers to the hounds.

Nor was this the only subscription to which he was glad to set his name; there were others where Mr. Dusautoy wanted funds, and Mr. Kendal's difficulties were lessened by having another lord of the soil on his side. Some exchanges brought land enough within their power to make drainage feasible, and Ulick started the idea that it would be better to locate the almshouses at the top of the hill, on the site of Madame Belmarche's old house, than to place them where Tibb's Alley at present was, close to the river, and far from church.

Mr. Kendal's plans were unpopular, and two or three untoward circumstances combined to lead to his being regarded as a tyrant. He could not do things gently, and had not a conciliating manner. Had he been more free spoken, real oppression would have been better endured than benefits against people's will. He interfered to prevent some Sunday trading; and some of the Tibb's Alley tenants who ought to have gone at midsummer, chose to stay on and set him at defiance till they had to be forcibly ejected; whereupon Ulick O'More showed that he was not thoroughly Anglicised by demanding if, under such circumstances, it was safe to keep the window shutters unclosed at night, Mr. Kendal's head was such a beautiful mark under the lamp.

If not a mark for a pistol, he was one for the disaffected blackguard papers, which made up a pathetic case of a helpless widow with her bed taken away from under her, ending with certain vague denunciations which were read with roars of applause at the last beer shop which could not be cleared till Christmas, while the closing of the rest sent herds thither; and papers were nightly read; representing the Nabob expelling the industrious from the beloved cottages of their ancestors, by turns, to swell his own overgrown garden, or to found a convent, whence, as a disguised Jesuit, he meant to convert all Bayford to popery.

As Albinia wrote to Genevieve, they were in a state of siege, for only in the middle of the day did Mr. Kendal allow the womankind to venture out without an escort, the evening was disturbed by howlings at the gate, and all sorts of petty acts of spite were committed in the garden, such as injuring trees, stealing fruit, and carrying off the children's rabbits. Let that be as it might, Genevieve owned herself glad to come to hospitable Willow Lawn, though sorry for the cause.

Poor Mr. Rainsforth, after vainly striving to recruit his health at Torquay during the vacation, had been sentenced to give up his profession, and ordered to Madeira, and Genevieve was upon the world again.

The Kendals claimed her promise of a long visit, or rather that she should come home, and take time and choice in making any fresh engagement, nay, that she should not even inquire for a situation till after Christmas. And after staying to the last moment when she could help the Rainsforths, she proposed to spend a day or two with her aunt at the convent, and then come to her friends at Bayford.

Mr. Kendal drove his ladies to fetch her. He had lately indulged the household with a large comfortable open carriage with two horses, a rival to Mr. O'More's notable car, where he used to drive in an easy lounging fashion on one side, with Hyder Ali to balance him on the other.

This was a grand shopping day, an endless business, and as the autumn day began to close in, even Mr. Kendal's model patience was nearly exhausted before they called for their little friend. There was something very sweet and appropriate in her appearance; her dress, without presuming to share their mourning, did not insult it by gay colouring; it was a quiet dark violet and white checked silk, a black mantle, and black velvet bonnet with a few green leaves to the lilac flowers, and the face when at rest was softly pensive, but ready to respond with cheerful smiles and grateful looks. She had become more English, and had dropped much foreign accent and idiom, but without losing her characteristic grace and power of disembarrassing those to whom she spoke, and in a few moments even Sophy had lost all sense of meeting under awkward or melancholy circumstances, and was talking eagerly to her dear old sympathizing friend.

There was a great exchange of tidings; Genevieve had much to tell of her dear Rainsforths, the many vicissitudes of anxiety in which she had shared, and of the children's ways of taking the parting; and of the dear little Fanny who seemed to have carried away so large a piece of her susceptible heart, that Sophy could not help breaking out, 'Well, I do think it is very hard to make yourself a bit of a mother's heart, only to have it torn out again.'

Albinia smiled, and said, 'After all, Sophy, happiness in this world is in such loving, only we don't find it out till the rent has been made.'

'And some people can get fond of anything,' said Sophy.

'I'm sure,' said Genevieve, 'every one is so kind to me I can't help it.'

'I was not blaming you,' said Sophy. 'People are the better for it, but I cannot like except where I esteem, and that does not often come.'

'Oh! don't you think so?' cried Genevieve.

'I don't mean moderate approval. That may extend far, and with it good-will, but there is a deep, concentrated feeling which I don't believe those who like every one can ever have, and that is life.'

Perhaps the deepening twilight favoured the utterance of her feelings, for, as they were descending a hill, she said, 'Mamma, that was the place where Maurice was brought back to me.'

She had before passed it in silence, but in the dark she was not afraid of betraying the expression that the thrill of exquisite recollection brought to her countenance; and leaning back in her corner indulged in listening to the narration, as Albinia, unaware of the special point of the episode, related Maurice's desperate enterprise, going on to dilate on the benefit of having Mr. O'More at the bank rather than Andrew Goldsmith.

'Ah!' said Genevieve, 'it is he who wants to pull down our dear old house. I shall quarrel with him.'

'Genevieve making common cause with the obstructives of Bayford, as if he had not enemies enough!'

'What's that light in the sky?' exclaimed Sophy, starting up to speak to her father on the driving seat.

'A bonfire,' said Mr. Kendal. 'If we had remembered that it was the 5th of November, we would not have stayed out so late.' The next moment he drew up the horses, exclaiming, 'Mr. Hope, will you have a lift?'

Mr. Hope, rather to the ladies' surprise, took the vacant place beside Sophy, instead of climbing up to the box. He had been to see his intended parish, and was an enviable man, for he was as proud of it as if it had been an intended wife, and Albinia, who knew it for a slice of dreary heath, was entertained with his raptures. Church, schools, and parsonage, each in their way were perfection or at least promised to be, and he had never been so much elevated or so communicative. The speechless little curate seemed to have vanished.

The road, as may be remembered, did not run parallel with the curve of the river, but cutting straight across, entered Bayford over the hill, passing a small open bit of waste land, where stood a few cottages, the outskirts of the town.

Suddenly coming from an overshadowed lane upon this common, a glare of light flashed on them, showing them each other's faces, and casting the shadow of the carriage into full relief. The horses shied violently, and they beheld an enormous bonfire raised on a little knoll about twenty yards in front of them, surrounded by a dense crowd, making every species of hideous noise.

Mr. Kendal checked the horses' start, and Mr. Hope sprang to their heads. They were young and scarcely trustworthy, their restless movements showed alarm, and it was impossible to turn them without both disturbing the crowd and giving them a fuller view of the object of their terror. Mr. Kendal came down, and reconnoitring for a moment, said, 'You had better get out while we try to lead them round, we will go home by Squash Lane.'

Just then a brilliant glow of white flame, and a tremendous roar of applause, put the horses in such an agony, that they would have been too much for Mr. Hope, had not Mr. Kendal started to his assistance, and a man standing by likewise caught the rein. He was a respectable carpenter who lived on the heath, and touching his hat as he recognised them, said, 'Sir, if the ladies would come into my house, and you too, sir. The people are going on in an odd sort of way, and Mrs. Kendal would be frightened. I'll take care of the carriage.'

Mr. Kendal went to the side of the carriage, and asked the ladies if they were alarmed.

'O no!' answered Albinia, 'it is great fun;' and as the horses fidgeted again, 'it feels like a review.'

'You had better get out,' he said; 'I must try to back the horses till I can turn them without running over any one. Will you go into the house? You did not expect to find Bayford so riotous,' he added with a smile, as he assisted Genevieve out.

'You are not going to get up again,' said Albinia, catching hold of him, and in her dread of his committing himself to the mercy of the horses, returning unmeaning thanks to the carpenter's urgent requests that she would take refuge in his house.

In fact, the scene was new and entertaining, and on the farther side of the road, sheltered by the carriage, the party were entirely apart from the throng, which was too much absorbed to notice them, only a few heads turning at the rattling of the harness, and the ladies were amused at the bright flame, and the dark figures glancing in and out of the light, the shouts of delight and the merry faces.

'There's Guy Fawkes,' cried Albinia, as a procession of scarecrows were home on chairs amid thunders of acclamation; 'but whom have they besides? Here are some new characters.'

'Most lugubrious looking,' said Genevieve. 'I cannot make out the shouts.'

'It is the Nabob,' said Mr. Kendal. 'Perhaps you do not know that is my alias. This is my execution.'

The carpenter implored them to come in, and Mr. Hope added his entreaties, but Mr. Kendal would not leave the horses, and the ladies would not leave him; and they all stood still while his effigy was paraded round the knoll, the mark of every squib, the object of every invective that the rabble could roar out at the top of their voices. Jesuits and Papists; Englishmen treated like blackamoor slaves in the Indies; honest folk driven out of house and home; such was the burthen of the cries that assailed the grim representative carried aloft, while the real man stood unmoved as a statue, his tall, powerful figure unstirred, his long driving-whip resting against his shoulder without betraying the slightest motion, neither firm lip nor steady eye changing. Genevieve, with tears in her eyes, exclaimed, 'Oh! this is madness! Will no one tell them how wicked they are?'

'Never mind, my dear,' said Mr. Kendal, pressing the hand that in her fervour she had laid on his arm, 'they will come to their senses in time. No, Mr. Hope, I beg you will not interfere, they are in no state for it; they have done no harm as yet.'

'I wonder what the police are about?' cried Albinia, indignantly.

'They are too few to do any good,' said Mr. Kendal. 'It may be better that they are not incensing the mob. It will all go off quietly when this explosion has relieved their feelings.'

They felt as if there were something grand in this perfectly dispassionate reception of the outrage, and they stood awed and silenced, Sophy leaning on him.

'It will soon be over now,' he said, 'they are poking up the name to receive me.'

'Hark! what's that?'

The mob came swaying back, and a rich voice swelled above all the din, 'Boys, boys, is it burning your friends you are? Then, for the first time, Mr. Kendal started, and muttered, 'foolish lad! is he here?'

Confused cries rose again, but the other voice gained the mastery.

'So you call that undertaker-looking figure there Mr. Kendal. Small credit to your taste. You want to burn him. What for?'

'For being a Nabob and a tyrant,' was the shout.

'Much you know of Nabobs! No; I'll tell you what it's for. It is because his son got his death fighting for his queen and his country a year ago, and on his death-bed bade him do his best to drive the fever from your doors, and shelter you and save you from the Union in your old age. Is that a thing to burn him for?'

'We want no Irish papists here!' shouted a blackguard voice.

'Serve him with the same sauce.'

'I never was a papist,' was the indignant reply. 'No more was he; but I've said that the place shan't disgrace itself, and—'

'I'm with you,' shouted another above all the howls of the mob. 'Gilbert Kendal was as kind-hearted a chap as ever lived, and I'll see no wrong done to his father.'

Tremendous uproar ensued; then the well-known tones pealed out again, 'I've given my word to save his likeness. Come on, boys. Hurrah for Kendal!'

The war-cry was echoed by a body of voices, there was a furious melee and a charge towards the Nabob, who rocked and toppled down, while stragglers came pressed backwards on all sides.

'Here, Hope, take care of them. Stay with them,' said Mr. Kendal, putting the whip into the curate's hand, and striding towards the nucleus of the fray, through the throng who were driven backwards.

'O'More,' he called, 'what's all this? Give over! Are you mad?' and then catching up, and setting on his legs, a little fallen boy, 'Go home; get out of all this mischief. What are you doing? Take home that child,' to a gaping girl with a baby. 'O'More, I say, I'll commit every man of you if you don't give over.'

He was recognised, and those who had little appetite for the skirmish gave back from him; but the more reckless and daring small fry began shrieking, 'The Nabob!' and letting off crackers and squibs, through which he advanced upon the knot of positive combatants, who were exchanging blows over his prostrate image in front of the fire.

One he caught by the collar, in the act of aiming a blow. The fist was instantly levelled at him, with the cry, 'You rascal! what do you mean by it?' But the fierce struggle failed to shake off the powerful grasp; and at the command, 'Don't be such a fool!' Ulick burst out, 'Murder! 'tis himself!' and in the surprise was dragged some paces before recovering his perceptions.

The cry of police had at the same instant produced a universal scattering, and five policemen, coming on the ground, found scarcely any one to separate or capture. Mr. Kendal relaxed his hold, saying, 'You are my prisoner.'

'I didn't think you'd been so strong,' said Ulick, shaking himself, and looking bewildered. 'Where's the effigy?'

'What's that to you. Come away, like a rational being.'

'Ha! what's that?' as a frightful, agonizing shriek rent the air, and a pillar of flame came rushing across the now open space. It was a child, one mass of fire, and flying, in its anguish, from all who would have seized it. One moment of horror, and it had vanished! The next, Genevieve's voice was heard crying, 'Bring me something more to press on it.' She had contrived to cross its path with her large carriage rug, and was kneeling over it, forcing down the rug to smother the flames. Mr. Hope brought her a shawl, and they all stood round in silent awe.

'The poor child will be stifled,' said Albinia, kneeling down to help to unfold its face.

Poor little face, distorted with terror and agony! One of the policemen recognised it as the child of the public-house in Tibb's Alley. There were moans, but no one dared to uncover the limbs; and the policeman and Mr. Hope proposed carrying it at once to Mr. Bowles, and then home. Mr. Kendal desired that it should be laid on the seat of the carriage, which he would drive gently to the doctor's. Genevieve got in to watch over the poor little boy, and the others walked on by the side, passed the battle-field, now entirely deserted, too much shocked for aught but conjectures on his injuries, and the cause of the misfortune. Either he must have been pushed in on the fire by the runaway rabble, or have trod upon some of the scattered combustibles.

Mr. Bowles desired that the child should be taken home at once, promising to follow instantly; so at the entrance of Tibb's Alley, the carriage stopped, and Mr. Hope lifted out the poor little wailing bundle. Albinia was following, but a decided prohibition from her husband checked her. 'I would not have either of you go to that house on any account. Tell them to send to us for whatever they want, but that is enough.'

There was no gainsaying such a command, but as they reached the door of Willow Lawn, Mr. Kendal exclaimed, 'Where is Miss Durant?'

'She is gone with the little boy,' said Sophy. 'She told me she hoped you would not be displeased. Mr. Hope will take care of her, and she will soon come in.'

'Every one is mad to-night!' cried Mr. Kendal. 'In such a place as that! I will go for her directly.'

'Pray don't,' said Albinia, 'no one could speak a rude word to her on such an errand. She and Mr. Hope will be much more secure from incivility without you.'

'I believe it may be so, but I wish—'

His wish was broken off, for his little Albinia, screaming, 'Papa! papa!' clung to him in a transport of caresses, which Maurice explained by saying, 'Little Awkey has been crying, mamma, she thought they were burning papa in the bonnie.'

'Papa not burnt!' cried little Awkey, patting his cheeks, and laying her head on his shoulders alternately, as he held her to his breast. 'Naughty people wanted to make a fire, but they sha'n't burn papa or poor Guy Fawkes, or any of the good men.'

'And where were you, Ulick?' cried Maurice, in an imperious, injured way. 'You said once, perhaps you would take me to see the fire; and I went up to the bank, and they said you were gone, and it was glaring so in the sky, and I did so want to go.'

'I am glad you stayed away, my man,' said Albinia.

'I did want to go,' said Maurice; 'and I ran up to the top of the street, and there was Mr. Tritton; and he said if I liked a lark, he would take care of me; but—' and there he stopped short, and the colour came into his face.

Albinia threw her arm round him, and kissed him, saying, 'My trusty boy! and so you came home?'

'Yes; and there was Awkey crying about their burning papa, and she would not go up to the garret-window to see the fire, nor do anything.'

'Why, what is the sword here for?' exclaimed Sophy, finding it on the stairs.

'Because then Awkey was not so afraid.'

For once, Maurice had been exemplary, keeping from the tempting uproar, and devoting himself to soothing his little sister. It was worth all the vexations of the evening; but he went on to ask if Ulick could not take him now, if the fire was not out yet.

'Not exactly,' said Mr. Kendal, drily.

'I beg your pardon, Mr. Kendal,' said Ulick, who had apparently only just resumed the use of speech; 'don't know what I may have done when you collared me, but I'd no more notion of its being you than the Lord Lieutenant.'

'And pray what took you there?' asked Mr. Kendal. 'The surprise was quite as great to me.'

'Why,' said Ulick, 'one of the little lads of my Sunday class gave me a hint the other day that those brutes meant to have a pretty go to-night, and that Jackson was getting up a figure of the Nabob to break their spite upon. So I told my little fellow to give a hint to a few more of the right sort, and we'd go up together and not let the rascals have their own way.'

'Upon my word, I wonder what the Vicar will say to the use you make of his Sunday-school. Pretty work for his model teacher.'

'What better could the boys be taught than to fight for the good cause? Why, no one is a scratch the worse for it. And do you think we could sit by and see our best friend used worse than a dog?'

'Why not give notice to the police?'

'And would you have me hinder a fight?' cried Ulick, in the most Irish of all his voices.

'Oh! very well, if you like—only there will be a run on the bank to-morrow.'

'What has Ulick been doing, Sophy?' asked Maurice.

'Only what you would have done had you been older, Maurice,' she said, in a hurt voice; 'defending papa's effigy, for which he does not seem to meet with much gratitude.'

'Well,' said Mr. Kendal, who all the time had had more gratitude in his eyes than on his tongue, 'if the burning had had the same consequence as melting one's waxen effigy was thought to have, it might have been worth while to interfere, but I should have thought it more dignified in a respectable substantial householder to let those foolish fellows have their swing.'

'More dignified maybe,' smiled Albinia, 'but less like an O'More.'

'No, you are not going,' said Mr. Kendal; 'I shall not release my prisoner just yet.'

'You carried off all the honour of the day,' said Ulick. 'I had no notion you had such an arm. Why, you swung me round like a tom-cat, or—' and he exemplified the exploit upon Maurice, and was well buffeted.

'That's a little Irish blarney to propitiate me,' laughed Mr. Kendal, who certainly was in unusual spirits after his execution and rescue by proxy, but you wont escape prison fare.'

'There's no doubt who was the heroine of the day,' added Sophy. 'How one envies her!'

'What! your little governess friend?' said Ulick. 'Yes; she did show superior wit, when the rest of the world stood gaping round.'

'It was admirable—just like Genevieve's tenderness and dexterity,' said Albinia. 'I dare say she is doing everything for the poor little fellow.'

'Yes, admirable,' said Mr. Kendal; 'but you all behaved very creditably, ladies.'

'Ay,' said Albinia; 'not to scream is what a man thinks the climax of excellence in a woman.'

'It is generally all that is required,' said Mr. Kendal. I don't know what I should have done if poor Lucy had been there.'

Thereupon the ladies went upstairs, Maurice following Sophy to extract a full account of the skirmish. The imp probably had an instinct that she would think more of what redounded to Ulick O'More's glory than of what would be edifying to his own infant mind. It was doubtful how long it would be before Guy Fawkes would arrive at his proper standing in the little Awk's opinion, after the honour of an auto-da-fe in company with papa.

Mr. Hope escorted Genevieve home, and was kept to dinner. They narrated that they had found the public-house open, and the bar full of noisy runaways.

The burns were dreadful, but the surgeon did not think they would be fatal, and the child had held Genevieve's hand throughout the dressing, and seemed so unwilling to part with her, that she had promised to come again the next day, and had been thanked gratefully. There seemed no positive want of comforts, and there was every hope that all would do well.

Genevieve looked pale after the scene she had gone through, and could not readily persuade herself to eat, still less rally her spirits to talk; but she managed to avoid observation at dinner-time, and afterwards a rest on the sofa restored her. She evidently felt, as she said, that this was coming home, and her exquisite gift of tact making her perceive that she was to be at ease and on an equality, she assumed her position without giving her friends the embarrassment of installing her, and Mr. Hope was in such a state of transparent admiration, that Albinia could not help two or three times noiselessly clapping her hands under the table, and secretly thanking the rioters and their tag-rag and bob-tail for having provided a home for little Genevieve Durant.

There was indeed a pang as she thought of Gilbert; but she believed that Genevieve's heart had never been really touched, and was still fresh and open. She thought she might make Mr. Kendal and Sophy equally magnanimous. Perhaps by that time Sophy would be too happy to have leisure to be hurt, and she had little fear but that Mr. Kendal's good sense would conquer his jealousy for his son, though it might cost him something.

Two lovers to befriend at once! Two desirable attachments to foster! There was glory! Not that Albinia fulfilled her mission to a great extent; shamefacedness always restrained her, and she had not Emily's gift for making opportunities. Indeed, when she did her best, so perversely bashful were the parties, that the wrong pairs resorted together, the two who could talk being driven into conversation by the silence of the others.

Of Mr. Hope's sentiments there could be no doubt. He was fairly carried off his feet by the absorption of the passion, which was doubly engrossing because all ladies had hitherto appeared to him as beings with whom conversation was an impossible duty; but after all he had heard of Miss Durant, he might as a judicious man select her for an excellent parsoness, and as a young man fall vehemently in love. Nothing could be more evident to the lookers-on, but Albinia could not satisfy herself whether Genevieve had any suspicion.

She was not very young, knew something of the world, and was acute and observing; but on the other hand, she had made it a principle never to admit the thought of courtship, and she might not be sufficiently acquainted with the habits of the individual to be sensible of the symptomatic alteration.

She had begged the Dusautoys to make her leisure profitable, and spent much of her time upon the schools, on her little patient in Tibb's Alley, and in going about among the poor; she visited her old shopkeeper friends, and drank tea with them much oftener than gratified Mr. Kendal, talking so openly of the pleasure of seeing them again, that Albinia sometimes thought the blood of the O'Mores was a little chafed.

'There,' said Genevieve, completing a housewife, filled with needles ready threaded, 'I wonder whether the omnibus is too protestant to leave a parcel at the convent?'

'I don't think its scruples of conscience would withstand sixpence,' said Albinia.

'You might post it for less than that,' said Sophy.

'Don't you know,' said Ulick O'More, who was playing with the little Awk in the window, 'that the feminine mind loves expedients? It would be less commonplace to confide the parcel to the conductor, than merely let him receive it as guard of the mail bag and servant of the public.'

'Exactly,' laughed Genevieve. 'Think of the moral influence of being selected as bearer of a token of tenderness to my aunt on her fete, instead of being treated as a mere machine, devoid of human sympathies.'

'Sophy, where were we reading of a nation which gives the simplest transaction the air of a little romance?' said Ulick.

'And I have heard of a nation which denudes every action of sentiment, and leaves you the tree without the leaves,' was Genevieve's retort.

'That misses fire, Miss Durant; my nation does everything by the soul, nothing by mechanism.'

'When they *do* do it.'

'That's a defiance. You must deprive the conductor of the moral influence, whether as man or machine, and entrust the parcel to me.'

'That would be like chartering a steamer to send home a Chinese puzzle.'

'No, indeed; I must go to Hadminster. Bear me witness, Sophy, Miss Goldsmith wants me to talk to the house agent.'

'Mind, if you miss St. Leocadia's day, you will miss my aunt's fete.'

Mr. O'More succeeded in carrying off the little parcel. The next morning, as the ladies were descending the hill, a hurried step came after them, and the curate said in an abrupt rapid manner, 'I beg your pardon, I was going to Hadminster; could I do anything for you?'

'Nothing, thank you,' said Albinia, at whom he looked.

'Did I not hear—Miss Durant had some work to send her aunt to-day?'

'How did you know that, Mr. Hope?' exclaimed Genevieve.

'I heard something pass, when some one was admiring your work,'he said, not looking at her. 'And this—I think—is St. Leocadia's day.'

'I am very much obliged to you for remembering it, but I have sent my little parcel otherwise, so I need not trouble you.'

'Ah! how stupid in me! I am very sorry. I beg your pardon,' and he hurried off, looking as if very sorry were not a mere matter of course.

'Poor man,' thought Albinia, 'I dare say he has reckoned on it all this time, and hunted out St. Leocadia in Alban Butler, and then tried to screw up his courage all yesterday. Ulick has managed to traverse a romance, but perhaps it is just as well, for what would be the effect on the public of Mr. Hope in *that* coat being seen ringing at the convent door?'

'Well, Miss Durant,' said Ulick, entering the drawing-room in the winter twilight, 'here is evidence for you!'

'You have actually penetrated the convent, and seen my aunt? Impossible! and yet this pencilled note is her own dear writing!'

'You don't mean that you really were let in?' cried Sophy.

'I entered quite legitimately, I assure you. It was all luck. I'd just been putting up at the Crown, when what should I see in a sort of a trance, staring right into the inn-yard, but as jolly-looking a priest as ever held a station. "An' it's long since I've seen the like of you," says he aloud to himself. "Is it the car?" says I. "Sure it is," says he. "I've not laid my eyes on so iligant a vehicle since I left County Tyrone."'

'Mr. O'Hara!' exclaimed Genevieve.

'"And I'm mistaken if you're not the master of it," he goes on, taking the measure of me all over,' continued Ulick, putting on his drollest brogue. 'You see he had too much manners to say that such a personable young gentleman, speaking such correct English, could be no other than an Irishman, so I made my bow, and said the car and I were both from County Galway, and we were straight as good friends as if we'd hunted together at Ballymakilty. To be sure, he was a little taken aback when he found I was one of the Protestant branch, of the O'Mores, but a countryman is a countryman in a barbarous land, and he asked me to call upon him, and offered to do me any service in his power.'

'I am sure he would. He is the kindest old gentleman I know,' exclaimed Genevieve. 'He always used to bring me barleysugar-drops when I was a little girl, and it was he who found out our poor old Biddy in distress at Hadminster, and sent her to live with us.'

'Indeed! Then I owe him another debt of gratitude—in fact, he told me that one of his flock, meaning Biddy, had spoken to him honourably of me. "Well," said I, "the greatest service you could do me, sir, would be to introduce me to Mademoiselle Belmarche; I have a young lady's commission for her." "From my little Genevieve," he said, "the darling that she is. Did you leave the child well?" And so when I said it was a present for her saint's day, and that your heart was set on it—'

'But, Mr. O'More, I never did set my heart on your seeing her.'

'Well, well, you would have done it if you'd known there had been any chance of it, besides, your heart was set on her getting the work, and how could I make sure of that unless I gave it into her own hand? I wouldn't have put it into Mr. O'Hara's snuffy pocket to hinder myself from being bankrupt.'

'Then he took you in?'

'So he did, like an honest Irishman as he was. He rang at the bell and spoke to the portress, and had me into the parlour and sent up for the lady; and I have seldom spent a pleasanter hall-hour. Mademoiselle Belmarche bade me tell you that she would write fuller thanks to you another day, and that her eyes would thank you every night.'

'Was her cold gone? Did she seem well, the dear aunt?'

Genevieve was really grateful, and had many questions to ask about her aunt, which met with detailed answers.

'By-the-by,' said Ulick,' I met Mr. Hope in the street as I was coming away, I offered him a lift, but he said he was not coming home till late. I wonder what he is doing.'

Albinia and Sophy exchanged glances, and had almost said, 'Poor Mr. Hope!' It was very hard that the good fortune and mere good nature of an indifferent person should push him where the quiet curate so much wished to be. Albinia would have liked to have had either a little impudence or a little tact to enable her to give a hint to Ulick to be less officious.

St. Leocadia's feast was the 9th of December. Three days after, Genevieve received a letter which made her change countenance, and hurry to her own room, whence she did not emerge till luncheon-time.

In the late afternoon, there was a knock at the drawing-room door, and Mr. Dusautoy said, 'Can I speak with you a minute, Mrs. Kendal?'

Dreading ill news of Lucy, she hurried to the morning-room with him.

'Fanny said I had better speak to you. This poor fellow is in a dreadful state.'

'Algernon!'

'No, indeed. Poor Hope! What has possessed the girl?'

'Genevieve has not refused him?'

'Did you not know it? I found him in his rooms as white as a sheet! I asked what was the matter, he begged me to let him go away for one Sunday, and find him a substitute. I saw how it was, and at the first word he broke down and told me.'

'Was this to-day?'

'Yes. What can the silly little puss be thinking of to put an excellent fellow like that to so much pain? Going about it in such an admirable way, too, writing to old Mamselle first, and getting a letter from her which he sends with his own, and promising to guarantee her fifty pounds a year out of his own pocket. 'I should like to know what that little Jenny means by it. I gave her credit for more sense.'

'Perhaps she thinks, under the circumstances of her coming here, within the year—'

'Ah! very proper, very pretty of her; I never thought of that; I suppose I have your permission to tell Hope?'

'I believe all the town knew it,' said Albinia.

'Yes; he need not be downhearted, he has only to be patient, and he will like her the better for it. After all, though he is as good a man as breathes, he cannot be Gilbert, and it will be a great relief to him. I'll tell him to put all his fancies about O'More out of his head.'

'Most decidedly,' said Albinia; 'nothing can be greater nonsense. Tell him by no means to go away, for when she finds that our feelings are not hurt, and has become used to the idea, I have every hope that she will be able to form a new—'

'Ay; ay; poor Gilbert would have wished it himself. It is very good of you, Mrs. Kendal; I'll put the poor fellow in spirits again.'

'Did you hear whether she gave any reasons?'

'Oh! I don't know—something about her birth and station; but that's stuff —she's a perfect lady, and much more.'

'And he is only a bookseller's son.'

'True, and though it might be awkward to have the parson's father-in-law cutting capers if he lived in the same town, yet being dead these fifteen or eighteen years, where's the damage?'

'Was that all?'

'I fancy that she said she never meant to marry, but that's all nonsense; she is the very girl that ought, and I hope you will talk to her and bring her to reason. There's not a couple in the whole place that I should be so glad to marry as those two.'

Albinia endeavoured to discuss the matter with Genevieve that night when they went upstairs. It was not easy to do, for Genevieve seemed resolved to wish her good-night outside her door, but she made her entrance, and putting her arm round her little friend's waist, said, 'Am I very much in your way, my dear? I thought you might want a little help, or at least a little talk.'

'Oh! Mrs. Kendal, I hoped you did not know!' and her eyes filled with tears.

Mr. Dusautoy told me, my dear; poor Mr. Hope's distress betrayed him, and Mr. Dusautoy was anxious I should—'

Genevieve did not let her finish, but exclaiming, 'I did not expect this from you, madame,' gave way to a shower of tears.

'My dear child, do we not all feel you the more one with ourselves for this reluctance?' said Albinia, caressing her fondly. 'It shall not be forced upon you any more till you can bear it.'

''Till!' exclaimed Genevieve, alarmed. 'Oh! do not say that! Do not hold out false hopes! I never shall!'

'I do not think you are a fair judge as yet, my dear.'

'I think I am,' said Genevieve, slowly, 'I must not let you love me on false pretences, dearest Mrs. Kendal. I do not think it is all for—for his sake—but indeed, though I must esteem Mr. Hope, I do not believe I could ever feel for him as—' then breaking off. 'I pray you, with all my heart, dearest friend, never to speak to me of marriage. I am the little governess, and while Heaven gives me strength to work for my aunt, and you let me call this my home, I am content, I am blessed. Oh! do not disturb and unsettle me!'

So imploringly did she speak, that she obliterated all thought of the prudent arguments with which Albinia had come stored. It was no time for them; there was no possibility of endeavouring to dethrone the memory of her own Gilbert, and her impulse was far more to agree that no one else could ever be loved, than to argue in favour of a new attachment. She was proud of Gilbert for being thus recollected, and doubly pleased with the widowed heart; nor was it till the first effect of Genevieve's tears had passed off that she began to reflect that the idea might become familiar, and that romance having been abundantly satisfied by the constancy of the Lancer, sober esteem might be the basis of very happy married affection.

Mr. Hope did not go away, but he shrank into himself, and grew more timid than ever, and it was through the Dusautoys that Albinia learnt that he was much consoled, and intended to wait patiently. He had written to Mdlle. Belmarche, who had been extremely disappointed, and continued to believe that so excellent and well brought up a young girl as her niece would not resist her wishes with regard to a young pastor so respectable.

Sophy, when made aware of what was going on, did not smile or shed a tear, only a strange whiteness came across her face. She made a commonplace remark with visible effort, nor was she quite herself for some time. It was as if the reference to her brother had stirred up the old wound. Genevieve seemed to have been impelled to manifest her determination of resuming her occupation, she wrote letters vigorously, answered advertisements, and in spite of the united protest of her friends, advertised herself as a young person of French extraction, but a member of the Church of England, accustomed to tuition, and competent to instruct in French, Italian, music, and all the ordinary branches of education. Address, G. C. D., Mr. Richardson's, bookseller, Bayford.

CHAPTER XXX.

Miss Goldsmith went to spend Christmas with an old friend, leaving Ulick more liberty than he had enjoyed for a long time. He used it a good deal at Willow Lawn, and was there of course on Christmas-day. After dinner the decoration of the church was under discussion. The Bayford neighbourhood was unpropitious to holly, and Sophy and Genevieve had hardly ever seen any, except that Genevieve remembered the sooty bits sold in London. Something passed about sending for a specimen from Fairmead, but Albinia said that would not answer, for her brother's children were in despair at the absence of berries, and had ransacked Colonel Bury's plantations in vain.

The next day, about twilight, Albinia and Sophy were arranging some Christmas gifts for the old women, in the morning-room; Genevieve was to come and help them on her return from the child in Tibb's Alley.

'Oh, here she comes, up the garden,' said Sophy, who was by the window.

Presently Albinia heard a strange sound as of tightened breath, and looking up saw Sophy deathly pale, with her eyes fixed on the window. In terror she flew to her side, but Sophy spoke not, she only clutched her hand with fingers cold and tight as iron, and gazed with dilated eyes. Albinia looked—

Ulick had come from the house—there was a scarlet-berried spray in Genevieve's hand, which she was trying to make him take again—his face was all pleading and imploring—she turned hastily from him, and they saw her cheek glowing with crimson—she tried to force back the holly spray—but her hand was caught—he was kissing it. No, she had rent it away—she had fled in through the conservatory—they heard the doors—she had rushed upto her own room.

Sophy's grasp grew more rigid—she panted for breath.

'My child! my child!' said Albinia, throwing her arms round her, expecting her to faint. 'Oh! could I have imagined such treason?' Her eyes flashed, and her frame quivered with indignation. 'He shall never come into this house again!'

'Mamma! hush!' said Sophy, releasing herself from her embrace, and keeping her body upright, though obliged to seat herself on the nearest chair. 'It is not treason,' she said slowly, as though her mouth were parched.

'Contemptible fickleness!' burst out Albinia, but Sophy implored silence by a gesture.

'No,' she said; 'it was a dream, a degrading, humiliating dream; but it is over.'

'There is no degradation except to the base trifler I once thought better things of.'

'He has not trifled,' said Sophy. 'Wait! hush!'

There was a composure about her that awed Albinia, who stood watching in suspense while she went to the bed-room, drank some water, cooled her brow, pushed back her hair, and sitting down again in the same collected manner, which gave her almost a look of majesty, she said, 'Promise me, mamma, that all shall go on as if this folly had never crossed our minds.'

'I can't! I can't, Sophy!' said Albinia in the greatest agitation. 'I can't *unknow* that you have been shamefully used.'

'Then you will lead papa to break his promise to Genevieve, and lower me not only in my own eyes, but in those of every one.'

'He little knew that he was bringing her here to destroy his daughter's happiness. So that was why she held off from Mr. Hope,' cried Albinia, burning with such indignation, that on some one she must expend it, but a tirade against the artfulness of the little French witch was cut off short by an authoritative—

'Don't, mamma! You are unjust! How can she help being loveable!'

'He had no business to know whether she was or not.'

'You are wrong, mamma. The absurdity was in thinking I ever was so.'

'Very little absurd,' said Albinia, twining her arms round Sophy.

'Don't make me silly,' hastily said Sophy, her voice trembling for a moment; 'I want to tell you all about it, and you will see that no one is to blame. The perception has been growing on me for a long time, but I was weak enough to indulge in the dream. It was very sweet!' There again she struggled not to break down, gained the victory, and went on, 'I don't think I should have dared to imagine it myself, but I saw others thought it, who knew more; I knew the incredible was sometimes true, and every little kindness he did—Oh! how foolish! as if he could help doing kindnesses! My better sense told me he did not really distinguish me; but there was something that *would* feed upon every word and look. Then last year I was wakened by the caricature business. That opened my eyes, for no one who had *that* in him would have turned my sister into derision. I was sullen then and proud, and when—when humanity and compassion brought him to me in my distress— oh! why—why could not I have been reasonable, and not have selfishly fed on what I thought was revived?'

'He had no right—' began Albinia, fiercely.

'He could neither help saving Maurice, nor speaking comfort and support when he found me exhausted and sinking. It was I who was the foolish creature—I hate myself! Well, you know how it has been—I liked to believe it was *the thing*—I knew he cared less for me than—but I thought it was always so between men and women, and that I would not have petty distrusts. But when she came, I saw what the true—true feeling is—I saw that he felt when she came into the room—I saw how he heard her words and missed mine—I saw—' Sophy collected herself, and spoke quietly and distinctly, 'I saw his love, and that it had never been for me.'

There was a pause; Albinia could not bear to look, speak, or move. Sophy's words carried conviction that swept away her sand castle.

'Now, mamma,' said Sophy, earnestly, 'you own that he has not been false or fickle.'

'If he has not, he has disregarded the choicest jewel that lay in his way,' said Albinia with some sharpness.

'But he has not been that,' persisted Sophy.

'Well—no; I suppose not.'

'And no one can be less to blame than Genevieve.'

'Little flirt, I've no patience with her.'

'She can't help her manners,' repeated Sophy, 'I feel them so much more charming than mine every moment. She will make him so happy.'

'What are you talking of, Sophy? He must be mad if he is in earnest. A man of his family pride! His father will never listen to it for a moment.'

'I don't know what his father may do,' said Sophy; 'but I know what I pray and entreat we may do, and that is, do our utmost to make this come to good.'

'Sophy, don't ask it. I could not, I know you could not.'

'There is no loss of esteem. I honour him as I always did,' said Sophy. 'Yes, the more since I see it was all for papa and the right, all unselfish, on that 5th of November. Some day I shall have worn out the selfishness.'

She kept her hand tightly pressed on her heart as she spoke, and Albinia exclaimed, 'You shall not see it; you overrate your strength; it is my business to prevent you!'

'Think, mamma,' said Sophy, rising in her earnestness. 'Here is a homeless orphan, whom you have taught to love you, whom papa has brought here as to a home, and for Gilbert's sake. Is it fair—innocent, exemplary as she is—to turn against her because she is engaging and I am not, to cut her off from us, drive her away to the first situation that offers, be it what it may, and with that thought aching and throbbing in her heart? Oh, mamma! would that be mercy or justice?'

'You are not asking to have it encouraged in the very house with you?'

'I do not see how else it is to be,' said Sophy.

'Let him go after her, if there's anything in it but Irish folly and French coquetry—'

'How, mamma? Where? When she is a governess in some strange place? How could he leave his business? How could she attend to him? Oh, mamma! you used to be kind: how can you wish to put two people you love so much to such misery?'

'Because I can't put one whom I love better than both, and who deserves it, to greater misery,' said Albinia, embracing her.

'Then do not put me to the misery of being ungenerous, and the shame of having my folly suspected.'

Albinia would have argued still, but the children came in, Sophy went away, and there was no possibility of a tete-a-tete. How strange it was to have such a tumult of feeling within, and know that the same must be tenfold multiplied in the hearts of those two girls, and yet go through all the domestic conventionalities, each wearing a mask of commonplace ease, as though nothing had happened!

Genevieve had, Albinia suspected, been crying excessively; for there was that effaced annihilated appearance that tears produced on her, but otherwise she did her part in answering her host, who was very fond of her, and always made her an object of attention. Albinia found herself betraying more abstraction, she was so anxiously watching Sophy, who acquitted herself best of all, had kept tears from her eyes, talked more than usual, and looked brilliant, with a bright colour dyeing her cheeks. She was evidently sustained by eagerness to obtain her generous purpose, and did not yet realize the price.

The spray of holly was lying as if it had been tossed in vexation upon the marble slab in the hall. Albinia, from the stairs, saw Sophy take it up, and waited to see what she would do with it. The Sophy she had once known would have dashed it into the flames, and then have repented. No! Sophy held it tenderly, and looked at the glossy leaves and coral fruit with no angry eye; she even raised it to her lips, but it was to pierce with one of the long prickles till her brow drew together at the smart, and the blood started. Then she began to mount the stairs, and meeting Albinia, said quietly, 'I was going to take this to Genevieve's room, it is empty now, but perhaps you had better take care of it for her, out of sight. It will be her greatest treasure to-morrow.'

Mr. Kendal read aloud as usual, but who of his audience attended? Certainly not Albinia. She sat with her head bent over her work, revolving the history of these last two years, and trying to collect herself after the sudden shock, and the angry feelings of disappointment that surged within, in much need of an object of wrath. Alas! who could that object be but that blind, warm-hearted, impulsive Mistress Albinia Kendal?

She saw plain enough, now it was too late, that there had not been a shadow of sentiment in that lively confiding Irishman, used to intimacy with a herd of cousins, and viewing all connexions as cousins. She remembered his conversation with her brother and her brother's impression; she thought of the unloverlike dread of ague in Emily's moonlight walk; she recalled the many occasions when she had thought him remiss, and she could not but acquit him of any designed flirtation, any dangerous tenderness, or what Mdlle. Belmarche would call legerete. He could not be reserved—he was naturally free and open—and how could she have put such a construction on his frankness, when Sophy herself had long been gradually arriving at a conviction of the truth! It was a comfort at least to remember that it had not been the fabrication of her own brain, she had respectable authority for the idea, and she trusted to its prompter to participate in her indignation, argue Ulick out of so poor a match, and at least put a decided veto upon Sophy's Spartan magnanimity—Sophy's health and feelings being the subject, she sometimes thought, which concerned him above all.

Ah! but the evil had not been his doing. He had but gossiped out a pleasant conjecture to his wife as a trustworthy help-meet. What business had she to go and telegraph that conjecture, with her significant eyes, to the very last person who ought to have shared it, and then to have kept up the mischief by believing it herself, and acting, looking, and arranging, as on a certainty implied, though not expressed? Mrs. Osborne or Mrs. Drury might have spoken more broadly, they could not have acted worse, thought she to herself.

The notion might never have been suggested; Sophy might have simply enjoyed these years of intimacy, and even if her heart had been touched, it would have been unconsciously, and the pain and shame of unrequited affection have merely been a slight sense of neglect, a small dreariness, lost in eagerness for the happiness of both friends. Now, two years of love that she had been allowed to imagine returned and sanctioned, and love with the depth and force of Sophy's whole nature—the shame of having loved unasked, the misery of having lived in a delusion—how would they act upon a being of her morbid tendency, frail constitution, and proud spirit? As Albinia thought of the passive endurance of last year's estrangement, her heart sank within her! Illness—brain-fever—permanent ill-health and crushed spirits—nay, death itself she augured—and all—all her own fault! The last and best of Edmund's children so cruelly and deeply wounded, and by her folly! She longed to throw herself at his feet and ask his pardon, but it was Sophy's secret as well as hers, and how could womanhood betray that unrequited love? At least she thought, for noble Sophy's sake, she would not raise a finger to hinder the marriage, but as to forwarding it, or promoting the courtship under Sophy's very eyes—that would be like murdering her outright, and she would join Mr. Kendal with all her might in removing their daughter from the trying spectacle. Talk of Aunt Maria! This trouble was ten thousand times worse!

Albinia began to watch the timepiece, longing to have the evening over, that she might prepare Mr. Kendal. It ended at last, and Genevieve took up her candle, bade good-night, and disappeared. Sophy lingered, till coming forward to her father as he stood by the fire, she said, 'Papa, did you not promise Gilbert that Genevieve should be as another daughter?'

'I wish she would be, my dear,' said Mr. Kendal; 'but she is too independent, and your mamma thinks she would consider it as a mere farce to call her little Albinia's governess, but if you can persuade her—'

'What I want you to do, papa, is to promise that she shall be married from this house, as her home, and that you will fit her out as you did Lucy.'

'Ha! Is she beginning to relent?'

'No, papa. It will be Ulick O'More.'

'You don't mean it!' exclaimed Mr. Kendal, more taken by surprise than perhaps he had ever been, and looking at his wife, who was standing dismayed, yet admiring the gallant girl who had forestalled her precautions. Obliged to speak, she said, 'I am afraid so, Sophy and I witnessed a scene to- day.'

'Afraid?' said Mr. Kendal; 'I see no reason to be afraid, if Ulick likes it. They are two of the most agreeable and best people that ever fell in my way, and I shall be delighted if they can arrange it, for they are perfectly suited to each other.'

'But such a match!' exclaimed Albinia.

'As to that, a sensible, economical wife will be worth more to him than an expensive one, with however large a fortune. And for the family pride, I am glad the lad has more sense than I feared; he has a full right to please himself, having won the place he has, and he may make his father consent. He wants a wife—nothing else will keep him from running headlong into speculation, for want of something to do. Yes, I see what you are thinking of, my dear, but you know we could not wish her, as you said yourself, never to form another attachment.'

'But *here*!' sighed Albinia, the ground knocked away from under her, yet still clinging to the last possible form of murmur.

'It will cost us something,' said Mr. Kendal, 'but no more than we will cheerfully bear, for the sake of one who has such claims upon us; and it will be amply repaid by having such a pair of friends settled close to us.'

'Then you will, papa?' said Sophy.

'Will do what, my dear?'

'Treat her as—as you did Lucy, papa.'

'And with much more pleasure, and far more hope, than when we fitted out poor Lucy,' said Mr. Kendal.

Sophy thanked him, and said 'Good-night;' and the look which accompanied her kiss to her step-mother was a binding over to secrecy and non-interference.

'Is she gone?' said Mr. Kendal, who had been musing after his last words. 'Gone to tell her friend, I suppose? I wanted to ask what this scene was.'

'Oh!' said Albinia, 'it was in the garden—we saw it from the window— only he brought her a bit of holly, and was trying to kiss her hand.'

'Strong premises, certainly. How did she receive the advance?'

'She would not listen, but made her escape.'

'Then matters are not in such a state of progress as for me to congratulate her? I suppose that you ladies are the best judges whether he may not meet with the same fate as poor Hope?'

'Sophy seems to take it for granted that he will not.'

'Irishman as he is, he must be pretty secure of his ground before coming to such strong measures. Well! I hope we may hear no more of brow-ague. But —' with sudden recollection—'I thought, Albinia, you fancied he had some inclination for Sophy?'

Was it not a good wife to suppress the 'You did'? If she could merrily have said, 'You told me so,' it would have been all very well, but her mood would admit of nothing but a grave and guarded answer—'We did fancy so, but I am convinced it was entirely without reason.'

That superior smile at her lively imagination was more than human nature could bear, without the poor relief of an entreaty that he would not sit meditating, and go to sleep in his chair.

Albinia thought she had recovered equanimity during her night's rest, but in the midst of her morning toilette, Sophy hurried in, exclaiming, 'She'll go away! She is writing letters and packing!' and she answered, 'Well, what do you want me to do? You don't imagine that I can rush into her room and lay hands on her? She will not go upon a wishing-carpet. It will be time to interfere when we know more of the matter.'

Sophy looked blank, and vanished, and Albinia felt excessively vexed at having visited on the chief sufferer her universal crossness with all mankind. She knew she had only spoken common sense, but that made it doubly hateful; and yet she could not but wish Miss Durant anywhere out of sight, and Mr. O'More on the top of the Hill of Howth.

At breakfast, Sophy's looks betrayed nothing to the uninitiated, though Albinia detected a feverish restlessness and covert impatience, and judged that her sleep had been little. Genevieve's had perhaps been less, for she was very sallow, with sunken eyes, and her face looked half its usual size; but Albinia could not easily have compassion on the poor little unwitting traitress, even when she began, 'Dear Mrs. Kendal, will you excuse me if I take a sudden leave? I find it will answer best for me to accept Mrs. Elwood's invitation; I can then present myself to any lady who may wish to see me, and, as I promised my aunt another visit, I had better go to Hadminster by the three o'clock omnibus.'

Albinia was thankful for the loud opposition which drowned the faint reluctance of her own; Mr. Kendal insisting that she should not leave them; little Awk coaxing her; and Maurice exclaiming, 'If the ladies want her, let them come after her! One always goes to see a horse.'

'I'm not so well worth the trouble, Maurice.'

'I know Ulick O'More *would* come in to see you when all the piebalds for the show were going by!'

'Some day you will come to the same good taste,' said his father, to lessen the general confusion.

'See a lady instead of a piebald? Never!' cried Maurice with indignation, that made the most preoccupied laugh; under cover of which Genevieve effected a retreat. Sophy looked imploringly at Albinia—Albinia was moving, but not with alacrity, and Mr. Kendal was saying, 'I do not understand all this,' when, scarcely pausing to knock, Ulick opened the door, cheeks and eyes betraying scarcely repressed eagerness.

'What—where,' he stammered, as if even his words were startled away; 'is not Miss Durant well?'

'She was here just this moment,' said Mr. Kendal.

'I will go and see for her,' said Sophy. 'Come, children.'

Whether Sophy's powers over herself or over Genevieve would avail, was an anxious marvel, but it did not last a moment, for Maurice came clattering down to say that Genevieve was gone out into the town. In such a moment! She must have snatched up her bonnet, and fled one way while Ulick entered by the other. He made one step forward, exclaiming, 'Where is she gone?' then pausing, broke out, 'Mrs. Kendal, you must make her give me a hearing, or I shall go mad!'

'A hearing?' repeated Mrs. Kendal, with slight malice.

'Yes; why, don't you know?'

'So your time has come, Ulick, has it?' said Mr. Kendal.

'Well, and I were worse than an old ledger if it had not, when she was before me! Make her listen to me, Mrs. Kendal, if she do not, I shall never do any more good in this world!'

'I should have thought,' said Albinia, 'that an Irishman would be at no loss for making opportunities.'

'You don't know, Mrs. Kendal; she is so fenced in with scruples, humility —I know not what—that she will not so much as hear me out. I'm not such a blockhead as to think myself worthy of her, but I do think, if she would only listen to me, I might stand a chance: and she runs off, as if she thought it a sin to hear a word from my mouth!'

'It is very honourable to her,' said Mr. Kendal.

'Very honourable to her,' replied Ulick, 'but cruelly hard upon me.'

'I think, too,' continued Mr. Kendal, stimulated thereto by his lady's severely prudent looks, 'that you ought—granting Miss Durant to be, as I well know her to be, one of the most excellent persons who ever lived—still to count the cost of opening such an affair. It is not fair upon a woman to bring her into a situation where disappointments may arise which neither may be able to bear.'

'Do you mean my family, Mr. Kendal? Trust me for getting consent from home. You will write my father a letter, saying what you said just now; Mrs.

Kendal will write another to my mother; and I'll just let them see my heart is set on it, and they'll not hold out.'

'Could you bear to see her—looked down on?' said Albinia.

'Ha!' he cried, with flashing eyes. 'No, believe me, Mrs. Kendal, the O'Mores have too much gentle blood to do like that, even if she were one whom any one could scorn. Why, what is my mother herself but a Goldsmith by birth, and I'd like to see who would cast it up to any of the family that she was not as noble as an O'More! And Genevieve herself—isn't every look and every movement full of the purest gentility her fathers' land can show?'

'I dare say, once accepted, the O'Mores would heartily receive her; but here, in this place, there are some might think it told against you, and might make her uncomfortable.'

'What care I? I've lived and thriven under Bayford scorn many a day. And for her—Oh! I defy anything so base to wound a heart so high as hers, and with me to protect her!'

'And you can afford it?' said Mr. Kendal. 'Remember she has her aunt to maintain.'

'I can,' said Ulick. 'I have gone over it all again and again; and recalling his man-of-business nature, he demonstrated that even at present he was well able to support Mdlle. Belmarche, as well as to begin housekeeping, and that there was every reason to believe that his wider and more intelligent system of management would continue to increase his income.'

'Well, Ulick,' said Mr. Kendal at last, 'I wish you success with all my heart, and esteem you for a choice so entirely founded upon the qualities most certain to ensure happiness.'

'You don't mean to say that she has not the most glorious eyes, the most enchanting figure!' exclaimed Ulick, affronted at the compliment that seemed to aver that Genevieve's external charms were not equal to her sterling merit.

Mr. Kendal and Albinia laughed; and the former excused himself, not quite to the lover's satisfaction, by declaring the lady much more attractive than many regularly handsome people; but he added, that what he meant was, that he was sure the attachment was built upon a sound foundation. Then he entreated that Mrs. Kendal would persuade her to listen to him, for she had fled from him ever since his betrayal of his sentiments till he was half crazed, and had been walking up and down his room all night. He should do something distracted, if not relieved from suspense before night! And Mr. Kendal got rid of him in the midst of his transports, and turning to Albinia said, 'We must settle this as fast as possible, or he will lose his head, and get into a scrape.'

'I do not like such wild behaviour. It is not dignified.'

'It is only temperament,' said Mr. Kendal. 'Will you speak to her?'

'Yes, whenever she comes in.'

'I suspect she has gone out on purpose. Could you not go to find her at the school, or wherever she is likely to be?'

'I don't know where to find her. I cannot give up the children's lessons. Nothing hurts Maurice so much as irregularity.'

He made no answer, but his look of disappointment excited her to observe to herself that she supposed he expected her to run all over the town without ordering dinner first, and she wondered how he would like that!

Presently she heard him go out at the front door, and felt some contrition.

She had not the heart to seek Sophy to report progress, and did not see her till about eleven o'clock, when she came in hastily with her bonnet on, asking, 'Well, mamma?'

'Where have you been, Sophy?'

'To school,' she said. 'Has anything happened?'

'We have had it out, and I am to speak to her when she comes in,' said Albinia, glad as perhaps was Sophy of the enigmatical form to which Maurice's presence restrained the communication.

Sophy went away, but presently returning and taking up her work, but with eyes that betrayed how she was listening; but there was so entire an apparent absence of personal suffering, that Albinia began to discharge the weight from her mind, and believe that the sentiment had been altogether imaginary even on Sophy's side, and the whole a marvellous figment of her own.

At last, Mr. Kendal's foot was heard; Sophy started up, and sat down again. He came upstairs, and his face was all smiles.

'Well,' he said, 'I don't think she will go by the three o'clock omnibus.'

'You have spoken to her?' cried Albinia in compunction.

'Has Maurice finished? Then go out, my boy, for the present.'

'Well?' said Albinia, interrogatively, and Sophy laid down her work and crossed one hand over the other on her knees, and leant back as though to hinder visible tremor.

'Yes,' he said, going on with what had been deferred till Maurice was gone.

'I thought it hard on him—and as I was going to speak to Edwards, I asked if she were at the Union, where I found her, taking leave of the old women, and giving them little packets of snuff, and small presents, chiefly her own work, I am sure. I took her with me into the fields, and persuaded her at last to talk it over with me. Poor little thing! I never saw a more high-minded, conscientious spirit: she was very unhappy about it, and said she knew it was all her unfortunate manner, she wished to be guarded, but a little excitement and conversation always turned her head, and she entreated me not to hinder her going back to a school-room, out of the way of every one. I told her that she must not blame herself for being more than usually agreeable; but she would not listen, and I could hardly bring her to attend to what I said of young O'More. Poor girl! I believe she was running away from her own heart.'

'You have prevented her?' cried Sophy.

'At least I have induced her to hear his arguments. I told her my opinion of him, which was hardly needed, and what I thought might have more weight— that he has earned the right to please himself, and that I believed she would be better for him than riches. She repeated several times "Not now," and "Not here;" and I found that she was shocked at the idea of the subject being brought before us. I was obliged to tell her that nothing would gratify any of us so much, and that this was the time to fulfil her promise of considering me as a father.'

'Oh, thank you,' murmured Sophy.

'So finally I convinced her that she owed Ulick a hearing, and I think she felt that to hear was to yield. She had certainly been feeling that flight was the only measure, and between her dread of entrapping him and of hurting our feelings, had persuaded herself it was her duty. The last thing she did was to catch hold of me as I was going, and ask if he knew what her father was.'

'I dare say it has been the first thing she has said to him,' said Albinia. 'She is a noble little creature! But what have you done with them now?'

'I brought him to her in the parsonage garden. I believe they are walking in the lanes,' said Mr. Kendal, much gratified with his morning's work.

'She deserves him,' said Sophy; and then her eyes became set, as if looking into far distance.

The walk in the lanes had not ended by luncheon-time, and an afternoon loaded with callers was oppressive, but Sophy kept up well. At last, in the twilight, the door was heard to open, and Genevieve came in alone. They listened, and knew she must have run up to her own room. What did it portend? Albinia must be the one to go and see, so after a due interval, she went up and knocked. Genevieve opened the door, and threw herself into her arms. 'Dear Mrs. Kendal! Oh! have I done wrong? I am so very happy, and I cannot help it!'

Albinia kissed her, and assured her she had done nothing to repent of.

'I am so glad you think so. I never dreamt such happiness could be meant for me, and I am afraid lest I should have been selfish and wrong, and bring trouble on him.'

'We have been all saying you deserve him.'

'Oh no—no—so good, so noble, so heroic as he is. How could he think of the poor little French teacher! And he will pay my aunt's fifty pounds! I told him all, and he knew it before, and yet he loves me! Oh! why are people so very good to me?'

'I could easily find an answer to that question,' said Albinia. 'Where is he, my dear?'

'He is gone home. I would not come into the town with him. It is nothing, you know; no one must hear of it, for he must be free unless his parents consent—and I know they never can,' she said, shaking her head, sadly, 'but even then I shall have one secret of happiness—I shall know what has been! But oh! Mrs. Kendal, let me go away—'

'Go away now?' exclaimed Albinia.

'Yes—it cannot be—here, in this house! Oh! it is outraging your kindness.'

'No,' said Albinia; 'it is but letting us fulfil a very precious charge.'

Genevieve's tears flowed as she said, 'Such goodness! Mr. Kendal spoke to me in this way in the morning, when he was more kind and patient than I can express. But tell me, dearest madame, tell me candidly, is my remaining here the cause of any secret pain to him?'

With regard to him, Albinia could answer sincerely that it was a gratification; and Genevieve owned that she should be glad to await the letters from Ireland, which she tried to persuade herself she believed would put an end to everything, except the precious remembrance.

Sophy here came in with some tea. She had recollected that Genevieve had wandered all day without any bodily sustenance.

There was great sweetness in the quiet, grave manner in which she bent over her friend and kissed her brow. All she said was, 'Papa had goes to fetch him to dinner. Genevieve, you must let me do your hair.'

It was in Genevieve's eyes an astonishing fancy, and Albinia said, 'Come away now, my dear; she must have a thorough rest after such a day.'

Genevieve looked too much excited for rest, but that was the more reason for leaving her to herself; and besides, it was so uncomfortable not to be able to be kind enough.

However, when people are happy, a little kindness goes a great way, and there was a subdued lustre like a glory in her eyes when she came downstairs, with the holly leaves and berries glistening in her hair, the first ornament she had ever worn there.

'It was Sophy's doing,' she said. 'Naughty girl; she tried to take me by surprise. She would not let me look in the glass, but I guessed—and oh! she was wounding her poor hands so sadly.'

I must thank her,' said Ulick, looking ecstatic. 'Why does she not come down?'

As she did not appear, Albinia went up, doubtful if it were wise, yet too uneasy not to go in quest of her.

It was startling to have so faint an answer on knocking, and on entering the room, she saw Sophy lying on her bed, upon her back, with her arms by her sides, and with a ghastly whiteness on her features.

Scarcely a pulse could be felt, and her hands were icy cold, her voice sank to nothing, her eyelids scarcely raised, as if the strain of the day had exhausted all vital warmth or energy, and her purpose accomplished, annihilation was succeeding. Much terrified, Albinia would have hurried in search of remedies, but she raised her hand imploringly, and murmured, 'Please don't. I'm not faint—I'm not ill. If you would only let me be still.'

Albinia teased her so far as to cover her with warmed shawls, and force on her a stimulant. She shut her eyes, but presently opened them to say, 'Please go.'

She was so often unable to appear at dinner, that no observation was made; and it was to be feared that her absence was chiefly regretted by the lovers, because it prevented them from sitting on the same side of the table.

Always frank and unrestrained, Ulick made his felicity so apparent, that Albinia had no toleration for him, and not much for the amusement it afforded Mr. Kendal. She would have approved of her husband much more if he had put her into a great quandary by anxious inquiries what was the matter with his daughter, instead of that careless, 'O you are going up to Sophy; I hope she will be able to come down to tea,' when she left him on guard over the children and the lovers.

'So it is with woman's martyrdoms,' said she to herself as she walked upstairs, chewing the cud of all the commonplaces by which women have, of late years, flattered themselves, and been flattered; 'but at any rate I'll have her out of sight of all their absurdity. It is enough to kill her!'

Sophy hardly stirred at her entrance, but there was less ghastliness about her, and as Albinia sat down she did not remove her hand, and turned slightly round, so as to lose that strange corpse-like attitude of repose.

'You are not so cold, dearest,' said Albinia. 'Have you slept?'

'I think not.'

'Are you better? Have you been comfortable?'

'Oh yes.' Then, with a pause, 'Yes—it was like being nothing!'

'You were not faint, I hope?'

'No—only lying still. Don't you know the comfort of not thinking or feeling?'

'Yes; this has been far too much for you. You have done enough now, my generous Sophy.'

'Not generous; one can't give away what one never had.'

'I think it more gracious to yield without jealousy or bitterness—'

'Only not quite base,' said Sophy. Then presently, turning on her pillow as though more willing to converse, she said, 'I am glad it was not last year.'

'We had troubles enough then!'

'Not for that—because I should have been base then, and hated myself for it all the time.'

'That you never could have been!' cried Albinia. 'But, my dear, you must let me contrive for you; I would not betray you for all the world, but the sight of these two is more than you ought to undergo. I will not send Genevieve away, but you must go from home.'

'I don't think I shall be cross,' said poor Sophy, simply; 'I should be ashamed.'

'Cross! It is I who am cross, because I am to blame; but, dearest, think if you are keeping up out of pride; that will never, never do.'

'I do not believe it is pride,' said Sophy, meekly; 'at least, I hope not. I feel humiliated enough, and I think it may be a sort of shame, as well as consideration for them, that would make me wish that no difference should be made. Do you not think we may let things go on?' she said, in so humble a manner, that it brought Albinia's tears, and a kiss was the only answer. 'Please tell me,' said Sophy; 'for I don't want to deceive myself.'

'I am sure I am no judge,' cried Albinia, 'after the dreadful mischief I have done.'

'The mischief was in me,' said Sophy, 'or you could not have done it. I saw it all when I was lying awake last night, and how it began, or rather it was before I can remember exactly. I always had craving after something—a yearning for something to fix myself on—and after I grew to read and look out into the world, I thought it must be that. And when I knew I was ugly and disagreeable, I brooded and brooded, and only in my better moments tried to be satisfied with you and papa and the children.'

'And the All-satisfying, Sophy dear.'

'I tried—I did—but it was duty—not heart. I used to fancy what might be, if I shot out into beauty and grace—not admiration, but to have that one thing to lean on. You see it was all worldly, and only submissive by fits—generally it was cross repining, yielding because I could not help it—and so, when the fancy came the throne was ready made, empty, swept, and garnished, for the idol. I wont talk of all that time; but I don't believe even Genevieve, though she knows she may, can dwell upon the thought as I did, in just the way to bring punishment. And so I thought, by-and-by, at the caricature time, that I was punished. I looked into the fallacy, when I had got over the temper and the pride, and I saw it all clear, and owned I was rightly served, for it had been an earthly aim, and an idol worship. Well, the foolish hope came back again, but indeed, indeed, I think I was the better for all the chastening; I had seen grandmamma die, I was fresh from hearing of Gilbert, and I did feel as I never had done before, that God was first. I don't believe that feeling had passed, though the folly came back, and made me feel glad to love all the world. There were—gleams of religions thought'—she spoke with difficulty, but her face had a strange beauty—'that taught me how, if I was more good— there could be a fulness of joy that all the rest flowed out from. And so when misgivings came, and I saw at times how little he could care for me—oh! it was pain enough, but not the worst sort. And yet I don't know—' She turned away and hid her face on the pillow. It was agony, though still, as she had said, not the worst, untempered by faith or resignation. What a history of that apparently cold, sullen, impassive spirit! what an unlocking of pent-up mysteries!

'It has been blessed to you,' said Albinia, affectionately. 'My dear, we always thought your character one that wanted the softening of such—an attachment. Perhaps that made me wrongly eager for it, and ready to imagine where I ought not; I think it did soften you; but if you had not conquered what was earthly and exaggerated in it, how it would be hardening and poisoning you now!'

'I hope I may have,' sighed Sophy, as if she were doubtful.

'Then will you not listen to me? You have done nobly so far, and I know your feelings will be right in the main; but do you think you can bear the perpetual irritation of being neglected, and seeing—what I *must* call rather a parade of his preference?'

'I think it would be the best cure,' said Sophy; 'it would make me feel it real, and I could be glad to see him—them—so happy—'

'I don't know how to judge! I don't know whether it be right for you to have him always before your mind.'

'He would be so all the more while I was away with nothing to do,' said Sophy; 'fancy might be worse than fact. You don't know how I used to forget the nonsense when he had been ten minutes in the room, because it was just starved out. Now, when it will be a sin, I believe that strength will be given me to root it out;' her look grew determined, but she gasped for breath.

'And your bodily strength, my dear?'

'If I should be ill, then it would be natural to go away,' said Sophy, smiling; 'but I don't think I shall be. This is only the end of my fever to see it settled. Now I am thankful, and my heart has left off throbbing when I am still. I shall be all right to-morrow.'

'I hope so; but you must spare yourself.'

'Besides,' she added, 'one of the worst parts has been that, in the fancy that a change was to come, I have gone about everything in an unsettled way; and now I want to begin again at my duties, my readings and parish matters, as my life's work, steadily and in earnest.'

'Not violently, not to drive care away.'

'I have tried that once, and will not again. You shall arrange for me, and I will do just as you tell me;' and she raised her eyes with the most deep and earnest gaze of confiding love that had ever greeted Albinia from any of the three. I'll try not to grieve you, for you are too sorry for me;' and she threw her arms round her neck. 'Oh, mamma! nothing is so bad when you help me to bear it!'

Tears fell fast at this precious effusion from the deep, sincere heart, at the moment when Albinia herself was most guilty in her own eyes. Embraces were her only answer, and how fervent!

'And, mamma,' whispered Sophy, 'if you could only let me have some small part of teaching little Albinia.'

A trotting of small feet and a call of mamma was heard. The little maiden was come with her good-nights, and in one moment Albinia had lifted her into her sister's arms, where she was devoured with kisses, returning them with interest, and with many a fondling 'Poor Sophy,' and 'Dear Sophy.'

When the last fond good-night had passed, and the little one had gone away to her nest, Sophy said in a soft, natural, unconstrained voice, 'I am very sleepy. If you will be so kind as to send up my tea, I will go to bed. Thank you; goodnight.'

That was the redrawing of the curtain of reserve, the resignation of sentiment, the resumption of common life. The romance of Sophia Kendal's early life had ended when she wounded her fingers in wreathing Genevieve's hair. Her next romance might be on behalf of her beautiful little sister.

Albinia was cured of her fretfulness towards the new order of events, and her admiration of Sophy carried her through all that was yet to come. It was the easier since Sophy did not insist on unreasonable self-martyrdoms, and in her gratitude for being allowed her purpose in the main, was submissive in detail, and had mercy on her own powers of endurance, not inflicting the sight of the lovers on herself more than was needful, and not struggling with the languor that was a good reason for remaining much upstairs. She worked and read, but without overdoing anything, and wisely undertook a French translation, as likely to occupy her attention without forcing her to over-exert her powers. Not that she said so; she carefully avoided all reference to her feelings; and Albinia could almost have deemed the whole a dream, excepting for the occasional detection of a mournful fixed gaze, which was instantaneously winked away as soon as Sophy herself became aware of it.

Her trouble, though of a kind proverbially the most hardening and exacerbating, had an entirely contrary tendency on her. The rigidity and harsh judgment which had betokened her states of morbid depression since she had outgrown the sulky form, had passed away, and she had been right in predicting that she should not be cross, for she had become sweet and gentle towards all. Her voice was pitched more softly, and though she looked ill, and had lost the bloom which had once given her a sort of beauty, her eyes had a meek softness that made them finer than when they wore the stern, steady glance that used to make poor Gilbert quail. Her strength came not from pride, but from Grace; and to her, disappointment was more softening than even the prosperous affection that Albinia had imagined. It was love; not earthly but heavenly.

If her father had been less busy, her pale cheek might have alarmed him; but he was very much taken up with builders and estimates, with persuading some of the superfluous population to emigrate, and arranging where they should go, and while she kept the family hours and habits, he did not notice lesser indications of flagging spirits, or if he did, he was wise, and thought the cause had better not be put into words.

Albinia had brought herself to give fair sympathy to the lovers; and when once she had begun it was easy to go on, not as ardently as if she had never indulged in her folly, but enough to gratify two such happy and grateful people, who wanted no one but each other, and agreed in nothing better than in thinking her a sort of guardian angel to them both.

Genevieve had assuredly never given her heart to Gilbert, and it was ready in all the freshness of maidenly bliss to meet the manly ardour of Ulick O'More. He was almost overpoweringly demonstrative and eager, now and then making game of himself, but yet not able to help rushing down to Willow Lawn ten or twelve times a day, just to satisfy himself that his treasure was there, and if he could not meet with her, catching hold of Mr. or Mrs. Kendal to rave till they drove him back to his business. Such glee danced in his eyes, there was such suppressed joyousness in his countenance, and his step was so much nearer a dance than a walk, that his very air well-nigh betrayed what was to be an absolute secret, till there had been an answer from Ballymakilty, until which time Genevieve would not rest in the hope of a happy future, nor give up her fears that she had not brought pain upon him.

In he came at last, so exulting and so grateful, that it was a shock to discover that 'the kindest letter and fullest consent in the world,' meant his father's 'supposing he would do as he pleased; as long as he asked for nothing, it was no concern of his.' It was discovered, by Ulick's delight, that he had expected to have a battle, and Albinia was scandalized, but Mr. Kendal told her it somewhat depended on what manner of father it was, whether an independent son could defer implicitly to his judgment; and though principle might withhold Ulick from flat disobedience, he might not scruple at extorting reluctant consent. Besides his mother, whom he honoured far more really, had written, not without disappointment, but with full confidence in his ability to judge for himself.

Mr. Kendal and Mr. Ferrars both wrote warmly in Genevieve's praise, and certainly her footing at Willow Lawn was the one point d'appui in bringing round the O'More family; so that as Ulick truly said, 'It was Mrs. Kendal whom he had to thank for the blessing of his life.' Had poor Miss Goldsmith's description of Miss Durant's birth, parentage, and education been the only one that had reached Ballymakilty, a prohibition would assuredly have been issued; but he was left sufficiently free to satisfy his own conscience, and before Genevieve had surmounted half her scruples, the whole town was ringing with the news, though no one could guess how it had got wind. To be sure the Dusautoys had been put into a state of rapture, and poor Mr. Hope had had the fatal stroke administered to him. He looked so like a ghost that Mr. Dusautoy contrived to release him at once, whereupon he went to try the most unwholesome curacy he could find, with serious intentions of exchanging his living for it; but he fortunately became so severely and helplessly ill there, that he was pretty well cured of his mental fever, and quite content to go to his heath, and do his work there like the humble and earnest man that he was, perhaps all the better for having been personally taught something more than could be gained from books and colleges.

Miss Goldsmith was the most to be pitied. She would not hear a word from her nephew, refused to go near Willow Lawn, packed up her goods and went to Bath, where Ulick promised the much distressed Genevieve that she would yet relent. Genevieve was somewhat consoled by the increasing cordiality of the Irish letters, and was carried along by the extreme delight and triumph of her good old aunt. By some wonderful exertion of Irish faculties, Ulick succeeded in bringing mademoiselle to Bayford in his jaunting car, when she laughed, wept, sobbed, and embraced, in a bewilderment of transport; pronounced the trousseau worthy of an angel of the ancien regime; warned Genevieve against expecting amour to continue instead of amitie, and carried home conversation for the nuns for the rest of their lives.

That trousseau was Sophy's special charge, and most jealous was she that it should in no respect fall short of that outfit of Lucy's for which she had cared so little. A hard task it was to make Genevieve accept what Lucy had exacted, but Sophy held the purse-strings, wrote the orders, and had her own way.

She and her little sister were the only available bridesmaids, since Rose O'More was not allowed to come. Having made up her mind to this from the first, when the subject came forward, her open, cheerful look and manner were meant to show that she was not afraid, and that her wish was real. Freely resigning him, why should she not be glad to join in calling down the blessing?

The wedding was fixed for Easter week, which fell early, and Albinia cast about for some excuse for taking her away afterwards. An opportune occasion offered. Sir William Ferrars wrote from the East to propose the Kendals meeting him in Italy, and travelling home together, he was longing, he said, to see something of his sister, and he should enjoy sight-seeing ten times as much with a clever man like her husband to tell him all about it.

Mr. Ferrars strongly seconded the project! Clever fellow, not a word did he say; but did not he know the secrets of that household as well or better than the inmates themselves?'

Now that Tibb's Alley was deserted, and plans fixed, architect and clerk of the works chosen, March winds ready for building and underground work to begin at once, what could be more prudent than for the inhabitants of Willow Lawn to remove far from the disturbance of ancient drains and no drains, and betake themselves to a purer atmosphere? Mr. Kendal was of no use as a superintendent, and needed no persuasion to flee from the chance of typhus.

As to the children, the time had come early when Maurice's whole nature cried out for school. He was much improved, and there was that real principle within him which made it not unsafe to launch him in a world where he might meet with more useful trials than those of home. Child as he was, his propensities were too much limited by the bounds of the town-house and garden, and the society of his sisters, one too old and one too young to serve as tomboys. He needed to meet his match, and work his way; Albinia felt that school had become his element, and Mr. Kendal only wanted to make his education the reverse of Gilbert's; so he ran nearly frantic between the real jacket and the promise of going to school with Willie. He knew not, though his mother mourned over, the coming heart-sickness and mother-sickness of the first night, the first Sunday, the first trouble. It was sure to be very severe in one of such strong and affectionate feeling, but it must come sooner or later, and the better that it should be conquered while home was still a paradise. Fairmead was not so far from his destination but that his uncle would keep an eye on him; and Winifred held out a hope that if the tour lasted long enough, he should bring out both boys to spend their holidays with them. A very good Winifred!

Albinia the Less was to become a traveller, for the good reason that nobody could or would go without her. They were to go direct to Lucy, who was at Naples with a second boy, and pining for home faces and home comforts—the inducement which perhaps worked most strongly to make Sophy like the journey, for since her delusion had been swept, away, a doubly deep and intense feeling had sprung up towards her own only sister, whose foibles had been forgotten in long separation.

CHAPTER XXXI.

The Lake of Lucerne lay blue and dark in the shade of the mountains, on whose summits the evening sunshine was fast mounting, peak after peak falling into purple shadow.

There was a small inlet where a stream rushed down between the hills, and on the green slope stood a chalet, the rich red of the roof contrasting with the green pasture. A little boat was moored to a stump near the land, and in it sat Sophia Kendal, her hat by her side, listening to and answering merrily the chatter of Maurice, who tumbled about in the boat, often causing it severe shocks, while he inspected the cut of the small sail which she was making for the miniature specimen, which he often tried in the clear cold water.

Farther off, a little up the hill-side, Willie Ferrars was holding the hand of the chestnut-curled, black-eyed fairy, 'little Awk,' who was impressing him by her fluency in two languages at once, according as she chattered to him in English, or in French to a picturesque peasant, her great ally, who was mowing his flowery crop of hay, glancing like an illumination, with an under- current of brilliant blossoms among the grass.

Wandering with slow conversational pace up and down the beach of the lake, were Mr. Kendal and Sir William Ferrars, conversing as usual; the soldier, with quick alert comprehension, wide observation, and clearness of mind, which jumped to the very points to which the scholar's deeply-read and long-digested arguments were bringing him more slowly.

On a projecting point sat Albinia, her fair hair shaded under her dark hat, beneath which her English complexion glowed fresh and youthful, as with flat tin box by her side, and block sketch-book on her knee, she mixed and she painted, and tried to catch those purples and those blues with unabated ardour. Suddenly a great trailing frond of mountain fern came over the brim of her hat from behind. 'Oh, Maurice, don't!' Then, looking up and laughing, 'Oh, it is you, is it? I knew Maurice would do, whichever it might be; but see, the other is quite out of mischief.'

'Unless he should upset Sophy into the lake.'

'He can't do that, the rope is too short. But is not he very much improved? He has quite lost his imperious manner towards her.'

'Nothing like school for making a boy behave himself to his sisters.'

'Exactly, as I learnt by experience long ago. I am glad William did not see him till he had learnt to be agreeable. How he does admire him!'

'You'll never make anything of that sketch; the mountain is humpbacked, and the face of that precipice is exactly like Colonel Bury;' and he caught up a pencil to help out the resemblance with nostril and eyebrow.

'For shame, to be so mischievous; such a great boy as you.'

'Well, we all came out here to be great boys, didn't we? I am sure you look a dozen years younger than when I last saw you, Mrs. Grandmother. By-the-by, it was a bold stroke to encumber yourself with that brat; what's become of him?'

'Susan has taken him in asleep. You see, Maurice, I really could not help it, the poor little thing was so sickly, and had never thriven; but when they were a little while in bracing air, Lucy was longing to have him in England, and his father, who never believes in anything but what he likes, *would* not see it, and what with those Italian servants, and Algernon hunting Lucy about as he does, it would have been the death of him. Susan, good creature, had taken to him of her own accord the moment we came to Naples, and could not have borne to leave him, and you know the Awk is almost off her hands now, and Sophy, who first proposed it, or I am sure I should never have ventured, is delighted to do anything for either of them, and always has her little sister in her room. As to papa, he was very good, and the child is very little in his way, and has been quite well ever since we have been in this delicious air.'

'How did you get Lucy to consent?'

'Poor dear, it was a melancholy business; but she had so often been in alarm about him, and had suffered so much from having to leave him with people she did not trust, that she caught at the proposal before she fairly contemplated what the parting would be; and when she did, Algernon was too glad to be relieved from him not to keep her up to it, but it wont do to think of it, she has her baby, who is healthier, and if they remain abroad, I suspect we shall keep little Ralph altogether; he is a dear little fellow, and Sophy has so taken possession of Albinia, that I should be quite lost if I did not set up a private child.

'What do you call him? I thought his name was Belraven.'

'I could not possibly call him so; and his aunts, by way of adding to the aviary, made him Ralph the Raven, so I mean it to stick by him; I believe papa has forgotten the other dreadful fact, for I caught him giving his name as Ralph Cavendish Dusautoy. How the dear vicar of Bayford will devour him! and what work I shall have to keep him from being spoilt!'

'Then you think they will remain abroad?'

'Algernon hates England; and all his habits are foreign.'

'Did he make himself tolerably agreeable?'

'He really did. One could bear to be patronized by one's host better than by one's guest, and he was in wholesome awe of William. Besides, he is really at home in Italy, and knows his way about so well, that he was not a bad Cicerone. I am sure Sophy could never have done either Vesuvius or Pompeii without his arrangements; and as long as he had a victim for his catalogue raisonnee, he was very placable and obliging. That was all extracts, so it really was not so bad.'

'So you were satisfied?'

'He has a bad lot about him, that's the worst—Polish counts, disreputable artists and poets, any one who has a spurious sort of fame, and knows how to flatter him. Edmund was terribly disgusted.'

'Very bad for his wife.'

'You see, she is a thorough-going mother, and no linguist. She really is improved, and I like her more really than ever I could, poor dear. I believe her head was once quite turned, and that he influenced her entirely, and made her forget everything else; but she has a heart, though not much of a head, and sorrow and illness and children have brought it out, and she is what a 'very woman' becomes, I suppose, if there be any good in her, an abstract wife and mother.'

'Was it not dangerous to take away her child?'

'There was another, you know, and it was to save his life. The duties clashed, and were destroying all comfort.'

'How does he behave to her?'

'I believe she has all the love he has to spare; he is proud of her, and dresses her up, and has endless portraits of her. Luckily she keeps her beauty. She is more refined, and has more expression; one could sometimes cry to watch her, and he likes to have her with him, and to discourse to her, but without the slightest perception or consideration of what she would prefer, and with no notion of sacrificing anything for her or the children. I know she is afraid of him; I have seen her tremble if there were any chance of his being annoyed; and she would not object to any plan of his if it were to cost her life. I believe it would be misery to her, but I think she would resist—ay, she *did* resist, and in vain, for the sake of her child.'

'Does her affection hold out, do you think?'

'Oh, yes, the spaniel and walnut-tree love, which is in us all, and doubly in the very woman. It is very beautiful. She is so proud of him and of her gilded slavery, and so unconsciously submissive and patient; but it is a harder life, I guess, than we can see. I am sure it must be, for every bit of personal vanity and levity is worn out of her; she only goes out to satisfy him; dresses to please his eye, and talks, with her eye seeking round for him, in dread of being rebuked for mistakes or bad French. And for the rest, her joy is to be left in peace with little Algernon upon her lap. Yes, I hope living in all womanly virtues may be training and compensation, but the saddest part of the affair is that he does not think it fashionable to be religious, and she has not moral courage to make open resistance.'

'May it come,' fervently.

'It is strange, how much more real and good a creature she is now, than when at home in the midst of all external observances. Yet it cannot be right! she surely ought to make more stand, but it is too, too literally being afraid to say her soul is her own, for she is unhappy. She does the utmost she can without offending him, and feels it as she never did before.'

'There is no judging,' said Maurice, as his sister looked at him with eyes full of sorrowful yearning. 'No one can tell where are the boundaries of the two duties. Poor girl! she has put herself into a state of temptation and trial; but she may be shielded by her exercise of so much that is simply good, and her womanly qualities may become not idolatry, but a training in reaching higher.'

'May it be so, indeed!' said Albinia. 'Oh, Maurice! how I once disdained being told I was too young, and how true it was! What visions I had about those three, and what failures have resulted!'

'Your visions may have vanished, but you did your work faithfully, and it has not been fruitless.'

'Ay, in shipwrecked lives. Mischiefs wherever I meant to do best! Why, I let even my own Maurice grow unmanageable while I was nursing poor grandmamma. The voluntary duty choked the natural one, and yet—'

'And yet,' interrupted her brother, 'that was no error.'

'Oh, no! I would not have done it for anything.'

'Nor do I think the boy the worse for it. I may venture now on saying he was intolerable, and it hastened school, but though your rein was loose, you never let it fall; and maybe, the self-conquest was the best thing for him. If you had neglected him wilfully for your own pleasure, nothing but harm could have been expected. As you were absorbed by a sacred act of duty, I believe it will all be made up to you in your son.'

'Oh, Maurice, if I might trust so! I believe I am doubly set on that boy doing well, because his father must not, *must* not have another pang!'

'I think he knows that. I do not imagine that he will never be carried astray by high spirits; but I am sure that he has the strength, honour, and sweetness that are the elements of greatness!'

'Nothing we did so changed him as the loss of his brother. Oh, Maurice! there was my most earnest wish to do right, and my most fatal mistake!'

'And greatest success. Gilbert owed everything to you.'

'Had I but silenced my foolish pride, he might have been safe in India now.'

'We do not know how safe he might be. I did indeed think it a pity your influence led the other way, but things might have been far worse; if you made some blunders, your love and your earnestness were working on that susceptible nature, and what better hope can we wish to have than what rested with us at Malta? what better influence than has remained with Maurice or with Fred?'

Albinia had not yet learnt to talk calmly of Gilbert's last hours, so she put this aside, and smiling through her tears, said, 'Ah! when Emily writes to Sophy, that their boy is to have his name, since they can wish nothing better for him than to be like him.'

'The past vision always a little above what is visible?'

'Hardly, Emily and Fred are as proud of each other as two peacocks, and well they may be, for—stoop down, 'tis an intense secret; but do you know the effect of their Sebastopol den?'

'Eh?'

'Lieutenant-General Sir William Ferrars is going out in quest of Emily's younger sister.'

'You ridiculous child! That's a trick of yours.'

'No, indeed. William was surprised into a moment of confidence, walking home in the moonlight from the Coliseum. En vrai militaire, he has begun at the right end, and written to Mr. Kinnaird to ask leave to come and try his luck; and cool as he looks, I believe he would rather prepare for Inkermann.'

'Well! if he be not making a fool of himself at his time of life, I am sure I am very glad!'

'Time of life! He's but three years older than Edmund. If you are not more respectful, we shall have to go out to Canada to countenance him.'

'I shall be rejoiced to see him with a home, and finding life beyond his profession; but I had rather he had known more of her.'

'That's what he never would do. He cannot talk to a young lady. Why he admires Lucy a great deal more than Sophy!'

'Well, judging by the recent brides, I think if it had been me, I should have gone in search of Mrs. Ulick O'More's younger sister.'

'Ah! I wanted particularly to hear of your visit at the bank. You had luncheon there, I think. How do they get on?'

'It is the most charming menage in the world. She looks very graceful and elegant, and keeps him in great order, and is just the wife he wanted—a little sauciness and piquancy to spur him up at one time, and restrain him at another, with the real ballast that both have, makes such a perfect compound, that it is only too delightful to see anything so happy and so good in this world. They both seem to have such vivid enjoyment of life.'

'Pray, has any one called on Genevieve? though she could dispense with it.'

'Oh, yes; Bryan O'More spent a fortnight there. And see what a moustache will do! The Osbornes, Drurys, Wolfes, and Co., all dubbed themselves dear Mrs. O'More's dearest friends. I found a circle of them round her, and when I observed that Bryan was not half such a handsome fellow as his brother, you should see how I was scorned.'

'I hope Bryan may not play his father's game again. Do you know how she was received in Ireland?'

'The whole clan adore her! Ulick, with, his Anglo-Saxon truthfulness, got into serious scrapes for endeavouring to disabuse them of the notion that she was sole heiress of the ancient marquisate of Durant. I believe Connel was ready to call Ulick out for disrespect to his own wife.'

'And was she happy there!'

'Very much amused, and treated like a queen; charmed with his mother, and great friends with Rose. They have brought Redmond home to lick him into shape, and I believe Rose is to come and be tamed.'

'Always Ulick's wish,' said Albinia, as her eye fixed upon Sophy.

And her brother, with perhaps too obvious a connexion of ideas, said, 'Is *she* quite strong?'

'Very well,' said Albinia. 'I am glad we brought her. The sight of beauty has been like a new existence. I saw it on her brow, in calmness and rest, the first evening of the Bay of Naples. It has seemed to soothe and elevate her, though all in her own silent way; but watch her as she sits with her face to those mountains, hear her voice, and you will feel that the presence of grandeur and beauty is repose and happiness to her; and I think the remembrance will always be so, even in work-a-day Bayford.'

'Yes, because remembrance of such glory connects with hope of future glory.'

'And it is a rest from human frets and passions. She has taken to botany, too, and I am glad, for I think those studies that draw one off from men's works and thoughts, do most good to the weary, self-occupied brain. And the children are a delight to her!'

'Sophy is your greatest work.'

'Not mine!' cried Albinia. 'The noblest by nature, the dearest, the most generous.'

'Great qualities; but they would have been only wretched self-preying torments, but for the softening of your affection,' said Maurice.

'Dear, dear friend and sister and child in one,' cried Albinia. And then meeting her brother's eyes, she said, 'Yes, you know to the full how noble she is, and how—'

'I can guess how imprudent a young step-mother can be,' said Maurice, smiling.

'It is very strange. I don't, know how to be thankful enough for it; but really her spirits have been more equal, her temper more even than ever it had been, and that just when I thought my folly had been most ruinous.'

'Yes, Albinia. After all, it is more than man can hope or expect to make no blunders; but I do verily believe that while an earnest will saves us, by God's grace, from wilful sins, the effects of the inadvertences that teach us our secret faults will not be fatal, and while we are indeed honestly and faithfully doing our best, though we are truly unprofitable servants, that our lapses through infirmity will be compensated, both in the training of our own character and the results upon others.'

'If we are indeed faithfully doing our best,' repeated Albinia.

THE END.